THE SECRET BOOK OF
GRAZIA DEI ROSSI

Also by Jacqueline Park

The Legacy of Grazia dei Rossi: Book Two

PRAISE FOR JACQUELINE PARK AND
THE SECRET BOOK OF GRAZIA DEI ROSSI:

"A sprawling historical novel that boasts its research on every page." — Elizabeth Renzetti, *Globe and Mail*

"Park has fashioned a dense, sweeping narrative of Renaissance Italy." — *New York Times*

"It is a rich Italian tapestry of human vices and virtues...in fact, all the irresistible elements of a fairy tale." — *Toronto Star*

"Possessing a precise eye for detail and a superb sense of time and place, Park has produced a remarkable saga about life during the Renaissance...An imaginative work deserving a wide audience." — *Winnipeg Free Press*

"A historical novel with a Renaissance Jewish heroine as captivating as Scarlett O'Hara. Simply irresistible." — *Newsday*

"Jacqueline Park's novel illuminates with remarkable accuracy the Italian Jewish world of the High Renaissance...[and is] firmly grounded in historical documentation. Park has demonstrated that she is a historical novelist of very high calibre." — Norman Cantor, Professor of History, New York University, Fellow of the Royal Historical Society, and author of *The Sacred Chain*

"One is reluctant to close this window on a dramatic chapter of the distant past, or to part company with a woman so full of grace and gumption." — *San Francisco Chronicle*

"Wonderful. An absolutely fascinating, compulsively readable novel about a sixteenth-century woman who would be considered outstanding in any era." — *Miami Herald*

"An epic book...Park's picture of the Renaissance is as incandescent as Italy's frescoes." — *Detroit Free Press*

"Rich and impressive. Park has written a vivid novel of the dawn of modern times. Subtly complex and intensely readable, it is also very wise." — *Philadelphia Inquirer*

"Park has written a superior piece of historical fiction, rich in Renaissance detail." — *Dallas Morning News*

"Subtle and seductive...Park has created a lively, courageous, and introspective heroine. Through Grazia, she elucidates the intricate and perilous world of Italian Jews during the Renaissance, telling her spellbinding story with honesty and humour and meticulous historical accuracy." — *Publishers Weekly* (starred review)

"An exquisitely crafted evocation of Renaissance Italy. An engrossing and illuminating chronicle of one woman's lifelong quest to maintain a delicate balance between faith and expediency." — *Booklist*

"The splendour and tumult of the Italian Renaissance live *con brio* in this page-turning tale...A story as rich as Raphael's tapestries...A genuine Renaissance woman memorably struts her stuff in a first novel that consummately mixes fact and fancy. Historical fiction at its best." — *Kirkus Reviews*

"Reading Jacqueline Park's superbly realized novel threw me back into the mesmerized pleasure I used to feel in adolescence, when I adored historical novels that were thick with details of place, intrigue, and fierce emotion. *The Secret Book of Grazia dei Rossi* is a superb work of scholarship and imagination, written with such smooth authority, one would swear the author knew everyone personally. I am so admiring, and so jealous." — Sandra Scofield, author of *A Chance to See Egypt* and *Plain Seeing*

The
SECRET
BOOK
of
GRAZIA
dei ROSSI

BOOK ONE

JACQUELINE PARK

ANANSI

First published in the United States in 1997 by Simon and Schuster, Inc.

This edition published in 2014 by
House of Anansi Press Inc.
110 Spadina Avenue, Suite 801
Toronto, ON, M5V 2K4
Tel. 416-363-4343
Fax 416-363-1017
www.houseofanansi.com

Distributed in Canada by
HarperCollins Canada Ltd.
1995 Markham Road
Scarborough, ON, M1B 5M8
Toll free tel. 1-800-387-0117

Distributed in the United States by
Publishers Group West
1700 Fourth Street
Berkeley, CA 94710
Toll free tel. 1-800-788-3123

House of Anansi Press is committed to protecting our natural environment.
As part of our efforts, the interior of this book is printed on paper that contains 100%
post-consumer recycled fibres, is acid-free, and is processed chlorine-free.

19 18 17 16 15   2 3 4 5 6

Library and Archives Canada Cataloguing in Publication

Park, Jacqueline, author
The secret book of Grazia dei Rossi. Book 1 / Jacqueline Park.

Issued in print and electronic formats.
ISBN 978-1-77089-889-9 (pbk.).—ISBN 978-1-77089-890-5 (html).

I. Title.

PS8581.A7557S43 2014   C813'.54   C2014-901916-5
C2014-901917-3
Library of Congress Control Number: 2014935632

Book design: Alysia Shewchuk
Map design: Jeanette Olender • Family tree design: Jeff Ward

Canada Council   Conseil des Arts
for the Arts   du Canada

ONTARIO ARTS COUNCIL
CONSEIL DES ARTS DE L'ONTARIO

We acknowledge for their financial support of our publishing program
the Canada Council for the Arts, the Ontario Arts Council, and the Government of Canada
through the Canada Book Fund.

Printed and bound in Canada

RECYCLED
Paper made from
recycled material
FSC
www.fsc.org   FSC® C103567

This book is for my granddaughter,

Molly Egan,

whose early enthusiasm gave me the heart to persevere, and for

Ben Park,

my constant reader, lexicographer, grammarian, and much-loved husband, who saw me through to the end.

CONTENTS

THE FAMILY TREES

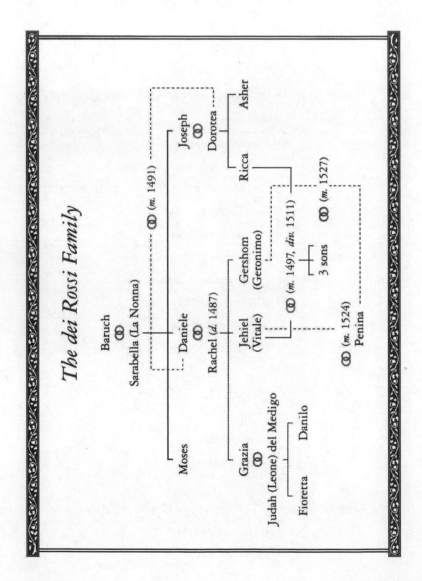

The dei Rossi Family

Baruch ⚭ Sarabella (La Nonna)

Daniele ⚭ *(m. 1491)* ── Joseph ── Dorotea ⚭ ── Ricca ── Asher

Rachel *(d. 1487)*

Jehiel (Vitale) ── Gershom (Geronimo) ⚭ *(m. 1497, div. 1511)* ── 3 sons ── ⚭ *(m. 1527)*

Penina ⚭ *(m. 1524)*

Moses

Grazia ⚭ Judah (Leone) del Medigo ── Fioretta ── Danilo

The Gonzaga Family

Federico I (1441–1484)
∞
Margarete of Bavaria (1442–1479)

- Chiara (1464–1505)
  ∞
  Gilbert de Montpensier
  |
  Charles, Connétable de Bourbon (1482–1527)
  ∞
  Susanne de Bourbon

- Sigismondo, Cardinal (1469–1525)

- Elisabetta (1471–1526)
  ∞
  Guidobaldo, Duke of Urbino

- Francesco (1466–1519)
  ∞
  Isabella d'Este (1474–1539)
  - Leonora (b. 1493)
    ∞
    Francesco della Rovere, Duke of Urbino
  - Margherita (d. 1496)
  - Livia (d. 1508)
  - Ippolita (1503–1580)
  - Federico II (1500–1540)
    ∞
    Margherita Paleologa
  - Ercole, Cardinal (1505–1563)
  - Ferrante (1507–1557)
    ∞
    Isabella di Capua
  - Paola (1508–1569)

- Maddalena (1472–1490)
  ∞
  Giovanni Sforza

- Giovanni (1474–1525)
  ∞
  Laura Bentivoglio
  - Alessandro (b. 1497)
  - 7 other children

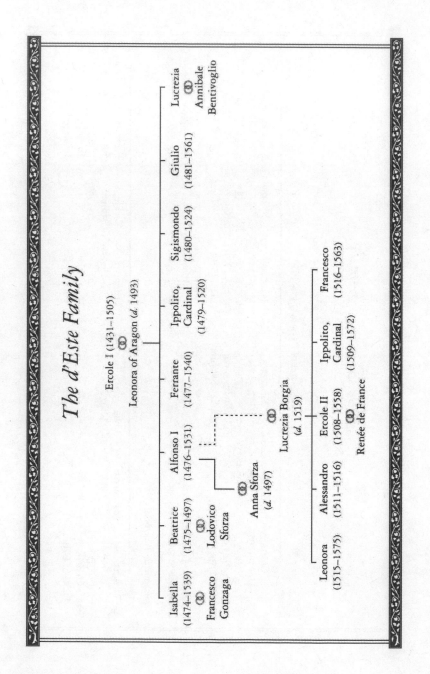

The d'Este Family

Ercole I (1431–1505)
∞
Leonora of Aragon (d. 1493)

Isabella (1474–1539) ∞ Francesco Gonzaga

Beatrice (1475–1497) ∞ Lodovico Sforza

Alfonso I (1476–1531)
- ∞ Anna Sforza (d. 1497)
- ∞ Lucrezia Borgia (d. 1519)

Ferrante (1477–1540)

Ippolito, Cardinal (1479–1520)

Sigismondo (1480–1524)

Giulio (1481–1561)

Lucrezia ∞ Annibale Bentivoglio

Children of Alfonso I and Lucrezia Borgia:

Leonora (1515–1575)

Alessandro (1511–1516)

Ercole II (1508–1558) ∞ Renée de France

Ippolito, Cardinal (1509–1572)

Francesco (1516–1563)

Northern and Central Italy
in the Sixteenth Century

Cadore

Trent

Bergamo

Brescia Vicenza Treviso

Milan Verona Padua Venice

Turin Piacenza Mantua

Mirandola Ferrara

Parma

Genoa Modena Bologna Ravenna

Savona Faenza

Forli Rimini

Lucca

Pisa Florence Urbino

Siena Perugia

Orvieto

Rome

N

Naples

0   25   50   100 mi.

PROLOGUE

THE ROMAN PORT OF OSTIA, OCTOBER 17, 1526
The ship's bells clang out their signal: Andrea Doria's four-master the *Triton* is about to set sail for Constantinople. With an earsplitting screech the winch swings the anchor up out of the muddy Tiber and drops it onto the deck. The great ship slips her moorings and edges away from the quay. At the prow stands an imposing figure of a man wrapped in the austere black affected by the scholars of the Pope's university. He is waving.

On shore, a smart-looking woman in good boots and a miniver-lined cloak raises her hand in a ragged salute to the departing vessel. At her side stands a boy. Together they watch the *Triton's* sails billow out in the stiff wind. Suddenly, the boy leans far over the edge of the quay in a perilous effort to catch one last sight of the figure at the prow of the disappearing ship. He is Danilo del Medigo. The woman beside him is his mother, Grazia dei Rossi del Medigo. The passenger at the prow of the *Triton* is her husband, Judah del Medigo, journeying to Turkey to take up the post of body physician to Suleiman the Magnificent.

In moments the *Triton* and its passenger are lost in the Tyrrhenian mists. Grazia turns to her son. It is time to leave. With obvious reluctance he follows her back to the carriage that brought them from Roma.

To the denizens of the port of Ostia, this carriage is a thing of wonder. It runs on wheels like a cart. But the driver, dressed in livery like a house servant, is perched on a box. And behind him, raised high above the wheels on four coiled springs, sits a little enclosed room with glazed windows cut out of its crested doors.

A few of these so-called coaches have been seen in Roma but this is the first one to make an appearance in Ostia. It is the year 1526. Gentlemen still ride about on horseback as they did in the Dark Ages. Pregnant ladies and old men are carried through the streets on litters. And the poor convey themselves on what God has provided — their feet.

From the moment of its arrival on the quay, the exotic conveyance has been the cynosure of all eyes. Not so a certain Nobilia, one of the girls who caters on the sailor trade. What takes her fancy is not the coach but one of its occupants, the boy she takes to be the lady's page. A juicy boy, she thinks. Not yet quite a man but close enough, with a man's shoulders and strong, shapely legs. And got up like a prince in a velvet doublet and parti-colored hose. A striking contrast to Nobilia's usual clients.

She pushes forward and positions herself, hand on hip, to bar the page as he enters the coach. "Sir, if you please, sir, whose carriage is this?" she trills.

"This rig belongs to Marchesana Isabella d'Este of Mantova," he answers good-naturedly. "It's not mine, if that's what you're thinking." And with a jaunty grin, he steps into the coach and is gone.

SPEEDING TOWARD ROMA ON the Via Appia Antica, the iron-bound wheels of the coach raise a racket almost loud enough to drown out the silence of the occupants. The boy, Danilo, has been keeping to himself since the journey began, but he is not a natural dissembler and cannot hide his feelings. His bowed head and slumped shoulders give mute evidence of a deep sadness.

His mother reaches across and takes his hand. "Believe me, Danilo, it is your destiny to stay in Roma with me."

"I believe you, Mama," he replies. But as he says the words he withdraws his hand.

"Your life in Roma will be wonderful," she persists. "And someday soon—"

"We will go to Constantinople and be with Papa again?" he interrupts.

"No. We will not go to Constantinople. But you will grow older and learn to accept the rightness of this decision."

Impatient with her efforts to cure his pain with platitudes, he wrenches his hand out of her loose grasp, and they ride on in silence.

Roma at last. The rattle of the wheels changes to an even series of jolts, indicating that the coach is traversing the ancient metal bands of the Ponte Sisto. The journey from Ostia, which has seemed so slow and tedious, is now moving swiftly. The Palazzo Venezia is already behind them. Just ahead lie the massive outer gates of the Palazzo Colonna. They have arrived at their destination.

Inside the palace an order is given to unbolt the lock. The great studded door swings open. A light appears in the lunette above the portal.

Danilo offers his arm. Together the mother and son pass slowly under the Colonna arms emblazoned on the arch. The great wooden door shuts behind them with a heavy thud.

Lit only by two flickering torches, the long reception chamber stretches ahead like a cavernous hole. The click-clack of their two pairs of heels reverberates in the silence. There are three hundred rooms in this palace, but at this hour not a soul is stirring in any one of them save the watchman. Madonna

Isabella tends to wind down at the close of day; unless she is revived by the promise of some captivating evening's entertainment she retires directly after vespers. Naturally her courtiers follow suit. Even the little dogs she dotes on are asleep in their baskets by the third hour.

At the foot of the broad staircase a figure emerges from the darkness rubbing his eyes. He is familiar to Grazia as no less a personage than Marchesana Isabella's major domo, Alessandro. "I will conduct you to your rooms, signora."

He motions her toward the staircase. She steps forward. Beneath her feet the red and black mosaic, a zigzag flash of color by day, has turned to streaks of blood and bile.

How could she ever have agreed to live here? To bring her son here? Already, as if infected by the protocol of the palace, he is mounting the stairs one step behind her.

As they round the corner of the landing, the light of another torch can be seen slithering along the covered loggia of the *piano nobile*. It is borne by Costanza, Madama's own maid. "Bidden by my mistress to stay alert for the arrival of the lady Grazia," she announces, and without ceremony, grabs Grazia's traveling bag and leads the way down the long corridor.

"This way, young sir. We have a fine light chamber for you up on the top story." Before she can protest, Grazia sees her son disappearing up the staircase in the firm grasp of the steward. Too fast. Too fast. She opens her lips to call him back. But it is too late. The boy is out of her sight, snatched from her by that brute of a butler.

Almost at once her common sense reasserts itself. What after all did she expect? That she and Danilo would live cozily side by side in this great house as they had in Judah del Medigo's modest establishment across the Tiber? Grazia has spent enough time in palaces to understand the arrangements. Children and servants go under the eaves. Even married couples are scattered about with fine disregard for their pleasure in the matter. If their rooms happen to fall a hundred doors apart, more's the pity. What could have led her to assume that she and her son would be treated differently from courtiers and relatives?

Costanza stops to wait for her at a doorway halfway down the hall. With a dramatic flourish the maid throws aside the heavy velvet curtain.

"This is your room, signora," Costanza announces. "It is called the Room of the Fishes. See?"

Grazia looks up. Above her on the ceiling schools of painted marine creatures swim about as if suspended in an upside-down sea.

"Madama chose it for you because you were born under the sign of Pisces," the maid explains.

"How kind," Grazia answers with automatic courtesy. But how much kinder Madama would have been, she thinks, to have allotted her a small room under the eaves close to her son and other unimportant people of the household. Of course such a thought would never occur to Madonna Isabella. To such a lady the marks of her favor are like jewels to be received gratefully and worn proudly whether desired or not.

Grazia sighs at the prospect of the envy sure to be evoked by this sign of preferment. And Costanza shakes her head in bewilderment at how a no account Jewess can remain so unmoved by the favor of such an exalted personage as Madonna Isabella d'Este da Gonzaga, Marchesana of Mantova.

On this note, the maid is sent away.

Grazia is finally alone. One by one she turns out the contents of her handbag—two linen towels, a manuscript of Maimonides' *Guide for the Perplexed* in velvet covers, a miniature jewel chest, a somewhat larger box filled with cosmetics, a hand mirror, a bottle of musk scent—and lays them away in the coffered chest that was her wedding *cassone*. It is the single piece of furniture she has brought with her from the old life. Now it sits against the wall of the Room of the Fishes, a powerful reminder of the deep past and of the rocky path that has led her to this day and to the sad farewell at Ostia.

It has been a long, dreary ride from the seaport in Madama's coach, so graciously lent for the occasion and so punishing on the back. Even so, she holds herself straight as she walks toward the writing table. Like all products of a humanistic education, she is a bear for posture.

She seats herself, adjusts her chair. Then, in a wonderful free gesture, she pulls off the golden filet that keeps her coif in place and releases a cascade of wine-dark hair that reaches her waist. Grazia always lets her hair down when she sits to write.

She reaches for a quill and dips it into the inky innards of the silver fish that Madama has provided as an inkwell. A further example of the lady's exquisite tact.

A stack of vellum sheets lies at hand. Nothing but the best for the Marchesana of Mantova, or for her confidential secretary. Grazia lays out a sheet of the precious parchment and begins to write in her immaculate hand: "I dedicate this book to my son, Danilo, to be read when he crosses the threshold of manhood..."

Grazia's Book

I dedicate this book to my son, Danilo, to be read
when he crosses the threshold of manhood.

*I*F I WERE A QUEEN, MY SON, I WOULD GRANT YOU VAST
lands and great wealth. If I were a goddess, I would bestow upon
you an honorable wife and a tribe of healthy children—female
as well as male. But I am a scholar and a scribe, so the best I have to
offer you is a document.

For generations, Florentine merchants have kept secret books—
libri segreti—which they leave behind for the edification of their
sons. I have seen one such book, inscribed by my old Florentine friend
Isaachino Bonaventura to his son, as follows: "So that you may know
whence you come and take benefit from the experience of those on
whose shoulders you stand, as your own sons will someday stand
upon the foundations you have laid."

What I propose to compile for you is such a document, a libro
segreto *in the Florentine manner, so that you may know whence you*
came and on whose shoulders you stand. But in one important respect,
I will depart from the Florentine model. To the Florentines everything
begins and ends with profit. What they reveal are the secrets of the
ledger. What I propose to set down for you are the secrets of the heart.

I will tell it all, from the long-ago days of my childhood in Mantova
to the moment of our arrival at this palace tonight. This I vow to do

no matter the press of work, the seductions of court life, the distractions of court intrigues, or the lure of romance—yes, romance; your mother may be an overblown rose but she has not entirely lost her pungency or her hue.

As I write, you will come to know my innermost thoughts and feelings along with the facts. Here, I vow to shun the florid style and to follow Judah's wise precept: "There is a morality in authorship as in all things," he said to me in my early days as an author. "For the author, true morality lies in accuracy of observation and clarity of statement."

Tonight I have made a beginning. Pray God my hand remains steady and my will firm. If I succeed, this document will dispel your confusion and ease the pain that is in store for you. Parting from your father has wrenched your young heart. But believe me, my decision has been made with your happiness uppermost in my mind. Not that I do not wish for my own happiness as well. I am no martyr. But your well-being is my first concern. There are reasons why you have been torn from the arms of a father you love dearly and brought to live in this great, cold, drafty, intrigue-ridden palazzo, reasons of justice and of love. Believe me, I love you more than I love my life, Danilo, my beloved son.

Grazia dei Rossi del Medigo, 17th day of October, 1526, Colonna Palace, Roma

MANTOVA

I

I WILL BEGIN ON HOLY THURSDAY IN THE CHRISTIAN
year 1487, Eastertide for the Christians, Passover for the
Jews, a perilous time for all. Until that day I had lived the
eight years of my life in a child's paradise. On Passover eve Fra
Bernardino da Feltre preached an Easter sermon in the town
of Mantova. After that day nothing was ever the same again.

The day began for me and my little brother in the ordinary
way. Awakened at cock's crow by the slave girl Cateruccia, who
slept at the foot of our bed, we washed up, said our prayers, and
went on to Mama's room for a sweet bun and some watered
wine. This repast had been added to the household routine the
year before on the advice of the humanist physician Helia of
Cremona. According to him a small amount of bread and wine
at the beginning of the day gave protection against the plague
by heating the stomach, thus strengthening it against disease.
Since few of our neighbors ever served a morsel of food until
dinnertime, this extra meal gave our *famiglia* a certain notoriety among those whose minds and habits were mired in the
Dark Ages. But our parents were adherents of all things modern and humanistic. They believed in the superiority of the

ancients, the beauty of the human body, and the new educational methods of Maestro Vittorino. Not for them the rabbinical axiom "First the child is allured; then the strap is laid upon his back." Our tutor was never permitted to use the rod.

Out of respect to the wisdom of the ancients, daily exercise was as faithfully adhered to as daily prayers. *Mens sana in corpore sano.* Even on Passover eve, we made our daily pilgrimage to the Gonzaga stud where our family had permission to ride, Jehiel and I on our pony, Papa on a black Araby stallion looking every bit the great lord in his sable-trimmed cloak. We often saw the young Marchese, Francesco Gonzaga, gallop by although he rarely troubled himself to acknowledge us. However, that morning he stopped to have a private word with Papa, whom he called Maestro Daniele, a term of some respect.

It was not a long audience. Francesco Gonzaga always preferred to converse with dogs and horses rather than people. But his demeanor that day was remarkably agreeable. He even had a smile for us. I thought he must be amused by the way we rode our pony, I in the saddle and Jehiel on pillion, contrary to the usual arrangement for boys and girls. Whatever his reasons, to me it was as if one of the gods had descended from heaven and smiled on us. I didn't even notice how ugly he was.

To my surprise, Papa introduced Jehiel to the Marchese by the name Vitale. I now know that Vitale is what Christians call all Jews named Jehiel, in the odd belief that they are translating the name directly from Hebrew into Italian, since Jehiel means "light" in Hebrew and Vitale means "light" in the Italian vernacular. My name, as is almost always the case with women, remains Grazia to both Jews and Christians. Apparently precise distinctions are not necessary in the naming of girls.

As for Jehiel, he was as perplexed to hear himself called Vitale as I. I think my brother had never heard his Christian name before. But he responded with a modest bow like a perfect little gentleman. And I bowed too since no one had taught me how to curtsy while seated on a pony. Again, the Marchese smiled. A fine beginning for Passover eve.

But on the way home, when we attempted to cross the Piazza delle Erbe, three barefoot Franciscan brothers appeared out of nowhere to bar our way, cursing us for infidel Jews. The sainted Bernardino da Feltre was preaching in the square that day. How dare we trespass on this holy Christian event?

We looked to Papa to put these cheeky priests in their place. Instead, he nodded courteously, reversed his mount, and led us home by way of San Andrea. As we approached our stable, he did make a halfhearted jest about barefoot priests but I caught a glint of something like fear in his eyes.

The maids had worked far into the night cleaning and plucking chickens and fowl and skewering them onto the great spit. And when we entered the house, the steaming kettle was beginning to release into the air that heavenly scent of figs and cinnamon that issues from the Passover pudding and fills the house with its fragrance as it cooks.

Dinner consisted of *minestra* and bread—scanty fare at our table, but no one complained. They knew they would feast that night at the seder. But as the soup was being served, Monna Matilda, the *shohet's* wife, rose to her feet, her beard hairs bristling, to challenge my father.

"Why were we not told that da Feltre was engaged to preach in our city this day, Ser Daniele?" she demanded on behalf of the assembled household. "And what is being done to protect the safety of this *famiglia*?"

I swear to God if the geyser at Vesuvius had erupted, that woman would have blamed it on the dei Rossis. But Papa, not always the most tolerant man, kept a special store of patience in reserve for Monna Matilda.

"I well understand your fears, good woman," he began sweetly. "Remember, I have little ones of my own and a wife in a delicate condition."

"Exactly." Monna literally preened her breast with pride at having been vindicated.

"I know you will be pleased to hear that this very morning I held a discussion on the matter with Marchese Francesco."

A restrained gasp went up among the diners at the mention of the title. True, Marchese Francesco Gonzaga was yet young, but in the Mantovan territory he shone with a luster equal to that of the Pope, the Emperor, or the great kings of Europe.

"The young Marchese was most gracious, as always," Papa reported. "He understands our unease. He is aware of what happened at Trento, even though he was a boy at the time."

At the mention of Trento, all heads dropped into a prayerful pose and murmurs of "God guard us from it" were heard all around.

"At the same time," Papa continued, ignoring the bowed heads, "the Marchese urges us to remember that his family has a long and close association with Fra Bernardino. Thus, to use his own words, he must pick his way carefully between his loyalty to a valued family friend and his duty to preserve the civil peace of Mantova."

"Does that mean," Davide, our tutor, asked in a quavering voice, "that the Marchese will allow this friar to preach against us in Mantova as he did at Trento?"

"Not a bit of it," Papa answered with a smile of satisfaction. "He has given me his personal assurance that the friar is strictly prohibited from preaching against the Jews in this territory. In his own words, 'There will be no rabble-rousing in Mantova as long as Francesco Gonzaga rules here. Nor will we permit anyone to interfere with *our* Jews.'"

"And do you take this declaration to be sincere, Ser Daniele?" asked the old rabbi.

"I do, Rov Isaac," Papa replied respectfully.

"Christians have broken their promises in the past..." the old man reminded him.

"So they have," interrupted Dania, the tutor's wife.

Rabbi Isaac silenced her with a glare. The old man had no regard for the opinion of any woman. "I was inquiring of Ser Daniele, who knows the Gonzagas well—the late father as well as this young son—if he rests content with their assurance of our safety."

"I have a particular reason to depend upon the protection of the Gonzaga family, Rov Isaac," was Papa's reply. "A reason that extends beyond their promises."

In fairness to Papa, he did have a good reason—a hidden reason—to put his trust in the Gonzagas' promise of protection. It seems that the young Marchese's grandfather, Lodovico Gonzaga, had initiated the practice of investing a sizable sum of ducats with the dei Rossi *banco* for the purpose of sharing in the high interest rate that he permitted us to charge. Put bluntly, the Gonzagas were silent partners in our *banco*.

Now bear in mind that the Pope only allowed Jews to lend money at interest in order to prevent Christians from committing the sin of usury. Imagine then the extreme displeasure of his Holiness were he to discover that one of the great soldiers in his Christian service, such as a Gonzaga or a Bentivoglio, was using Jewish partners to cover over his own dealings in usury. It was clearly in everyone's best interests that such partnerships remain "silent." But whether secret or open, being a partner in our *banco* gave the Gonzagas a close, personal interest in the safety of the establishment. That reasoning lay behind Papa's confidence in the Marchese's promises.

And perhaps another thing. There lives within some of us Jews—especially the *banchieri* and the physicians—a powerful pull toward the Christian princes. Because of the intimate nature of our dealings with them, we are brought close enough to the perimeter of their lives to see into their very hearts. Yet no matter how close we get, no matter how many privileges we are accorded, no matter that we are invited to their fetes, permitted to ride our horses in their parks, made party to their secrets, we can never truly be a part of their world. Their sphere becomes a charmed circle; they themselves a breed apart. And no amount of contrary evidence, of brutal acts, coarse habits or broken promises can quite vanquish the charm they hold for us.

I believe that this aura wrapped the Gonzaga court in a kind of veil that obscured its all too human aspects from my father. He was a very clever man, and worldly enough to know that the gracious young man who welcomed him at his court, who called him maestro, who saluted him when we passed each other on our morning canters—that this prince was quite capable of maintaining his pledge to protect the goods in our warehouse while, at the same time, withdrawing his protection from our persons...which is precisely what Francesco Gonzaga did to us on the eve of Passover in the year 1487.

The first hint of this betrayal came in the form of three wagons and a teamster that clattered into our *vicolo* just after dinner. They had been sent by Marchese Francesco, the wagon master announced, to transport the valuables in our warehouse to the Carmelite convent in the Via Pomponazzo for safekeeping.

From the astonishment on Papa's face, it was clear that this was an aspect of Francesco Gonzaga's gracious benevolence he hadn't counted on. Still he could hardly refuse the proffered help without offending the man. Hiding his distress under a flinty smile, he offered his arm to the factotum and led the way to the warehouse.

I remember asking myself, as I watched them turn the corner, why if we were so safe under the Marchese's protection, must our valuables be sequestered elsewhere "for safekeeping"? But something else bothered me even more. I could not get out of my mind the moment at dinner when everyone fell silent at the mention of Trento. What had happened in that place? I had to know.

I could not have chosen a worse time to trouble my father with my perturbation. But, to his credit, he put aside his own worries and responded to my question. "The events at Trento are among the blackest ever recorded," he advised me. "You are a maiden. Do you have the stomach for a diabolical mix of horror, lies, and slaughter?"

I did.

"Very well." He laid down his papers and took me up into his lap. "I suppose a girl who has weathered the *Odyssey* is ready for Trento. But you must agree to stay with me till the end of the story."

I agreed. And he began. "Twelve years ago, the Christian Easter coincided exactly with the Jewish Passover."

"As it does this year?"

"Exactly. And it so happened that the preacher who came to Trento to preach a course of Easter sermons that year was —"

"Bernardino da Feltre!" I knew it.

"Now before you jump off into a sea of analogy, daughter, bear this in mind: That was Trento and this is Mantova."

'Analogy is milk for babes but reasoned truth is strong meat,' I quoted proudly.

Papa sighed. Why was it that everybody always sighed when I quoted the ancients? "Now can we get on with Trento?"

"Yes, sir."

"Very well. In the year 1475, Fra Bernardino was still merely one of a legion of itinerant preachers who roam the peninsula in bare feet exhorting Christians to revenge Christ and kill the Jews. But by the time he had delivered the last of his sermons, titled 'The Sins of the Jews'" — here Papa's voice took on a deeper timbre — "his name was inscribed in the Book of Infamy."

"What did he say, Papa, that was so evil?"

"The libel is breathtaking in its malevolent simplicity," Papa answered in the same stentorian tone. "He told the people of Trento that there was a secret ingredient in the matzoh that the Jews baked and ate at Passover time. And that this secret ingredient was human blood. Now here is the real cunning of the man. This blood, he told the people of Trento, was no ordinary blood, mind you, but the blood of Christian babies stolen from their mothers' breasts by the blood-hungry Jews, crucified in a mockery of the suffering of our Lord, and finally disemboweled, their tiny limbs torn from their bodies and their hearts milked for blood."

"But that isn't true!" I burst out.

"It is a falsehood so monstrous that it has achieved its own cognomen: the Blood Libel of Trento." He shuddered slightly as he spoke the word. "Now you, my daughter, are schooled enough in the law of Moses to appreciate the magnitude of the falsehood. You know well the categorical prohibition in the Mosaic Code against the consumption of blood in any shape, form, or quantity. You know that a Jew would rather die than eat blood, so repugnant is it to his faith. But how were the people of Trento to know this? Their saintly friar had verified the libel as true.

"On fire with blood lust, the crowd streamed out of the church bent on vengeance. In the street where they lived, the Jews of the town were conducting the first seder, celebrating the escape of their ancestors from bondage in Egypt. As the Jews bowed their heads in prayer, the crowd of Christians stormed the street like an enraged beast, shouting, 'Burn the Jews! Avenge the children!'"

"No!" I did not want to hear any more. But Papa plunged on as if unable to stop himself.

"The people of Trento put the houses of the Jews to the torch one by one. Then they lay back and waited, the way hunters wait for their dogs to flush out the prey. And after not too many moments, the Jews began to emerge, choking, from the fiery furnaces that moments ago had been their homes. As they came out, the Christians cut them down one by one. It is said that no one there got out alive. Women, children, the old, infirm, all perished."

He leaned back, exhausted.

And I kept silent, thinking that the same preacher who had exhorted the people of Trento to a crime too vicious to imagine would, this day, be preaching in my town, in my square. And I knew why a roomful of people had lowered their heads in desperate prayer and why Papa shivered at the mention of the name Trento.

2

AS I WRITE OF THE OLD DAYS IN MANTOVA, THE people appear to me like characters in a masque. My brother Jehiel becomes a little boy again. My father is young and handsome and hopeful, unpricked by Fortuna's poisonous arrows. My mother glides gracefully through the scene, always dainty no matter the extra girth her pregnancy has brought her. And Zaira...ah, Zaira...my nurse, my comfort, my friend. She had arrived at our gate only a few weeks before, forced to flee from her town of Modena by the same threat that now menaced Mantova: Fra Bernardino.

Papa, always ready to help a coreligionist in trouble, introduced her into our *famiglia*, explaining to us that her profession—she was a dancing teacher—made her a prime target for those *ignoranti* who use the death of their Savior as an excuse for riot and violence. Later, I asked Zaira why the *ignoranti* picked on dancing teachers in particular. I suppose I expected a show of emotion when I mentioned the subject...anger, distress, even tears. Instead, she favored me with a perfectly composed countenance and, without a trace of bitterness or malice, explained the behavior of her persecutors.

"It has to do with what they call consanguinity—closeness. When we teach our pupils to dance, we lay our hands on them, like so," she explained, clasping my waist to illustrate the point. "And from there it is but a short step to casting spells, laying down curses, and other witches' tricks, you see."

I knew enough about the punishment inflicted on witches to find the thought terrifying. But Zaira was not easily frightened. In her, nature had combined two qualities not often found together: an ability to see the world without illusions and, along with it, a readiness to accept the misery and injustice of that world without complaint or cynicism.

The ladies in my mother's sewing circle saw none of Zaira's virtues. A bird of exotic plumage, she was completely out of place in Mama's nest of brown wrens. No matter how diligently she plied her needle or how high she buttoned up her chemise, she could not hide the curve of her breast or the length of her legs or the girlish dew of her complexion. She made them all seem doughy and pale and for that they could not forgive her.

But my mother befriended and defended Zaira and thus gained her undying loyalty. Beset by the fevers and ague of a difficult pregnancy, my mother sorely needed a nurse. And in quick time Zaira fell into that role, warding off the least hint of ill humor, bad tidings, or any other threats to Mama's peace of mind.

But even constant vigilance cannot prevent domestic calamities on feast days. Shortly after dinner a loud crash from the top of the house followed by a terrible cry alerted the household that disaster had struck the kitchen.

Now my mother was not a woman given to sudden fits and tempers. Yet it was exactly in such a state that we found her when we dashed up to the kitchen. All activity had ceased. The roasts had stopped turning on the spit. The broth boiled over onto the fire, unstirred. The servants stood transfixed by what lay on the floor at Mama's feet—a small pile of shards which I recognized at once as the shattered remains of a dish from the gorgeous blue and yellow service that was the pride of her dowry. Zaira had her arms around my mother and was waving a small vial of smelling salts under her nose, while off to one side stood the culprit—our Tartar slave girl, Cateruccia—her arms folded, chin thrust out, more defiant than penitent.

Behind her on the plate rack was lined up the set of portrait plates of heroes and heroines of the Pentateuch. David was there. And Noah. And Miriam. Moses, of course, and Joshua with his trumpet, each of them identified by his name in Latin script. We were a very advanced Jewish family to name our heroes in the language of the humanists rather than the language of our ancestors. And, indeed, to go beyond the first five books to search out suitable subjects for the maker's superb portraiture.

I always tried to position the plate of Judith holding up the head of Holofernes next to my place when the Passover table was laid. It was my favorite. And now it lay in a hundred pieces, the general's severed head watered by Mama's tears.

Once I knew the cause I did not wonder at my mother's distress. The dishes had been ordered by her papa from the Castel Durante kiln of the elder Giovanni Maria, surely the finest maker of tin-glazed ware in the peninsula. The brilliance of the blue that came to life in Messer Giovanni's kiln was enough to make the sky sigh with envy. Indeed, it was said that no one in Mantova save the Gonzagas themselves owned more elegant tableware than Rachel dei Rossi.

What happened next needs little explanation. Mama was not herself, being within weeks of her lying-in. Cateruccia had to be gotten out of the kitchen before she caused more damage. Also someone had to watch over Jehiel and me. I spoke up for Zaira as our child minder, but a piteous look from Mama told her she could not be spared. So, in a moment of rash expedience, Mama sent us away in care of the slave girl with strict orders not to venture out into the street. How could she have known that Cateruccia had other plans for herself, plans which she neatly expanded to include us?

When the time came to fetch the matzoh from the communal *forno*, the slattern ordered us to come along. She was a strapping Tartar with a bullying way that we found hard to resist. Besides, the bakehouse was only two houses away from ours. Such a brief passage hardly seemed to fall under Mama's interdiction to stay off the street. And, indeed, our *vicolo*— more of a lane than a street—presented the perfect picture of serene seclusion when we walked out into the crisp March day.

At the *forno*, an equal tranquillity prevailed, if anything an unaccustomed tranquillity. Generally the place buzzed like a hive with the gossip and greetings of servants, slaves, and housewives. But that afternoon we were the only customers.

Zoppo, the lame baker, greeted us with his usual disagreeable wheeze, muttering as he removed the round, flat biscuits with his long-handled paddle. What vexed him today was that his customers were tardy in picking up their matzoh. No one ever considered the baker, he grumbled. He too had a family, he reminded us. He too must make preparations for the seder. It would serve them all damn right, he snarled—blasphemy on the eve of Passover!—if he shut up shop there and then and left them without.

Thinking back, it strikes me that the reason Zoppo's customers hadn't picked up their unleavened bread for the evening service was that many of them had heard about Fra Bernardino's permission to preach and were already on their way out of town.

When we had filled our hamper with matzoh and climbed up the steps of the *forno* onto the *vicolo*, we were once again subjected to Cateruccia's blandishments, this time sugar-coated. "They say there is a juggler in the piazza today who throws balls of fire in the air and catches them with his bare hands," she coaxed. "And a dancing bear who performs the *moresca* in time to a drum."

I might have been able to resist the juggler. But I had never seen a dancing bear. And your Uncle Jehiel knew no better, at the age of six, than to follow his foolish sister in her pursuit of novelty.

The first sight to greet us when we turned the corner into

the Via Peschiara was a woman walking down the street on her hands, accompanied by a dog walking on his hind legs, the two of them dressed alike in white and red squares. Then, before we had time to absorb the wonder of their appearance, the woman flipped herself upright and began a series of amazing somersaults, the dog all the while jumping up and down and barking his encouragement. Jehiel clapped his dimpled hands in glee and wanted to turn and follow them, but Cateruccia pushed him firmly ahead, straight into the arms of a beggar staggering along the street presumably in the grip of "divine inspiration." And this *felso* was only one of several specialists in the art of begging who lined the street. There was a *testatore*, pale and shaking and looking to be very ill, chanting his promise to leave all he possessed to anyone who would help him in his final hour. And several rogues in chains jabbering nonsense and showing off wounds supposedly received at the hands of the Saracens. And an extraordinary *allacrimanto*, who kept tears flowing from his eyes in a never-ending stream.

There is truly no end to the ingenuity of our Italian beggars. How rich they would be if they put all that effort and cunning into an honest trade! Or do I malign them by excluding begging from the "honest trades"? Grant them their due. They give the gullible donor a good show for his money. Little Jehiel was ready to give up a treasured ducat to the *allacrimanto*, but Cateruccia kept prodding us on to the piazza with promises of sweetmeats and jesters.

With great poise, she shepherded us along the arcades that line the piazza, set aside this day for the jongleurs, acrobats, troubadours, and mountebanks who always appear on the fringes of any public spectacle. At the end of the arcade, there was a gambler's booth. Here, Cateruccia took the trouble to introduce the gambler to us as a friend of our father. This outlandish announcement was accompanied by an odd, lopsided grin that stirred up misgivings in me. For the first time since we started off, I set myself against the Tartar and advised her as smartly as I could that we were expected at home. But she insisted that we must stay just a little while, for a great saint was about to arrive. Completely in charge now, she hustled us through the gathering crowd and into the piazza itself, where a temporary pulpit had been erected at the north end. A low partition of white cloth ran the full length of the square. Its purpose was to separate the men from the ladies, Cateruccia explained to us. The farther we got from the Casa dei Rossi, the less muddle-headed she became. Either the proximity of her sainted friar performed a true miracle and cleared her head of its habitual confusion, or her stupidity was a veil she donned at home in order to hide her thoughts from us. Whatever the reason, she certainly did come to life, Lazarus-like, that morning. Her slit-eyes opened wide. Her slack body stiffened to alertness. And her craven manner gave way to assurance.

Without our noticing it, the holiday spirit had undergone a change in the few moments since we entered the piazza. The gay babble had quieted down to a hush. Many of the people around us were standing with eyes closed and hands clasped in silent prayer. I looked up and saw Cateruccia's lips moving in rhythm with the click of her rosary beads, suspended above my head like a hanging rope. Across the aisle in the men's section, a young father was giving his son a breathless report of a miracle that the sainted *frate* had performed that very morning.

"When he found there was no boat to carry him across the Mincio, do you know what he did? Can you guess?"

"No, Papa," we heard.

"He laid down his cloak as if it were a raft, and sailed across the river on it," the unseen father explained to his child. "And never got wet."

Jehiel looked up at me, his eyes wide. "It is not true," I wanted to tell him. "Men do not float across rivers on cloaks, except in fairy stories." But as I bent down toward his ear, my whisper was drowned out by a roar louder than a hundred lions. Fra Bernardino da Feltre had arrived.

I should have guessed that da Feltre would be Cateruccia's

holy man, but somehow, in the excitement, it failed to register with me. Then, looking up at her, I caught the end of a small but triumphant smile and I knew she had lured us to this place in anticipation of this moment. But by then all possibility of escape was cut off by the hundreds of bodies that surrounded us on all sides.

To my surprise the friar did not in any way resemble the devil I expected him to be. He was, in fact, a frail man with a soft voice and a gentle manner. And as he joked and jested, I felt the tension slowly leave my body and began to enjoy the afternoon exactly as I and all the others in that crowd were meant to do.

"Behold Monna de la Torre" — he pointed out a woman with a very elaborate headdress — "with a tower on her head as tall as that one." Here he turned and pointed at the Tower of the Cage behind the piazza. Then he whirled back to fix his chosen victim with his bright eyes.

"Monna Vanitas, you have made a god of your head. Deny that false god. Pull down that proud tower. For I see upon its battlements the devil's banner." And, would you believe it, the woman rose to her feet and began to tug at her hair and to pull it down in full view of the crowd.

Now Fra Bernardino began to intone the litany of women's vanities — from the *ale*, those wide sleeves which he called wings and warned would be clipped, to the *pianelle*, the foot coverings that have a pointed heel and many layers of leather beneath the sole to make women appear taller.

"God has made a woman small, and you put stilts under her to make her tall," he berated them. "He has made her dark and you smear her up with lead to make her pale. He has made her yellow and you paint her red. Do not try to improve on God," he admonished sternly. "He is the best painter."

By the time Fra Bernardino left off talking of clothes and started in on *delicatura*, I had fallen into a drowse, lulled by the heat of the March sun and the buzz of the crowd. So I was caught quite off guard by his first mention of Jews. The *frate* did not speak loudly and I was not certain if I had heard him right, but a look from Cateruccia told me I had.

"Listen! Listen to the saint!" She grasped me in her sturdy arms and, with a great grunt, yanked my hand from Jehiel's and hoisted me onto her shoulders.

"...If only you spent as much time beautifying your souls as you do beautifying your bodies." There was no censure in the *frate*'s tone, only infinite regret. "But no. Instead you invite Jewish witches into your houses with their ass's milk and sulfur paste and promises of beauty.... How many of you are guilty of consanguinity with Jews?"

Here and there the odd reluctant hand was raised.

"Confess it," he urged sweetly. "Confess and you will be forgiven."

A few more hands.

"I command you," he roared in a completely different voice. "Tell the world that you have been a dupe of Jewish witches. Shout it out so God can hear you."

This brought the required screams and faints, which the friar allowed to run their course before he returned to his theme,

"Some there are among you whose mouth stinks from their cosmetics. Some of you reek of sulfur and smell so foul in the presence of your husbands that you turn them into sodomites. In this you are urged on by these domestic enemies who weasel their way into your houses to work their evil..."

Behind us a cry went up: "I repent my vanity, O blessed friar."

Now, many of the women around us began to strip themselves to the waist and scourge themselves with small whips passed around by the friar's boys, his so-called Army of the Pure in Heart, along with flacons of wine and wine-soaked cloths to ease the wounds of those who were scourging themselves. The sun was high in the sky and its penetrating rays, together with the fragrance of the wine and the sight of blood, must have driven me into something of a delirium. I only came to my senses after repeated pokes and pinches from Cateruccia. There was something she wanted me to hear.

Love. The friar was speaking of loving kindness. "See to it that there is nothing in your heart but *caritas*—charity. And remember," he warned, "the greatest sins are sins against *caritas*: avarice, blasphemy, witchcraft, and usury."

"For these sins you will go to the hot house. To the devil's house..." A great moan went up. "And you will have many a visit from Brother Rod." Another great moan.

Then suddenly, a different tone, thoughtful, almost pedagogical. "Money is the vital warmth of a town. Usurers are leeches who draw the blood and warmth from a sick limb with insatiable ardor. And when the blood and warmth leave the extremities of the body to flow back toward the heart, it is a sign of death. Do you understand?" I didn't. Not a word made sense to me, but Cateruccia shook her head up and down in a positive frenzy of comprehension.

"And it is not enough that you do not commit these crimes yourselves. You must cleanse your town of those who do. You must destroy the usurer in your midst, for he is the enemy of Christian charity."

From some dim, arcaded corner, an unseen voice boomed out, "Kill the Jews." The phrase echoed eerily across the piazza.

All at once the white curtain was down and all around us men, women, and children were crowding toward the pulpit, many of them with a wild light in their eyes, like mad people.

Cateruccia put me down and began to chant, "*Dio! Dio!*" quietly at first, then louder and louder. All around us people took up the cry, "*Dio! Dio!*" It seemed that the entire crowd was shouting "*Dio! Dio!*" Carried away completely, Cateruccia let go of Jehiel and began to throw her arms up into the air as if she were reaching for heaven. "*Dio! Dio!*" she shouted, her eyes closed tight, her body jerking convulsively with each repetition of the sacred word.

I saw my chance. Yanking my brother from between her legs, I made for the arcades at the side of the square, pulling the poor child, half dead with fear, past the friar's boys now brandishing knives, along streets echoing with fearful shouts, and finally through our portal, where I fell headlong into Zaira's arms, panting and weeping.

3

"Upstairs, quick, and clean up before your poor mother sees you looking like a pair of little Gypsies...and on the night of the first seder..." Zaira's sole concern was to save Mama from any further perturbation. She didn't even inquire what mischief we had been into to get ourselves so bedraggled. In fact, no one had even noticed we were gone.

"Look there. Your cheek is all mottled. What have you been leaning on? Here, let me..." As she dabbed away, I told myself it would be best for Mama if I kept silent about what we had witnessed at the Piazza delle Erbe. Perhaps I lacked the courage to take the punishment for my disobedience. Whatever the reason, I dressed for the seder in silence and arrived at the table loaded down with my guilty knowledge of what was happening in the town.

Seated at Mama's sumptuous table, lit by the glow of pure white candles and swaddled against the winds of the world by the comfort of the ritual, everyone—even the servants—had managed to forget the unease stirred up by Monna Matilda and had entered fully into the spirit of the Passover. Everyone except me. And Cateruccia. Wherever I moved in the room, I felt her eyes on me, gloating. When Papa called us to take our places for the seder, she placed herself modestly at the foot of the great table, from which vantage point she could look directly into my face without being observed. To a casual eye, she was her usual sleepy, slow-witted self. But, even though I tried to keep my eyes on the prayer book, I could feel her eyes boring into mine, taunting me with the secret we shared.

Finally we came to the climax of the ritual, that moment when the youngest of the house rises to ask his father the Four Questions. Jehiel stood tall at Papa's side, his tiny waist encircled with a gold link belt and his sturdy little body encased in a padded velvet doublet. He had a taste for red, and Papa had ordered him a pair of *borzacchini* which the cobbler swore were the smallest pair of trimmed boots he had ever made, ever so fetching in soft black leather with a turnover cuff of red velvet and a rosette of green and peacock ribbons fastened to the right boot. Since the time of our first *condotta* with the Gonzagas, they had permitted the dei Rossi men to display their colors.

To complete Jehiel's ensemble, Mama had fastened to his hair just above the widow's peak a pearl which nestled there amid the chestnut curls like a glowing charm. He was a prince that night. He made our house a palace. My father was a king and all of us were members of a royal family.

And when that little boy took hold of our precious illuminated Haggadah with its velvet and filigree cover, and began to read the ancient questions in the ancient tongue, he was letter-perfect. Nothing about his manner suggested that he had been through the most terrifying experience of his short life a few hours before. Not the slightest hesitation or stammer marred his performance.

"Wherefore is this night different from all other nights?" His reedy boy's voice sang out like Pan's pipes.

As he and Papa went through the ancient dialogue, my memory of the afternoon retreated. Somehow our *famiglia* would be saved from the *frate's* marauding boys just as the Jews had been saved from Pharaoh centuries before.

By the time we got to counting the ten plagues which were inflicted on the Egyptians—frogs and gnats and mullein (whatever that was)—I was spilling out the droplets of wine that marked each plague with the same gleeful abandon as the other children.

Now it was my turn to glower at Cateruccia. "See, you slut, what happens to those who persecute the Jews! Flies and dust and boils and mullein."

But my happiness was short-lived. Halfway through the meal, a loud ringing of the outer bell announced a visitor. At first I thought it was Elijah, for whom a silver cup is always placed in the center of the table in the unlikely event that he decides to make a miraculous appearance. But the adults of the *famiglia* knew that trouble comes to the door in the dark night far more often than a miracle. And indeed, the messenger, a distant Gonzaga connection by the name of della Valle, had brought evil tidings.

He held in his hand a *grido* issued by the Marchese that very hour warning the Jews of Mantova to remain in their houses for their own safety. A disturbance had broken out in the Gradaro district. Rulers never use the word "riot" unless they have to. "But the Marchese has instructed me to advise you that your family has no cause for worry," the equerry assured Papa, with the excessive condescension that courtiers always use when addressing those they consider their inferiors. "The dei Rossis occupy a particular place in my lord's heart," he intoned, as if conferring a benediction. "As a mark of his affection Marchese Francesco has sent with me two carts to carry your *famiglia* to the Porto Catena and an armed escort of ten men to see you safely aboard a boat bound for Ferrara, where you will be safe in the bosom of your family until the unnatural fever of our people has burned itself out." No mention was made of how many Jews might be consumed in this fire.

Papa was the first to recover his equanimity. Having thanked the equerry profusely, he turned to his *famiglia*.

"As you hear, the gracious Marchese has sent wagons to take us to the port. Let us therefore stanch our tears"—this advice was accompanied by a stern look at Dania and Cecilia, two young women of the *famiglia* who had embarked on a fortissimo duet of weeping and wailing—"and with all good haste, make our preparations."

"Pack no *cassones*. No boxes. Nothing that will impede our flight," he cautioned them. "Each bring your own bedsack and put on all your warm clothes. Be quick. Time is our ally. We must not betray him with tarrying."

Still old Rabbi Isaac stood, supported by his son, as if fixed to the floor. And Davide, our tutor, appeared dazed beside his weeping wife and as short of will as my Aunt Sofronia. But Monna Matilda had will and energy enough for all.

"Get on, you lot," she ordered. "You heard Ser Daniele. Time is our ally. We must not betray him." And to emphasize the point, she sent the rabbi flying out the door with a great shove. Then, turning back into the room, she headed for the table in a most resolute way and proceeded to wrap up the leftover cakes of matzoh in a cloth.

"We will carry our matzoh as we make our escape just like the Jews of old." Then she gathered up her twins and took her leave.

Meanwhile, Papa had bade our servants to fetch our clothes and mattresses, for he wished us to remain with him.

Now Papa inquired of the equerry how many horses the barge might accommodate, for he did not wish to abandon his animals.

"None, I am afraid," was the answer. "The boatmen of the Mincio have little taste for nocturnal voyages. We could commandeer but one vessel to carry you to Governolo and that one too light to carry animals." Then, seeing the distress on Mama's face, the gentleman quickly added, "I am certain that when you reach the Po, there will be no shortage of comfortable barques to carry you on to Ferrara."

Having thus smoothly disposed of the Jewish problem, he

turned to take his leave. But something stopped him.

"About the animals..." He hesitated, no longer the patronizing flunkey but a man with fellow feeling. "I share your concern for them. Knowing my lord's nature, I feel he would wish me to offer the hospitality of the Gonzaga stud to your horses. Yes, indeed he would. And believe me, Maestro Daniele, they will be cared for as if they were the Marchese's own precious Barbary steeds." They love horseflesh in that family.

Mama kept her composure during the equerry's visit, but the minute the door closed behind him her lips began to quiver.

"They were only concerned to protect the contents of our warehouse," she cried. "Now that the goods are safely put away at the monastery, they will abandon us."

"You forget, my Rachel, that I am a sharp Jewish gambler," Papa replied with a smile. Papa a gambler? We had never before heard such a thing mentioned.

"Oh yes, my dears," he went on, including us now in his audience. "Your father has been cursed as a damned Jew cardsharper. And you know that the cardsharper always has a knave up his sleeve... or under his shirt..." Whereupon he reached under the strings of his *camicia* and drew forth a small dun-colored bag of some undistinguished cloth.

"Daniele," Mama rebuked him, "this is no time for games."

"And this is no game, my dear," he retorted, as he loosed the cord around the little bag and poured out onto the table a cornucopia of jewels. Diamonds and rubies and pearls tumbled onto the tablecloth, shooting out into the room a corona of red and green and clear white shafts that made our eyes blink. And when that brilliant stream ceased, Papa shook the bag and out rolled two great green emeralds the size of plover's eggs.

"By Saint George and Saint Stephen," Papa shook his head in imitation of some desiccated cleric, "I seem to have forgotten to send these treasures to the monastery for safekeeping. Where can my poor memory have wandered?"

Pretending to search for his lost wits in the folds of his *camicia*, he drew out a large leather purse which must have been hanging from an inner belt. "What have we here?" he asked.

This time what poured out onto the table was a shower of gold—chains, buttons, rings, and plaquettes.

"What to do? What to do?" Papa wrung his hands. "So much treasure. We cannot leave it behind for the barbarians, can we?"

He held up a rope of large, creamy pearls. "The young Marchese would never forgive me for neglecting the care of this necklace. It belonged to his dear mother, the Duchessa Barbara of sainted memory, and is destined to grace the pretty throat of his intended bride, little Isabella d'Este. He has told me that he intends to redeem it in time for her thirteenth birthday, this very year..."

He paused as if to consider what course to take, then picked up the matched emeralds and held them aloft. "And what are we to do with these, pledged only last month to tide the treasury over until the spring taxes are farmed." Very gently, he cupped Mama's delicate hand and placed the huge gemstones in her palm. "I appoint you guardian of the Gonzaga emeralds, my dear Rachel. Let us hope we will not have need of them to buy our safety. But, if we do..."

At last, Mama smiled. Jehiel, who had been looking on gravely until then, quickly reached out for a small gold rabbit he had spotted. Squirreling it away inside his *borzacchino* before anyone could stop him, he announced, "I shall be the guardian of this."

I took nothing. In the Holy Book, we are told to carry forth naught of the flesh abroad out of the house, not even a bone. I was not certain if the prohibition against bones included jewels, but I was taking no chances. For I had persuaded myself that if I followed God's instructions to the letter, He might bring us forth safely on this Passover as He brought forth the Jews out of Egypt in bygone days.

IN ALL OUR LIVES in Mantova, neither Jehiel nor I had ever been to the port. One look was enough to tell why. It was a sewer of a place, the stink of the air exceeded only by the squalor of the denizens. In the midnight darkness—it was six of the clock by then—the odd flickering candle disclosed a litter of layabouts, women as well as men, huddled on the steps. Many of the women wore the yellow badge of the prostitute.

There is an inn at the top of the steps where sailors go to game and carouse. There went Papa, leaving us huddled at the shore in the feeble hands of Rov Isaac and Davide, the tutor—poor Davide almost as close to tears as his wife, Dania. But Jehiel and I, more through innocence than bravery, danced about the piers investigating the various crafts and speculating which one we would be boarding.

The Marchese's golden bucentaur lay at anchor there and Jehiel believed that it would carry us to Ferrara. Being two years closer to cynicism than he, I was certain that the gilded barque was not for us. But there were at least five worthy crafts tethered to various poles, any one of them spacious enough to accommodate our *famiglia* plus the ten or more oarsmen needed to power the craft along the river should the wind fail.

However, when Papa returned after a while with a half-drunken barge captain in tow, we were led around the bend of the river, away from the Marchese's barque and the fishing fleet, to where a single open boat lay at anchor without so much as a canopy to protect the passengers from the wintery winds.

Seeing it bobbing up and down forlornly, Mama uttered a piercing "No!" Jehiel ran to her side and began to cry. How could we survive the chill of the river in that scow? As if to emphasize our peril, a light snow began to fall. Dante's ominous warning came to my mind: "Abandon all hope, ye who enter here."

Only Papa kept countenance. He detached his *borsa* from his belt, withdrew from it a thick rope of gold, and held it out to the captain. Grabbing it, the captain lurched off.

Moments passed. Then, out of the fog, a second craft emerged looking for all the world like the ghostly boat that Dante tells us plied the River Styx. This one had sails, but they were so tattered and frayed that I could not believe them capable of containing any wind stronger than a breeze. However, the barque also possessed a skimpy canopy, and because of that slim protection, Papa selected it.

Thus our pathetic armada set sail for Governolo, the town just beyond that crotch where the Mincio joins the Po, and where, Papa reassured us, we would most certainly find a comfortable bucentaur to carry us the rest of the way to Ferrara. But, from the looks on the faces around me, I could tell that nobody believed him. And I wonder if any of the party besides me were haunted by Dante's vision as we set sail across the foggy vastness of Lago Minore under the venomous gaze of that drunken navigator. Wrapped in a gray shroudlike cloak, he did indeed resemble the dreaded boatman, Charon, as he thrust his head into the fog, red-eyed and blinking. It took very little power of invention to imagine that the water washing across our bow was that of Dante's river and that this ghostly craft was heading straight for the ninth circle of Hell.

I could feel the presence of spirits all around us in the water—a flash here, a leap there. I even saw the spirit of Fra Bernardino rising out of the water, his magic cloak floating behind him. And, floating in his train like a school of sea monsters, his white-clad boys drifted by brandishing their knives.

I must have screamed, although I had no awareness of it. For I felt a hand across my mouth and, looking up, saw the face of Monna Matilda, for once not angry but kindly.

It was but a flash. The very next instant, the old puckered-up frown returned. "Ser Daniele..." She plucked at Papa's cloak and whispered loud enough for all to hear. "I fear that the Lord is not looking kindly on this craft."

Surely she was not going to blame that on the dei Rossis!

"And just what," Papa inquired with more than his usual asperity, "would you suggest we do about that, respected madama?"

"I would suggest," she replied, bold as ever, "that we complete our ritual of thanks, so rudely interrupted by these distressing events."

"Here? In this boat?"

"Here is where the good Lord has placed us. Here is where we must complete our prayers. Is that not what the Jews did during their flight from Egypt?" she asked, quite mildly. "And are we not also in flight from a cruel oppressor and saved from destruction by the grace of God?"

Her logic was, in a certain sense, unassailable. And it did have the virtue of taking our minds off our troubles. I, for one, had quite forgotten my fears, so intrigued was I by the proposal to conduct a seder on a barge in the middle of the night.

"But we have no—"

Without allowing Papa to finish, Monna Matilda pulled out of her tattered *borsetta* a small, misshapen piece of tallow.

"I have brought this candle. It will stand for two," she announced firmly. "The Lord will understand."

At this, Rov Isaac, who had remained quite speechless with astonishment, rose to his feet to object. But the virago was not to be gainsaid.

"Abraham! Jacob!" she called out to her boys.

From somewhere deep in the pocket of his cloak, Jacob drew a folded napkin and handed it to his mother. The afikomen!

A ragged cheer went up.

Rov Isaac reseated himself.

Papa's eyes crinkled. "We have indeed been saved through the Lord's goodness, Monna Matilda," he said. "And we owe Him thanks. Yes, we will say our last blessing and eat our last morsel and then..." Here, he took a breath and looked straight at the lineup of cowed women huddled together against the railing. "And then," he repeated, "we will sing our praise of the Lord."

And so we did. We sang the *Kiddush* and the *Hallel* and then we moved on to the old Passover question-and-answer songs, *Had Gadya* and *Ehad Mi Yodea*. We sang them in Hebrew; then we sang them in the Italian vernacular, one voice rising above all—the deep, strident basso of Monna Matilda, resonant with ardor, every note off pitch.

We sang ourselves hoarse.

In the end, we sang ourselves to sleep.

I woke up when someone shouted, "Land ahoy!" We were approaching the town of Borgoforte, where the Mincio meets the Po. Half asleep, I heard Mama whispering urgently in Papa's ear that we must dock at once. Her pains had begun. There could be no waiting for Governolo. The barque lurched sharply as it heeled over in midstream, and when I looked up, we were in a small side canal lit by torches that bathed the quay ahead in a greenish-yellow light. Behind me, Mama rose unsteadily to her feet, as if she could not even wait for the craft to be properly moored.

Our captain hurled the landing rope onto the dock and shouted to the mate to jump up and fasten it. But before the fellow could obey, a giant figure emerged out of the yellow light bellowing at the sailor to keep his hands off the bollard if he valued his life. "I am Pietro, the dockmaster," he roared. "Who the hell are you?"

To protect himself from the bully's wrath, Old Charon, as I had taken to calling our captain in my mind, immediately disowned us and all our works. He was simply a sailor for hire, he whined, and the Jew in the back of the boat had ordered him to put in at Borgoforte, for what purpose he did not know.

"Where is this Jew? Why does he not show himself?" the bullying dockmaster demanded. "Is he afraid to reveal the horn that grows out of his head?"

My father stood up, removed his *berretta*, and bowed low. "I am the Jew, dockmaster," he announced. "Daniele dei Rossi traveling under safe-conduct from the Marchese of Mantova with a wife about to give birth any moment."

"Not here she don't," was the reply. "We will welcome no Jews in our town on the eve of Easter day."

And nothing would budge the brute. He waved aside the Marchese Francesco's safe-conduct pass contemptuously. "Try the dockmaster at Governolo called Pepino," he advised Papa with a twisted grin. "They say he is not unwilling to soil his

hands with Jewish gold. But here at Borgoforte we fear God
and love Christ."
Wait. I hear footsteps...

Dio, I AM SUMMONED. Forgive the hasty departure, my son. I
am not my own person in this palace.
What keeps Madama awake this late? I wonder. Have the
Imperial troops launched an offensive against France? Has the
King of France caught Madame d'Etampes in flagrante delicto?
Or does Madama simply feel the need to hear the poetry of the
ancients issuing from my golden throat? I leave you to wonder
while I answer the summons.

LATER. BEFORE I SLEEP, a quick report on the urgent matter
that interrupted my *ricordanza*. A midnight courier had arrived
with a letter from Madama's son, the Marchese Federico. A
new threat of trouble in Mantova which had to be addressed
at once, even if at once occurred in the middle of the night.
Madonna Isabella and her son may be at odds over the matter of his mistress but she still stands guard over him like a
tigress protecting her cub. And a good thing for him. Month
by month, the battle lines become sharper and tighter between
Francis, the King of France, and Charles, the Holy Roman
Emperor. The issue: which of these titans will achieve domination over the Pope and, by extension, over all Christendom? In
this struggle little Mantova, pledged at one and the same time
to both the French king and the Emperor, finds itself not only
powerless but pulled tighter and tighter in opposite directions.
When a man is stretched long enough on such a rack, he dies.
Is it the same with a state?

TONIGHT I COPIED TWO letters that made me wish you had
been a fly on the wall of Madama's *sala*. Then the thought

occurred, why not make copies for you, in my immaculate hand? Why not put aside, even search out, documents in which you will hear these people speak in their own voices as I do?

Tomorrow I will purchase a fine wooden box with two locks in which to keep my purloined documents, singular ones winnowed out of the vast number that pass through my hands, which I trust will amuse, entertain, even edify you. Thus begins Danilo's Archive, a scribe's gift to the son she loves more than her own life.

TO ISABELLA, DOWAGER MARCHESANA OF MANTOVA AT ROMA
Honored and Most Illustrious Mother:

I send you this by a courier with orders not to stop riding until he reaches Roma. A dependable witness advises that Georg Frundsberg, the Emperor's German feudatory, has gathered together an army of thirteen thousand landsknechts from Swabia, Bavaria, Franconia, and the Tyrol. He proposes to duplicate Hannibal's feat by crossing the Alps of Savoia into Italy. He rides with a golden garotte swinging from his saddle which he swears he will use to strangle the Pope with his own hands. But before he can accomplish that he must pass through our territory.

To be blunt, Madama, these damn Germans threaten to bring the Emperor's war to our doorstep. If they succeed in crossing the Alps, they will surely pass through the Mantovana on their way to join with Bourbon's forces at Milano. I ask you, respected mother, what am I to reply to this Frundsberg when he asks for safe passage through my lands?

Only last week the Holy Father wrote to remind me that, as gonfaloniere in his army, I am bound to serve in his League if needed. Does his Holiness not understand that I cannot go to war against the Emperor who is my liege lord? Can you perhaps explain it to him?

I blame the whole mess on that German priest, Luther. It is he who fired up the Germans and set the Emperor against the Pope and left me in the middle. How will I persuade them

to leave us in peace, mother? Do you have a plan? I await your
words of wisdom.

> *Your most respectful and admiring son,*
> *Federico Gonzaga.*
> *Encoded in cipher at Mantova. October 21, 1526.*

TO MARCHESE FEDERICO GONZAGA AT MANTOVA
Most Illustrious Marchese and Loved Son:

You must know out of your own wisdom that if Count Frundsberg does prove himself a second Hannibal and manages to present himself at your doorstep, you have no choice but to grant him safe passage through the Mantovan territory. If you do not, he will march across you anyway. But, by giving the permission freely you will be in a position to extract guarantees of safety for our towns and our people.

If he calls on you for men and arms, promise whatever satisfies him — troops, barges, cannons, anything. But make sure these are delayed in their delivery, indefinitely. It may help to send ahead to his camp small tokens of your friendship, but in untraceable form. Those you choose to bear your gifts must swear to die rather than reveal the source. Above all, do not allow yourself to be recruited. In a similar predicament your father availed himself of the assistance of a trusted physician and the blood of a pig. Need I say more?

Remember this. Stay above the fray no matter what means you must resort to. Strict neutrality is the rock on which the safety of our state rests. Stand firm on that rock.

> *Your mother, whose love for you is the first thing in her life,*
> *(signed) Isabella d'Este da Gonzaga,*
> *Roma, October 28, 1526.*
> *Written in the hand of her secretary, Grazia dei Rossi.*

4

"**I**N THESE TIMES, SO TRYING TO THE SOUL, EVERYONE
needs to divert himself occasionally, do you not agree,
Grazia?"

Madonna Isabella's question does not require an answer.
Whenever she feels the chill breath of danger, she plans a party.
It is second nature to her. It is also in her nature to explain away
these occasions as acts of charity.

"This city is in the grip of a languor, a choler. Our friends
have need of tonic. We will have a fete. Next week. Invite all
of our friends."

"And what shall we give as the reason for this fete?" I ask.

The question displeases her. "Must there always be a reason?" she demands.

"We could tell them that we want to gather up the latest
intelligence on Commander Frundsberg and his army of
German landsknechts," I think to say, knowing this to be the
true reason for the fete.

From the moment she heard that Mantova might be threatened, Madonna Isabella took up the challenge as if she were
still Marchesana there instead of mere Dowager. As I watch

her marshaling her forces and planning her strategy, Madama reminds me of no one so much as the great warrior queens of legend. Mind you, she does not buckle on a sword. Instead, she wields a pen—in *my* hand. Nor does she mount a Barbary steed. Her gilded coach serves her purpose better. It carries her around Roma like a festooned battlewagon proclaiming her grandeur and her invincibility. And when it comes to fighting for her land and her family in hand-to-hand combat, she is as deft in the joust and as ruthless at the kill as any great champion, man or woman. Of course, being a woman, and the defender of a very small and vulnerable state, she is forced to mask her courage with cunning. Other captains do battle. She does parties.

"Since you seem to think it necessary, why do not you find a pretext?" she prods me, then goes on without waiting for my answer. "Perhaps a celebration of the winter solstice...with the dancers all in white as snow maidens....My honorable father, may his noble soul rest with the angels, had a way to make the most convincing snow. I do not doubt he passed on the secret to my brother, Duke Alfonso. See you ferret it out. And be quick..."

Details do not concern her. They are my job. "And be certain you do not forget to invite the Venetian ambassador...and all the cardinals..." She pauses. "Why do I always have to do everything myself?"

In fact, the winter solstice is a fine pretext. The dancers will be charming, all in white. And the gathering most distinguished, as always. All Madama's friends from the Curia will be there. No one in Roma ever refuses her invitations. There will be too many cardinals to mention—even Farnese. Paolo Giovio, of course. He goes anywhere he is invited. The Venetian envoy, Domenico Venier (do not forget him; the Venetians are in the northern war theater up to their ears). And our good friend, the amorous ambassador Landriani of Milano.

Ah, the wine that will be drunk and the geese consumed and the secrets exchanged and the lies that will be told before the evening is out. That is what passes as high life for the powerful. There is no honor among the great.

Tonight as I sharpened my quill, I thought of my father, who could not believe that his prince would cast us out into the Mincio without a care if we lived or died. And I saw before me the face of my mother, Rachel dei Rossi, and the despair in her eyes when the dockmaster, cursing us for Jews, refused to let us disembark in the town of Borgoforte.

I can still hear that rasping voice: "Here at Borgoforte we fear God and love Christ." I can see that grinning, pockmarked face as clearly as if he were in this room with me. And the look on my mother's face, contorted, terrified, when that pious Christian drove us back into the river to seek refuge at a more distant port.

There was murder in Papa's eyes but he contained it. In a dead calm voice he ordered our boatman to head for Governolo, a night's journey away. Then he set about to comfort Mama.

"There are Jews at Governolo. We will be safe there," he reassured her. "They will take us in. Keep courage."

At first, Mama smiled back at him, pretending to a confidence she could not have felt. But as our forlorn craft inched its way along the banks of the Po, she smiled less and less. And for the last hours of the journey, silence commanded our party.

True to his reputation, the Governolo dockmaster called Pepino was not too proud to soil his hands with Jewish gold. He allowed us to land at his dock. But our expectation of finding a community of helpful Jews in the town was quickly shattered. The torn locks and gaping windows of the Gallico *banco* stood mute testament to a hasty departure and the looting that followed it. On the outside wall was drawn a crude representation of a child held upside down in the air by a small bearded man in a pointed hat. In one hand, the bearded Jew held the child's feet. In the other, he brandished a heavy scimitar. Under it, someone had written, "Simon of Trent was disemboweled by Jews. Remember him!" Fra Bernardino's message had reached Governolo.

For a time, we stood huddled together in front of the wreckage of Gallico's *banco*, too stunned by the vastness of God's indifference even to speak.

Papa was the first to break the silence.

"There is an inn in this town, not luxurious but habitable, called The Ox. We still stay there," he announced. "Follow me." Thank God for his fortitude. Everyone else had run out of hope.

The Ox was a small inn opposite the quay, a place so mean that, as the innkeeper put it, he wouldn't turn away a monkey with ducats enough to pay for his bed. That host must have been cousin to the Pepino who was not above soiling his hands with Jewish gold. His avaricious fingers scooped up Papa's coins as if they might fly from his grasp; and he made certain to pack them away in a strongbox before he informed us that he had but one room to offer.

"One room? But we are eighteen souls!" Papa cried.

"Then you will have to take turns at sleeping," the host replied with an unctuous smile. "The bed is large enough to accommodate four—two at each end—if they sleep still."

"But my wife..." Papa pointed helplessly at the litter

"It's one bed or none for you," the landlord replied, the smile never leaving his face. "But if my humble establishment is not fine enough..."

Of course we took the room. As he said, it was either that or nothing. At least it had a roof, however leaky. And a bed, no matter it housed more fleas than I reckon ever resided within a single mattress.

Only a Dante could do justice to the horror of that place. It was completely dilapidated and ruinous, the veranda black as soot, every room holed, fallen down, and shored up with timbers. We were all faint with hunger, not having eaten for twelve hours—and that only a morsel of the afikomen and a sip of wine. But one look at the table was enough to poison all appetite. It was worm-eaten inside and out and greasier than a butcher's slab, the saltcellars held together with wires and wax, the goblets stemless, the jugs cracked. And the cloths! Purple wine stains and the greenish marks of spoiled soup covered those rags like giant buboes. Around the edges of these islands of festering slop, vermin were dining daintily, undisturbed by any effort of the landlord to dislodge them. His eyes, so sharp to catch a glint of gold, were apparently blind to both dirt and pests.

Poor as it was in every other respect, the place abounded in animal life. The first sight to greet us when we climbed the rickety stairs to our room was a huge, black rat. When Papa opened the door, this creature scurried out from under the bed as if to take stock of the new tenants, and continued to sit there on the rushes, completely unafraid, taking our measure.

Aunt Sofronia screamed and went into a swoon. Papa cursed. Zaira, the most worldly of us all, began to flap her cape at the creature, shouting, *"Vata, vata, vata!"* at the top of her lungs. And, to be sure, Signore Topo paid her the respect of crawling back under the bed.

A fitting testament to the hellishness of this place were the countless obscenities that spattered the walls, scrawled there by travelers such as ourselves.

"This place stinks like a broken piss pot!" It did.

"The lousiest inn in Lombardia!" It must have been.

My favorite was a long poetic curse which almost ran off the wall: "God damn the bells of hell rung by this devil of a landlord. May he fall into a lake of shit with Christ and all His angels!"

Once the twins had carried the litter upstairs and laid Mama down on the bed, they retired to a corner with their father, the *shohet*, and sat there cowering under his cloak. Monna Matilda settled meekly beside her husband and sons, still and gaunt. She had left Mantova a strong hulk of a woman with a will of iron. Two nights on that horror ship had transformed her into a vacant-eyed crone. Aunt Sofronia, always a slight, frail woman, seemed to have lost whatever little blood and guts she had. Without Mama to turn to, she was lost. A wraith.

Zaira was the only one of our party with any spirit left.

While the others sat frozen, she took off her cloak, rolled up the sleeves of her *gamorra*, and stepped into the breach. With a wag of her finger, she ordered Davide, our tutor, to go out and scour the town for a doctor or a midwife. When his wife, Dania, refused on his behalf—"Because the streets in this town are alive with danger"—Zaira gave that young woman a talking-to that would have singed the hide of an elephant.

"You speak of danger!" she admonished the timid Dania. "What about this woman here?" pointing dramatically at my mother's inert form. "What about her danger? Is she to be abandoned by those who owe her the most loyalty? Tell me, *signora*"—her voice fairly dripped with sarcasm when she pronounced the respectful title—"will you see her die here and no hand raised to save her?"

A gasp went around the room at the word "die." That possibility had not been spoken aloud, even though it was uppermost in everyone's mind. Zaira not only spoke it, she proclaimed it, with her hands on her hips and great anger flashing in her eyes.

"Tell me, signora"—once again, she flayed Dania with a contemptuous look—"when the Day of Judgment comes, how will you face the Lord to whom you pray so sweetly at every turn, knowing that you abandoned your patroness in her hour of need? This woman still lives. I pledge my all to help her but I am no midwife. I have no bag of remedies. Nothing but my hands and my willing heart. These I offer her without reserve. And I expect the same of you. *And* your husband. Now, be off with you and find a doctor! Go!" She pointed to the door with an imperious gesture. And Davide and Dania wrapped their cloaks around themselves and crept down the stairs, shamed as she meant them to be.

Zaira's performance with Davide and Dania not only forced those two into action, it also brought Monna Matilda back to life. As Zaira's harangue rolled on, the old woman's head slowly lifted from her breast. When the tutor and his wife left, she rose to her feet, somewhat shaky but a woman of spirit once again. Wearily but with deft, precise gestures, she rewrapped her head scarf and began to rummage in her *borsa*. At length, she drew forth a small flat package wrapped in a cloth. The afikomen!

Carefully, she broke the round wafer into four equal pieces. Then, with some creaking and cracking of her old bones, she went round the room placing each piece on a lintel or window ledge. We all watched, uncomprehending. But no one said a word. When she had finished the task, she turned to us, more her old self with every passing moment, and announced, "It will give the little one sustenance."

This blatant show of superstition brought the shadow of a smile to Papa's face. In Rabbi Isaac, it produced a deep scowl of disapproval. That worthy, who had not opened his mouth yea or nay through all of our travails since he made his blessing that morning on the boat, was jolted into speech by this misuse of the afikomen.

"It will give the little one no such thing, woman," he began to remonstrate.

But Papa laid his hand on the old man's arm. "She means no disrespect, Rabbi," he explained. "She is praying in her own way."

"But what she is doing is barbaric. It is witchcraft and heresy. The Talmud tells us, 'No talismans, no charms.'"

"No talismans or charms, true," Papa riposted, with a glint of his old spirit. "But it never says, 'No matzoh,' does it?"

As the afternoon rolled by, our *famiglia* was restoring itself. As if in tune with the change, Mama began to stir. We saw her foot move under the blankets, irritated no doubt by one of the colony of fleas that inhabited that ancient mattress. But she *had* moved.

Seeing Mama stir, Monna Matilda pulled her boys up from the floor with a quick yank and sent them off for fresh water. They must find it at any cost, she told them. She also found a moment for a reproachful look in the direction of Rov Isaac, as if to say, "What do you think of my talismans now?"

Just after that, Dania and Davide crept up the stairs and into the room for all the world like thieves or criminals. Their only crime: failure to find help. One of the midwives told Dania that she could not touch Jewish flesh for fear of warts which would never heal. The proof of this, she explained through a crack in her door, was the odor that emanated from Jewish bodies, which showed them to be contaminated.

The local physician was less fanciful and more practical. He simply informed Davide that he could not risk attending a Jewess. The temper of the town was such that he feared for his own and his family's safety if he were known to consort with Jews. But as Davide and Dania were telling us their miserable tale, a boy arrived with a pot of unguents from that same doctor with instructions to rub the paste on Mama's belly to ease her travail and bring it to a quicker conclusion. Zaira set to work at once to comply with his instructions—without any effect—and the vigil continued.

All through the afternoon Jehiel and I swatted flies with a will. But new cadres appeared as quickly as we demolished the old ones. Leaving Jehiel to that thankless task, I took up a position at the top of the bed to ward the beastly things off Mama's face. I wanted to be there when she opened her eyes and saw her baby. I was pleased that she no longer suffered the periodic spasms that had racked her body the night before. I did not read jeopardy in the cessation of her birth contractions. To me, she had simply fallen into a peaceful sleep out of which she would arise at the appropriate moment and somehow produce a baby. My mind did not make a connection between the pains of labor and the birth of a child. My only anxiety was the fever of impatience I suffered as the long day wore on. I could not wait to see if I was to have a sister or brother.

Late in the day, I recall seeing our manager and his wife go off in search of food for our supper. And I have a very clear picture of Aunt Sofronia floating around the room wiping at the walls with her chemise—a futile effort. To cleanse that chamber for the birth according to custom was an impossible task. I honestly believe the walls had never been cleaned since the place was built; nor the mattress aired; nor the floor rushes changed.

Zaira set the clerk and his family the task of disposing of the old rushes. Even a bare floor, she said, would serve us better than those flea-bitten husks. But lifting them only exposed additional hordes of lice. Naked to the dim light, they jiggled up and down in a dizzy dance that made the tiles seem alive. Seeing this bizarre galliard, Cecilia, the clerk's daughter, who had been pressed into this service with the utmost reluctance, promptly fainted, putting an end to *that* effort.

Has anyone ever explained why God made fleas? I know that every creature on earth is presumed to have a purpose. But what is the use of fleas except to make us itch and scratch? Judah is of the opinion that they do us a further ill. He theorizes that these fleas carry disease with them, a fanciful notion which no one takes seriously. For myself, I discount none of Judah's opinions. Of all the clever men I have ever known, he is the most original.

I sigh. I sip. Not for the first time, I wonder if Judah has reached his Turkish haven; and why I am here in this palace among these strangers. Why am I hounding myself to set down this eccentric history? I say it is meant for your eyes when you reach your manhood. Will you ever read it? I wonder. Will you see things as I do?

I am remembering Mama, her curls loose and spread out on her pillow like a great dark halo. Monna Matilda sits at her right, wiping the beads of sweat from that sweet face. Somehow the old woman manages to keep her hold on a piece of jasperstone which she firmly believes will ease Mama's birth pangs.

On the other side sits Papa. He could not be dissuaded away, even though the women insisted this was no place for a man. So there he sits, calm, quiet, impassive.

It was Jehiel who got Papa started talking about his childhood. The rest of us were too overcome by the gravity of Mama's plight to attempt conversation. But his child's mind was already moving past this crisis toward the life ahead of him.

"How is it in Ferrara, Papa?" he wanted to know. "Is it like Mantova? Will it be spring when we arrive? Does La Nonna have a dog?" His questions went on and on. Finally, Papa had to respond, if only to stop the chatter.

"Sad to say, Ferrara is *not* a beautiful city," he explained. "Its streets are mean and its buildings old-fashioned. But Duke Ercole has grandiose plans for improving the city—"

"Is he a handsome duke? Like our Marchese Francesco?" Jehiel interrupted, ever concerned with the handsomeness of men and the beauty of women. "And does he ride a Barbary horse?"

"He does ride a horse," Papa answered. "For he is a soldier, a great *condottiero*, like our Marchese Francesco. But the Estes do not care as passionately for horses as the Gonzagas. Duke Ercole is more interested in beautifying his city. He is even now building a new addition to Ferrara which will have the broadest streets in Europe. People have begun to call it the Herculanean Addition since Duke Ercole is named after the god Hercules. One of these days, Ferrara may be the most modern city of all."

Jehiel was not interested in town planning or in any duke who was. He quickly switched his attention to a new subject: his grandmother and grandfather and aunts and uncles and cousins in Ferrara.

"Is La Nonna a very beautiful lady, Papa?" he asked.

Papa smiled broadly. "I wouldn't exactly call your grandmother beautiful, Jehiel," he answered with a smile. "Dignified, yes. Imposing, perhaps. But, much as I love my mother, I cannot call her beautiful."

"Is she clever?" I asked, intrigued in spite of myself. "Does she read Latin?"

For some reason I could not understand, my question brought forth an even broader smile from Papa than Jehiel's. "No, my dear." Papa patted my hand gently. "I am sorry to say that your grandmother is not a great believer in scholarship for women."

"She is a perfect Jewish matron, the soul of piety," Monna Matilda muttered without looking at him.

"Indeed she is that," Papa agreed in a somewhat wry tone.

"And the house," I asked, "what is the house like?"

"It is big. A tall house," Papa answered. "With four stories and many rooms. In fact, it is a palace."

"A palace!" Jehiel's eyes widened. "Does it have beautiful stables with pictures of horses on the walls?" He had once seen Marchese Francesco's stables with a fresco on the wall of each stall and had never forgotten the sight.

"No pictures in your grandfather's stable," Papa answered. "Sorry."

"But there *are* ponies, aren't there, Papa?"

"There were ponies when your Aunt Sofronia and I were children," Papa answered. "And I daresay there will be ponies again. But you must remember that this is your grandfather's house. And La Nonna's of course. They are the ones who decide things there, not like at Mantova where your mother and I—" He broke off, looked down at Mama, and was abruptly silent, putting an end to conversation for the afternoon. The day was dying and our hope with it.

Just then the manager and his wife came bounding up the stairs, breathless and red-faced but smiling. Tucked away in a back street, they had found a shopkeeper who either had never heard of Fra Bernardino's interdiction or, like Pepino the boatman, loved Jewish gold more than he loved his eternal Christian soul. From that lapsed Christian they had gleaned a bountiful harvest—armfuls of fresh bread, sacks of cheese and two kegs of wine! If I close my eyes and concentrate, I can smell the yeasty fragrance of that bread even now. What a perfume!

Everyone smiled. Jehiel cheered. Zaira laid out her cloak on the worm-eaten board atop the trestles and prepared to divide up the bounty.

Suddenly, a powerful voice arrested her with a terse command. "Stop, woman!" It was Monna Matilda, back in full form. "Cease your preparations for this heathen feast!"

Cecilia began to cry, closely followed by Dania and, I must admit, me and Jehiel. Not a morsel of food had passed our lips for almost a full day. Were we now to be denied the very staff of life by this virago?

"Have you forgotten the Passover? The Lord's prohibition against unleavened bread?" she berated us. Next, she would prevent us from drinking the wine because it had been handled by an uncircumcised person, and the cheese because the goats had slept next to pigs.

The first to speak out was Rov Isaac. "Woman..." he began. But the virago overwhelmed him with a bellow of "Godless priest!"

Just in time to save us all, a new opponent entered the lists: Zaira. Tearing off a piece of the loaf, she began to wave it in the air like a banner and shouted, even louder than the old woman, "This bread is as bitter to us as matzoh was to the Jews of Egypt."

"Hear, hear!" we all shouted.

"Have we not been driven from our homes?" Zaira continued. "Are we not homeless? Behold this woman..." She pointed down at Mama. "Are not suffering and humiliation her lot?"

Monna Matilda lowered her head, in silent confirmation of that assertion.

"Well then," Zaira concluded triumphantly, "this bread is *our* bread of affliction. And we *will* eat it!"

Without another word, she began to tear off pieces of the loaf and hand it around. When she reached Monna Matilda, everyone held his breath. Zaira held out the morsel with a deferential air. A long look passed between the two women.

Monna Matilda hesitated. But at last she stretched out her hand and took the bread from Zaira. Then, all of us together, as if we had rehearsed it, the company began to recite: "*Baruch ato adonai, elochenu melech holum...*" "Blessed be He, O Lord, our God, King of the Universe, Who hath given us matzoh..."

5

TOMORROW IS THE ANNIVERSARY OF CHRIST'S BIRTH-
day in a manger. There was no room for His mother at
the inn. Is it not fitting that I recall for you on the eve of
that day the birth of my brother Gershom, to whom the world
also denied its bounty?

Admittedly, we did have our room at The Ox, that one
small, smoky, smelly, scabrous chamber. But, like the Christ, my
brother came into this world poorer than the poorest peasant
babe, without a drop of sweet oil to cleanse him or a soft cloth
to swaddle him or a dram of honey to rub on his gums for his
appetite's sake.

By then, two nights and one day had passed since my
mother felt the first stab of pain at Borgoforte, and the hours
had bleached her face to a chalk white and smudged her eyes
with smoky circles very like the eyes that Maestro Raffaello
Santi gives the Christ children he places in the arms of his
beautiful sad Madonnas. Pretty as those children seem at first
glance, if you look at them carefully you cannot help but note
the presentiment of death in their black-rimmed eyes. That is
the aura I saw circling my mother's eyes. But she acted out the

charade of hope until the end for our sake.

That morning she allowed the women to prop her up at the side of the bed in the traditional position for birthing. And she endured patiently the poking and prodding which accompanied Zaira's and Monna Matilda's efforts to discern the state of the child within her. From time to time, Zaira took advantage of the space between the pangs to put her ear to Mama's belly and report to the assembly that the child's heart was beating strongly. Each time she did it, Papa grasped Mama's hand tightly and gazed fervently into her eyes.

The pains were coming regularly now but not any closer together than three Paternosters and an Ave Maria. I took this as a good sign for I saw that the long pauses allowed Mama to recoup her strength betweentimes. In truth her sighs of relief presaged difficulties to come. These birth pains had now been going on for almost two revolutions of the sun with very little progress toward the actual moment of birth. And with each hour that passed, Mama's strength ebbed away.

But that secret was artfully hidden from us children and Papa by the women present. With exquisite tact, they lent themselves to Mama's masque of high hopes and optimism.

In this improved climate, the manager and his wife went out foraging again, this time in search of gifts for the infant about to be born. But they returned empty-handed, having failed to coax so much as a rag of clean cloth out of the townspeople.

Mama bore the news with composure and Papa did manage to contain himself—for her sake, no doubt—for several minutes. Then some barrier within him gave way. Raising his fist to heaven, he began an impassioned oration to the Almighty such as none of us had ever heard from him.

"Why, why, O Lord?" he groaned. "Why punish her for my sins? Surely she has done no evil. Punish me." He began to tear at his garments with wild, violent gestures. "I am the sinner. Send *me* naked into the world. But not an innocent babe . . ."

To everyone's astonishment, this outburst brought Mama to her feet. For a moment, she simply stood—a column in the room. Then she spoke. "We must accept the will of God," she said. "God is just and everything He does is for the best."

So saying, she placed a restraining hand on Papa's forearm, and with her touch a calmness descended upon him. He ceased his ranting and lowered his fist. "It is your suffering that I cannot endure..." he explained meekly.

"But *I* can," she answered. "And you must, for my sake. There will be an end to this suffering," she comforted him, as if he and not she were the sufferer. "Like Job, I know that my Redeemer liveth and that after my skin is destroyed, I shall stand without my flesh and see Him. Yes, Daniele, I will see God for myself..."

At which point her sudden burst of strength failed and she placed her hand on Papa's shoulder to be lowered down onto the bed. And from that position, in a voice barely audible to the rest of us, she continued, her eyes caressing my father lovingly as she spoke.

"My dear, you yourself must go into the countryside and find what is necessary for our child. Swaddling bands and sweet oil and salt to rub on him and honey and a wet nurse for him. He will be tired after his long travail..." She patted her belly as if to comfort the little one. "He will need richer sustenance than my poor breasts can give him in my wretched state."

I saw Papa open his mouth as if to protest leaving her. Then, most amazing, I saw my mother place her hand over his mouth to silence him. "Do this for me, Daniele," she requested politely, as one might ask for a draft of wine or some such small service. "Do it for the love you bear me and for our son."

Like every other expectant mother in Mantova, she had paid a secret visit to the pure spring at the very moment she felt the child's first stirrings. And there she had squeezed a drop of her blood in the spring to test if the droplet would sink or rise. And indeed, that droplet had sunk, foretelling the birth of a son.

Once Papa understood that he had no choice but to go, he lost no time about it. A quick kiss for Mama, for me, for Jehiel, and he was off.

"Wait!" Mama held up her hand. "Take the boy. He needs air. Grazia will stay with me."

Without a word, Papa whisked Jehiel up in his arms and went clattering off down the steps—the sooner gone, the sooner to return. I remained, amazed and proud to be chosen to stay at Mama's side.

Mama lay still, listening to the echo of the footfalls on the stairs until they faded to nothing. Then she beckoned to Rov Isaac and the *shohet*.

"Come," she said. "We must talk." And to Zaira and Monna Matilda and me: "Take a cup of wine and bathe your foreheads. I will need you soon."

Everyone obeyed her quiet commands without demur. Zaira drew me over to the wine cask, leaving Mama and the men to their privacy. They spoke too quietly to be overheard. Yet, from time to time, a phrase came to our ears.

"Wait for the master, I beg you, madonna," we heard the rabbi plead.

And, more than once, from the *shohet*: "No, I cannot. I cannot do it."

And, quiet but with a steely edge that cut through the silence in the room, we heard Mama's voice, cold as a tomb: "You *can* do it. And you *will* do it."

Then she turned to me and the two women. "We are going to take the baby from my womb," she announced. "For I am dying..."

Dying! "Mama..." I threw myself upon her, heedless of her great belly and her pain.

Very gently, she raised my head and looked into my eyes. "I chose you to stay with me, little Graziella, because I need one of my own loved ones to give me strength to bear what must be borne," she said. "You are young for the task. But then..." I swear I saw the shadow of a rueful smile cross her face. "I am young to die." She was twenty-eight years old.

Having prepared herself like a sacrificial offering, Mama instructed Zaira to fetch a small vial of clear liquid from the pocket of her cloak. To me, she gave the task of tearing a small, clean piece from the hem of her chemise. Rending that garment was as painful to me as if I had been ripping the flesh from her bones. But I persevered and was able, without help, to rend the linen and present the piece to Mama as she bade me.

"Now," she ordered Zaira, "soak the linen in the potion and give it back to Grazia."

Zaira did so.

Then Mama spoke to me. "This is my last medicine," she explained in the light, clear voice which had returned to her in this extremity. "When I raise my hand like this"—she held up her left hand—"I wish you to squeeze the cloth a drop at a time onto my tongue. One drop at a time. On my tongue. Do you understand?"

"Yes, Mama."

Then she very carefully removed the betrothal ring from her second finger and held it out to me.

"Put this on your finger," she said. "It is a token of my trust in you. If your courage fails you, look at this ring. It has never left me since the day your father placed it there. It will give you strength."

I slid the ring onto my finger, hardly feeling the weight. For a numbness had settled in me, and my gestures proceeded without my will.

"Now take your place at the top of the bed," Mama instructed me, as quietly and calmly as if ordering me to take my seat at the table. "And remember, you are my strength. Do not cry out. No tears. Only love and strength." Then, leaving me to my duty, she addressed the others.

"Are you ready, Ser Moses?" she asked the *shohet*.

"Oh, madonna, I cannot..."

Mama's silent reproach stopped him like the flick of a whip. With a slow, shuffling step, he made his way over to the corner where the boxes had been piled. With tears coursing down his face, he peered into the depths of his box and at length brought out a long, narrow tooled-leather sheath. One twist of the hand

and the *mohel's* knife—his circumcision tool—glinted in the dusty gloom like a silver ribbon.

Slower than ever, the *shohet* made his way back to Mama's side, the unsheathed knife in his hand. He motioned to Monna Matilda to pour some water over his hands. Then, without being asked, she held out a beaker of wine. He plunged the knife into the beaker up to the hilt. Then he drew it out and stood waiting, holding up the knife dripping purple.

"Uncover my belly," Mama ordered Zaira. It was swollen, blue-veined. I felt I could see the baby's heart pulsating under the mottled skin.

"Pray for me, Rabbi," Mama asked in a humble tone.

The rabbi opened his prayer book and began to fumble for his place with trembling hands.

"Kiss me, Grazia."

I bent and kissed her mouth. It was dry to the touch and cold.

"I am ready, Ser Moses," she stated calmly.

"Oh, madonna..." the poor old man wailed.

"Do it now!" Mama ordered in a voice which shook the room.

The knife flashed through the air. I saw it make a slice in Mama's flesh. Then another. Another. I thought, Where is the blood? There was so little blood.

Then I heard a terrifying wail from my mother and a last whispered instruction. "Quick. Quick. Save my baby."

Her arm went up. My signal. True to my task, I began to squeeze the saturated cloth onto her tongue drop by drop. She swallowed those drops in greedy gulps, as if they contained the stuff of life itself instead of what I suspect was the stuff of death. I never knew for certain that there was poison in that vial. Whatever it was, it brought her peace.

My brother was born quickly and without mishap. The *shohet* exposed the birth cavity with the first cut. Then, out of the corner of my eye, I saw him reach into Mama's open belly and pull out the bloody, mucused ball of humanity that was my beautiful brother Gershom.

One smack from Monna Matilda and the tiny creature emitted a howl quite out of proportion to his diminutive size. My eyes leapt up toward the sound. Until that moment, I had not betrayed my charge by so much as a single moment of inattention. But that first howl of fury and delight struck a chord in me deeper than duty.

I do not know what I expected to see when I lifted my eyes from Mama's face. Something splendid, I suppose. Certainly not the squirming spidery creature that I now beheld. As I watched, Monna Matilda measured out four lengths of her finger on a long loose string of flesh that hung down from the baby's belly. At a nod from her, Zaira took the *shohet*'s knife from his hand and, with one quick slash, severed the cord and tied it around itself, pulling it taut with a jerk as one secures a rope.

I looked down at Mama to see if she was as disappointed as I was in the miraculous child. Her eyes were wide. Staring. I whispered in her ear. "Mama..."

She did not answer.

Zaira leaned over and pulled Mama's eyelids down over her eyes. Then, looking straight into my eyes and speaking slowly and clearly, as if to make certain I did not misunderstand, she said, "She is dead, Graziella. Your mother is dead."

FERRARA

6

T HE VIA GRANDE GAVE US A FORETASTE OF WHAT OUR
life was to be in Ferrara — narrow, confining, mean, and
muddy. One feature alone added a dash of interest to this
moldy morass: a series of overhead fly bridges that connected
the fine houses of the Via Grande with their servants' quarters
across the way. Mantova contained no such passages, not even
in the oldest quarters of the town. As we made our way along,
the tip-tap of footsteps and the echoes of laughter in the covered passages above our heads did add a certain charm to the
surroundings. But in no other way did Ferrara compare favorably with Mantova in my young eyes.

My grandmother had not met us at the dock. Nor did she
come out to the courtyard to greet us. She chose instead to
welcome us formally in her reception room, her *sala grande*,
and thence we were conducted by a liveried porter up a staircase broad enough to accommodate three stout men abreast.
When he threw aside the curtain, what greeted my eyes was
an Aladdin's cave of a room, every meter of wall space covered
with a tapestry or a fine Persian carpet, every surface crowded
with gold and silver bowls and pitchers and ceremonial cups

and wonderfully carved crystal vessels and cameos in frames and all manner of expensive stuff. In the midst of this grandeur stood my grandmother dei Rossi, an incongruity among her treasures—short, squat, and squinty, with beady black eyes and skin that hung in leathery furrows like the skin of a toad.

Her first words to us were: "Take off your boots, children. The carpet under your feet cost your honored grandfather three hundred gold ducats at Constantinople."

As she led us through room after luxurious room, every object and artifact was catalogued for us as if in a ledger. This plate had cost so many ducats at the kiln of Maestro Orazio in Deruta. The marble for that mantel had been hauled from Toscana at a cost of so many ducats per wagonload. The vault that covered the grand staircase had been painted by a pupil of Cossa, the favored artist of the Este dukes, a rascal who charged four forms an ounce for the ground lapis he used to make the ultramarine color of the vault and fifteen ducats for the measly handful of golden stars.

Only once was she distracted from her single-minded concentration on the price of things. It happened after we had climbed the staircase and were about to begin our procession through the balance of the private rooms. Using her walking stick as a pointer, she drew our attention to the delicate Roman-style decorations that adorned the portal ahead of us.

"This is my *sala di giustizia*," she announced. Hall of justice? "Now tell me, what do you see carved here on the portal, children?"

As these were the first words she had addressed directly to us since she ordered us to take off our boots, both Jehiel and I were too surprised to reply as quickly as we might have. Whereupon she repeated her question, this time reinforced by a sharp poke at Jehiel with the end of the stick.

"Fruits..." he blurted out. "And plants and designs...and... and..." Another poke with the stick.

"Monsters..." I interrupted. "Images..."

"Graven images?" She spoke the phrase in such ominous

tones that I knew I had fallen into some kind of trap, but, for my life, I could not discern where the danger lay. They *were* images, I reasoned. And they *were* graven on the portal.

"Yes," I answered.

"Wicked girl. Do you accuse your grandparents of breaking the second commandment?"

"No, madama."

"Madonna La Nonna," she corrected me. Then she turned to Papa and announced, "This girl needs lessons in deportment. She has no respect."

"She meant nothing by it..."

His reasonable tone was drowned out by her forceful croak. "Never let it be said that the dei Rossi house dishonors the Lord in any way, nor that we break commandments here. If you look at these *grotteschi*, you will observe that they resemble nothing to be seen in the sky, on earth, or in the seas. For that reason, they do not fall under the interdiction against making graven images. Do you understand?" She fixed her beady eyes on me.

"Yes, honored Madonna La Nonna," I answered.

"This disrespect is what comes of teaching girls pagan languages," she informed my father.

I looked to him for a denial of this insult to the humanistic creed, but he remained silent and the procession moved on.

After showing us the family rooms and our own rooms— Jehiel and I were each to have our own bedroom—and introducing us to our body servants—one apiece, quite in the style of little royals—and having dispatched Zaira up to the top floor with an impatient wave of the hand and instructions to find herself a little room near the kitchen maids, my grandmother conducted us back down the grand staircase through the courtyard and into the *banco*, to be presented to the lord of this domain, my grandfather.

My first impression was of a striking resemblance to my father: the same thick, shiny brown hair—although my grandfather's mane did show quite a few strands of silver by then. But this cavalier made no concession to his advancing years.

No coarse or dun-colored cloak for him. His everyday garment was a velvet tunic lined in red satin. And I noticed that his sleeves were lined with sable fur that perfectly matched his eyes.

Even Papa was intimidated by this exalted being. The moment he entered that room and laid eyes on his father, he became a boy again, shy, withdrawn, stammering when asked to account for the state of his health.

"F-f-fine, Signore Padre," he replied, in a weak tone such as I had never heard issue from his lips.

"And the children?" the old man asked, turning his hard stare on us.

"We are well, sir," I replied quickly. "As well as can be expected after our ordeal and the terrible loss we have suffered."

Grandfather fixed his eyes on me, squinting as if he couldn't quite make me out. Then he turned to my father and asked, "Is there anything you will be needing for these children?"

"Yes, sir, there is," Papa replied, slightly stronger this time. "They are accustomed to taking their exercise each morning on horseback. I wondered if our family still possessed the right to ride in the Este park and whether there would be suitable mounts for Grazia and Jehiel in our stable."

"We haven't kept ponies in years," my grandmother burst in impatiently. "And I doubt that Nachum would take kindly to that idea." Nachum was the stableman.

"He is most irascible these days," Grandfather added.

"The children are accustomed to their ride," Papa replied mildly. "And I do believe the exercise keeps them free of coughing and phlegm. Besides, I myself enjoy a brisk canter."

"I daresay you do, my son," my grandmother rejoined in a scathing tone. "But I think you will find yourself too occupied with responsibilities to have time for courtly affectations. Is that not so, Honored Signore?"

"Quite so," my grandfather agreed. "You must bear in mind, my son, that the Ferrarese *banco* is the mother of all the dei Rossi branches. We carry a heavy responsibility here." He shook his head gravely. "Even I do not find time for recreation."

"But the children..." my father protested.

"Their cousins, Asher and Ricca, have managed to remain quite healthy without careening all over the countryside on wild animals, and I am certain that your children will too, Daniele," my grandmother announced firmly. And thus the matter was settled.

WE WERE GIVEN TWO days to settle ourselves and unpack our possessions. On the evening of the second day, La Nonna ordered Jehiel to present himself in the schoolroom at a goodly time before sunrise the next day. Although she did not address me directly, I took myself to be included and made my preparations accordingly. I awoke in the dark, dressed, washed my face and hands in the icy bowl at my bedside, and went in search of my brother.

There was no "little meal" to ward off the plague in this austere household. Wary as forest creatures, Jehiel and I padded through attics and storerooms, picking our way among the servants, many of them still sleeping against sacks or in stairwells. At last we reached the schoolroom, which was situated at the southern end of the house so as to catch the first rays of daylight from the east.

There I stood in the gloom beside Jehiel, my writing case under my arm, my pens and powder and quills and vellum prepared as I learned to do in our Mantovan schoolroom.

Jehiel tapped lightly on the portal.

After a moment or two, the curtain was drawn aside and Nataniele, the tutor, took his arm to usher him in. But when I stepped forward the fellow pushed me back.

"No, no." He shook my shoulder impatiently. "No girls in this schoolroom. This is for serious work."

"But I am serious," I replied.

He smiled one of those patronizing smiles that stupid adults reserve for children. "Run along now. Off to your sewing.

There's plenty of women's work to be done."

"Women's work?" Having been nurtured on Vittorino's humanistic theories, the idea of denying learning to anyone — even a girl — came as a heresy.

"Women's work," the tutor reiterated. "The duties of the household: to make bread, dress the capon, sift the flour, make the bed, spin, darn stockings. These are the skills you must learn so that when you marry it will not be said of you that you come from the woods."

"What about Latin?" I inquired, still not understanding the full import of what he was telling me. "I have already committed to memory Virgil's *Eclogues* and have begun Cicero's *Epistles*..."

At the mention of Virgil, his hand fell from my shoulder. Cicero brought a gasp of horror such as one might emit at the first sight of buboes on a plague victim. He fell back, his arm holding me at its full length as if to escape the contagion, and intoned in a quivering voice, "It is not proper for a devout Jewish maiden to read Latin."

"Why, that is the most foolish thing I ever heard in my life," I shot back, without thinking. My impudence gave him all the provocation he needed.

"Do you call me foolish, girl?" he thundered, and began to shake me vigorously back and forth. "Do you dare to insult me?"

"It is not your person that I impugn, sir," I explained, with as much dignity as I could muster between shakes. "It is your ideas."

Whereupon the man slapped me.

That was the first slap I ever received in my life and it took the juice out of me. Shocked and humiliated, I fled.

How I found myself in my grandfather's *studiolo* I cannot tell you. Perhaps the smell of the books lured me in. However it happened, that is where my feet landed me and that is where I was discovered fondling a Greek manuscript that had been left on the lectern, by my grandmother's steward, Giorgio.

The moment he recovered from his shock at finding me in Grandfather's study—*sitting on Grandfather's chair, touching Grandfather's book!*—he picked me up as if I were a sack of flour and dumped me down on the floor, not seeming to care if I landed head or feet first. Then he picked me up and dragged me along the corridor to my room and ordered me to stay put until I was called. And there Zaira found me licking my wounds, which, motherly creature she was, she set about to soothe. To the ugly redness on my cheek, she applied a sweet-smelling unguent. To my wounded spirit, soft words of comfort.

But, like a good mother, she had more than sympathy and poultices to give. After she had tidied me up and heard the tale of my misadventures to the end, she stood me up straight and announced that I must seek out the tutor and make my apologies to him, as soon as possible.

"But he told me that I was tainted by reading Latin," I protested. "How can I agree..."

"Shush, child," she silenced me. "Of course the fellow's an ass. But since when did a woman ever win a case against a foolish male? Give it up, Grazia. Make your peace with him."

"Must I?"

"Absolutely." Then, taking my face in her hands as my mother used to do when she had a lesson to teach me, she continued, "We are all of us on very rocky terrain here in the Casa dei Rossi. New habits. New rules. And you must learn them quickly. If you cannot—or will not—I cannot protect you."

"Do you want me to play false, then? To pretend a regard for cant and idiocy?" I demanded, stiff-necked to the end.

"This is not a debate, Grazia," she answered with a sad shake of her head. "This is the game of life, where only those who play by the rules survive. In your mother's house, God bless her name, justice and kindness ruled. Here, respect is the first principle. You must learn to show respect for those who are deemed to be above you—fools included—whether or not you feel it in your heart. For my sake, will you promise me to try?"

For her sake, I promised.

By now, the dinner bell had rung and the *famiglia* were already seated when we entered the *sala*. But before we could take our seats, we were stopped by my grandmother's commanding croak. "What brings you here, Grazia? Were you not told to wait for me in your room?"

Zaira stepped forward, as if to shield me. "She asked me to bring her, madonna, so that she could pay her respects and apologize for her—"

"And who gave you authority over this child, signora?" The old woman's wattles were beginning to quiver. "Do you take her for an orphan, like yourself, with no family of her own to teach her right and wrong?"

"But madonna..." I had never before seen Zaira nonplussed.

"Release my granddaughter's hand, signora, and take your assigned place at the table." In these moments, she rolled on like a battlewagon, flattening everything in her way. "Go, go." She waved Zaira out of her sight the way we ward off troublesome Gypsies in the street, then turned her attention to me. "You, Grazia, will accompany me to my *sala di giustizia*. I will require your services, Giorgio." She nodded to her beefy steward. "And you, Rabbi. Move along, Grazia."

I turned to Zaira for a gesture, a sign. But all I got were tears and a helpless shrug.

In spite of its formidable name, the *sala di giustizia* was not an imposing room. Nothing but a bare trestle table, three crude chairs, and a small washstand with a basin on it. Nor was my grandmother's manner calculated to cause alarm. She simply took a seat behind the table, beckoned me to approach and began to speak to me across the table in a low, conversational tone.

She talked of the natural depravity of children—imps, she called them, "imps with folly tied onto their backs"—and the double depravity of children of the female sex.

"Beginning with Eve," she explained, "women have followed the paths of curiosity and pleasure, with what sad results you know well, for you are an educated girl. You remember, do you not, what wise King Solomon told the Queen of Sheba?"

I did remember only too well and intellectual pride compelled me to confess my knowledge. "He wrote that while one might find one good man among a thousand, he had never found among all women even one who was virtuous," I reported.

For this, I got a rare, pinched smile. "Well then," she resumed, "you can understand that women are in the greatest danger of falling prey to sloth and corruption. That is why we have a special duty to little girls to keep them from such folly in the tenderness of their youth, while the twig is still pliant."

To this awkward metaphor, the rabbi, who until then had remained seated quietly beside her, nodded his bobbing assent.

Now it was his turn. He took as his text the line from Genesis: God formed the rib he had taken from the man into a wife. Staring fixedly into my eyes, he asked, "Why was Eve not formed out of man's head?"

Then, before I had a chance to open my mouth, he answered his own question. "In order that she might not be clever and learn more than was good for her," came his reply.

Beside him, La Nonna nodded her approval.

"And why not out of his eye or ear?" he continued. Then again without waiting for my answer: "So that she should not be curious, wishing to see and hear everything."

As before, La Nonna shook her wattles in furious approval.

"And why was she not formed out of his mouth?" Again he answered his own question. "She was not formed out of his mouth so that she might not be too talkative. Or out of his heart so that she not be passionate. Nor was she formed out of his hand or foot. And why? In order that she might not touch everything nor go everywhere. It was to avoid all of these pitfalls that Eve was formed out of Adam's rib, a part that is hidden from sight and must serve as an emblem of modesty and virtue. Forget the mind," he concluded, waving his ignorance like a banner. "Women do best to keep their bodies in continual travail. Work, work, and more work. Make use of the needle and go to the loom for your recreation. Too much learning has already led you to pride and disrespect. Now you must learn to subdue the flesh."

With this he leaned back in his chair, exhausted from the expenditure of such profound mentation.

But my grandmother had barely begun to exhaust her intellectual resources. "It is books and study that have corrupted your virtue, child," she explained in a quiet, even sympathetic tone. "Books destroy a woman's brains, who has little enough to begin with. And it is the solemn duty of all who are entrusted with the care of little girls to minister to them with the rod..." Here she nodded in the direction of a clutch of birch rods hanging on a hook behind her. "Yes, the rod," she gestured to Giorgio—"applied in the greenness of their years so as to refashion their evil nature into a mold more pleasing to Him."

On cue, the steward, a strapping fellow with a forearm as big as a ham hock, stepped forward and took me from the rear, pinning my arms behind me. I did manage to get in one good kick, which made him curse but gained me only further binding, this a rope he kept dangling from his belt that he employed to tie both my ankles and my wrists.

So now I was bound hand and foot, immobilized, with no recourse left me but to shout. And that I would not do. For I feared that once I opened my mouth, I would release a flood of tears. So I simply glared silently at the old woman, whose eyes glittered now with all the zeal of one of the Pope's inquisitors. "Bring her to me, Maestro Giorgio," she ordered.

Now, Giorgio dragged me across the floor and laid me against Grandmother's bony knees. Then, as majestically as if he were a king, that monster turned to the wall and, making certain that he was in my full sight, selected one from among the birch rods hanging there and held it up.

My grandmother refused his choice with a decisive shake of her head. Thus he was encouraged to select a heavier stick.

This one must have measured at least the girth of a man's ring finger.

Having selected the whip, Giorgio then dipped it into a basin filled with salted water, the better to make the welts sting. Again La Nonna nodded her silent approval.

He stood waiting his final orders.

When they came, the import shocked all other thoughts out of my mind.

"Strip her," the old woman ordered.

"Papa. Mama. Save me," I shouted, but to no avail. The steward, well practiced in this procedure, neatly took up the hem of my *gamorra* and raised it high over my head, exposing my bare back to the rod.

Now I did indeed feel the symptoms of terror: a falling of the stomach as if to the center of the earth and a terrible shortness of breath.

After an eternity of time, I heard my grandmother order, "Stroke the first."

The first stroke hit my back. A scream escaped me inadvertently.

The second stroke drew blood. As I crouched there against my grandmother's knees, I felt a rivulet of the warm stuff trickle down between my legs.

More than anything I wanted to fall in a swoon and lose my senses. But God showed me no mercy. I remember it all: the terrible third stroke, more painful than the other two in that it intermingled its own pain with that of the two before it; the untying of the rope and the modest drawing of my chemise over my bloody ass; no word from either of those two monsters but for a curt "Off with you now" from La Nonna; and finally the painful limp down the corridor to my room, where I burrowed deep into the pillows of my grand canopied bed like a wounded cur.

After some time Papa found me out. Even though some part of me longed for comfort, I could not bear to be looked at, and when he made a move to pull back the coverlet I screamed out a "No!" so piercing that he stopped the effort at once and crept out.

Later that evening he returned, with questions. But I had no heart for a dialogue. I merely placed my hand on his mouth to silence him as I had seen my mother do. I had nothing to say to him. He who should have protected me against his bullying parent had left me instead to her mercy. I never forgave him for it. I do not say that I never loved my father after that. Or even that my love for him lessened. But never again was he a god to me or any kind of a hero.

Each evening he would come directly from prayers and sit silent, squeezing my hand from time to time in a mute plea for forgiveness. But I, stony-hearted, withheld it.

One evening, he brought with him a pearl pendant that had belonged to Mama and fastened it around my neck on a gold chain. Whereupon I unlatched the clasp and placed the offering back in his hand without a word.

Zaira was the one who rescued us from this sad impasse. It was she who suggested to Papa that he ought to read to me. Of course, he took up the suggestion with alacrity — anything to avoid my reproachful eyes. And I responded in spite of myself for he had cleverly selected my favorite — the *Aeneid*.

"This is a tale of arms and of a man,
   The first to sail from the land of Troy,
   And reach Italy, displaced by destiny..."

At first I remained aloof. But by the time Papa reached Juno's declaration of war against Aeneas, a passage dear to me, I found myself reciting along with him.

"I, vanquished? I, abandon the fight?
   The fates forbid me. They never stopped Minerva
   from gutting the Argives' fleet by fire
   and drowning all of them..."

Who could resist Virgil's oratory? By that conduit the terrible silence between me and my father was bridged and we took to passing the book back and forth and reading alternate passages to each other every evening.

It was during one of these readings that I first noticed Papa stealing glances at Zaira and she at him. Through my sleepy eyes and ears, I discerned the current that flowed between them, sluggish at first but rising to great turbulence as the weeks went by.

Alert behind my closed eyes, I could feel on my own skin the flush that suffused Zaira's flesh. And my sharp ears caught the crackling hush in the air between their murmurs.

I never saw them touch. I do not believe they ever did embrace. For two worldly people—and both had seen and done much in their lives—they were remarkably innocent in pursuit of their love... much good it did them. All kinds of lewd behavior was later hinted at by La Nonna and her cohorts. But that was yet to come.

For the time, the affair was secret to all but me. In my dreams I saw Zaira lying beside Papa in Mama's old bed in Mantova, the two of them as beautiful as ancient statues in their nakedness. Those were sweet dreams to me.

But by day my spirit languished. Since the day of the beating I had been possessed by intermittent nausea and an inability to keep solid food on my stomach. Never a plump child, I had begun to resemble a wraith clad in my black mourning garment. Still, I could not abide the thought of being seen by one of La Nonna's doctors. Each time Papa brought up the subject, I wept so wildly that he did not have the heart to pursue it.

My salvation came from a most unexpected quarter: Papa's ailing brother, Joseph, whom I hardly knew as he had been confined to his room by chronic ill health since we arrived. Then one day he took a sudden turn for the worse and on his account the finest doctor in all of Italy was invited to attend him. "The finest." That is how my grandmother characterized the prodigy when she requested the entire *famiglia* to be present for his examination of my uncle.

As long as he was not about to lay hands on me, I was eager to get a good look at this paragon reputed to combine the genius of physician, philosopher, and scholar within his one sagacious person. I had heard him lauded for the philosophical *dispute* he engaged in all over the peninsula as frequently as for his miraculous cures. And all this was doubly amazing since he had not yet attained the age of thirty years.

The prodigy did not disappoint. A giant of a man, his *berretta* barely cleared the lintel when he entered the sickroom. Even La Nonna's hefty Giorgio, who ushered him in, was dwarfed by the august presence presented to us as Leone del Medigo.

His first move, after making a courtly bow to the crowd assembled to see him do his magic, was to stride to the window and throw open the shutters. The effect was as if a thunderbolt had hit the room. Everybody knew that Uncle Joseph's windows must never, never be opened for fear that in his weakened state a chill might carry him off.

Aunt Dorotea rushed across the room and fairly threw herself at the window in an effort to shut it tight once more. But the great physician prevented her by simply placing his massive girth between her and the opening and thus barring her way to the shutters.

"But he will die, he will die of the chilly air," she cried.

"Nonsense, woman," he corrected her, leaning out to fasten the shutters so that they would stay open. "The fetid air in this room will kill him faster than any draft. Let the poor man breathe."

"But maestro, my husband's weak chest..." she protested.

"No buts, madonna," he cut her off. "God has given us the early-morning air so that we may breathe in its freshness. We must allow the patient to do God's will. From now on, Joseph is to sit in a chair outside in the morning sun each day for an hour."

"But he cannot walk," Aunt Dorotea protested.

"My son's limbs are weak," La Nonna added.

"He can walk if you help him to walk," the physician retorted firmly. "What you are helping him to do now is to become an invalid by keeping him a prisoner in this bed. Like all other members of the human body, the limbs are meant to be used. When Nature sees that any member no longer serves the body, she causes that useless thing to atrophy. If you wish to keep your faculties, you must exercise them. Use it or lose it," he quoted from the Latin, then immediately focused his penetrating stare upon La Nonna once more and asked in his most stern manner, "Why do you suppose that men no longer have tails or horns?"

"That is God's doing, maestro," she replied. "And not for us to question. But I hear little of God from you. Where is He in all this talk of Nature?"

"Remember that He created Nature in all of her wonder in six days," the physician replied patiently, as if instructing a backward child. "And that He looked around on the seventh day and was pleased with what He saw. What He saw, madonna, was Nature. And, since Nature pleased Him so well, do you not agree that Nature should please you and me equally well?"

After that a small, almost cursory nod was all it took to clear the room. Aunt Dorotea was allowed to stay, and one serving maid. The rest of us filed out obediently, my grandmother as meek as the rest.

The moment we were alone together, Zaira embarked on a paean of praise to the great physician—his sagacity, his kindness, his authority. "If ever I have need of a doctor, I pray to God to send me Messer Leone. Did you see his eyes, Grazia? So wise. So kind."

Of course I had noticed those extraordinary eyes. But what impressed me most was the way he stood up to La Nonna, and I said so. "He wasn't disrespectful, either. Nor disputatious. Yet he made her look a perfect fool," I noted.

"Such a giant of a man he is, yet so gentle." Zaira continued her rapture. "I wager you he has the touch of a woman."

"How can you tell that?" I inquired.

"Did you see the way he held his hands? Drooping slightly. That always indicates a gentle touch in a man," she informed me. "A doctor like that would never hurt his patient. And they say that when it comes to diagnosis he is the finest physician in all of Italy. It was Maestro Leone, you know, who treated Lorenzo dei Medici in his last attack of gout and stopped the pain. Such an honor for the Jews." She paused and stared at me fixedly. "Yes, Leone del Medigo is a physician I would trust with my life."

Her words echoed a chord already plucked within me. This amazing giant would cure me of my dyspepsia and melancholy. I knew it.

"I would indeed be a fool to refuse if he agrees to see me," I told her with full confidence. "Please take him the message that I humbly request his attendance."

Then I sat back to await the prodigious physician in whom I had recognized my guardian angel.

7

T HE RENOWNED LEONE DEL MEDIGO ARRIVED AT MY
sickroom followed by a much smaller retinue than had
accompanied him on his visit to Uncle Joseph. Only my
father and La Nonna, Aunts Dorotea and Sofronia, two servants, and Zaira accompanied him.

Taken by a fit of shyness, I buried my head in my pillows at
the sight of them.

"I hear you have not been well of late, Madonna Grazia." His
voice came to me in a tone quite unlike the resonant one he
had employed when addressing the *famiglia*, a low tone meant
for my ears alone, which won me over at once.

Without being asked, I turned my face from the pillow and
looked up into those heavy-lidded, all-seeing eyes.

"May I try to help you overcome your debilitation?" he asked
with an air of grave courtesy owed to a duchess at the very
least.

I bobbed my head up and down to signify my agreement.

"Very good. Now then…" He turned to the assembled company. "You may go about your business, all of you. But you…"
He pointed to Zaira as if he had selected her quite at random.

"You will please stay in the room for modesty's sake."

They stood rooted to the spot, not so much recalcitrant as stunned. To dismiss La Nonna in such a manner was unheard of. But he appeared to be quite unmindful of the irregularity of his behavior. He simply repeated, "Go now, all of you. Out!" — like a kindly schoolmaster shooing his charges out to play.

Of course, they went. Certainly his fame as a healer lent him authority. But it was his fame as a scholar that gave him *gravitas*. Why else do we train physicians at universities but to add wisdom to their skills and thus to distinguish them from surgeons, who are, after all, nothing more than butchers of human bodies?

Mind you, it did not detract from the great man's presence that he knew how to dress to perfection the part of the celebrated physician-scholar. No shabby or threadbare dog fur for Messer Leone. Only the finest ermine trimming for his capacious robe, a full-length garment of rich black stuff trimmed with bands of scarlet. On his fingers, heavily begemmed rings. And on his feet, gilded spurs like a knight's. This was the imposing personage who sat down beside me on the bed and asked after my state of health.

"Do you suffer pain?"

I answered shyly that I did not suffer pain.

"Lassitude? Cramp in any limb? An ache in the belly?"

"Only this wretched nausea," I explained. "And then I vomit."

"In the morning or evening? Or at dawn?" he asked, waiting patiently for my answer and listening attentively when I gave it. This scrupulous attention to the patient formed the core of Judah's famous "bedside manner," sought by princes and kings, an intensity of interest rivaled only by the rapt attention of a lover in contemplation of his love. And, as with all Judah's patients, it brought out such trust in me that I found myself blurting out before I knew it the fear that had been gnawing away in me since my malady began, and which I had confided to no one.

"Do you think I have gravel and stones like Uncle Joseph?" I asked him. "Or a tumor in my belly? Is that why I am wasting away?"

"A tumor? Not likely. Growths and crystals rarely appear in people as young as yourself. How old are you, little madonna?"

"My name is Grazia, sir," I replied, as I had been taught to do. "And I am nine years old... almost."

"My name is Judah." He did not volunteer his age. No matter. Anyone over fifteen years of age was old to me.

"Now that we have introduced ourselves," he resumed, "we will get down to business. In a moment, I will ask for a sample of your urine. There is much to be learned from that..."

"And my blood, sir. Will you bleed me?" I asked, uninhibited now in the expression of my secret fears. "Will you cut into my veins..."

"I don't believe so," he answered quite matter-of-factly. "The urine sample will tell me what I need to know. And an examination, of course." He gestured to Zaira to pull back the coverlet. "You have my word, I will not hurt you."

The examination was indeed painless. Even more remarkable, it was not humiliating. Judah did not touch my body with love, as the sentimental would have it, but with respect. And even when he probed my most intimate orifices, he performed that examination with such care that I did not—as is almost always the case with medical examinations—feel I had been violated.

When he finished, he ordered Zaira to cover me again and asked for a basin so that he might wash his hands. Now we were ready for the next phase: giving up the urine sample. Another potential humiliation. For try as I may, I could not squeeze out more than a drop or two. The damned stuff settled tenaciously in my bladder, refusing to come out no matter how I exhorted it. With a delicacy uncommon in physicians—or in men in general, for that matter—Judah chose that moment to leave the room, ostensibly to see to a remedy for Uncle Joseph but, in truth, to spare me the embarrassment of voiding my bladder in the presence of a stranger. Once he left, the task was accomplished expeditiously and I was able to greet him on his return with a full yellow beaker.

He went about his analysis of my urine in the same careful, patient manner that he had adopted when examining my body. First he placed the beaker directly under his nose and inhaled its aroma deeply. Next he dipped his finger into the liquid and dabbed a taste of it on his tongue; then another; and then another, licking his lips after each taste as if searching for some hidden essence.

Next, he poured a dram of it into a crockery dish and, withdrawing from his bag a vial of deep purple stuff, carefully poured exactly two drops of the purple liquid into the yellow. And he smiled when the mixture went green, just as the magician does when his turn is brought to a successful conclusion.

"I can assure you there is no tumor," he announced after all this was done. "Nor is there gravel or stone in your belly."

"But why then do I vomit up my food?" I asked.

"Ah, my dear." He sat down beside me once again. "If I knew the answers to all the questions beginning with 'why,' I would be Jehovah Himself and not a humble physician."

"But if you do not know what ails me, sir..." My voice trailed off. It seemed tactless in the extreme to say what was in my mind, that is, if he did not know the cause of my ailment, how could he cure it?

"Not to know the cause does not mean that one cannot effect a cure," he admonished me.

This was a form of thinking I understood well from my study of Aristotle's logic.

"How then shall you cure me, sir?" I asked, bolder by the minute.

"For one thing, I will prohibit all nasty-tasting medicines. No purges are to be allowed in this room. Not so much as a drop of cassia or rhubarb." Now a pen was secured, and ink and vellum, and I was ordered to copy my own diet. It was my first task as a scribe. And I still remember how he led off, almost gravely, as if to underline the importance of the undertaking. Item—a daily addition of *galinga* for its stimulating and heating properties and to warm and comfort the brain. Item—cinnamon in the wine, for it greatly comforts both a cold and humid stomach and a cold liver and expels the humors of the stomach.

Here he added in his most matter-of-fact tone that a liberal intake of cinnamon would encourage menstruation. "And the sooner the better for your health and spirit, little woman." I had no idea what he was talking about, never having heard the word "menstruation" before—it certainly had not come up in Aristotle, Cicero, and Pliny—and I was too embarrassed to ask the meaning of it.

There was also to be ordered for me a comfit from the apothecary called *tregea*. One dose a day, he explained, would encourage the flow of urine.

"Do you like fruits?" he asked.

I confessed that I did, mightily.

"Well then, write this: Almonds fresh and dried, as many as you will. Fresh and dried figs before a meal. Also grapes. But not afterwards. Melons in season before a meal. But"—he held his hand up in a commanding gesture—"be so courteous to me as to cast aside the fruits which are harmful—*baccelli*, apples, chestnuts, and pears."

I gave him my solemn word never again to so much as look upon a podded bean or an apple or a chestnut or a pear, a vow which I have since broken more times than I have honored it; for I believe that no fruit of this earth is harmful in moderation, a point of contention between me and the great physician.

But at that first meeting there was nothing in him or his prescriptions that did not command my fervid obeisance. My faith was rewarded almost at once by a dramatic improvement in my well-being. And in addition, the effects of his visit continued to brighten my life long after his departure.

As if by magic, four new horses appeared in the stable and our daily rides resumed. The oiled cloth that covered the schoolroom windows was removed, letting in the sounds of birds and the rays of the sun and the whispers of the breeze. I was witness to that dramatic moment, for La Nonna, in a sudden reversal, decreed that henceforth the girls of the household were to be instructed in the Hebrew language and Judaic history and practice. Not Talmud, mind you. Girls had no use for the sacred law. And there was to be no Latin. Certainly no Greek. Nothing so arcane as Aramaic nor as frivolous as French. Those romances which Dante calls "the most beauteous fables of King Arthur" were condemned out of hand by my grandmother as "incredible French lies." But I was back in the schoolroom. And, to add to the bouquet of my delights, La Nonna engaged that most excellent dancing master, Messer Ambrogio of Pesaro, who had served at the courts of Milano and Pesaro and had even been lauded in a terza rima poem by Filelfo of Firenze. The maestro came to us directly from the Estense *castello*, where he taught dancing to the Este children, Isabella, Beatrice, and the ducal heir, Alfonso.

Mind you, this particular blossom had its thorny side; for the appointment of Maestro Ambrogio was, in an offhanded kind of way, an insult to Zaira. She too was an experienced dancing teacher. And she had earlier offered her services to the household and been turned down.

My grandmother was nothing if not deliberate in her actions. She must by then have sniffed out the growing affection between my father and Zaira and I have no doubt that the wound to Zaira's pride in the matter of the dancing lessons was the opening feint in a farther-reaching plan to sever this threatening appendage from our family group.

But La Nonna was a shrewd old campaigner. Secure in the knowledge that nothing could come of the affair until Papa's year of mourning was up, she bided her time, waiting for the right moment to strike.

8

EVERYONE KNOWS THAT JEWISH PARENTS ADORE their firstborn son, often to the detriment of their other children. Yet, in the dei Rossi family it seemed that my father, the eldest, was despised by his parents almost to the point of loathing. I sensed that this unnatural malice had been provoked by an event of which I was ignorant. And to be sure, not long after we arrived at the Casa dei Rossi, my Aunt Dorotea inadvertently revealed in a dinnertime conversation that my father was not, after all, the eldest dei Rossi son. There had been another boy — the true firstborn — who died young.

Later my cousin Ricca, loose-lipped like her mother, let slip that a weakness for gambling had clouded Papa's early life in Ferrara, culminating in some dreadful catastrophe she could not bring herself to speak of. But all the pieces did not fall into place until a crisis in the lives of Mantova's Jews erupted which tore aside the curtain of secrecy that had hidden my father's early life from my view, and exposed the entire sordid mess.

Duke Ercole d'Este was at the center of it. Just before the celebration of Chanukah, he decided, after several decades of benign tolerance, to reinstate the wearing of the yellow badge by the Jews of Ferrara. This badge, a large circle of cloth sewn to the outer garments of Jews to signify their race, was meant to warn the Christian population against the temptations of consanguinity.

Why did the Duke choose that moment to reintroduce the hated thing? More than likely, sheer whimsicality. I can attest to the vagrant impulses that run riot in the blood of the Estes. Our patroness has inherited a sufficient measure of the family capriciousness to give me ample proof of it. Or perhaps there was an actual cause. The rains had hit our territory with unaccustomed force that autumn, flooding the forests and ruining the hunting season. That whim of nature could easily have moved a prince who loved the hunt to vent his spleen on whatever target came to hand, such as the Jews. Whatever the cause, a *grido* reinstating the wearing of the badge was promulgated and the *parnassim* of the Jewish community of Ferrara were soon at our portal begging my father to intercede for them.

To my surprise, my grandfather refused even to consider the proposal. "If the Duke will not be moved, he will not. And that is the end of it," he announced to the five men and the rabbi who had come to beg help.

"All very well for you, Ser Baruch, since you and your family are exempt from wearing the hated thing," one of the five snapped back. "But for us it is an unbearable mortification."

"To be marked with the same brand as the whores," added another. Indeed, it is the deepest of all humiliations for Jews to be forced to wear the same mark of identification as prostitutes.

"I will leave this town forever and migrate to the Holy Land rather than ask my wife to sew that accursed badge on my garments," one of the younger *parnassim* burst out.

"The Duke has retired to Belriguardo to wait out the rain," the rabbi explained in a more conciliatory tone. "We need someone to travel there who can command an audience... someone who has a way with him—"

"Not my son," Grandfather interrupted heatedly. "Not Daniele. I forbid it."

"He is our only hope," the rabbi responded gravely.

"Our children will be spat upon and cursed in the streets," cried the old man, on the edge of tears.

Once again the rabbi spoke: "The wearing of the badge always leads to trouble. It gives succor to those who believe that anything is allowable."

"There is no trouble in Ferrara." La Nonna's voice rose firmly over all. "And there will not be if you stick to your prayers and behave yourselves."

But the rabbi was not to be bullied. "You know, madonna, that Fra Bernardino is back in the district," he reminded her. "He surely will take this action of the Duke as a sign that Ferrara is a fertile ground on which to spread his slanders. And we all know what happened in Mantova this very year, when the Gonzagas gave the *frate* his way."

That arrow hit home, leaving La Nonna silent and my grandfather gazing heavenward, looking for guidance from above.

After allowing them a few moments to contemplate the possibility of another of Fra Bernardino's spectacles, the rabbi broke the silence. "We have collected a sum of ducats." He stepped aside to reveal two strongboxes at his feet.

"How many ducats do you have there?" Grandfather asked.

"Five hundred gold ducats," the rabbi whispered. "Enough to buy the Duke five altarpieces by the finest masters."

"I will match that sum with five hundred more," Grandfather offered, as easily as if he were offering them a barrel of oil or a packet of spices. "But I cannot allow my son to go to Belriguardo. That is asking too much."

"I will pray with him before he goes," the rov offered. "I will pray all night."

"And I."

"And I too."

"He will be purified by prayer," the rabbi went on. "He will go into the den of vipers and walk through it without being tempted."

"Amen," echoed throughout the room.

Now the rabbi strode forward and, placing his hands on Papa's shoulders, pronounced over him the ancient words of the benediction, "May God bless you and guard you..." *"Yiv aresh icha adonai..."*

When he finished, Papa turned to my grandfather and said, "I must go, Father. I must."

But Grandfather held back, refusing his permission.

Then, just when it appeared to me that we would all turn into stone waiting for some resolution, the rabbi beckoned to me, of all unlikely people. Wordlessly, he led me up to the bimah at the front of the synagogue, where women never dare to tread, and stood me before the Holy Ark. Was he planning to make a human sacrifice of me right there in my grandparents' private synagogue on an autumn day in the month of Ab?

Of course I knew that Jews have never countenanced human sacrifices, at least not since the binding of Isaac. But the pagans had reached deep into my imagination and although my mind knew that what I feared was impossible, my body trembled.

Seeing this, Papa rushed to my aid. "What are you doing to my daughter?" he demanded, pushing the rabbi aside. "Have you no better stratagem than to toy with the fears of a child?"

"I am not toying with your daughter, Daniele," the rabbi replied calmly. "It is the fate of this community that I seek to influence. And the Lord in His wisdom has shown me the way. I see now that this child is the key."

"You intend to send my granddaughter to plead with the Duke?" Grandfather demanded.

"No, sir," the rabbi retorted. "I mean to send this child and her brother along with their father to petition the Duke. For if anything will secure Daniele's honor, it is the witness of his little ones."

This bizarre idea, completely incomprehensible to me, was greeted by others in the gathering with loud approval. This time Grandfather did not instantly declare his opposition but instead pulled on his beard thoughtfully, as if the idea was worth considering.

But as always, it was my grandmother who finally decided. After waiting a few moments for her husband's response and seeing that none came forth, she strode up to the bimah and, placing her hand on my shoulders, announced, "So be it. The children will go with Daniele. We have wasted enough time. It is already two hours since the rising of the sun and the *banco* is not yet open. Let us all go to our tasks and be done with this."

THE ROAD TO BELRIGUARDO lies along the tops of the dikes that line the Po. From that vantage point the verdant fields of grain rose to meet us and wave us on our journey. In the year 1487 the devastation of the Venetian war was only a year past, yet already the natural fertility of the Po Valley had reasserted itself. Where else in Italy could one ride through league after league of fields burgeoning with grain a scant year after they had been burned to the ground in a devastating war?

Sited on a commanding rise in the midst of this paradise stood Belriguardo, built in the last century by an Este ancestor as an outpost in Ferrara's defense system. Rising out of the mist, it was a structure from the *Reale di Francia* come to life. Everything about it spelled romance: the four tall towers from which a maiden might gaze wistfully down at her paladin; the long approach lined with an unbroken row of tall poplars, stiff as sentinels; the great surrounding wall that Papa told us measured 383 steps around and was still unbreachable. And, most wonderful to our eyes, an enormous rectangular fishpond, whose length matched the row of poplars on the opposite side of the approach, illuminated, as it were, by the flashing silvery tails of its fishy inhabitants as they scurried and jumped in the clear water.

Now, I thought to myself, I know why they call these places *delizie*, for this fanciful approach was truly a delight.

The huge entrance gate displayed a different facet of the Este style — majesty. Intricately wrought of iron, it was sheltered by a terra-cotta roof mounted on four columns, two of white marble, two of red. These embellishments, Papa explained to us, had been added recently by Duke Ercole, whose taste ran heavily to columns. Ferrara was stuffed with them during his rule. I found them most imposing.

We made our entrance, still mounted, through the west tower and thence into a courtyard as big as a meadow, with a paved brick road running through it. On this path, we dismounted. And there we stood—*inside the castle*.

Papa took it all in stride. Showing his familiarity with the place, he pointed out to us the features of the ground floor: on our left the wine cellars and the *cancellaria*; on our right the kitchens, dispensary, and barbershop. Above us the *piano nobile* was bordered all around by an open loggia which, Papa told us, gave access to the family's rooms and seven guest suites with servants' quarters attached. That servants should have their own quarters was a new notion to me. In the houses in which I had lived servants slept where they could—on landings or in corners or if lucky on trundle beds in our rooms. As I had suspected, life in castles was of a very different order from life in houses, even grand houses like the Casa dei Rossi.

In due course the illustrious Duca himself came forth to greet us. To me he was a fabulous presence so beyond my world that I failed to notice his ordinary human flaws, such as his limp or the sardonic curl of his mouth. He was all in black, the better, I daresay, to display the magnificence of his jewelry: a long heavy gold chain (which must have been worth a thousand ducats); a pendant carved from a giant pearl and set with what seemed to be a thousand sparkling diamonds; innumerable rings; and most impressive of all, a little clock he wore on his wrist. As the child of *banchieri*, I was not unaccustomed to the sight of jewels but I had never seen anything like that little wrist clock.

Noticing my fascination, the Duke beckoned me closer so that I might have a good look at it. He even took it off his wrist and invited me to hold it in my hand, the better to watch the time go by. However capricious the man was, he was also capable of true kindness. In that, his favorite daughter, our Madonna Isabella, takes after him.

Now came the time for Papa to explain the purpose of his visit. He began by lauding the Duke for his bounty, his goodness, his generosity and most especially his generosity to his Jewish subjects, a piece of flattery which to me rang false, although it did get Papa to his point: the hated yellow badge.

"I suspected that might be the matter which drew you to me, Daniele." Although the Duke's lips widened in a smile, his eyes remained cold. "But much as I might wish to please you, I cannot rescind my order. I have given my sacred word to Fra Bernardino. It was he who prayed for our cause night and day and turned the tide for us against the Venetians. In return I promised to grant him any wish his heart desired. And what he desired of me was the restoring of the yellow badge."

On the face of it, this unequivocal rejection put an end to the dialogue. But no. It turned out to be only the beginning of the negotiations. After a few more rounds of the polite palaver that passes for conversation in courts, Papa stopped himself in midsentence, slapped his thigh, and cursed lightly. "*Dio mio, the gift. I have forgotten the gift.*"

At the word "gift," the Duke brightened considerably.

"The community of Jews wishes to make a tribute to Your Magnificence," Papa announced, as he summoned the grooms who stood behind him with the saddlebags. "A reminder of our service to you in the past and of our wish to serve you in the future."

"There are those who might say this was a bribe to persuade me to rescind the *grido* of the badge," the Duke commented.

"We live in corrupt times. Men are cynical today." Papa paused to sigh for the loss of innocence in our time. "It would pain me to take these casks full of golden ducats back to my people and tell them that their gift has been spurned."

"Nor would I for the world offend my Jews, who, as you rightly say, have often come to my aid in times of trouble." He paused. "Do you have a solution to offer, Daniele?"

"No, sir," Papa replied. "Unless..."

"You are thinking what I am thinking, are you not, my little son of Israel? A wager? Your gift against my *grido*? That way, fate will decide and no human agency can be called to account. What say you, Daniele? Do you have the nerve for it? Is luck on the side of the Jews today?"

"Whether luck is on our side remains to be seen, sir. But in answer to your first question, yes, I do have the nerve."

"I heard you had taken a pledge never to gamble again." The Duke smiled that sly smile of his.

"Like your vow to Fra Bernardino, that pledge must give way to a higher purpose, sir," my father answered smartly, causing the Duke to laugh out loud.

"By God and by Jesus you are quick, Daniele. I have missed your wit since you took that oath, indeed I have."

"And I have missed the honor of basking in your sun, sir," Papa answered gallantly.

"Well." The Duke sat up in his velvet chair, sprightly now and full of cheer. "Shall we begin?"

"At your command, sir," Papa answered.

"And what's your game? Still Zara?" the Duke asked, with what I felt to be a new malevolence in his tone.

"Zara, yes," Papa answered quietly. "Let it be Zara." It was the first time in my life I ever heard the word "Zara," but I knew from the moment it reached my ears that it was cursed.

A trestle table was assembled and covered with a green baize cloth like the one in the gambling booth at the market. At Duke Ercole's nod a silver cup and set of dice appeared.

The Duke shook out his hand a few times as if to limber his wrist. Papa remained still as a well. Then the Duke broke the silence with a curse.

"Damn the devil. We cannot play Zara, my friend. For we have no *barratiero*."

"Then we must find another game," Papa suggested.

"No. Zara it is," the Duke insisted. "That game has brought me luck before and will do so now. Here, you..." He beckoned to Jehiel, who was standing by quietly.

"No." Papa reached out and drew Jehiel to him protectively. The Duke's eyes widened. "Do you fear that the boy may catch your contagion, Daniele?" he asked, with the malevolent edge that had come into his tone since the dice were brought.

"Not my son," Papa replied quietly.

"Then who?" the Duke inquired.

"I will do it, sir," I volunteered, with no clear idea of what I was volunteering for.

"You?" The Duke laughed.

"Yes, sir," I answered. "I am almost nine years of age, sir. And I can quote all of Cicero's orations to the Romans *senza libro*."

"Is it true that the girl can recite all of Cicero without the book?" the Duke asked Papa, momentarily distracted.

"I believe so," Papa replied.

"Well in that case she is a rival to my illustrious daughter Isabella. And do you know Greek?" he asked me.

"No, sir," I answered. "I would dearly love to learn it but La Nonna, my grandmother, prefers us to study Hebrew."

A quick flash of the Duke's eyes told me that he understood something of my tribulations in the Casa dei Rossi.

"Well, my little prodigy." He beckoned me close. "Do you think you can perform the tasks of a *barratiero*?"

"I will try my best if such is needed by Papa...and by you, *illustrissimo* Duca." I had never addressed a duke before, but that seemed to be the way to do it.

"Even though you don't know what a *barratiero* is?"

"As Publius tells us, 'No one knows what he can do until he tries,'" I replied.

That made him laugh out loud and agree at once that I must be the *barratiero*, which I discovered meant the croupier. Then he put the three dice into the cup and instructed me how to run the game, not a complicated task but one that demanded good nerves and perfect control, as I was to find out. After a few practice rolls of the three dice, the Duke instructed me to begin. "And remember," he admonished me, "a vast fortune rides on your throw."

I placed the three dice in the cup and began to shake it. "Place your bets, gentlemen," I chanted in a shaky voice. "What numbers will you have?"

"Seven," Papa announced firmly.

"Nine!" the Duke snapped back. "Roll out the dice, girl."

With a trembling hand I shook the cup and threw the dice onto the green cloth. Out they rolled: a four, a second four, and a one.

"Zara!" The Duke's shout reverberated through the echoing audience hall.

Papa's shoulders sagged slightly. Beyond that I saw no sign that he was distressed or even disappointed. But the Duke gave free rein to his delight, clapping his hands and crowing over my father as if he had bested him in the most grueling joust.

"Too bad, Daniele. Too bad for the Jews. But you cannot deny I won fairly with your own daughter as the *barratiero*."

"Indeed I cannot, sir," Papa answered calmly. "The ducats are yours. You won them fairly."

"And the *grido* stands," the Duke reminded him, rubbing salt into the wound. "Now what say you to a drink of wine to celebrate my victory?"

"I would be honored, sir," Papa replied.

"And while we drink I will send a page to show the little ones my menagerie," said the Duke, once again the soul of kindness.

A snap of his fingers brought a pretty page, and before we knew it we were whisked up to the *piano nobile* on a staircase so grand—Jehiel counted forty-seven steps in all—that we had to stop for breath on the colonnaded landing. Still winded, we were hustled through a series of painted rooms, all with windows of glass, stuccowork fireplaces, and frescoed ceilings. This efflorescence of *lusso* brought a glow of excitement and pleasure to my little brother's face. His feet fairly danced along as we descended into the open fields behind the villa. But I had lost my spirit back in the Duke's *sala*. My mind kept returning to the fateful game of Zara and to what lay in store for Papa, an expectation so grim that I hardly noticed the exotics in the

Este menagerie—a tame wolf walking free, a panther in a cage, a giraffe.

It took a physical blow to jar me out of my preoccupation with Papa's fate, a sudden thwack to the kidney that knocked the breath out of me and sent me sprawling onto the grass. At first I thought I had been attacked by some wild thing. But when the page boy held up the cause of my discomfort, I managed a weak smile. What had laid me low was nothing but a small hard globe of skin—a tennis ball.

"The young princess has a strong stroke but a poor aim," the page remarked, indicating a green meadow beyond the menagerie where stood three young people with tennis rackets, two girls and a boy, lit by the sun. The boy interested me not at all—I cared only for princesses in towers—but I was fascinated by the smaller girl, the dark one, who had a quite un-princesslike petulance about her. By contrast the taller one shone in the sun like a true princess on account of the shower of red-gold hair that cascaded down her back, and her gracious smile.

Jehiel and I must have presented a strange sight to them: two small figures all in black from head to toe. But their ordinariness was even more incongruous to me. I could not accept what my eyes had told me: that, up close, princesses and princes were children just like ourselves.

"What did you think they would be?" Zaira asked when I confided this to her later. "Do you think they rise full-grown from the sea on the half shell like gods and goddesses?"

I admitted to some such expectation.

"Princes are not gods," Zaira stated firmly. "Nor even kings. Their children are born of as much travail as the children of lesser persons. And I daresay they bring their parents as much heartache and disappointment."

"No!" I protested. The notion of trouble in this paradise was not acceptable to me.

"Why no?" Zaira challenged me. "All parents love their children, expect much of them, and are doomed to be disappointed in them, royal or not. In fact children are valued by dukes much in the same way as they are by us Jews. Boys come first with them as with us. For it is the sons who carry on the family business, just as the sons of the *banchieri* do. And if you think the boys in Jewish families are spoiled," she went on, warming to her subject, "you should see the fuss they make in these castles when an heir is born. That boy Alfonso that you saw today was welcomed into the world as if his arrival were the coming of the Messiah."

"What about the princesses we saw?"

"The older one got quite a celebration, I hear," she replied. "Her name is Isabella and she is the firstborn. But when her sister, Beatrice, was born—that's the little dark one who hit you with the tennis ball—not a bell was rung. Furthermore, her mother, the Duchessa Leonora, took the children away to visit her father, the King of Napoli, when the little one was still a babe and left her there for seven years."

"Seven years!" That was a much longer exile than the one meted out to my baby brother, Gershom, removed to the care of a wet nurse but whom La Nonna promised back to us at the end of our year of mourning.

"So you see it isn't all sweetmeats and satins for these royals," Zaira pointed out.

But I did not believe her for one minute. Nor do I to this day. For I observe that the great ones of the world, for all that they endure certain miseries, are better clad, better fed, live longer, stay healthier, and in the main have a much happier time in life than do the common people. They say justice is more evenly dispensed in the next world. We shall see.

We found the Duke and Papa as we had left them, sipping wine, laughing and chatting. No question about it, my father possessed in abundance that *virtu* so prized in aristocratic circles: I saw not a shred of evidence of his terrible loss at the gaming table. At his prompting we thanked the Duke for his hospitality and prepared to take our leave. But before we had reached the portal of the *sala*, the Duke beckoned us back with an imperious gesture.

"Daniele, halt a moment." His voice rang out. "I have a proposal for you."

What now?

"It grieves me to see you return to your people with such a sad message. I am inclined to give you a second chance. What say you to one more round of Zara?"

"By all means," Papa agreed, without a moment's hesitation.

"Double or nothing." The Duke's words floated from his lips with the lightness of a feather.

"Double or nothing, sir?"

"If you win this time, I rescind the *grido*," the Duke explained.

"And if I lose?" Papa inquired mildly.

"Why, then you pay me two thousand golden ducats."

"It's a bet!" Papa's voice seemed to jump out of his throat of its own accord.

"You have a gallant heart for a Jew, Daniele." The Duke nodded his approval.

"Thank you, Excellency." Papa bowed.

Once again I was handed the three dice and the silver cup. This time my voice trembled when I called for the bets. And my hand shook as if palsied. And I could barely hear the numbers that they called for—the same seven and nine.

At the Duke's nod, I rolled out the dice.

Four dots. Then three dots. Then...

In my fear I must have thrown the cubes too fast. The last die went off the table and onto the floor.

"A seven! A seven!" Jehiel shouted. "Papa wins!"

"Not so fast, my boy." The Duke held up his hand in an imperious gesture. "This throw does not signify. For all three dice are not upon the table. We must play the turn again."

We turned to Papa for confirmation.

He bit his lip—just once. Then quietly he said, "So be it."

The Duke turned to me, a man of bronze. "This time take care, girl. You may have cost your people dear by your carelessness."

"It was but an accident such as I have witnessed many times

in the gaming booths," Papa contradicted him, heedless of protocol. Then to me: "Pick up the dice, Grazia."

I did so.

"Now announce the play," he ordered.

"Place your bets," I intoned.

Again Papa picked seven and the Duke nine.

Again I released the dice onto the cloth at the Duke's signal. But with perfect control this time.

The dice rolled out smoothly onto the cloth.

Two dots.

Three dots.

Two dots.

A total of seven, my father's number.

Across the table, he leaned forward and, in a husky whisper, pronounced the magic word: "Zara!"

With poorly disguised ill humor the Duke ordered the two small chests to be returned to Papa. But my father demurred.

"The gift was a sincere token of gratitude from the community of Jews, *illustrissimo*," he informed the Duke in honeyed tones. "I am certain they would wish you to keep it."

The Duke smiled a half smile. "A fine gesture, Daniele," he said. "Worthy of an honorable and ancient people. Tell them for me that I love my Jews as I love myself and that they have nothing to fear in Ferrara while I rule here."

"They will be gratified to hear it, sir," Papa replied. And with that final bit of rampant hypocrisy we took our leave.

Deceit is bred in princes. It is as much a part of their nature as breathing. I whose work it is to inscribe and archive Madonna Isabella's confidential correspondence, relearn this lesson each time my services are solicited to express her thoughts to her son Federico or convey his to her. The correspondence between this mother and son constitutes a veritable lexicon of double-dealing, evasion, and betrayal.

It is difficult to understand these people. So much of life is a game to them. Madama assures me that the discord between the Pope and the Emperor is only a family squabble between a loving father and his loving son. Remember, she counsels me, that the Holy Father is Christ's vicar on earth and that Charles V, even though he be Emperor of all the German lands and King of Spain as well, remains a devout son of the church. He has only unleashed Frundsberg to warn the Pope against an alliance with the French.

But try as I may, I cannot see this Charles V as a loving son to anyone. To me he seems obsessed by Francis of France and has shown himself quite prepared to beat the Pope into submission in order to secure him as an ally against France. To send a hardened campaigner like Frundsberg across the Alps—a military exploit not even attempted since the days of Hannibal—counts for more than a mere warning, I think. But what do I know of the minds of these high Christians who say one thing and do another and then refer to their religion as the justification?

I think you are more at home with them than I. As I see you making the rounds at Madama's soirees, bowing and bantering with such elan, I wonder if I have done right to bring you into this world. Ought I to follow Judah's pleading and send you off to Turkey where you will learn high principles and exemplary behavior at his knee? Do I, by keeping you here with me, risk turning you into one of them, into another Federico Gonzaga?

FROM DANILO'S ARCHIVE

TO MARCHESANA ISABELLA D'ESTE DA GONZAGA, PALAZZO COLONNA, ROMA
Most Illustrious Lady and Dearest Mother:

Frundsberg has done the impossible. He arrived at Brescia with his landsknechts two days ago. If Fortuna smiles on us he will choose to approach Milano by the northern route. If not, he will be in my territory within two days.

You advise me to remain above the quarrel between the Pope and the Emperor. But neutrality is easier to preach than to practice, Mother. I would gladly adulterate my urine with pig's blood in order to substantiate a claim of illness and thus avoid the demand for my services. But unfortunately my honorable father's success with that stratagem has, by now, been widely circulated. I fear that even a dull German would recognize the ploy. And I would become the laughingstock of the peninsula.

But never fear, I will find a way out of this dilemma. I am not my father's son for nothing.

Your son, Federico. (Written in cipher in his own hand) Mantova, November 21, 1526.

TO MARCHESANA ISABELLA D'ESTE DA GONZAGA, PALAZZO COLONNA, ROMA

Salute me, Mother!

I have walked into the lion's den. I have put my head into the lion's mouth. Fortune favors the bold. The lion did not eat me. Our neutrality is preserved.

It was but a day's journey to the Imperial encampment south of the Po. I traveled with only a few men, none of them armed, and carried in my wagons gifts of oil, wine, cheese and gunpowder, modest gifts befitting a pauper prince. Frundsberg was grateful for the food but seemed most impressed by the gunpowder.

At his request I granted him permission to pass unmolested through the Mantovan territory and declared myself willing to share what little stocks we have. But I warned him that we have suffered two crop failures in the past two years and that our own people are going hungry.

In these delicate negotiations I did my best to emulate my honored father. I pronounced myself desolated by my inability to respond more generously. I lamented the dilapidated state of our palaces, the infertility of our fields, and the barrenness of our flocks. I confessed that all of our plate and most of our treasures were in pawn with the Jews.

My confessions touched the old man's heart. I became like a son to him. He assured me he has no designs on our state. He

asks only for enough to feed his men as they march through on their way to Lombardia.

I have written to the Holy Father to acquaint him with my version of this meeting before he hears of it from someone not well disposed toward us. I added my advice—and I solemnly urge you who have the Pope's ear to press this point upon him yourself—to make his peace with the Emperor and pay off these German landsknechts now. If he is as hard-pressed for ready money as he says, let him sell off a few red hats. But let him not hesitate. He must act before this new Imperial army is grafted onto Bourbon's force at Milano.

You have known my cousin, Bourbon, since he was a child. You know he is not a man to be contained by any siege for very long. Sooner or later, with or without Frundsberg's aid, he will break through the Milano blockade and the two halves of the Emperor's army will be joined. From that moment on, all Italy stands in peril, even the holy city where you now reside. Believe me, Roma carries no sacred weight in the hearts of the landsknechts. They call themselves Christians but what they are is Lutherans who hate the Holy Catholic Church and mean to bring it down.

Most respectfully, Excellency, it is time for you to think of returning to Mantova, before any of these dire possibilities come to pass. This suggestion comes from one who cherishes you and would not for all the world see you exposed to danger.

Your loving son, Federico. (Written in cipher in his own hand)

Mantova, November 25, 1526.

9

L A Nonna was not one of those who perpetrate cruelty for its own sake, nor was she uncharitable. She and my grandfather tithed themselves rigorously to help poor Jews, widows, and orphans. Her harshness came not out of a lack of generosity but out of an excess of zeal in the cause of righteousness.

A humanist education might have taught her to heed the old Greek motto "Above all, no zeal." But she was uneducated and priest-ridden. To her the Greeks and Romans were degenerate pagans and Moses' law was revealed truth. With the conniv-ance of the ignorant rabbis with whom she surrounded herself she came to feel that she was one of those chosen to regulate, judge, and punish those who came under her scrutiny.

Had she been less resolute she would have been less effect-ive — thus, less cruel. But alas, nature had endowed her with a strong will and a shrewd mind. When she undertook a cam-paign she was invincible. What a general she would have made! Her strategy was faultless, her timing impeccable. She did not need Caesar's *Commentaries on the Gallic Wars* to tell her that spring is the best time to launch an offensive.

Come back with me now to the spring of the year 1488 and watch her battle plan unfold . . .

We are at morning prayers in the women's gallery of the dei Rossi private synagogue. Below us, half hidden by the punched brass screen, a bright yellow turban stands out in a sea of black skullcaps.

Who is the owner of this exotic headdress? I ask my cousin Ricca. She knows everything that happens in this house.

"He is Maestro Gedaliah, a *penumbra* from Roma."

"A *penumbra*?"

"A marriage broker. One of those who works the northern fairs looking for husbands for Jewish brides."

"Oh, a *shadchan*," I say.

"Haven't you heard, stupid? *Shadchans* are out of fashion. A *penumbra* charges a percentage of the dowry and he guarantees satisfaction or your money back. A clever one can find a husband for any girl, even a goose like you."

"Me?" La Nonna's plan revealed itself to me in an instant. She hated me and wished me gone. What better way to rid herself of me than through an early marriage, arranged by a Roman flesh peddler who guaranteed satisfaction or your money back?

Goose. Ricca's word stuck in my head. Like a goose before the skewering, I was to be cleaned and stuffed for presentation at the marriage table.

All through the day I felt Maestro Gedaliah's eyes following me. When we came back from our morning ride, he was at the door of the *banco* peering out as if searching for me. Halfway through our lessons, he appeared in the schoolroom.

Now there were many cozier places in the dei Rossi house. Why else had Maestro Gedaliah elected to climb up to the attic and visit the schoolroom but to scrutinize me? All through my recitation from the *Kiddushin* I felt his hovering presence, an angel of death preparing to carry me off.

Due to our mourning we did not celebrate Purim with the usual games and plays that year. But at the modest supper La Nonna put out in honor of Esther's triumph over Haman, I noticed that Maestro Gedaliah had been accorded a place of honor between my grandparents, a clear indication that they had serious business with him...such as the marriage of a granddaughter. And sure enough, halfway through the meal I heard my name called out by my grandmother. *Dio*, I was about to be auctioned off at Lübeck like a cow or a pig. My life would be over before it had begun, terminated in the marriage bed of some old, smelly German.

I walked the length of that table feeling like Persephone being borne off to the underworld, with the sound of Ricca's giggle filling in for the call of the Sirens. Desperately, I cast about for someone to save me. But Papa was absent in Padova that week. And my next-best comfort, Zaira, was helping in the kitchen.

"Grazia, my dear." My grandmother's hand fell on my shoulder like an iron weight. "Maestro Gedaliah is most impressed by your accomplishments." The little man bobbed up and down in energetic agreement. "He tells me that your mastery of the Hebrew tongue is quite remarkable for a girl of your age."

This may have been the first time in my life—it certainly was not the last—that I wished myself rid of my damnable brains. What good were my accomplishments if all they did was raise my value in the matrimonial marketplace?

"And of course, she will be a beauty in her time...just give her a year or two." At this, the *penumbra's* little red beard actually twitched.

"Grazia..." La Nonna poked me in the ribs. "Do you not thank Maestro Gedaliah for the compliment?"

Now it was my turn to bob up and down. That done, I was dismissed to wallow in my misery.

Later, when Zaira appeared, she too was summoned to an audience with the *penumbra*. I was unable to hear from my place at the table. But what I saw was a dumb show that told its own story: the little Roman sniffing Zaira like a dog in heat; my grandmother, her beady little eyes narrowed with calculation; and, standing between them, Zaira, shuffling from one foot to the other with uncharacteristic want of balance and staring fixedly at the floor, almost in the style of Rabbi Abramo's ideal Jewish maiden who never lifts her eyes to search for her beloved until he is presented to her by her father. Somehow, in the past months, the Casa dei Rossi had subdued her proud spirit.

When Zaira was dismissed, La Nonna and Maestro Gedaliah turned as one to look after her. La Nonna was smiling a thin smile. The *penumbra* was eating up the retreating figure as if she were a succulent roast...legs, breast, cheeks. I saw Zaira consumed by that old pimp and hated him.

That night I cried for my mother and prayed to God to take me up to heaven to be with her. I must have cried out loudly in my sleep, for when I awoke, I was in Zaira's arms and she was crooning softly to me.

In that moment of intimacy, I blurted out all my fears of the day. "They mean to marry me off to a German and send me away and I will never see you again or my brothers..."

"Wherever did you get such an idea?" She seemed genuinely puzzled.

"That's why they called Ser Gedaliah. To find me a husband..." I babbled on.

"No, Grazia, no. It is I who am to be married."

"To Papa?" Now it was my turn to be confused.

"No." She shook her head as if to shake off the thought. "I am to be married to a stranger. Maestro Gedaliah will find me someone suitable. That is why your grandparents brought him here."

"For you?"

She nodded. "It is all arranged."

I must admit that my first reaction was a deep surge of relief that I was not the object of the *penumbra*'s services. But it was quickly followed by an equally intense surge of compassion for Zaira.

"But you don't have to do it," I insisted. "You can refuse."

"No, no," she replied. "It is all arranged."

"But I want you to marry Papa," I insisted.

"That is not to be. Your grandmother will not have it."

"And if you refuse?" I asked again.

"I cannot. It is all arranged. They have given me a dowry of five hundred ducats, enough gold to buy me a lawyer or a doctor—a rabbi at the very least, so Maestro Gedaliah says."

"You'd rather have a lawyer than Papa?"

"Oh, Grazia..." She paused as if about to confide in me, then shook her head again and repeated, as if she had memorized the words, "I am to be married. It is a wonderful opportunity for me, an orphan and a widow, to be endowed with such a dowry and a fine new wardrobe. Your grandparents have been most generous. They are my benefactors."

Sending her off to some foreign place to marry a stranger did not seem to me such a benefaction, but something in Zaira's eyes told me that she was not an entirely unwilling victim of my grandmother's "generosity." Perhaps she was overwhelmed by the forces arrayed against her. Perhaps she had used up her reserves of strength during our harrowing escape from Mantova or, since then, defending us against the cruelties of the dei Rossi household. However it had happened, we dei Rossis had, I believe, taken the spirit from her and, in return, had proffered five hundred gold ducats.

AFTER THAT, NOTHING WENT as I had hoped. The evening trysts in my bedchamber between Zaira and my father ceased. Now, Zaira contrived to be otherwise engaged when Papa came to bid me goodnight. Had it not been for the air of sadness that enveloped them both, you might have concluded that they cared not a fig for each other.

I told myself that Papa was obliged to live out the mourning period in unimpeachable correctness and that everything would change when the year was up. This fiction sustained me through the early months of spring. But although hope springs eternal in the breasts of the young, patience does not. In spite of my efforts to submit to the delay of my gratification, my soul cried out for release from the joyless prison that La Nonna had made of the Casa dei Rossi.

By her order our seder that year ran its course unenlivened by so much as a single song. Seeing Jehiel all in black when he asked the Four Questions—he was still the youngest in the company and thus the honor remained with him—reminded me of his gorgeous appearance the previous year at Mantova in his little red boots. Gazing around to see if anyone else shared my nostalgia, I noticed for the first time that our Mantovan *famiglia* had eroded gradually within the year, the way a promontory falls into the sea, stone by stone.

Davide, our old tutor, sat even more silent than usual, barely mouthing the prayers and invocations. Dania, at his side, had grown yellow and old, humiliated by her husband's diminished status as a tutor of girls. No longer did she interrupt Papa—for Papa himself rarely spoke. Nor was Monna Matilda there to put her in her place. That lady had died of a terrible headache early in the year and her twins had been separated—one of them sent off as apprentice to a wool merchant in Reggio, the other soon to begin his clerk's apprenticeship at our family *banco* in Ostellato. Deprived of his helpmeet and about to lose the company of his last child, the *shohet* shuffled about the place, bewildered and out of the stream of life.

A happier fate had visited Cecilia, the clerk's daughter. She got her wish—a husband, one of the couriers who carried the family's messages and goods from branch to branch. She complained bitterly that he was never home, but we had ample evidence that he must have managed to come to earth at least once, for when she left to take up residence in the Venetian territory, she was manifestly pregnant.

Sitting at the long Passover table in the grand *sala* surrounded by strangers, I was overwhelmed by a terrible sense of loss. Mama, of course. Mama first. And Monna Matilda. And Cecilia, off to the Veneto. And the twins, who had never spent a night apart, torn asunder. Who would be the next to go?

Late one day in June, Maestro Gedaliah reappeared at our gate all smiles. That evening in the garden, La Nonna made her announcement. Her "adopted daughter" Zaira was officially betrothed to a merchant of Ratisbon.

No time for long goodbyes. The horses came to fetch her and Ser Gedaliah before sunup. La Nonna's work was accomplished. Overnight, the last and strongest link with our Mantovan past was severed from our *famiglia* as neatly as if the public executioner had done the deed with his axe.

Stunned by the suddenness of the maneuver, I stood mute as the groom boosted her up onto the saddle. She raised her arm in a salute. Then all at once, her horse reared and, although she managed to keep her seat, her riding hat, a fine, rust-colored felt with a red plume, fell to the ground. The groom reached to pick it up. Too late. The horse's hoof claimed it first, smashing it into the mud. Zaira looked down, shrugged, dug in her spurs, and galloped off.

All I had of her now was the hat. I grabbed for it greedily and bore it away upstairs, vowing to myself to keep it always as a memento of one who had loved me so valiantly. But the next day it disappeared from my room. I never saw it again.

IO

ONCE ZAIRA WAS GONE, MY FATHER REFUSED TO speak of her. My questions about her met with cold rebuffs. When her name was mentioned in company, his face went masklike, as if she were dead. And very soon he began to frequent the Duke's court as he had in bygone days. He was at Belriguardo. At Belfiore. At the Schifanoia Palace on the edge of town. He was once again a part of the Duke's inner circle. And the Duke and his *intimati*, as everyone knew, had nothing better to do with their time than to ride around the park, dabble in astrology—and gamble.

When the calamity came, it blew up like one of those violent tornadoes that afflict the Tuscan plains, gaining intensity slowly as the skies darken until at last they swallow up all the land and everything on it.

This whirlwind began early one morning, before the three iron locks on the front door had been unlatched, with a barrage of knocks and shouts from the street below. The shouting was so loud that even up in the schoolroom we heard the gravelly male voices below shouting, "Open up, you Jews, in the name of the Duke."

Famiglia and servants alike streamed down the main stairway, garments unbuttoned, faces unwashed, to discover the cause of the commotion. We reached the *cortile* just in time to see three armed brutes from the *bargello's* department lay hands on my grandfather and accuse him of crimes against the Duke.

When my father pressed them to name the charge, one of them raised a short dagger and threatened to cut off his Jewish nose for his insolence. Then they were off, dragging my dignified grandfather after them as if he were a sack of millet.

My grandmother was the first to regain composure. Within moments, she had Giorgio ring his bell for silence, and after the din had subsided, she walked up a few steps of the great stair with her accustomed bold step, and from there addressed the gathering in a loud, unwavering voice.

"I order you all—family and servants—to go to your accustomed tasks at once. The *banco* will open on time. The children will attend their lessons. Dinner will be prepared as usual. And I will get to the bottom of this matter. Go now and shush your chatter." She gathered up the folds of her *gamorra* and ascended to the *sala* followed by her steward, her rabbi, and her retinue of ladies. Almost as an afterthought, she beckoned my father to follow.

That was the last we saw of Papa for two days. He simply dropped out of sight without an explanation or even a goodbye. When we inquired, we were put off by vague admonishments to "be good children and pray"—a poor substitute for the assurance we so desperately wanted that our only remaining parent was not gone forever.

The result? We became prey to my cousin Ricca's wicked inventions. The evening after Papa's disappearance, she beckoned us into a dark corridor and informed us that she knew why Grandfather was taken and our father fled.

"Uncle Daniele has committed a terrible crime," she whispered with a wicked gleam in her eye, "but don't ask me to speak of it. It is too terrible..."

"You must tell us, Ricca," I begged. "He is our father."

"No." She shook her head vigorously. "No. I cannot speak of it for shame."

Jehiel was the more effective persuader. "If you don't tell us at once, I'll wring your neck until you choke," he warned her, with all the assurance of someone who meant what he said.

To my astonishment, Ricca's courage collapsed at the threat. "Very well," she conceded. "I'll tell you." Then she added, with a dash of malice, "But you'll wish you hadn't heard. Your father has run away. And poor Grandfather is being held hostage for him in the dungeon of the *castello*."

"Why has he run away, Ricca?" Jehiel pressed her. "What terrible crime has he committed?"

"That's the shameful part." She lowered her eyes. "It pains me so to speak of it."

Jehiel took her by the shoulders and gave her a little shake. "Speak of it," he ordered.

"Your father has been keeping a woman—*a Christian woman!*—in a house near the public baths."

"I don't believe you," Jehiel announced. "Who told you?"

"Our porter heard it from the *bargello's* man," she replied, then added, "I suppose you know that last year a Florentine Jew was beheaded and burned in the Piazza della Signoria for only one encounter with a Christian woman. So you can imagine the punishment for keeping a Christian woman all the time ..."

Had we had the wit to think, we would have recognized her story as a fabrication. If Papa had been found out keeping a Christian woman, then he, not Grandfather, would have been arrested. But reason had fled our minds. That night, I dreamed of a headless body trussed and roasting on a spit, while a fat woman with huge, pendulous breasts and a cross around her neck slowly turned the handle.

It was my grandmother who finally, after two days of silence, rescued Jehiel and me from this miasma of rumor and fear. Dour and harsh as always, she wasted no time on words of sympathy. But, say this for her, you could believe what she told you.

"You will want to know that your father is safe. He is," she began. "But he has gotten us all into serious trouble. Once again his cursed gambling is at the root of it."

This explanation had the ring of truth to it.

"It appears that he is heavily in debt to his patrician friends, and has resorted to that most heinous of all crimes — coin clipping."

At least he was not keeping a Christian woman in a house near the baths.

"That is not the worst of it," my grandmother went on. "The manner in which your father committed this offense has tarred many innocent victims with his guilty brush. Every Jewish business in Ferrara is closed by the Duke's order. Your grandfather languishes in the dungeon at this very moment for his part in the mischief, even though he knew nothing of it and passed the coins in perfect innocence. Your father has gone to see the Duke at Belfiore and confess his guilt."

Was this really true? Had Papa allowed Grandfather to take the punishment rightly coming to himself? I could not believe it.

"Do you doubt my word, Grazia?" I hung my head.

Now came a quiet mutter from the other side of the table. "My papa would not do such a thing. My papa is an honorable man."

"Some fine gentleman to let an old man take his punishment for him. And that man his own father." La Nonna's pockmarks were showing dangerously white against her flushed skin.

Dio, I thought, she is going to beat us. But no. The accusation with the ring of truth about it was punishment enough.

My father returned from his audience at Beiriguardo the next morning. He galloped into the *cortile*, sweated and filthy from riding all night, but triumphant, having achieved Grandfather's pardon. The old man would be released from the dungeon that afternoon. And the next morning the Jewish *banchi* and shops would be permitted to reopen. Papa himself was, he explained to us, "the most fortunate of men." The Duke had granted him full clemency—an unprecedented act of mercy.

"I told them you were not a cheater." Jehiel danced along happily at Papa's side. "I knew you would never do a wrong thing, Papa."

"Ah, but I did, my son. I am guilty of coin clipping. Furthermore, I allowed my father to go to prison for it. It would be wrong of me to deny my guilt. And useless. For I am to be tried for my crime."

"But you said 'full clemency,'" I interrupted heatedly. "And that means you are forgiven, does it not?"

"By the Duke, yes. But he has remanded me to my own people for justice and punishment. I am now bound over to the Wad Kellilah."

"That is not fair!" I cried. "He gives with one hand and takes away with the other."

"Stop your ranting," Papa ordered me severely. "I have done a grievous thing. I deserve to be punished."

"Just for clipping a little bit of gold off the edge of some coins?" I asked.

"In any other city in Italy I would have lost my head for clipping that little bit of gold. Or at least had both my hands cut off. Here, look at this." He reached into his pocket and handed me a gold coin. "What do you see?"

"I see a ducat," I answered stupidly.

"Give it to Jehiel," he ordered me impatiently. "Maybe he has better vision. What do you see, my son?"

"I see a strange bird, an eagle with two heads and two bodies," the little boy replied.

"That is the Este double eagle," Papa explained. "Now turn the coin over and tell me what you see on the other side."

"I see a picture of the Duke, the one who taught us how to play—" He stopped short before uttering the cursed word.

"So we have the Duke's emblem and the Duke himself. Now, Madonna Grazia . . ." He turned to me, still stern. "Why do you suppose the Duke's picture is on the coin?"

"Because he is vain," I answered, which earned me a smile.

"That picture stands for the Duke himself, who guarantees personally the amount of gold the coin contains. Now reverse the metaphor. When I tamper with the Duke's currency it is akin to tampering with the man himself."

This line of reasoning baffled me and I must have shown it, for Papa once again turned irritable. "Sit still, Grazia, and listen carefully. The Emperor himself granted to the Duke's ancestor the privilege of minting Ferrarese coins. From that time on, the Estes' lifeblood—their credit—has depended upon the integrity of the coinage. Do you know what that means?"

"It means that the coin is exactly what it pretends to be—no more, no less. Like a man of integrity," I replied readily.

"That is why I tell you that to clip the Ferrarese ducat is like taking a piece of flesh out of the Duke himself," Papa explained. "Do you understand now why my crime is so serious?"

I did. But what he called my "lawyer's mind" began to search for a loophole in his logic. And, to be sure, I found one.

"But Papa, even a stern jurist like Seneca makes it a condition of any crime less than murder that the first offense is to be treated lightly. For, having not committed the crime before, the perpetrator should be given the benefit of the doubt that he did not, the first time, understand the gravity of his offense..."

He held up a hand to silence me. "Unfortunately for your case, daughter, this is not my first offense," he advised me in a much gentler tone.

"You have clipped coins before?" I asked.

"No, daughter. But I have gambled before to excess and, in my passion, caused untold havoc for myself, my family, and for all the Jews in Ferrara. They forgave me then. But to allow the same passion to drive me into crime for a second time—that is not forgivable."

"What did you do that other time, Papa?" I asked. And when he remained silent, I added, "We must know."

"Very well." He nodded. "Since you share my disgrace, it is only just that you should share my secrets. Come." And he led us up the staircase to my sleeping room, where he settled us on the bed, one on each side. Then he began his confession.

"The events I speak of took place in Ferrara when you, my daughter, were still a babe in swaddling clothes and you"—he drew Jehiel closer to him—"were only a hope in my heart. It was that season when *carnevale* fever takes hold, those weeks before Lent when even princes give themselves over to feasting and wenching and whatever else satisfies their appetites.

"Now, Duke Ercole d'Este never was a womanizer. Nor a glutton. Nor a brawler. But, as you children have cause to know, he does have one besetting vice..."

"Gambling," I whispered.

Papa nodded his confirmation and continued: "How else does such a man choose to indulge himself during *carnevale* but in an orgy of gambling? And what better place for it than on his golden bucentaur, where the guests can be sequestered from the eyes of the curious?

"We gambled for three days and three nights. As the gilded boat wound its way slowly up the Po, the stakes gradually mounted," Papa continued. "On the final day hundreds of ducats were being wagered on each throw of the dice. By the time the ship sailed into port one man, a merchant named Ambrogio, had been ruined. And a young Jew 'with golden hands' had won three thousand gold ducats."

Papa paused to allow us to digest the magnitude of the numbers. Then he continued.

"The following day, Ambrogio's son, crazed by the overnight disappearance of his inheritance, 'stolen' (as he believed) by a cheating Jew, made his way to the *banco* owned by the Jew's family. He stormed into the place waving an unsheathed dagger, and before anyone knew what was happening, he fell upon the first young Jew he encountered and stabbed him to death."

Instinctively, I covered my eyes with my hands as if to block out the terrible picture. But Papa gently reached over and took away my blindfold, as if to say, "You wanted the truth. Now you must face up to it." And there was more to come.

"The worst of it was," he continued, "that in his rage for vengeance the young Christian had mistaken his victim. The Jew he killed was not the dealer with golden hands. The Jew who went down was his innocent brother. In case you have not already guessed," he went on in a low voice, "I am the Jew with the golden hands. The boy who went down in my place was my brother, Davide, the true dei Rossi firstborn."

The revelation struck me dumb. I looked at Jehiel. He too was speechless. But Papa had one more thing to tell, and he gathered himself together to give us the coda of his tale.

"In time the tempers of the citizens cooled. But not the bitterness of the slain son's family toward his slayer, the gambling son with the golden hands. The daily sight of those cursed hands served only to remind them of the dead firstborn on whom all their hopes had centered. With each day that passed their loathing of the living son mounted. His very presence in the room raised a stink in their nostrils. Driven by rage and grief, they decided to cut him off from the family, as a surgeon amputates a gangrenous limb so that it will not infect the healthy part of the body. The gambler was exiled from Ferrara, sent off to a distant branch of the family bank in Mantova with his wife and his infant daughter. Before he left in disgrace, he took a solemn vow never to gamble again in this life."

But he *had* gambled again. With terrible consequences. And now "the Jew with the golden hands" — my father — was about to be judged by the *Wad Kellilah*. What punishment they might choose to inflict, we dared not wonder.

II

WITHIN A DAY OF MY GRANDFATHER'S RELEASE from the Duke's dungeon, the *Wad Kellilah* assembled in the dei Rossi private synagogue to judge my father. As they shuffled through the courtyard, I recognized many of them as the same people who had come a few months before to plead for Papa's help in the matter of the Jewish badges, and later, when he had performed so excellently on their behalf, had returned bearing sweetmeats and trinkets. Now, they stared through him as if he were a pane of Venetian glass. Where was their gratitude? I berated Jehiel, having nowhere else to vent my spleen.

"It seems, sister," he replied in his grave little way, "that gratitude is like the butterfly. It bursts out of its chrysalis, flutters, and dies within a day." (That child knew his Pliny.)

Lest I slander the members of the council, I should point out how ill prepared they were to deal with my father's case. Their true function was to arbitrate the civil disputes that plagued the Jewish community — mainly to allocate liability for the tax burden imposed by the Estes on the community. On the criminal side, their jurisdiction held sway over paternity suits, divorce settlements, and such domestic matters deemed sufficiently minor by the Christian authorities to leave to the Jews to settle among themselves. To stage the trial of a serious crime — and to arrive at their judgment with all Ferrara watching to see what constituted Jewish justice — must have weighed heavily on those reluctant Solomons. Certainly they hardly appeared to look forward to their task as they filed past us in the *cortile*.

The *banco* was closed that day. No lessons were given. Jehiel and I hung about the chamber as silent as two shadows, waiting for the verdict of the council. Only when the council members finally emerged at dusk did we give vent to our feelings, rushing forward to throw ourselves into Papa's arms, weeping and hugging him with abandon. We knew such displays to be odious in that household but we were beyond caring.

Papa kept countenance through it all. With solemn dignity he gathered us into his arms and gently conducted us into a small side room that we might speak together privately.

"What I have to tell you children is not something you will wish to hear," he began. "Nor do I wish to tell it." Then he took a moment to wipe away my tears before he told us the verdict. "I am to be put under a *cherem*. Do you know what that means?" We did not.

"It is an excommunication from the faith — the community — the family," he explained.

"Is it like a *niddui*, Papa?" I asked. Once in Mantova the silk merchant Mordecai had been placed under a *niddui* for forging a receipt, and I remembered the poor man clad in black from head to toe and ignored by everyone for an entire month.

"No, my daughter," Papa replied. "The *cherem* is a longer punishment and more severe. By its terms, I am banished from all concourse with the synagogue, even denied a place in consecrated ground should I die. And you along with me, unless ·you agree to renounce me."

"Renounce you?" I placed my hand on my heart, à la Dido. "Never!"

Jehiel did not even dignify the idea with a response. To him, our refusal of the offer was a foregone conclusion. "What will happen to us under this *cherem*, Papa?" he asked.

"You will be banished from Ferrara along with me. Like me, you will be prohibited from entering the sacred precincts of any synagogue for any purpose. And, like me, you will suffer the contempt of your fellow Jews. *If* you cleave to me."

"Of course we cleave to you," Jehiel answered with just a trace of impatience in his high, boy's voice. "Who else would we cleave to? Poor old Uncle Joseph or Grandmother or—"

"All right, all right," Papa cut him off. "You are decided then not to renounce me?"

We nodded solemnly.

"In that case, I must explain to you what will happen tomorrow. Since I cannot keep you from it, I had best prepare you..." Yet he did not speak.

In that moment of silence, the question that had been bedeviling me rose to my tongue. "Why did you do it, Papa?" I found myself asking.

"Why indeed?" he asked of the air.

"We wonder why you had to steal gold from the edges of the coins when there is so much of it in the strongboxes of the *banco*," Jehiel explained.

"I've wondered about that too, my son," Papa replied. "Why did I choose to rob the Duke rather than my parents?" He paused, bemused by his own question, then continued in a much brisker tone. "What I do know is that I was a double-damned fool to make such a choice. The Duke forgave me," he added.

"I knew he was a good man when I played Zara with him," Jehiel announced. Then, realizing that he had trodden on forbidden territory, he quickly added, "I never speak of it, Papa. Never."

"Good," Papa commended him. "Keep your silence. And stay away from dice. If I were you, I would prefer *calcio*—kicking the ball is better for your muscles *and* your purse."

"Very well, Papa," Jehiel agreed. "But who am I to play *calcio* with? Grazia is the only person who can kick hard enough. Asher dribbles the ball like pee-pee. And—"

"Enough!" Papa held up his hand. "Let me speak of tomorrow while I still have the heart for it. What you will see may seem cruel to you. But remember, the civil punishment for the crime of coin clipping is death by dismemberment. Do you know what quartering is?"

We were not certain that we did.

"When a man is quartered, his body is chopped into four pieces by the executioner." Jehiel buried his face in my shoulder when he heard this. But Papa would not stop. "After his body has been divided by the axe, the head is mounted on a pike and displayed for all the world to see atop the town walls. *That* might have happened to me, had not the Duke forgiven me, as you put it. *That* is the fate I escaped. Whatever you see and hear in the community's synagogue tomorrow, remember that I deserve it all—and more."

We both agreed to remember. But, of course, with no clear idea of what we were about to witness.

"One last thing," Papa went on. Would there be no end? "I have inflicted grievous shame on my parents by my folly, and not for the first time in my life. For this, I must also pay a penalty, and this time, the penalty falls upon you two as well."

Dio mio, I thought, we are all going to be beaten together in La Nonna's *sala di giustizia*.

"What are they going to do to us, Papa?" asked Jehiel.

"Banishment is their judgment, my son," he replied. "It is at their request that the *Kellilah* has banished us from Ferrara."

"Where will we go, Papa? Who will take us in?" Jehiel bit his lip to keep from crying.

"We will go to Bologna," Papa answered. "I have been offered a post there. As a clerk in the *banco*."

"A clerk?" I could not imagine it. Clerks were inferior beings, only a jot above servants.

"A clerk," Papa repeated forcefully. "But a clerk with two

hands and two feet and two beautiful children. I call that a gambler's luck."

Of course he was right about everything—the seriousness of his crime, the extent of his folly, and the magnitude of his good fortune. Nonetheless, the next day when they led him forward in the synagogue, hooded like a blind leper, I froze with dread. And when they pulled off the hood and revealed his head completely shaven, I could not stifle a scream.

After that he was paraded up and down the aisles barefoot and shirtless while the congregation cursed him and slapped at him and spat upon him. Yes, Danilo, they spat upon my father. And I sat up in the gallery and watched the wads of spittle thicken on his bare chest.

After two full rounds of this, some of the meaner ones began to aim higher...at his checks...his eyes. He could do nothing to cleanse his face for his hands were bound behind his back.

When they were done spitting and cursing they sat him down to listen to the terms of the *cherem*. Words upon words washed over him. But no one of all those believers made a move to wash away the clots of yellow phlegm that covered his face.

After what seemed like hours the time came for the actual ritual of excommunication. A funeral bier was brought in. Then the cantor came down the aisle and laid upon the bier a dead cock, which continued to drip blood down the front of the casket as the ceremony progressed.

Next, a fringed tallis was laid upon the bier. With a gasp, I recognized it as Papa's prayer shawl, the one my mother had embroidered for him with her own hands. With slow deliberation the *shammash* lit four white tapers and placed them at the four corners of the bier as is done at funerals. Then suddenly a weird cacophony broke out—a din of chanting and dancing around my father while the rabbi and his minions tossed burnt ashes over his head and rubbed them into his cheeks, all this accompanied by the cantor blowing the great ram's horn over and over, each time louder and wilder than the last.

When the adults had worn themselves out, the children got their turn to dance around Papa, chanting curses and forcing bursts of noise into his ears from inflated bladders.

At last, the lust for spectacle having been satisfied, Papa was led to a seat below the ark. And there, the recentor, standing over him with the scroll of the law in his hand, pronounced the prayer for the dead:

Yisgadal v'yiskadash, Shmay rabo.
Byolmo dee v'hir usay...

As the rabbi repeated the ancient words, Papa was led out followed by his bier, the dead cock dripping blood on the feet of the pallbearers.

As far as the Jews were concerned, my father was now dead.

BOLOGNA

12

FOUL WEATHER, DOUBLE-DEALING BARGE CAPTAINS, rapacious innkeepers, treacherous waterways—these are but a few of the conditions of the journey from Ferrara to Bologna that have been known to reduce strong men to tears. They say there is not a captain on the Reno canal who will budge from his moorings until every cubit of deck space is covered by the behind of a paying customer. I had heard tales of travelers forced to sit out days in the foul inns of Malalbergo (well named) until their vessel was full up. Not to mention the wicked currents of the Reno canal and the treacherous mud flats of the Ferrarese marshes into which whole boatloads of passengers have been known to sink without a trace. Yet to us those treacherous marshes presented their most benign aspect that day, a thick greenish-gold carpet of undulating reeds as far as the eye could see, crisscrossed by narrow waterways that seemed to be incised on the marsh like *graffiti* patterns.

And the very moment our mule train reached the terminus of the canal at Malalbergo and clambered up the slippery bank onto the barge mooring, we were hailed by a captain eager to be on his way who needed just four more passengers to make up his complement. And there we were, Papa, Jehiel, myself, and Gershom's wet nurse. (Gershom, a baby, rode free.) In that happy event, we embarked on our journey along the notorious canal, where the pilgrims' motto is: "Every man for himself and God against us all."

But God took pity on us that day. At the first sluicegate, where the passengers are forced to debark with all their baggage while the barge is hauled through the gate by a team of horses, one of the passengers actually offered to help with our boxes. And this priest continued to act as our porter throughout the voyage. He was a true Christian.

Another remarkable surprise. When little Gershom began to wail, a Lombard merchant sitting near us wet his own shirttail with his own wine so the babe could suck some comfort from it. (And you know the Lombards are not known for their generosity.)

As we skimmed along the Corticella road on the final lap of our journey to Bologna, Jehiel stood up in the hired wagon and announced that our period of misfortune was over. "Our guiding planet has come to rest in a new, serene orbit," he augured with supreme confidence. And I believed him.

He was the one who first spotted signs of the city. "Look, Grazia! Look, Papa! Crooked towers! They tilt like men walking on stilts." And to be sure the towers that thrust up crookedly into the sky did resemble stilt-walkers with their bases swathed in mist and their tops emerging out of the fog all askew.

At a distance, the red brick of the buildings made Bologna look like a city on fire — not so much blazing as glowing, the way embers do. The closer we got, the warmer it seemed. Beauty is in the eye of the beholder. Places in which we have been miserable, no matter how gorgeous, appear cold and lifeless in retrospect. Places that offered us comfort, solace, and hope take on an air of beauty. So it was with me and Bologna.

Such bustle. Such shouting. So much laughter. Even Papa regained some of his spirit as we rode through the teeming streets. Every day was like this in Bologna, he explained, it being the seat of a great university—in fact, the mother of all universities. There were upwards of five thousand students living there. And they were the cause of the shouting and japing in the streets. Students were the main clientele of the dei Rossi *banco*, he added, temporary impoverishment being their natural condition. But they looked so gay in their colorful clothes and so free that I longed to be one of them and to share in that carefree life, impoverished or not.

"Could I?" I asked Papa. "Could I someday be a student?"

For answer, he pointed into the crowd jostling us from all sides. "Look carefully at the students, Grazia. What do you see?"

"These students are all boys," Jehiel interposed. "And you can never be a student here, Grazia, because you are not a boy."

"Is it true?" I turned to Papa.

"I fear so, my little scholar," he allowed. "The university was founded by men to further their own learning. And it remains a male preserve."

"But *I* can come here, can I not, Papa? When I am older. To the university?" Jehiel demanded

"Yes, my son, if you prepare yourself properly. And Grazia can learn as much—or more—at home. In fact"—he paused to capture a thought—"I myself will be her tutor. Yes I will."

AS WE MADE OUR way across town I found nothing to displease me and much to delight in. Best of all were the arcades that extend over the street from every structure and make Bologna into one continuous protected cloister. Even Jew Street, cramped and crowded though it was, was arcaded. And the minuscule Casa dei Rossi, wedged in between its neighbors like a plump pillow, looked to me like a dollhouse.

The *banco* itself was so tiny that when we tried to enter as a group, we could not all stand in it at the same time. As it was, the manager was forced to rest his old bones on the *cassone* that held the day's pledges, because there was only room for a single chair to accommodate both him and his clerk. But he greeted us kindly, and despite his sciatica, insisted on showing us around himself.

The house was arranged so that children and servants occupied the top floor and adults the *piano nobile*, just as in grand establishments. But here everything was reduced in size, so much so that when Papa stood in the center of the *sala grande* and stretched his arms wide, his fingers almost reached the walls.

What a steep descent this was from the life he had lived up until then, a man with his own *studiolo*, his library of books, his fine clothes, and all the accoutrements of the rich life. But to me, the little house offered the cozy nest I had longed for ever since we left Mantova, and I danced through it curtsying to the cook, Tasha, and to the two daily maids who, with the addition of our wet nurse, Gelsomina, composed the entire domestic staff. Three men completed the *famiglia*: a clerk, a porter-cum-messenger, and the manager, whom we called Zio Zeta since he was our uncle by marriage. Even with the addition of Papa, that still did not give us enough male adults for a *minyan*, which tells you how unimportant the Bolognese *banco* was in my grandfather's eyes. Any self-respecting *banco ebreo* made certain to include at least ten male adults to provide the minimum number needed for daily prayers. As it was, the men of our *famiglia* were forced to go elsewhere to make their observances.

This hardship did not affect Papa, excommunicated as he was from participation in any Jewish ritual. But it would have wrung your heart to see old Zio Zeta limping his way up the street twice a day to attend prayers with the Meshullam *famiglia*. We also depended on their *shohet* to butcher our meat. And on their tutor to instruct Jehiel in Jewish ways. Imagine the proud dei Rossis agreeing to accept such largesse from a rival family.

We quickly settled into a daily routine. Each morning at cock's crow, I woke Jehiel — we were back to sharing a room, as in the old days at Mantova—and helped him to dress for school. No body servant to dress us. And no pony ride. Papa simply walked Jehiel to the Meshullam *casa* at the near end of Jew Street and I tagged along for the exercise and the company. Papa and I were always back in our own little house long before the great bell of San Petronio rang out the call for matins, and hard at work by the time the Christians passed by on their way home from early mass. Since Tasha would not allow me near the cooking pots, I busied myself playing housekeeper during the morning hours. And Papa very soon took old Zio Zeta's place on the *cassone* behind the counting table. Having begun his apprenticeship with the dei Rossi *banco* at the age of fifteen, the old man was entering upon his fiftieth year of service to the family and felt, quite rightly, that the time had come when he might be spared the exertions of the banking business and allowed to live out his remaining days in peace.

In the old man's own words, Papa dropped in upon him "like an angel from heaven." No matter that Zio was called "manager" and Papa, "clerk." The old uncle was ready to be saved and he recognized Papa as his savior.

Once Zio Zeta had abdicated the space beside Papa, it seemed natural that I should take his place. I say natural because I soon realized that the maids did a much better job of shaking the blankets and wringing the wash than I did. But although I had no vocation for the housekeeping trade, loan-banking ran in my blood. I learned the abacus in record time, quicker than any boy, Papa said. And after dinner when business was slow, I took my afternoon plunge into the labyrinth of Greek grammar. For Papa proved as good as his word. He did begin to teach me Greek there behind the counting table.

Since you, my son, have also put in time sweating over a Greek grammar, you can guess what sweet relief Jehiel brought with him when he returned home at the end of the afternoon and interrupted our labors. Oblivious to our studies, he would settle himself beside me on the *cassone* and launch into a rambling account of the tribulations of his day. Do not fault him. He was only eight years old. And in addition to the usual insolence of street urchins, whose favorite pastime is to harass Jewish children, he was also subject to the taunts of his Jewish classmates on account of Papa's disgrace. To his credit he learned to bear the abuse with fortitude. But every so often his courage failed him, more often on account of a curse than a blow.

One such day, the accusation had to do with usury, a word linked in my mind to Fra Bernardino and our harrowing exodus from Mantova. Jehiel had again been accosted on his way home, this time by a new set of ruffians who cursed him as a "little imp of usury," an epithet new to him — and to me.

"Is it true, Papa?" he asked in a thin, sad voice. "Do we Jews draw all the good out of the poor and give back only gall?"

"No, my son, that is not so," Papa answered forthrightly.

"But Papa," Jehiel persisted, "those boys told me that gold is barren and performs no function and that those who collect interest upon money are but thieves under another name."

"I know what you hear, my boy," Papa replied patiently. "But remember that it is borrowed money lent out at interest by so-called usurers that finances the importation of goods, the seeds for next year's crops, and the wars of kings and dukes and popes. And before your sister reminds me that we might be better off without wars, let me remind you that without loans of money *at interest*, we would have no spices from the Indies, nor would the peasants of Europe be warmed in winter by their Florentine woolen cloaks."

"And jewels, Papa, what about jewels? Would we have ballases and emeralds..." Jehiel never failed to introduce some form of *lusso* into any discussion.

"And beautiful, painted manuscripts..." I added. For I never failed to take a turn on my pet pony either.

"The list of all the things that are brought to us by ship and mule and cart and for which money must be advanced would fill quartos," Papa agreed. "But that is not the whole of it. For you might well contend that money does not, in fact, create these goods but merely facilitates their transport, might you not?"

We nodded our understanding.

"What these pietists and preachers neglect to attend to in their diatribes is the element of *risk* that is involved in these transactions. Interest is our payment for the risk we take. We risk losing all our money every time we lend it out. Caravans are robbed regularly. Ships are attacked and often sunk by pirates, whence the entire cargo is lost. As for these vast war loans, kings as a group are neither more nor less honorable than other men. And the heirs of kings have a most unfortunate disposition to forgive themselves the debts of their fathers."

"Kings do not pay their debts, Papa?" Jehiel asked, astonished.

"Someday I will tell you the sad tale of the great banking families of Firenze, the Bardi and the Acciaiuoli, who were ruined—wiped out—by the English monarch Edward the Third when one day he declared himself bankrupt and unable to repay his debts to them."

"Did they cut off his hands and feet and lock him in the stocks in the town square?" Jehiel asked.

"Oh no, my dear." Papa smiled. "Kings are not pilloried. The poor are pilloried. And the Jews. Kings are forgiven. Apparently it is part of their divine right."

"But that is not fair . . ." I protested.

"The next time you take tea with a king, tell him so," Papa answered me. "But I wouldn't advise you to talk justice with a king if you value your head."

That day marked the beginning of our instruction in the skills of a *banchiere*. Each day, Papa would bring in from the warehouse two or three diverse items—a dog collar perhaps, and a lamp and an ivory comb—and invite us to evaluate them. At the end of the year, I was able to judge the values of hundreds of items with great accuracy. Jehiel never got the point of the exercise. If the crimson silk of a pillow cover caught his fancy, he would inflate its value beyond all sense; whereas a dull-looking article such as a cooking pot seemed worthless to him even if it be cast from solid copper. Since he always lost at this game which gave me such delight, it quickly lost its charm for him; and after a few months, Papa and I were left to ourselves to pursue the twin intricacies of Greek grammar and loan-banking.

Then, in the second year of our stay in Bologna, an event happened that transformed me overnight from a mousy, domestic creature into a positive monster of worldliness and vanity. All it took was a short letter. The news it contained snatched me up out of exile and disgrace. Within days after that letter arrived, I was bound for glory.

13

ALTHOUGH THE DEI ROSSI COURIERS PLIED THE CANals between Ferrara and Bologna regularly on banking business, we had received only one personal message during the first year of our exile. On that occasion, Papa opened the envelope joyfully, hoping, no doubt, for some word of forgiveness. Instead, what he read to us was a brief, cold note to the effect that his brother, our Uncle Joseph, had been called to God, leaving my Aunt Dorotea widowed and my cousins fatherless. Having lost a parent myself, I knew I ought to feel compassion for their loss, but when I sat down to write my condolences (at Papa's instruction) I found it difficult to pretend a warmth I did not feel. Jehiel wrote too, as did Papa himself. None of us received the courtesy of an acknowledgment.

The next personal document arrived at the beginning of the second year of our Bolognese exile—January of 1491. Who had been called to God now? I wondered as we stood by waiting for the solemn announcement. But this time Papa's face brightened as he read. And by the time he reached the end of the letter, he was smiling.

"Well, my dear," he addressed me. "It seems that you are about to be honored by the Jews of Ferrara."

"Do not josh me, Papa," I begged him. "Tell us what has happened. Who else is dead?"

"No one is dead," he replied. "This letter concerns you, Grazia. It seems that you have been selected to portray Esther, Queen of the Jews, in the wedding procession of young Alfonso d'Este next month."

"What about *me*, Papa? What part do I play?" Jehiel asked.

"No mention of you, my boy," Papa answered. "Nor of me. Only your sister is to be honored."

"If you and Jehiel are not included, then I won't go either," I announced.

"Now, now, let us not be precipitate," Papa cautioned. "It will only be for two weeks — three at most."

"I don't want to go," I answered. "Not even for three days. I hate that house and I hate —"

Papa's warning look stopped me from finishing the sentence.

"Allow me to tell you how this invitation came about," he coaxed with what was, for him, remarkable patience. "Then you may take a decision. But remember this, my daughter..." I heard an unmistakable trace of the old steel in his voice. "No matter what you decide, it will be up to me, finally, whether you go to Ferrara or no."

I knew him too well to resist when he took this tone. Meekly, I answered, "As you wish, honored Signore Padre," and took my place on the stool at his side.

"In two months' time," Papa resumed, "the Duke's eldest son, Alfonso, is to be married to young Anna Sforza, the bastard daughter of the Duke of Milano."

"I remember this Alfonso d'Este, Papa," Jehiel interrupted. "He was playing tennis with his two sisters the day we went with you to Belriguardo."

"You remember them, do you?" Papa seemed surprised.

"Of course we do, Papa," I assured him importantly. "We saw them playing tennis the day you played Z—" I caught myself short and Papa continued with his explanation.

"Well, the boy you saw is getting married on the twelfth of February and this letter says that the Duke has asked the *Wad Kellilah* for a Jewish queen to grace his son's procession as one did his own wedding procession some twenty years ago."

"But why me, Papa?" I interrupted. "Why must I go? Can they not get some other girl to play the queen?"

"Reading between the lines, I gather that the elders of the community have proposed other maidens for the honor, but" — he turned to read directly from the letter—"'...no other maiden will suit the Este duke but Grazia dei Rossi. And it is to enable said Grazia to reenter the Ferrarese community that we hereby offer amnesty from her excommunication.'"

"I do not want their clemency if it does not include you and Jehiel and little Gershom. Either forgive us all or none," I declaimed in my most Didoesque fashion.

But Papa was having none of it. "Does it occur to you, my dear," he inquired derisively, "that there are more consequential matters in this world than what you wish or do not wish... such as what the Duke wishes, who holds the lives of two hundred Jews in his hands?"

"I do not trust those elders, those *parnassim*," I muttered. "That letter is probably a counterfeit."

"No matter what you think of them, daughter," Papa replied evenly, "I cannot imagine them to have concocted this scheme out of cunning; for surely their last wish is to pay respect to the daughter of a man so disgraced as myself. No. The Duke's will is what prevails here. And, as I have reminded you many times, Jews do not say no to dukes."

"I understand, Papa. But I still do not wish to go. I am afraid."

"Afraid? You?"

"When we traveled here from Ferrara, you and Jehiel and Gelsomina were with me. But now I will be alone...."

"You have a point there." Papa thought for a moment. "Yes, we must find you a companion. A protector."

Jehiel sprang up at once and stood on his toes as tall as he could make himself. But Papa squelched the idea with a shake of his head.

"I have it," he announced after several moments of thought. "We'll send Zio Zeta along with you. He is the logical one."

"*Lo zio?*" I couldn't believe my ears. "But he can hardly see and he can't hear without his trumpet."

"He is good and kind and loves you as he loves himself," Papa replied firmly.

When the old man was told the plan, he jumped as if stung by a bee, clasped his hands to his breast, and cried, "*Ferrara mia!*" with such a mixture of joy and pathos that there was no way to tell whether he was happy or sad to be going to the place.

When Papa brought out from the warehouse a monk's habit and an ebony cross for him to wear as a foil against highwaymen, the old man donned it readily, twirled about daintily as if quite delighted with his new identity, and then suddenly clapped his hands to his breast and cried, "May God forgive me for my sin!"

My protection against thieves and rapists was a boy's outfit concocted out of odds and ends of Jehiel's wardrobe. Although two years younger than I, he was a sturdy boy almost up to my height, so that his shirt and trunk hose fitted me without a pin. But I refused the generous offer of the red *borzacchini* which he had kept with him long after he outgrew them. Knowing his great affection for those elegant boots, I contented myself with a pair of rough clogs that some poor boy's mother had left in pawn with us and never returned to claim.

Thus disguised, Zio Zeta and I were mounted on a pair of mules one wintry morning bound for the southern terminus of the Reno canal. *Lo zio* jogged along the rutted road without a word of complaint. But when we reached the mooring dock at Corticella, he slid down off his mule, crawled onto the deck of the closest barge, and collapsed like a bag of bones, hugging the coal burner on the deck and refusing to eat, drink, even to relieve himself or move his bowels.

In vain did the barge captain warn him that we still needed

many souls to fill the craft and that we might be moored there all the balance of the day—or longer. "You had better take refuge at the inn with the other passengers, Signore Padre," he advised Zio respectfully. "There is a warm fire at the inn."

But the old man refused to move. "No inns, for God's sake," he moaned, and curled himself up even tighter in his cassock.

By a stroke of good fortune, this standoff was interrupted when a pair of those religious women called Poor Clares who follow the teachings of Saint Francis approached the barge seeking passage along the canal. Now, with them to augment the group of pilgrims waiting at the inn, we constituted a party sufficient to fill up the vessel to the captain's satisfaction.

Taking lo zio for a monk on account of his dress, these two nuns instantly dedicated themselves to the care of the old man, insisting that he share the soup they kept hot on a brazier and later covering him with one of their own blankets when the northern winds reached down into our bones.

At the sluiceways, when we were all forced out of the barge so that it might be towed through the locks by a team of horses—there seemed to be several more of these than I remembered from the previous time—the two sisters carried old Zio up and down the banks, an act of compassion I remind myself of when I become outraged by the bigots and seducers who display the underside of Christian monasticism.

There was no difficulty filling empty seats on the next lap of the journey. The slim barques that ply the shallow marshes cannot accommodate more than six on their two boards, and those are made sittable only by squeezing the passengers together like peas in a pod. Heedless of the shouts of the bargemaster, lo zio's guardian angels bundled him aboard the sturdiest of the crafts and laid him down for a nap across the full horizontal expanse of one of the boards, leaving the other for themselves and me. Then, having said their beads, they wrapped their shawls around themselves and went off into a snooze, leaving the pilot furious but helpless to dislodge the old man from three paying seats and leaving me to my fancies.

That Duke Ercole d'Este had remembered me kept intruding on my thoughts. If he remembered me, he must be kindly disposed toward me. If kindly disposed, he might be amenable to an entreaty...

A plan began to take shape in my mind. I would contrive somehow to petition the Duke on Papa's behalf. I would move his capricious heart and get him to force Papa's reinstatement as he had mine. Quite taken with the role of Papa's rescuer, I began to compose an oration that would capture the Duke's attention with classical allusions and, at the same time, win his fickle heart with flattery as I had seen Papa do.

I must compare him with gods and heroes. But which ones? Caesar? Pompey? Hercules? Of course. Ercole is our Italian transposition of Hercules. That god was his namesake. Now what I needed was an instance of the god's clemency; better yet, a moment at which he set himself against the world to right a terrible wrong. But all I could dredge up was a printed image seen fleetingly in some marketplace or other of the nude god posed between two half-dressed women, making his choice between pleasure and duty. Hardly apt for my purpose.

I never did find a suitable analogy. But the search through memory served to hold my attention for the journey through the bog, and before I knew it, we were being borne along the icy ruts of the road into Ferrara on a litter with runners—a sled.

It had been a frigid journey, especially the least piece on the sled, but no chillier than the welcome that awaited us when we arrived at the Casa dei Rossi after almost three days of arduous travel. We were hungry and stiff with cold. But neither food nor a warmer were offered by La Nonna's steward, Giorgio. Taking his cue from his mistress, old Giorgio would do his duty by us but nothing more. So I crawled under the silk coverlet racked by hunger pangs and flooded with pity for poor little Graziella, scorned by her family, cast off like a leper without even a crust of bread for her supper.

Curling myself up into a tight ball, I squeezed my eyes shut and willed myself to sleep. But before Morpheus responded to my summons I heard a rustle, then a soft pitter-patter, then a whispered shush, and there in bed beside me was a little girl I had never seen before.

"I am your cousin Penina," she introduced herself. "I have brought you something to cheer you. Courage must be rewarded." Whereupon she held out a handful of sweetmeats, all of which she fed me without reserving even one for herself. Younger than I by two years, she had recently been adopted by my grandparents, she told me. "So now I am your cousin," she informed me. "But, if you agree, we can also be friends." And friends we became.

She had heard horrific reports of the rigors of the journey through the Ferrarese marshes—told with relish, she informed me, by various members of the *famiglia*. "They do not wish you well, Grazia," she reported sadly. "But you will have your day when you ride through Ferrara on that elephant and leave them on the ground gaping."

Elephant? Nowhere in the letter of invitation had there been mention of an elephant. But Penina assured me that the Jewish queen would indeed ride on one.

"The Duke insisted upon it," she explained. "Years ago the Jews of Ferrara contributed some biblical queen on an elephant to his wedding procession and he wants nothing less for his son. Your grandfather ordered the beast all the way from Constantinople, together with its keeper," she added. *Dio!* What was I in for?

Penina did not stay long with me that first time, but after that came to me every night, often carrying with her some tidbit from the kitchen. How she contrived to smuggle the stuff out I cannot imagine—La Nonna's larder was better policed than the *podesta*'s prison. But Penina was full of spirit, and having picked me as a friend, stuck by me at great risk to her position in the *famiglia*. La Nonna, who had taken her in on a whim when her parents died, was quite capable of throwing her out if she did not suit the role of the grateful orphan.

Between my grandmother and me the old war continued as before. This time what brought us into contention was my costume. La Nonna and her ladies had strong opinions on color, trimming, accessories, caps, hair arrangement, and every other aspect of female fashion. Just as it should be, since none of them had ever been seen in anything but black bombazine since the day she was married—a fashion experience which fitted them uniquely to select a costume for a queen.

What they concocted was a shapeless, dowdy outfit in shiny gray satin which they thought to spice up by tacking onto it hundreds of little red satin bows. I knew that this mismatched creation would make me into a figure of fun. And when I asked to see myself in a mirror, my worst fears were confirmed. All that was needed to complete the picture of a fool was a cap and bells. And so I informed my grandmother.

The aspersion on her taste sent her spine—never notably pliant—into a spasm of rigidity. "This is the garment you will wear, my dear," she informed me in her most steely tone.

"No, I will not, Grandmother," I replied, equally obdurate. "For it is tasteless and vulgar and stupid and silly and makes me look more a fool than a queen."

There we stood, centurions of the sewing room, neither willing to give a cubit. Luckily, at that moment, a referee appeared, none other than Maestro Ambrogio, our old dancing master, who had been hired for the day to give me lessons in how to turn and make a low bow without tripping over my train. He took one look at me and erupted into a flourish of giggles, pointing at me as if I were a buffoon in a clown suit. I could not have coached him better for my purpose.

"What is this apparition supposed to represent, Madonna Sarabella?" He inquired between hoots.

"It is the Jewish queen, maestro," La Nonna replied sternly, drawing herself up into her most regal attitude, the one where her ample breasts pointed straight out like twin *bombarde*.

But the maestro had seen too many displays of female armamentaria to be intimidated. "This girl is supposed to be a queen, madonna, not Punchinello," he admonished her.

"But we thought the satin would do..." I had never seen my grandmother so out of countenance.

"Well, you people can practice whatever foolish economies you wish." The maestro dismissed her creation with a contemptuous wave of his hand. "But don't be surprised if the Duke has you all on the rack for mocking him with this travesty. He expects something rich and regal from the Jews. Pearls, he said. And velvet. And jewels out of your strongboxes, fit for a queen."

A new costume was begun that very day, the most beautiful gown I had ever seen. Where they found the stuff to make it, I do not know. It was a velvet so thick that even the February cold did not penetrate its great heft. And the fur that lined my cloak was the most excellent miniver. They piled gold on me until I felt faint from the weight of it. And then finished by placing on my head a tiara so thickly studded with emeralds and carnelians that you could hardly see the gold mounting beneath.

But all this splendor was laid upon me so coldly and with such disdain that had it not been for the warmth I drew from Penina, I think I would have perished from the frigidity of my surroundings in spite of my miniver cloak.

Fortunately I had little time for hurt feelings. I had to learn how to walk in a train almost two meters long without tripping myself, how to curtsy to the floor in a very low-cut dress without exposing myself immodestly, and most important, how to mount and dismount an elephant.

At our first meeting, the beast, whom Penina and I named Sarabello on account of his resemblance to my grandmother, proved no challenge to my courage. A special pen had been set aside for him just north of the city gates and there he sat on his huge haunches, his eyes closed as if in a stupor, refusing to budge. If elephants can be said to have moods, I would have said Sarabello was morose. Penina surmised that he missed his mother. Whatever the cause of it, Sarabello demonstrated a most peaceable nature that first day. His keeper, a strange little brown man in a huge white turban, had him already saddled in anticipation of my arrival. Now all I had to do was mount the beast, sit balanced on his back under a *baldacchino* for a few moments, then dismount.

Eyes firmly shut, I ascended the ladder that my cousin Asher, appointed as my groom, balanced against the beast's side. I was terrified. However, the ascent was accomplished without incident. Then began the effort to force the beast to stand up so that I might get the feel of riding him. In vain did his little keeper prod and poke him. No reaction from the beast. As a last resort, the keeper picked up a pail of water standing nearby and threw it full force into the elephant's face. All it got him was a high toot and a blast of wind. The beast had made up his mind to stay put and no power on earth, it seemed, would make him move.

With a shrug, the keeper beckoned me to descend. I did so thankfully. And no sooner had my feet touched the ground than Sarabello slowly but not ungracefully raised his great bulk into a standing position. Whereupon all those assembled applauded wildly and the elephant curtsied daintily. A charming performance but not one to bolster my hopes for the actual wedding procession two days hence.

THE DAY OF THE wedding dawned clear and very cold. As a concession to the weight of my costume, I was carried on a litter to my rendezvous with the elephant. My grandmother and her ladies and several of the *parnassim* walked behind me in a solemn procession. Every expression, every look in that morose group foretold disaster. I kept my spirits up by fastening my eyes on the shining countenance of my friend Penina, who had vowed to follow the procession on foot for its entire length.

Finally we reached the appointed place. Once again my cousin Asher took hold of the ladder to balance it up against the side of the elephant so that I might mount. But this day, our beast was disinclined to make himself agreeable. With one tremendous throw of his huge body, he shunted the ladder to the ground. And then, as if to make his intention clear, he smote it into splintered sticks with one stamp of his great foot.

I saw myself lying dead on the Ferrarese cobbles, thrown down by this ferocious jungle creature and trampled by him—just as the ladder had been—before anyone had a chance to drag me to safety...if, indeed, anyone made the effort, an unlikely possibility since all my *famiglia* wished me dead.

I looked to Penina for reassurance. She cast a weak smile in my direction. Even she had lost faith in the enterprise.

Meanwhile, Asher had been sent off for a new ladder, leaving me to saturate my eyes with the sight of the unruly beast and fill my ears with the raucous trumpeting that filled the air.

Just then, my attention was arrested by the fast clip-clop of a horse approaching from the direction of the *castello*. Could this be a messenger from Duke Ercole canceling the appearance of the Jewish queen? Had God taken pity on me?

When the rider rounded the corner and made straight for me, hope flooded my being. His velvet doublet and heavy golden chain marked him as someone more distinguished than a mere page. And the manner in which he dismounted and strode toward me, straight as a rod, marked him as some sort of knight. Despite my agitation, I also managed to observe that he was very young and that his legs and thighs were most beautifully formed.

Now he stood before me, this knight, the Este colors streaming from a plaquette pinned to his *berretta* marked with the initials PG. Every inch the courtier, he thrust one elegantly shod foot forward and, sweeping his cloak behind him, bowed low.

"Respects, ma'am," he began. "The Duke sends his best wishes to the Jewish queen for a safe journey atop the beast. And the bride, Madonna Anna, begs her to accept these colors as a token of gratitude for the fine wedding offering."

Thereupon, he brought out from under the folds of his cloak a carved wooden box and opened it to reveal ribbons to match his own—one red, one purple, one black, held together by a small gold plaquette in the shape of an elephant.

"May I?" The young cavalier held out the plaquette with the intention of pinning it to my breast. I had but to lean forward to receive the attention. Would that forward gesture make me appear bold and common to him? For a moment I stood poised on the decision. Then, I chanced to look up and found myself staring directly into his eyes. They were the color of cornflowers, clearer than the most perfect sapphire stone.

As they say of such encounters, the world stopped turning at that moment. God knows how long we would have stood there with our eyes locked in embrace had not Sarabello chosen that moment to relieve himself at our feet.

Jarred into action, the young cavalier neatly sidestepped the cascade and, without waiting for my permission, fastened the colors over my shoulder and across my breast. He managed to avoid looking any longer into my eyes; he also managed to brush the tip of my breast with his hand. Oh, the touch!

Then, before I had the chance to utter a word, he was off. I watched him stride across the square to remount his jennet and jump directly onto his horse from a standing start. The last impression I had of him was a black velvet *berretta* streaming ribbons among a shower of copper curls.

My fears forgotten, I mounted the elephant lightly, as if wafted up by a zephyr, and proceeded to drift through the streets of Ferrara on the back of the beast, oblivious of the tumultuous crowd, the spectacular floats, the gorgeous costumes, and the decorations that transformed Ferrara into a garlanded fairyland. All I heard was the sound made by the beaded fringe of the canopy as it swayed from side to side—a soft repeated click—and all I saw before me was the remembered vision of a pair of cornflower-blue eyes, a slightly off-center nose, and a devil-take-it grin. I passed that ride in a dream of love.

When the procession reached its destination at the Reggio, darkness was beginning to descend. There I said farewell to

Sarabello and swept into the *castello* on Asher's arm. Would my Knight of the Este Colors be at the feast? I wondered. Would he speak to me? Would he even recognize me?

He seemed not to be present at the banquet, a sumptuous repast featuring tables piled with capons, fish, pies, and the most elegant pastries cunningly molded into figures and glazed with colored sugar to resemble polychromes. Nor did I find him in the audience for the masked dancers who entertained the gathering after supper nor among those who crowded the floor for the common dancing. I did, however, recognize the young princess, Isabella, come from Mantova for her brother's nuptials and looking every inch a marchesana in black velvet — the better to display her infinite pearls. Her head swathed in a huge turban, her hair pulled tight back in the *scortino* style, she captivated me with her aura, a mixture of the majestic and the exotic.

Even in the bloom of her youth Madonna Isabella was never truly beautiful. The Sforza bride had a longer neck than she and a smaller waist. But our Madama far outshone the pallid bride, waxen with fatigue after the long day's exertions, who approached each step with a deep sigh. By contrast, Madonna Isabella had plainly thrived on the events of the day. The Estes are relentless processionists. Any one of them, even the fat cardinal, is capable of riding a caparisoned horse for leagues on end, tossing out sweetmeats or coins and smiling, always smiling.

Like most of the Ferrarese who were invited, Asher and I did not presume to dance but only stood by and watched. And at last, I did catch a glimpse of the young knight who had brought me the colors that morning. Seeing him whirl by with this great lady or that, I did not expect him to notice me. But I would have eagerly given ten years of my life — no, twenty — for just one turn around the floor in his arms.

Beside me, Asher jiggled his foot impatiently. The gaiety and music that fed my fantasy gave him vertigo. Could we not, he pleaded, make our bows to the Duke and go home? The tinge of green that tinted his cheeks spoke eloquently in his cause. I agreed.

Without much difficulty we found the Duke seated in a robing room, his gouty foot propped up on a stool.

"Sir..." I greeted him with the curtsy I had practiced.

"Ah, the little Jewess... Grazia, is it not?"

"Yes, sir. And this is my cousin Asher dei Rossi." Asher managed an unsteady bow.

"You have done your people proud today, Grazia. You made a courageous queen." He reached out and patted my head. This was the time to plead for my father. I would never have a better opportunity.

"Excellency, is it appropriate for me to beg a great favor of you on this happy day?" I asked in my humblest manner.

"Ask away."

"It is about my father, sir. He longs to be restored to the light of your sun."

"Daniele's exile is no doing of mine, child. It is a matter for the Jewish council to settle."

Did I sense a lowering of the temperature? No matter. Once begun, I must finish my task. "But your word carries such weight, Excellency," I continued.

"You want me to intervene with the Jews for Daniele—is that what this is all about?" His manner was suddenly brusque.

"Yes, sir." I took a deep breath and launched into my oration. "It would seem a hard thing to an ordinary man to take the part of one who had injured him as my father injured you, sir. But to men of generosity and greatness of soul such as your Magnificence, it is a natural and easy thing to forgive a crime and to go beyond even that largeness of spirit and befriend the criminal. I beg you, sir, to shower your compassion on my unworthy father."

With this, I prostrated myself at his feet and crouched there waiting for his response. It was not long in coming.

"Get up, girl," he ordered me gruffly. "You take a great liberty to bother me with such a sordid matter on this happy occasion."

"I chose the occasion because I knew that your heart would be full this evening and hoped it might be full even to the overflowing."

"Hmm." He sniffed and looked about. "Full to the overflowing, is it? Where did you learn to speak so glibly?"

"I speak what is in my heart, *illustrissimo*," I answered.

"You speak what you learned from Cicero," he corrected me. "Has your father been teaching you Latin?"

"No sir, Greek. I learned Latin from my tutor before my grandmother..."

"Well, you are quite the little rhetorician, Signorina Grazia."

"Rhetoric is cold porridge if it cannot warm the hearts of the hearers," I answered boldly.

"Not only a rhetorician but an aphorist as well." The Duke was smiling once again. Beside me, Asher's breath was coming in quick, nervous gusts.

"What ails the boy?" the Duke asked.

I took a deep breath and asked God's forgiveness for the *nahora* I was about to cast upon my poor cousin. "He has a breathing disease, sir. Asthma. A family trait."

"Well, in that case, you had better get him home at once and under some warm blankets."

I knew I was being dismissed, but could not bring myself to give up on my mission. After a long silence he spoke again.

"You have brought us much pleasure today, riding on the elephant." His tone was kindly. "If the decision were mine to make, I would forgive Daniele everything in acknowledgment of his having trained you so well. But I do not interfere in the internal affairs of my Jews."

I rose slowly to my feet, desperate for an idea, a ploy.

"You could bring him back, sir, to perform some special service, just as you brought me here to ride upon the beast..."

For a moment I thought I had reached a place in his heart. But his next words disabused me of that hope. "Unfortunately, my child, there are no more elephants to be ridden." He leaned over and patted my head. "And so goodnight."

As we made our way down the great staircase and across the piazza past the huge equestrian statue of Duke Borso, I recognized the strains of Josquin's lively "Scaramella." Quite suddenly, Asher paused, bowed low and took my hand, and, with flushed cheeks and a new-inspirited gait, led me in a dainty galliard around the stone Duke perched on his stone horse above us. And somehow I knew that word of my bold intercession with the Duke would never reach La Nonna's ears—at least not from Asher's mouth.

My journey back to Bologna was not a happy one. Even Duke Ercole's compliments could not disguise the fact that I had failed to rescue my father. Of what use were my rhetorical flourishes if they could not persuade him to champion my cause? Of what use was my daring if I could not evoke his sympathy? The one bright memory I took away from Ferrara was of the young cavalier I dubbed my Knight of the Este Colors. And even he was driven into the shadows by the sense of failure that followed in the wake of the Jewish queen.

14

ALTHOUGH MY ABSENCE FROM BOLOGNA WAS BRIEF, it was long enough to provide a fresh look at the familiar when I returned; more precisely, a fresh look at my father.

Most striking was the contrast between Papa and Zio Zeta. The day after we arrived home, old Uncle Zeta was back at his hearthside post looking neat and trim after a walk to the barber's. Somehow he survived those frigid hours on the deck of the barge. And here he sat dipping his gnarled, blue-veined fingers into his food and carrying each morsel to his mouth with the aplomb of a courtier. Whereas when Papa used his fork—an old affectation of his—bits of food fell onto his lap, which he often did not even bother to brush off.

Furthermore I noticed with shame that there was dirt under Papa's fingernails. And when he bent forward, his *lucco* showed a greasy rim around the collar. Gradually, without my being aware of it, my elegant papa had been turning into a ragpicker.

At least a part of the answer was to be found in the wine barrel. Even before our departure for Ferrara, Papa had taken to absenting himself from the *banco* on the occasional afternoon.

Now, he almost never came back to his seat behind the money-changing table after dinner. Our afternoon lessons petered out. Supper became a miserable thing, since by then even I could not ignore the thickness of his speech.

One day after dinner, without saying a word, Papa handed me the heavy iron ring that held the keys to the front door, to the warehouse, and to the ironbound strongbox that sat against the back wall of the little *banco*. Inside that strongbox lay the ten thousand ducats that guaranteed our *condotta* for the next five years. He had entrusted to me the very life of the business, an awesome responsibility, but not without its compensations.

I set out at once to survey my domain. It was a wondrous place, that warehouse, lit only by the glints of sunlight that sneaked in through the chinks between the heavy wall planks, and festooned with booty like the hold of a pirate ship. There I stood, mistress of it all—baskets and boxes and trunks overflowing with silks and ribbons and chains and velvet-covered breviaries and coarsely bound printed books and boots and hats and cloaks and towels and sheets and balls and ropes and flowing curtains and embroidered pillows in every hue.

My eye fell upon an object suddenly illuminated by a glint of the sun—red and covered with stones. Mesmerized by its brilliance, I went toward it and discovered it to be a red leather belt, embossed and embroidered in gold and plastered with green, amber, and blue stones. Papa's training enabled me to tell at a glance that the leather was worn, the "gold" thread of the embroidery was shot through with telltale rust, and the stones, alas, made of glass. But the knowledge of its relative worthlessness in no way diminished its charm for me. I *had* to have it.

I reached for the ticket. "Donna Claretta," it read. Beside her name was written the expiration date of the pledge: 10 March 1491. My own birth date, only four days hence. I tried the belt around my waist. It fitted perfectly.

Each day after that I made the trip to the warehouse to assure myself that the girdle had not somehow slipped through my fingers. But it remained safe on its hook, shooting out colored rays like a corona, and on the day of my birth, it reverted to the *banco*, a gift to me from the gods.

From that day forward, I was never seen without it around my waist. As if to enhance its importance, I took to hanging from it a small *scarsella* such as I had seen the ladies wear at the Este wedding; and I kept a few *bolognini* in the little purse so as to make a nice jingle-jangle when I moved. I subsequently added one final piece of affectation: a small bit of linen to be used as a *fazzoletto*. This I waved about languidly with what I hoped was a ladylike air, putting it to my nose from time to time to dab daintily or pressing it to my mouth to spit in as I had seen my mother do.

Whereas previously I had aspired to a neat respectability in my appearance, I now fell into fantasy, slipped into it unknowingly, much as I daresay Papa had slipped into squalor. With the warehouse stores under my control, I ransacked the place for any bit of finery or fluff that lay there abandoned and took to wearing two, then four, then five rings and a pearl necklace that anyone could have known at a glance was concocted entirely out of paste.

Each afternoon, I took my seat behind the money-changing table, adorned by my many rings and my jeweled belt, and from my dais dispensed coins to this poor wretch or refused the pledge of that one. In some strange sense, I actually became the Jewish queen, with a clerk to do my bidding and no one to say me nay. Only one element of the picture was missing: a handsome and faithful courtier. And that requisite was very soon supplied by bountiful Fortuna. I cannot remember if it was sunny or cloudy that morning or if the *banco* was full or empty. If there were clients around they faded into oblivion the moment I caught sight of those sky-blue eyes.

He entered the *banco* clad in the sober garb of a student, come to borrow a few ducats until the end of the university term. No horse. No plumed velvet *berretta*. No initialed plaquette. But I knew him at once. And he knew me.

"As I live, it is the Jewish queen ruling the roost in Bologna," he observed the moment he saw my face.

My mouth opened to riposte but no words came out.

"What has happened to your elephant, Sheba?" he asked lightly. "I hardly knew you without him beneath you."

"He is back at the pyramids, sir," I gulped, then added, still breathless, "Resting."

"Were the wedding festivities too much for him then?" he inquired with mock courtesy.

"I fear so," I replied.

"I am saddened to hear of the fate of your elephant," he went on in the same tone. "For I did think him a handsome specimen . . . almost as worthy to grace the princess's wedding as his rider."

Barely sixteen years of age, he already knew how to turn a pretty compliment. But I, at thirteen, did not know how to accept one. I simply reddened and busied myself with extricating my *fazzoletto* from the *scarsella* at my waist. Perhaps if I blew my nose he might credit my weak voice to a malady of the chest.

But when I had managed to get out the wretched cloth and cough into it, the effect was quite the opposite from what I had intended.

He drew back from the table and inquired suspiciously. "What is the purpose of that rag, Jewess?"

Stung by his insolence, I was also made bold by it. My shyness forgotten, I replied angrily, "This is no rag, sir. This is a *fazzoletto.*"

"I care not for the name but for the purpose," he answered impatiently. "Tell me true, do you put a Jewish curse on me when you wave it in my eyes?"

The idea of myself as a Jewish witch so diverted me that I burst out laughing. "It is meant to wipe the nose, sir, and nothing more."

He stepped a step closer to the table.

"But why the rag?" he asked, still not satisfied.

"Because certain fastidious persons prefer not to wipe their noses on their sleeves," I explained. "This *fazzoletto* is a civilized thing, sir."

But I could tell from his eyes that he continued to harbor suspicions of the thing. So, taking my courage into my hands, I walked around from behind the counting table and placed myself nose to nose with him, so close that there was barely room for a hair between us. Then, staring at him straight, I asked, "Tell me, sir, do I look like a witch to you?"

The ploy worked. He threw back his head and began to laugh. "In truth you do," he answered cheerfully. "A Gypsy witch. But I do not believe you would harm me."

A Gypsy witch! Was that what I appeared in my finery? To mask my hurt at this unintended insult, I went straight to the business at hand.

"Now then," I began in the honeyed tone I had often heard my father use when dealing with a highborn client, "how can we serve you today, young gentleman?"

In answer, he placed a large, cloth-covered packet on the table and explained as he untied the strings, "I wish to leave these books in pawn with you. I have used up all my allowance and am awaiting a fresh remittance from my lord father."

The bantering manner was gone now. When it comes to money, patricians never jest.

Taking my cue from him, I set about to examine the merchandise for telltale signs of rot and misuse the way Papa had taught me. As I thumbed through the vellum leaves in search of tears, stains, and mold, the words jumped off the page:

Come Lesbia, let us live and love,
Nor give a damn what sour old men say.
The sun that sets may rise again
But when our light has sunk into the earth
it is gone forever...

Who was the author of this marvelous verse? I turned to the frontispiece. Catullus: *Poesia*, a work forbidden to all virtuous women for fear that its contents would overheat our blood.

With great reluctance I tore myself away from the Roman poet and directed my attention to the second volume, a smaller book, not illuminated but copied onto fine vellum with an elegant hand.

"But this is your Latin grammar," I exclaimed upon reading the title page.

"So it is," the young man replied cheerfully.

"How will you study without it?" I asked.

He rubbed his chin and furrowed his forehead. Apparently, he had not foreseen that predicament.

"You must not place this book in pawn," I ordered him, quite unconscious of the impropriety of my address, not to mention my lack of business acumen.

"Oh, must I not now?" he joshed. The dancing devil in his eyes brought me back to myself. Blushing deeply, I begged his forgiveness.

"What do I have to forgive?" he inquired, the soul of geniality.

"My impertinence, sir," I answered prettily. "It is not my place to instruct you. I only know that, for myself, I could not get from one day to another without my Greek grammar, and I know it is the same in studying any language. The grammar book is the base on which the entire edifice stands."

"You are a scholar, then?" he asked.

"In a small way," I answered modestly.

"I find nothing small about Latin and Greek, lady," he rejoined. "In truth, I find them mountainous and far too elevated for my poor understanding."

"It is the same with my brother," I told him, more familiar as the minutes went on. "He is very clever at science but cannot digest a single Latin conjugation without choking on it."

"A man after my own heart." He smiled.

"I believe it is often the case," I ventured, made bold by his amiability, "that boys cannot command the patience for the study of languages, especially active boys such as my brother Vitale, and—yourself." Here I felt myself blush to a flaming red.

"Whereas girls..." he encouraged me.

"If girls were given an equal chance, they would take over scholarship in a single generation," I stated flatly.

But he did not take my words ill. Instead, he smiled broadly. "I wonder what my teacher will have to say when I tell him that," he teased.

"Oh sir, please..." I begged. God knows what reprisals might come back to me from my careless boasts.

"Never fear, little one," he consoled me. "I would not dream of repeating your remark, not only for your sake but for my own. If I were to make such a statement to my teacher—or even in his hearing—I should surely feel the touch of the rod for it."

"He beats you?" I asked.

"For such an impertinence, he might. For he never tires of warning us against women, their wantonness, inconstancy, and proneness to folly. Women have their being in this world, he claims, for no other purpose than to serve men and to bear them many children."

"And do you agree, sir?" I asked.

"I have before me in my family the example of women of great learning and virtue," he replied, suddenly serious. "I would betray their trust if I did not espouse the cause of female scholarship."

The sweetness of his countenance when he spoke of these kinswomen melted my heart. Until then I had dreamed of him as a phantom lover; now, I began to see him as a young man—a man of sentiment and honor.

"But if I do not put my books in pawn, what must I do for my living?" he inquired of me. "For even a student must eat, lady."

"Have you not some articles of equal value but of more trivial importance?" I asked. "Search your mind."

"I could bring my silver bowl and pitcher. But then I might never wash myself. Do you believe cleanliness to be trivial?"

"Not at all, sir. Our Jewish sage Maimonides tells us that

hygiene is a sacred duty. Have you no tapestries or fine garments that you can spare for a few weeks?"

"Not my clothes, lady. Spare me nakedness and the chill."

"If you were a woman, you would have a needle case," I persisted.

"Alas, I am no needleman...but I do believe..." And in a moment he was out the door, gone without a word of explanation.

He returned within the hour, carrying an inlaid ivory box. This he set upon the table and with a flourish raised the top to reveal an exquisite set of chessmen, each group of pieces carved from a different gemstone. The bishops were fashioned from a dull onyx as befitted their solemnity, the knights from an elegantly striated sea-green malachite matching their occupational flamboyance; the queen was chalcedony and the king carnelian. They all stood on little gold feet. Taken as a whole, that set was an object of grace such as we rarely saw in our small *banco*. "But this is magnificent!" I exclaimed.

"Magnificent, yes," he replied. "But as you say, lady, trivial compared to the pursuit of Latin."

Thus we made our contract: twenty gold ducats at twenty percent for the chess set, to be reclaimed within a year or else sold with all profit accruing to the *banco*.

"But of course such a thing cannot happen," he assured me, "for I mean to reclaim my chessmen within the month. Meanwhile, take care of them for me. This set was a gift from my kinsman Alfonso d'Este for my service at his wedding. I treasure it above all my other goods and trust you not to sell it out from under me."

I promised faithfully to keep the chessmen under my eye, and since we had no more business to transact, made as if to bid him farewell.

But he was not done with me yet. "One thing more," he insisted. "You have given me a lesson today, lady, for which I am grateful. And I should like to do some small service for you in return."

"Your kind words, sir, are payment enough," I replied.

"Is there no small thing I can do for you? Think on it..."

"There is a thing..." I hesitated. "But no...I dare not..."

"Out with it!" he boomed. "The lady who does not dare to utter her own thoughts will never take over the world of scholarship."

Reassuring words. "You are a student at the great University of Bologna, are you not, sir?" I ventured.

"Indeed I am," he replied.

"I hear much of this university," I told him. "But we live very retired and I go out rarely..."

"You wish me to show you the university?" he asked.

"I long to see it and to pay my respect to its great fame," I replied.

But dare I risk the scandal? Dare he? Jewish girls had been burned for doing not much more than taking the arm of a Christian gentleman on a public street. Certainly young men had been expelled from the university for the offense of keeping company with "Jewish whores." I could tell from his gaze that these dangers occupied his mind as they did mine. But none of this was spoken of. He simply bowed to the floor and announced, "Lady, you have but to speak your will and it shall be done. I am at your command."

Within moments, I had bidden the clerk watch over the *banco* and was out in the *vicolo* at the side of my knight.

I had never before walked out in a public street unaccompanied by some relation or servant. That first moment of freedom loosened the bonds that held me to the earth and I fairly flew along beside him under the sheltering arcades of the town.

Before long we entered into a narrow street, where he stopped before an imposing house decorated with what I recognized as the Gonzaga *imprese*: a dove on a dead tree trunk with the motto *Vrai amour ne se change*. The door was unlocked by a page who flashed the Gonzaga colors on his sleeve. Could this be the famous University of Bologna? It looked much more like an opulent private house.

Leaving the page behind, we walked through two reception rooms and a library to a large lozenge-shaped room that ran the full width of the house at the back. The frescoes that adorned the walls and ceiling and the emptiness of the place marked it as a ballroom. But, to my surprise, my companion presented it as a lecture room. "Here is where the professor dispenses his wisdom," he told me.

"And where do the students sit?" I asked.

"The lucky ones on chairs and benches. The rest on the floor," he answered, then added, "Bleeding piles are the occupational disease of the university student, you know. It comes from sitting for hours on cold tiles."

"How long then are these lectures?" I asked.

"They seem to last an eternity," he answered.

"And how often are they given?" I asked.

"All depends on the fancy of the professor. Sometimes we do not see him for weeks on end. Then all at once he will turn up daily at the crack of dawn and devil us until the sun sets and expect us to learn the stuff overnight into the bargain."

"Where then do you study?" I asked.

"Come." He beckoned me on. "I'll show you."

Onward he led me through a sweet little courtyard, up an imposing marble staircase, and thence, straight up to the third story of the house, the kitchen floor. There we made for a series of small rooms, one giving onto the next, until we came to the last one. "Here we are," he announced.

It was a sparsely furnished room with a bed, a chest, and a trundle meant for a servant but currently occupied by a small brown and white mongrel on a satin pillow.

"This is my study," he informed me, "and that," pointing at the dog, "is my tutor, Fingebat." At the sound of his name the little dog sprang to life and began to prance on his hind legs.

Now ordinarily the diminutive performer would have delighted me. But in this setting he only confirmed my suspicion that I had been taken in by a ruse.

"Where am I?" I cried. "Where have you brought me to?"

"I have brought you to my cousin's house, to my chambers where I live. Did you not see the Gonzaga colors painted on the doorpost?"

"But you promised to bring me to the university and this is not the university at all." I was beginning to repent my impulse. "And the *sala* is not the lecture room either."

"But it *is*," he insisted. "You can depend upon it. I am no liar, lady. Perhaps a bit of a trickster but no liar. You see, what we have here is a jest. Better still a conundrum. The university is both here and not here."

"But that is impossible. Your own Thomas Aquinas tells us that no thing can be both here and not here," I reminded him.

"Well, this university both can be and is both here and not here," he responded confidently, quite unimpressed by the learned Christian. "Forget Aquinas and think for yourself. What if it is elsewhere?"

"Then it cannot be here," I replied, firmly committed to the Christian position.

"But what if sometimes it is here and sometimes it is elsewhere?"

"The university is a movable feast!" I finally grasped what he had been getting at.

"Bravo!" He clapped me on the back heartily. "You've guessed the riddle. In truth, the university is no place. Or every place. We gather where we can. If there are too many students for anyone's salon, we meet in a field. Or we meet in the professor's lodging. Some days, you will find us in the Piazza del Nettuno or here in my cousin's palace..."

"You mean that this famed University of Bologna has no buildings of its own?"

"As I am the son of my father, Luigi Gonzaga," he swore.

As soon as he spoke the phrase, I realized that we had never been introduced. "You are cousin, then, to the lords of Mantova?"

"I am descended from the cadet branch of the family, the Gonzagas of Bozzuolo. Allow me to introduce myself, lady. Pirro Vincenzo Gonzaga, at your service."

He then conducted me on a whirlwind tour of the university which was, in effect, a tour of the city, for the University of Bologna is indeed everywhere, just as he said.

That hour of freedom in the streets, with Fingebat dancing along beside us while we joked and laughed and dared the powers that be, gave me a tantalizing view of what life must be like for those less hampered than myself.

It is a hard thing to relinquish one's freedom after such a brief taste. When we reached the *banco* I scooped up little Fingebat and hugged him to my breast for comfort. And, do you know, that clever fellow repaid me with a shower of wet kisses and an outpouring of sympathetic whinnies.

It took an effort of will to hand him back to his master. And when I did, to my delight the young lord waved me off. "You keep him, madonna. An impoverished student makes a poor master. Besides, I can see how happy he is in your arms."

Then, before I had time to think it over, my knight had tipped his hat and was whistling off down Jew Street. "Fingebat will guard my chess set until I return for it," he shouted over his shoulder as he rounded the corner. "Within the month."

I stood for many minutes at the door with the dog in my arms, reluctant to reenter our tiny dwelling. From the first day I saw that house I had loved it. Now, I felt the tiny structure close in on me as if to smother me. All at once, I knew the doll's house for what it was, and what it must have seemed to Papa—a prison.

FLY. FLY. BIRDS ARE pushed out of the nest. Cubs are tossed out of the lair. But girls never leave home. And Jewish girls rarely venture beyond Jew Street. During the days after my escapade, I could think of nothing but the wind whistling through the arcades and the strength of my cavalier's forearm as he danced me along the streets. Nights I snuggled next to Fingebat, my token for his master's return. Within the month, he had said. But many things can happen in the space of a month.

March brought another letter from Ferrara. This time, Papa did not read it aloud. But he was smiling when he finished the letter. And his good humor continued through the days that followed.

That same week, he took himself to the barber and had his unkempt beard shaved off. We had not seen his countenance exposed for more than a year, and what we saw when it was revealed by the razor caused me more than a few pangs. His round cheeks were sunk in; deep furrows drew the corners of his mouth down toward his chin, what the face readers call lines of disappointment. In less than two years, my father had turned the corner into old age.

But he himself was not at all sad. He ceased to frequent the wine cupboard in the afternoons. His step lightened day by day. Finally, on the day that the purpose of the letter was revealed to us, he appeared to be absolutely jaunty.

It was late on a Friday afternoon, always a hectic day in any *banco*, for on Fridays Christian clients suddenly need cash to finance their weekend festivities and, at the same time, we Jews are pressing to close shop in good time for our Sabbath meal. Thus the *banco* was in the usual state of hubbub this Friday and all of us too busy to pay much attention to the cart that pulled up outside. Only when the door opened and the visitor stood before us did Jehiel and I recognize him as our cousin Asher.

I could not have been more astonished if he had descended from the sky in a chariot. On the other hand it was plain that Papa had been forewarned, for he greeted my cousin with great aplomb and seemed overjoyed to see him.

After the Sabbath supper, we sat by the light of the candles and took turns reading from the Holy Book under Papa's direction. It was the first time we had observed a religious ritual since arriving in that house. This gesture led me to believe that my cousin had brought with him some promise of reinstatement for Papa. But he made no mention of it. And I held my questions.

The week that followed passed peaceably and amicably. Asher drifted into the *banco* each day to assist as he could.

Seeing him ill at ease, I offered him my seat on the *cassone*. He accepted it gratefully. Now I was the odd man out. But it was only for the duration of the visit. So I thought. However, on the following Sabbath eve Papa summarily informed us that he was about to journey to Ferrara and that our cousin Asher would stay on to supervise the *banco* in his absence. Early the next morning, a mule arrived at the door to carry Papa off and we were left behind with our new master.

It was not in Papa's character to move so swiftly nor so secretively. He was the most forthright of men. But he was also as malleable as wax in the hands of his family. Mind you, none of this occurred to me at the time. For one thing, life went on very pleasantly in the little house after Papa left. I resumed my place on the *cassone*. Only now, I sat there beside Asher.

Another thing. My cousin was quite taken with me. I would often catch him looking at me with something close to longing. And once or twice, he even made a clumsy move to touch my hand.

Here is a fact of life for you, my son. No woman can resist being adored. Consistent, abject worship is a more powerful ploy in the game of love even than brute force. A man of strength can force a woman to submit to his advances. But he cannot compel her to give herself over to him. Whereas the constant pressure of unalloyed adoration never fails to call forth surrender.

First comes irritation. "Will he never leave off this milksop gazing?"

Then comes pity. "The poor thing is dying of love for me."

Next, impatience, a very important part of the process. "Why doesn't he *do* something about it, for God's sake, before we both die of boredom?"

After that, guilt. "How can I be so cruel? He asks so little. One smile would give him happiness for a whole day..."

At last, the lady relents. She smiles invitingly. Still he is too shy to do more than blush and look at his feet. Now, she is determined to put some starch into him. Bold, she looks into his eyes. He trembles. She is touched. Was ever a woman held so dear? At last, she takes his hand in hers. She fondles it. She presses it to her bosom. The courtship has been accomplished. She is his. Believe it.

People wonder how so-and-so can capture the hearts of so many women. He is pale, skinny, pockmarked, bandy-legged, and cross-eyed. What do women see in him? I asked one such unlikely cocksman in Madama's circle (discretion forbids me to mention his name, but he is high in the church and notorious for his great success with ladies) what accounted for his prowess. His answer was a statement you can ponder. "I simply put my limp member in her hand and start to cry," he told me.

Of course, my cousin Asher did no such thing. He was not a practiced seducer. His shyness was honest and natural. And when I finally did take his hand in mine (thinking to alleviate the misery of his unrequited passion for me), he literally ran out the door and into Jew Street. But that evening when we lit the candles he suggested boldly that we might essay something a little more secular than the Holy Book. "My education has been sadly neglected by that German ignoramus Rabbi Abramo," he told me, "and I feel the need to improve my understanding of the world." It was the longest sentence I had ever heard him speak.

I wasted no time in rushing up to my room to retrieve my copy of the *Aeneid* from under my pillows. And that night, we stayed up until the candles sputtered down to their ends, reading to each other out of my favorite chapter, in which Dido laments her lost lover. It was a most romantic moment, our two heads leaning in toward each other in order to share the light and the text. And we might as well have been alone, since although Zio and Jehiel stayed until the bitter end, they both slid into slumber shortly after the reading began, leaving us with no reminder that we were chaperoned other than an occasional snore.

At the end of the evening, Asher accompanied me to the door of my room and even got up the courage to lean forward as if to embrace me. But then his prudence took over and he slunk away down the hall without even saying goodnight.

The next day Papa returned full of schemes. His trip to Ferrara had succeeded beyond his dreams. The *cherem* had been lifted. He was once again a Jew among Jews.

"And that is not half of it, children," he informed us with shining eyes. "We are to leave this insignificant outpost and return to Mantova where our old friends, the Gonzaga princes, are pleased to welcome us."

"Will we have our old home back? And our ponies?" Jehiel wanted to know.

"For a certainty," Papa answered with confidence.

"And our beautiful garden?" I asked.

"Only if you agree to tend it, little Graziella," he replied. "For your Aunt Dorotea, I fear, is no gardener."

"Aunt Dorotea?"

"Yes, my dears." Papa scooped us up and sat us down upon his lap with unaccustomed familiarity. "I have saved the best news until the last. Now that I am reinstated, I am able to take my brother's place as I am ordered to do by the laws of Israel."

"Take Uncle Joseph's place?" I did not follow his meaning.

"Yes, my dear. It is written that after a suitable period of mourning, the observing Jew, if he be unmarried, must take the place of his dead brother, marry the widow and adopt her children." Then, turning to Asher: "You are my son now, as dear to me as Jehiel and Gershom. And Ricca is my daughter, as dear to me as Grazia. And Dorotea is my wife. I married her this week in your grandmother's house in Ferrara."

MANTOVA
REVISITED

15

MY FATHER'S MARRIAGE AND OUR MOVE BACK TO Lombardia brought our odyssey full circle, from Mantova to Ferrara to Bologna and, now, back to the town of my childhood. But we were in a different house this time. And with a different mother. Never were two women less alike than my mother and Dorotea.

At dinner, my new stepmother imposed an iron discipline completely at odds with the free exchange that had always prevailed among Papa, the boys, and myself. There was little laughing and no leaning at Dorotea's table. Jehiel and I were not permitted to speak until spoken to. And God help poor little Gershom if he reached out for a bit of bread before the "honored Signore Padre," as Dorotea insisted we call our father, had raised his cup.

She was also, like her mother-in-law, a great believer in purges, which she dispensed to us every Sabbath eve before bedtime so that our bodies would be, as she put it, clean inside and out. We had been raised in a more modern school of medicine, where fresh air, exercise, and plenty of fruit did the work of cleansing the gut. But we swallowed the vile stuff she dished out and endured the cramps that inevitably followed without protest.

I think we were waiting for Papa to step in and set things right. But as the weeks lengthened into months, not a word of objection was heard from him. Instead I found my prerogatives disappearing one by one. The first to go was my place in the *banco*. Dorotea claimed, with some justice, that my presence was much more urgently needed in the *casa* than behind the counting table. With a large household to run and two young boys to raise, she needed every spare female hand. And there went my chiefest freedom.

Next came the matter of books and learning. We had no tutor in residence — Dorotea had as yet been unable to find one to suit her — so that in order to pursue my studies, I would have had to attend the synagogue school with my brother Jehiel. But girls were not welcome in the school. I begged Papa to solicit special permission for me. Dorotea pointed out that it would be unseemly for me to be seen walking back and forth in the public streets every day, like a common tart, as she put it. Once again, Papa withdrew from the contest. Even more than my seat at the *banco*, my pursuit of knowledge had given me a window on the great world. Now a shade was drawn over that window.

But I did find a chink of light in the gloom. Denied a tutor, I set out to school myself. Each day after dinner, I sequestered myself in my bedroom, pleading a headache. And there, in the autumnal afternoon light, I pored over my old Cicero, parsing and analyzing just as I would have done under the direction of a teacher.

Made bold by Cicero, I soon ventured farther into forbidden territory. I had always wanted to sample the worldly pleasures of La Nonna's "French lies," and one afternoon, I sashayed through the kitchen, across the backyard, and into the warehouse in search of enlightenment and sin.

Any loan-banker always held in pawn dozens of copies of the *Reale di Francia*. It was far and away the most popular book in Italy—still is, I believe—read by the educated class in the original French and by the less cultivated in vernacular Italian. According to the plan I had formulated, I would steal one copy of each version and, by going from the one language to the other, would teach myself the French tongue while I reveled in the forbidden pleasures of romance.

As I had anticipated, the warehouse held in pawn more than half a dozen versions of the *Reale* in the French language, two of them beautifully illuminated. But I chose a cheap printed copy with only two woodcuts for illustration, reasoning that the more valuable items might occasion a more serious search if their owners should return to claim them. Likewise with the vernacular translation. I picked the most dog-eared, shabby one of the lot, reasoning that the owner of such a poor thing was unlikely to recoup his fortunes sufficiently to reclaim it.

As Madonna Isabella is fond of saying, no one who reads books and collects them is ever totally bereft of comfort in this life. Books made my early days in Dorotea's household bearable. They also kept me out of sight and out of mischief. But books were never all of life for me. I was also attracted to the glitter of the great world. And when a communication came inviting the dei Rossi *famiglia* to attend upon Marchese Francesco Gonzaga and his Marchesana at the Reggio, I put away my books and entered into the plans for the audience as eagerly as everybody else in our household.

It had been the old Marchese's custom to reaffirm his *condotta* with his Jewish *banchieri* each autumn—a not so subtle reminder that October was traditionally the month for giving gifts. During the first years of his rule Marchese Francesco had allowed this custom to drop from use, largely because the harvest time coincided with the major *palios* of the year and he far preferred galloping around racecourses winning ribbons to staying home and entertaining packs of Jews. But after he married Madonna Isabella in 1490, life at the Reggio became more courtly. And one of the customs Marchese Francesco revived in honor of his Este bride was the annual reception of his Jews.

On the day of the harvest reception we joined the five other Jewish banking families of Mantova and marched together into the Gonzaga stronghold: women, children, rabbis, *shohets*, clerks, and serving maids — all polished up for the occasion and dressed so grandly you would have thought we were en route to meet our Maker rather than a minor Christian prince — and only a marchese at that, not even a duke.

Mind you, the Gonzagas disported themselves like kings. The Marchese and his bride had set themselves up on identical gilded armchairs in the center of a large, formal garden under a white silk *baldacchino* that fluttered in the breeze. What a sight they presented to us on their twin daises, surrounded by courtiers and dogs — lean, rangy hunting dogs for him, small squeaky lapdogs for her — and two or three of their favorite dwarfs tumbling around at their feet. Glowing mistily in the autumn sun, they seemed posed, as if waiting for Maestro Mantegna to immortalize them with his brush as he had Marchese Francesco's grandparents on the walls of the Camera degli Sposi.

All that was missing was an appreciative audience. And that we Jews supplied when we were pushed forward into the presence, en masse, by a pair of turbaned body servants, garbed to resemble Janissaries with balloon trousers and scimitars hanging from their waists — a marvelous exotic touch.

Madonna Isabella had chosen blue for her summer *gamorra*. Seated there against the red cushions, framed in gold and clad in the Virgin's own color, her golden hair streaming down over her shoulders, she bore an eerie resemblance to the Queen of Heaven, for she was barely eighteen years of age, with the fresh skin and clear eyes of youth.

As for her husband, Marchese Francesco — whom I had seen only at a distance at the Este-Sforza wedding — up close he was an amazingly atavistic creature, squat and swarthy, with thick lips and an abnormally low-slung jaw. But power and presence fairly radiated out of that sullen face.

I found it astonishing that his young wife appeared to be

completely unintimidated by him. When he rose to give his welcoming address, she hardly bothered to feign interest. She simply sat there, playing with the gold bracelets that lined her bare arm. Then again, why should she be cowed by the likes of him? She was, after all, an Este—a clan with far deeper roots in Italy than the upstart Gonzagas.

The Marchese had chosen as his subject the *monte di pietà*—the Christian loan bank—that he had recently authorized in Mantova, at the request of Fra Bernardino da Feltre (yes, the same). An invention of the Franciscan friars, these *monti* were springing up wherever the brotherhood held sway. Their capital came not from savings or risk but from the charitable contributions of wealthy Christians. Thus the *monti* were able to lend to the poor at a much lower rate than the Jews—sometimes as low as five percent. And what had been virtually a Jewish monopoly of the pawnbroking trade was being seriously threatened up and down the peninsula.

With farming, landowning, commerce, and almost all civic employment forbidden to Jews, pawnbroking stood as the last bastion of an independent life for them. The alternative was penury. Do you wonder that the Mantovan Jews listened attentively to Marchese Francesco when he spoke to them of the imminent opening of a *monte di pietà* in Mantova?

It was an unusually hot day for October. The air, heavy with the sweet odor of the trumpet-flowered vines that hugged the atrium's pillars, resonated with the buzz of hummingbirds and the croaking of crickets. In this thick, heavy air, the Marchese's words reached my ears as if from a great distance. After a time, I heard him call out for an equerry, but the name he shouted hung in the air and did not reach me.

The equerry entered from a side portico, so that only his profile was visible to those of us facing the princes. Punctilious in his court etiquette, he bowed first before the young Marchesana, then made the same obeisance before his liege lord, the Marchese. That courtesy accomplished, he turned to survey the assemblage of Jews spread out before him. Poised confidently with his hand on his hip, a living reproduction of some contrapposto Greek hero, he slowly fanned the half-circle of Jews with a languid gaze. To me, seeing him through the heavy mist and heat of the false summer, he appeared as if in a daydream. But when his eyes came to rest on me, I knew that this was no fantasy. Without doubt, my Knight of the Este Colors was standing before me in the flesh.

He held my eyes with his and slowly lowered his left eyelid in a sly wink, as if daring me to lose countenance. I rose like a poor fish to the bait and sniggered aloud.

"You find my address amusing, signorina *ebrea*?" The Marchese was speaking to me. "Does it appeal to your wit?"

Dead silence in the garden now. All eyes on me. Then, out of the silence came a voice: "I cannot attest to the lady's wit, sir, but I can bear witness to her courage."

It was my young knight speaking up for me.

"Cousin." The lady turned to the young lord. "How is it that you know this Jewess?"

"She was the Jewish queen at your honored brother's wedding," he replied easily. "Perhaps you do not recognize her without her elephant."

It was not a first-class jest but it did turn Madonna's frown to half a smile.

"Come, Signorina Grazia." Lord Pirro took my hand and led me toward her. "Allow the *illustrissima* to look at you up close."

His touch bolstered my courage. Assuming the regal carriage of the Jewish queen, I honored her with the deep curtsy I had learned from Maestro Ambrogio.

As I rose she nodded approvingly and, turning to her consort, addressed him: "We have heard excellent reports of this young girl's ride through the streets of Ferrara. Being at the head of the procession myself, I was not witness to it, but your kinsman, I believe, will bear me out that she was reported by my honored father to display great poise and true courage riding the beast."

"She was magnificent," the young lord affirmed with a long

look in my direction. Whereupon I flushed.

"Look how she blushes." Madonna Isabella laughed. "A girl who can master an elephant has no need to be shy of a few Gonzagas." She turned to her husband. "Is that not true, sir?"

But the Marchese was not into the spirit of the jest. He never did like me. Not from that first moment. At the same time, Madonna Isabella made her judgment and came to a completely different conclusion. If a great Christian princess can be said to befriend a Jewish pawnbroker's daughter, she showed every evidence of befriending me. Yet I hung back, still not recovered from her husband's malevolence.

"Sit here, donnina." She patted the stool at her feet. "Let us talk. You have nothing to fear from us. We are Christians here, not savages. We don't eat young Jewish maidens for supper." She turned to Lord Pirro. "Do we, cousin?"

"Only when we are very, very hungry." At this, he bared his teeth, made a lunge as if to grab my arm and take a bite of it. Of course, I screamed. And all the assemblage collapsed with giggles. All except one. The Marchese was not amused.

"Enough of this jesting." He raised his hand in command. "Lord Pirro, fetch me the documents relating to the *monte di pietà*." And to his young wife: "Honored lady, you will repair with the Jewish ladies and children to the summer sitting room whilst I continue my business with the *signori ebrei*."

I did not see Lord Pirro again that day. Nor did he seek me out at the *banco* in the days that followed. But I felt certain that he would come someday soon, if only to reclaim his chess set, which lay sequestered in my *cassone* under the two forbidden volumes of the *Reale di Francia*. And to be sure, not many days went by before he arrived at our *banco*. I was not there. I only learned of it from that most unlikely of Cupid's messengers, my cousin Ricca.

"Asher tells me that the princeling who kissed your hand so boldly at the Reggio was sniffing around after you at the *banco* yesterday," she whispered to me as we knelt at prayers.

My delight must have registered for she instantly added, "If you take my advice you'll avoid him like the plague. Christian princelings bring nothing but trouble to Jewish girls."

"But what have I to do with him or he with me?" I asked, making a poor effort to hide my excitement.

"He came looking for you, didn't he?"

"For me? Did he ask for me?"

"No, stupid. Nothing that obvious. He made as if he had come to place a book in pawn, but it was really you he was after."

"Why, Ricca, wherever did you get such an idea?" I temporized, searching my mental library to find some tale that would distract her mind from these dangerous suspicions.

"I saw the wink he gave you at the Reggio. You ought to know better than to try and fool your wise cousin Ricca." She smirked.

Now I am not a natural liar nor a practiced one. But something told me that if ever there was a time to break the eighth commandment, that was it. I had to find some way to rid Ricca's mind of its suspicions.

"Well, this time, wise cousin, you are off the track." I took a deep breath and silently asked God to forgive me for the libel I was about to commit. "Did you not know that young Lord Pirro is the favorite of Cardinal Monsanto? They say at court that he is the old man's bum boy."

It was an inspired invention. You could almost see her salivate when I laid the choice morsel before her. "You mean he's a...I cannot speak the word."

"Life in these courts is not like life in our *casa*, cousin," I assured her airily. "They practice vices that you and I have never even dreamed of."

"Such as?" Her eyes widened avidly.

"Oh, Ricca, those vices are unspeakable. I couldn't soil my tongue with them."

And with that, I enjoyed the satisfaction of having her, for once, begging me to tell her a secret—a plea to which I, of course, remained deaf. For, truth to tell, I had not the least idea what I was speaking of. My total knowledge of "the unspeakable vice" was all ill-digested reading of Alcibiades' defense of his intercourse with Socrates, hardly a fruitful source of information on the subject. But my invention did serve to put Ricca off the scent and left my mind free to concoct wild schemes to seek out my Knight of the Este Colors.

In the *Reale di Francia*, the old nurse always serves the lovers as a go-between. But in our house the closest thing to a nurse had been Gelsomina and she was dismissed by Dorotea on Gershom's first school day. My brothers would willingly have done me courier service but their lives were even more circumscribed than my own, since they left for school each day before sunrise and only returned after dark. However, having established the custom of retiring to my room with my afternoon headache, I myself was free between dinner and evening prayers. If I could somehow breach the defenses that Dorotea had erected around our *casa*, I could act as my own messenger.

In my mother's time, our doors had been left open during the day and members of the *famiglia* came and went freely. Under Dorotea's regimen both great portals, front and back, remained bolted at all times. And the keys to those locks never left their place at Dorotea's waist. In the *Reale di Francia*, the heroine or her knight solved such a problem by dosing the villainess with a sleeping potion and stealing the keys from her while she sat snoring in front of the fire. But Dorotea never slept by the fire. And the wizards who turned up so conveniently at French castles to peddle lotions and potions never seemed to stop by our house.

Desperate for instruction, I turned to Caesar, who had breached so many walls in the course of his Gallic campaigns. And to be sure, he advised me that every citadel has its weak spot, even the most impregnable. Find that place and sneak in through it, he counsels; for it is no less honorable to breach a wall surreptitiously through a chink than to scale it heroically with a ladder. His exact words.

If anyone had bothered to notice, which of course no one did, that person would have been mightily amused to see me sneaking stealthily around the grounds, rattling the locks, pushing at the gates, searching fruitlessly for one of those chinks that Caesar claims no citadel is without. Obviously, he never ran up against a castellan like my stepmother.

But in the end he justified his reputation as a tactician. One morning when I slipped into the stable yard to examine the huge wooden doors one more time, there stood a horse and cart come to bring firewood from the nearby woods. A chink in the citadel. If what goes up must come down, I thought, then surely what comes in must go out.

Sounds of conviviality told me the muleteer was enjoying a bowl of cheer in the stable. Familiarity with Dorotea's ways told me he would not be long consuming that small portion.

Carpe diem. Horace's exhortation sprang to mind. Seize the day, Grazia. Darting across the muddy yard, I hurled myself into the wagon and pulled a rug over me. No time to plan how I would get back into the fortress once I had gotten out. No time for thought at all.

Almost at once I heard the jingle of keys. It was Dorotea come to open the great doors. How kind of her to arrange for my visit to the Reggio, I thought.

Very soon, the creak of rusted hinges moaned in the damp air and slowly the old door swung open. Then a shout from the muleteer, a crack of his whip, and out we sailed, past the gate and into the Via San Simone.

I leaned forward to try for a glimpse of something familiar—the old Baptistery or the Palace of Matilda of Toscana—but could see only ruts. Then just as I spotted the facade of San Andrea ahead, I heard a tremendous crack—a broken axle—and next thing I knew, I was tossed out of the back of the wagon with a great splatter of mud.

There I sat in the middle of the Piazza San Andrea at nones. We were enjoying a January thaw, which turned the square into a stinking marsh. On either side of me ladies in fine attire, assisted by their maids, were carefully negotiating wide slabs of board laid across the square to protect them from the mud. Between these I sat, flat on my rear, facing the stream of worshippers emerging from the church. My chemise was wet and filthy. My bottom was one great mud cake. My face was spattered like a raisin tart. One of the worshippers, taking me for a beggar girl, flipped a coin my way. He had just attended mass. His Christian spirit was aroused.

I sat in the mud, disdainful of his charity, and watched the coin sink slowly out of sight. With it went all my hopes for this wild adventure.

"May I be of assistance?"

I recognized the voice. It had a particular lilt, as if laughter was lurking around the edges of it.

He bowed gracefully. "May I know what has brought a queen down so low?"

As the longtime companion of a man of science and logic, I disdain magic in all its forms. But with a gambler for a father and an astrologer for a brother, I incline to a belief in spells, curses, signs, and auguries. Things do happen outside the bounds of reason. Against all reasonable expectations, my wild, imprudent adventure had landed me in the muddy center of the Piazza San Andrea looking up into the eyes of Pirro Gonzaga, my Knight of the Este Colors. It was, as the Jews say, *beshert*—foreordained.

With one strong pull he had me on my feet.

"May I conduct you to your house before you take a chill?" He offered his arm.

"Oh no, sir, that will not do. For you see, sir, I am gone without permission and if my stepmother finds out..."

"Say no more." He nodded understandingly. "I have been in similar straits myself. Although, I must admit, such predicaments are more common to members of the male sex than—"

"I know it is unseemly of me, sir. But I had no other way to deliver my message than to bring it to you myself."

"And was your message so important, then?" he asked.

"It is about your chess set, the one you put in pawn, the one you love more than you love your own life."

"Ah yes, my chess set. I fear I have not yet scraped up the ducats to reclaim it."

"But you have no need of ducats," I was happy to reassure him. "For I brought it with me from Bologna and the pieces reside at this very moment in a safe place unknown to anyone but myself and Fingebat... and now, you."

By then several passersby had stopped to stare and point at us. We must have made a strange pair, the young cavalier in his ermine and velvet and the shivering girl with the muddy behind.

"I fear we are beginning to attract attention." He held out his arm once again. "Not a wise move for either of us."

Whereupon he conducted me across a plank to the other side of the square and thence into a *vicolo* behind the shop that announced itself as the *monte di pietà*, the Christian loan bank.

"What sort of jest is this, sir, to bring me here?" I asked, suddenly suspicious.

"No jest at all," was his answer. "I would have taken you more readily to a Jewish loan bank, perhaps even to the dei Rossi *banco*. But from what you tell me, that would not be prudent. And we must find you a fresh garment, for you are shivering."

Then, seeing me still reluctant, he whispered into my ear most sweetly, "Surely a girl who could stand up to an elephant cannot fear to face an insignificant priest."

His whisper tickled my ear in a most delightful way. His grasp on my arm drew me close to him. We stepped in.

Not surprisingly, the Christian loan bank presented almost a mirror image of our little *banco* in Bologna — same weighing scales, same green cloth, same *cassone*. One difference: in place of my cousin Asher there stood a thin young man in clerical garb. But as the bargaining began he proved even more aggressive than most Jews would have dared to be with a Christian nobleman.

In the end I emerged in a decent plain back woolen *giornea*, acquired for one ducat, placed gently around my shoulders by my companion. No cloak of satin, or even miniver fur, could have seemed more luxurious.

Unremarked now, we strolled through the Piazza delle Erbe past Virgil's statue and thence around the back of the Reggio to a private gate where I was greeted with a perfect view of the majestic Castel San Giorgio and a heavy whiff of horse manure. Who but the Gonzagas would choose to stable their horses cheek by jowl with their residence?

Leaving me with orders not to budge, my cavalier disappeared in the fragrant direction of the stables. He was not gone long. After a few moments, he emerged leading a handsome chestnut stallion.

"This is Capotasso." He patted the animal affectionately. "We have enjoyed many a campaign together. With his help, I plan to smuggle you past that stepmother of yours and safely home."

"Home?" The thought that we must part so soon filled me with dismay.

"You do not wish to return?"

"Of course I must. I know I must," I answered, sad to say it.

"But do I understand that there may be time for a *brief* detour?" His blue eyes crinkled ever so slightly.

"A very brief detour," I replied, hoping that my lowered gaze would hide my most unmaidenly readiness.

In no time, we crossed the Ponte di Mulino and were in the countryside. Here frost had covered the earth with a white carpet. Looking down, I could see Capotasso's hoofprints etched on the pale surface. But the air felt balmy against my cheek, perhaps because the sun, which almost never shines in Mantova in winter, came out for us while we rode, as if to emphasize Fortuna's favor.

When we came to stop at last in a forest glade, I fairly floated off Capotasso's back into my lover's waiting arms, as if my body had no weight at all.

Without a word, he slipped the cloak off my shoulders and

pressed my body to his. Then putting me from him a little ways, he looked deep into my eyes and very slowly began to kiss me—my forehead, my cheeks, my chin, my eyes, and finally, my mouth, which had been longing for his all through the weary months.

Poets speak of the first kiss as sweet and dewy, dewy as a rose petal. Perhaps for some it is. For me, that first kiss was dark and moist and laced with fire. I felt myself sinking, drowning in sensation. Glorying in it.

There was no seducer in that wintry glade and no victim caught in his wily toils; only two young bodies intoxicated with yearning. The penetration of my hymen gave me one short stab of pain, but ah, the reward. Waves of passion washing over me like a vast sea. I did not yield my body to him. I gave it over as willingly and as wantonly as he gave his to me. Touch for touch. Stroke for stroke. Bite for bite. Suck for suck.

At length, I opened my eyes and became aware of the surroundings. We were in a large glade circled on all sides by waving aspens. Beside us there was a small stone basin—not more than eight of a man's arms in diameter. At its center, a bubbling little spring. Somehow, I knew at once where we were. "This is the Bosco Fontana," I cried. "The magic fountain."

"You have been here before?"

"Never."

"Then what makes you think—"

"I do not think, sir. I know it. My heart tells me."

"What have we here? Another Cassandra?"

"God forbid, sir. She is my least favorite character in all the ancient world. If there is anyone I would choose not to resemble, it is that cow."

"In that case, forgive the analogy. Would you like to know why I brought you here?"

Delighted at the prospect of hearing something other than a jest or a gallantry from his lips, I cried out, "Indeed I would, sir."

"Very well, I shall tell you. But on one condition."

"And what is that?"

"That from this moment you do not call me sir."

"But sir... what must I call you then?"

"Anything you wish. Call me Capotasso if you like. But no more sirs."

"But I am a lowly Jewess and you are—"

"Do not tell me who I am, lady. I know who I am. I am Pirro Vincenzo Gonzaga of Bozzuolo, the second son of Lord Luigi of the cadet branch of that illustrious family. And you..." He took my face into his gentle hands. "You are a brave, wild, beautiful young lady who has twice now risked life itself to come out with me." Then, as if so much talk had used up his supply of words, he turned away from me to face the little spring.

When next he spoke, the sound of his voice barely rose above the burble of the spring. "This fountain is said to be the remnant of an ancient temple dedicated to the goddess of love. They say that lovers who anoint themselves here will be under the special protection of Venus from that moment on. I brought you to this place because we are in need of all the protection we can enlist. We have entered upon a dangerous game this day, lady."

So saying, he dipped his hand into the icy water of the magic fountain and anointed my forehead. And I, in my turn, performed the same rite for him.

Then he lifted me up to the saddle, hopped on in front of me, and after a shout of "Hold on!" carried me swiftly through the wood, back across the Mulino bridge, and finally through a series of tiny *vicoli* and garbage-strewn *piazzette* that brought us to the Via San Simone. There, some fifty steps from the doors of our stable yard, he put me down with the terse instruction "Stay here. When you next see me, these doors will open and I will come out, possibly followed by a stableboy or one of your relations. Then, a ruckus will ensue that will take everyone's attention. When that happens, you must slide in unobserved and secrete yourself in one of the horse stalls. I will come to you there."

After he had seen me safely hidden in the shadow of the wall, he tethered his horse to one of the rings on the side of the building. Then, whistling happily as if he had no care in the world, he made for the front door of the *banco*.

Faithful to my orders, I waited as I had been told to do. Some moments later the great doors did indeed swing open and he came out, followed by Sandro, the cross-eyed stableboy. Then all at once Capotasso began to rear and neigh and set up a most terrible clamor, causing much shouting and running about.

During this diversion, faithful to my orders, I took the opportunity to slide into the yard through the open door and thence into the first horse stall. After some moments I was joined by Capotasso, meek as a lamb now. Then, following close behind the mount, his master.

When I saw him standing there, framed by the arch in silhouette like an angel, my heart jumped with such force that I thought it would raise me from the ground. And as he approached me, his fingers to his mouth to warn me into silence, a most violent surge of heat suffused my body. Without a word, he pulled me gently to my feet and, as he slipped the cloak off my shoulders, pressed my body to his. It was dark and humid in that stall and heavy with the pungent odor of horse droppings. But I swear to you that when he pressed his lips against mine, the damp and stench fell away and I was transported to another place, warm and soft and smelling of jasmine. Truth to tell, I would happily have gone on to taste the ultimate bliss for a second time. But my gallant love showed more care for me than I did for myself.

"You must go before you are missed," he warned me. "Be off now, lady. We cannot have you missing your evening prayers — or being missed at them."

Still I tarried, reluctant to leave the warmth of his arms.

"We must be strong, my love," he admonished me gently, "so that we can be weak another day. How does next Wednesday suit you?"

"I fear I cannot," I replied sadly. "Today was a fortunate

accident. Most times this place is locked and bolted like a jail."

"Then I must come and rescue you. I will come on Wednesday in the afternoon just after dinner," he announced, quite matter-of-fact. "Let us meet here in this horse stall. It will be cozier than your stepmother's *sala*, do you not agree?"

I laughed. We kissed one last time. Wednesday was only a week away.

16

FORTUNE FAVORS THE BOLD. ALTHOUGH I WAS TEASED for having slid so clumsily into the mud in the yard, a much more consequential event happened the same afternoon that drew attention away from my mishap. It seems that a member of the Gonzaga clan had appeared at the *banco* just before evensong with a lame horse.

"He came to me," Asher reported, "and reminded me that we had met twice before—once at his kinsman's wedding in Ferrara and once recently at the Reggio."

"You must have made a good impression, my son," Dorotea remarked, her pigeon breast swelled with satisfaction.

"He asked to be remembered to you as well, cousin Grazia."

I felt a kick under the table from Ricca's direction. "What did the fellow want with us?" she inquired, all innocence.

"There was some trouble with his horse, a loose shoe or some such thing," Papa answered. "He wished to stable the animal with us until one of his grooms could be brought to tend it. Of course, we obliged. The animal is quartered in the first stall at this very moment. I myself saw to it— although I cannot for the life of me find anything wrong with his shoes," he added with a puzzled look.

"And what of the young prince?" Ricca asked.

"He is no prince, daughter," Papa corrected her. "This young fellow is merely the son of a lord . . . Luigi Gonzaga of Bozzuolo, who is uncle to our Marchese Francesco."

"Prince or lord, it's all one to me." She shrugged.

"He's still out there, fussing over his animal. Those Gonzagas are mad about horses, you know. We used to meet them in the old days, when we all rode in the park together. Do you remember, children?"

It was still a fond memory to him.

"I have been wondering if we could not take up that custom again, Papa," I ventured.

"Such habits are for little children and patricians with nothing but time on their hands," Dorotea sniffed. The older Dorotea got, the more of a sniffer she became. Judah once explained to me that there is some organ behind the nose that can cause it to drip constantly, like a faulty pump. This was the malady to which he attributed Dorotea's sniff. And he must have been right, for you could often see a small bubble of moisture forming at the tip of her nose just before she sniffed it up her nostril. Whatever the reason for it, the habit of sniffing gave her an air of perpetual disdain; and since she found much to be disdainful of, this ailing organ provided her with a gesture quite in keeping with her nature.

While Dorotea sniffed, I pursued my cause. "Might we have our horses back, do you think, Papa?" I asked.

"Out of the question," Dorotea answered for him.

"Then perhaps I could ride one of our regular horses," I suggested. "As you point out, stepmother, I am a woman now, so I ought to be able to control the likes of Tamarindo."

The very mention of the name excited Asher's concern — honest enough, however misguided. "Oh, do not ride that beast, I beg you, cousin," he cried. "He is a terror, even to Sandro."

"I have little doubt Grazia could handle the bay, my son," Papa replied with, I think, a touch of pride. "The true questions are: Can Sandro be spared to care for the animal? And who is free to accompany Grazia on these daily rides?"

"The groom has his hands full as it is," Dorotea answered. And, as usual, Papa deferred to her judgment. But I did manage to establish my intention of getting to know Tamarindo — "as if he were a human being," scoffed Ricca — and of taking over the task of grooming him, which she pronounced disgusting. To her, it was. But for me, that stall was redolent with memories, and Tamarindo a perfect confidant. Having no words, he mostly listened and occasionally neighed sympathetically. We had some fine conversations.

"Did you notice the way Lord Pirro sits his mount, Tamarindo? Is he not made in the mold of Apollo?"

A loud whinny from my horsey friend.

"And his eyes. Are they not a blue to rival the vault of heaven?"

Two neighs.

"And am I not the most fortunate of girls to find such a gallant cavalier?"

A resounding affirmative stamp of the hoof.

Nights, I gathered up poor, patient Fingebat into my bed and pressed on him the same questions I had asked Tamarindo that day. And he, equally well suited to the role of confidant, never failed to respond with an appropriately affirmative yelp. So the week passed.

By the following Wednesday, my daily presence in the stable was so much a part of the life of the household that I was able to make my way to the horse stalls unremarked. The cook even gave me a sweet bun on my way out "to share with Tamarindo." Sandro the stable hand was another matter. A hulking, slow-moving brute of a fellow, he was further cursed with a defect of vision. His eyes, one blue, one brown, were completely crossed. When he "looked you in the eye," so to speak, his left eye looked to the right, and his right eye to the left. Such people are often made sport of in the street. And indeed, they do present a comic spectacle. But they are also inscrutable, for one cannot tell whether one is being observed or not.

That was my difficulty with this slave Sandro. The ill-made creature had been a wedding gift to Dorotea from La Nonna— and a very generous gift it had seemed, since male slaves were, at that time, going for ten ducats or more. But his handicap, added to the slowness of his brain, made him unfit for service in the house. Thus he became a stable hand by default. From my first afternoon in the stable, I felt his eyes on me as I worked over the horse. Yet, when I turned to catch him out at spying, I could not know for certain if it was at me he was staring so fixedly or some object on the other side of the yard.

Wednesday dawned a crisp, brilliant February day, not the best day to sneak about undetected. For that, fog is one's best ally. But I knew Lord Pirro would find a way to come to me.

And sure enough, when I came into the stall that afternoon with my horse-grooming tools, there stood my cavalier leaning against the wall, still as a statue. Silently he indicated the broad ledge above our heads where the hay was stored. It was a perfect hiding place. Making a stirrup of his cupped hands, he offered me a boost up. I hesitated. The shelf was at least six hands above my head. Did I have the strength to catapult myself so high?

With great firmness, he placed my two hands on his shoulders and my right foot in his cupped hands.

"*Uno, due, tre . . .*" he muttered. And, whoosh, I was up in the loft spitting straws out of my mouth. A second later, his face popped up over the ledge. But when I rushed to embrace him, he held me off, muttering, "We must talk," through a stern mouth.

"Of what?" I demanded, peevish at being denied.

"Of love," he answered, grim as death.

As yet I did not intuit the direction he wished the conversation to take and I persisted in my petulance. "Why talk of love when we can do it?" I demanded.

"Because, hussy, if we continue to do it and get caught at it, we may both burn. For sure, you will."

I must admit this thought sobered me down. "What then

do you have to say to me of love, my love?" I inquired, more humble now.

"First, that I have come to cherish you. Second, that I have confided this passion to my kinswoman Madonna Isabella."

Whatever I expected, it certainly was not such a declaration.

"I told her that you are dearer to me than my life," he went on, "and that, although you were willing to risk all for me, I could no longer expose you to such danger as we have been courting."

"You knew that I loved you?" I asked naively.

"Of course," he answered, with that serene confidence that marks men of his rank. "Why else do women take great risks except for love?"

I could not deny it. Nor did I wish to play coy. For he had confessed his love in such an open way that I could not do less.

"You read me right. I do love you," I answered, as candid in my confession as he had been in his. "But was it wise to admit the Marchesana to our secret? What if she should tell the procurator, or her confessor—those priests are a menace to us Jews, you know."

"It was a calculated risk," he answered. "My kinswoman is young like us and a great believer in romance. I doubt she would ever betray us. And I hoped she might be persuaded to help us."

"Was she persuaded?" I asked.

"She offered to take us under her protection."

"Would that keep us safe?"

"Oh yes, her power is absolute in Mantova, second only to her husband's."

"Then it is settled. We can meet and go about as—"

"Not quite so easily, my Grazia. She will take us under her protection and in due course she will give us permission to marry, on one condition."

I knew before he spoke what the words would be. "She wants me to become a *conversa*..."

He nodded. "That is her condition."

"Oh no, I could not. I could never..." was my first reaction.

"I am a Jewess, my lord. How could I suddenly change?"

"You would have to take instruction. Madonna Isabella has spoken to her confessor—mentioning no names—who is in charge of the *casa dei catecumeni*. He is willing to take you in and teach you himself."

"The *casa dei catecumeni* in the Via dei Grechi?"

The so-called House of Converts was well known to every Jew in Mantova. A small, dark place adjoining a Dominican convent, it sometimes served as a refuge for renegade Jews, frequently criminal types who preferred to convert rather than face the justice of the *Wad Kellilah*.

"But bigamists and cheaters and wife-beaters go there," I told him. "Those *conversos* are an unsavory lot, my lord."

"It will only be for a short while until you learn the catechism and a few other things. Then, Madonna Isabella has offered to stand sponsor for your baptism. And once you are baptized, we will join ourselves in a Christian marriage." He took my hand and looked deep into my eyes. "I understand what a sacrifice this will be for you..." He was talking as if my mind was already made up. "But a Christian marriage is the only course open to me if I am to remain an honorable man. Otherwise we will both end up dishonored—and you, I fear, more harmed than I."

"But I would never see my family again. My brothers...my father..."

He placed his fingers gently over my lips. "Say no more. Think. Consider. Madama has given me a letter for you. Read it. Perhaps it will provide counsel. We have a week. Madama has told me that either I must bring you into the *casa dei catecumeni* or give you up by *carnevale*. If you decide against me, I have agreed never to see you again."

I gasped.

"It is for your protection more than my own, my love. I have seen a woman burned, Grazia. I have seen her flesh sizzle on the faggots. I cannot face that prospect for you. Now you know all. Let us make love."

Was ever there born a creature more perverse than woman? The moment the invitation formed on his lips, my passion fled. The great ardor in me gave way to timidity—even fright. Of its own volition, my mouth closed tightly against his insistent tongue and I slowly withdrew my body from his embrace.

A coarser or more brutish man would have had his way in spite of my opposition. Such men—stuffed with pride and *virtu*—take any sign of resistance as caprice, perhaps because it has no equivalence in their experience. But Lord Pirro is a peerless lover who understands the natural perversity of women. He simply left me to myself. And before long, I found myself edging through the straw back into the curve of his arm. Still he made no move toward me. Ever so cautiously, I placed one of my legs over his thigh. I could feel his muscles hard against mine through the silken *calze* he wore. Then very slowly he began to stroke my hair, my cheek, my shoulder. Everywhere he caressed me tingled as if touched by a magician's wand.

Patiently and tenderly, he led me through the age-old dance of love, serenaded by cicadas, with the swish of the horses' tails for an accompaniment.

Suddenly, the rhythm was broken by a faint movement of the air, not menacing but an interruption nonetheless. I saw the ladder describe an arc above me before I heard it land against the attic shelf. Then I saw Sandro's hand—unmistakably his, for no one in our household had a paw that brown and that huge—flailing about in the darkness, searching for something to grab onto. Then a heavy grunt. Then the face with its crossed eyes.

Lord Pirro had fallen into a crouch behind me, so what Sandro saw when he pulled himself up to eye level was Madonnina Grazia sitting in the shadows on a pile of straw, looking, I hoped, furious at being intruded upon.

After blinking for some time, the brute was able to focus his wandering eyes on me.

"Sandro, what in the name of God and his saints are you

doing up here?" I was easily as alarmed as he but determined not to show it.

"A n-n-noise...I her-her-heard..."

He heaved his huge body up onto the ledge.

"Go back!" I ordered.

But he made no move to obey. He simply crouched there, blinking.

"Down!" I pointed in the direction of the ground. Behind me, a hidden presence reached for my hand.

"Down, Sandro! Go!" As I gave the order I felt a handle being placed in my fist, a pitchfork from the feel of it.

"If you do not turn and go back down that ladder..."

The brute sucked in a great bellyful of air and lunged. And, gathering all my strength, I raised the heavy pitchfork and plunged it straight into his head.

The blow must have stunned him. He whirled half a turn, then stood with his back to me, swaying and moaning.

"I'll finish him off." Behind me, a hand took the weapon out of mine and lunged. Over and over I saw the tines of the fork raised in the air and plunged into the giant's backside. The pain must have been excruciating, for it seemed to knock his eyes back into his head. I saw a pair of white eyeballs, then a glimpse of a torn *camicia* streaked with blood, then heard a deafening shriek as the slave hurled himself off the open shelf and onto the stable floor. There followed a series of groans that finally subsided into whimpers. And at last, silence.

Beside me, Lord Pirro stood tense and wary, straining for some sound to indicate that the giant's screams had aroused the household. But no indication was forthcoming. Only the buzzing of the flies and the swishing of the horses' tails.

Motioning to me to stay still, he laid the pitchfork down, walked softly to the edge of the loft, and looked down.

"He's gone," he whispered.

"Gone?"

"Come and see for yourself. The ground is bare."

I approached and peered over the edge cautiously. Nothing

but a stray bucket and a pile of horse manure.

"I must go down and see what's become of the villain," he announced.

"No, no. I shall go. I must," I insisted, albeit weakly. "For if I am found, I can fabricate some pretext. But if you are discovered, we are both undone."

"I doubt you can get down the ladder without taking a tumble. Look at you. You are trembling like an aspen leaf."

"I *am* frightened," I admitted. "But you mistake yourself, sir, if you think me a coward. I will descend the ladder and find the brute."

"And if you find him dead—with a broken neck?"

"Why, then I shall faint," I replied, "and you must risk all and come down and carry me back up."

Down I went, quivering, as he said, like an aspen leaf in fear of what I would find. But to my astonishment, there was no sign of Sandro in the yard nor in any corner of any of the stalls. The brute had disappeared. This I reported to my lord when I once again ascended the ladder.

"Then we are in luck. But we must not press it," he said. "I shall be off. And you, to your room to read Madonna Isabella's letter. Watch me leave you for the last time. When next I depart this paradise of straw, I will carry you with me."

So saying, he grasped two heavy iron rings lying flat on the ground and, uttering a fierce grunt, pulled them up in one tremendous heave, creating a hole in the floor of the loft that gave directly down into the *vicolo* below. As I watched, he jumped down into the lane with perfect grace, untethered his horse, and rode off, jaunty as ever, his honorary Este colors streaming out behind him in the wintry wind.

The Sandro affair ended most mysteriously. That monster was never seen again in the environs of Mantova. Although my father put out notices of a runaway slave, he never did turn up at any of the slave markets on the peninsula. Nor was his bloated body ever washed up on the shores of the Mincio, as I dreamed it would be. He simply vanished. And truthfully, I did not dwell overmuch on his disappearance. What took over my mind from that day on was Madonna Isabella's offer with its nonnegotiable terms.

What was it to be? A life without love or a life without family and religion? I had one week to decide.

FROM DANILO'S ARCHIVE

TO GRAZIA DEI ROSSI, THE MANTOVAN JEWESS

The fame that resounds in my ears about your virtue and goodness prompts me to offer the hand of friendship. Listen to my advice. Convert to Christianity and live your life illuminated by the Holy Spirit. For the one flesh-and-blood mother that you renounce, you will find ten more through the love of Jesus Christ. The Madonna of Mantova will be a mother to you. My sister, both my sisters-in-law, and myself will be mothers to you. Nor will you lack a gracious husband. Lord Pirro Gonzaga longs for you so much that the wretched man is at risk of losing his head for the love of you. The poor little thing is falling apart like a snowflake that the sun has discovered.

Come to see me within the week. We will debate. I will pull the scales from your eyes. The blindness of the Hebrew faith will become clear to you. Trust me. I speak to you in perfect faith. I have read in the book of the Jews called The Sanidrin that the Messiah was born the same day the temple was destroyed. Do not allow yourself to be deceived any longer by your doomed rabbis ignorant of both human and divine doctrine. Instead, join me in Christian fellowship where you will enjoy a husband who is wise and courageous and neither importunate nor wearisome. Every time I hear his witty narrations I am afraid I will die laughing as Philomene, the poet, or Philistione, the actor, did. No melancholy humor will ever reside in your house. Sad thoughts will keep far away from you. I assure you on my faith that you will be more loved by him than Euridice was by Orfeo, than Aspasia was by Pericle, than Orestia was by M. Plautio.

Think and examine well what I've told you. Come to me as a sister in Christ. Beautiful and pleasant thoughts to you. May God illuminate you with the living rays of the Holy Spirit and guide you to do the right and wise thing.
Isabella d'Este da Gonzaga

17

A CLOSE READING OF MADONNA ISABELLA'S LETTER left no room for doubt. Although it was couched in the scholarly style of a *disputa* putting forward the superiority of Christ's religion to the religion of Moses, the true message was that I must convert or sacrifice her support.

As Plautus's jest goes, it was not difficult to make up my mind; I made it up several times every day. Each time one of my brothers sought me out for heart's ease or protection, I knew I must stay for their sake. The next minute, having forgotten to bow or ask permission to leave the room, I would suffer such a stinging rebuke from Dorotea or my father that I knew I must flee from this tyranny to the kinder arms of strangers.

Then, on the very day of decision, Papa summoned me to his *studiolo* to tell me that he had acquired a fine new jennet for my use. This gift of love came to my troubled spirit like a message from the angels. Papa did love me. He had opposed his wife for my sake. I could not betray his trust. I would sacrifice love for duty.

But no sooner had I decided than Virgil's words came back

to me, the words spoken by Anna to Dido when she decides to give up Aeneas.

Will you wear out your life, young as you are?
Will you live alone sorrowing and pining, never to know
The crown of joy that Venus gives?

Yes, Anna, I answered. I will give up my youth and the joys of Venus, which I have barely begun to enjoy. And I will live on alone, sorrowing and pining forever.

But the stoical mantle of Dido which fitted me so well on my walk through the house and across the yard was cast off the moment I stepped foot in the stable and beheld my lover. One look and I threw myself into his arms, weeping.

That is how we were discovered, there in the open horse stall where any passerby could see. By my cousin Ricca.

One shriek and she was off to alert the household. At my urging Pirro scuttled up the ladder to the hayloft. His presence could only embarrass him and harm me.

Moments later, they entered the yard like a trio of inquisitors: Papa, Dorotea, and Ricca, the informant.

"He was there with her in the horse stall," she announced, pointing to where I stood. "They were embracing. I saw it with my own eyes"

"Is this true?" Papa demanded.

"Yes, it is true, honored padre. I was about to —"

"Do not speak. You have nothing more to say to me. Go to your chamber. Go now. Go before I give in to a terrible urge to beat you until you bleed."

"For shame," Dorotea murmured under her breath as I walked by. No further words were spoken to me that day. No one came to my room, not even my brothers. I could only assume they were forbidden my company on pain of severe punishment.

I lay awake until the first hours of the morning living and reliving the day's events, flagellating myself for carelessness, folly, and self-indulgence. Toward the early morning hours I heard the rings of my bed curtains scraping on the rod and found myself looking into the watery blue eyes of Rabbi Abramo.

"Good morning, my daughter." The oily patina on his words told me he was in his pastoral mode. "I am here on behalf of your loving parents," he announced. Had they suddenly been struck by paralysis, I wondered bitterly, to have to send an emissary up the stair to speak to me?

"They are sorely tried by your betrayal of them," he went on. "But I have assured them that you cannot be held account- able for your actions. The evil that dwells in the hearts of all women has taken hold of you. Do not despair." He placed his soft, damp hand on my arm. "These devils that dwell in you — for that is what they are — can be exorcised."

"Of what does this exorcism consist, Rabbi?" I asked.

"Twice each day I will come to you and recite certain ancient prayers over you," he answered. "Words of God, which reduce the power of the devil over your corrupted mind. As for your body..."

I held my breath.

"You will be bled every morning, starting on the morrow. And purged every night. And the apothecary will administer a klyster twice each week to complete the cleansing."

Twice each week.

"How long..." I was too fearful to finish my question.

"One month will be sufficient. Of that I am certain. Of course, should the evil spirits prove to be obdurate..." He paused a moment to allow the implications of this threat to sink into my mind. "But let us not dwell on failure when suc- cess is assured. I never yet have failed with an exorcism. We will begin this evening after sundown." The tight set of his thin lips persuaded me that there was no appeal against his remedy.

"Can I see my parents now?" I asked.

"You will see no one save myself — and the surgeon and

the apothecary—for a full revolution of the moon. For the moment, your honored parents prefer not to see you. Think of the humiliation you have caused them and of the danger into which you have led this family. Begin your penitence by putting their feelings ahead of your own. And spend every minute of this day and the days to come transforming yourself into a virtuous daughter they can be proud of."

Anger, which is a sin, is also an antidote to despair. The anger that rose up in me gave me the strength to resist, that and the knowledge that I had a bed waiting for me at the *casa dei catecumeni* and friends eager to welcome me there. To give myself reassurance, I took Madonna Isabella's letter from its hiding place and read, "...wretched Lord Pirro is at risk of losing his head for love of you...he is falling apart like a snowflake that the sun has discovered." And, just above, "...my sister, both my sisters-in-law, and myself will be mothers to you..."

In those words I saw spelled out an entire new family—an adoring husband, a loving mother, loyal sisters. And, in time to come, children of my own, Gonzaga children, fair like their father and strong and fearless like him.

That evening the rabbi came to me as he had promised and chanted his ritual prayers and offered me his purge, for which I thanked him humbly. I even sank to my knees at the bedside so that his last sight of me that night would be of a penitent girl praying to God to help her fight off her devils.

"May the devil take you, Jehovah, you old whore," I mumbled silently to myself, as I gazed reverently up to heaven. "May you fall into a pit with your prophets and your angels together. And may you drink piss for wine and eat cow's dung for meat and may you choke on the shit sliding down your gullet as you descend into hell."

AT MIDNIGHT, THE WATCHMAN passed beneath my window. "Ring, oh ring, the heavenly bell," he chanted. "'Tis the sixth hour of darkness and all is well."

That chant was my signal. I must be packed and gone between now and the matins bell. Into my sack went Cicero's *Orations*, Caesar's *Commentaries*, and my "French lies." I hesitated over my Virgil—an illuminated manuscript that I had borrowed from the warehouse—for I was determined to take nothing of value that might brand me as a thief. But in the end I threw it in the sack. I could not bear to part with it.

I left no note. Instead I made a little pile on my pillow where it would be noticed, of my Hebrew grammar, Maimonides' commentaries, and my velvet-bound prayer book. Then I laid upon this stack of rejections all the pieces of jewelry that Papa had given me over the years—my pearl necklace, my ruby pendant, and my little diamond ear clips.

Down the corridor my brothers lay sleeping. Gershom's even breathing was in no way disturbed when I touched my lips to his. But as I bent down to embrace Jehiel for the last time, his thick, sweeping lashes fluttered and his eyes slowly opened. He intuited in a glance the reason for my midnight visit.

No cry escaped his lips. But his deep, dark eyes spoke their own language. He held out his arms, pleading to go with me. Reluctantly, I shook my head. Somehow he understood. Beckoning me back to his side, he reached up and, taking my face in his hands, drew me down to him and kissed me full on the mouth, as brothers and sisters are warned never to do. Then, he let me go.

All that remained now was to recross the *cortile*, gather up Fingebat and my few possessions, and slide down to freedom. But my feet, unbidden by me, made their way to the room where Papa and Dorotea slept. I found them in each other's arms tightly entwined, like twin snakes. That sight set my hesitant feet firmly and finally on their way.

Releasing Fingebat from his bondage to the pillar was easy work. The heart of a champion was buried in the salt-and-pepper coat of that small fur ball. At first sight of me, he did give out with one delighted yip, but a single "Shh!" stilled his bark. Prohibited from barking, he made his pleasure known by covering my face with eager little licks as we climbed up the ladder to the loft. And he applauded my efforts to lift the trapdoor by jumping up and down in a frenzy of encouragement. The trapdoor was beyond my strength, but miraculously it slowly yielded to my muscles. One last hoist and it fell back with a clatter, revealing the *vicolo* below. I slung my sack over my shoulder, clasped Fingebat tight against my breast, and leapt to freedom.

ANY CITY ASSUMES DIFFERENT guises according to the season and time of day, but none more so than Mantova. At sunup, the moisture that rises from the surrounding lakes burns off and reveals the place for what it is—a small, neat town of no particular distinction except for the Reggio (and the most distinguished thing about that collection of palaces and gardens and fortresses is the question of how so many of them can be crammed into a space not much bigger than Campo Marzio). That is Mantova by day.

But in the hour before dawn, with only the occasional torchlight to penetrate the mist, a wavering diaphanous fog obscures the outlines of the buildings, and Mantova is a city out of one of Maestro Piero's magic landscapes. As I walked through it, this landscape came to life before my eyes—a figure here, a rustle there, the unmistakable odor of a gutted animal wafting past my nostrils. Each of these small assaults upon my senses nudged the still life into action.

My way to the *casa dei catecumeni* was strewn with memories. I passed the Via Peschiara, the fishmongers' street, hard by the house we had lived in, in happier times. And the Street of the Jewish Goldsmiths, where I had seen the dancing bear on the day of Fra Bernardino's sermon. And the Street of the Christian Goldsmiths, where I had seen the friar's boys brandishing their knives. That day I had been running away from Christians. This time, I was rushing headlong into their embrace.

The house set aside for converts was hidden away on a piazza between the Street of the Christian Goldsmiths and the Via Peschiara. It was not a formidable place, simply an ordinary two-story structure with a small cloister adjoining.

I peered through the iron pickets of the fence. The cloister looked green and peaceful. As I watched, a cleric all in black walked round and round under the colonnade, counting his beads. His hood was up, so I could not see his face. But he certainly did not swagger like a bully or a torturer.

I grabbed the bellpull and gave it three good tugs. The priest did not look up. But behind me, the main door opened and a voice inquired, "Can I be of service, signorina?"

The voice was eerily familiar. I did not turn around to face its owner but waited until she should speak again.

"Will it please you to state your business, signorina?" The words themselves fairly dripped sweetness but no amount of smearing with honey could disguise the rasping, guttural tone. I had heard that voice too often ever to forget it. "Listen to the saint," it had droned into my ear. "Listen! Listen to the saint!" No mistake about it. That voice was the voice of our old slave Cateruccia.

I ran from that place as if pursued by devils. Out into the piazza past the ancient Rotonda di San Lorenzo, smashing through the Piazza delle Erbe, heedless of the farmers who were just now beginning to set out their wares.

I believe I would have continued to race all the way to the city gates had not my strength given out. As it was, I did not pause until I had covered the entire length of the Palazzo di Ragione. There, under Dante's watchful eye, I ran out of breath in front of the old Mayor's House.

Once my pace slowed, so did the beating of my heart. The power of thought, which had deserted me in my panic, began to return. Cateruccia, the gatekeeper of my refuge! How could one explain her presence there but as a sign from God? The message was as clear as if He had come down from heaven and whispered in my ear. The *casa dei catecumeni* was the devil's stronghold. I must return to my own people and to the true faith. I must humble myself before Rabbi Abramo. I must acknowledge my transgressions with a full and open heart. I must prepare to take my medicine both literally and figuratively and to live out my miserable life without any hope of redemption.

I knew that I would never again find favor in my father's house. Nor could I look forward to escape by marriage. Once the word of my disgrace got out, no decent boy would ever marry me. The best I could hope for was that God, who had cared enough to give me this unmistakable sign, would take further pity on me and cause me to die young. It was a dismal prospect after only thirteen years of life on this earth, but just the kind of invention you might expect from an imagination fed by French romances.

I bowed my head in a prayerful pose and begged God for an early death, the sooner the better. Raising my eyes in supplication, I craned my neck upward toward heaven. But before my eyes reached the vault, they were arrested by a vision not of Jehovah, mind you, but of Virgil. There above me in his niche in the wall stood the great poet, no specter but a representation in glistening bronze, his arms resting on a stone lectern and a doctoral cap crowning his fine, shining head.

"Vergilius Mantuanus Poeterum Classimus," read the inscription. Virgil, son of Mantova, poet, seer, and sage.

Fortuna had stepped in. Who else would have led me to the very spot where, when I raised my eyes to God, I met the pagan poet in his stead? Perhaps, I thought, the great sage has some wisdom for me, some message of hope.

In my sack lay the precious manuscript I had snatched up at the last moment. Placing the volume in my lap, I riffled through the pages and let them fall open where they might, as I had seen Jehiel do when foretelling the future from the sacred book.

"Be not appalled by fear," I read. "Destiny will find a way for you. If you court her well, she will give you fair passage." Juno's advice to Aeneas. I read on.

But for you Italy is still far into the future
And lies at the end of a long voyage over uncharted
waters.
Your way will be blocked by Scylla on the right.
And on the left, by the never-pacified Charybdis who,
    Thrice in the day, drinks down the sheer depth
    of her engulfing abyss.

Like Dido, I too was caught between Scylla and Charybdis:
the *casa dei catecumeni* on one hand, the Casa dei Rossi on the
other.

Scylla hides in a cavern and sucks ships down
onto the rocks. Her upper half is as of a human
in the shape of a maid. But her lower part
is a monstrous whale.

What a perfect image for Cateruccia, half maid, half monster.
As for the never-pacified Charybdis, that had to be my relentless nemesis, Rabbi Abramo.

And how did the goddess advise Aeneas to make his way
between these twins of jeopardy? I turned the page, seeking confirmation of my memory. Yes. There it was, just as I
remembered:

It will be wiser not to hasten through the straight
    But rather to take a long and roundabout course.

All doubt dispelled and all fear quelled, I picked up my sack
and, holding Fingebat close, headed for the Reggio—making
certain not to hasten and to take a roundabout course by way
of the fish market.

IT IS NOT CUSTOMARY to call uninvited on princes. In all my
life, I had not heard of a Jew taking such a liberty. So it was

with some fluttering of the heart that I presented myself at the sentry box outside the great portal of the Reggio to ask if I might see Lord Pirro Gonzaga.

"And who shall I say is calling on the young lord so boldly this morning?" the guard inquired with a stern scowl.

"Say it is the lady Grazia dei Rossi," I replied in the strongest voice I could muster.

To my astonishment, his cloudy countenance turned immediately sunny and he took my arm in a most gallant fashion. "Where have you been, lady?" he asked, letting me through the gate as he spoke. "The Marchesana has been expecting you."

"There must be a mistake." I tugged myself free. "I am come to see Lord Pirro."

"Oh, there is no mistake, lady, unless you be not who you pretend to be."

"I *am* Grazia dei Rossi," I assured him.

"Grazia dei Rossi, the Jewess?" he asked.

"The same."

"Then you are expected for an audience with the Marchesana. See here." He pointed to a sheet of vellum pinned to the guardhouse wall. "These are the week's arrangements." And sure enough, written in bold letters below the name of Maestro Antonio, the goldsmith, and above that of Madonna Yseult Beau Tre, Princess of France, appeared the name of the lady Grazia, the Jewess.

"Hurry along, now. A page will take you to the Marchesana."

Still I hesitated.

"You are late, lady. The goldsmith and the French princess have long since been and gone." He pushed me again, not so gently this time. "Leave the dog with me."

"No! Madonna Isabella has requested that Fingebat accompany me," I heard myself say. "He is wanted at the audience."

And the gatekeeper gave way.

Now the page boy grabbed my free hand and proceeded to whisk me through corridor after corridor—each grander than the one before—and up and down stairways and across cloisters and gardens. Finally we crossed over a drawbridge and entered Saint George's castle, where the Marchese and his lady lived their private life.

Here the Marchesana did not sit upon a raised dais beside the Marchese, but alone, in a plain chair by the stove, with her dwarfs seated nearby on child-size stools, and a small dog in her lap. The moment this pampered animal caught a whiff of Fingebat, he leapt off his perch and lunged at my boots, biting and scratching to get at what he perceived as an enemy. Fingebat in his turn set up as noisy a caterwaul as the other dog, wriggling and squirming to jump out of my arms and down to the floor in order to do battle with his adversary. And the young Marchesana clapped her hands with delight and ordered one of her attendants to bring a juicy bone to the little Jewish cur, as she called Fingebat.

Then, turning her attention to me, she remarked, most pleasantly, "So you have brought your dog to the *disputa*, signorina *ebrea*?"

What *disputa*? I had heard of no *disputa*.

"Did you bring no documents to bolster your case?" she inquired. "I had hoped to see the dei Rossi volume of Josephus's *Jewish War*, for I hear it is the least corrupted translation of that work in all of Italy."

Confounded by her questions, I remained silent.

"Is there something amiss, lady?" she inquired, noticing my reticence at last. "Are you unwilling to engage in this *disputa* with me? Everything I know of you suggests that you would make a worthy adversary. And I do believe that for us women to stage such a battle of ideas would be most unusual and interesting. Do you not agree?"

It was not possible for me to keep still any longer without leading her to believe that I was either dumb, obdurate, or cowardly.

"I most humbly beg pardon for my ignorance, *illustrissima*," I answered, "but I know nothing of this *disputa*."

"What brings you here then if not my invitation?" she inquired, not quite so friendly now.

"I fear it was no invitation but rather desperation that brought me, *illustrissima*," I replied. "I came to your portal to throw myself on your mercy and to beg your *caritas*."

"*Caritas*? Desperation? What has desperation to do with my *disputa*?" Suddenly the gracious lady was a petulant child. I had witnessed an identical display of capriciousness by the lady's father the day Papa took us to Belriguardo. Papa had not lost countenance then and I must not allow myself to lose it now.

"Forgive me, *illustrissima*," I pleaded. "Not for all the world would I disappoint you — you who have shone your light so graciously on me, who have honored me with your attention to my plight. There has been some mischief at work here. For I misread your invitation. That is the reason I am ill prepared to engage in this *disputa*. But I assure you that if I am given a second chance..."

She was wavering. I could see the goodness and sweetness which is a genuine part of her nature doing battle with the petulance and quick temper which is also a part of her.

Then, as if he had been coached in his part by a master, little Fingebat let out a thin, pathetic whine. Never was a sound better timed. The dwarfs seated around Madonna Isabella's chair began to giggle. The little one called Crazy Catherine laughed so hard that she peed a stream upon the marble floor.

That lapse and the merriment it occasioned tipped the balance in my favor. Unable to resist the laughter around her, the Marchesana joined in and ended up laughing as heartily as any of her attendants, albeit with more control than the female dwarf.

At length, wiping the tears of glee from her eyes, she remarked, "The little Jewish cur is a fine performer. Perhaps we should include him in our revels at *carnevale*. For he is truly a most original clown." And would you believe it the little Jewish cur actually had the wit to bark out a thank-you.

Her temper softened by his tricks, Madonna Isabella agreed to postpone the *disputa* until the following day and allowed me to kiss her hand before I was excused. Courtiers who had looked down their noses at me when I entered now bowed me out with smiles. And the page who had conducted me to the audience with such ill grace now stepped along sprightly beside me, chatting me up as if I were a regular familiar of the court. In the circumstances, I had no hesitation in asking him to announce me to Lord Pirro. Nor did he display any hesitation in setting off to find that young gentleman for me. But first he insisted on settling me comfortably on a bench in the Guard's Hall. For a time I diverted myself by gazing at the amazingly lifelike portraits of the Gonzagas' favorite horses that decorated the walls above me. But the tumultuous events of the morning had worn me down and after a while I curled up on the bench with Fingebat in my arms and fell asleep.

I was awakened by a tap on my shoulder. Even half asleep, I knew the touch.

"Do my eyes deceive me? No. It is my sweet Grazia." Taking my hands in his, he raised me gently to my feet. "Oh, lady, you are a feast for my eyes. How come you here?"

I quickly related to him all the events that had transpired, up to and including my puzzling audience with Madonna Isabella, but coming back again and again to my fateful encounter with Cateruccia at the *casa dei catecumeni*. "It is an evil augury."

"You believe that?"

"There cannot be any doubt," I assured him. "If I go into that place, I will lose my soul. The One True God has put her there to warn me away."

"Which God is that? The God that you have this very day renounced by coming to me?"

In the confusion of the day I had forgotten what brought me to this place, what I had embraced, what I had rejected.

"You look stricken, lady. Is it regret that clouds your eyes? So soon?"

"Perhaps, sir," I admitted. "I never expected to find the like of our old slave Cateruccia at the *casa dei catecumeni*. She is my devil."

"She is a wretch of no importance, a gnat to be swatted if it presumes to light on you," he contradicted me firmly. "Think of your consequence in the world. You, my love, have this day become a protégée of the most powerful lady in Mantova as well as the beloved of her kinsman. This slave is beneath your notice."

From the moment I heard Cateruccia's voice that morning, she had taken the shape in my mind of a great and powerful being hovering above me like a huge black bat. As I heard her described so disparagingly, she began to lose both volume and power.

"Listen to me, Grazia." I was hearing a new Lord Pirro, a wise and worldly man. "It is not with some unimportant slave that we must concern ourselves but with this proposed *disputa* that you tell me about. For although the One True God, as you call Him, may be heating up some dreadful punishment for you in the great by-and-by, Madonna Isabella is here and now in this palace and is capable of considerable spite when she is crossed. It is the Este in her. We on the Gonzaga side tend to display more consistency. Now..." He was sounding more businesslike by the minute. "Are you prepared to debate with her the question of Jewish and Christian interpretations of the Messiah?"

The very idea filled me with trepidation. Only the wisest and most erudite Jews ever entered into such a *disputa*; for it takes a hand as practiced as Judah's to guide the discussion safely past the rocky shoals of heresy and blasphemy, offenses for which Jews have been known to burn.

"Oh, my lord, I could never...I could not possibly...I did not understand..." I floundered about in my fright.

"But now you do understand," he interrupted in a firm voice. "And now we must make haste to extricate ourselves from this treacherous trap of a *disputa*. For if we do not, it will snap shut on both of us tomorrow."

How clever he was. How knowing.

"Have you ever watched the hummingbird as she goes about sucking nectar from the blossoms?" he inquired.

Indeed I had. "My grandmother was cursed, as she put it, with a rampant trumpet vine that attracted hummingbirds in droves," I answered. "Although I could never see the plague in it. They are so agile, so delicate, so quick—quicker than Mercury."

"What you have limned there is a likeness of my kinswoman, the Marchesana," he said. "To her admirers, she appears to be a quicksilver creature, full of lightness. To her detractors, she is a species of freebooter, bent on extracting the last drop from every transaction. But there can be no disagreement about her quickness. She is one who tastes, sucks, and moves on with lightning speed. Like the hummingbird, my cousin flits quickly from blossom to blossom. For the moment, she fancies the prospect of this *disputa* with you. Given some number of days, she will find another great enthusiasm, I assure you. Eventually, she will discard the scheme altogether and it will be safe for you to appear at the Reggio. Meanwhile you will feign some female complaint and sequester yourself in the *casa dei catecumeni*."

"No," I cried out. "I cannot go back there."

"Yes you can," he insisted. "Believe me, the sight of you and Fingebat being carried by four of the Marchesana's liveried porters will put this Cateruccia on her knees before you."

He was right of course. The moment that slut saw me on the litter, protected from the elements by a curtain emblazoned with the Gonzaga arms, her mouth dropped open and she actually did fall to her knees.

Word of my arrival had been sent ahead, so all was in readiness for me, she announced, as obsequious now as she had been bold in other times. Fra Pietro extended his heartfelt welcome and would be in to see me before evening. This afternoon, he was at the Reggio conferring with Madonna Isabella. (Fra Pietro, the castellan of the *casa dei catecumeni*, was also the *illustrissima's* confessor.) Having delivered her messages, the girl waited awkwardly to see me to my chamber.

If anyone had told me that morning that I would end the day taking leave of my lover under the watchful eye of Cateruccia,

I would have pronounced him mad. Yet that is the way it happened. After a brief moment in the entrance hall Lord Pirro informed me with a trace of embarrassment that he must return the litter forthwith—that, in truth, he himself was overdue at the Reggio. "For my time is not my own, my love. I am entirely at the disposal of my cousin, the Marchese, being in his service. And he has excused me only until vespers," he explained.

"He seems as jealous of his prerogatives as his wife is," I remarked. "And as quick to take offense at any lapse in fealty."

"More so," the young lord answered tersely. "Madonna Isabella can be jollied but my cousin Francesco has no playful side to him. I dare not defy him on pain of my life." He told me this, not making a drama out of it but with a matter-of-fact acceptance that made it quite believable.

Heedless of Cateruccia's stolid presence, I begged a kiss of reassurance. And a kiss is what I got, that and no more. For my lover was visibly nervous now and eager to be gone to his master.

"When will I see you?" I called into the gathering dusk.

"I will send a note . . ." His voice trailed off.

I stood in the portal watching until he was long gone. Then, as the twilight gathered, I slowly and finally closed the door on my family, my religion, and my God whose most stern command I was about to defy.

18

THE ROOM ASSIGNED TO ME MORE CLOSELY RESEMBLED a cell than a chamber. No embroidered satin pillows here to caress my back. No feather quilt to buffer me from the winter's damp. No bed, in fact. Only a straw pallet on the floor. Plus a crude pine chest without a lock, a cracked pitcher, and a chamber pot. To complete this desolate picture, the room boasted but one window and that a tiny one, shuttered and beyond my reach. Would I ever hear a bird sing outside those shutters? I doubted it.

Not surprisingly, my thoughts turned to home—to my brothers. I called out for Cateruccia (no silken bellpulls in this monk's cell) and asked for a pen and some vellum. Quickly I penned a note to tell my family where I was. Given my address, they could easily deduce my intent.

When the note was done I called again for Cateruccia and ordered her to have it delivered. Hand on hip, she informed me in a most defiant manner that no letter could leave the *casa dei catecumeni* before it was read by Fra Pietro. In vain I protested that my parents would be worried about me. She would not be moved.

"Fra Pietro will attend to your affairs directly after matins. This is the hour he sets aside for *conversos*," she informed me. Now that I was locked up securely within the gates, her manner was not as deferential as it had been earlier. She did not completely discard the mantle of respect she had assumed in Lord Pirro's presence. She simply allowed me to glimpse flashes of the old insolence underneath, much in the way that wanton girls manage "accidentally" to display the red petticoats hidden beneath their sober gray *gamorras*.

Having defied me in the name of Fra Pietro, she went on to presume further in the priest's name. "We have our customs here, Donna Grazia," she simpered, "which I have come to know since I first entered this house as a *conversa*."

"You were not a Christian before?" I asked.

"Only in my heart," she replied with another arch little smile. "But when my master, your father, abandoned me, Fra Pietro took pity on me, God bless his pure white soul, and agreed to train me as a Christian."

Abandoned! The gall of the girl. Perhaps I ought to have challenged the slander of my father there and then. But my spirit was eroded after the long day and I must admit the wretch still exerted a vestige of power over me.

I felt her presence heavy and menacing in my tiny cell long after she had left me. It seemed that I had incarcerated myself in a prison as harsh and punitive as the one I had fled, without the comfort of my brothers to sustain me. I could not even turn for solace to my old friend Virgil, for the wretch had neglected to leave me a candle. Had it not been for Fingebat I believe I would have fallen prey to a true melancholic malady that night.

Contrary to my fears that my confessor would be a graybeard with a sepulchral voice and quivering jowls, when he appeared next morning Fra Pietro turned out to be a comparatively young man, light of step and slim of figure, with a winning smile and a solicitous manner. First off, he ordered Cateruccia to fetch a warm stone from the fire to place next to my belly in my distress (he must have had a report of my arrival on the litter). In addition he offered me a sip of wine—an unheard-of indulgence in that abstemious household, I was to learn.

Once the priest had made me comfortable, he hastened to reassure me that the letter to my parents had been delivered. They were entitled to supply me with food for the duration of my stay as I was still technically a Jewess, he reminded me. It would be some time before I could complete the training which must precede my baptism. Besides—he took my hand in his—we must all be certain that my desire to convert was sincere.

"Oh, I am sincere, Padre," I told him. "And I am most eager to get on with it."

"Good." He nodded approvingly but did not seem overwhelmingly impressed by my enthusiasm. "It is well that you begin at once. For there are trials of both spirit and flesh ahead for you."

"Trials of flesh?" The phrase brought to my mind the old medieval rites of trial, the thought of which made me tremble.

"Only the mildest mortifications, my child," he reassured me. "We Christians need not suffer severe trials of the body Christ suffered those for our sake." He stated this with such firm conviction that it was impossible not to believe him, and for the first time since I had left home I began to feel some confidence in this venture. So that when the priest asked if I would be well enough to take dinner with him that day, I pronounced myself willing to try.

The meal was execrable. I cannot remember ever having been served such poor fare or so little of it. A thin soup with a few potatoes to thicken it and some stale crusts floating on the top; a wine which burned the throat even though it was thoroughly watered; and a single fig. That constituted the whole of my first dinner at the *casa dei catecumeni*. As a side dish I was offered tidbits of Cateruccia's witless chatter, and for seasoning, the ripe odor of her unwashed body.

To these discomforts of flesh and spirit the priest remained admirably impervious. He drank Cateruccia's watery soup and inhaled the fumes of her sweat and listened to her banal chatter with amiable cordiality. I was unable to muster an equal Christian *caritas*. In the dei Rossi house, as in most households, the servants ate after their masters were done. Even lowly Jews did not force themselves to endure the stink of their servants' bodies while they ate. But although they ate second, I promise you that our servants dined forty times more delectably on leftovers than I did at Fra Pietro's egalitarian table. Our servants would have staged a revolt had they been given these meager crusts and this watery slop for their daily allotment.

I had come into this place prepared for conflicts of conscience and crises of the soul. I had never considered the possibility of having to starve for Christ.

Toward the close of the day, Fra Pietro came to my chamber to conduct me on a turn around the cloister—if I felt able. He was solicitous in speech and manner but not so concerned as to spare me the chastisement he had brought me there to administer.

I was about to face my first trial on the road to salvation, he explained. Starting now, I would be required to make ten rounds of the square each evening and to stop and repeat five times at each corner, "The meek shall inherit the earth." To expedite my comprehension of this basic Christian precept, I was to seek out Cateruccia and invite her to pace out the penance at my side. "For she is one of God's children just as you are, Signorina Grazia, and deserving of your pity," he explained.

"Take up her burden," he urged me. "Remember Jesus Christ, our Lord." He paused to cross himself and salute the Savior. "Think of Him pinioned to the cross suffering for our sins and think of the smallness of the sacrifice I ask of you now in His name." Again he paused to genuflect. "Drink in Cateruccia's ignorance, inhale her sweat as if it were ambergris and myrrh," he exhorted. "Is that too much to ask of one who professes to have heard His call?"

Up until that moment I could not truthfully have said that I had heard any such call. My presence in the House of Converts was certainly more an expediency than a vocation. But at that moment, standing in that little courtyard at dusk, facing that saintly man, overcome by the quiet force of his rhetoric, I did truly feel myself overwhelmed by grace. I threw myself at his feet, weeping.

He was a wise confessor. He allowed me time to cry out all the pent-up misery of the past days—the fear, the hurt, the loneliness—all. Only when my tears finally gave way to dry racking heaves did he speak.

"You feel yourself superior to the slave girl. You refuse to accept her as your sister in Christ, do you not?"

Miserably, I nodded.

"That is your pride speaking, the pride that will keep you from Christ."

"No."

"Yes." He was steel now, his touch cold as he dabbed at a tear on my cheek.

"The true tears of the penitent are cooled by remorse," he explained. "Those tears of yours are hot tears, tears of rage."

"But I am not angry, Father, I swear it."

"Then why do you weep so passionately? Why?"

"I am hungry, Father. My belly is empty. I am starving."

The moment the words were out, I wanted to bite my tongue off. What must he think of me, bawling after food like an infant? I needn't have worried. My outburst evoked no more distaste in him than did Cateruccia's stench. Nor did it evoke the slightest inclination to feed me. From Fra Pietro, I got neither bread nor a stone. I got a sermon.

"We Christians are congenitally abstemious and ascetic, after the way of our Lord Jesus Christ," he began. "Whereas your people..." A slight shiver agitated his body. "I do not wish to defame your people. I shall merely point out to you that whereas a Jewish priest would merely have satisfied your physical desire for food this evening, Christ will reward your fast with everlasting grace. Is not the sacrifice of a piece of bread a small price to pay for eternal salvation?"

Something of the sweetness of Christ's love was revealed to me at that moment and I was able to answer, with a full heart, "Yes, Father. It is a small price, to be sure."

For this, I was rewarded by a smile of delight such as one sees on the faces of Fra Angelico's angels.

"Now listen carefully to what I have to tell you, Grazia," he went on. "Nowhere more than in the food you eat, the pallet you sleep on, and the company you keep with lesser souls will you learn more quickly to grasp the heart of the Christian faith, the transformation of flesh into spirit. I will lead you. You must trust my way. I will teach you. You must learn. But learning is not enough. You must come to know Christ in your own blood and your own flesh. Only then can you truly embrace Him."

He took me in his arms like a lover and fixed my eyes with his own. "Embrace the bleeding, beating heart of Christ, my child, I implore you." Moved by some passionate religiosity, he fairly threw himself into a spasm of submission. "Il cuore del Cristo!"

With this final cry, he subsided into deep silence, and after a while, without another word, he released me from his embrace and left the cloister.

In due course, Cateruccia appeared. Inspired by Fra Pietro, I took her arm in the friendliest manner. Then we started off on our rounds, Cateruccia emitting hoarse sighs as she lumbered along beside me and I muttering, "The meek shall inherit the earth," five times at each corner. By the end of it my hunger pangs had subsided and I walked up to my cell with a firm tread and an inner assurance that I had chosen the right path.

19

L IFE IN THE *casa del catecumeni*. DREARY. HARSH.
Up before dawn in my cell. Most mornings a layer of ice
has formed in the jug. I crack it with my fist, splash the
frigid water on my face. (Jewish habits of sanitation die hard.)
I ask myself if the addiction to washing is another indulgence
of the flesh. Make a note to ask Fra Pietro. But I see him rarely.
He is in constant attendance on Madonna Isabella. The court
has moved to Marmirolo and he with it.

I have not seen Lord Pirro since the first day of my incarceration in this place. Nor have I heard a word from him. Or
from the *illustrissima*. The plan for the *disputa* must be forgotten. Have I too been forgotten?

I write every day to my love, but I know that these letters
are not delivered since Fra Pietro is not here to put his stamp of
approval on them. Kneeling on the cold stones of the Church
of San Andrea, which we do, Cateruccia and I, four times each
day, I do not feel Christ entering into me. I feel cold entering
into me. And hunger. And disappointment. And disgust. (I do
try to overcome my revulsion against Cateruccia but it retains
its hold on me.)

Food is delivered here for me every day — white bread and buttery cheese and figs. My family brings kosher food to the *casa dei catecumeni* to keep my Jewish soul free of the taint of the pig, should I change my mind about converting.

Every day at dinner this banquet of Jewish delicacies is put at my place beside the watery soup. So far, I have resisted eating it. But with every day that passes, my resolution weakens. I know it is only a matter of time before I give in to the cravings of my belly.

They have taken my Virgil away. Also my grammar books. In their stead, I find beside my bed a tattered printed version of *The Imitation of Christ*. I try to read it. The words of the saint make no sense to me. I make a note to ask Fra Pietro why he gave me this particular book. If I ever do see him.

What holds me in this place? Why do I not run off? Quite simply, I have nowhere to go. I have bound myself over. I am a slave to Christ.

Yet I am also, and always was, a creature of hope. And when, on an afternoon some two weeks after my incarceration began, Cateruccia informed me brusquely that I was wanted below, I took heart at once. My love had not forsaken me, after all.

No reproaches, I promised myself. I would exhibit only my most engaging face to him. I would hide my disappointment and express only my joy to see him again. Full of resolve, I passed through the portal that led to the cloister and searched in the dusky light for the familiar broad shoulders and the raffish *berretta*.

In the farthest corner my eyes discerned a shapeless form huddled against a pillar. Moving closer, I could see that it was not a single body but two. They were shrouded in dark cloaks and bent over as if they carried the world's troubles on their shoulders. I could not make out the faces. But as I approached, they revealed themselves to be my father and his wife, Dorotea.

"Papa!"

He turned, arms outstretched. He wrapped himself around me like a swaddling blanket and I snuggled into his body, a child again. Then I caught sight of Dorotea, her eyes reproachful, her stance rigid, unbending; and the bile began to course through my body, black and bitter. I withdrew from my father's embrace.

"We tried to come before, Grazia." Papa's tone was conciliatory, even suppliant. "But the visit took some arranging. Do you receive your food regularly?"

"I do, honored padre," I replied, every bit as respectful — and every bit as distant — as Dorotea's code of conduct demanded.

Her attention went to Fingebat. "They allow you to keep that flea-bitten mongrel in the house?" she inquired, pointing contemptuously at the little creature at her feet.

"Why yes, honored stepmother." I bent to pick him up. "Jesus loved all living creatures great and small. He placed them under the special protection of Saint Francis."

"What about those pigs they go around slaughtering by the hundreds? And the deer and the fowl they kill for the sport of it? Whose protection are they under?" she snapped back.

"Please, Dorotea...this is no way..." Papa placed his hand on her arm as if to restrain her nasty tongue, but he never was a match for her.

"You must take care not to place yourself beyond redemption by eating the forbidden flesh of the pig and other such unclean stuff." She wrinkled her nose in disgust. "If you set yourself against God's commandments, it will go all the harder for you when you return to us."

"I will never return to you. Never."

"You say that now..." She sniffed. "They will tempt you with dainty morsels." I smiled to myself at what Dorotea would make of the watery soup that constituted my tempting Christian diet.

"It is also very important that you do not eat fish without scales such as the eels these Christians dote on."

The more she hectored me, the more I became convinced that Fra Pietro was correct in his condemnation of the Jewish obsession with things of the flesh. Could the woman talk of nothing but food?

When she finally finished her peroration I got my chance to speak.

"What news of my brothers?" I asked. "Are they well?"

"As well as can be, considering the shame they feel—"

"They are well, daughter," Papa cut in. "But they miss you mightily. They ask every day when you will be home again."

"I miss them too," I answered. "Possibly even more than they miss me. For they have each other..."

"Why do you not come home with us now, daughter?" Papa reached out and took my hand in his. "Give your sad eyes the treat of the sight of those who love you so much."

Sadly I nodded my refusal.

"Why not, child? What have we done to make you so bitter and so obdurate? How can we make amends?"

Before I could even consider whether I might risk an honest reply, Dorotea made up my mind for me. "Do not lower yourself to beg her, honored husband. She is not worth it."

Those words concluded the interview. I quickly excused myself and left the cloister without even saying goodbye.

If Dorotea's intent had been to drive me farther into the arms of Christ, she could not have done a better job of it. The next morning, I fairly bounded out of bed in my effort to be first at the church, determined as never before to taste Christ's blood when I was offered the wine and to feel His flesh between my teeth when I chewed the consecrated wafer. If belief was a requisite for baptism, I would believe. If it killed me, I would believe.

Did this fit of faith come from the heart? Christ must have thought so. For not too long after my parents' visit, another visitor came to me in the cloister. Not shrouded or bent over, this one. Oh no, this caller shone with the aura of Saint George himself, decked out as he was in gold spurs and chains. My knight had come to fetch me.

But oh, I looked a fright. My newfound religiosity had led me to neglect my personal habits. I was dirty. My hair hung down greasy and lank. As for my garments, a coarse, black hooded cloak had become my second skin.

To my astonishment, my drab and disheveled appearance seemed to inflame my lover's ardor rather than to cool it.

"Look at you. So thin. So pale. Oh, my love, what you have endured for my sake. You have deprived yourself of all comfort, all adornment... Oh, my angel..."

Locked in my lord's arms, clutched, cosseted, kissed, and caressed, I fell back into the fleshly world without a backward glance. My only reverent thought—if you can call it that—was that all my sacrifices had been well worth this moment.

The visit was short. He had ridden more than twenty leagues at full gallop from the Gonzaga country place at Marmirolo and must return before sunset on pain of his kinswoman's extreme displeasure, "...for I am her favorite partner at *scartino* excepting only her sister-in-law, the Duchess of Urbino, who is not with us this season," he explained.

Still keeping a firm hold on my waist, he began quickly to tell me all that had transpired in his world since we parted.

"Since the court moved to Marmirolo I am expected to ride out with Marchese Francesco every morning... a pleasant duty, I must admit. Do you hunt, my love?"

I confessed that I had never had the opportunity

"But you do ride, do you not? Something other than elephants?"

"It is my greatest pleasure, after Virgil," I answered, happy not to disappoint him.

"After Virgil, of course," he repeated with one of those sly smiles of his. "I keep forgetting that in addition to your unbridled spirit and your hot passions you are also quite the lady scholar."

"Would you prefer me light-minded and bird-witted?" I inquired, with just a touch of the tartness I always felt when he teased me for my bookish preoccupations.

"Soothe those ruffled feathers, lady. I bring good tidings. Madonna Isabella has invited you to Marmirolo."

"For a *disputa*?" I asked anxiously.

"No. That is forgotten, as I assured you it would be. Now we are all agog for country pursuits—music, games, dancing, and the hunt."

"Oh dear. The hunt."

"Never fear, my love, you are not invited to that. To be offered a place close to the Marchese's dogs is the highest honor of all at the Gonzaga court. No, this is merely a fete. But Madonna Isabella herself issued the invitation and that counts for something. I will come for you at dawn on Saturday. Be ready."

But I could not be ready. Readiness was not possible. Tearfully, I told him that my attendance was out of the question.

"You refuse the Marchesana's invitation?"

"Oh sir, I know that Jews do not say no to princes. My father taught me that. But I cannot go to this party. You see, I have nothing to wear. They have taken away my clothes."

"Then they must bring them back."

"But my hair... there is no one to wash my head."

"The slave girl will do it."

"Oh no. I dare not ask Fra Pietro."

"Perhaps you do not dare, my love, but I do. Pta Pietro sits next to me every day at dinner in the country. It is his good report that has put you back in Madonna Isabella's favor. He tells us you are his most compliant *conversa*."

"He does?"

"Yes, my little scholar. You are not unobserved here. Or uncared for. Did you think you were?"

I hung my head. In truth I had thought just that.

"Now then, do we have any other problems to solve? For I must be off."

"So soon?"

"You know that my cousin the Marchese is a demanding taskmaster," he answered.

"Do you not sometimes wish to be free of this servitude?" I asked. "To be your own man rather than his?"

"Few of us are vouchsafed such liberty, my love," he answered. "Even my cousin is not his 'own man,' as you put it. He is the hired captain of the Venetians and that makes him their creature much as I am his. They pay his living just as he pays mine. Remember your Plato. No man is free. Is that not what the old Greek pederast taught?"

"If the revered sage ever said such a thing, I am not aware of it," I snapped back.

"'Destiny waiteth alike for them that men call free and them by others mastered,'" he quoted with perfect accuracy, putting my nose completely out of joint. Then he swooped me up in his arms and pressed me to him tight enough to squeeze all the starch out of me. Not content with mastering me in that way, he then whirled me around the little courtyard until my head swam with vertigo and, for a last tease, took a nip out of my ear that made me squeal with pain. In revenge, I had at his chin with the hard right fist I had cultivated wrestling with my brother. I wager that old cloister had never witnessed such merriment or such tumult. Oh, we were hellions, both of us, ready to jettison prudence at a moment's notice and abandon ourselves to our fancies and passions.

The next day a small *cassone* appeared beside my bed. When I looked inside, there lay my chemise freshly laundered and smelling deliciously of comfrey. Cateruccia had not forgotten the housewifely lessons she learned in my mother's house.

On Friday morning, Cateruccia lumbered up the stairs hauling a bucket of water on her head and carrying a flacon of liquid in the pocket of her apron.

"From the *illustrissima* Marchesana Isabella," she mumbled when she handed the bottle to me. "A hairwash."

The stuff inside the bottle, I discovered when I pulled out the cork and sniffed it, smelled unmistakably of chamomile; but there were other scents lingering around the edges of the herb that I could not so readily identify. Vinegar? Lettuce? The chemist who mixed the potion had disguised his formula well. But however confusing the chemistry, the message in the bottle was quite clear. For one woman to share her beauty potions with another could only be interpreted as a gesture of friendship.

The night before the fete, I made my first voluntary prayer to the Lord Jesus Christ.

"Sweet Jesus," I prayed, "let me be a success tomorrow at Marmirolo and find favor in Madonna Isabella's sight as I have in Yours. Please let my hair fall into soft curls and not stick up in spikes. And please make me graceful in the dance and witty in the talk. Amen."

20

ALL MY LIFE I HAD HEARD TALK OF THE PLEASURES of country living and of hunting lodges and various *delizie* where princes could shed the formality of court life and "be themselves," as the saying goes. What I quickly learned at Marmirolo was that grand people are always grand, no matter what the surroundings.

Even at Marmirolo the Marchese and his Marchesana seated themselves on a dais above everyone else. The ladies were just as corseted and as bejeweled as ever. There were as many courses at table, servants in attendance, and perfumed courtiers as in town. Everyone vied to sit closest to the Marchese, who, in the country as in town, clearly preferred the company of the pack of dogs with whom he carried on a continuous, barking sort of conversation and was permitted to be as rude and boorish as he chose, whereas for the rest of us, a rigid protocol reigned over all activities, even the games.

No sooner had we dismounted than we were ushered into the *sala grande*, where Messer Equicola, Madonna Isabella's Master of Revels, was in the process of expounding every detail of the rules of games to the players. We came in as he was winding down, to everyone's evident relief.

"Let me once again remind the gathering that a game suitable for noble company is neither cards nor dice nor athletics. It is discourse based upon some ingenious proposition that calls upon the quick exercise of wit and erudition." I repeated these words to myself in an effort to fix them in my mind.

"Remember," he went on, "no one can refuse to take part in the game if he is present and invited to do so. Nor should anyone play in a careless manner. Show interest in the game. Above all, everything that is said or done should tend toward joy and laughter and pleasure—but no buffoonery, mind."

"Hear that," the Marchese shouted over to Matello the dwarf, who stood in a corner sulking as he always did when he was not the center of attention. "We'll have none of your crude farting today."

Whereupon Matello let out a most odoriferous explosion of gas in a series of high toots. Not to be outdone, his companion, Crazy Catherine, rushed into the center of the floor and spewed out a river of pee to everyone's amusement save that of Messer Equicola, upstaged as he always was by the little people.

But he managed to get back the attention of the gathering by tapping several of them lightly on their heads with his *mestola*. That ladle signifies the office of Master of Revels, and Equicola wielded it majestically.

"Remember now, if a player has to do a thing that consists of acts, gestures, or signs, he should strive to do it gracefully — no jerking or twitching even in the Game of the Deformed." What on earth was that game? I wondered. "And be careful not to repeat the same proverb or device, even if it is apropos. For repetition makes tedium."

To this statement the Marchese interposed a loud grunt of assent which Equicola acknowledged with a graceful bow.

"Most important"—he cleared his throat to emphasize the importance of what he was about to tell us—"if you are questioned on the subject of love, your replies should show a certain loftiness. In your answers, be jealous of the honor of woman and admiring of her virtue and greatness. Couch your replies rather in the style of Petrarch than in the styles of Ovid or Catullus. Now, let us begin."

"Sooner begun, sooner ended," the Marchese mumbled.

The game that Equicola had selected was, he declared, brand-new and never before played in the whole of Italy. He called it the Game of Ships and swore he had made it up himself. In this game a lady is caught in a storm with two suitors chosen from among the company by the Master of Revels. She is forced to throw one of them overboard in order to save the vessel. When questioned by the Master, the player must give her reasons for the choice.

That was as far as we got. With a growl that came from somewhere deep in his bowels, Marchese Francesco heaved himself forward in his chair and ordered a change in the program. "This Game of Ships is too long to play before we eat," he announced. "I am hungry now. The game be damned. It's time to sup." And every toady there cheered him.

During the fish course, Lord Pirro brought over to meet me two ladies of the court, who seemed vastly unimpressed by the honor. Then, between the fish and the pie Madonna Isabella called out my name and bade me sit at her side for a while, a signal honor. My mastery of the classics had captured her interest, she said. Did I know Greek as well as Latin? And what about Hebrew?

At that moment I thanked God for those long afternoons at Papa's side in the Bologna *banco*, for I could reply in all candor that I did indeed know a little Greek and more than a little Hebrew. No knowledge is ever wasted.

Without doubt I had caught the light of the princess's eye. For a few moments, I even became the repository of her confidence. She confessed to me with disarming candor how bitterly she regretted being forced to abandon her own studies in the crush of court business. She had plans to commission certain works of scholarship, she told me, in emulation of her adored papa (yes, she used that familiar term in my presence that day!).

Perhaps I might be the one to help her begin this enterprise, she suggested. She did not say yes or no, only maybe.

Returning to my chair, I passed the two chilly ladies-in-waiting, who now seemed eager to engage me in conversation. Amazing what a touch of preferment can do to enhance one's charms.

The dinner ended with the passing of gorgeous platters of *confetti*, each sweet perched on a gold or silver leaf, each fashioned to resemble a different fruit and colored to its image — the grapes purple, the cherries scarlet, the lemons yellow. If the common people knew how these people eat, there would be an uprising.

After supper we danced under the stars with five musicians making music on a balcony hidden from view by billowing satin drapes. After offering his arm to Madama for the opening pavane, Lord Pirro gave every dance to me, twirling me around and around until the tapestries that covered the walls, the candles flickering in their sconces, the rouged cheeks of the ladies flashing by, the gorgeous fabrics of their costumes, the fast beat of the *frottole*, the crash of the tambourines, the musky perfume of civet (with which everyone there had doused himself except me), my lover's murmurs in my ear, his hot breath on my neck — all of this blended into a single sensation: rapture. Whirling around the floor in my lover's arms, lifted above all earthly concerns — the *casa dei catecumeni*, my family, Cateruccia, even God, forgotten — I was the happiest girl in the world.

Rapture by its own definition is finite. Inevitably it ends and the quotidian life recommences. The Game of Ships remained unplayed. Madama was, then as now, a pit bull when it came to having her way. At her insistence the game had to be played and played by all, ". . . for it will bring bad luck upon the entire company if any one of us breaks the circle before all disperse," she informed the gathering. So the musicians were dismissed; the dancing ended and the choosing began.

Of the dozen or so ladies present three others, including

the Marchesana, drew the Marchese as one of their suitors. All three were given their chance to choose ahead of me and all three chose to keep the Marchese and to throw his opponent overboard. Madonna Isabella gave as her reason that she had pledged her life to her honored husband before God. "And were I to betray him in front of Messer Equicola"—his rival in the game—"and this gathering," she added prettily, "I should not only dishonor myself here on earth but would surely suffer for all eternity in that fifth circle of Hell that Dante reserves for those who bear false witness."

Next to be called, Madonna Maria Pia, also chose Marchese Francesco in preference to his rival, a certain Fabiano. "For although Messer Fabiano is a man of virtue, Marchese Francesco is of noble ancestry and thus more worth saving in the eyes of both God and man," she reasoned. She was rewarded by an approving grunt from the Marchese.

The third lady who drew the Marchese and also chose to save him, this time at the expense of Fra Pietro, did so on the pretext that the man of God had already performed his portion of God's work on earth whereas the Marchese, still in the vigor of his youth, was needed down here to defend God with his sword. By now, the Marchese had lost himself in a tease with two of his dogs and had not even a grunt to spare for the lady.

Then came my turn.

"Signorina *ebrea*, here are your suitors: Marchese Francesco and Lord Pirro. What say you? Who lives and who dies?" he demanded.

I hesitated, for I could not find it in my heart to consign my beloved to a watery grave.

"What of Lord Pirro? Is he to be kept by your side safe in the ship or fed to the fishes? You know the rules. You must choose. I ask you for the last time, who lives and who dies?"

"Lord Pirro." I could hardly summon up the voice to reply.

"Fed to the fishes or kept?"

"Kept," I whispered.

Too late, I understood from the shocked faces around me

that I had made a devastatingly wrong choice. But now I could not take it back.

"And the Marchese?" the questioner pressed.

"He dies," I mumbled.

A disapproving murmur ran through the company. The only person in the room who appeared not to be affected was the Marchese Francesco himself. He simply sat upon his golden chair and picked his teeth.

I told myself that he was too worldly to take a silly game seriously. I reassured myself that if I came up with a flattering reason for making fish food out of him I could recoup my loss of favor. But deep inside, a wiser voice told me that princes do not appreciate being condemned to death, even in jest.

"And what do you give as the reason for your choice, signorina *ebrea*?" The Master tapped me lightly with his *mestola*.

I took a deep breath and plunged into an effulgence of flattery. "His Celsitude is much too far above me ever to be my cavalier. He is far too noble. Far too good. Too good even for this world. He is one of those whom, the poet tells us, the gods have picked out as their favorites. I take my reason from the poet." Then, placing my palms together in a worshipful attitude, I intoned the words of Plautus: "*Quem di diligunt, adolescens moritur.*"

"What's she saying?" The Marchese suddenly came to life.

"She quotes the Latin poet Plautus, honorable husband," Madonna informed him.

"And what does this poet have to say about me?" he growled.

"He says, 'Those whom the gods favor die in youth,'" she translated with deadly accuracy. "I recognize the passage," she added. "It is from *Bacchides*, a piece often performed at our court in Ferrara, for the Roman poet is favored by my honored father, the Duke."

Marchese Francesco mulled this over for several moments, masticating it with his mind as if to extract the full flavor. Then, he called up an enormous gob of spittle from deep in his chest and spat it across the room with terrific force. "That is what I think of your honored father's favorite poet, honored wife."

With that he strode out of the room. At his heels, the dogs, who had somehow caught the scent of his fury, set up a fearful clamor, circling him round and round as he made his way across the room and taking the opportunity to nip at my ankles as they passed.

21

A LTHOUGH I MIGHT HAVE BEEN EXCUSED FOR OFFEND-
ing the Marchese once, I could hardly expect to be forgiven a second time. The man hated me. And he was
the most powerful being in Mantova. I spent the days after the
debacle at Marmirolo waiting for the axe to fall. Instead, to my
surprise I received a courteous invitation to wait on Madonna
Isabella the very next week.

She received me in the first of her "three little rooms" —
her *camerini*, that suite of treasures for which she was already
celebrated throughout Europe. Having commanded me there,
she then kept me cooling my ardor for some considerable time
while she composed a shopping list to be sent to her agent
in Venezia. She needed *at once* blue cloth for a *gamorra*, an
engraved amethyst, a rosary of black onyx and gold, and anything else that was new and elegant in Venezia. She also *must
have* black cloth for a mantle such as should be without a rival
in the world even if it cost two ducats a yard — this at a time
when a master like Sandro Botticelli was paid no more than
thirty ducats for all the labor he lavished on the Bardi Chapel
in Firenze.

While my ears absorbed the details of *lusso* yet to come—each item to be found and shipped to her quickly, quickly—my eyes catalogued the treasure she had already amassed: crystal candlesticks with gold bases, blown at Murano and carved by Ragusa at Venezia; cameos and porphyry vases; books bound in velvet and gold or rich white brocade; portrait medals by such masters as Pisanello and Sperandio, including one of Madonna Isabella herself, cast in gold and ringed with diamonds.

At last her long list wound down and the lady dismissed her secretary and turned her attention to me.

"Now then, signorina *ebrea*." She beckoned me to join her. "Let us see your fair face. Let us look into your eyes." Whereupon she did indeed gaze steadily and at some length into my eyes.

"What do we see?" she mused. "Do we see faith? Purity of purpose? Dedication? Or do we see wantonness and desire?"

She laid her hand on my cheek. "Cool." She tilted her head to one side, thoughtfully. "And the flesh is pale, which would indicate serenity of spirit. But the eyes are cloudy." She shook her head disapprovingly. "I fear there is turmoil in the eyes."

"Oh no, *illustrissima!*" Without knowing why, I knew that my happiness depended on there being no turmoil in my eyes.

"Our illustrious lord, the Marchese, believes this conversion of yours has been planned for purposes other than good Christian ones. He fears that it is not Christ you have chosen to follow but the charm of a well-turned calf and a pair of blue eyes."

I could not look her in the eye and deny it.

"On the other hand, Fra Pietro assures us that you are sincere..." But would the *frate*'s commendation prevail over a great lord's vengeance? "And so I must make my own investigation. That is the reason for your presence here today. By the time we are done, I shall either stand sponsor at your baptism or wash my hands of you."

"And what must I do to win your—"

"Be sincere," she ordered coldly. "Do not play a part for me. For I always know when I am being deceived."

If that was so, my cause was lost. For, given Jesus Christ at one end of the room and Lord Pirro of Bozzuolo at the other, there was no doubt which one I would have chosen to spend my life with. Fearful that these thoughts might be read on my face, I turned aside and busied myself with the portrait medals. Thus I did not see but only heard her order to have Lord Pirro summoned at once.

I did not turn when I heard him enter the room. But I could hear him breathing behind me. And I swear to you I could feel Madama's eyes boring through my spine and straight into my heart.

Save me, Jesus. Give me the strength to dissemble, I prayed. Fancy the gall of such a prayer — to ask Christ to aid me in my efforts to disguise my preference for an earthly love over His!

"She is transported by Sperandio's portraits," I heard her whisper. "She does have a most keen appreciation of beauty for an ignorant girl."

"The better for us, madama. For we are her teachers. And what is more godlike in the world of mortals than to create a mind? Is that not what the esteemed Vittorino once wrote to your illustrious father?" my lord inquired with courtly grace.

"Cousin, you astonish me." Her tone became light and bantering, as it so often did when in his company. "No sooner do I begin to think of you as permanently attached to a sword and pike than you give me a peek into another side of your being."

"Not for all the world would I mislead you, madonna. I am a soldier by trade and in my heart like all the Gonzaga men. But I take as my model your husband's father, the late Marchese Lodovico, a great *condottiero* who took time between campaigns to search out Andrea Mantegna when that maestro was a stripling, and who rebuilt this city according to the dictates of no less a master than Leon Battista Alberti."

As I listened to this exchange, it occurred to me that courtly conversation is like a tennis game in which the conversational ball is always returned but never so far out of reach as to force a lady to run or otherwise extend herself in order to win.

I turned slowly, eyes downcast (just in case Madama could, as she claimed, read the turmoil in my soul), and interrupted their chitchat. "Forgive my inattention, madama. I was bewitched by the artistry of the medalist." Then, as if noticing him for the first time, I glanced up at my love. "Lord Pirro. What a surprise. It has been so long that I thought I might never have the pleasure of seeing you again."

"I have been at Venezia, lady, attending on the Marchese."

"Yet you are at Mantova today," I answered with every show of coolness. "For how long, I wonder."

"Only until this evening, lady," he answered. "Then I am off to Brescia to join my lord in the lists."

"The more reason for us to make the very most of this day," Madonna Isabella interrupted. "For I too am off with the sun to pay a delayed visit to my esteemed sister, the Duchess of Ban." (That must be the little dark one with the mean face, the one called Beatrice, I thought.)

"Cousin, bring out my silver lute and let us have some music." She waved him toward an *intarsio* lute, cunningly implanted in the door of a cabinet. And for a moment I believed he would attempt to dislodge it. But instead, he swung aside the panel of woodwork, revealing it to be no thicker than a finger's depth (amazing that it looked the full volume of the instrument from the distance of a few feet). Behind the panel in a niche lay the true instrument, not an illusion this time but a body of silver gilt complete with gut strings and ready to play. "Come, honored ladies," he invited us sweetly. "Follow me and I shall serenade you with the latest tune from France."

Madonna Isabella clapped her hands delightedly — reminding me that for all her imperious airs, she was still a young girl — and followed him into the larger adjoining room. There, he located a footstool, perched his left foot on it in the manner of a troubadour, swung the instrument into place, and began to strum.

The name of the air, he advised us, was "Three Maids and a Monk" and the lyric was enough to bring a blush to my cheeks.

In this ditty a priest manages to trap not one or two but three virgins in a chapel in the woods. Each in turn offers herself to him if he will spare the other two. But no! He wants all three. And take them he does, one after the other, then two together, one from in front and one from behind while the other is bade to "kiss me on the lips to sanctify the pleasure." In the last verse, the monk goes off unfrocked, his shirt and "other accessories" hanging between his legs and his habit under his arm.

The song ends with a warning to virgins not to pray in that chapel: "For, girl, although three Hail Marys may take away your sins, that monk will load you with three more before he has come to the end of his beads."

To this scurrilous lyric, Madama gave her delighted attention. And the pun at the end evoked a loud handclap from her and a demand for more.

"What ails you, signorina *ebrea*?" Madonna Isabella's voice cut off my thoughts. "Are you not amused or is it that you do not understand French?"

I understood French well enough, but it seemed wise to feign ignorance.

"Then Lord Pirro must translate for you so that you can share our mirth."

"Better still," he responded, "allow me to sing in Italian so that all may understand. A favorite of yours, madama," bowing, "with a verse by the magnificent Lorenzo dei Medici."

Until then I knew the Medici as bankers and patrons, not as poets. Yet this verse, which has since become as popular as any sonnet of Petrarch's, seemed wonderfully lyrical to me — and without the extreme coarseness that marked the French verse.

Youths and maids, enjoy today.
Naught ye know about tomorrow.
Fair is youth and void of sorrow
But it hourly flies away . . .

During the rendition of the many verses of this song, Madonna Isabella began to taunt me lightly with references to Lord Pirro. His charm. His looks. His sweet voice. "What do you think of your troubadour from Bozzuolo, signorina?" she crooned. "Does he not sing in the tones of an angel? Is he not fair? Do his eyes please you, lady? And his golden curls? Do they not curl their way around your heart?" Rising above the singer, her questions pricked at me like little daggers.

Was this the test I had been promised earlier, meant to take the measure of my wantonness and desire? If so, I passed but only just. Certainly Lord Pirro gave no indication of strain. He strummed away on the silver lute seemingly oblivious of the barrage of little pointed questions that punctuated his ditty. And when it was done, he asked permission to sing a song "for the lady Grazia," which Madonna Isabella graciously granted.

Then, looking deep into my eyes like a truly lovesick troubadour, he commenced his serenade:

Oh beauteous rose of Judea, oh my sweet soul,
Do not leave me to die, I beg of you.
Wretch that I am, must I perish
For serving well and loving faithfully?
Oh God of Love, what torture it is to love.
See, I am dying for the love of this Jewess.
Help me in my despair. Do not let me die.

As the last strum died away, he gave me one long, last look, made a deep bow to his kinswoman, and was off, leaving me exposed to Madama's pitiless gaze, my pose of indifference shattered.

"Now where do you suppose he picked up that strange little tune?" she inquired coolly. When I did not reply, she shrugged and, indicating a painted *cassone* against the wall, instructed, "Come over here. I have something to show you."

It was an exquisite piece of French lace fashioned into a cap, most delicate and expensive.

"Take this as a reaffirmation of my pledge to stand beside you at the font, signorina *ebrea.*" She tucked the gossamer thing into my pocket. "Wear it on the day of your baptism. Until then I urge you to attend faithfully to your instruction. Remember that when your course is done we will become sisters in Christ." She bent over to kiss me on the cheek.

I had passed the test of sincerity. I was to be the Madonna Isabella's sister in Christ. But would I also become her cousin in the world? Could I trust her to honor her undertaking to me? Or Lord Pirro himself?

During the days that followed, thoughts of my brothers intruded constantly. And of my father. Had I sacrificed every golden thing in my life for dross? Doubt joined with fear and regret to undermine my resolve. Put your faith in Christ, I told myself. Work. Study. Pray. Be patient and your prayers will be answered.

My dedication was rewarded. Within weeks Fra Pietro pronounced me ready for baptism. Next came news that Madama had returned from visiting her sister at Milano and would be pleased to audience me, not in private this time but at her weekly levee, the forum in which all manner of events — births, deaths, marriages, and betrothals — were announced.

In the way of such audiences, I was kept waiting while several petitions were heard. A wife-beater was let off with a warning. A certain Zoppo was granted fishing rights in the Lago Minore in exchange for half the catch. A fence was ordered torn down. Impatient as I was for her to get to my business, I had to admire the young Marchesana's conscientious conduct of her tasks. It is not amusing to sit for hours week after week adjudicating trivial disputes and judging minor offenses. But she betrayed no sign of boredom at the tedious parade, listening attentively as the petitioners gave their accounts, questioning the timid most gently, the bombastic with severe rigor, and rendering what seemed to me a series of just and compassionate judgments.

After an hour of this, many of the courtiers went into a doze but the lady seemed more wide awake than ever. Playing the role of ruler brought out the best in her.

Next she called upon Messer Equicola to assist her in enunciating the court calendar. My turn at last. But instead of my betrothal announcement, Equicola began to read out to the assemblage a long letter from one of the Gonzaga horse buyers at Cadiz. Each purchase was followed by a detailed description of the animal and its bloodline and each was greeted by enthusiastic applause. And the fervor of the assemblage did not abate when the letter went on to give a long report on the health and well-being of their Catholic Majesties King Ferdinand and Queen Isabella. Every royal cough was greeted by murmured expressions of sympathy, every menu and every gown with avid interest, and every *grido* promulgated by the Spanish crown as if the laws had issued from the mouth of God Himself... with Madonna Isabella the greatest sycophant of all. This indiscriminate worship of royalty—any royalty—is another side of her nature.

The levee had now been in progress for two hours and, although others had been greeted and smiled at, I had not received so much as a glance of recognition from the Marchesana. Instead, I was forced to suffer through the inventory of Barbary stallions and the Queen of Spain's raw throat. By the time they got to the final item in the horse dealer's communiqué—the return of an Italian navigator in the employ of the Spanish crown from a voyage across the great western ocean—my mind was frayed. All I got from the report was a jumble of exotic snatches—parrots as big as falcons and red as pheasants, sandalwood free for the chopping, rivers that run with gold and men like Tartars with hair falling over their shoulders who eat human flesh and fatten other men as we do capons. The astonishing fact that a new world had been discovered by this Cristoforo Colombo escaped me completely.

"Now then, signorina *conversa*..." At long last the horse trader's letter was done and Madonna Isabella acknowledged my presence. "We hear that you have completed your studies and are ready to join us in Christ's sisterhood. Congratulations."

Whereupon everyone applauded.

"I said that I would stand with you at the font, did I not?"

"You did, *illustrissima*."

"Then we must set a date. June would be a good time. For I am just now bound to visit Venezia and after that my honored parents in Ferrara."

"So long?"

"Ah, your eagerness is touching." She smiled sweetly. "You cannot wait to embrace the faith. Have you given thought to what name you will take when you are reborn as a Christian?"

"With respect, madama, I hope to take the name of my betrothed, Lord Pirro Gonzaga."

"Betrothed?" Her face took on a distracted air. "Well, I am afraid that is not to be, after all. My illustrious husband has made other plans for Lord Pirro."

Her cool tone cut through my heart as smooth as a knife through butter. "He has arranged a match with a princess of Savoia. She has a dowry of thirty thousand ducats and lands inherited from her illustrious mother."

I could feel myself trembling as I protested, "But I heard nothing..."

"Lord Pirro is prohibited from writing to you now that he is betrothed to another. His honor forbids it."

"And his promises to me? His sworn word?"

"Lord Pirro has but one sworn word and that is to his liege lord, my illustrious husband, the Marchese. And, of course, to God..." She crossed herself reverently.

These princes know no shame. They command God to appear on their behalf and then banish Him the next minute as if He were their servant.

"It is God's will, girl. Accept it. Come forward now," she commanded me. "I have words for you."

Even though my head was reeling and my gut in turmoil, I did step forward as I was bidden.

"Earthly delights are short-lived," the lady announced solemnly. "Christ stays with us forever. Even if we two are not fated to be cousins in the world, we shall still be sisters in Christ."

"No-o-o!" The long wail escaped my throat independent of my wish to utter it.

Abruptly the hand was withdrawn. Before me now stood a proud and angry woman.

"Does this mean you refuse baptism? Is my lord correct that this faith of yours was but a gambit to snag a fine husband? Are you refusing Christ, girl? Are you or are you not?"

Was I? I hardly knew, myself. A great weight was pressing upon me, urging me to sink. Christ, I prayed silently, take me from this place. Take me anywhere, even to hell, but take me from here...

"Perhaps I misunderstood you." Her voice came to me as from a distant shore. "You need time to pray for understanding and acceptance. You are excused..."

Purely out of habit I made a deep curtsy and began to back out of her presence. But before I reached the door I was arrested by the majestic voice.

"Take this thought with you, signorina *ebrea*. I will pray every day for the purity of your intention. And no matter that you waver up to the last moment, I will come from wherever I am to stand beside you at the font, even if I have to ride for a day and a night to be there. For I am a woman of my word."

The cloister was a bitter place for me that evening as I did my rounds with Cateruccia. No longer did I repeat my homily that the meek inherit the earth. I knew better.

As the darkness came down I continued to tramp around and around the tiny square, cursing God on the triangle and Jesus and Mary on the second turn. Dimly I heard the bells of San Andrea announce vespers. Then compline. Still I walked and cursed, chained to the motion of my own body like a galley slave to his oar. How long I might have stayed there I do not know. But sometime just after the prime bell I felt a gentle hand on my arm and looked up to see Fra Pietro's face gazing down upon me like an angel. Then I did sink. I felt myself falling into blackness.

22

F ROM THE DAYS THAT FOLLOWED MY ATTACK OF TER-
tian fever only a few fleeting impressions remain. A knife
at my foot. Someone pressing cups upon my chest. The
flickering lights of the little candles inside the cups. Darkness.
Sleep. Dreams.

Then in the midst of a dream, the clear sight of a beloved
face, the sound of a familiar voice. "Take a little of this *minestra*,
sister." A pair of steady young hands held the bowl to my lips.

My brother Jehiel came to me at the *casa dei catecumeni*
every day of my illness. He braved the terrors of that place—
of which he had heard the most frightening reports—to bring
me chicken soup and love. It was he who coaxed me to leave
there and who overcame my fears of the Casa dei Rossi with its
alarming memories.

"Do they not hate me?" I asked. "Have they not disowned
me?"

"Not at all. They are sad that you have left. Gershom and I
pray every night for you to come back. And Papa sits in his *studiolo* but he does not study. He only stares and sighs. We need
you, Grazia. Come home with me now."

"This moment?"

"When better?" he asked with perfect logic.

"But my fever. The weakness in my limbs..."

"You can lean on me."

OF OUR ARRIVAL AT my father's house I remember nothing. When I came to awareness, I was in my own bed. Above me loomed the pale, serious face of my little brother Gershom.

"Is she going to die?" I heard him whisper. "Is Grazia going to die like Mama?"

"No, brother." Jehiel entered my field of vision. "She is not going to die. Not unless you smother her with those wet kisses. Leave off, baby..."

My brothers were my only friends in that house. The rest of the *famiglia*, including my father, kept me at a distance. It was not difficult to understand the reasons. The whole household heard them enumerated every night after we had retired, reiterated by Dorotea in a piercing wail that penetrated every room in the house.

"Oh, the shame! Oh, the mortification that she causes us to suffer! My poor Ricca! Who will marry her now that Grazia has brought disgrace on us all? My poor innocent virgin is doomed to spinsterhood. Oh, the shame that Grazia has brought upon this house! Oh, the injustice!" And so on far into the night.

She had reason to despair of her daughter's chances. The Jews in Italy are small in number and ferocious in pursuit of gossip. The news of my near apostasy had surely spread north to Venezia and south to Napoli by now. And I daresay Ricca's chances for hooking a really fine fish in the marriage pond were lessened considerably by her sisterhood with a girl of little faith and even fewer morals such as I was perceived to be—and, by their standards, was. Bad enough to be in disgrace with God and man alike; but to know myself guilty made my remorse doubly bitter.

In that state, even Virgil lost the power to carry me out

of myself. But Jehiel, in whom Vittorino's teachings were grounded, hit upon a true humanistic remedy for my lassitude and weakness. *In corpore sano, mens sana.* My body must be made healthy, he announced to me, before my spirit could be healed. In that cause, he set about on a campaign to get our morning rides reinstated. And he hectored Papa so effectively that ponies were ordered in spite of Dorotea's opposition to the scheme.

Jehiel's remedy proved efficacious. Galloping full tilt, my hair loose and flying, the horse's mane flowing, the beat of his hooves pounding below, I felt strong again, young again. I came back to life on the back of a chestnut bay.

But with youthful zest comes youthful folly. Somehow Jehiel got it in his head that we must take a gallop in the Gonzaga park. "Just once," he pleaded. "It will be like the old days when we were little ... and happy."

I knew I should not go riding in the Gonzagas' park. My wounds at their hands were too raw to rub them with memories. But there was a part of me that also yearned to go back to that earthly paradise just one more time. I agreed.

As we galloped along the long, soft carpet of emerald green that led to the stables, memories of other rides began to flood my mind: the day I ran away and was carried home like a bride on Lord Pirro's steed, the way-stop at the Bosco Fontana where we pledged our love, the excitement of my ride to Marmirolo to attend Madonna Isabella's fete, and the ride back to the *casa dei catecumeni* after my dismal blunder in the Game of Ships. Then out of this sea of memory emerged a pair of riders, a lady and a gentleman coming toward us through the mist. As they approached I could see that the lady was wearing a hunting hat with a long plume that dipped in the breeze. When she turned her head, her sharp, pointed nose stood out in profile against the background of the sky. I did not recognize her.

But the other figure was only too familiar. I knew the tilt of that body in the saddle. I have never seen anyone ride quite the way Lord Pirro does—laid back like Triton astride his sea horse.

There were no byways leading off the tree-lined pathway. Approaching from opposite ends, we were like two knights riding into combat after the gauntlet has been thrown down. No avoiding the inescapable confrontation.

As the distance between us narrowed we all slowed our mounts to a polite pace as is customary for riders who must pass close. The lady was at hand. In spite of my inner turmoil a certain part of me observed when we came abreast that her skin had lost the bloom of youth.

Now came the real test. I took a deep breath to bolster my composure. Everything in me longed to cry out, to shriek betrayal, to wail my loss like a bereaved widow. What he felt, I do not know; for he bowed low just as we passed and his *berretta* covered his eyes.

Did I actually hear him murmur, *"Mi dispiace,"* as he bent low before me, or did I imagine it?

A moment later I was galloping wildly away from the scene headed I knew not where, with Jehiel at my heels shouting after me to hold up. Instead I threw the rein over my horse's head, a most reckless act as you know, and let the animal fly as he might. All I wanted was to be carried away out of that long green trap and into the open fields.

Then suddenly a fence loomed up ahead and a tall iron gate, shut against riders. Too late now to regain the reins. I lowered my head, dug into the animal with my knees, and prayed.

We sailed over the gate without a mishap.

It took no more than a few seconds for me to feel the prick of the first nettle. Brambles as high as my waist dug into my flesh. On we galloped, the horse tossing his head wildly from side to side to ward off the pain of the thorns but both of us too stubborn to slow down.

Just ahead on the edge of the thicket, there rose into the air a great buzzing cloud. Louder and louder it buzzed, like a demented sackbut. Then needles, fire, flashes of pain. The horse and I went down screaming. I had taken him into the center of a swarm of bees.

THE NEXT THING I remember is the taste of mud and the feel of it seeping into my ears and my nose. And the sound of a country voice, not unkind but rough: "'Tis the best remedy for the bee sting, master. It draws the poison." Then the pressure of a man's arms lifting me and Jehiel's voice saying my name over and over. "Grazia. *Povera* Grazia..."

I was awakened by the pain, a thousand little darts of it shooting through my head and face.

"The child is writhing in pain, Maestro Portaleone. Cannot something be done?" My father's voice.

"Indeed it can and indeed it shall. We need only draw out the poison. I have already sent my boy off for the remedy."

Let him come soon.

"As I told you, honored husband..." Dorotea's voice. "There is nothing to concern yourself about. Her wounds will heal quickly, mark me. Now, dinner awaits. And our guests are arriving."

I opened my lips to cry out for my father. But they were stuck together and the cry remained locked in my throat. In place of a gentle hand on my brow, I got the tip-tap of retreating footsteps.

Left alone, I tried to raise my eyelids. But narrow slits were all the swelling allowed and I saw little. I felt my nose. My ears. Fiery. Then I began to pry my lips apart with my fingers. They felt dry and puffy, like beached fish lying dead on the shore.

Footsteps again.

A boy's voice. "I brought it fresh from the cow's ass just as you ordered, sir. She plopped it right onto the dish for me, obliging as you please. See, it is still steaming."

"Good, good."

I brought my hand to my eyelid and lifted it to get a peek at Portaleone's remedy. As I did so, a most noxious odor filled my nostrils. The smell of ordure.

"No. No." A cry managed to make its way through my swollen lips.

"Quiet, girl. I am going to draw the poison out of those punctures." I felt his hands grasp my hair and pull it back. Then, the heat and stench of the stuff on my forehead.

Where does strength come from? As often from fear as from courage, I wager. I grasped the quilt and, with all the force in me, threw it over his head. In the confusion, I staggered off the bed and, naked as I was, fled down the staircase.

"Catch her, boy! Catch her!" Behind me I heard Portaleone and his boy clattering down the stairs, hot in pursuit.

It certainly was not forethought that led me to seek refuge in the dining hall but more like pure accident—or fate, if you please. I was well into the room before my half-blinded eyes even recognized the familiar trestle table with all the *famiglia* arrayed along its length. In the center, my father, looking down at me like Jehovah. And beside him...a face I knew...with deep-set, compassionate eyes and a full, generous mouth. It was to that forgiving presence and not to my father's frightened eyes that I appealed by throwing myself at his feet with a plea of "Save me, Maestro del Medigo!"

Such a caterwaul as then went up you cannot imagine. Portaleone and his boy arrived shouting and Dorotea went into a screaming tantrum which, in turn, gave rise to name-calling and even fisticuffs, for my brothers were always ready to defend me. My father's main concern seemed to be to cover my nakedness, which he accomplished by pulling the cloth rudely off the table and rushing around to wrap me in it.

In all that gathering only one person demonstrated concern for my well-being. Rising to his full stature, he came around the table and, pushing my father aside with a brusque "By your leave, sir," gathered me up and carried me through that squealing mob, brushing them away like so many gnats. When we gained the *cortile* he laid me very carefully upon a bench and, drawing up a bucket of water, proceeded to wash the filth off my face, using for a rag a piece of his fine embroidered *camicia*, which he tore off as if it were an old piece of linen towel.

Now, Portaleone staggered out of the dining room all puffed up and spitting. "Whoever you are, sir, I warn you that this girl is my patient."

In the commotion he must not have caught sight of Judah's

face. But the moment he did, all the puff went out of him and he began to gibber. "Forgive me, Maestro Leone. I did not recognize you. The girl had an encounter with bees. I was about to apply a poultice of cow ordure."

"A tried and trusted remedy, maestro," Judah replied in his most gracious manner. "And the very one I myself would have chosen up until a few months ago. But I have recently concocted an unguent for such emergencies and used it with success on a *bravo* or two in the Borgia circle. By good fortune there is a vial in my bag."

The name of the papal family acted upon Maestro Portaleone more efficaciously than an emetic. His rage voided, he immediately took on a tone of placation.

"Do you wish my boy to fetch your case, honored sir?" he sniveled, in what he doubtless took to be a courtly manner.

"He will find it under the chair in the center of the table where I was sitting," Judah replied graciously, showing no sign of impatience or disrespect. Then he turned to the boy. "It is black leather. With my initials stamped on it. J. del M."

"This gentleman is the eminent physician and philosopher Leone del Medigo, boy," his master instructed him. "Bow to him at once." Which the boy did. At once.

"Look for the initials J. del M.," Judah repeated for the boy's benefit. Then to Portaleone he added, "The Christians may choose to call me Leone for their own ignorant reasons but I never refer to myself except by my Hebrew name, Judah. They must take me as what I am or not at all. It is the only policy to pursue with these Christian baptizers. Do you not agree, maestro?"

During this dialogue he never for a moment ceased his gentle cleansing of my wounds, and with each soft stroke my pain lessened.

Portaleone's wounded pride had been assuaged. Now Dorotea made her entrance, dragging my father behind her. "I want that girl punished. Punished. We have been humiliated once again, mortified before our honored guest. Oh, Maestro Leone, I beg your indulgence."

"No indulgence necessary, signora." Judah did not even deign to look at her as he spoke. "This girl is wounded. I am a physician. My duty is clear. Unless you, sir..." He turned his gaze on Papa and added sternly, "Unless you object to my ministrations."

The idea of anyone objecting to the attentions of Maestro Leone was too absurd to consider.

"Now then, I wish to have brought to me a bowl of warmed water, straight from the well, and some fresh rose petals—a good handful," he instructed Dorotea. "And a few drops of sweet oil. Do you have that in your housewife's cabinet?"

"Yes, Maestro Leone," replied a newly compliant Dorotea.

"Very good. Have it brought upstairs together with clean linen. The good physician Portaleone will assist me so the rest of you can get back to your dinner."

"But what of *your* dinner, maestro? I have prepared a beautiful pie with special birds brought from the Bosco Fontana." Dorotea literally wrung her hands in her distress.

"I will dine with my patient when the treatment is over," Judah announced. "Plain broth. A pasta with good cheese. And a ripe melon. If one is not to be had, a few figs chopped fine and soaked in wine and sugar. Can that be prepared in your kitchen, madonna?"

Oh, how she must have hated me at that moment. I had interrupted her dinner, stolen away her celebrated guest, and now she was being ordered around like a publican. But Judah's authority being what it was, she dared not express her rage. She simply curtsied and went to the kitchen to transmit Judah's orders while he lifted me like a baby and carried me up to a clean bed.

The treatment, like many of Judah's treatments, was simple but exceedingly painstaking. When he had settled me down, he explained what he was about to do. First, he would remove the stingers one by one with a fine needle and apply a special unguent to the punctures to relieve my distress and to close up the little wounds.

"It will take time and it will hurt some," he warned. "But not more than you can bear, I promise."

He took from his bag a strange-looking piece of glass, framed in silver. It would magnify the wounds and help him to guide his needle, he told me. Then he went about his work, with me peering up at him from between my swollen eyelids. It was difficult and somewhat painful to open them, but the look in his eyes—those deep-set orbs of weariness, wisdom, and pity—was something I could not get enough of.

Occasionally the needle refused to do its work. When that happened, he would lay it aside, lean down, place his warm lips over the puncture, and suck the stinger out with his own breath.

I found myself imagining that those kind eyes and that soft mouth were the eyes and mouth of my father and that he was the one caring for me, not the great physician. But this man was not my papa much as I might wish it so. This man was a stranger. How fortunate his children were, I remember thinking, to have such a man for a father.

When the treatment was done dinner was brought. Judah fed me the soup himself, spoonful by spoonful with a smallish silver spoon he took from his bag. And then while I munched on the soft melon he had requested, we talked. To be accurate, he talked. He was in Mantova, he explained, at the invitation of the young Marchesana, who had requested him not for his talents as a physician but as a scholar.

"She has a manuscript half Hebrew, half Greek, called *The Sanidrin*, which she believes to be very ancient, and she wishes me to verify it since she herself is not at home in Hebrew."

"But you are, sir?"

"I was born in Greece and studied the ancient tongue as a child. Then in Padova the Latinists trained me in Latin and the rabbis in Hebrew," he answered. "Aramaic, I taught myself. And I do not know a word of French. Now why does that make you look sad?"

"Oh, I am not—" I stopped myself in the midst of the lie. He who had been so candid with me deserved the courtesy of a truthful reply. "I am envious, sir, of your opportunities and of your accomplishments. It is my heart's desire to master these tongues that you speak of and to unlock the mysteries that I know reside in the great books."

"Not to mention the delights," he added.

"Those too," I admitted. "But I do have enough Latin to read Virgil and"—here, I bent to whisper the forbidden tongue— "a little French, which I taught myself."

"You *are* a wicked girl," he remarked, and it took a moment for me to note the twinkle in his eyes that gave away the rebuke as a jest.

Made bold by his good humor, I ventured to ask, "If you do stay here to study the Marchesana's manuscript, would you..." I felt bolder saying it than I had riding atop the elephant or during any of my less admirable exploits. "Would you teach me, sir? I do so long to learn."

His reply was not encouraging. Much as he would have enjoyed tutoring such an eager mind, he said, his work on the manuscript was almost finished. All that remained was to inform his client that her document was spurious and that there was no record of any Hebrew text named *The Sanidrin*. Even now he was making preparations to journey to Firenze, where he had been appointed a member of the Platonic Academy by the son of the late and most lamented Lorenzo dei Medici, known as *il magnifico*.

"When the magnificent Lorenzo died, his son Piero dissolved the Platonic Academy," he explained. "But now Piero has had second thoughts and is about to reconstitute the charmed circle in an effort to emulate his revered father.

"Firenze is a place where I have been very happy," he added, speaking to me all the while as if to an equal and not being in any way condescending. "Besides, after the Medici, I find the Gonzagas more than a little..."

"Whimsical?" I inquired as he searched for a word. "Changeable? False?"

"Exactly," he agreed, smiling. "But then you know them at first hand, I hear."

"My true feeling, sir, is that they are a pack of pigs and whores wallowing in *lusso* and ready to sell themselves to the first corner with a handful of ducats in his pocket."

"They have disappointed you, then?" he asked lightly.

That mild question unleashed a flood that carried everything with it, facts, fantasies, and feelings, all in a rush—my infatuation with Lord Pirro, my betrayal by him and Madonna Isabella, the *casa dei catecumeni*, Careruccia, the chess set, the Game of Ships, every detail except one. What caused me to lower the veil over the Bosco Fontana? Modesty? Shame? Or was it a subtle transformation of my feelings for the listener? As I led him pell-mell through my life and felt the warmth of his gaze and the soft pressure of his hand on my arm, he slowly became more and more a man to me and less a god. And I became less a child and more a woman with a woman's jealousy of her heart's secrets.

23

THREE DAYS WERE ALL IT TOOK FOR JUDAH TO CURE me of the ill effects of my misadventure at the Gonzaga stud. The day after he extracted the stingers, he returned with a little pot of stuff to soothe and hide the blemishes as they healed. The day after that he came again to roust me out of bed and escort me on a stroll to the Pusterla Gate. A walk in the fresh air was the treatment that day—nothing more.

"Invalids make their own diseases," he explained as he conducted me homeward. "Bedsores, swellings, blood clots, and wheezing all come from recuperating in a prone position." When he repeated this to Dorotea, she was not impressed.

The following day he examined my little wounds with extreme care and announced me beyond his powers to help, since I was cured. The good news made me unaccountably sad, which I chose to attribute to fear of the punishment I was sure to suffer now that I was well enough to bear it.

As if to confirm my fears, the afternoon of the day I was pronounced well, I received an instruction to wait upon my father in his *studiolo*.

"Grazia...my dear little Grazia...I have been searching for

you all the afternoon. Come in. Come in."

Too astonished by this reception even to think, I stepped in obediently and stood before him.

"Sit down," he invited me with a smile. A smile. Almost as if he approved of me. "Now then, tell me, what are your thoughts about marriage?"

"Marriage?"

"Marriage."

"Well I...I understand, honored padre, that I must banish all such thoughts from my mind since I have disgraced myself much too far ever to hope for—"

"But let us suppose that, by some unexpected—astonishing—even miraculous intervention of God's charity, you were forgiven your transgressions..."

"I cannot imagine that, honored Signore Padre," I replied.

"Imagine it, Grazia," he ordered me, quite stern now. "Imagine yourself forgiven."

"I cannot, Signore Padre."

"What do you want, girl? A note sent directly from heaven and signed by God Himself?"

Before I could frame a suitable answer, he reconsidered the barb and returned to his earlier kindly tone. "You are forgiven, Grazia. Believe me. God has taken pity on you. He has given you more than a second chance. He has thrown your way a beneficence not vouchsafed many. He has sent you a husband."

"Who?"

"A fine man. An honored Jew."

Dio! It was Rabbi Abramo, pressed into service by La Nonna to erase the stain on the family escutcheon.

"No!" I cried.

"No?" he shouted, giving way at last to anger. "You say no to such an honor? Even before you know who has made the offer? Ungrateful brat! God knows why he wants you," he muttered, as much to himself as to me. Then, throwing his hands in the air, he ordered me to leave him and go at once to my stepmother. "She will explain. These matters are better left to women. Go now." He rose and gave me a push toward the door. "And I would not be so quick to answer no, young lady," he shouted after me as I scooted along the hall to the *sala piccola*. "You may never get such a fine offer again in your life. In fact, I'd be willing to bet on it."

In the kitchen I found a new Dorotea, solicitous, with a cup of spiced wine, "for you are shivering with cold, poor girl," and the offer of her own shawl.

Made bold by this welcome, I asked her straight out for the name of my suitor.

"Did not your father tell you?" she asked. "Oh, that foolish man. They are all hopeless when it comes to affairs of the heart." She nudged me conspiratorially.

"Will you tell me, then?" I asked. "Is it Rabbi Abramo?"

"Rabbi Abramo? Did your father give you that notion? Is it his idea of a joke?" She laughed. Then her face took on a look I cannot ever forget, a mixture of amazement and envy. "My dear, your hand has been requested by no less a personage than Leone del Medigo."

"Maestro Judah, the doctor?"

"Physician, scholar, philosopher. He has the ear of the Medici and the support of powerful Christians. He was tutor to Lord Pico of Mirandola, who seeks his counsel to this day."

"Is he rich?" I asked, as if I cared.

"He is rich in knowledge," Dorotea answered self-righteously. "Mind you, he does not lack for ready cash either. His great skill fetches high fees."

"He wants to marry me?" I could not believe it.

"He made his offer this morning. It seems he is about to leave for Firenze and he wishes to take you with him as his bride."

"Messer Judah wants to marry me?" I asked again, stupidly.

"He is coming to ask you himself this evening, with our permission, of course." Dorotea preened.

"Is it decided, then?" I asked.

"Why do you ask? Surely you do not intend to refuse the offer."

"He is not young..." I ventured.

"He has just passed thirty. Young enough for any normal purposes."

"He is not married, then?"

"Never had the time for it, he says, luckily for you. Do you have any comprehension what a blessing has fallen upon you? Your husband has an appointment in the Medici circle. You will accompany him to Firenze. It is a high honor. Do you not know anything about the world, girl?"

Oh, I knew many things about the world. "Perhaps I cannot believe in my good fortune," I answered truthfully.

"Understandable. And suitably modest for a Jewish bride. I shall tell your father of your reaction. It is most appropriate." Then she leaned down and whispered into my ear as I had seen her do with her own daughter so many times. "You have my permission to rub a little rouge into your cheeks. Just a little. Not enough to attract your father's notice. But you could use a bit of brightening up, Grazia. No man likes a pale woman. And it wouldn't hurt you to put on a bit of flesh around the bosom and the behind. From the side, you look quite like a boy." Oh dear.

"Don't pout now. You will manage these things beautifully with my help. All it takes is diligence and brains and you have ample amounts of both. You will make a fine wife, Grazia." It was the first compliment she had ever paid me.

"Always stay at home. Do not stand by the portal. Never look out the window. If your eyes wander fasten them at once on your needlework."

"Remember to water your orange trees every day in summer or the Tuscan heat will burn them up."

"If you need ask your honored husband for a courtesy or favor, wait until after dinner when he is well fed and content. Offer him a cup of sweet malvasa wine (always keep a vessel of it handy for this purpose), seat yourself on a stool at his feet, and from that humble posture,

making certain that your eyes express fully the reverence in which you hold him, make your request."

By the time Judah arrived that evening, I had mastered enough of Dorotea's marriage catechism to pinch my cheeks until they turned rosy and to lower my gaze in reverence for my bridegroom.

"Your face is flushed, Grazia. Let me feel your forehead." Those were his first words to me when we were left alone, hardly what Dorotea had led me to expect.

"Hmm. No fever. Why are you flushed?"

"I am blushing, sir. I am shy." Not entirely untrue.

"But we know each other so well."

"Oh no, sir, if you will forgive me ..." ("Never dispute your husband or deny him," was one of Dorotea's dicta.) "I do not mean to sound contentious, but everything is different now."

"That is where you are wrong," he replied. "Everything is exactly the same. We are still friends, are we not?" I nodded my agreement. "Well then, let us dispense with this idea of wife for a moment and talk of friends, loving friends." He took my hand in his. "Companions in learning and in life. Partners. Confidants. Walking along the road of life side by side, through sun and rain, offering each other help over the rough patches. I will soothe you with unguents. You will succor me with soft words. And we will read together. But above all, we will be loving friends. That is my proposal."

I knew he was not young. But my memory of love, young and eager and laced with fire, was still fresh and I could not help but wonder, need marriage be so bland, so passionless as Judah made it sound? Even Dorotea's diatribes held more promise of excitement.

"If he gives you a slave, watch her like a hawk. Tartars, especially, are beasts. You cannot trust the house to them."

"Be sure always to seize the Sabbath bread firmly with both hands. Ill fortune will dog you all the week if each one of your ten fingers is not touching the loaf when it is blessed."

"Keep on the alert for fleas. Search them out every day in the linens,

the garments, the heads of servants. Fleas can destroy your household and your happiness."

She fed me constantly, stuffing my mouth as conscientiously as she stuffed my head. My indoctrination did not cease until the day of my wedding. Occupied with feasts and fittings, I barely saw my groom after he made his proposal.

THE WEEK OF THE wedding a huge contingent of well-wishers arrived from Ferrara to be entertained and fed. They proved a welcome distraction from the pangs of unease I had begun to suffer. It was not only the spirit of the proposal that troubled me but the fast-approaching wedding night itself. When that moment came, there would be no way to hide my lapse from virtue at the Bosco Fontana. Would a man whose vision of love was a mix of unguents, soft words, and reading ever understand? Forgive?

It was not something I could discuss with my marriage mentor, Dorotea. Nor with any of the countless relations and friends who descended on us, arms laden with gifts and stomachs cursed by unappeasable hunger. They never stopped eating from the moment they arrived until the moment they departed. Fortunately, my grandparents had sent along sacks upon sacks of fresh fish, wagonfuls of capons, and enough sweetmeats to keep everyone happy.

The only bitter moment in these high spirits was occasioned by my marriage ring, of all things. I do not speak of the ceremonial ring. That I received by proxy on the day my marriage contract was read out and the rabbi himself placed a sprig of myrrh in the little golden temple at Jerusalem which traditionally decorates these heavy, unwearable amulets. My true betrothal ring, a gift from Judah, was also made of yellow gold but much more delicate and, if you recall, studded with a gorgeous, sparkling diamond.

By some ill fate, Rabbi Abramo happened to be standing by when the packet was unwrapped. The jewel shone so brightly in the morning light that the rays lit up the *sala piccola* the way a chandelier does, casting blue and silver shafts of light here and there as I moved it around on my finger.

"Is it a gem? Is there a gem embedded in that ring?" I heard the high-pitched whine of the rabbi's voice.

He shouldered his way past the women who had gathered around me to admire the ring, and pulled it rudely from my finger.

"This ring will not do," he announced abruptly. "You must return it at once to the bridegroom."

Dorotea was the one who came to my aid. "But why, Rabbi? It is so beautiful. And worth at least two hundred ducats." Her eyes glittered as brightly as the gem itself.

"Because the sages tell us that only a plain gold band will do as a wedding ring. No jewels. No gems. No decoration."

Within moments of the time the ring was returned, the irate bridegroom was at our portal pounding angrily and demanding to see my father.

We heard Papa called out of the *banco*. Then came a loud peremptory call for Rabbi Abramo, who scuttled out of the *sala piccola* like a ferret. There followed a most contentious affray conducted at an earsplitting pitch. Like most people who are slow to anger, when he finally succumbs Judah vents his rage with torrential force.

"Do you dare to instruct me in the interpretation of the Torah?" he bellowed at the cowering rabbi.

"With all respect, maestro..."

"With no respect at all, I say."

"Apologies, Maestro Leone..."

"Maestro *Judah*. What do you take me for, Rov? A *converso* with a new Italian name to go with my apostasy?"

"Oh no, sir..."

"I am Judah del Medigo and it behooves any Jew to address me by that name, no matter what the Christians choose to call me. To Christians I am transformed by my name, Judah, into the *Lion* of Judah. Hence their cognomen for me is Leone. It is as if they were to call you *Paternus* because your Hebrew name is Abraham and Abraham is the father of the race. Do you grasp the absurdity, man?"

"Oh yes, Maestro Leo — I mean Judah."

I edged myself out from behind the curtain to feast on the sight of Rabbi Abramo being brought low.

"Very well," Judah resumed sternly. "Now we will deal with your foolish and unsubstantiated objections to my bride's gift."

"It says clearly in the Talmud, maestro..."

"The Talmud says nothing *clearly*, fool. If any adjective in the world is inappropriately applied to the Talmud, it is the word 'clear.' As the great sage reminds us, the Talmud is a muddy sea which yields up its pearls with reluctance."

The rabbi bowed to this rebuke with a series of obsequious little nods, like a poor pupil being reprimanded by his tutor.

"Now then, having settled the matter of the Talmud, we will return to the insult you have perpetrated upon me, and what is much more important, upon my bride-to-be. Poor child, to be given a gift of love and to have it whisked away by an ignorant busybody. Listen now for I mean to say this only once..."

By then the courtyard was full of people — clerks and maids and porters and wedding visitors (who numbered near to one hundred souls), all attracted by the promise of a juicy family fight.

"The wedding ring is never mentioned in the Torah. Never mentioned," Judah repeated, in spite of his declaration that he would make his explanation only once. "Only one form of marriage is recognized in the Great Book — marriage by consummation. To be blunt, the only way in which the Torah tells us that a marriage is sanctified is by the act of copulation. Do you follow me?"

This time not only Rabbi Abramo but the entire assemblage bobbed their heads up and down. By some sleight of hand Judah had transformed an arena of domestic discord into a schoolroom and all the hungry gossips into wayward students.

"For those of you who are ignorant of the source" — he gave

a terrific glare in Abramo's direction on the word "ignorant"—
"I commend to you the Book of Genesis, Chapter Twenty-four,
in which we are told, if memory serves me, 'And Isaac brought
Rebecca'—his bride—'into his mother's tent and took Rebecca
and she became his wife and he loved her.' The 'taking' of the
woman was enough to sanctify that marriage in the eyes of the
Lord and should be enough to satisfy the rest of us, would you
not agree, Rabbi?" ·

"But it was the ring..." Abramo whined.

"Ah yes, the ring. Of what significance is the ring? If all it
takes to sanctify a Jewish marriage in the eyes of God is consummation, of what significance is the ring?"

No one dared to venture an opinion.

"The ring is of absolutely no significance whatsoever." Judah
answered his own question. "The only reference we have to
any ring is in the story of the messenger who comes to Nahor
to find a bride for Abraham's son Isaac. There"—he pointed
his finger at the little man—"in Genesis Twenty-four, I believe
verse twenty-two, we find reference to a *nazem*, which is indeed
a ring *but not a marriage ring*. Do you not understand the difference between a *nazem* and a *tabat*?" he thundered. But by then,
the rabbi was reduced to gibbering and shivering and the entire
gathering stood silent, as if they too had been rebuked for their
ignorance. All except Jehiel, the irrepressible questioner.

"What is the difference between a *nazem* and a *tabat*, Maestro
Judah?" he inquired, quite unintimidated by the maestro's display of ill temper.

"*Tabat* is the word for a finger ring, my son," Judah answered
him sweetly, now every inch the scholar/teacher. "But the
word in the text, *nazem*, is the word for a nose ring, which I
hardly thought suitable to bestow upon your sister." At which
my brother laughed heartily and the crowd, seeing that Judah
was not offended, joined in.

"What the messenger gives to Rebecca is a gift of jewelry,
a golden nose ring of half a shekel weight and two bracelets
for her hands of ten shekels weight. They are gifts, proposals

if you like, of marriage as is my gift to your sister. Nothing more. The marriage is sanctified by consummation. And the marriage contract is made binding by the bride's acceptance of the marriage contract, the *ketubah*. Neither of these long traditions has anything to do with rings. And let that be the end of the matter."

My wedding was attended by friends and neighbors from around the peninsula and several kinsmen of our family. Along with their prodigious appetites they brought gifts of a magnificence to equal our hospitality, all of which will come to you in the fullness of time. Among the treasure, I commend to your especial care a small porphyry bowl (easy to miss but very precious) etched with a profile of the Great Philosopher, sent to Judah by Count Pico of Mirandola and his fellow members of the Platonic Academy in Firenze, and six hand-painted plates, a gift from my dei Rossi grandparents, who found themselves too frail to make the journey, or so they said. My dear friend Penina brought with her from Ferrara a most beautiful embroidered coverlet in blackwork. "I was keeping it for my own wedding," she admitted to me. "But since that day may never come..."

Seeing her again was one of the most delightful aspects of the occasion. But my pleasure in her company was somewhat marred by her evident unhappiness. Our first night together, she confided in me that there was a young rabbinical student in my grandparents' service at Ferrara whom they had all but decided upon as husband for her and whom she, poor sentimental child, did not fancy, she told me, "...although he is very kindly, Grazia, but stooped, you know, and pale. And he has been trained at Padova by the Germans, so he never bathes."

Her lack of enthusiasm for the match had incurred my grandmother's wrath, doubly terrifying to an orphan without kin to defend her or fortune to protect her and whose entire happiness depended on the mood of a capricious old woman.

Now La Nonna had taken the opportunity to withdraw her offer of a dowry, saying that if the ungrateful girl did not appreciate her guardian's choice, then she could make her own— and make her own dowry as well. As a result Penina feared that she would never marry, for no man worth having would marry a girl without a dowry.

A lesser being than Penina might have succumbed to envy. If anything, she drew closer to me and even struck up a friendship with Jehiel, just a year her junior. At table they took to sitting side by side. At *calcio* he invariably kicked the ball in her direction and she in his. And at odd times of the day I would find them huddled in a corner, heads close together over a book, voices low. What they were planning or confiding I never knew. They always straightened up and became mute when I approached. Like conspirators—or lovers. But that was foolish. They were children.

The day of my wedding I awoke to find Penina at my bedside with a cup of spiced wine. "A libation for the virgin bride on her wedding day," she announced cheerfully. It was on my tongue to confess to her then and there that I was no virgin, as a sort of rehearsal for the confession I knew I had to make to Judah that night. But before I could get the words out, Jehiel made his appearance through the curtains. Forgoing the politeness of a salutation, he thrust Penina aside and demanded in a low, insistent voice, "Do you wish to give your husband mastery over you, Grazia?"

"What a question! Of course not." Of all times for him to interrupt with one of his bits of nonsense.

"Listen to me, Grazia. I know you think me young and foolish. But I have read forbidden books. And I know things..."

"He does. He does," Penina echoed behind him.

"What things?"

"While the seven blessings are being said, all your husband needs to do to attain mastery over you forever is place his right foot over your left foot."

"I have no time for superstitions, Jehiel. This is my wedding day."

"Exactly why you must pay attention. Once he has done it, there is no undoing it and he will rule over you all of your days and you will harken to all his words and bow to his will in all things whether you like it or not, for you will be under the spell."

"What must I do, then? Would you have me cripple him before the ceremony so that he cannot step?" I asked.

"All you need do is set *your* left foot over *his* right as soon as the rabbi begins to recite the blessings. Then you will rule over *him* all of your days. Will you do it, Grazia?"

"I am to put my right foot over his left..."

"Your left foot over his right," he corrected me. Then, to Penina: "It is no use. She will never remember. And he will have dominion over her all the rest of her days."

"Of course I will remember, Jehiel," I answered. "I am to put my..." But I had paid scant attention to his instructions and now could not remember them.

"*Dio*, what use is all my learning?" He raised his hands to God. "I am dealing here with a half-wit."

A clatter on the stairs interrupted this desperate prayer.

"Try to remember, sister," he urged me. "For your own sake...the left foot."

"Yes, sweetheart." By now the genuineness of his concern for my happiness had overcome my irritation.

"...even if you forget, all is not lost." His voice wafted back to us as he fled down the corridor. "You will have a second chance when the marriage is about to be consummated. At the certain moment you must ask him for a glass of water. That will give you dominion over him all the rest of your days..."

But what will I say to him when he sees no blood on the sheets? I thought. Instruct me on that trick, brother.

ON THE DAY OF my birth my parents had planted an acacia tree in our garden in Ferrara. It was this tree which provided the poles for my wedding canopy and at some cost, I can tell you, since the Christian to whom we sold that property became unaccountably attached to the tree the moment he knew the purpose for which it was wanted, and nothing less than twenty ducats could assuage his acute sense of loss when he sold it back to us. I would have taken the twenty ducats and been married under a canopy made of some old aspen growing by the roadside. But my father became intensely sentimental at the time of my marriage, talking often of my mother and the happy days of old, and it was he, actually, who insisted that my grandparents send us the tree from our former garden.

As soon as Judah took his place under the canopy, the rabbi showered ashes on his head—a reminder of the destruction of Zion—and then conducted me to my place at his right, facing Jerusalem. Then my brothers and some other men took the corners of Judah's hood and placed it over my head to form a second canopy. Whereupon the rabbi proceeded to read the seven blessings, during which Judah's right foot never came near my left.

Now came the wonderful moment. Having offered a sip of wine to Judah and then to me, the rabbi gave the cup itself over to Judah, who whirled about to face north and threw it with all his might against the wall, sprinkling wine everywhere and initiating an explosion of *"Chaim!"*'s and *"Mazel!"*'s.

Then came the feasting and the music. But at last the well-wishers saw us to our chamber and left us to ourselves. My moment had arrived.

"Sir, there is something I ought to have told you that I must tell you now," I began.

"A confession is it?"

I nodded my head, hesitant to begin.

"Perhaps you will allow me to speak first. For I too have something to say to you."

Again I nodded, only too happy for the reprieve.

"It is about the conversation we had on the day of our betrothal, about friendship," he began. "Do you remember?"

Yes, I remembered.

"I think that perhaps I did not make my proposal sufficiently clear in every aspect. Things were left unsaid, unexplained. Now that we are on the threshold of our marriage, I wish to rectify that omission." He cleared his throat—was he slightly uneasy, or was it my imagination? "You are delicate, child. And have been through a lot for one of your age. As a physician, my prescription would be rest, good care, peace...time for the wounds to heal..." Again he cleared his throat. "What I am proposing is that we delay our consummation of this marriage for a time. A few months, perhaps a year. Until you are ready."

How strange.

"You look puzzled, Grazia. Does not my solution suit you?"

"Oh no, sir," I assured him. "I am relieved."

"Good. Then it is agreed. For now, loving friends and nothing more." A nod of satisfaction. "I have brought with me a sack of cow's blood," he went on, once again his usual confident self. "Sometime in the night, as I cradle you in my arms, I will break open the sack to bloody the sheets for the benefit of the morning well-wishers. I suggest we keep this arrangement as our secret, do you concur?"

I fell asleep on my wedding night happy and contented in my husband's arms. Sometime before the first light I awoke to see him, a giant figure in the dim light, rummaging around in his bag. After a moment he returned to my side clutching a small soft sack. It felt cold against my back. Then I heard a thin pop as if a bubble had burst.

Why, I do not know. But when that vessel released its measure of cow's blood onto the sheet below me, I turned to face my husband and, in my most pleasing voice, asked if he would please fetch me a glass of water.

FIRENZE

24

F ROM THE MOMENT WE PUT MANTOVA BEHIND US
Judah did not cease to sing the praises of our future
home. Firenze was a model republic of scholars, built to
the measure of man, a symbol of the rebirth of knowledge and
culture, a new Athens. As we worked our way down the peninsula the classical perfection of Brunelleschi's dome, Giotto's
bell tower, Maestro Ghiberti's miraculous bronze doors, and
Ser Donatello's perfect figures played in my ears in *basso rilievo*
against the clip-clop of the mules' hooves.

Casting my mind ahead, I saw myself wandering through
classical temples dwarfed by majestic columns, and taking the
air in vast open forums. Encouraged by Judah's rhapsodies, I
created a city after Mantegna's model in his "Triumphs" and
named it Firenze. You can imagine my astonishment when we
first looked down on the actual place from the hills of Fiesole
and beheld a typical city of the old-fashioned kind with spiky
towers sticking up into the sky as a reminder that the world
was a dark and unsafe place and that man's first need was for
defense.

The closer we approached, the less Firenze resembled the

city of my dreams. Once inside the gates, we found ourselves traversing one mean little street after another, streets so muddy and rutted you would have thought yourself back at the beginning of the century rather than in its final decade. This was the year 1493. Already, in Ferrara, Ercole d'Este was ripping out the dark smelly hovels that surrounded his *castello* and had begun to lay out the Herculanean addition with its broad streets and spacious palaces. And I had counted more columns on my visit to Belriguardo—a mere hunting lodge—than I was able to locate in the whole of Firenze the first time I rode through it.

Yet the place put Judah into a state of rapture. When he pointed out Brunelleschi's dome his eyes shone. At Giotto's tower he bowed his head in reverence. And the facade of the Ospedale degli Innocenti brought tears to his eyes. To me a dome was a dome, and a bell tower a bell tower. I had seen plenty of bell towers in my short life. Every town I ever stepped foot in boasted more than one. And I, ignoramus that I was, could not perceive the difference between an indifferent example of the species and a sublime one.

Later, when my eye had been educated, the balance and harmony of Brunelleschi's facade for the Ospedale brought me to a stop every time I passed through the Piazza Santissima Annunziata. But when Judah took me by it that first day, I found myself forced to express an admiration I did not feel. All I saw was a low flat building—no towers—fronted by some skinny unimpressive little columns. I did find the swaddled infants in the roundels adorable—and expressed my approval in precisely those condescending words.

I was even less impressed by the Medici house in Via Larga. Small, I thought. Square. Plain. It certainly was austere compared to the Gothic piles that Biaggio Rossetti built for the Estes and the Gonzagas. It did not even have its own tower and could not have contained more than fifty rooms at most. Our Reggio at Mantova boasted more than six hundred rooms counting all of its additions. What did Judah find to admire in this small boxlike structure?

My eyes followed his pointing finger to rest in turn on the jutting cornice and the three registers below it. I especially detested the bottom register clad in massive blocks of unadorned, rustic stone. But I managed to disguise my lack of enthusiasm.

"Dismount, wife, and I will show you the Medici garden." Judah offered me his arm.

Only one garden? With my own eyes I had seen half a dozen gardens within the walls of the Reggio at Mantova. But I kept my counsel and followed his bidding, tethering my horse alongside his on one of the huge iron rings that together with a series of bulky torch holders constituted the only adornment on the facade of the Medici house. Where were the *putti* and the *grotteschi* and the carved fishes and lions, those embellishments that in my eyes gave a palace its air of splendor?

My disappointment grew deeper when, having been waved through the courtyard (lined with those skinny columns again), we stood at the threshold of the little garden behind it. Could this be the celebrated Medici garden where Lorenzo dei Medici, *il magnifico*, had gathered together the great philoso phers and scholars of the world to discuss the ideas of Plato and Socrates amid the most glorious sculptures of our time? At first glance there seemed to be no sculptures at all, unless you were to count a stone boy squeezing a fish that spouted water in the center of a small pool.

"Does the sculpture please you, little bride?" Judah asked me.

"It is rather small, honored husband," I replied, trying to find a phrase that would hide my disappointment without causing me to lie.

"Small. Yes." Judah pulled on his lower lip and said no more.

Donatello's rendering of Judith and Holofernes stood plainly visible on a plinth in one corner of the garden. But that piece of statuary is far from monumental and I had eyes only for the monumental, so I missed it. An even more egregious want of taste was my failure to notice the same master's wonderful David, that cocky boy in the ruffled hat who has changed the course of the art of sculpture forever. My eyes were blinded by the modesty of the scale.

It took many years for me to catch the secret of Florentine grandeur. This rich and elegant city does not reveal herself readily to the casual glance. The true Firenze conceals herself (ought I to say himself? Firenze is the most masculine of cities) behind the closed doors of churches and private houses. As a Jewess, churches were forbidden to me. And although Judah was at home among the merchant princes of the town, almost a year passed before I got a glimpse of the gracious city/country life enjoyed by the magnates in their town houses and country villas. Given Judah's preferred style of living, I might have lived and died in Firenze without penetrating the heart of the city.

Now understand, Judah was no jailor. He was simply unsociable. More precisely, he got all he needed of conversation and companionship at the Platonic Academy. That I had no such opportunity to mingle in society as he did at the Academy or that I might not be quite ready, at the age of fifteen, to dedicate my life to housewifery and discussions of the *Phaedo* did not, I am sure, enter his mind.

At the beginning of our marriage I lent myself with a will to the role of the exemplary wife who finds all the diversion she needs in tending her house. Each morning, I lined up my domestic troops in the kitchen and searched their heads for lice just as Dorotea had instructed me to do. Lice, you remember, can destroy your household. And dirt.

Was that a curl of dust under the credenza? Gimlet-eyed, I found it out. Then I went in search of Orlando and gave him a good tongue-lashing for having missed it.

Had I tasted an excess of pepper in the soup? Magliana was called to task. Pepper did not grow on a pepper tree in our garden, I reminded her. It had been carried across deserts and over seas *at great cost to her master*. Yes, I did say such things. Worse, I threatened to have her beaten or discharged. Dorotea would have been proud of me. I was a woman now, a member in good standing of the sisterhood of Jewish wives.

But despite my posturings in the kitchen and the larder, I was not a Jewish wife in every respect. In the bedroom Judah and I remained, to use his phrase, "loving friends." And I could not stop myself from wondering, as I lay in my marriage bed being cuddled like a child, what kind of marriage excluded the very act that sanctified it in the eyes of God. But I dared not question the arrangement; for I found myself much more in awe of Judah after our marriage than I had been before.

The humanistic circle in which he moved in Firenze brought out aspects of his nature never shown to me during the brief weeks of our courtship. Not unkindness certainly. Judah has never been unkind. Nor irascible or impatient. Pressed to describe to you the nature of the change in him, the best I can offer is "inattentive." Even when he sat opposite me at dinner and praised my table, his compliments were given with an abstracted air, as if he was forcing himself to pay attention. But after dinner, dressing to attend the Academy with his colleagues, he was another man — light of eye and springy in step. Some days I was convinced that he must be keeping a mistress somewhere, a luscious blonde with rosy cheeks and curves.

From the first night of our marriage, I had fallen asleep cradled in Judah's arms. After we settled into our own marriage bed in Firenze, he gradually retreated from that position until, within a few months, we were no longer sleeping spoon fashion — as loving friends — but back to back as if to signify that we no longer shared the same world of dreams. And indeed, as the months passed I did begin to dream dreams that I knew were shameful. But could not stop.

In these dreams I am dancing naked with a masked man, whirling madly in a candlelit ballroom. Suddenly, the music stops and there stands Francesco Gonzaga all in white. But no. It is not Francesco. It is Judah wrapped in his white prayer shawl, his arm raised like an avenging angel.

I bow my head, waiting for the blow to fall. He lunges forward and yanks off my partner's mask, revealing...Lord Pirro. I wake up. It is possible to purge adulterous thoughts in life. But in dreams?

These dreams which came and went became a guilty secret that intensified the increasing distance between me and Judah. Days would go by without a word between us except for the analysis of texts that now made up the conversational substance of our noonday meal together.

I felt I had done something wrong but could not find the courage to ask what. Books, my ultimate refuge, lost their appeal. I began to distract myself by gazing out into the street. Without my being aware of it, I was becoming that most despised of creatures, the wife who hangs out the window snooping.

Before long the prospect from the window no longer satisfied my curiosity. Seeking a less constricted view, I announced to my astonished servants that henceforth I myself would hang out the laundry on the upper loggia and bring it in at sundown. Not coincidentally, the loggia gave a wide view of the comings and goings in the street below all the way down to the Arno.

Our house was situated in the Oltr'arno, a district that stands in relation to the heart of Firenze as Trastevere stands to the heart of Roma. Both are separated from the center by a river. But there the similarity ends. In Trastevere you find the Street of the Tanners, the Street of the Dyers, the Street of the Bankers, each street restricted to a single trade according to the fashion of the Dark Ages. By contrast, on the streets of the Oltr'arno the shoemaker cobbles beside the butcher and the rich man gorges himself next door to the half-starved porter. At the top of our street a tailor plied his craft on the ground floor of a typical Florentine craftsman's house, no wider than four spans of a man's arms by law. Close at his hand stood a farrier's shop. Next to it, a wood-carver. Then came our house, wider by twice than any of the tradesmen's houses and all the more commodious because we had no shop on the ground floor and were free to use all three stories for living in.

Directly across the street from us, a baker and a pork butcher nestled side by side, offering an ever-present temptation to our servant Orlando, who loved the meat of the hog better than life itself and could never be made to understand why he might not bring it into our house.

Just past us at the point where the road pitched down toward the riverbank, three quite grand gentlemen's houses took up most of the frontage. But at the bottom where the street slid into the muck of low-lying lots beside the river, the houses became smaller once again.

It took me a few weeks of diligent observation between the clotheslines to sort out the inhabitants of these diverse establishments. The cobbler was easily identifiable by his leather apron, the baker by his tall white hat, and the pork butcher by his blood-spattered coat. With a little effort I managed to distinguish those who lived in the grand houses from those who lived in the mean ones and to recognize which were the servants and which the masters. But even after several weeks of careful observation, I still could not account for a tight clique of dark-complexioned people dressed alike in black cloaks who never passed in ones or twos but always in a gaggle.

They could not be members of a monastic order, since the men and women mixed freely and there were children in the group. Something told me they were Moors. I had never actually seen a Moor, but there was a tinge of Africa in those sallow faces and a flavor to their embroidered garments which I recognized as Byzantine from having seen books illuminated by Sienese artists in what was termed the *maniera greca*. But, to confuse the issue, the women were veiled below the eyes like Turks or Persians. What manner of people were they? This puzzle became the focus of my empty mind and would likely have continued to do so had not a peremptory demand for Judah's services disturbed the pattern of our days.

Young Count Pico of Mirandola, Judah's former pupil and now his sponsor at the Platonic Academy, had been taken by a high spiking fever and was calling for his old master.

I have never seen Judah move so fast as he did in response to that summons. More like a general than a physician, he instantly deputized Orlando to hire a pair of horses and me to fasten his *camicia* and lace his boots. Then, after only the briefest of farewells, he and the servant disappeared into the falling dark.

He did not come home the next day. Or the next. On the third day of his absence—a Thursday—Orlando returned briefly to retrieve certain supplies from his master's laboratory. But he brought no word for his master's wife. When I asked for a report, all I got from that half-wit was a melange of the gold service at Count Pico's table, the Persian shawls that covered him ("Softer than duck down, lady, and made of a million colors"), the gold braid on the servants' liveries, and other nonsense. My questions about the Count's condition met with dumb incomprehension. As for when I could expect my husband home—not a clue.

Normally Friday was the day Judah devoted himself to supplying the household with its weekly needs. In his absence, the cook presented me with her list of necessaries—a capon, fresh fish, makings for a salad, goat's-milk cheese, and so forth.

To be honest, I could have made do without fresh stuff. Nobody ever died on a diet of bread and beans. But that prospect did not tempt me. Besides, a far more appealing alternative began to suggest itself to me. What if I were to go to the market myself? I knew that no respectable woman would be seen in the street unaccompanied. But I told myself...Does it matter what I told myself? Fortuna had opened the door of my cage and I simply donned my bonnet, picked up a basket, stepped out into the sunlight, and soared over the Ponte Vecchio to the market square.

Give them credit, all the merchants dealt with me most courteously. I found everything I needed with no trouble, except for the fish, which smelled spoiled to me and which I refused to buy at stall after stall. After an eternity of poking, sniffing, and looking into the eyes of a legion of carp and tench, I was about to give up when who should come alongside me but an old gentleman I recognized as Messer Bonaventura, head of a large clan of Jewish *banchieri*. He was one of perhaps three or four souls I had been introduced to on a rare visit to the synagogue.

"Good morning, sir," I greeted him.

"Eh?" He motioned to his servant to hand him a little golden horn, which he put to his ear. "What's that again?"

"I said good morning, sir," I repeated.

"And good morning to you, madonna," he replied agreeably. "But may I know who is bidding me good day?"

"It is Grazia dei Rossi, wife of Judah del Medigo," I answered.

"So it is. So it is. And where is your august husband, lady?" he asked.

"Up in the hills of Fiesole with a sick patient," I replied.

"Then who brought you here to the market, lady?"

"I have brought myself, sir," I answered. "We were in need of supplies."

"Come to the market yourself you say?" He pushed the trumpet up against my lips as if somehow the proximity of the instrument would rephrase my words.

"Yes sir, quite alone," I assured him.

When the full impact of my statement had sunk in he insisted that I could not possibly return home alone. Out of the question. I must come with him to his own house to recover from my ordeal in the streets, and later, after I had rested, he would have me accompanied across the river to my home. But now I must—must!—put myself under his protection.

Seeing no courteous way to resist this deaf and determined old man, I agreed.

The visit did not begin auspiciously. Madonna Regina, the old man's wife, turned quite pale when he reported finding me alone in front of the fishmonger's stall, and insisted on pouring into me cup after cup of borage tea to counteract whatever malady I might have contracted in such gamey surroundings. After that I was put to rest in her second-best bed to recover from my ordeal. (No amount of nay-saying from me could lessen her conviction that my adventure at the market had been an arduous trial.)

The old woman was full of apologies that her daughter-in-law Diamante was not there to receive me. "She is on her horse again." She shook her head disapprovingly. "Always bouncing her belly around on the back of that animal. Just like the Queen of Portugal. And you know what happened to her."

With that enigmatic hint she was gone, taking my boots with her to be cleansed of whatever disgusting stuff they may have picked up in the market.

Next thing, the bouncing Diamante herself appeared at the door still dressed for hunting in a hat with a magnificent red plume. She was a true Diana. Tall. Long-necked. Golden-haired. Everything I longed to be and was not. Had you told me at that moment that we two were destined to become friends, I would have staked my entire fortune against it.

"Here." She held out my boots to me. "You'll need these to make your escape."

When I failed to grasp her meaning she went on to explain. "If I were you I'd put the boots on before my mother-in-law finds another reason to take them away. Believe me, the old parties would like nothing better than to keep you locked up here on some pretext or other."

"Locked up?" Surely she was joking.

"Not with a key and bars," she explained. "With kindness. Because the streets are dangerous. And horses are dangerous. Very dangerous. And young women are reckless..."

"Like the Queen of Portugal?" I asked.

"Precisely. If you take my advice you will get going while my esteemed mother- and father-in-law are taking their rest. I will send your goods on with a lackey. Go now."

It sounded like good advice. I donned my boots at once and with Diamante's help slipped down the broad staircase and into the courtyard.

Then I belatedly remembered my manners. "I haven't even said thank you —"

"Write them a note," she cut in. "I hear you're a practiced scribe."

There was not much to do but thank her and be on my way. But although I knew myself to be well rescued from the strangling embrace of the senior Bonaventuras, I did suffer a pang of regret at leaving this bold Diana of the *banchieri*.

UNTIL HIS ABRUPT FLIGHT TO FIESOLE I HAD known Judah only as a dignified, slow-moving, deliberate sort of man—the soul of *gravitas*. The haste with which he made his departure to attend Count Pico astonished me. But even more of a surprise was the limping, bleary-eyed, disheveled Judah who staggered into our bedroom five nights later, barely able to croak out a greeting before he collapsed beside me in a deep sleep.

I concluded that he had not slept much these past five nights, and indeed, when he awoke, he confirmed my diagnosis. "Count Pico was in the grip of a raging fever and I could trust no one to care for him but myself," he explained.

"Is he so important a personage, then, to require a body attendant?" I inquired.

"Important?" Judah pondered my question. "Who is to be the judge of a philosopher's importance? He is much admired in the Medici circle. Yet he himself would be first to admit that he is no Plato."

"Why then..."

"Why then what?"

· 284 ·

"Why could you not trust a servant or another friend to spell you at his bedside?"

"He was my pupil in Padova, the most brilliant I ever had. I taught him to read and write Hebrew in the space of eight months, if you can believe it. And when he—somewhat rashly I thought—concocted his sixty-eight propositions for the papal Curia, he called upon me to assist him—me...Leone the Jew."

"And did you assist him, even though you thought him rash?" I asked.

The reply I got was roundabout. "Pico della Mirandola has a touchingly innocent belief in the power of cabala, which I do not share."

"Then he would get on with Jehiel, for Jehiel is always babbling about mystic numbers and seraphim and the like." Judah's countenance clouded over, as it often did at the mention of my brother.

"Surely you are not comparing Count Pico of Mirandola, famed in all countries where scholarship is valued, to your mischief-making brother," he retorted.

"It was an ill-placed remark, honored husband," I replied as coldly as he. "But I fear I still do not understand just what it is about this Pico that caused you to give up five consecutive nights of sleep for him and risk your own health."

"He is my benefactor, my colleague, and my friend," Judah answered. "When Lorenzo the Magnificent was alive Pico introduced me into his circle. Since then he has never ceased to bring me fortune and favor. Without his intercession we would not be living here now in this great city in this fine house as pensioners of Piero dei Medici."

"And would that be such a tragedy?" I queried, as much to myself as to him.

"Are you not enjoying your life here in Firenze?" he asked quietly, then quickly added, "We must talk, Grazia. I have had a letter at Fiesole from Ser Bonaventura. Some reckless escapade in the marketplace."

What was I to say?

"I am on my way back to Fiesole now. But I will return before vespers. Let us meet then in my *studiolo*. A proper setting for a serious conversation, do you not agree?"

I nodded my head but said nothing.

"Good. And tell Orlando to put out a tray of sweetmeats for us. And some spiced wine. A talk can be serious without being bitter, you know."

As vespers approached I found myself digging furiously into a little bronze cask that Dorotea had given me on the eve of my marriage and that I had never yet opened. One by one I drew out the tools of the trade, assembled for a woman who felt herself no better than a wanton.

First the ambergris, which I slathered on my bosom with such abandon that the entire room smelled like a whorehouse. Then the white paste for the face. Then the kohl around the eyes. Then the rouge. Never forget the rouge. "They do not like us pale." Dorotea's words came back to me. "It is not the most... what shall I say... stimulating color."

That night I went to meet Judah in his *studiolo* painted and rouged and smelling like a harlot. The sight so unnerved him that for several moments he was unable to utter a word. Instead, he poured himself a draft from a bottle he kept beside his lectern and swallowed it in one gulp. Even then he seemed not to know how to go on, but cleared his throat several times and lapsed into silence.

"Put him at his ease," I heard Dorotea whisper in my ear. "Remove his shoes and let the blood flow through his limbs."

I knelt down at his feet and began to pull off his boot.

To my astonishment he jerked his foot back.

"Why are you groveling down there, Grazia? Is this some jest?"

"Oh no, sir." I bobbed up as quickly as I could.

"And why is your face so white today? Are you constipated? Come closer." I edged toward him. "Surely it cannot be that damned pumice?" He rubbed at my cheek harshly. "Aha! Dye!"

"Does it displease you?" I asked.

"Displease me? Indeed it does. This stuff is poisonous. Next thing we will have you breaking out in little red spots. What possessed you to put it on?"

"I was told that by such means I could entice you to look favorably upon me," I admitted.

"Do I not look favorably on you?" he asked, softer now.

"You rarely look on me at all, honored husband," I replied truthfully.

"I see." He paused. "Come here, little wife." He indicated a small stool that I was to pull up at his side. "Here by me." He leaned down and turned my face toward him. "Now then," he began. "Perhaps you have forgotten that I am a physician trained to see not only what lies on the surface of the skin but also what lies under it. I am proof against your poor efforts at illusionism, child. What my eyes see is the true Grazia, the Grazia you have taken such pains to hide under the layers of powder and pigment. And I am distressed, because I love that little Grazia dearly. You need never poison yourself or whiten your face to seem beautiful to me. I find you beautiful just as you are." He stroked my cheek gently. "Besides, if you begin now with paint and powder, you will be a crone by the time you are thirty. Look at the way your stepmother has ruined herself with her potions."

"It was she who gave me the powder and the scent," I admitted.

"You must be more discriminating in your choice of tutors. For the present I would suggest you make do with me, since I am at hand and willing. What say you to that?"

"Oh, I would be grateful, sir. For everyone knows you are the wisest of counselors. But I never knew you dealt in beauty remedies."

"It is time you found out what I deal in, wife. I have kept you too far from my affairs, leaving you on your own here to while away your hours with potions and peeking. Oh yes, I know where you have been spending your afternoons."

I hung my head.

"Now then, look up and let us agree on a new regimen. What is done is done. We have both been in error: you for acting like a fool, which you are not, and me for treating you like a settled old matron, which you also are not. On your feet, wife. Smile. Let us both thank God that there is time to make a fresh start."

The next morning changes were begun that altered the pattern of my life. A dancing master was engaged and a new pair of slippers ordered. Judah himself conducted me up the street to the cobbler's shop to be fitted for them and allowed me to pick the leather.

All my life I had wished for shiny black slippers with a red leather trim such as I had seen on the feet of Madonna Isabella at the Este wedding. But when I was told to make a choice, did I ask for them? No. With a deep sigh I pointed to a pebbled black leather made from the skin of a buffalo—heavy, mottled, serviceable.

"Those will last a good while," I commented.

"But will they put wings on your feet, Grazia?" Judah asked.

"Wings?" I shook my head sadly. Those boots would not put wings on my feet.

"Then they will not do at all for dancing slippers. I expect to see you flying about the room like a beautiful bird." He turned to the cobbler. "Have you something finer in a dancing slipper for my wife?"

"Shiny?" I added, encouraged now to voice my true sentiments. "And trimmed all around the ankle with a red leather ruffle."

"Anything for a price," the cobbler replied equably. "But the red will cost you something extra. And a ruffled trim...on shiny leather..." He shook his head dolefully in contemplation of the astronomical cost of such a creation.

"How much?" Judah demanded.

"Two gold forms," the man answered.

"Sold!"

The new regimen did not stop with boots and dancing lessons. Just after dinner Orlando announced that a visitor was waiting in the *sala*. The only visitors we ever had were the friends and relations of sick people come to beg Judah to call on their ailing loved ones, only to be disappointed—for he had refused consistently to see patients since we came to Firenze. Excepting for Count Pico of Mirandola.

I naturally assumed that this caller was simply another suppliant whom Judah would end up turning away, and since I saw no purpose in remaining, excused myself. But Judah urged me to stay. "There is someone I want you to meet," he whispered, as he conducted me into the *sala*.

My first sight of the young man who stood waiting for us told me that he was one of the mysterious people who lived at the bottom of our street near the river. His sallow skin and embroidered black cloak identified him unmistakably.

"Honored wife, meet my new apprentice, Medina de Cases. Medina, your mistress, Madonna Grazia."

The boy was clad from head to toe in black with only the white of his linen for contrast. How different from the style of our Italian boys, who deck themselves out in four-colored hose and crimson jackets and plumes of all colors, their *berrettas* fastened, when the wearer can afford it, by jeweled plaquettes.

In response to the boy's gallant bow I knelt low in my most graceful curtsy, wondering as I executed the movement what he was doing there. Judah had never expressed a need for an apprentice before. Why now? And why this wan exotic?

"How does he strike you, wife? Do you think he will make a good student?"

A strange question. I stepped closer, the better to probe the eyes, those mirrors of the soul. Deep-set and rimmed with dark circles, they seemed to me to reflect some inner anguish. As for intelligence, I could not make a guess. Whatever lay behind that impassive gaze was hidden from me.

"As you see, Medina, my wife is a serious young woman not quick to make decisions." Judah put his arm around the boy in a fatherly manner. "Run along now, but make sure to be on hand tomorrow morning before the bell tolls matins." And with a gentle pat from his new master the boy was gone, leaving me full of questions.

I did not have to wait for an answer. Judah was only too eager to tell me the story of the de Cases family, and took it up the moment the boy had left us.

These unfortunate people were a remnant of that horde of Jews exiled from Spain the previous year by King Ferdinand and Queen Isabella of Spain, he told me.

"A group of these refugees has settled at the bottom of our street in one of those tiny houses on the riverbank," he explained. "Many of them had risen high in the Spanish realm not only as physicians but as tax-farmers and advisers and familiars of the court itself. They were caught completely unprepared when the order came to expel the Jews."

I found it difficult to believe that these refugees had no notion of their impending disaster—particularly if they had been so close to the court—and said so.

"No doubt they fell into the trap of believing that such a thing could not happen to them. To other Jews, perhaps. But not to them," he responded. "The tide of Jew-hating rises and falls like the sea itself. When it floods we Jews ask ourselves, Why me? Why here? Why now? Whereas the real question is how can any Jew who makes his home upon a Christian promontory ever believe himself beyond reach of the tides?"

"I have never seen a Spanish Jew before," I remarked. "Are they all so sallow? And do they all wear black and smell of garlic?"

"They are Spaniards, my dear," Judah answered with a smile. "Garlic is like mother's milk to them. But out of deference to you I will give Medina some powerful mint to chew when he is in your presence. Will that suffice to raise him to your standard?"

"My remark was not intended as a criticism, honored husband," I lied. In truth there was a smell about the young Spaniard much more subtle than garlic that went against me.

"I am delighted that you find him pleasing..." (I had never said I found him pleasing.) "For you and he have much to offer one another."

"Is he to teach me to eat garlic and look solemn?" I asked.

"It is you who are to teach him," Judah answered, as pleased as if he had presented me with a bauble. "He is to be your pupil. The boy is all but unemployable here from his lack of training in vernacular Italian and I cannot imagine a better tutor for him than your learned self, my little wife. You are to teach him Italian."

Until that moment, I had gobbled up whatever texts came my way like a starving man who fears he may never get another meal. But the true scholar consumes a text the way a deer ruminates her food, chewing it slowly, regurgitating it, reflecting upon it, and only then consuming it. That done, he takes the process one step farther, and after he has analyzed his food for thought, finds ways to manifest its essence to others. This I would try to do for Medina de Cases.

Now as you know, there are but two masters of the vernacular language: Dante Alighieri and Boccaccio. I leaned toward Dante, the loftier poet. But Judah persuaded me that Boccaccio's more earthy tales might have a greater appeal to Medina than Dante's terza rima. And his judgment proved doubly apt. Not only did Medina take to Boccaccio at once but the first text we chose, Boccaccio's tale of the merchant Landolfo who is taken by pirates en route to Amalfi, described almost precisely the ordeal that the de Cases family endured during their flight from Spain.

As the boy explained to me, his family too had set sail on a fragile craft—a mother, father, and three brothers forced aboard at sword point by Spanish soldiers with neither food nor water enough to feed them. En route to the Amalfi coast, they, like Landolfo, ran into a great storm which made the waves run mountains high. Forced into a tiny cove, they too were taken over by the Genoese, "a race by nature rapacious and greedy of gain," according to Boccaccio. By then the de Cases family was reduced to a father and two sons, one brother having died of drowning and the mother of a fever at sea. Now these three survivors were robbed of the last of their ducats and every other small thing that they possessed by the Genoese pirates. They themselves were locked into the hold of the pirate carrack to be sold as slaves when the ship reached the slave market at Constantinople.

In Boccaccio's tale, there comes a violent spasm of the sea which, he tells us, smites the carrack with great force against a shoal, cracking her apart at midships. And after a long night clinging to a plank in the raging sea, the merchant Landolfo is rescued by the old women of Corfu.

"But that is what happened to us," Medina gasped. "We too were captured by the Genoese, then a great storm cracked their ship in two, just as the poet tells it. And the Corfu women rescued us from the sea. That poet is a great seer." Either that or, what seemed likely to me, the rough waters off the coast of Amalfi attracted pirates in Boccaccio's time as they do now. And the old women of Corfu are not unaccustomed to finding human flotsam on the beach when they go out to gather firewood in the morning. Still, the eerie similarity between the tale I had selected and the true tale of the de Cases' escape from Spain did promise a comradeship I had not anticipated when I first met Medina. In that spirit I presumed to ask after his brother, Bartolomeo. "Where is he now?" I inquired.

"Dead," he answered. "Killed here in Firenze last year at Passover for desecrating a statue of the Virgin. The doctor told us that he was out of his head when he smeared the Virgin with shit. The seawater had infected his mind. But the *bargello* said that Christ could forgive anything except an insult to His Mother. They brought my brother to the *bargello*'s jail and hung him out the window by his feet. My father took me to see him hanging. He had no ears, no hands, only holes with blood dripping out of them onto the stones."

This horrific tale he related to me as if giving street directions or enumerating an inventory, without a tear or a break in his voice. Thus died my hopes of camaraderie with Medina de Cases.

Happily, Judah's next effort to provide me with companionship proved much more successful. From the first day we settled in Firenze, invitations had arrived constantly for us to dine with this one or to attend the bar mitzvah of that one's son or the wedding of the other's daughter. All these Judah refused without consulting me. Now, in an abrupt shift, he announced that we would be going to the country villa of the Bonaventura family to celebrate the feast of Purim, a feast often referred to as the Jewish *carnevale*. What I discovered at the Bonaventura celebration was that in Firenze, Jews who follow the humanist way have added their own pagan coloration to the feast of Purim, making it as much a celebration of Bacchus as of Queen Esther.

Much as he loathes strange beds, Judah agreed to depart for the Bonaventura villa in the afternoon before the feast and remain through the following night, a huge concession for him. In addition, he had himself fitted for a mask. When Medina saw his master put the thing up against his face I thought the boy would faint from astonishment. Apparently Spanish Jews do not indulge themselves in the *carnevale* revels that Italian Jews enjoy. Judah says it is because we are so much closer to the pagan culture that spawned these rites. I say it is because the Spaniards are a low, doleful people who dress in black, never smile (even when smiled at), and glory in pain rather than in delight, and that like us the Spanish Jews emulate their Christian hosts. So it is, I say, that our Purim resembles *carnevale* and theirs an auto-da-fé.

THE BONAVENTURA FAMILY KEPT their farm—the Florentines all call their country villas "farms"—in the Mugello district about half an hour's brisk ride from the city. As we rode, Judah kept up a running commentary on the sights as we passed them.

"The villa on the crest of the next hill is the Strozzis' place." He indicated a rambling group of low buildings ahead. "Look to the right. See the little shrine. It marks the beginning of Pala Strozzi's farm."

"But it is no farm. It is a vast holding. It is a grand estate," I protested.

"The Florentines prefer to call their estates farms. They find it less ostentatious. Besides, these villas are genuine agricultural enterprises. This place of Strozzi's is no idle hunting fief like those *delizie* you see in Lombardia. A place like this yields more than enough wine and oil to supply all the family's needs, with plenty left over to sell for profit."

Indeed, the land on both sides of the road stretched out as far as I could see in straight rows of espaliered grapevines and even the groves proved to be of olive wood. Very neat. Doubtless very profitable. But I preferred the dense hemlock growths of the Mantovana, whose only profit was to give shade and shelter, and the bosky perfume of the deep forests of Lombardia. Where were the birds and snakes and rabbits and all the other creatures who find refuge in the wild? And where were the secret springs, once sacred to the gods?

"But where is nature in all this?" I asked, half to myself.

"What you see is nature tamed," Judah answered, his eyes bright with enthusiasm. "This is nature as the ancients treated it. Horace's Sabine farm, Cicero at Tusculum taught us to civilize nature in just this way."

Like many other things Florentine that excited Judah's admiration, the charm of the idea eluded me. I could find no relation between these well-run agricultural enterprises and Horace's farm or Cicero's. What was so noble about transforming wild nature into a grubby commercial enterprise for the profit of people who already had too much money?

Mind you, not all the farms in the Mugello were equally sumptuous. As we rode along the quiet country road, Judah pointed out to me a small property called La Costa that belonged to Cristoforo di Giorgio, the doctor, and another more modest one belonging to Nando, the stonemason.

"Only in Firenze does every citizen have his chance at the good life," he intoned as he swayed from side to side on the donkey the Bonaventuras had thoughtfully provided for him.

On this point I did not find it difficult to meet him. I have never lived in a place where Jews were treated more equitably than in Firenze under the Medici. Judah and I were provided for as well as any scholar and wife in the peninsula. And the Bonaventura family was permitted to live the life of the aristocracy in every respect. As evidence I give you the grandeur of their "farm" as it presented itself to my eyes that day.

The Bonaventura villa was an imposing brick structure with a colonnaded central portico which qualified as a farmhouse, I suppose, by virtue of its lack of turrets, gun emplacements, and the other military accoutrements of a castle. It was bordered by a meadow on one side, a vineyard on the other, a fenced kitchen garden behind, and, Judah pointed out, several hectares of hunting land beyond that. Apparently the Florentines did admit wild nature to their world, but only on condition that it occupy its proper place in the balance of things and suffer itself to be rigidly contained.

The entire Bonaventura clan was on hand to meet us: Diamante; her husband, Isaac (whom she called Isaachino in a most familiar way straight to his face); his parents; and several aunts and cousins and brothers and sisters I never did succeed in getting to know. Diamante took me in tow the moment we arrived, linking her arm with mine in a most sisterly fashion, and barely gave me time to visit the water closet before she spirited me off on a tour of the place. The plumbing astonished me. To have a private water closet piped out into the yard is extraordinary enough, but to have one in the country!

The estate was palatial, but palatial in that sly Florentine way that makes them refer to their *delizie* as farms and to their princes as ordinary citizens. In just that spirit, Diamante's proudest exhibit turned out to be not the stables or the horses or even her pet falcon but her market garden.

"My husband gave this garden to me as my own territory," she announced proudly as she led me into the walled enclosure. "And I also claim the profits from my little holding. For, as I said to Isaachino, if I am to have the responsibility then I must also reap the benefit. Here, taste this." She pulled up a bunch of spinach. "Have you ever tasted spinach crisper or more mild?"

I confessed that I had not.

"That is because I use sheep manure on it. Horse manure turns vegetables strong. Did you know that?"

I confessed that I did not.

"You northerners do not love the land as we Tuscans do," she declared, as if stating an incontrovertible fact.

"But that is not true."

"Oh yes it is. My husband, Isaachino, has been all over Europe and he tells me that only here in Toscana do patricians toil on their land the way we do." Then to demonstrate she yanked up her brocade *gamorra*, fell down to the earth on her knees, and began to dig around two long lines of slight green blades that had just begun to poke up through the soil. "When these ripen I shall send you some."

"Thank you," I replied courteously. No doubt about it, the girl was sincere. But I could not reconcile this peasant grubbing in the earth with the elegant huntress who had recently abetted my escape from her gilded prison.

"You do know what this is, do you not?" she teased, holding up a bit of green she had plucked.

"To be candid I do not."

"Come down here with me then. Smell and you shall know. Come now. Do not be concerned about your skirt. Hike it up, like I do. That way the only thing to suffer will be your knees and you can get the soil off in your bath. You do bathe, do you not?"

"What do you take me for?" I challenged her. "A German?"

I could not have chosen a quicker route to her heart.

"Caught me out there," she admitted cheerfully. "I suppose I thought that since you Lombards live so close to the Germans, you may have taken up their habits."

"You have a wrongheaded idea of Mantova, Diamante," I advised her. "In fact, I would say you know as little about life in the north of this peninsula as I do about growing vegetables."

"Touché," she replied amiably. "Want to taste a turnip? They are not bitter, I promise you. I freeze them over the winter to take the bite out of them."

And so it went until she had plucked a sample of everything growing in that garden: her little onions — sweeter than mother's milk, she insisted — and her sage and her marjoram and her borage — nothing like it to take the red out of the eyes — and her lavender, row after row of it — to keep all things sweet-smelling and repel the moths. You would have thought she was showing off her children to me. In truth, as I discovered over those two days, her garden was much more precious to her than her children. To them she displayed an astonishing degree of indifference, leaving the older boy, Bubu, entirely in the charge of his wet nurse all the time we were there. His younger brother, only a few months old — whom his mother never called by his name but only "the little boy" — had been shipped off to a nearby farm to live with his nurse for the first year of his life, just as Bubu had been. "For they do create such a ruckus with their teeth cutting through and their stomach complaints," Diamante explained. As an afterthought she added, "I fear I am a better gardener than a mother. But fortunately we have plenty of servants to see to the little ones and as long as I drop a litter regularly, Isaachino is content to leave me to my other pursuits."

These pursuits, as I discovered that day, were multifarious. Once she was able to tear herself away from her garden, Diamante took me straight to the stables, and there I saw another aspect of her nature — her deep love of animals. At least here we were of one mind.

"Well, what think you of my prince?" she inquired, pointing toward a handsome chestnut stallion. "I call him Suleiman for he is a true Turk in his temperament. Is he not handsome? Is he not the finest steed you have ever seen, Madonna Grazia?"

"Certainly he is as handsome a horse as I have ever seen, Donna Diamante," I replied as tactfully as I could.

"As handsome as but not the handsomest? You have seen

better, then?" she pressed. "Look here. Look at this mouth— how soft it is. Here, put your hand in." I did as I was bid and had to admit that the horse had a sweet soft mouth.

"And his color. A burnished strawberry."

"He is very beautiful," I agreed.

"But not the most beautiful?" she pressed.

"Madonna, you are worse with your animals than with your vegetables. You are as bad as Francesco Gonzaga."

"You have seen the Gonzaga horses?" She gripped my sleeve urgently.

"In Mantova we had permission to ride at the Gonzaga stud. We were in and out of the stables often as children," I replied.

"Ah, what a sight they must be." She sighed. "Marchese Francesco rode two of his Araby stallions here at our *palio* last year and took away all the prizes. No wonder you hesitated when I asked you if my Suleiman was the most handsome. But Grazia, if you rode every day, you must be a horsewoman. Is that so?"

"I do love to ride," I answered, "although I have had no opportunity for it in Firenze. We do not keep horses."

"But *we* do! Both here and in town!" She clapped me on the back. "And I invite you to ride with me any day you choose. Any day at all. In truth, much as I love to ride it gets to be a lonely business without a companion. And Isaachino is much too occupied with his business to accompany me."

To my eye Isaachino Bonaventura did not possess either the appearance or the temperament of a horseman. Tall and shambling, with shaggy dark locks and bent shoulders, I would have bet it was lack of inclination rather than pressing business that held Isaachino Bonaventura back from his daily ride. And further acquaintance with the couple proved me correct.

In the course of that long afternoon, Diamante and I embarked on our lifelong friendship. Our mutual love of horses gave us common cause. But she was more than simply a comrade to me. God knows she was no intellectual. Her penmanship was appalling, as I discovered after we took to writing each other notes; her understanding of the ancients was virtually nonexistent; and her want of feeling for her own children was incomprehensible to me. But when it came to friends, animals, servants, and the insulted and injured of this world, she had a ready heart.

By the time we had tramped through the vineyard and the orchards and come to the winery, we had reached the next stage of intimacy for women—our husbands. Once again Diamante led the way.

"Let us sit here by the casks where it is cool and talk a bit," she began, as if we had not been chattering our heads off for the entire afternoon. "Now then..." She patted a place beside her on a bench against the rough earthen wall of the cave. "Tell me, how do you like married life?"

What did she mean by married life? Did she mean what I thought she meant? I could not imagine myself responding to her engaging frankness with obfuscation. Yet it did seem to me woefully indiscreet and somehow disloyal to Judah to tell her the truth of my situation.

"I like my house well enough," I answered, "Although I find the servants lazy and dirty, just as my stepmother said I would. And to be truthful, my life is rather lonely. I miss my brothers."

"But does not your husband compensate for the loss of your brothers? I find I have all I need of men in Isaachino."

"You do?"

"Oh, he is a demon in the bed, my Isaachino. Do not let that shy exterior fool you. My husband is a regular Etna. He erupts almost every night." A coarse metaphor but, you must admit, a telling one.

"How about yours? He is so big. A giant. Is he like that... all over?" She nudged me and giggled. "Do not fear to confide in me, Grazia. I am like a tomb, I promise you. All my secrets will die with me." And when I did not reply she added anxiously, "Have I offended you with my coarse talk? The old hag says I have become as common as a whore from hanging about the stables. Is it true? Am I offensive in my bold talk?"

"Of course not," I assured her. "Words do not a lady make. It is by her actions that we know her. To me, you are made honorable by your noble heart. And to prove it I will confide in you. But you must not ask me for more than I can tell. For I am bound by a pledge not to speak of it."

"A pledge? To whom?"

"No questions." Her unrelenting curiosity reminded me of myself. "I will make one statement and after that, no more talk of it. Agreed?"

"Agreed!" She held out her hand to confirm the arrangement.

"Very well. This is something I have never told a living soul, Diamante, not my brothers or even my best friend Penina. The truth is my husband and I have not yet consummated our marriage. He believes that I am too young for those responsibilities and prefers to wait."

"*Dio*, what refinement!" She shook her hand back and forth in the air in that gesture the peasants make when they are overwhelmed by some piece of news or other. "But of course such delicacy is to be expected from a man of discernment and learning like your husband. My Isaachino never had such a thought in his life. He told me he expected to make a son with me on our wedding night. And so he did."

"Did you always love Isaachino...from the beginning?" I asked, hoping to elicit some guidelines for my own initiation when it came.

But Diamante was never one to appreciate the nuances of feeling. "Love him?" she repeated, puzzled by my question. "Of course I loved him. He was my husband."

She made it sound so natural. Would I too learn to love Judah simply because he was my husband?

Night was falling fast by the time we began our tramp through the vineyards back to the *casa*, a mighty distance to cover on foot. Diamante offered to send one of the cellar porters for a pair of mules to carry us back, but I assured her that exercise would serve better than any potion to give me a good night of sleep. "A long walk before bedtime is Judah's prescription to his patients when they complain of restless nights," I told her. "And I have found him in this as in all things to be a most excellent physician."

"But surely you are not planning to go off to bed without your supper, my dear Grazia," she demanded.

I replied that such had always been my custom.

"Then you must change your custom as long as you are under the Bonaventura roof." She wagged her finger with mock severity. "My husband's honored parents would take it as a slight were you to forgo supper. And besides, you will miss half the fun."

"But it will be dark by the time we arrive," I answered, still not understanding her meaning fully.

"And since when did darkness undo hunger? My belly is fairly groaning with it. Is not yours?"

Mine was not. It had not been trained to sup. We served but one meal each day in our household and that by the brightest light of day—at high noon. The only people I knew of who took more than a morsel of bread in the evening were gluttons and princes. Excepting for feast days of course. But the way in which Diamante expressed her appetite led me to believe that the Bonaventura family supped luxuriously every evening—like princes.

Later when we sat down at the long table that had been laid in the grand salon, we not only enjoyed three courses after the fish; we were also serenaded by a group of musicians. And just as the roasts were being brought in, who should appear as a guest of the house but Maestro Ambrogio of Pesaro, done up just as I had seen him at the Sforza wedding in a gold-embroidered jacket and red satin hose turned up at the ends with little silver bells attached to his toes.

To my surprise he recognized me, even going so far as to regale the company with an account of my exploit as the Jewish queen and to praise my dancing to the heavens, which although it made me blush did not displease me (for such a compliment is no mean thing coming from the foremost dancing master in Italy). Encouraged by the senior Bonaventura, I was prevailed upon to dance with Ser Ambrogio for the delectation of the company, and although my step was not perfectly practiced, I managed to acquit myself creditably enough to bring a proud smile to Judah's face.

After that Diamante took her place with the musicians to entertain us on the harp, which she played with uncommon skill. Then, although it had become very late, she insisted that the entire gathering must dance one final galliard, which she initiated by leading off on the arm of Isaachino in the Christian manner. Never before had I seen a Jewess dance publicly with a man other than a dancing teacher. Even at my wedding I was not permitted to dance with my own brothers. But the Bonaventuras' rabbi looked on complaisant while men danced with women. He even clapped his hands in time to the music!

When we at last retired and I was alone with Judah, I asked his opinion of this astounding display. "Mixed dancing." He shrugged. "It is one of those trivial issues that keep idle rabbis scribbling *responsa* who could better spend their time invigorating their sodden minds with the writings of Maimonides." Then, having thus condemned out of hand a goodly percentage of the rabbis in the peninsula, he quickly moved on to hints of a surprise that awaited me the following day.

"You will see that I too have a taste for pleasure, even a small talent for it," he announced with the smug self-consciousness of a boy. Then, with a tender kiss, he begged off further conversation.

I did not need more clues to the nature of the surprise he was planning. These hints and winks and tender kisses could only foreshadow one thing. No doubt about it, the time had arrived for our marriage to be consummated. The last thought that crossed my mind before I fell asleep that night was, What an original way to celebrate the feast of Purim.

26

I T WAS A NOVELTY WHEN I DRESSED THE NEXT MOR-
ning to find a maid at my elbow with a cup of spiced wine
and a biscuit. Her blunt, flat fingers appeared more suited
to the plow than to the buttonhook, but when she began to
lace up my bodice those same fingers moved from grommet to
grommet as lightly as a butterfly.

As I stood being tied into my *gamorra*, the maid's touch on
my skin brought back memories of another touch — light, gentle, loving; and for the first time in many years I allowed my
mind to dwell on Zaira and to feel afresh the pain of losing her.

But my reverie ended abruptly when Judah stepped out
from behind the dressing screen wrapped in black from neck
to ankle, and pressed me to put away my doleful thoughts and
follow him without delay to the *sala grande*.

"This is Purim, not the Day of Atonement, wife." He
smacked me smartly on the rump. "You have long deserved
some gaiety in your young life and today you will have it."

As he strode off I could have sworn I saw a dash of purple
on his toenails. But the idea was so preposterous that I quickly
explained it away as a trick of the light.

When I arrived at the *sala* a few moments later, Judah, whose social reserve made up a good part of his dignity in my eyes, was standing with Isaachino Bonaventura and his father, greeting the guests as if they were long-lost friends. In quick order he introduced me to a Jewish dentist named Mantino with a face like a fox (he was custodian of the Medici family teeth) and a crowd of Jewish loan bankers all accompanied by their families, many of them costumed the way Christians get themselves up at *carnevale*, the men as women, the women as men.

"A woman shall not wear articles proper to a man nor shall a man put on woman's clothing... for it is an abomination to the Lord." So it is stated in Deuteronomy, Chapter Twenty-two. I learned this when I was dressed as a boy for the journey from Bologna to Ferrara. That was for safety's sake. Even so, I had to get special permission from a rabbi to transgress the prohibition against cross-dressing. What excuse had these Florentines given their rabbi? I wondered. Or had the entire crowd been granted a dispensation by the Florentine rabbi solely for the purpose of diverting themselves?

My musing was cut short by the arrival of a second group of guests. These did not stop to dismount at the portico but instead galloped straight into the courtyard, causing those of us gathered around to dash for the safety of the arcades. Only after they had frightened us all to death did they rein their horses in. What manner of maniacs were these?

Christian maniacs, it turned out, owners of the large estates that adjoined the Bonaventura farm—the men adorned with heavy gold necklaces that identified them as Florentine citizens of importance and the ladies laden down with golden caps and hair ornaments and rings and bracelets.

Now our host stepped up to introduce the day's Master of Revels, the Purim rabbi. Like the others, I crowded in to see who had volunteered to play the fool. Maestro Judah del Medigo, did he say? Surely my ears were playing me tricks. But no. The buffoon who stepped forward to receive the scepter of

Purim rabbi was unquestionably Judah. And when he ascended the makeshift pulpit to begin his sermon, there was no mistaking that he was enjoying himself hugely.

It was then that I caught sight of the prayer book dangling between the folds of his costume. Seen briefly, it appeared to be a mean, ragged printed book. You know how much Judah detests the printed book. His prayer books are all illuminated, hand-printed, and covered in velvet. What business had this ratty volume to be hidden away on the person of Judah del Medigo?

He commenced his sermon with a reference to the ancient gods, as befitted a Florentine Platonist. "You all know that great Zeus assembled twelve gods in his pantheon," he began. "But how many of you know which of the gods he placed in the seat of honor at his right hand?" A short, embarrassed silence.

"Let me tell you then. Great Zeus chose as his most valued and chiefest adviser none other than Dionysus, the god of wine."

This announcement was greeted with a huge cheer, as if Dionysus had won his seat in the pantheon just yesterday and not thousands of years before.

"Why pay the god of wine such respect, you may ask." He continued when the din had died down. "I offer you this exegesis: When the world was young cannibalism and ritual murder ran rampant. Zeus himself could not stamp out the horrid practices. It was Dionysus who found the cure, for he understood that no man can live every day of his life in Apollo's blinding light. There are dark forces in his nature that will out. In giving us the wine cult, Dionysus provided the instrument to channel man's natural, brutish blood lust into a harmless annual feast of abandoned revelry. It is for that great service to mankind that he was rewarded with the place of honor at Zeus's table. And it is for that same great service that we will honor him at our table tonight."

He raised his glass. "In the name of Dionysus I urge you to carouse and sing and dance and drink until you drop, so that you may go forward to live a restrained and prudent life for the three hundred and sixty-four days that follow. That is my sermon. Will you have me for your Purim rabbi?"

To this question there arose a shout of affirmation unequaled, I would guess, even in the days of the wine cult.

"Very well then. Let us begin our revels," he concluded. And with that, he threw open his black *lucco* to reveal a gorgeous purple toga, sashed in bright green.

Had I been rocked by a thunderclap I could not have been more stunned. But the pagan sermon and the flamboyant costume were only the beginning for this Purim rabbi.

Now he called out in a booming voice for Haman to be brought in—a great ugly puppet meant to be kicked and battered by the children until the Purim rabbi pronounces it dead—and insisted on exercising his prerogative to be the first to attack the creature, which he did by turning on one foot like a discus thrower, twirling the poison green ruffle of his toga far above his thighs and kicking out his balance foot like some Attic dancer. It was when he did this that I caught my second sight of his toenails, painted bright magenta to match his toga, not a trick of light after all but a carefully planned effect.

So it went, one shock after another. The reading of the *megillah*, that age-old tale of Queen Esther's heroism that normally occupies the most sacred part of the Purim feast, was relegated to a quiet mumble while Judah, the Purim rabbi, roared around the courtyard swatting people with his scepter and castigating them for not being drunk.

"Here it is almost nones and you are still sober enough to stand upon your feet, Maestro Chaim," he berated the dentist. Whereupon he dragged the poor man over to the fountain, shoved his face under the spigot, and would not let him up until he had consumed several mouthfuls of wine.

At last Judah announced we could begin the feast. And sure enough, he reached into the folds of his costume and drew out the scabby prayer book I had noticed earlier, a dilapidated Haggadah held together with sisal and made of thin, printed pages, quite unlike the hand-lettered, illuminated prayer books that ornamented his *studiolo*. From this he proceeded to read the opening blessing of the feast.

But wait. The words I heard were the words of the Passover blessing. And we were celebrating Purim. Yet no one challenged the error. Nor was there a voice of dissent when the Purim rabbi proceeded from the false blessing to the Four Questions, another rite of Passover suddenly transferred over to Purim.

By custom, the asking of the questions was an honor reserved for the youngest child at the table. But Judah pointed straight to the foxy dentist, who, swaying from the effects of wine, rose unsteadily to his feet and squeaked in a high-pitched voice, "Wherefore is this Purim night different from Passover night?" Then he giggled, farted, belched loudly, and fell back into his chair. And the crowd roared approval.

Now Judah, holding his cup in one hand and reading from the raggedy little Haggadah, answered the drunken dentist's question as follows: "On Passover we drink only four times but on Purim we are obliged to drink ten times—nay, twenty — until we fall down in drunkenness. Fill the cups!" And all the company drained their glasses with alacrity.

By then, there was no mistaking that the little prayer book was a parody of the Passover ritual known as the *Masachet Shikurim*, "The Drunkards' Treatise," and that what I was witnessing was the enactment of a blasphemous Purim ritual conducted by my august husband.

When the dentist reached the fourth question his speech was so slurred that he had to repeat it six times before he got it right. And each attempt drew louder and more prolonged laughter from the guests than the one before. Finally, before Judah even had time to answer the final question, the poor man fell face forward into his soup and passed from this world for the remainder of the celebration.

By sunset, the ground in the courtyard was littered with celebrants passed from consciousness and the hallways of the villa smelled quite odorous from the vomit of those who had driven their stomachs beyond endurance. Truly, in Toscana, Purim becomes the Jewish version of *carnevale*.

For my part, I had had my fill of the high life of the Florentine Jews. The prospect of a long night of dancing and revelry promised only more weariness and a headache to me. But the arrival of the musicians for the night's dancing had quite the opposite effect on Judah. He instantly proposed to partner Isaachino in the first galliard, and by the end of the long evening he had managed to partner every Jewish man and boy in the place at least once. As is their custom, the Christian men danced with their Christian ladies. But, unlike the night before, the Jews reverted to the traditional custom, men dancing with men, women with women.

Without a curtain to hide behind, I took refuge in a dark corner of the *sala* hoping to escape notice. But Diamante's sharp eyes sought me out.

"A dance or two is exactly what you need," she insisted. "The motion will stir up your brains and let out the noxious air. Besides, I wager there is no woman here who can dance the galliard with your speed or grace and I do so long for a sprightly partner. Come, Grazia. Be my sister."

A moment later she had me twirling around the room on her arm at a speed that made my head swim. Whether or not the noxious fumes in my brain were released by all the twirling, I cannot say. But my headache did subside, and gradually, its place was taken by an exhilaration of spirit that I had not felt in many a month.

Something of the same emotion seemed to take hold of Judah. As the dancing progressed he less and less resembled the dignified scholar and more and more took on the unfamiliar coloration of a febrile youth, his wig askew, his toga crushed and wine-stained, his sharp eyes glazed over. Not that he ever lost countenance completely. But I who knew him well—or so I thought—perceived a look of wild longing in his eyes that I had never seen before.

Did this signal that the moment for the consummation of my marriage had come? As I followed him up the staircase and into our chamber I persuaded myself that it did. But I could not have been more mistaken. While I was brushing my hair he threw himself over on the bed and began to snore. By the time I had folded my garments away and crept in beside him, I was assailed by a roar louder than the trumpeting of a pack of elephants. I raised myself on my elbow and looked down upon my husband splayed out on his back, the painted nails on his toes flashing red in the moonlight. (He had, of course, neglected to close the shutters.) Lying there beside him trying to shut out the great snorts, I remember thinking to myself that drunkards go to bed in such a state every night of their lives. And thinking further that if I were married to such a one, I would surely poison him.

27

A FTER THE BITTER DISAPPOINTMENT OF PURIM night and the prospect of returning to the emptiness of my life in Firenze, an invitation to stay on in the country with the Bonaventuras came to me as manna from heaven. Judah, although quite willing to allow me the visit, was baffled by my enthusiasm for the Bonaventura clan and for Diamante in particular.

"She is barely literate. Even young Medina de Cases has more love of learning. What can you have to talk to her about?" he inquired with genuine puzzlement.

Had I chosen to reply, my answer would have been: "Yes, husband, Diamante is uneducated as you point out. But she knows how to be mistress in her own bedroom, which is more than can be said for clever Grazia, and because she is generous and forthright, I know she will gladly share her womanly wisdom with me."

What I did not take into account was that, having lived a totally unexamined life, my friend was unable to formulate ready answers even to the simplest question about her own conduct. So that when I asked her how she went about pleasing her husband, she simply repeated, "How I please him?" as if such an idea had never entered her head. Which it hadn't.

"Do you feed him some potion or wear a special perfume?" I persisted.

"Perfume on me?" She laughed delightedly. "I am lucky if I can get the manure out from under my fingernails. No, Grazia, if you are looking for such secrets you have come to the wrong person. I am no Delilah."

"Oh, I did not mean . . ."

"Yes you did, my love." She cuffed me under the chin as if we were two boys together. "And I shall make inquiries for you if you like. We live in the midst of the whores and witches in the Jewish quarter, you know. It will not be difficult."

"I would appreciate it," I replied with a blush. And then because I felt the need to clarify my concern I added, "It is not only the secrets of the bedchamber that I seek, Diamante. Isaachino talks to you, does he not? He tells you about his business, his inner feeling, his life outside the family."

"And does not your august husband talk to you? I am told he spends each noonday alone with you in conversation."

How do these tales get around? "Judah never speaks of his life outside our walls to me," I told her honestly.

"Do you ever ask?"

I was ashamed to admit that I held my husband too much in awe to initiate any topic of conversation.

"What do you talk of when you dine together?" she inquired.

"Some problem of interpretation from the *Phaedo*," I replied. "Or perhaps a *responsum* from one of the Jewish sages. Often we are silent at the table. Judah detests trivial talk and gossip."

"What a pity! I find gossip the spice of life. Every noon when Isaachino comes in from the *banco* for dinner, I wring him dry of every drop of news."

"How do you do it?" I asked.

"Do what?"

"Wring him dry?"

"Oh . . ." She pondered the question thoughtfully. When at

last she answered, it was with regret. "I declare I do not know how I do it. Or even *that* I do it."

In the end Diamante's secret turned out to be no secret at all. It took but a single dinner table conversation to give me the answer to my question. If you want a talkative man, marry a blabbermouth. Isaachino Bonaventura was a born talker. All anyone had to do to tap the contents of his mind was to sit in his presence with a silent tongue and out would pour a stream of anecdotes, events past, present, and future, speculation, and opinions, most of them shrewd, some manifestly sagacious. And all this without the slightest encouragement from anybody.

I learned more of the goings-on in Firenze at my first dinner with the Bonaventuras than I had in over a year in the company of my reticent husband.

"Things are coming to a head in town, I fear," Isaachino informed the assemblage. "The monk from Ferrara has come into collision with the Pope, and our Medici is about to be squeezed between the two of them."

"But does not the Christian pope command the loyalty of all Catholics?" I inquired. "How can a mere monk defy him?"

"For one thing, this monk is no ordinary street beggar with dirty feet," Isaachino replied, delighted to have his conversational pump primed. "Girolamo Savonarola is a dangerous man."

"As dangerous as Fra Bernardino da Feltre?"

"Worse."

"Oh no. Forgive me, Ser Isaachino, but he could not be worse than that villain. No one could be worse," I assured him earnestly. "Have you not heard of the Blood Libel of Trento?"

"Believe it or not, Madonna Grazia, I have heard of the Blood Libel," he replied. "And I also have heard of your family's expulsion from Mantova at Fra Bernardino's instigation, and still I say that this Savonarola is the more dangerous. The Jews here think of him as just another anti-Semitic priest, and he is that, of course. But he is far more clever, far more powerful than any of the others. Do you know that when Lorenzo the Magnificent lay dying he sent for this bastard of a priest to grant him absolution for his sins? Think of it. Lorenzo dei Medici felt the need of Savonarola's blessing before he could pass securely into the next world. Count Pico of Mirandola was sent to the convent of San Marco to bring the priest to the *magnifico's* bedside. You do know that Mirandola is a follower of Savonarola's, do you not?"

"But Count Pico is a Platonist," I protested. "A philosopher, a humanist." That much I did know.

"He is also obsessed by cabala. He spends his days searching for the universal truth in numbers, signs, and tongues. That is why he employed your honored husband to teach him Hebrew. So that he could ferret out the secrets of cabala."

"Judah does not believe in mysticism," I assured him. "He thinks it is all nonsense."

"Heaven forbid I should slander such a jewel in the Jewish firmament as Judah del Medigo," he answered graciously. "But when I refer to Count Pico of Mirandola I know whereof I speak. He comes often to the marketplace, especially in the melon season, for he is very fond of melons and prefers to select them himself. And he talks to everyone. Especially Jews. Because of his obsession with cabala."

"But Judah despises the cabalists," I repeated weakly.

"I tell you only what I heard from the lips of Count Pico himself. Oh, he was eloquent, lady, when he spoke of cabala, that ancient and mysterious text which contains the most secret revelations of all and which will resolve every problem of mankind." Here Isaachino made his eyes wide with wonder in imitation of Mirandola's manner. "With his own mouth he assured me that the sage who learns the alphabet of God in the correlation of letters and numbers will discover the hidden harmonies between different levels of being, between heaven and earth, between man and the world. And that sage will have the method of reducing all faiths, all doctrines, all languages of the Lord to one unity — one *Christian* unity. These Christians are all proselytizers in their hearts," he added. "He would turn us all into Christians."

"Count Pico told you he would turn us all into Christians?"

"No, he only said 'one unity.' But whose unity do you think he has in mind? Do you imagine he wishes to unite the world under the laws of Moses?"

I kept my own counsel on that question and Isaachino moved to another subject. But I did resolve to question Judah on the subject of his patron at the first opportunity, and indeed I brought the subject up the next day when I was seated opposite him at our own table.

I began the conversation by inquiring about the Count's state of health—not a subject that had ever interested me before, nor did it then except as a means of arriving diplomatically at my point.

"Count Pico is not well. Not at all well," Judah responded. "He still suffers from a recurrent tertian fever against which all my remedies do not avail. But whatever brought Count Pico to your mind? I have not spoken of him to you in some time."

"He was the table subject at the Bonaventuras' villa," I replied. "Ser Isaachino believes that Count Pico is after the deep secrets of cabala in the cause of the Christian church."

"Isaachino Bonaventura is an overgrown baby with an abacus where his brain should be," Judah replied crossly.

"Perhaps. But is what he says the truth? Does your patron the Count seek out the secrets of the cabala from you?"

"He does have a great interest in cabala," Judah admitted ruefully, "for which I must take part of the blame. Years ago at Padova—he was only a boy when he came there to study, not more than fourteen years old, with a mind like a diamond— he sought me out. He wished me to translate for him from Averroës and to teach him the Arab tongue. I introduced him to cabala merely as an oddity. A distraction. I never thought for a moment it would beguile his mind. Plato and Socrates were my mentors. But Pico fell under the spell of the mystics and has remained there, I fear, ever since."

"But you tell me he is a Platonist. How can he give his allegiance to both a pagan philosopher and Jesus Christ?"

"He believes that every way is the way to the One Truth," Judah answered simply. "It is not easy to estimate how much soothsaying and magic operate in his brain. But I do know that fruitful aspirations animate his mind. His great dream is of religious harmony. Peace among men. He seeks to find the method for reducing all faiths, all doctrines, all languages of the Lord to one unity." Precisely Isaachino Bonaventura's phrase, I noted. "As I say, he believes that every way is the way to the One Truth, if we could but find it."

"Including the way of Savonarola?"

"What do you know of Savonarola?" Judah whirled on me.

"Isaachino Bonaventura was saying—"

"Do I have to tell you again that Isaachino Bonaventura is an *ignorante*, that he knows nothing but the numbers in his ledger?"

"He knows what is happening in the city," I answered boldly, in defense of my new friends.

"Does he now?"

"He told us that this priest Savonarola is in correspondence with the French king against the Pope. And that he intends to bring the French army into Italy to cleanse us of heresy and corruption."

"Hmm." Judah pondered this thought. When he spoke again, the petulance was gone from his tone. "I cannot but agree with Isaachino Bonaventura that Fra Savonarola is playing a perilous game. It is foolish of me to plead his cause. This flirtation of his with the French is mad. He is a dangerous man. A fanatic."

"Does not that make him a strange companion for a Platonist?" I asked, trying to keep the pride out of my tone, for surely Judah had made my point for me with this admission.

"You are quite the little logician, my Grazia, are you not?"

"I do not aim to be clever, sir. I only try to understand the mysteries of the human heart," I replied, with what I hoped was suitable modesty. "And I find it incomprehensible that a Platonist like Count Pico cultivates a fanatic such as you say this priest Savonarola is."

"So do I, little wife, so do I." The man who gave this soft answer was a different Judah, a seeker who, as he confessed his incomprehension, nodded his head from side to side like a bewildered child. "These divided souls among whom I have spent so much of my life are still a mystery to me after all these years."

"The Christian Platonists, sir, and their search for One Truth?"

"Exactly." I had never seen him like this. Humble, puzzled, and somehow innocent. "Is it possible to fuse Christianity and paganism without making one the handmaid of the other, even for the most brilliant mind?" He stopped suddenly as if shocked by the sound of his own doubts. Then, turning his full gaze on me, he uttered an amazing confidence. "Sometimes my own Pico astonishes me with his interpretations. Last week, he plunged into Virgil's *Eclogues* and emerged with the poet's forecast that a Golden Boy would come to earth and inaugurate a Golden Age. And who do you suppose he interprets that Golden Boy to be?"

I knew at once who that Golden Boy had to be. "He interprets the pagan boy to be Jesus Christ."

"How did you know that?"

"I knew it because of what Isaachino said about Pico della Mirandola. The Platonists· might be searching for One Truth but it is still One Christian Truth. Because these Christians are all proselytizers at heart. I know it from my dealings with Madonna Isabella. Tell me true, sir, has this Pico never tried to convert you?"

With this bold query, I went too far. At the hint of an attack on his pet, the doubting, confiding, companionable Judah vanished, giving place to the man of *gravitas*, sure of himself, proud, defended by his superior knowledge and wit.

"Of course Lord Pico tries to convert me," he answered loftily, making nothing of my accusation. "It is a game between us. He swears he will make me a Christian before he dies, and I swear he never will."

But I would not be deterred. "Tell me this, then," I challenged. "How long a step is it between your amiable game with
the Count and the forcible conversion of Jews, as has happened
in Spain?"

What made me adopt this accusatory stance? God only
knows. Whatever the reason, my contentiousness completely
destroyed the congress that had been building between me and
my husband. When he answered my question about forcible
conversion, it was as my enemy.

"I see you are determined to mark my patron as a Jew-hater.
Isaachino Bonaventura has poisoned your mind."

"Isaachino has brought certain facts to my attention."

"Did he bring to your attention that Count Pico was con-
victed of heresy by the Roman Inquisition for the crime of
encouraging the obstinacy of Jews and of being a Jew-lover and
of Judaizing?"

"Did he burn for it?" I inquired, dripping acid.

"Fortunately he escaped Roma before the sentence could be
pronounced, and was taken under the protection of Lorenzo *il
magnifico*."

"When we Jews are accused of heresy, we burn," I responded,
making no attempt now to hide my anger. "When Medina's
brother was accused of heresy, he was put to the torture, his
arms torn from his body, and hung like an animal from the
bargello's tower, for he had no powerful friends to shield him
from the Christians' wrath."

"Are you blaming Lord Pico for having friends, Grazia?"

"I am simply saying, sir," I replied, "that it is easy to hold
two opposing ideas in your mind at the same time and to keep
a foot in each camp when you have powerful friends on either
side to make certain you do not fall into the chasm between
and break your bones."

"Some are blessed by fortune with good friends," Judah
answered smoothly. "I for one. So if it is your intention to
condemn Count Pico for having friends in high places, then
you must surely condemn me along with him. How else do

you suppose I hold my position here in Firenze except by the intercession of Count Pico and the acquiescence of Piero dei Medici? And what enables your lady friend Madonna Diamante to caper around the countryside on a blood stallion with a groom in attendance like a princess? Powerful friends, Grazia. Any Jew in this country lives happy and free only through his powerful friends in the Christian community." And without another word, he got up, turned on his heel, and left the room.

I had driven him away with my anger. Why? Was I jealous of the Count, of Judah's obvious preferment of his company to mine, of the way Judah's eyes lit up when he spoke of his old pupil's quicksilver intelligence. If so, the sentiment was unworthy of me. If Judah found more stimulation in the company of Count Pico of Mirandola than with me, who could blame him? I was impulsive and willful, fit only to gallop and giggle.

Thus began my self-castigation. Judah was my savior. He was endlessly forgiving, always eager to please me. On my account he had brought Medina de Cases into our house to provide me with a pupil and thus to occupy my time in something better than gazing out the window. He had forsaken his distinguished colleagues at the Platonic Academy for a group of provincial Jewish bankers in order to introduce me into a social milieu where I might feel at home. For my amusement, he had acted the fool at a *Shikurim* Purim. All this for my happiness. And I had repaid him by repeating slanders against his beloved pupil and patron, Count Pico.

If I had failed to find a community of interest with Medina de Cases, whose fault was that but mine? If I had found Judah's performance as the Purim rabbi disappointing, my own priggishness was the cause. If I did not fill him with desire, my skinny, flat, boy's body was at least partly to blame. If he did not choose to confide in me, no doubt my own shrewishness had marked me as unsympathetic.

The facts led to only one possible conclusion. I must work

and study to make myself a fit companion for a wise man. I must keep my temper in check and bite my hasty tongue. And I must somehow make myself lovable.

28

G IROLAMO SAVONAROLA. IF THE SOUND OF THAT name echoes into future centuries, how will he be remembered? As a villain? As a saint? As a hero? As a heretic? He was all these things and more to the Florentines in the brief span—less than eight years—of his rise and fall in the city.

After first hearing the name from Isaachino Bonaventura, I now seemed to hear it wherever I turned. Like a cancer that grows from a single lesion, his following (dubbed *piagnoni*—"weepers"—for their ostentatious piety) quickly spread from the monastery at San Marco into all the districts of the city. A good number of these *piagnoni* were children, young boys—shades of Fra Bernardino da Feltre's Army of the Pure in Heart—who clothed themselves in white cassocks in imitation of monastic novices. At first they merely importuned passersby, crying of the scourge to be unleashed upon the Florentines if they did not repent their godless ways. But very quickly their harangues assumed a physical aspect as well—grabbing women's necklaces off their throats and snatching furs from their shoulders, knocking down merchants who dealt in *lusso* goods, and increasingly provoking sword and dagger fights with Savonarola's opponents.

In this climate of escalating passions the magnificent Lorenzo's heritage of liberality quickly gave way to Savonarola's harsh orthodoxy. Public punishments of the cruelest sort supplanted the pageants and feasts of Medici times; and the pursuit of pleasure yielded to the search for sin.

As always, the first victims of the heresy hunters were the insulted and injured of this world—Gypsies, the mad, whores, and Jews. And the first among the first were Jewish whores, who bore a double stain.

I came to know this persecution because by chance a cousin of Diamante's chose that season for her wedding. It was May in the year 1494, a fine day for the procession that wound its way through the Duomo Square on the way to the synagogue. Suddenly the peace of the occasion was shattered when a boil of citizens spilled over into the square from one of the adjoining streets, shrieking curses and tossing small stones at an unseen victim. Then all at once the crowd parted to reveal the cause of the uproar: a woman, chained to a cart and wearing the yellow badge of the prostitute, being whipped along the street by the *bargello*.

"*Dio*," Diamante muttered beside me. "It is the Jewish whore caught out at last, damn fool. She has been warned against cohabiting with Christians. See, there is her client behind the cart with his privates exposed. He's lucky they didn't cut them off."

Now the whole ugly procession moved into full view before us: the woman, her chemise torn from neck to thigh so as to expose her beaten body, her back a river of blood; the *bargello* standing high on his little cart like a Roman charioteer whipping her on; the Christian shorn of his hose, his cock and balls tolling a warning to the spectators. Still he was not the one being whipped. It was the woman who took the punishment, not only from the *bargello* but from the crowd as well. The sting of the whip as it fell on her seemed to excite some animal memory in them. Every time the lash drew blood, there were shouts of vicious obscenities, all directed at the woman.

"Don't look, Grazia. Cover your eyes." Diamante turned to veil my face with her cloak. And I took advantage of this merciful blindness and did not look. But as the cart came abreast of us I began to hear the woman's cries, hardly stronger than the yelp of a puppy, and suddenly aware of my cowardice, I pushed aside Diamante's cloak and looked straight at the poor creature.

At that moment she threw back her head to toss aside the dark curls that fell across her face, and our eyes met. I knew those flashing eyes. I knew this woman. *And she knew me.* It was Zaira.

I jumped forward but Diamante grabbed me with her strong arms and barred my way.

"What do you think you're doing?" she whispered urgently. "You must not take notice. We are all in danger here. She is a Jewess, remember. If you make any more gestures toward her the *bargello* will take you too. Perhaps all of us."

The *bargello's* whip whirred through the air. Zaira's eyes widened with terror. I screamed as if the lash had fallen on my own back.

Diamante's hand closed over my mouth. "Let them pass, Grazia. She deserves what she's getting. She was warned."

I made another effort to free myself. But years at the reins had given Diamante the muscles of a muleteer, and to be perfectly truthful, I did not struggle against her with all my might. I let them take my beloved Zaira to the torture. I jettisoned her for the same reason that sailors jettison heavy cargo in a storm — to save their own skins. Diamante had provided me with the perfect excuse. I must not endanger the safety of "all of us."

But my conscience could not abide the evasion. Before the sun was up I plucked an unwilling Medina out of his hiding-hole in Judah's *studiolo* and ordered him to accompany me on an errand across the river. He grumbled, but in the end, he did accompany me across the Ponte Vecchio. However, when we turned away from the market and toward the Piazza della Signoria he began to hang back.

"Where are we going, madonna?" He tugged anxiously at the sleeve of my *gamorra*.

"I have an important task to do," I replied.

"Where? Where are you taking me?" His voice began to rise.

I strode ahead decisively, hoping to encourage him by example. But after some steps I sensed he had not followed me, and indeed, when I turned around I discovered that he had removed himself to the wall that held back the Arno at that point and was clinging to it like an ivy plant. I knew Medina for a fainthearted whiner. But never until that moment had he actually refused to obey me.

Back I went, prepared to slap him if necessary. But when I stood close to him I saw a look on his face of such misery that my heart was touched and I opted for a more compassionate style of persuasion.

"Why so obdurate, naughty boy?" I wheedled. "What is troubling you? Tell me now."

"There are places I cannot go in this city," he mumbled.

"Where? What places?" I asked.

"In the Via Calzaiuoli..." He spoke so quietly I could barely make out his words. "There is a church they have made out of an old granary."

I knew the church. I had seen it on the day we first entered Firenze. "That is the church named after Saint Michael, is it not?" I asked.

"That is it. Orsanmichele." As he intoned the name of the church his eyes widened. "In the wall of that church, in a niche, stands the Virgin that was smeared with shit."

"By your brother Bartolomeo?"

"I beg you, madonna, do not make me go near that place. The Virgin is waiting for me. She has put the curse of death on me. Let me go home."

To force him on would be cruel indeed. Still, no amount of pity would bring back his brother. Bartolomeo de Cases was dead. But Zaira was alive. I made my choice. I smacked him, hard.

Then I held out my hand. "Take it," I ordered him. "Now pull yourself up, cleanse your mind of ghosts, and gather your courage together. For I am going to the *bargello* this day. And you are going with me."

And to be sure, he put forth one foot. Then another. And he walked at my side across the Piazza della Signoria without too much trembling. When we passed the Chiesa Orsanmichele he did turn his face away. But he did not falter and we passed that obstacle safely. However, when the forbidding tower of the Bargello's Palace loomed up in our path he began to shake. Who can blame him? The Bargello's Palace was designed to put fear into the hearts of the boldest men. How could it not paralyze the will of a terrified boy—and a boy with such memories of it as Medina's? Lucky for me I had to put on a brave front for him. Otherwise I might not have had the courage to approach the guard myself. But, forced to act the part of a virago, I carried it off, as one almost always does when life offers no other choice.

"I seek to see the Jewish whore who was brought here yesterday," I informed the guard with as much authority as I could command.

"Do you now, little lady?" He had a twinkle in his eye and an obvious weakness for pert girls, a good omen for my mission.

"Yes, I do, sir," I replied. The man was so tall that I doubted my reedy voice would reach his ears if I did not shout.

"And may I know your purpose?" he inquired, still twinkling.

"I believe I recognized her as one who served my family long ago and I wished to bring her what comfort I could as she often comforted me when I was a child," I answered, forgoing guile for truth and sincerity.

"I see you have a good heart, madonna. And an honest tongue. So I will not turn you over to the captain for questioning as my orders direct me to do." At the mention of the captain I felt Medina's arm grow weak beneath my hand and I gave him a quick kick in the shins to bolster his courage.

"Your kindness marks you as a compassionate man and a true Christian, sir," I replied. "May I see the woman?"

"You may for all I know. But not in this jail."

Was I too late? "Is she dead?" I asked.

"Ought to be after what she's done. But she's one of those who step in shit and come up smelling roses. Her Christian client turned out to be a Turkish Mussulman, so she's free, sent back to her house with a warning to leave Firenze at once. You've seen the last of her, lady, and just as well for you. A nice little lady like yourself needs have no traffic with a slut. It doesn't do. Tell your servant to see you home." He turned to Medina. "See your lady home, lad. On your way now."

And before I knew it Medina was fairly dragging me along the street toward the Ponte Vecchio and home. But I could not let the matter rest. Calling up all my strength, I turned the wretch around toward the Bonaventura house so that I might learn from Diamante where I would find "the Jewish whore."

When I told her my mission she warned me that I was on a fool's errand. But her loyal heart could not long withstand my urgent pleas for help, and I left her accompanied by two armed porters to show me the way to the house of whores and to watch over me if I insisted on entering.

"But beware, Grazia, these places are not filled with the betrayed and the innocent as you seem to think. There isn't one of those sluts who wouldn't slit your throat for the scarf around your neck." This firm judgment was followed by a final warning from my friend to her *bravi* that if any harm should come to me they would pay dearly for it.

The street they led me to was not more than a hundred small steps from the Bonaventura mansion. But what a distance we traveled in that hundred steps.

From the outside the house seemed no worse than the house of any Florentine silkworker or artisan—three stories high and four *braccias* wide. Not until we stepped inside did the truly hellish character of the place emerge. Normally in these narrow Florentine houses the ground floor serves as a shop or *bottega*, stuffed with hides or woolens or statuary or tinware as the case may be but rarely used by more than three or four persons at one time. In this infamous den the tiny area had been divided by thin curtains into cribs. There must have been twenty of them, no one larger than was absolutely necessary to accommodate the thin straw pallet that along with a metal pitcher and a stool constituted the totality of the furnishings of each cubicle. By comparison, the most austere monk's cell is a palace.

All this came to me in a glance, for many of the cribs were open to reveal the human merchandise offered for sale in this infamous *bottega*—women in various states of undress, legs splayed, breasts flopping down to their knees, many sucking on bottles of wine like babes on the tit.

And the stench!

"Watch your feet, madonna," one of my escorts warned just in time to save me stepping into a pile of feces. Apparently the denizens scattered their leavings around like animals. No. Not like animals. Animals do not befoul their own nests. Not even the despised and unclean pig.

Everything in me wanted to bolt, to run back to my friends in their fine clean house. But I had gone too far to turn back.

"Ask who is in charge here," I instructed my escort.

Behind me a strong husky voice spoke out. "I am, madonna."

Then the curtain was drawn and out stepped a veritable giant (or giantess) almost a head taller than Lord Pirro, with fluttering hands and a full purple mouth, opulently dressed in a jeweled turban. "How can I be of service?"

"A woman...a Jewess..." I barely knew where to begin.

"You wish to enjoy a woman?" The heavy voice took on a musky flavor.

"I wish to find someone," I replied in a voice I had never heard myself use, a tight prissy voice cut off from feeling. "I saw this woman yesterday in the piazza in the custody of the *bargello*. They tell me she stays here."

"Ah, the Jewish whore. The little dancer with the taste for wine. Believe me, madonna, we can do better for you than her. I have one from Alexandria with a tongue like a snake and hands to turn your body to water."

"I want the Jewess." Where I got the breath to speak I do not know, for the stench was choking me.

"We have better, believe me...sweet and young and juicy with hot little mouths...big ones with arms like pillars to lift you up to paradise."

"I want the Jewess," I repeated. "Is she here?"

"Answer the lady's question, pander," my escort prodded the giantess (by her gestures I now took her for a woman).

The purple mouth, pursed up until then, oozed out into the face, loose and vulnerable. "I was only trying to serve the lady, sir." The deep voice quavered. "But the Jewish wench is gone, with her pimp and her wine bottle. And good riddance too. She's a wild one. Always laughing. Life is not a dance, you know."

"She had a good heart," I heard myself say. In spite of my resolve not to speak to this scum, I could not let an insult to my old friend pass unchallenged. Of course the gesture was futile. What place have hearts in these so-called palaces of love?

I cannot write further of Zaira tonight. The shame of each word as I lay it down on the page burns into me like a branding iron. Madonna Isabella would disdain that sentence as a wallow in Jewish guilt. Her Christ forgives her everything. But my God, whatever little piece of Him I cling to, offers me no such comfort. We have only one obligation to God and man: to act up to the best that is in us. When I turned my back on Zaira, I succumbed to the weakest part of my nature. In betraying her, I betrayed myself, an act that has diminished me forever in my own eyes.

As I pronounce this harsh sentence, Sappho whispers in my ear the words she wrote to Athis, who had loved and betrayed her:

...the memory is still dear.
Look deep into my eyes
And keep the dead past clear
of all regret...

To keep the dead past clear of all regret is a piece of advice that might have issued from the mouth of Zaira, that generous spirit who, I know, forgives me everything. But although I have learned with the years to forgive those who have done me ill, I still have not achieved that high and confident state of forgiveness for my own transgressions.

29

I N HIS HISTORY OF FIRENZE, FRANCESCO GUICCIARDINI proclaims the year 1492 as the last of Italy's good years. Above all other things, he attributes the subsequent decline of the city to the early death of Lorenzo dei Medici, eulogized by the poets as the laurel that sheltered the birds who sang in the Tuscan spring.

I too mourn that cultivated, wise, and generous heart. But with due respect to Lorenzo's diplomacy, I tell you that it was not the loss of a good man but the active presence of a bad one that plunged Italy into shame and misery. If you would know how this villain affected my life and your own, I beg you to come back with me to 1493, the first of the bad years for Italy.

Lorenzo il magnifico is dead. His son Piero rules in Firenze as the first among its citizens. In Lombardia, Lodovico Sforza has usurped the dukedom of Milano from his nephew Gian Galeazzo. This piece of treachery is in itself no cause for alarm. It is a family matter between the Sforzas. However, Lodovico happens to be married to the granddaughter of the King of Napoli. And the King of Napoli is a touchy Spaniard who does not take kindly to having his granddaughter unseated.

Meanwhile, in faraway Paris, the scion of the house of Anjou has come to the throne of France. Named for Charlemagne, he is the eighth Charles to rule France. Small and bent over, with a huge nose, huge feet, and a convulsive twitch, his extreme ugliness is matched only by his appetite for women and victories.

There you have the main characters in the Italian drama—Charles VIII of France, mad for glory; Ferrante, King of Napoli, intent upon revenging his granddaughter's humiliation; Piero dei Medici of Firenze, a pale counterfeit of his magnificent father; and Lodovico Sforza, Duke of Milano, a usurper. They comprise a volatile group, proud, ambitious, quick to take offense, every one sly. And the slyest of all is Lodovico Sforza, the Duke of Milano.

Casting about for a way to deflect the ire of Napoli, Lodovico Sforza happens on the idea of distracting King Ferrante with a new enemy. In Charles VIII Lodovico sees a willing pawn. Perhaps the impetuous French boy can be persuaded to attack Napoli rather than Milano. After all, the house of Anjou does have an ancient if groundless claim to the throne of Napoli. Lodovico sends ambassadors to invite the young French king to come to Italy and press his claim to the kingdom of Napoli.

Perhaps Lorenzo the Magnificent—the peacemaker and diplomatist—could have persuaded Lodovico Sforza away from his shortsighted ploy. But Lorenzo was dead, and without his presence, the Florentine delegation that rushed to Milano hoping to dissuade the Duke carried less weight than a feather.

In vain they warned against the danger of inviting foreign troops onto Italian soil. Remember what happened to us in the year 410 when the barbarians swept down over the Alps, they reminded him. But Lodovico Sforza was fixed on using the French as food for the consuming wrath of Napoli.

In a final appeal to Lodovico's better nature, the Florentines unfurled the tattered flag of the motherland.

"Think of Italy," they begged him.

His answer rings in my ears as I write it, resonating the dim-sightedness and arrogance not only of Lodovico Sforza but of all the other tin-pot Italian princes.

"Italy? Italy?" Lodovico looked here and there about the room as if pursuing a phantom. "Where is this Italy you speak of? I have never looked her in the face."

Thus was the stage set for the first foreign invasion of Italy in a thousand years.

BY THE END OF the summer of 1494 word came to us in Firenze that Charles VIII of France had crossed the Alps with a force of twenty-two thousand infantry and eighteen thousand cavalry and was gliding over Piemonte and Monferrato like one of God's angels. Before we knew it, the French king had reached Asti and settled in as guest of the Duke of Milano and his wife, Beatrice (whom I always thought of as Madonna Isabella's mean little sister). Two weeks later he was felled by a mysterious ailment. Noblesse oblige. Piero dei Medici ordered Judah del Medigo to Asti to minister to the King, which I took to be a high honor. Not so, Judah.

"It is never an honor to be ordered about like a lackey," he advised me as he tossed his garments angrily into a *cassone*.

"How long will you be at Asti?" I asked.

"Until the King gets well. Or dies, I suppose."

"Is he so unwell then?" I asked.

"Who is to know? He took to his bed two days ago with a mysterious ailment—maybe the pox, says Lodovico Sforza's astrologer, who seems to be serving as the King's physician. Possibly the monarch has worn himself raw with sexual exertion. I understand that Lodovico's notion of hospitality is to provide a new lady of the court every night for the King's pleasure, with a substitute standing by should one partner prove insufficient to satiate the satyr. A regimen like that could kill a man. Mind you, it would not stop the gossips from crying poison as they always do."

"In that case you had better make certain to cure your patient, maestro," I joked. But the jest died on my lips. We knew of physicians who had literally lost their heads in punishment for the death of important patients.

With Judah gone, the notion of writing a *ricordanza* seemed at worst a harmless way to pass the time, at best intriguing. In Firenze even a shoemaker felt entitled to take some moments of each day to enter the events of his life in his *libro segreto*. The merchants did so as a matter of course. Isaachino Bonaventura, the least poetic of men, would not have dreamed of settling into his bed at night without making a daily entry. If he could write his life, so could I.

Thus began my first efforts toward literature. In no time I found myself composing the occasional passage in terza rima. Then one day a whole poem. After not too long I was producing a poem a day, all of them pallid echoes of Virgil, all sentimental, flowery, mushy as a rotten peach. I must have filled thirty quarto pages while Judah was absent. When I learned he was on his way home I quickly burned the lot. But I had made a beginning.

It was a pale and haggard Judah who staggered into our house after an absence of twenty days at Asti. Nonetheless he refused tea and a warm bed, taking time only to bathe before he was off again, this time to Fiesole. Lord Pico had taken ill again, he explained as I scrubbed him down. To my questions about Charles VIII he replied coolly that there was nothing to tell. Reports of the King's ailment had been greatly exaggerated. "All his Majesty needed was a physic and some hand-holding," was how he put it, and then he turned away from me and called for Medina to assemble a list of necessaries for his visit to the ailing Count.

After that the subject of Asti was closed, much to my disappointment and that of Diamante, who had counted on hearing all the details of the French court at first hand.

"How otherwise will we know what transpired at Asti?" she pressed.

"We may not, my friend," I replied.

"But I shall die if I don't have every single detail. How do the French ladies dress? Do they cut their necklines down their navels like the Venetian ladies do? Does the King really kiss everybody of both sexes that he meets? You must ask your husband these things, Grazia."

"I tried to but he yawned and patted me on the head and went to bed."

"Ask him again. Pinch him if you must."

"I could never pinch Judah," I replied. "Never."

In the end, Diamante and I did discover many of the details of the French king's stay at Asti, but not from Judah. The Bonaventura agent at Milano was our source. From him through Isaachino we learned that Lodovico's Duchess, Beatrice d'Este, brought eighty beautiful young women and forty musicians with her to Asti to welcome the French king and keep him amused; that she obliged the monarch by dancing for him in the French manner; that he, flattered by the delicate compliment, had her portrait taken on the spot by his own painter, Jean Perreal, to send to his sister the Duchess Ann; that even though the King called Lodovico "cousin," he had the keys to his residence delivered into his own royal hands each night after lockup and the gates to his palace guarded by twenty of his own French hussars.

I made a few feeble attempts to use these details to start Judah reminiscing about his sojourn in the King's entourage. But they came to nothing. All of his attention was reserved for the ailing Pico della Mirandola.

Everything else, even his work at the Medici library, was forgotten. When I mentioned one day that he had not visited the library since his return from Asti, he replied irritably that the library would doubtless be there long after we were dead. It was a shocking statement from a man who treasured books and scholarship above all else. I watched, mystified, as each morning before the matins bell he shook himself awake in the dark to spend hours locked in his laboratory concocting new remedies for his patient. After dinner he would mount a horse — a pair of them was kept at a stable in the next street — and travel up to Fiesole, accompanied by Medina. Most nights I was asleep by the time he returned, worn out, to fall into bed beside me.

I feared that he would collapse from exhaustion. But he seemed to gain strength from his exertions. His eyes burned with an almost manic zeal when he spoke to me of his fight to keep the Count alive. And one night I awoke to find him kneeling on the cold floor praying, "Find me a way, God. Lead me to the remedy."

Had I been forced to depend solely on Judah for my view of events I might easily have supposed that the fate of the world hung on the survival of Pico della Mirandola. Only the reports passed on by Isaachino told me that the fate of our city—and perhaps of all Italy—hung on an equally precarious balance: the mercurial relationship between the King of France and Piero dei Medici.

Three times that summer King Charles sent ambassadors to Firenze to request safe conduct for his army through Toscana on his way to Napoli. Three times Piero forced the Florentine Council to refuse. Having thrown in his lot with Napoli early in the game, Piero now felt he could not move from the position for fear of being judged weak. His *bella figura* was at risk.

After that the storm clouds gathered over Firenze with amazing speed. In a series of quick moves, Charles and his troops decamped from Asti, passed Genova, and began to move south toward Firenze. Unopposed, the French army sped over the desolate Garfagnana and made camp in the little town of Fiorvizzano, as close to us as cheek to jowl.

"The occupation of our city is now a certainty," Isaachino told me. "Only the moment of it remains in doubt. You must prevail on Maestro Judah to leave town with us." But when I told Judah that the city might be under siege any day, he ridiculed me. "The Florentines are not stupid enough to get into a pissing contest with the King of France. If he does come they will pacify him. It is good for trade. And the Florentines always do what is good for trade."

He was not entirely wrong. One fine day Piero dei Medici

came to his senses and galloped off to Fiorvizzano to pacify the King. Too late. Piero emerged from the audience room stripped of Livorno, Pisa, and Sarzana. What it had taken his father, Lorenzo, a lifetime to amass he gifted away in a day.

Back in Firenze, Fra Girolamo Savonarola publicly cursed Piero and extolled the French king as the living incarnation of the Sword of God, urging him to come quickly and scourge the wicked Florentines for their sins. With a savior like that, who needs a devil?

Mesmerized by Savonarola's rhetoric, the Florentine *signoria* declared Piero a traitor and banished him. That night his brother Cardinal Medici escaped the city hidden in a wagonload of hay. It took only two days to wipe out sixty years of Medici rule.

Within hours of the bloodless coup, a cadre of French billeting officers arrived from Fiorvizzano and took over the city of Firenze by the simple expedient of marking each house with the name of whoever was to be billeted there. Not a shot was fired, not a protest uttered. Rodrigo Borgia summed it up neatly: The French captured Firenze with a box of chalk.

I was at the Bonaventura house the morning the French advance party came to Jew Street. Without a by-your-leave, they entered every room, assigning this one to Baron so-and-so and that one to Count thus-and-so. They gave it to be understood that they meant to pay. But, as Isaachino predicted, when they offered to settle up, they paid for the horns and ate the ox, as the saying goes.

On my ride home, an eerie quiet pervaded the streets of the city. Not a sign nor sound of resistance. Only the jingle of spurs as the King's men walked from house to house with their wands of white chalk. Was this a siege, a pageant, a quadrille, or what?

"The Bonaventuras are leaving for the Mugello tonight," I told Judah, hunched over his burners and retorts as usual. "We must go with them."

"Out of the question," he muttered.

"The French are commandeering houses—"

"If you are apprehensive it is best you leave," he interrupted. "Go along with the Bonaventuras if you wish."

"And you? Will you come with me?"

"Certainly not." He turned the burner up and began to stir the contents of the beaker furiously.

"You refuse the offer, then?" I pressed him.

Now he turned to face me. "Grazia, I hold the life of a desperately ill young man in my hands. Have I not made that clear to you?"

"You have, sir. And I tell you that we are in a precarious position here with the French at the gates."

"Twaddle. Your friends the Bonaventuras are in a precarious position. They run the risk of having their fortune confiscated. You and I have nothing to lose. You forget that I am in high favor with the French king since I treated him at Asti. I am now his physician. His confidant. His savior." He allowed a wry smile to crease his lips when he pronounced the word "savior." "If you like, I will write to him in the field and ask him to place this house under his special protection. Still, perhaps you should go to the countryside with your friends."

"And leave you here?"

"Medina will see to my needs."

Medina take my place? Never. "I do not believe that a wife should leave her husband when danger threatens. My place is by your side." I drew myself up to my full height and began to quote: "'Entreat me not to leave thee and to return from following after thee. For whither thou goest I will go. And where thou lodgest, I will lodge—'"

"Enough, Grazia." He raised his hand as if to command me. "Spare me your erudition. If you wish to go, go. If you wish to stay, stay. But for God's sake leave me to my work."

The King's billeting officers came into our street early the next afternoon. As they moved down the street closer and closer to our house, the blows of the halberds resounded against the portals as if struck by Thor's hammer. When I heard them at the next house I smoothed my hair, stiffened my spine, and walked down, trembling, to greet them. I heard the clatter of their spurs on the cobbles as they approached our portal. Then: *"Allons-y, Allons-y!"* An order to move on. *"Le médecin reste ici. Le roi commande."*

The doctor's house was to be spared. No more than a just reward for saving the King's life, I thought, and so remarked to the physician when I reported the day's events to him on his return from Fiesole.

"Who says I saved the King's life?" was the response I got.

"Why, everyone in Firenze knows he was ailing from the pox. The Bonaventura agent in Milano wrote in his report—" I began.

"The French king no more had the pox than you did." He cut me off, impatient once again. "I tell you that and I am the man who cured him. Now whose word do you take? Mine or that of your mentor, Isaachino Bonaventura?"

"Yours of course, honored husband," I answered quickly. Then I added, "But if you did not cure him of the pox, sir, then what did you cure him of? Please tell me, husband. For I long to know."

"I cannot break my oath by disclosing a patient's confidence, even though my little wife longs to know. However, I will tell you that the French king himself is the author of the fiction that he had a touch of the pox."

"He invented an illness? Why?"

"Think, Grazia. Logic will tell you."

I thought. "If the King had injured his bow arm or for some reason was unable to sit his mount he would be unable to lead his troops. And since he came to Italy to make war..."

"He would rather have it put out that he had gotten the pox than that he was rendered powerless in war. Is that your line of thought?"

I nodded. It was my reasoning exactly.

"Fine deduction," Judah congratulated me.

"In that case, I will guess his malady to be hemorrhoids."

"Wrong."

"But you said..."

"I congratulated you on your deduction, not on your conclusion. You have left out a most important variable in this equation."

"And what is that, sir?"

"You forgot that the King is also a man. And that a man does not only see his power in terms of his ability to make war."

"How then does a man see his power?" I asked.

"How then?" Judah echoed.

"A man perceives his power in his cock," I answered, certain as I spoke that I had it right. "At least an Italian *bravo* does."

"And believe me, my dear, so does a French king," Judah answered. "For a king to lose his potency strikes twice as deep as for an ordinary mortal. Being a man, his sexual prowess must support the pride of a man. But being a king, it must also support the line of succession to the crown."

The King of France impotent. What a scandal!

"Now you understand that this information which you have ferreted out of me under duress is for your ears alone." Oh, Judah, how well you knew me! "Swear to me that you will tell no one. Ever."

"I swear. But honored husband, Diamante would keep the secret to the grave if I—"

"She must not know, Grazia." From his tone I understood this prohibition was not to be breached. "Being my wife, you are a part of me as Adam's rib was a part of him. But if the truth were to spread beyond that boundary, and this king who now holds me dear should find that I had betrayed his secret weakness, we would be finished, Grazia. Finished."

"Does it really matter all that much?" I asked.

"More than you can imagine, little wife. Much as it pains me to admit it, my present position in this treacherous world depends almost completely on my secret cure for impotence."

"But you are a scholar as well as a physician. You have other strings to your bow," I pointed out.

"Italy is not what it was in the time of Lorenzo *il magnifico*," he answered sadly. "Scholarship and learning are fast losing their luster. We are entering a new age of barbarism. Mark me, wife, this Charles the Eighth of France is only the spearhead of a barbarian assault that will equal the sack of Roma in the fifth century. By the dawn of the year 1500 the legacy of the past will have been spent up to its limit. The forces of reason will be routed and brutal power will constitute the law of this sweet land. In such times a strong arm and a potent cock count for all. Now then..." He took my face in his hands as he had used to do and added in a gentle tone, "Is that serious enough for you?"

"Oh sir, I am ashamed." No pretended modesty this. I truly did feel shame for my empty-headedness.

"No need to be ashamed, wife. But you must keep my confidence. My skill in this highly specialized branch of medicine will not only put bread but sweetmeats and melons in our mouths. Already the King rewarded me well for his 'cure.'"

"How well?"

Judah smiled a self-satisfied cat's smile that I had never before seen on his countenance. "Let us say, handsomely."

"How handsomely?" I pressed him. "One hundred gold ducats?"

"Would you believe five times that much?"

"Just to help him fuck again?"

"And to swear on a bust of Hippocrates that no one would ever know from my lips the nature of his true ailment. I was also obliged to report to Piero dei Medici that I had cured the King of pox. Anything but the true malady."

"Better a fatal disease than a soft cock?"

"Precisely," Judah answered.

30

THE FRENCH MONARCH'S REPUTATION PRECEDED HIM. Monstrous ugly, they said; so unlettered that at the age of twenty-four, when he came down into Italy, he could barely write his own name. Two passions fired the spirit of this royal homunculus: women and conquest. Judah explained to me that to Charles the conquest of Napoli would yield up a double prize because whoever is crowned King of Napoli also inherits the accompanying title of King of Jerusalem, meaningless though it is. Titles were like women to little Charles VIII. He could never get enough of them.

Two days before the King's triumphal entry into Firenze, a communication arrived at our door via a liveried footman—a beautiful piece of rag vellum with the most extravagant rippled edges, composed by some traitor's fine Italian hand—inviting *Médecin Leone et femme* to sit with the King's party in the Piazza del Duomo to welcome *le roi*. Thus did we come to be seated under the canopy that sheltered the King's most favored guests, between the exquisites of the French court and the Florentine traitors who followed Savonarola's teachings, each group determined to outdo the other in their enthusiasm for the conqueror of the once-proud commune of Firenze.

The French gave us a spectacle to cheer: five thousand Gascon infantry; three thousand Swiss infantry; and three thousand cavalry in engraved armor with brocade mantles and velvet banners embroidered in gold. At the sight of the horses the French officer on my right exploded with such a forceful clamor that I feared he might rupture himself. Beside me Judah sat glum and unimpressed, impatient to be gone to his patient in Fiesole. But of course the King's invitation could not be refused. Nor could his procession be hurried.

After the cavalry came the archers. Four thousand Bretons. Next, the crossbowmen, two thousand Scots, bows at rest but menacing all the same. It is truly a monstrous thing, that crossbow, equal in height and girth to its marksman, a veritable killing machine. And on this occasion the menace of these weapons was emphasized by the relentless beat of the drums, which did not stop nor vary until the King made his entrance.

Hail the conquering hero! The ugliness of Charles VIII was legendary, but nothing could have prepared me for the misshapen creature who passed before me that day, close enough almost to touch. His body was small, his head overlarge, with a beak nose even longer than Savonarola's and thick lips that hung open like an engorged vulva. This obscene suggestion was intensified by his beard, a scraggly reddish mess more like pubic hair than the coarse whiskers that generally adorn a man's face.

As he rode past us his head and hands twitched so that I whispered to ask Judah if the King did not suffer from some brain disorder. But Judah said no. "The king is not well coordinated," was his quiet comment.

Not well coordinated! The poor man jerked around on his horse like a puppet on a string. He was everything they said and more. A botched thing. An abortion. But a king for all that. Glittering like one of Fra Angelico's angels in his gold armor, he lit up the day. And when he passed from sight it seemed as if the sun had left the world, even though everyone knew him to be a mere mortal and a poor specimen of the breed at that. But I was given little time to reflect on the attributes of kingship. As soon as the King disappeared from sight Judah grabbed my hand and pulled me through the milling crowd into a nearby stable yard, where he had rented a pair of mules for the ride up to Fiesole. To escort me home would have robbed him of precious time with his patient. Willy-nilly I must accompany him to Count Pico della Mirandola's villa on the Fiesole heights.

Midway up the path, swaying from side to side as one does on muleback, Judah turned to me and announced, "He is dead." How he knew, I cannot guess. But his intuition was verified by the servant who met us at the portal. The brightest ornament in the humanistic diadem had lost his light that morning in the thirty-second year of his life. "Too young. Too soon," Judah muttered as we passed into the *sala grande* where the body lay.

Savonarola was not present. No doubt he and his cohort were occupied honoring the triumph of their hero, the Sword of God, Charles VIII. So the members of the Platonic Academy had their Phoenix—as Pico was called by his intimates—all to themselves. They stood around the bier like a coven of Platonic witches dressed in black *luccos* talking of Pico, extolling his virtues and mourning his loss, while the flickering candles caught the glint here and there of the jewels that adorned their expressive fingers.

When Judah conducted me forward so that we might pay our respects, I noted that at the foot of the coffin stood a bust of Plato mounted on a plinth where the Count might contemplate it through his dead eyes.

Seeing his face—the noble forehead, the straight nose, the golden hair spread out on the pillow—I could not help but feel a pang. I had not expected him to be so young, nor so beautiful...nor so benign in death. But even as I sighed, a small voice in me inquired what this Pico della Mirandola was to me that I should weep for him. And I left the bier dry-eyed.

Once all were assembled, various members of the Platonic circle rose to give account of the dead man's last days and of his great deeds. The first to speak was Marsilio Ficino, come from a distance to be with his beloved Phoenix in his final hours. It was his fourth bedside vigil in a year. First, Lorenzo *il magnifico*, dead at forty-three. Then, Barbaro. Then, only two months previous, Poliziano, age forty. And now, Pico. Humanists die young. Except for Ficino.

The revered graybeard spoke of the past sentimentally, of how this beautiful, good, and learned being had dropped into his *studiolo* one day like an angel from heaven. "He praised my translation of the *Dialogues* and urged me to crown my labors by performing the same office for Plotinus as I had for Plato," the old man recalled in his deep resonant voice. "I was weary. But I felt that the visitation of this angel must be a divine monition and I undertook to begin a translation of Plotinus at once."

He stopped a moment to clear his throat, then continued in his perfectly articulated Italian. "I was to him in years as a father, in intimacy as a brother, in affection as a second self," he went on. "Now he is gone from us, our Phoenix of the Wits, as Poliziano truly dubbed him." He heaved a deep sigh. "For he will rise from the ashes. He will never be forgotten as long as men treasure learning, wisdom, and goodness."

Then he pronounced a long Latin benediction and sat down.

Next came members of Pico's family and finally Judah, seeming much at home among the party in spite of the little Jewish cap which set him off as not one of them. He did not stand beside the bier as the others had done. He merely glanced for one poignant moment at the beautiful face and then looked away, as if he could not bear the sight. But what a world of love there was in that look.

"I sat at his side for three days before the end, I whose profession it is to sit at the side of the dying and to comfort them," Judah began. "And I am witness that his dying was like no other I have ever seen. For he lay always with a pleasant and merry countenance, embarrassed almost to be causing inconvenience to others by his leaving, as a gentleman would be who must make an awkward or precipitous exit. Not once did he cry out.

Nor did he speak of pain except to reassure me that he felt none. How can one describe so kindly and modest a spirit? If there are words, it needs a poet, not a physician, to voice them. Even with the coming of those twitches and pangs which foretell the end, he never spoke of despair or fear but only the opposite. Yesterday, after an exhausting seizure, he whispered to me that he beheld the heavens opening to receive him. Today he is with the angels. But he is with us in spirit. He lives in our hearts, may God bless his soul."

After that, someone said a prayer in Latin and then the group dispersed, leaving Judah to sit the night out in watch, as he had requested. I left him hunched over a slim morocco-bound volume of the *Phaedrus*, his lips repeating the words so dear to his young patron and himself, more shrouded in his black cloak than the bright figure on the bier in his white linen.

A maid saw me to my room, a chamber stripped bare of all excepting the essentials. There were no furnishings beyond the bed, a single *cassone*, and the candles. No furs, no hangings, tapestries, or wall decorations, not even rushes. But what little was there was of the finest quality, the coverlet woven of a linen thread so fine that it felt like satin to my hand, the candles pure white and smokeless, the crucifix on the wall facing my bed studded with large rubies and emeralds. The floor beneath my feet was bare. But it gleamed as wood will that is lovingly polished with beeswax. And the single pillow was stuffed to its limits with softest down—no feathers or other cheap stuff here. And I was brought two bricks wrapped in towels to warm my hands and feet.

In such a fresh, luxurious surround I ought to have drifted off at once. The silence all around told me that everyone else in the household had done so. Yet, much as I wished to lose myself in sleep, I could not. The body below haunted me. The rumors of Pico's comeliness had not prepared me for the great beauty of that face. In every way this Pico had been the perfect model of a prince, a stunning contrast to the live king I had seen earlier that day propped up on his charger.

My mind wandered back to the procession, to the Florentines shouting "Francia! Francia!" to welcome their conquerors. What awaited us there on the morrow? Thus far the French had behaved well. But how long could such a motley collection hold together? The Scottish bowmen especially had frightened me. So tall and so savage. I needed to see Judah—to get his reassurance that all would be well with us. That we would not be seized, robbed, tied, raped...Throwing off the quilt, I quickly dove into my *gamorra* and crept out into the corridor.

It was a long, cold, unfriendly space lit only by a flickering candle positioned to illuminate a small panel of the Virgin in the Sienese style. A forbidding sentinel of the staircase, her wide, unseeing eyes stared out at me from her niche at the end of the corridor. Instinctively I crouched down as I passed beneath her, as if to avoid that reproachful gaze.

Down the staircase I crept, stealthily so as not to wake the dead, across the vast reception hall hung with ghostly tapestries that muffled all sound, and cold enough to chill your blood. At the portal of the room where Count Pico's body lay, I hesi tated for a long moment, reluctant to violate the eerie silence that enveloped the place. But I had come too far to turn back.

I thrust aside the heavy drapery. The scene drew me toward the bier, closer and closer, unable to resist the sight: Judah, unconscious of my presence, on his knees at Pico's side, his tears falling unchecked on the dead face like a soft salty rain. He was mumbling, muttering, keening, clasping and unclasping the dead hands in his own, swaying back and forth over that dead body as Jews do when they recite the prayer for the dead. But what Judah was whispering was no prayer for the dead.

"My beloved..." I heard. "There is no sun without you and no moon. Only grayness. And tears." And, sobbing: "Speak to me one last time. Tell me I am forgiven. That you love me. Oh, speak..." And I saw him raise one of those dead hands to his lips and cover it with kisses. Then, as if the hand was not enough to feed his great hunger, he laid it aside and fell upon the face, covering it with kisses, lifting the head to gaze into the closed eyes and kissing the dead mouth as passionately as if he held a woman in his arms.

He saw me then, turned and saw me. And with an agonized groan, he heaved himself to his feet and staggered from the room, clutching his head in his hands like a great wounded beast.

31

ILENCE HUNG OVER JUDAH AND ME LIKE A HEAVY cloud as we plodded homeward from the Fiesole heights. Even the horses became sullen and skittish. Judah came close to being thrown when his mount unaccountably shied at a crossing. And twice he had to dismount and lead the neighing horse across the stream on foot. That animal has caught the contagion from us, I thought. He knows we are descending into some kind of hell.

But Judah, who must have been gathering his courage all through the tortuous descent, finally found the will to break the silence when we stopped outside the city walls to water the horses.

"Grazia, I understand how you feel. You feel lied to, betrayed. But I swear to you there has been nothing between him and me since our marriage."

I felt the pressure of his hand on my arm and shook it off. "Don't touch me!" The words leapt from my throat.

"Very well. But may I speak?" The question was put in a pitifully suppliant voice I had never heard before.

I nodded my assent.

"I swear by all that is holy to me that when I married you I believed it was over. But then the fever got its hold on him and I thought he might die..." He hesitated, hoping no doubt for an encouraging word from me. But I had no encouragement to give him.

"This passion was not a thing that either he or I pursued," he went on. "Like the Furies, it pursued us."

"When men succumb to weakness, they blame the gods," I told him. "I thought you were above such self-deception."

"Have it any way you wish," he replied. "Call me a weakling—"

"Worse, a deceiver," I cut in, showing my anger now. "The deception is what hurts the most. Calling me your little wife when you never meant to make me wife. Blaming my youth for our barren bed when it was your love for another that kept us apart."

"But I did believe we would take up a life as man and wife someday..."

"Someday," I echoed.

He buried his head in his hands, and only after a long wait did he lift his eyes to meet mine. "My nature is flawed, Grazia, deeply flawed. I am a sinner. A deceiver. But I never meant you harm." Again he touched my arm, but this time he withdrew it before I could throw it off. "I am what I am, Grazia. Knowing that, will you still have me for your husband?"

"No!" My pride had been stomped on and I could not rise above my wounds. "No," I repeated, "I will not be your wife."

"Do you wish a divorce, then?"

"No." As before, the words issued from my throat unwilled.

"What then?"

"At this moment I do not feel you are my friend. Friends do not lie to one another. And love does not betray," I told him, speaking the words just as they came to me. "After what I saw last night the role of wife seems to me a travesty. I am no wife to you nor are you husband to me or ever have been. But I have known you as friend and perhaps I can again. Let us go back to the time before our marriage. You spoke to me then of being loving friends and nothing more. Maybe we can regain that friendship. I will try. But this time, no lies, Judah."

In that understanding we took up our life together once more. But now it was Judah who moved toward me at night in bed, looking for warmth, while I turned my back and retreated into my own world of dreams. And he was the one who kept his vow to be a loving friend whereas I, in spite of my resolve, found myself dishonoring my pledge every day. Sometimes I betrayed myself with a bitter word, sometimes with a look, often with a gesture of dismissal if Judah dared even the slightest evidence of tenderness toward me. An ice crust had formed around my heart that would not melt.

Servants are the most accurate gauge of domestic discord, the first to know when it heats up and when it cools down. So it was not entirely surprising to me when one day in the midst of our perusal of Boccaccio, my pupil, Medina, broke off his translating and asked, "Is something wrong, madonna? You speak so coldly these days. Is it my fault?"

I had become so flooded with bile that even this boy could sense it. "I do not hate you, Medina," I answered softly. "But I am very sad. I have suffered a deep disappointment."

"I know, madonna."

What did he know? I bent down, lifted his chin in my hands and set his face at a level with mine. The almond eyes were half closed as usual. His breath smelled of cloves, an expensive remedy against the garlic breath I had complained of.

"Where did you get the cloves, Medina?" I asked.

"From the master, madonna."

"Four of those must have cost you a month's wages."

The long, curled black lashes swept over his face coquettishly. "They were a gift, madonna." Then he added, "The master loves you more than his own life, madonna."

There it was again, that insinuating intimacy, as if he had been present at Fiesole.

"Leave me now, Medina," I ordered him. "There will be no lesson today."

But he did not obey. He stayed there kneeling at my feet, smelling of cloves.

"Go now," I repeated.

Still he did not move.

"What is it, Medina? Speak or get out."

"I no longer wish to study Maestro Boccaccio, madonna. I wish to study the poet Terence."

I was prepared for any insolence but not for this strange request. "You have never displayed the slightest interest in the ancients," I answered. "Why now?"

"We can all learn from Terence, madonna. It was he who said, 'I am a man and nothing human is alien to me.' Which means that we must forgive and pity. My master says that justice is a brutal whip in the hands of someone untouched by *caritas*."

"He is not the first to make that observation, Medina," I commented. "The Christian apostle Mark made the same point more than a dozen hundred years ago."

"Which only strengthens the case, madonna. All of life is a revelation of the one perfect truth, madonna. All earthly faiths are imperfect strivings after that perfect faith and thus resemble each other more and more, the closer we come to the perfection of perfect love — *caritas*."

"What has all this to do with Terence, Medina?"

He shook his head, confused for the moment by the necessity to explain himself. Then, he simply resumed his oration. "I speak of harmony, madonna, and the divinity of man. As the great Pico has written in his oration on the dignity of man, (Did I see a sly grimace pass over his face when he spoke the name Pico?) all is the word of God, the stars in the heavens, the elements of the earth, the voices of nature, the *senses* of men..."

"Enough!" I had had a gutful of this prattle. "What are you getting at, Medina? Spit it out!"

Whereupon he took a deep breath, leaned forward, and pointing his finger at me like an avenging angel, intoned in a manner worthy of Savonarola himself, "I am a man and nothing human is alien to me. We can all learn from Terence, madonna."

Then, as if his courage had left him in one great voiding, he scurried to the door and fled.

I never saw that boy again. When Judah returned home for dinner I asked him to dismiss Medina at once. An insolence too humiliating to repeat, I told him. I did not offer the details. He did not press me.

By evening, the boy's few belongings were packed and sent off. He did not appear the next morning nor ever again at our portal. But every time I saw Judah leave our house and head in the direction of the river where the Spaniards lived, I wondered if he was gone to visit his boy Medina with a little packet of cloves tucked into his pocket or a small book of verse — perhaps Pindar's odes to the athletes, their backs arched like bows.

I never asked Judah where he went when he turned left instead of right. And the name of Medina was added to the name of Count Pico della Mirandola on the unwritten list of names not to be mentioned in the arid conversations between us.

Poor Judah. Everything in his life went wrong at the same moment. He lost the man he loved. His comfortable charade of a marriage was shattered. Piero dei Medici's exile wiped out the Platonic Academy, his haven of camaraderie and intellectual delight. The dispersal of the Laurentian Library robbed him of his sinecure as librarian of the now-scattered Medici collection. Deprived of friends, work, and love, he was left stranded on an island of domestic discord with a shrew for company.

But Fortuna, who has always kept a weather eye out for Judah, looked down, and seeing one of her favorites brought so low, determined to end his penance. This she did in her usual whimsical way, by granting him the least of all his heart's desires. She enlisted him again into the service of the King of France, now firmly established as the conqueror of Napoli and an avid student of Neapolitan *dolce far niente*. With this shining example before them, his troops, loyal Frenchmen every one, set about to follow their sovereign's dalliance along the prim-rose path. And soon there appeared among the soldiers a virulent new affliction known by the French as "the love disease" and by the Neapolitans as "the French boils." By whatever name, it seriously threatened the health of the King's army. Once again the French monarch had need of his specialist in diseases below the navel. Judah left at once for Napoli.

Less than a week later I received a letter from my stepmother, Dorotea, urging me to come to Mantova without delay. Some trouble with the Gonzagas, so horrendous in its consequences that she could not write of it.

Her letter left me as ignorant of the nature of the impending catastrophe in Mantova as Judah was of the nature of the mysterious love disease that had disabled the French army in Napoli. But we each of us answered the call and took off, Judah to the south, I to the north. Fortuna had willed it.

MANTOVA
AGAIN

32

MY FATHER'S NEW HOUSE WAS SITUATED ON THE western edge of Mantova hard by the Porta Mulina. Riding in through that gate, I was spared the sight of the places that might desolate my spirit with reminders of loss: our old home near the fish market, where I had left my childhood; the Piazza delle Erbe, where I lost my innocent belief in the world's goodwill; the Reggio, where I had been severed from the man I loved.

Moments after we had passed through the gate, we headed into a street lettered "Via San Simone," and our porter called out to me to halt my horse. This was it, he shouted, number five, the number Dorotea had written in her letter. I had noted the house as we turned the corner—a strikingly angled building on the corner with a most beautiful carved balustrade around the loggia—and had ridden on past it, never for a moment thinking that this palazzo could be my father's house. It was much too grand. Almost twice the width of our old house, with a polychromed facade and in a very exposed location for the house of a Jew.

"Are you certain this is it?" I asked doubtfully. Then I heard,

"Here she is! Here she is! It is Grazia come home!" and out into the street poured my family: Dorotea, her features composed into a false smile; at her side, Ricca, still lumpish like her mother; Asher, fat and bashful; standing modestly to one side, my darling Penina, thin and bent like a bamboo reed; dodging in and out among them, Jehiel, showing the beginnings of a barrel chest; and Gershom, a pensive seven-year-old with a perfect oval face and black coals for eyes. As I embraced him I vowed to take him back to Firenze with me and teach him how to smile.

But where was my father?

"Your father is resting," Dorotea volunteered before I had a chance to ask. "I would not wake him even for you, Grazia, he sleeps so fitfully."

My father a fitful sleeper? He always slept like a stone.

"What ails him, Dorotea?" I asked her directly. "Your letter was marvelously vague."

"I did not have the heart to write it," she answered. For once, I believed her. There were black smudges under her eyes that often come from sleepless nights.

"I want to know what is happening here, Dorotea," I pressed her. "Why have I been called?"

What I got in reply was a prolonged sigh and a quiver of the lower lip. "Take me to him," I instructed her. Better to make my own investigation than try to penetrate a veil of tears.

"I will take you, cousin." Asher stepped forward. What a kind, open countenance he had. Why had I never noticed?

We found my father in his *studiolo* wrapped in a blanket, dozing in a chair, lost in it, small and shrunken in his shawl, and with a yellowish tinge to his skin. Liver, I thought. Then I stopped thinking and simply threw my arms around him and hugged him with all my strength.

At first, he struggled against my embrace. I had surprised him in his sleep. But then, I heard him mumble, "Graziella *mia*," and felt his arms close around me. And we stayed there clasping each other for God knows how many minutes until I became aware of a discreet clearing of the throat behind me and realized that Asher must still be with us. I released my hold on Papa—he seemed so light in my arms—and calling up my utmost courtesy so as not to insult the good fellow, I asked my cousin if he would be good enough to leave us.

He bobbed one of his awkward little bows and made haste to oblige me. Obviously, the role of eavesdropper was uncongenial to him.

I must remember, I thought, not to lump him together with his mother and sister; for he is a completely different article.

As if to reinforce the thought, he mumbled shyly as he passed me, "I am glad you have come, Grazia." And was gone.

"Asher has grown into a fine fellow," I remarked to my father.

"He is my right hand, only steadier," Papa answered, holding up his trembling right hand to prove the truth of the metaphor. "I could not have got on without him these past weeks."

"What about Jehiel? Is he too young for the *banco*?" I asked.

"Your brother will always be too young." Papa smiled indulgently. "He is a tinkerer. A dreamer. Perhaps someday he will make an engineer. But a banker, never. Now, the little one is another story."

"Gershom?"

"He took to the abacus like an infant to the tit. Thrives on it."

"He looks so solemn, Papa. Does he ever smile?"

"He is a worrier like you, daughter."

"But not such a trial as I was?"

"Few children are." Again, the indulgent smile. Who was this stranger with the low voice and air of resignation? What had happened to my contumacious father?

"What is wrong with you, Papa?" I asked him.

"Some months back, there was an episode out in the street. Ruffians, *ignoranti*. In the melee a stone struck me on the back. Maestro Portaleone says it caused a tumor to grow on my kidney. He has prescribed a poultice to ease my discomfort."

A poultice for a tumor? What nonsense was this? And what was the meaning of this "discomfort" he spoke of? *Dio*, I do hate it when physicians refer to pain as "discomfort."

"Are you in pain, Papa?" I asked.

"A little. Sometimes when I change my position..." He shifted his body to show me and grimaced noticeably from the exertion.

"You *are* in pain."

"My pain is eased by the sight of you," he replied. Eased, perhaps, but not removed. The tight creases at the corners of his mouth told me that much. Clearly I must get Judah to come at once. At once.

Meantime I must not continue to aggravate the patient's misery by interjecting my unease into his tranquillity.

"What can I do to aid in your convalescence, Papa?" I asked, putting on as cheerful a face as I could. "Is there some special thing I can cook that might whet your appetite? Or would you like me to read to you? Virgil, perhaps."

"Perhaps. In the evenings."

"This very evening if you like, Papa. But what of the days? I have come all this way to serve you. You must give me something to do."

He sighed and paused, a pause so long that I thought he might have let go the thread of our conversation. But at length, he picked it up. "I hate to ask this of you, Grazia. You are a married woman now. With a position to uphold. The wife of a great scholar..."

"Tell me, Papa," I interrupted him. "Whatever it is, tell me and I will do it. I assure you Judah would want me to."

"I do not wish you to demean yourself. Your position in the world..."

"Anything, Papa," I insisted. "Do you wish me to wash your feet? Comb the lice out of your head? The lowliest task would give me pleasure..."

He held up his shaking hand to stop me. "Nothing like that, daughter. It is the *banco* I am concerned about. Francesco Gonzaga is about to be reappointed Captain-General of the Venetian army. He will need ready cash to tide him over until the Venetian gold starts to flow. The Gonzagas are shrewd bargainers, especially the wife, Madonna Isabella. And I fear I have not the strength for a battle. I am asking you to take my place in the *banco* and deal with him when he comes to us, which he is sure to do. Asher is a fine young man and willing, but inexperienced. You are the only one I can trust to deal with the Gonzagas."

"But I will adore to do that, Papa. Am I not a pawnbroker's daughter born and bred and trained by you?" As I spoke I could feel the weight of the coins in my fingers and the itch of the horsehair cushion I sat on in the little *banco* in Bologna where I had been daughter, student, helper—everything—to my father.

"I will miss you at my side, Papa," I told him.

"And I you, daughter." He reached up and touched my cheek. "So beautiful." His fingers felt dry and cold on my flushed skin. "You have become such a fine woman. Your mother would be proud of you."

"You would not always have said so, Papa," I chided him gently.

"Oh yes I would," he corrected me, more spirit in that one denial than in all his conversation with me thus far. "Many times in the past you have rubbed my patience like a rough burr. But you have never shamed me."

Unthinking, I bent on one knee and lowered my head before him as I had been taught to do by the Christians when blessed. Indeed my father's benediction was to me as hard-won as God's and twice as treasured.

When I left him a few moments later, I found my friend Penina waiting for me on the landing.

"Come." She took my hand and led me up a narrow flight of stairs to her attic chamber. It was a room with rafters so low that even I, who am not a tall woman, could hardly stand straight without bumping my head on them. "My bed is yours to share if you wish it, Grazia," she offered.

It was a tempting offer. But I knew that if I was to achieve any authority in this house, I must command a space in which I could stand tall. A household is like any other establishment, be it a royal court or a chicken house. Certain stations count for more than others. The place one occupies at table, the place one sleeps—these bespeak authority more eloquently than words. In case you have not noticed, duchesses do not sleep in attics. With heartfelt regret I refused Penina's offer and set forth to pick myself a fine bed and a proper place to put it.

The bed I chose with Asher's help was only the second-best one in our warehouse. The best bed was a heavily carved thing from Marchesana Barbara's time, when things German were the fashion in Mantova. My choice was more modern but with enough gilt carving on it to proclaim its owner's consequence.

The next decision: Where should I establish my command post? After considering the possibilities I chose the *sala piccola* where Dorotea sat to her sewing with the women of the household. How better to establish one's place in another woman's house than to take over her sitting room?

Leaving a porter to see to the hauling, I then went to search for some fine linens and a coverlet. A red satin one caught my eye at once, but I resisted—I was growing up—and selected a cover of Persian wool from the place they call Cachemire. Very soft and elegant. And warm too.

When I returned to the house with my treasures, I found Dorotea standing in her *sala* beside my bed, hands on hips, shouting at the top of her voice for the porter who had put it there to take it away.

"I ordered it put here," I informed her sweetly. "It is my bed. And this is to be my room as long as I live here."

No explanation did I give. No excuse. No apology. Time had taught me something about dealing with bullies.

That afternoon, I resumed my old seat in the *banco*. For a moment when I first climbed onto the strongbox to sit behind the green-covered table, the years fell away and I was again that raggedy creature girdled in paste jewels who sat dreaming that a knight would stride in and carry her away to an earthly paradise. But one look at the faces around me wiped that image from my mind. What I saw reflected in their admiring eyes was a fashionable young woman in a fine wool *gamorra*, low-cut in the Florentine style, her hair caught up in a golden filet — a gift from Diamante — gathered on her forehead by a fine, large pearl — a gift from Judah. And in truth, I was an ornament in that dreary little provincial *banco*. The envy in Ricca's eyes when she came in and beheld me enthroned on my high banker's chair was especially delectable to me.

In the evening, old doctor Portaleone came at my bidding, bringing along his fellow croupier in the game of life and death, Rabbi Abramo. The interview was protracted and acrimonious. Taking the longest way around, they informed me that my father was suffering from an incurable tumor and that he would die within the year. Perhaps within months. That from the physician. And from the other one, a reworking of the old saw "God is just and everything He does is for the best."

Every time I hear that phrase I could spit in God's eye. My father was a man who had never harmed a soul intentionally. I could not accept the sentence so easily pronounced on him by the very ones charged with saving his life. I ranted. I raved. In the end I told them both to go to hell and wrote off a long letter to Napoli begging Judah to come at once and save my father from the jaws of death, because this doctor and this priest together would surely kill him.

There remained Dorotea to deal with and I proceeded to the task with relish. I found her in the garden.

"Why did you not tell me that my father was knocking on death's door?" I berated her.

"I did not have the heart." She sniffed and dabbed at her nose.

"You did not have the wit is more like it. What if we have left this tumor to fester there too long? What if he could have been saved?"

"Maestro Portaleone told me that there was no hope. It is God's judgment on us for our sins. This house is cursed," she went on. "I castigate myself every day that I agreed to move here."

"It was not your wish?" I asked.

"Your honored father was bound to have it. And you know him when he sets his mind on something." Indeed I did. All it took was a nudge from the right elbow to dislodge him. The woman was lying in her teeth.

"Well, it seems Papa is being repaid for his obduracy," I remarked, baiting the trap. "And I shall chide him for it when I see him."

"No. Do not do that." She clasped my sleeve urgently. "Do not mention this cursed house, please, Grazia. It will only add to his misery."

Now I was in no doubt that this grand house had been bought at her instigation.

"Tell me about this curse," I urged her.

"It is a long terrible story..." she temporized.

"Start," I ordered. And after some sniffing of the bubble on the end of her nose, she began.

"This house was the property of a Christian silk merchant called Pagano. His business fell on evil days. He needed money, hundreds of ducats to cover his debts. He came to the *banco* to borrow it. But he had no security, only this house. So I said to Daniele—" She caught herself short and started again. "I said to Daniele, 'Do not buy the silk merchant's house, honored husband. It is out of the district of our friends where we are safe. And much too visible a residence for a family of Jews.'"

"But he insisted?" I prodded.

"Yes," she sighed, and moved on quickly. "Now, this Pagano was one of those Christian scoundrels who steal and cheat all week, then light expensive candles on Sundays for forgiveness. *You* know how they do it, Grazia..." I let the comment pass.

"Well, Pagano must have pulled off some monstrous cheat," she continued, "for not only had he given money to all the convents in town, he had hired an apprentice from Messer Andrea Mantegna's workshop to paint a likeness of the Virgin over his door with a little shrine under it. That was the one thing about the house that your father disliked."

What about the marble halls and the carved friezes above the portals? Had my father suddenly in the thirty-eighth year of his life developed a taste for ostentation? I doubted it.

"Daniele swore he would not live under the sign of the Virgin even if he were offered the entire Reggio as his palace," she went on. "He said that to do so was a double offense to God since it broke two of His commandments."

The reference to the commandments sounded as if it had come out of my father's mouth. It was her way to weave in a strand or two of truth with the lies so that one could not pick them apart.

"And what did you answer to that, Dorotea?" I asked innocently.

"I told him we must take steps to remove that Virgin," she replied.

"Easier said than done," I remarked.

"We sought permission directly from the Marchesana Isabella so that there would be no trouble afterwards." Again Madonna Isabella. Would I never be free of the woman?

"Why did you not approach Marchese Francesco?" I asked.

"He is rarely at home these days. He is raising an army to fight the French king. The Venetians have named him General of the Holy League."

"And does he leave all decisions to his wife, then?" I asked.

"The girl rules Mantova like a queen. Imagine a twenty-year-old lording it over all the graybeards at the Reggio. It's amazing."

Knowing Madonna Isabella, I was not amazed at all. She certainly had the bearing for it. And the nerve.

"And what did the *illustrissima* say to your petition?" I asked.

"She sent us to the bishop and he gave us permission on the spot to have the image erased, in return for several fine chalices we held in pawn."

"And plenty of ducats into the bargain, I'll wager."

"How clever of you to guess that, Grazia."

No guesswork was needed. Everyone knows that all priests have their price.

"So what is the great commotion about, Dorotea? You got the permission, erased the Virgin, and moved in. Whence comes this nonsense about a curse?" I asked. "All you've told me so far is a simple tale of greedy Jews who lust after *lusso* and fall victim to blackmail on account of it. The only mystery is how this happened to the dei Rossis. I had thought we were above such vulgarity."

"Oh, Grazia, I fear you blame me for our misfortunes." Good. She recognized the portrait of her that I had just drawn. "But you are quite wrong," she went on. "I could not have known that this house had a curse on it."

"What curse?" I asked.

"The Virgin's curse. That is what the men shouted when they attacked this house and stoned us and wounded your father. That they were avenging the Virgin."

Finally I understood her mysterious letter. My father's wound, the evasions and lies that had met me at every turn, all centered on this accursed house and this accursedly acquisitive woman. "Look at me," I ordered. And she complied.

"It was not my father but you who wanted this house, Dorotea." She hung her head, a tacit admission.

"You worked on him as you know how to do. And to his discredit he gave in and agreed to buy a house he never wanted and that he must have known would bring only trouble and misery to his family. Well, now you have your heart's desire and my father lies upstairs in what you call this cursed house, dying for your covetousness. Oh, this house is cursed all right, Dorotea. Not by the Christian Virgin. By you." And fed to the teeth with the sight of that duplicitous face, I turned away from her and headed for the door.

"Oh, Grazia, I fear you hate me," she wailed.

"No, Dorotea. When I was weak and powerless I hated you. Now that I am a woman with my own place in the world, hatred is beneath me. Now, I merely despise you."

33

J UDAH RESPONDED TO MY DESPERATE SUMMONS AT
once, as I knew he would. But Napoli is a far way from
Mantova and I spent the weeks between my confrontation
with Dorotea and Judah's arrival suspended in time like a fly
in amber, waiting, watching, hoping, and praying.

The *banco* became both my fortress and my comfort. Its only
defect was the constant presence of Ricca, who made herself at
home there, galloping through the place like a baby elephant,
braying loudly and knocking things over with her wide sleeves.

Once I began to take notice of her presence, I observed
that somehow she always managed to bump into Jehiel on her
peregrinations. And then to blame him loudly for the collision
and to poke and prod him until they both exploded into fits of
giggles.

High spirits, I told myself. Pranks. But one night something
happened that forced me to acknowledge what I had been
unwilling to admit. After putting Papa to bed for the night, the
famiglia had gathered to enjoy the cool of evening in the garden.
Jehiel was sitting on the bench next to me with Ricca on his
other side. The days are long in June and dusk comes late. In

the half-light, I saw him reach over and press his index finger into the nipple of one of Ricca's half-exposed breasts, laughing while he did it. And she laughed too. They must have thought themselves hidden by the gathering dark. But Penina, sitting beside me, gasped. And I saw Asher, who was sitting on a little bench some distance off, half rise in response to what he had seen, then sink back into the shadows. But Dorotea did not sink back. She smiled.

After that, there was no way for me to avoid the truth nor, I felt, my responsibility to act on it. As we were leaving the garden I grasped Dorotea's hand tightly and asked her to stay behind. I think she knew she had gone too far in so openly encouraging what could only be construed as lewd behavior. She pleaded a headache and made as if to take her hand away. But I held firm.

"It is important, Dorotea," I told her. "Your headache will have to wait. Something must be done about Jehiel and Ricca."

"Why so?" she asked, forcing her heavy-lidded eyes into an openness that would convey innocence. "I believe it is a matter for rejoicing that they get on so well. A brother and sister. Just as it should be."

"A brother and sister on the verge of tumbling into bed together," I advised her. "Perhaps you mistake where you are. This is the household of Daniele dei Rossi, not Rodrigo Borgia."

"You shame yourself to say such things, Grazia." Her thick eyelids made a clumsy attempt at a flutter. What do men see in these coarse-grained vulgar women? One look at the swing of those plump asses tells the whole story. In some sense all men are bulls and all women cows.

"Jehiel has become a true brother to my Ricca," she advised me proudly. "Your honorable father and I take that as a blessing."

"For Jehiel to be a brother to Ricca certainly is a blessing," I replied. "To be a lover is incest." There, I had said the word. To my surprise she took it most mildly.

"They are cousins, not brother and sister," she informed me.

"First cousins," I added. "And Ricca is three years older than Jehiel. He is a child. A boy."

"He is close to fifteen years old. Old enough to marry."

"Marry!"

"You forget that time passes, Grazia," she went on. "Boys grow into men. If anything were to happen to your honored father, Jehiel would be the head of this family."

So that was the strategy. To wait until my father was dead, then to marry Jehiel off to Ricca so that she and her mother might enjoy the lion's share of Papa's estate.

I left that garden saddened and dismayed. Of course, I would attempt to talk some sense into Jehiel. But what proof were my arguments against Ricca's bulging breasts and hot lips? As I mounted the stairs to Papa's room I heard a scuffling sound from under the stairwell. Then a moan of pleasure. It was my brother and his whorish cousin, for sure. I turned back, intending to upbraid them for their wantonness, then stopped myself. Anything I did now to deprive Jehiel of his pleasure would only exacerbate his appetite for it.

Wearily, I trudged up the stairs to look in on my father. He lay still. But as I watched, he turned slightly and the wrench of that turn forced a moan of pain from between his lips. Down the stairs the son moaned with pleasure. Upstairs the father moaned in pain. And I stood suspended between the two, powerless to hinder or to help. Come soon, Judah, I thought. For I cannot bear this alone much longer.

Judah rode into Mantova within a week, a ghostly apparition, his black cloak grayed with dust, his face pale with fatigue and pain. For my sake, he had forsworn his mule in favor of a horse, a way of sitting that always anguishes his backbone.

As I sat beside his bath pouring warm water over his head, I observed that his hair had turned quite white. And the heavy lines in his forehead had deepened into furrows. With a great toss of his giant frame, he called for a towel and within minutes was combed, dried, and dressed in clean linen, ready to visit my father.

It was a most peculiar examination even for a physician with unorthodox methods. Judah did not so much as touch my father except to kiss him on the cheek. Nor did he inquire after Papa's condition but merely passed the time in idle chat, talking of the French king's pursuit of pleasure in Napoli, and of the new papal alliance that was forming against the foolish Frenchman, instigated by, of all the unlikely supporters, the King's sponsor and best friend, Lodovico Sforza of Milano. "Apparently the Duke's eyesight has been restored," Judah commented wryly, "and he can now recognize the face of Italy." Which brought a smile to Papa's wan countenance.

That smile—so rare with Papa those days—captured far more of my attention than Judah's clever talk of affairs. And I was only half listening when he went on to predict that from this league would arise a wave of violence that was sure to wash over all of Italy. What was Italy to me compared with Papa's illness?

"Now, wife..." Judah turned to me when we had taken our leave of my father. "Will you do me the honor to walk out with me into the town? I have need of your company for I am bound on a delicate diplomatic errand at the Reggio."

What of Papa? I wanted to know.

"We will speak of that in good time, I promise you," he answered. "But for now, do me a good turn and get out that beautiful silk *gamorra* that you wheedled out of me for your birth gift. And all your jewels. I do not wish the doctor's wife to take second place to Lady Chiara."

"Lady Chiara? Who is she?"

"Sister-in-law to Madonna Isabella. Sister to the Marchese Francesco. Married to the French king's nephew on the Bourbon side. His name is Gilbert de Montpensier."

"But what business do you have with—" Before I could finish, he placed his fingers gently over my mouth to cut off my question. "If you accept my proposal to walk out with me I will tell you *all* on the way to the Reggio."

He did not need my company on his errand. In all likelihood he could have managed the interview better alone. But he knew the news in store for me, had known it, he told me much later, after one look into Papa's eyes. And he had concocted his need for my company to prop up my spirits before he laid the burden on me.

As we stepped out of the Casa dei Rossi into the sunlit day he took a deep lungful of air, held it, expelled it, and then demanded that I do the same. "Let us enjoy to the full this glorious day that God has given us. He would fault us if we were to tarnish His golden light with dark thoughts of what tomorrow might bring," he instructed me.

If Rabbi Abramo had heard such pagan sentiments attributed to his God, he would have damned the speaker as a heretic there and then. But Judah's God was a humanist's God for whom all things move from goodness to goodness and Who commands us to rejoice in the present. Taking my cue from Judah, I set about to exercise my lungs in the fine air and to satisfy my curiosity as to his business with Chiara Gonzaga, wife to Gilbert, Duke of Montpensier, nephew of the King of France. It was not like Judah to take up intimacy with either foreigners or Christians. With a certain notable exception, I reminded myself. Could it be that this Montpensier had become the successor to Pico della Mirandola?

His next remark disabused me of my suspicions. "We have found common cause, the Frenchman and I," he explained as we walked. "Both of us are far from home, both lonely, both exiled by the whim of the King. And both our wives have taken refuge in Mantova. Besides, he is quite civilized for a Frenchman. Eats with a fork just as we do. And worries about his little son and what will become of the boy should he be left fatherless with only an Italian mother and his negligent uncle, the King, to protect him. Part of my charge is to bring the little fellow a gift from his papa's own hands."

Part of his charge? "And the rest?" I asked.

But by then we had reached the Reggio and I had to rest content with a muttered "Later" for my answer.

The Duchess of Montpensier did not look Italian. Her years in France had transformed her in a way difficult to pin down,

yet quite unmistakable. What had she gained there? A languid-
ness of gesture, a rarefied elegance, a contemptuously arrogant
expression that Italian women—including princesses—do not
cultivate. What had she lost? Vitality. Her eyes had a faraway
look. Even as she listened she appeared not to hear what was
said to her. Either she was stupid or the lassitude of the French
courtly style had weakened her strong Gonzaga blood.

"Maestro Leone, how kind of you to come," she trilled in her
French-accented Italian.

"My pleasure, ma'am." Judah bowed low. I have always been
surprised at how well he can play the courtier when he must.
"I bring regards from your illustrious husband and gifts from
his own hand." Reaching under his cloak, he drew out a small
cloth bag and a rather larger wooden cask. "The jewel is for
you, madonna. The *cassone* is for your honorable son Charles."

She clapped her hands together, as delighted as a girl.

"Do let me see the jewel."

Silence as she opened the bag and spilled out of it a coral
bead framed in diamonds. "How beautiful!" she exclaimed,
and held it up to her bosom at the place where it might properly
hang from a chain. "Is it not beautiful, is it not a masterwork?"

"The Neapolitans are renowned for their cameo carvings,"
Judah agreed. "Come and look, Grazia." He beckoned me.

"Oh yes, do," the Duchess added agreeably, although until
that moment she had made no sign to acknowledge my
presence.

"May I present my wife, ma'am."

I made the obligatory low curtsy.

"Have you ever seen anything more exquisite?" she asked
me. Then, without waiting for a reply, she bubbled on: "My
sister-in-law, Madonna Isabella, will envy me this treasure.
She does love jewels. Now then..." The lady looked up briefly
from her perusal of her treasure. "Will there be anything else?"

"About the gift for your son Charles, ma'am..." Judah
handed her the *cassone*. "They are toy soldiers and the Duke
most particularly asked me to have his son receive them in my

presence. There are two sets in this box—one molded in metal and one carved in wood by a most skilled Neapolitan master. His father wishes him to choose."

"I believe he is in his room with his tutor, ma'am." The maid spoke up. "If you recall, he was suffering from toothache . . ."

"Oh yes. Toothache. Well, see if he is well enough to join us, Mathilde." Then, turning to Judah: "I beg you, Maestro Leone, do not report this toothache to the Duke. My honorable husband takes every sniffle of that child as seriously as a death rattle. Believe me, the boy is perfectly sound."

"I do believe you, ma'am. And of course I will refrain from referring to this toothache if you wish it."

"Oh, you are everything they say of you, Maestro Leone— kind, discreet, and skillful. We must all be grateful for the service you rendered to our cousin the King. We are told that you cured him of the pox when all other efforts availed nothing."

Judah lowered his head modestly. "I was honored to be of service, madonna."

Now the little boy Charles was brought in, a handsome enough child with a thin intelligent face and a brooding air.

"This is Maestro Leone Ebreo and his lady, Charles." His mother presented us. "He has brought you something from your father."

"Papa? You have seen my papa?" The child's eyes lit up.

"I see your honored parent every day, sire," Judah replied. "And he has commissioned me to present you with the contents of this box. May I?"

Judah reached for the little cask which the boy's mother had not even troubled herself to look into. "*Voilà!*" He pushed a concealed button on the underside of the box and the top sprang open, a trick which brought a most delicious sparkle into the boy's eyes and a bored yawn to his mother. No doubt about it, the woman had spent too long in France.

"May I take them out?" the boy asked eagerly, looking from Judah to his mother and back as if uncertain where the authority lay.

"Your honorable father has some choice in mind for you. The gentleman will explain it." The Duchess waved her hand vaguely. "Now I fear you must excuse me. Stay with him, Mathilde, and take him back to his tutor when this matter is settled." And out she floated, back to whatever far-off country she inhabited in her mind.

Before long, Judah and little Charles Bourbon had all the soldiers out of the box and were engaged in a life-and-death struggle — metal against wood — on the floor. Poor little boy, I thought to myself. Locked up here with this vapid mother and cut off from the father he obviously adores.

The afternoon at the Reggio ended oddly and in retrospect very interestingly. Little Charles begged Judah to stay on and on — how that boy longed for his father. But we did have to go. And at the end of the visit Judah told the boy he must make his choice between the wooden and the lead soldiers. Until then, he had behaved quite normally for a five-year-old boy. But faced with the necessity to make a choice, he became a different child.

"But I love them both, maestro. I cannot choose. I cannot," he cried out with real anguish.

"Perhaps if you consider what you like about each set…" Judah suggested sympathetically.

"No, I cannot. I must have both." The boy was working himself into a most unhealthy state.

"But the Duke most particularly wished you to have a choice."

"No." The child was crying now and holding his head. "If I cannot have both I shall have none."

"Is it that you love them both so much?" I asked.

"No."

"Then why?"

The child leaned forward toward me and in a voice that was almost a whisper confided, "I like the wooden ones, madonna. But I am afraid that my honorable father would have me choose the metal ones. Because they are so strong, you see. And I do not want to make the wrong choice and displease him."

I was left wondering, What happens to a child so fearful of losing his parent's approval that he cannot summon the will to choose one toy over another? The answer is he grows up to be Constable Bourbon, who as a grown man with a choice to make could not decide whether to obey his King, to defy him, or to betray him.

I was astonished when, as we made our way out of the Reggio, Judah, who abhors tittle-tattle, turned to me and asked, "Did you notice anything peculiar about that interview, Grazia?"

"Aside from the fact that the woman seems to suffer from some kind of sleepwalking disease, you mean?"

He smiled. "Perhaps that accounts for it."

"Accounts for what?"

"She never asked a word about her husband," he replied.

"Exactly!"

"You noticed it too."

I nodded. "Even if she hated him, she would want to know..."

"And I was not certain as to how I would answer the woman."

"He is ill, this Montpensier?"

"Yes, he is," Judah answered. "I am treating him. With mercury. Very dangerous. It may not work."

"He has the love disease," I guessed.

"He and two thousand other Frenchmen."

"And how does one get this disease, Judah?"

He hesitated a moment. "I will be delicate, Grazia. It takes more than kissing."

So that was the love disease. I ought to have guessed from the name. No wonder the Neapolitans called it the French boils. Fuck a whore, get infected, blame it on the French. That was the Italian *bravo*'s style.

Now I understood Judah's predicament. How do you tell a wife that her husband is ailing without disclosing that the disease was caught from another woman? Fortunately the wife hadn't cared enough to ask. A strange woman, Chiara Gonzaga, Duchess of Montpensier.

Her husband did die in Napoli as Judah feared he might, and his little son was immediately shipped off to France with his tutor. From what I can piece together of his story, he never saw his mother again. She lived out her days in Mantova an embittered, poor, neglected widow.

A sad little story, is it not? But before you heave too deep a sigh for the widow and her son, let me remind you that this fatherless French boy has grown up to be the same Constable Bourbon who betrayed his King and country to put himself at the service of France's great enemy, Emperor Charles V; that he is also the same Constable Bourbon who leads the barbaric Imperials toward Roma as I write, the same Constable Bourbon who menaces this city—and those of us in it—as no force has done since the Huns poured over the Alps to sack Roma in the year 410. In great measure, my son, we sit shivering here in this palazzo, fearing for our very lives, because of that little boy grown up.

OUR VISIT TO THE Reggio was a respite for my fretful soul, but only that. The same evening, Judah undertook a full examination of my father, purely to confirm what the first look had already told him. "It is a bad tumor, Grazia," he explained to me when we were alone in our chamber. "One of those that duplicates itself within months. That old fool Portaleone was right for once. A surgeon is of no use here. Cut this growth out and two more will appear to take its place."

"Are you telling me there is no hope?" I asked.

"You know that is not my judgment to make. Only God decides who lives and who dies."

"I hate God," I muttered.

"Grazia!"

"He is so unjust. So arbitrary! At least Christ has some compassion."

"So they say," he answered mildly. "But I have yet to see the proof of it. Christians die as suddenly and as cruelly as we do. Like us, they are stricken by plague. Their babies are born dead, their children maimed. I do not see any particular compassion being lavished on Christians. Except perhaps for rich Christians. There I see a difference. Observation has taught me that the poor of all religions suffer more grievously in this life than the rich. If you wish to eat injustice, chew on that for a time."

I had irritated him with my blasphemy. Worse, I had blamed him for God's will after he had traveled over sea and land to come to my father's aid.

"Please forgive me, honorable husband," I asked humbly. "Perhaps what we need is a surgeon to cut out my sharp tongue."

"No surgeons," he answered, his anger gone. "This will be a hard time for you, Grazia. To see someone you love wasting away is one of life's great trials. But you have the strength for it. And the love your father needs. Now, may I give you some advice?"

"Please . . ."

"Come close to me." He beckoned me to move toward him in the bed and placed his arm around my shoulders. "If Danicle's case follows the usual course, he will weaken and lose weight. These tumors seem to gobble up all the nourishment we feed the patient and leave none for the rest of the body. I have spoken frankly to your father. He does not fear death. He has given himself over to the disease. He is prepared to die. And you must help him do it easily. Are you up to the task?" I nodded, mute.

"Good. Prepare yourself then. Soon he will begin to refuse food. Do not force him to eat. As the end approaches he will spend most of the hours in a doze."

"And when will that be, Judah?" Whose voice was this, calmly requesting a deathbed schedule?

"No man can predict the moment of death," he answered. "I would judge a few months. Mind you, I have been wrong before."

A few months. I could bear that, I thought.

"I will leave you a vial of powerful medicine. Should he be in pain a drop or two on the tongue will ease it. Three may kill him. It is that powerful. Do you understand?"

I nodded my understanding.

"I would stay and see you through this if I could," he went on. "Believe me, I do not willingly burden you with this responsibility. But my patron the King of France demands that I return to Napoli. I believe he is planning to battle his way back to France. And I hear the Venetians have hired Francesco Gonzaga to cut him down en route."

"We hear the same. These wars never end?" I asked, half to myself.

"Not until the money runs out," he replied cheerfully. "Bravery and honor have their place. But it takes cash to field an army. And even more cash to incite them to fight bravely." Charles VIII had turned Judah into a cynic.

Next morning the mules were at our door at matins, and before I knew it, Judah had paid one last visit to Papa, donned his traveling cloak, and was at the portal ready to mount.

There we stood alone in the misty morning, just the two of us — and the unspoken matter that lay between us.

"When this is over..." Judah began.

"Yes?" I encouraged him.

"There will be time enough to talk. In Firenze. When we are alone."

"We are alone now," I reminded him.

"But time is short. And the shadow of death hangs over us."

Exactly the time, I thought, to speak of the future and of happiness. However, the habit of compliance was etched deep in me, so I did not insist. And so the moment passed.

FROM DANILO'S ARCHIVE

Honored Wife and Consort:
   *We have news that the French king is about to retire from
Napoli and to make for the Alps and thence back to France.
Our plan is to head him off at the Taro River. For this we will
need the reinforcement of the Swiss stradiots. As always, they
are insisting on payment in advance. Here is the problem I
face: Once again, the Venetian signoria procrastinates with
its payments and I am left to equip my cohort out of my own
treasury. I need seven thousand ducats at once. Do anything
you must to raise the money. If necessary place your jewels in
pawn with the Jews. You will have them back in due time. The
Venetians always pay their debts eventually. But I need ducats
now. These stradiots do not unsheathe a weapon until they see
the color of money. Be quick.*

Written in haste by my own hand . . .

Most Honored Lord:
   *I am of course always ready to obey your Excellency's com-
mands, but perhaps you have forgotten that most of my jewels
are at present in pawn at Venezia, not only those you have
given me but those I brought with me as a bride to Mantova or
have bought myself since my marriage. I say this not to make
a difference between yours and mine but to show you that I
have parted with everything and have only four jewels left in
the house—the large balas ruby which you gave me when we
married, my favorite diamond, the small diamond I received
from my mother, and one other. If I pledge these I shall be left
entirely without jewels and shall be obliged to wear black,*

because to appear in colored silks and brocades without jewels would be ridiculous.

Your Excellency will understand that I say this out of regard for your honor and mine. On this account I will not send away my jewels until I have received your Excellency's reply.

By her own hand.

FROM THE MARCHESE FRANCESCO GONZAGA IN THE FIELD
TO HIS WIFE, MARCHESA ISABELLA D'ESTE DA GONZAGA,
AT MANTOVA
WRITTEN ON THE 19TH OF MAY, 1495.

Pawn the jewels and be quick about it!
(signed with his initials, F.G.)

34

PEASANTS CUSTOMARILY ARRIVE TO BORROW MONEY at our *banco* with sacks containing their pitiful capital: two pots, five linen towels, a few worn garments. Princes send emissaries bearing their treasure in gilded casks to demand outrageous sums for allowing Jews the honor of taking their goods in pawn. The Gonzagas sent us a swaggering courtier with a long plume in his hat and an arrogant expression on his face.

"Fetch me Maestro Daniele, girl," he ordered me. Not a greeting, not a "good day." This fellow needed taking down.

"Maestro Daniele is indisposed. I am his daughter and his deputy," I replied softly.

"No, girl. Get the Jew."

"I do apologize, sir," I answered, even more compliant than before. "But my father is ill. If you would be gracious enough to tell me the nature of your business with him..."

"Regular banking business," he replied, with that particular disdain that Christian knights take on when they lower themselves to dabble in commerce. "Her Excellency the Marchesana Isabella wishes him to take some articles in pawn. She has temporary need of fifteen thousand ducats."

Beside me Asher paled at the mention of so large a sum. But I remembered the lessons learned at my father's knee and kept myself from displaying anything more than a routine interest in the transaction.

"May I see the contents of the cask, sir?" I inquired humbly.

"They are for the eyes of Maestro Daniele," he insisted.

"My father has instructed me to handle all business that comes to our door," I answered. "So I fear, sir, that either you conduct your business with me or not at all." And I turned away to other business to drive my point home.

Of course, after a moment or two of indecision he opened the little box and turned out the contents.

Taking my time about it, I began to inspect the treasures one by one. Two immense diamonds, one with a flaw visible with a jeweler's glass but the other seemingly perfect. Madonna Isabella must have paid dearly for that one. Five thousand ducats at least. And a thousand, I would have judged, for the other. She had also sent five large rubies, unset. Ten thousand for those on the open market. And these were not the whole of it. There were also a few small pieces — one I especially remember, an amazing Saint George paved with diamonds, riding astride a dragon carved from a single pearl with a glittering tail of emeralds wound around the saint's foot. But most valuable of all was the necklace, a masterpiece of the goldsmith's craft forged from links so cunningly entwined that no one without a glass could ever know where they were joined. This must be the *illustrissima*'s Necklace of a Hundred Links, celebrated as a triumph of the art of Maestro Fidele, the Jewish goldsmith who glittered up half the princes of the peninsula with his inventions. I daresay so much wealth had never resided at one time in the dei Rossi Mantova branch as did that morning.

"Nice little trinkets," I commented to the courtier. "But not worth anything like fifteen thousand ducats to us. Take them back to your mistress. Tell her we cannot supply her with the money she requests. With regrets." And to underline my point

I began to place the stones back in their satin bags.

"But madonna..." I had suddenly come up in the world. "The stones alone are worth at least twenty thousand ducats and the necklace is priceless," he sputtered.

"As a sentimental piece, of course," I replied. "But when it is melted down we are not likely to extract more than a few hundred ducats' worth of gold from the thing."

"Melted down!" He was genuinely horrified by the suggestion. "This is the *illustrissima*'s Necklace of a Hundred Links, famous throughout Europe. Copied by queens and empresses."

"That may be, but to us it is merely gold." I threw the thing on the scale as if it were a dead fish. "No more than three hundred ducats' worth there. See for yourself."

"You will not take these pieces, then?" he asked, by now quite drained of his arrogance.

"Not for fifteen thousand ducats. Five perhaps. Eight at most."

"Eight thousand ducats for all of this?"

"Maybe," I answered. "You may tell the great lady that Grazia dei Rossi is managing the *banco* due to her father's indisposition and that she knows her father would never countenance the payment of a penny more than eight thousand."

"Well..." The fellow began to gather up his baubles. "I certainly cannot accept eight thousand ducats for this lot. The lady would have my head for it." He scratched his pate, perplexed. "I might take twelve..." he ventured.

"Do not bargain with me, sir." I fixed a steely eye on him. "Eight I said and eight it is." I could hear a little hiss of astonishment from my cousin behind me. But I knew Madonna Isabella and the sharp bargaining for which she is as celebrated as for her marvelous collections. And I did not doubt that she had primed this jackanapes for just such a contest as we were now engaged in.

"Eleven?" he asked, diffident.

"Eight," I answered, implacable.

"Ten?"

"Nine," I offered. Now that I had him in my territory, it was time to give a little. By my most conservative estimate, the stuff was worth at least forty thousand ducats. So we stood to lose nothing should the Gonzagas default. And to gain thirty-five percent in interest should they not.

"I cannot go below ten." He squared his shoulders. And then, in an attack of candor, he added, "Those are my orders."

"Very well." I turned away, as if bored by the entire procedure. "I know that my father bears nothing but the most loyal feelings for the Marchese. I think he would not object too strenuously if I were to extend myself beyond what is prudent in this case. We will give the ten. Asher..."

The plump face bobbed up from behind me.

"Make a receipt for this gentleman," I instructed him. "Jehiel!"

"Yes, Grazia." My brother bounced out from behind the door to the strong room.

"We will need to count out ten thousand ducats in coin. Can you and the clerk manage it?" I knew him to be an accurate counter, albeit no bargainer.

"You will have your ducats within the hour, sir," I advised the courtier. "Would you care to sip a glass of wine while you wait? With a biscuit?"

"Thank you, madonna." He was tame as a house cat by now, bargained down to his absolutely final position. And he would report the interview to his mistress, laying much stress on the little Jewess with the small stature and the will of steel. Had I known that the money was needed to equip the Marchese's men for the battle so soon to be joined at Fornovo, I would have shaved my offer even finer. But I had not yet received Judah's letter telling me that the King of France had left Napoli and was marching north.

FROM DANILO'S ARCHIVE

TO GRAZIA DEI ROSSI AT MANTOVA

Dearest wife:

The King departed Napoli this day without me in spite of

my pleas to accompany him. I have doctored the man too well. He no longer needs my help to shoot off his pitiful cannon. My reward is to be left in this pestilential sink to minister to two thousand ailing and unpaid men while he fucks his way back to France, accompanied by the portion of his army that has been spared by God—and with all modesty, by my ministrations—from the crippling effects of the love disease.

As I write, Montpensier—another who has been left behind by the careless King—is scouring the Calabrian hills for a safe bivouac in case his pitiful remnant of an army is forced out by the Neapolitans. They now hate the French as much as they loved them six months ago. "What's to become of my men?" Montpensier asks me. "The King has left us no money, no food, no tents... We will end our days here foraging for food and living in caves like animals."

Poor Montpensier. His case is too far gone to respond to my mercury treatment, and the best comfort I can offer him is to audience his reminiscences of his little son, the child to whom we brought the toy soldiers.

"Does he not resemble me?" he asks. "Can you not see the soldier in him?"

I nod my acquiescence and refrain from expressing my hope that if little Charles Bourbon does become a soldier, he will find a better master than his namesake, the King of France. We are told that the whimsical Charles VIII has washed his hands of Italy. How can a king worthy of his title abandon half an army to wait endlessly for reinforcements that will never come, because he has lost interest in war?

I had hoped to make one last visit to Daniele before his end. Now it appears you may have to face the sad moment alone. Be brave, good wife. Dip into your well of courage which is boundless. I am with you in spirit.

Your devoted husband, J.

Napoli, May 12, 1495.

Darling Grazia:

Your favorite mare, Carlinga, foaled last night and you not here to celebrate because poor Daniele is dying. It is all too sad. Sad. What a weak and puny word! Damn it, Grazia, your friend and comrade Diamante misses you. For the rest of my feelings, I have no words. Pity? Ugh! Admiration? Too stiff. Maybe I can cheer you up with the news of the day. You always did appreciate Isaachino's gossip.

You must know from Judah that Messer Charles VIII of France has left Napoli and turned tail for France. And that his former allies are lying in wait to trap him along the Taro River at Fornovo. Poor little king, about to be chased out of Italy by the very friends who imported him, with nothing to remind him of his Italian campaign but a record book of the ladies he has fucked.

Next a marriage announcement. I include it because Isaachino urges me to pass it on to you. Last week Philip the Handsome, son of the Emperor Maximilian and known to his admirers as the Burgundian Stud, was married to Joanna, the daughter of King Ferdinand and Queen Isabella of Spain. It is a marriage made in heaven. He is a reprobate; she is mad.

These names mean little to me. But Isaachino says you will understand that this marriage is certain to have far-reaching dynastic consequences. A child of this union, he says, stands to inherit not only the crown of Spain but also the vast Habsburg holdings in Burgundy and Germany. If this charming couple perform their dynastic duty satisfactorily, the fruit of their labors may well become a future Charlemagne, God help us all.

Why do sensible nations entrust themselves to these royal monsters and half-wits? You must instruct me at length on this subject during our next canter over the Tuscan countryside.

I miss you too much, Grazia.

Your loving sister, Diamante. (Written in her own hand at Firenze, May 15, 1495.)

35

AT FIRST THE BATTLE OF FORNOVO WAS CELEBRATED in Mantova as a personal triumph for the Marchese. Bonfires were lit in every square and the people danced in the streets. But as time went on we began to hear a different story. More than one foot soldier reported that their own cavalrymen used their horses to make off with booty while they stood firm awaiting reinforcements. From others came tales of Swiss stradiots more devoted to raping whores than to fighting the enemy. And from every quarter we heard reports of League soldiers running for their lives. Running for their lives? Who in the history of warfare ever ran away from a victory?

At best the outcome of the battle was equivocal. But the Gonzagas needed Fornovo to be seen as a triumph. Why else had the Venetians hired the Marchese as their Captain-General but to win? And how could the Mantovan exchequer survive without infusions of cash from the exploits of its invincible *condottiero*? The stability of the little state depended on a glorious victory. If Fornovo proved to be something less—as indeed it did—then they would damn well make it a victory. With the help of his advisers, Francesco Gonzaga devised a distracting public spectacle together with a plan to get it paid for by that never-failing source of cash, the Jews.

The letter that came addressed to my father was short, curt, and brutal. Daniele dei Rossi's insult to the Virgin, it said, had not been satisfied by a mere apology. Her glory must be restored in a more palpable form. In furtherance of this high purpose, Daniele, the Jew who had shamed Her, was ordered to commission from the finest artist in all Italy an altarpiece to memorialize and celebrate the victory gained in Her name at Fornovo, this tribute to be presented to the city in a public ceremony.

The second paragraph of this document instructed the Jew to carry fifty-five ducats to the home of Maestro Andrea Mantegna without delay as a down payment on the final price for the altarpiece of one hundred ten ducats.

My first thought was to keep the affair from my father. The second was relief that we were to be let off with nothing more than the loss of a hundred ducats. The third was that there was a proud obverse to the humiliation. Not everyone got the chance to become a patron of the celebrated maestro Andrea Mantegna.

Before the *banco* closed that day I took my cousin Asher aside and showed him the letter. No further words were needed. He understood at once what had to be done. I slept with fifty-five golden ducats under my pillows that night. At dawn Asher met me at the front portal and together we went in search of Messer Andrea's house near the Pusterla Gate.

I had heard tales of the aftermath of the battle at the Taro, but nothing prepared me for the misery that saturated the streets. Beggars in torn uniforms grabbed at us pitifully, many armless or legless. Crippled men lurched about drunkenly, cursing the Marchese and the Venetians and the French in one breath. And there were women everywhere — respectable-looking women — holding up fatherless babes to ask for a few pennies to feed them. No wonder the author of this disaster had chosen to placate the Virgin. It would take a blessing from above to redeem this poor city.

Mantegna's dwelling was not hard to find. There was no mistaking it. Designed by his own hand, the maestro's house resembled no other house in the world. From the outside it was a perfect cube. But inside, one stepped into a circular atrium — a perfect circle described within a perfect square. Not a statue, not a fountain, not a tree or bench, marred the austerity of the circle. And the effect was amplified by the pattern of the terrazzo floor, an eight-pointed star set so that four of the points led to four arched portals leading to four of the rooms on the ground floor. To stand in that space was like inhabiting geometry.

"What are you gaping at? Have you never seen a circle before?"

The maestro was an ugly little monkey of a man with a harsh voice and leathery skin. But he did have an air about him.

"I am struck dumb by the symmetry, maestro," I answered, determined not to be cowed. After all, I was the patron here.

"The symmetry, eh?"

"Yes, maestro. I have long admired your work but I did not know you were also an architect."

It was meant as a compliment but he took it ill. "I have built many buildings in my time, lady. Have you not seen them, you who are such an admirer of my work?"

"No, I have not, sir. I have only seen your 'Triumphs' and the Camera degli Sposi in the old Saint George Castle."

"And when you were in the Camera, did you find the *putti* on the ceiling adorable?" Every question was like a prod with a pointed stick.

"No, sir," I answered. "'Adorable' was not the word I would use. I found them miraculous for I felt that, at any moment, they might fall over the railing and bash me on the head."

This answer seemed to please him for he nodded and replied, quite pleasantly, "It is a trick. A way of fooling the eye."

"I have never seen anything like it, maestro," I said.

"Live long enough and you will, lady, you will. How old are you now?"

"Seventeen years old, sir," I answered, adding more than a few months to give myself additional dignity.

"Mark me. Before you die, you will see such ceilings everywhere in Italy. In every church, in every castle. A little false oculus in every cupola looking up to a piece of false sky. And around the edge a painted railing with all manner of creatures hanging over it, looking as if they were about to fall over and bash you on the head."

"But none will equal yours, maestro," I made bold to say.

"That depends," he corrected me, "on who paints 'em. If that fellow from Vinci takes it into his head to do one, he might give me a contest. But he won't. He's too proud to imitate me. And the rest aren't good enough. But that won't stop 'em from trying. Have you brought the money?"

I motioned to Asher to present the bag of coins. "We will need a signed receipt, sir," I told him, fearing his displeasure, which indeed was forthcoming.

"And I shall need to count these. One is never sure with pawnbrokers." He might as well have said Jews. It was what he meant. "Come…" He gestured toward one of the arched portals.

The entry led directly into a large messy room jammed with bits of old masonry and sarcophagi and damaged stone busts, a disposition of antiquities not dissimilar to the arrangement in the Medici garden. Only in this house the garden was empty and the great pieces of stone were jumbled together inside. What a strange fancy to pack the house with garden decorations and the garden with nothing at all!

"Give me the purse, boy," the maestro instructed Asher. Then we stood while he seated himself at a trestle table and carefully counted out the fifty-five coins, one by one.

"Are they all there, maestro?" I could not resist the dig.

"Yes," he answered coldly. "Did you bring the receipt?"

· How embarrassing. I had not written up the receipt as I might have done. "I have not brought one," I answered. "But if you can spare a small piece of paper I will write on it here and now and you can sign it."

"Paper costs money, you know." He slid out a sheet of vellum and scrawled the receipt. "Bring a replacement next time." Then, without a pause: "Stand over there." He pointed his finger at a part of the room where a shaft of sunlight made a wide triangle on the floor. "There in the light. And take your cap off."

I did as I was told. Whereupon I was subjected to the most intense scrutiny I have ever faced, even including Judah's examinations. Maestro Mantegna's eyes not only pierced me, they illuminated me as if he were blazing a trail into my soul. When he had finished he picked up my hands one by one and examined them in the same way. Then he tugged a piece of my hair out of its ribbon and frowned over the strand intensely. When that was over he stood back and squinted at me the way men do at horse auctions. All this without saying a word. When at last he spoke, he was curt and to the point.

"I want to paint you from life."

Too astonished to reply, I simply gaped.

"Don't look so frightened. I have no designs on your body. Except to immortalize it." A gasp from Asher caught his attention. "You can bring your servant along for a chaperon."

"He is not my servant," I stammered. "He is my cousin."

"Well then, don't bring him. Bring your husband. Or your mother. Anyone you like. But only one. I cannot bear chatter."

"But I did not say—"

"Think before you turn me down, young lady," he interrupted. "This country is full of women who would give their teeth to be painted by Andrea Mantegna. You are being offered a chance to live forever, girl. Don't you understand?"

From behind me Asher's voice stammered weakly, "It is against our religion to make graven images, sir."

"You won't be making the graven image, boy. I will. And it is not against *my* religion, so we are both safe from burning." Then, turning to me: "Is that what frightens you, young lady?"

"No, maestro." I was determined not to be ridden over like some serving wench. "I am afraid that you will make me ugly."

He laughed. Out loud. Not a giggle but a great roar of a laugh. "Afraid I will make you ugly! Where did you ever get such an idea?"

"I heard that you painted the *illustrissima* Isabella and that you made her fat."

"And you are afraid that I will defile your beauty as I did hers?"

"I am not beautiful, sir," I answered. "But I fear that if you made Madonna Isabella, who *is* beautiful, ugly, then maybe you will make me, who am not beautiful at all..." I could not find the words to finish the thought. But he understood.

He walked toward me and once again took my face in his gnarled, paint-stained hands. "I do not find Madonna Isabella beautiful, although I would prefer you not to tell her that." He spoke quietly. "But I do find *you* beautiful. And that is why I am asking you to sit for me."

Whereupon I agreed. On the spot.

All the way home Asher pleaded with me to change my mind. The sitting would cause a scandal; it might get back to Marchese Francesco and make him angry. The more he spoke, the more eager I became to have my portrait.

Asher's reproofs were a mild prelude to the shrieks and laments that greeted me at home. "He will ask you to take your clothes off," Dorotea wailed. "And dishonor you forever." She even went so far as to solicit my father's support—which necessitated my showing him the Marchese's letter and distressing him unnecessarily. Had I been able to strangle that woman every time I had the whim, she would have died a dozen deaths.

To my surprise, Papa sided with her although for different reasons. "Who will manage the *banco* in your absence, daughter?" he asked. How quickly one becomes indispensable.

I put his agitation to rest with a promise not to do my sitting in business hours. But Dorotea's objections were not so easily overcome. Only my husband had authority over me, I informed her, whereupon she insisted that I must get Judah's written permission for the sitting.

Days went by. I saw my chance at immortality slipping away. "Why cannot they leave me alone?" I beseeched Penina. "What I am proposing is blameless. The words of the commandment are very clear. Thou shalt not make a graven image or bow down to a graven image. Nobody is bowing down. And as for the making of the thing, it will be Maestro Andrea who will be making the image, not I. And his God lets him do it, so neither of us will burn," I quoted.

"Sometimes you seem so harsh that I become frightened of you, Grazia." She shook her head dolefully.

"I fight for what is my right," I answered heatedly. "Some of us do, you know."

The moment I uttered the words, I wished them back behind my tongue, for the tears that came to her eyes told me that I had hurt her deeply. "I have not your spirit, Grazia," was all she said.

Her humility was worse than a reproach. Of all people in the world, she least deserved my scorn. "Oh, Penina *mia*..." I ran to embrace her. "I am sorry. Forgive my hasty tongue."

"There is nothing to forgive. You spoke the truth, Grazia. I lack courage. I know you would like me to do battle with La Nonna and Dorotea as you do. But we are not made the same, cousin."

"And thank God for it," I cried, meaning it. "If you were me, what would I do without you, the sweet and gentle influence on my hot temper? Who would I choose to accompany me when I go to sit for Messer Andrea?"

"Me?" Her eyes widened.

"Of course you. How else will I prove to you that Maestro Andrea is not the old goat you think him? That his eyes seek out beauty, not lechery. You will see for yourself."

The next day after dinner, without asking or telling anyone, I set off with Penina for Maestro Andrea's house. We were met at the front portal by a servant who led us immediately across the empty atrium and into the cluttered room with the trestle table. But now there were three large pieces of heavy beige-colored canvas hanging on each wall. Blank canvas.

"You took your good time coming," was the only welcome we got. The maestro sat me down at once on a chair in the same corner of the room where he had put me before.

"Get rid of those plaits," he ordered.

"But—"

"You can bind them up again when we're done. Now let 'em loose."

I saw Penina's eyes widen. What wildness did this presage?

She soon learned. As I carefully unbraided my hair, the maestro began to drag a heavy plinth across the floor, cursing it at every push. "Move, you son of a whore," he panted as he wrestled the thing into position opposite me. Then when he had the little pillar in a place that suited him, he gave it an affectionate pat and left the room without a word.

"He is a madman," Penina whispered. "A maniac."

"He is the finest painter in all of Italy," I told her. "Except perhaps for the one called Leonardo from Vinci. And that one never finishes anything."

"Does he not frighten you, Grazia?"

"No," I answered truthfully. "For there is no malice in him."

Just then the maestro returned, followed by a young man carrying the stone bust of a woman.

"I want Faustina up there on the top of the plinth in profile, facing the girl," the painter ordered, indicating the bust.

"Yes, Father." Turning to look at me from time to time to make certain that my head and the stone head were at the same angle of profile, the young man set the head on the plinth.

"Will that do, Father?" he asked.

"Yes, yes," the old man answered impatiently. "Now get back to work. The Marchesana wants her birth tray in time for the christening. At the rate you are going, it won't be ready until the child is weaned. Go! Work! Call me when it is time to put in Abraham's face."

"And the boy? Isaac?" his son asked timidly.

"I leave that figure to you, my son. Just remember, his father has a knife at his throat and is quite prepared to use it. Just like me. Ha ha ha." I swear the old man enjoyed frightening people. He certainly took pleasure in his son's discomfiture. Well, he was not going to frighten me.

"Who is the stone lady?" I asked, even though his manner did not invite conversation.

"Who do you think?" he growled.

"She looks Roman to me. Perhaps the wife of some Caesar."

"She is Faustina, wife of the Emperor Marcus Aurelius. He loved her so much that he could not be without her. He even took her with him on his northern campaign."

"They say he took her with him because he couldn't trust her. That she was faithless and immoral," I answered.

"Faithless and immoral, perhaps," was his answer. "But beautiful." He drew his hand over the stone cheek, following its contours lovingly. "She is my muse. I would give all I own in the world for her. My house, my children, all." Then, without missing a beat, he asked, "Did you bring the sheet of vellum you owe me?"

Luckily, I had remembered that infinitesimal debt.

"Good." He nodded with satisfaction as he took the sheet from my hand and rubbed it between his fingers. "This will do nicely for a beginning."

So saying, he picked up a quill and began to draw on the paper with quick, scratchy strokes. I never knew drawing could be such a noisy activity. Scratch. Scratch. Scratch. The sound put my teeth on edge. But I said nothing of it and the room remained silent except for the rasp of the pen on the vellum.

After a time my neck began to cramp and I raised my hand to rub it, only to be stopped midway by the stern order "Stay still, damn it. I will tell you when to move."

By the time the triangle of light in the corner of Maestro Andrea's studio had shrunk to a sliver, my neck felt like a cushion stuck full of pins. Still, I forbore and kept my pose. And at last the painter suddenly cried, "Enough!" and with a grand flourish, waved the vellum sheet through the air in a series of swirls and brought it to rest before my eyes.

"Madonna Grazia..." He bowed low.

There I was to the life. Sitting face-to-face with Faustina, who bore a startling resemblance to me. How do they do it, these great ones?

"I shall call the painting 'Faustina and her Double,'" he announced. "And I will put some buildings in behind for you."

I turned to my friend. "Penina, come and look."

"No!" He quickly withdrew the sketch and clamped it into a tin box on his table. "No one sees my sketches..."

"But she is my—"

"Your cousin. So you told me. You have too many cousins."

"But she is also my friend, maestro. Please let her see it."

"She can see the painting when it is done. I do not show my sketches. Not like those who make a sketch or two to tantalize the eye, then never do more."

Plainly he would not be moved.

"When shall I come again, maestro?" I asked.

"Tomorrow early. I only work here in the studio in the mornings. Afternoons I give over to my workshop. It is birth trays and costumes and gewgaws that keep food on the table, you know. And they all want evidence of the master's hand for their five ducats."

"But I cannot come in the mornings, for I must work in the *banco*."

"Ah yes, the loan bank." He did not bother to disguise his contempt.

"Loan-banking is my family's profession, one of the few open to us Jews in this world," I reminded him.

"So it is." A great veil of indifference fell over his eyes. "Very well then. You may come on Tuesday afternoons. One afternoon out of the week is the most I can spare from my workshop. It will delay the portrait, but..." He shrugged, threw up his hands, and was gone.

It was almost dark by the time we arrived home. The sitting

had taken longer than I thought. Surprisingly, I heard not a word of rebuke from Dorotea.

Instead, she simply reached down into her workbasket and handed me a small packet without a word. It was a letter. With the seal broken. So she had already read the contents. They must not have pleased her, for her pale face fairly quivered with fury when she handed it to me.

"Most treasured and beloved wife," I read.

"Vis-à-vis your request for guidance in the matter of having your portrait made by Maestro Andrea Mantegna: I have consulted the rabbis of Napoli on their interpretation of the second commandment. They are divided. In the face of this official confusion, I advise you to follow the dictates of your own conscience, which, I have cause to know, is a sterner taskmaster than any rabbi.

"Tell anyone who questions your decision that you act with my blessing.

"My most devoted felicitations to your honorable father. Remember my prescription: gentle hands, warm smiles, soft voices, and no spicy foods. Bear in mind that you are the chiefest among my concerns and that I am prepared to come to your aid in spite of my duties if I am badly needed. You must be the judge of that. In this, as in all matters great and small, I place my full confidence in your wise and prudent judgment. I hold you dearer than life itself, my little wife."

It was signed, "Your most respectful and loving husband."

Now it seemed that nothing stood in the way of my portrait. Even Penina agreed. But we were soon to learn that the project had a much more potent enemy than my stepmother. That revelation came at my fourth or fifth sitting when the door to the studio flew open and the maid rushed in, flushed and flustered.

"I am sorry, sir, but the Marchesana insisted..."

She had barely gotten the words out when in swept the *illustrissima* herself—Madonna Isabella. "Why, Grazia, what a surprise to find you here. We had been informed that you were managing the loan bank."

"So I am, *illustrissima*."

"Then what brings you to Maestro Mantegna's studio?" Out of the corner of my eye I saw the maestro, with great casualness, throw a sheet over his easel. "Have you come to inquire after the progress of our altarpiece to the Madonna of the Victory?" Then, in the same breath: "How does the work go, Maestro Andrea?"

"Slowly." His tone was gruff as ever.

"We are sorry to hear that. May we see it?" she asked, ignoring the roughness of his reply.

"You are looking at it." He waved his hand to indicate the three lengths of canvas fabric hanging on the opposite wall.

"Is this a jest, maestro?"

"Not at all, my lady. You ordered a triptych, did you not?"

"That is correct."

"Well then, there is your triptych. Panel one, the commander in full regalia — but without his horse — kneeling reverently at the left hand of the Holy Mother with his honorable brothers behind him. Across from him kneels his lady — that is you, *illustrissima* — with her patron saint, Elizabeth, behind her. Panel two" — he waved at the second piece of blank canvas — "presents the patron saints of Mantova, Saint Andrew and Saint Longinus. Each bears a distinct resemblance to the honorable brothers of the victorious commander. And on panel three we see the heavenly warriors, Saint George and Saint Michael..."

"Stop this nonsense at once! The truth is that you have not even begun your work on the altarpiece. Is that not so?"

"No, lady. I have begun. I sketch. I think. The real work of painting is in the mind."

"For my purposes, the real work is in the brush, maestro. And I see no brushwork on these canvases."

"But to plan a triptych, my lady, with so many figures to be included, and such exacting terms of execution... that the ultramarine for the vault must be purchased for four forms an ounce, that I must use forty forms' worth of gold —"

"How long will it take?" she cut him off.

"Possibly a year."

"Out of the question."

"The muse cannot be rushed, madonna."

"How do you think the muse would enjoy a stay in one of our dungeons?" Her eyes flashed with a fury she was now making no effort to disguise. "You are welcome to bring her to spend a night there and see how the accommodations suit her."

"As you wish, my lady." He held out his muscled brown arms. "Shall I go shackled?"

For this retort he was rewarded with a smile and the appearance of a new Madonna Isabella, a lady with a soft, teasing voice. "Let us stop this charade, maestro. You know we love you far too much ever to punish you, as well as you know that a year is out of the question. The altarpiece must be ready by the anniversary of the victory at Fornovo. Beyond that date everyone will have forgotten the purpose of it."

"Perhaps another artist..." he purred, matching the sheen of her tone with his own. "My esteemed brother-in-law might possibly—"

"Giovanni Bellini? He's even slower than you are." A stray twinkle in the maestro's eye told me he had been aware of this facet of his brother-in-law's temperament when he made the suggestion.

"No, no. You are the only artist my esteemed husband wants for this commission. No other will do. And it must be finished by June. What you need, maestro, is encouragement. Perhaps we should take a hostage. One of your children. Your son Orsino..."

"Welcome to him, madonna."

"Mmm. Not the best hostage." She rubbed her nose thoughtfully. "What about her," pointing in my direction.

"The girl?"

"Me?"

"Not you, Grazia. No, it is Faustina I have in mind. I know how you treasure her, maestro. Sometimes I think you love that stone woman better than you love your own wife."

"Better even than that, madonna," he answered, deadly quiet now. "For she is more perfect than any woman nature can show. The master who made her borrowed from all living women for his creation. She is my inspiration."

"She does not seem to have inspired you to work on my triptych," she answered.

"You are impatient, madonna."

"It must be done by June," she insisted.

"Forgive the interruption, *illustrissima*..." My interjection went into the silence as into a void.

I cleared my throat and tried again. "There may be a way to resolve the problem," I said.

"There is," she answered without looking at me. "The maestro must paint faster."

"Impossible," from the other side. "When I painted the San Zeno *pala* it took over my life for three years."

More silence and murderous looks. Dare I jump into the void one more time? "Maestro Andrea." I picked him as the less menacing of the two. "There are six panels in the San Zeno altarpiece, are there not?"

"Three large ones, three small in the predella," Madonna Isabella answered for him. "Each one a jewel."

"That means it took you roughly six months to finish each panel." I pursued my thought.

"We do not measure our art the way a pawnbroker counts out his ducats, lady," he sneered. "How long do you think it took the master who made my Faustina to create such perfection of form? Two weeks? Two years? What matters is that we stand here today, hundreds of years later, enthralled by her. Our measure is eternity, do you not understand that, ignorant fool?"

Oh, he had a whip for a tongue. But I was quite inured to his lashes by then and went right on with my scheme.

"I merely mean to demonstrate that it is possible for you to create a single work of genius within six months, maestro," I answered sweetly. "How large are the biggest panels at San Zeno?"

The question drove him even deeper into his fury. "Here..." He threw a ball of string at me, narrowly missing my eye. "Use this. Take it to Verona. Measure the *pala*. How can I remember after all this time? *Dio*, it is at least thirty years since I made the thing. Do you not understand that I do not measure out the works of my hand by the yard?"

Perhaps not, old man, I thought, but you certainly do charge by that measure. However, I kept my temper and continued in the same bland tone as before. "I am merely trying to make a point, maestro," I said.

Meanwhile, as we bickered on I saw Madama turn toward the draped easel. Like a bird dog sniffing her quarry, she quivered a little and began slowly to move in on it. Now I understood Maestro Andrea's haste to conceal the work. It was on account of my portrait that he had fallen behind. He had been painting me instead of the Madonna of the Victory. *Dio!*

"Please, maestro, I beg you to tell me the size..." The urgency in my voice must have come through, for he finally responded.

"Perhaps three *braccias* in height," he answered.

"And the width?" I asked.

"Some two-thirds of that."

"The *illustrissima*'s panel must be larger than that," I announced. "Much larger. Is that not so, madonna?"

"I have agreed to nothing," she answered sternly. "But if I were to consider a single panel..." A slight, tight smile crossed her lips. "If I were to agree, as I say, certainly the panel would have to be much larger than any one of the San Zeno panels."

"And would not a panel of that size be the largest panel you had ever executed in your long and illustrious career, maestro?" I asked. By now my nervous glances at the easel must have warned him, for he answered quite politely, "Certainly the largest."

"How would it compare with your other large pieces such as your Florentine circumcision?"

"The Florentine panels are small in comparison." He was clearly onto the game now. "One might almost say inconsequential."

That, I thought, was going too far. But contrarily, the answer seemed to please Madama. And the sarcasm in his reply, thinly veiled as it was, escaped her completely. For her it was enough that her panel, should she agree to it, would be larger by twice than the one Maestro Andrea had executed for the Medici family.

"What will become of the figures in the side panels—the Beata Orsanna and our noble brother-in-law, the Protonotary Sigismondo—*if* we should agree to the plan, maestro?" she asked. "Can they still be included within the confines of one large panel?"

"They cannot. Not unless we float them up above the fruit and flowers," the painter replied with a wicked grin. "Or unless you are prepared to give up your place opposite your illustrious consort at the Virgin's left hand."

"Would you have *me* floating above the fruit and flowers, maestro," she inquired with a sour sweetness.

"It *is* closer to heaven, *illustrissima*," he answered, deftly dodging the arrow.

"No, maestro. I fear I am slightly too heavy to float. Indeed, if you go ahead with this plan, I will be forced, albeit reluctantly, to relinquish my position at the left hand. Yes, I will be forced to yield to Beata Orsanna." She paused. "But now I think of it, the place of honor ought more properly to go to that holy woman in any case. For there is no doubt that her intercessions with our Lady were instrumental in bringing about the great victory at the Taro River." And she smiled a most complacent smile, as if she had won a vital point in a *disputa*.

"But will his Excellency, the Marchese, approve?" I asked. "Did he not intend to share the honor with you who stayed bravely at home and conducted the affairs of Mantova so nobly in his name?"

"His honor on the battlefield he shares with no one," she answered sharply, as if irritated at being held back in this new plan. "Nor need he share his piety. It was he who entreated the Holy Mother, he whose courage She rewarded with victory. I see now that Fra Redini was mistaken in his program. Neither I nor the Protonotary should be included. Only the saints, the Blessed Mother, and my noble consort. For they are the chiefest actors in this wonderful drama." She nodded with satisfaction at her own mental process. "It is all quite clear to me now. Not only need I not sit for this portrait, I must not sit. All the honor goes to the commander. I shall send off a letter to him at once explaining our inadvertent insult to his glory. I am sure he will understand."

Then, without taking a breath, she turned to Mantegna and asked, "What are you hiding under that sheet, maestro? Something you do not wish me to see?"

"It is a portrait of Faustina," he answered, truthful to a point. "Not yet finished."

She stepped forward and grasped the corner of the sheet between her thumb and her forefinger. "Not even a peek, maestro?"

"I cannot forbid my princess," he answered, suddenly altogether a courtier. "But I guarantee she will not like what she sees. And I beg her humbly not to look. For I prefer to show her only works that bring her joy and satisfaction."

"Very well then. I will wait." She dropped the cloth. "But, mark you, I will return one month from today to see how far you have progressed with the Madonna of the Victory. And I will send a message to Beata Orsanna to expect you at the convent tomorrow."

"At the convent?"

"Surely you do not expect the sainted woman to come to you for her sitting?"

"Of course not." He knew when he had been bested.

"Very well." She turned to me all haughty once again. "My regards to Maestro Daniele, and tell him how pleased we are that he is recovered enough to run the *banco*."

"But he is not recovered," I answered. "Not at all."

"Really?" she drawled. "Then who takes care of business?"

"I do, madonna."

"In that case, if I were you I would stick closer to my tasks at the loan bank. It is not seemly for a young woman to be sprawling about with her hair down in an artist's studio. Believe me, no good will come of it."

And with that she swept out, leaving both the maestro and me on notice that we shoemakers had best stick to our lasts: he to his altarpieces, I to my counting table.

Without any discussion we agreed that work on the portrait must cease at once. "But never fear, Madonna Grazia," the old man assured me, with a touch of courtliness he must have had left over from his encounter with Madonna Isabella, "I am no Leonardo da Vinci. I finish what I start. You will yet see yourself immortalized by the greatest master in Italy."

36

THE YEAR 1496 BEGAN WITH A SERIES OF BAD OMENS. In the midst of a hailstorm it had rained blood over the gates of Siena. In Ferrara, Duke Ercole, seized by a late-in-life burst of religious fervor, once again ordered the Jews to wear the obnoxious yellow circle on their breasts. This time, the dei Rossis were not excluded. To Mantova, an early spring thaw and freeze brought ruined crops and the threat of empty stomachs; while upstairs in our fine house my father began to refuse food, a step in his slow separation from those of us who loved him.

God must be on holiday, I thought, to permit so much misery all at once. However, it was not God but the Gonzagas who launched the final thunderbolt at our sorrowful household. The telling blow was delivered by two gentlemen of the court, a friar and an architect. They oozed in through the door of the *banco* one morning, the friar thin and oily, the architect fat and twitchy.

"Maestro Daniele?" The friar spoke in a high whine.

"My father is ill," I answered. "I am Grazia dei Rossi. What can I do for you?"

"We are here to see Maestro Daniele." The other spoke this time. "These papers are for his eyes only."

"I am his eyes," I answered. "And his ears and his hands as well."

"Is there no man in the family? An uncle? A brother?"

"I am the manager in my father's stead. Please show me the document." It was all I could do to be civil. Blackmailers and pirates who hide themselves in holy garb bring out my worst.

"Very well then." The friar turned to the fat one. "Messer Ghisolfo, the document."

While the fat one was fussing with his case, the priest explained, "Messer Bernardo Ghisolfo is the Marchese's architect."

Architect? What a strange person to dun us for money, I thought.

"And you, Father? May I know your name?" I asked.

"I am Fra Redini. Fra Girolamo Redini of the Eremitani order. Adviser to the honorable Protonotary, Sigismondo Gonzaga."

So this was Redini, the inventor of the program for the Madonna of the Victory; also, I suspected, the author of the plan to get Daniele dei Rossi to pay for it. He certainly had the face for chicanery: a mouth like a viper and a tongue that worked constantly. And when he held out his cursed document I could tell by the proprietary way he handled it that he had devised this new ruse, and shuddered to think what we were in for.

The document was short and clear. Daniele the Jew was to be honored once more. His house had been chosen as the site for a small chapel to house the Madonna of the Victory, an altarpiece being made even now by Maestro Andrea and dedicated to our Lady by Her grateful son Marchese Francesco Gonzaga, in praise and gratitude for his glorious victory at Fornovo.

"Our house ... this house ... is to be a chapel?" I stammered, for I did not completely understand what was intended.

"Not this structure, lady," the architect explained. "Merely this site. The house which stands here now will of course have to be razed to accommodate the new chapel. Razed to the ground."

"Razed to the ground?"

"It would hardly redound to the glory of our Lady to worship Her image in the house of a heretic Jew, now would it, madonna?" The sarcasm fairly dripped from the friar's thin lips.

"But this is our house," I mumbled stupidly.

"No longer," the friar replied. "As of this morning, the twelfth day of April, it belongs to the Holy Virgin. But you seem not to be sensible of the honor."

"To have our house razed to the ground is an honor?"

"To provide a shelter for our Lady is more honor than any Jew ought to expect in a lifetime. You should be down on your knees thanking the Marchese for allowing you to make such a noble contribution in his cause."

"I am honored," I answered, hardly aware of what I was saying. "I am truly honored. We are all truly honored. And where would you suggest we take our honored selves and our honored business, having given over our house and shop in the Marchese's cause?"

"God will provide," he answered airily. Then, in a more urgent tone: "You must be out by Tuesday next. Five days from now."

"The work of demolition begins on Wednesday," the architect chimed in. "The date is registered with the guild."

"Over my dead body," I answered, without thinking. Then added quickly, to cover up my lapse: "My father is ill, gentlemen. Very ill. He cannot be moved."

"Sick or well, he will rejoice when he knows the purpose of his removal. He may even rise and walk from his sickbed a new man. I have seen it happen. God works in mysterious ways. And do not forget, madonna," he reminded me gaily, "that on the sixth day the *bargello's* men will be at the door with their pikes. You have five days." Five days to pack up a business, a household, and a dying man.

I kept the visit and its purpose to myself all day, but at sundown, with no solution in sight, I decided that I must consult my father. So, while the others were sitting in the *sala*, I excused myself and climbed the stairs to his room.

As always he smiled at the sight of me. "Take my hand, Grazia," he invited me. "Tell me what happened today in the world."

I would never get a better opening for the terrible story I had brought to him, so I took a deep breath and began to report the events of the morning as I have told them to you. And he followed my words most attentively, like a child listening to a cautionary tale, never interrupting, not even to ask a question.

When I was done, he nodded sadly and said, "I see." That is all. "I see."

"What shall we do, Papa?" I asked at last. "Please help me. Tell me what to do."

Not a word from him. Only a tear at the corner of his eye. Then another. Then a blink. Then a flood onto the pillow. He was weeping silently. Where was my sense? How could I have put this burden on him?

"I am so sorry, Papa." I took him up in my arms. He felt lighter than a feather tick. My husky father, his once-ruddy skin now as transparent as parchment and his once-sparkling eyes cloudy behind the tears.

"Only one thing, Grazia..." He spoke haltingly.

"Yes, Papa."

"Let me die here. In my own bed. In my own house."

"Yes, Papa."

"Don't let me die on the street, daughter. Or in the house of strangers. That is all I ask. Let me die in my own bed."

"Yes, Papa."

"Will you swear it?"

"Yes, Papa." What was I swearing to? How could I swear it?

"Listen to me, Grazia..."

"Yes, Papa."

"You must not cry for me."

"Yes, Papa."

"I am not afraid to die. Or even sorry. My life—what I have made of it—is not such a field of roses. My best days are behind me...the days with your mother when you and Jehiel were young and we used to ride together. Do you remember?"

"Oh, Papa..." How could he think I would forget?

"No tears. Do you hear me, daughter?"

"Yes, Papa."

"Life has been good to me. I have had many good times. I was given two fine sons. And you, my treasure, to stay beside me at the end. No man could ask for more than that." He stopped, opened his eyes wide, and then, looking deep into my eyes, spoke in a much stronger voice. "But I do ask for more. I ask for this one thing. Only this. To die in my own bed. Not in the street, Grazia. Do not let me die in the street."

I wrote to Madonna Isabella that night requesting an urgent audience, and charged our porter to be at the gate of the Reggio when it opened in the morning to present my petition.

What I wrote would have choked your throat with bile. So servile was I. Such a sycophant. I named her saint, angel, Diana, Minerva, every flattering epithet in both the Christian and pagan lexicons. A man's life was at stake, I wrote her. And only she—the *illustrissima*, the Celsitude, the beneficent—could save him. That much at least was true. She was my last chance.

I waited all day Thursday for a reply. Early Friday morning I received my answer, a letter from Madama by the hand of her private secretary. The message, in sum: She did not hold court on Saturdays. However, on account of her love for our family, she would audience me privately in her suite the following morning. Be early and wait patiently, she advised. Your petition will be heard.

I entered the *illustrissima*'s presence much more of a soggy rag than I would have liked. She on the other hand appeared radiantly cheerful and almost happy to see me. Perhaps it was simply the prospect of an admirer for her new *camerini*, the suite of "little rooms" she had moved into in the Domus Nova since my last visit.

"What think you, Grazia? Is this not an improvement over that dreary old castle across the moat?" she asked.

I agreed that these *camerini* were a vast improvement over her old suite. In fact, the rooms were smaller than her old *camerini* and even more cluttered with the cameos and coins and medals and paintings she had acquired. There were now so many paintings that many had to be placed on easels, since there was no room for them on the walls. Yet there were many more to come, she told me, "... for I mean to have the finest collection of treasures in all Italy." (And so she does.)

Although for once I was not captivated by the trappings of *lusso*, I managed to make a good show of interest in her plans for the *camerini*. Impatience to get to the point is the prerogative of princes. Patient humility is the lot of Jews and other negligible persons. Surely the honor of being admitted to the princely presence is reward enough for the lowly. Must they also insist on being heard?

At length, I got my chance. The letter. Ah yes, my letter. Someone dying? Who, pray?

"It is my father, *illustrissima*."

"Daniele? I had heard he was improved."

I almost corrected her but caught myself. Be sensible, Grazia. What does a Jewish pawnbroker mean to her that she should remember the latest bulletin on the state of his health? I went on with my plaintive report. His pallor. His loss of weight.

"And is there nothing your distinguished husband can do? We have heard that he performs miracles for the French." From her sister-in-law Chiara, no doubt.

"Judah says the end is very near, madama. The tumor has eaten him away. My honorable husband is a great physician but no miracle worker, as he would be the first to acknowledge."

"Well then, if your celebrated husband can do nothing for Daniele, what do you want of me? Am I a miracle worker?"

"Yes, madonna." I knelt at her feet and kissed her hand. "You have the power to grant him his dying wish."

She withdrew her hand as if she suspected poison in my kiss.

"And what is that?"

"You can allow him to die in his own bed," I answered.

"There is a document. Signed by your hand, madonna."

"My hand?"

"Yes, madonna. An order to destroy our house."

"I thought so. It is Ghisolfo's chapel you've come about then."

"We will gladly give up our home to your husband's cause, madonna. All I ask is that you wait until my father has breathed his last."

"And when is that likely to be?"

"He is very weak, madonna."

"He has been weak for many months." Her tone had proceeded from quite warm, to lukewarm, to cool, to cold and was now bordering on icy.

"He is close to the end, madonna."

"But how close? You cannot tell me, can you? How do I know that you and Daniele between you did not concoct this dying wish as a ploy to keep from losing your house?"

Monstrous woman, I wanted to shout. Are you asking me for a guarantee that my father will be dead by Tuesday?

But I did not shout. Instead, I changed my tack.

"We will start to move the family immediately, madonna. And to disassemble the *banco*."

"If you wish I can make arrangements for space at the convent in the Via Pomponazzo."

"Thank you, madama. We already have an offer of space with the banker Davide Finzi." We had no such offer, but I was not so far gone in desperation that I would entrust my valuables to this lady. That would have been leaving the wolf to guard the chicken house.

"It is not the valuables or even the children that bring me here, *illustrissima*. It is my father. If you could see him, so frail, so resigned. He asks nothing, only to die in his own bed. Have mercy on him, madonna. Delay the eviction."

"Impossible. Redini's plan for the chapel has been accepted. Our honorable consort has approved the plans and given

the orders that construction is to begin at once. He is commander here as he is in the field. It is not my order. I am but his
lieutenant."

"For mercy's sake."

She waved away my plea as if it were a bothersome fly. No
use. She would not be moved. Yet I could not give up. Try
something else. An appeal to her cupidity, perhaps. But how to
get to it without impugning her honor?

"The necklace, *illustrissima*, the Necklace of a Hundred
Links..."

"Yes..." At least I had her attention back.

"We know how dear to you it is. I wish to assure you that it
has been sent to Ferrara for safekeeping."

"I am pleased to hear that."

"An arrangement could be made, madonna..." I dropped my
head in embarrassment. How I wished Papa had been there.
He was so clever at these kinds of negotiations. "An arrangement that I believe is called a *quid pro quo*."

"Something for something?"

Why must she make it so difficult? She knew damn well what
I was after. "We will return your necklace at once, madonna,
and forgive the interest on the loan if you allow us to stay in our
house until my father dies. Not a day longer."

There was a moment when her eyes lit up and I knew she
was tempted. But the moment passed and instead I got my final
rejection. "What you ask is impossible. I can give you two days
of grace, no more. This Friday coming, the *bargello* will be at
your gate to pull down the house. If Daniele is as close to the
end as you say, he will be dead by then and his dying wish will
have been honored. Otherwise, he moves. He has five days to
die. One of my men will see you home." And she turned away
from the reproach in my eyes.

At least I had gained two more days. After that if Papa was
still alive I would throw myself in the way of the *bargello*'s men
and give the last thing I had to give for my father—my life.

My mind was teeming with such wild fancies as I left that

room that I barely heard Madama's last words, hurled at me like a thunderbolt as I passed through the portal.

"Why are our dealings with you dei Rossis always so contentious?" she shouted. "Why can you not be gentle?"

WALKING BACK FROM THE Reggio in the gathering dark, I pondered what course I must take. It was one thing to offer myself as a victim to the *bargello's* sword but quite another to sacrifice my brothers and cousins in the cause. They must be gotten away safely. Then there was the *banco* to deal with. My father had honored me by placing his trust in me; but he had laid me low with the weight of it.

My brothers looked so very young to me that evening, sitting around the trestle table playing some silly game. Even Asher, a full-grown man, clapped his hands together delightedly like a child when his counter took the rest. I left them there and went off to my bed to plan our evacuation feeling at least twice my seventeen years.

By morning my plans were made. I would send the *famiglia* on to Ferrara at once. And the *banco* must be dismantled quickly. I instructed Asher to begin packing up the contents of the warehouse and went off to arrange for the transfer of our goods to a safe place. Messer Davide Finzi, our old neighbor and fellow loan banker, bore no great love for our family; but I had been told all my life that in times of trouble Jews stick together. The time had come to test the truth of that axiom.

The old man agreed at once to make room in his warehouse for our goods—at a fee, of course, and a fee which I had to negotiate at that. But business is business, as I had also heard all my life. What surprised me was that, without my asking, the old man offered my family one of his *bravi* as their escort to Ferrara. He even bent his stiff old neck so far as to volunteer himself and his sons as pallbearers at Papa's funeral, a most considerate gesture since all the men in our family would be gone by the time of that unhappy event if my plan went well.

My next stop was the posthouse. There I hired enough horses and carts to carry everyone in our household to Ferrara, excepting only my father and me. If it must be done, it had best be done quickly.

That afternoon I gave orders for the *banco* to be closed and called a family meeting. As accurately as I could, I relayed to them the substance of my meeting with Madonna Isabella. "I will stay with Papa," I announced, "as I gave him my word I would. It is best that you all go on to Ferrara now. There is no need for anyone else to stay behind but me. There may be trouble here with the *bargello's* men and—"

"If there is trouble, we must be here to fight off the devils," Jehiel broke in heatedly. He never was short on courage. And little Gershom added, "We can get swords out of the warehouse. I have seen them there."

"Quite right, cousin," Asher agreed. "A woman alone . . ."

"A woman alone has a better chance than a group of unarmed boys," I answered him. "I have my tears to protect me."

"But we cannot abandon you, Grazia," Penina insisted.

"You will not be abandoning me," I answered. "You will be doing me a service. I must keep my vow to Papa. If you go, you will leave me free to do my duty. Don't you see?"

"But I do not want to leave you, Grazia." Gershom threw himself into my arms, a child still in spite of his efforts at manliness. "Must I go?"

I nodded sadly. "Yes. It is best for all of you and for me. Now it is time for you to begin packing. I have ordered the horses for tomorrow."

Through it all not a word from Dorotea. Now, she spoke. "You have arranged all this without consulting me?"

"The sooner we get our gold and valuables out of the city, the better," I explained, with as much patience as I could muster. "Already the *illustrissima* has offered to 'protect' them for us. And you can guess what that means."

"But should not our honored parents be consulted?"

"There is no time for that, Dorotea. They will be happy to

see their strongboxes safe, believe me."

"All this comes too fast for me..."

"For me too," I answered tartly. "And I daresay for Papa. I do not believe he was counting on leaving this world quite so hurriedly."

"Oh, Grazia, what a thing to say..." And she flew from the room, weeping. I still do not know whether she intended to stay on with Papa or go to Ferrara with the rest. God knows, I did not want her. Still, I could hardly forbid a wife her place at her husband's deathbed.

I needn't have worried. After the children were asleep, she came down to the *banco*, where Asher and I were packing up, and beckoned me to one side. "I must speak to you, Grazia..."

"Speak."

"Not here. Not in front of Asher."

"Dorotea, I have enough work to keep me here all night. And I must try to sleep a little to keep strong for my father. So, whatever you have to say, you will have to say it here or not at all."

She now went into a little song and dance of whining and truckling as she always did when I spoke curtly to her. "Oh, Grazia, have pity on me," she whined. "I have an important decision to make and who else do I have to turn to? Your honored father on whom I depend for counsel is..." She snuffled up the bubble at the end of her nose. "Asher is meant to take the place of his father but he has not your strength, Grazia. He is delicate like me."

And what am I, I thought, a pack mule?

"I know that your honorable father would understand, but I fear that you will never forgive me," she wailed.

"For what?" I demanded.

"For going ahead to Ferrara with the children." She pulled a handkerchief out of her sleeve and dabbed at the end of her nose. "I would be no use here, Grazia. Soldiers frighten me. And you know I always faint at the sight of blood."

"But Papa isn't bleeding, nor is he expected to," I reminded her.

"He cries out in pain," she answered. "I cannot bear the sound of his screams in the night." How could she speak with such indulgence of her own gutlessness?

"What about me, Dorotea?" I taunted her. "Am I to be left alone with a dying man in a house under siege?"

"You can manage it, Grazia." She reached over and patted my arm with her hand. "You have the strength for it."

Using every bit of self-control I possessed, I very carefully detached her hand from my sleeve. It felt clammy and boneless, like an eel.

"Have you told Papa you plan to leave him?" I asked.

"Would you tell him for me?" Once again she placed her hand on my sleeve. This time I made no attempt to disguise the disgust I felt when I picked her fingers off me.

"Yes, Dorotea, I will do your dirty laundry for you. I will tell Papa that I have begged you to go with the children for their protection. I will do it not for you but to save his feelings. I cannot bear to see him so bitterly disappointed in these last days of his life as he would be if he knew what a craven, gutless, crawling, cringing, fawning bitch he picked to take my mother's place. Now get out of my sight."

And the poor wretch crept out into the dim of the courtyard.

But don't you think she was back in five minutes, pulling at my sleeve again?

"What now, Dorotea?" This time, I all but shoved her aside.

"A little thing..." She hesitated. "When you speak to your father, had you not best find out from him where he keeps his will? To make certain that his wishes are carried out? I have looked high and low for it."

"Why don't you ask him yourself?" No reply. "Or have you already?" Silence. How strange that he had not confided in her.

"Very well. I will ask him," I agreed, for it was important to me too that my father's wishes be known and carried out.

"Tonight?"

"When I see fit," I answered brusquely. Then, beyond patience, I added, "Do not worry yourself, lady. I will worm the secret of his will out of him before he breathes his last."

"Oh, Grazia, how cruel you are…" And she was gone, this time not to return.

As Asher and I worked on wrapping and packing and checking our inventories the matter stuck in my mind. It was unlike her not to know what was in Papa's will. If I knew her, she had dictated it.

Then, as if he had been reading my thoughts, Asher spoke suddenly. "My mother fears that Uncle Daniele has made a new will these past few weeks."

"Is it true?" I asked.

"Just before you arrived he had Ser Natale the lawyer here three days running. The lawyer had never stepped foot inside this house before, Grazia. But he came three times and brought documents and he called for a quill and some hot wax. Your father must have signed something official."

"It could easily have been *banco* business," I suggested.

"Yes, it could." He considered my suggestion. "But I do not believe it was. For after the lawyer left the last time, my uncle called me to him privately — I have told this to no one, Grazia — and spoke to me most affectionately. He said he wanted to assure me that I would be taken care of, that he had arranged it. He told me that when he took me to his bosom after my own father died, it was not only an act of charity but also an act of love." He turned his head away and pulled out a raggedy *fazzoletto* from his sleeve. "And he thanked me for my service to him. And called me his own son. And he kissed me…" No longer able to stifle his sobs, he turned and buried his head in my breast. "Oh, Grazia," he sobbed. "I will miss him so. He was like a father to me."

Then I broke down as well and we let our tears mingle and were finally the brother and sister that my father had so long wished us to be. Together, we finished fastening the last chain around the last *cassone* just as the watchman passed by chanting matins. We had inventoried and packed the entire contents of the warehouse within one revolution of the sun. We had done Papa proud.

"Wakey, wakey, rise and shine for matins time." The watchman's rough voice rang out in the street below.

"I must admit I was never certain we could accomplish the task," I confessed to my cousin. "I could not have done it without your strong right arm," I told him.

"My strong back is more like it, cousin." He smiled. "But this is only the beginning of the task. It is far easier to dispatch trunks and cartons than people."

"Oh, we will get them off safely, never fear," I assured him.

"About my honorable mother..." He hesitated.

"Yes?"

"I beg you not to judge her too harshly, cousin. In many ways she is a child. Often she does not know what she is saying."

So she would have you think, I said to myself. But I held my tongue. No matter how indefensible her conduct, she was his blood mother and there was something upright and admirable in her son's defense of her.

Then on a sudden impulse I turned to him. "Stay with me, cousin," I urged. "Dorotea can take care of the children. I need you more than they do. Next to my honorable husband, you are the strongest and most loyal man I know."

How eagerly he responded to the compliment! "At your service, madama." He sprang to his feet and executed an awkward bow. True, he almost toppled over on his way up from the floor. But if gallantry begins in the heart as they say it does, my cousin Asher had all the makings of a true gallant. What a fine husband he will make for someone, I thought to myself. How perfect for Penina. But I quickly reminded myself that La Nonna had other plans for her and no doubt for Asher as well.

The next morning the children lined up at my instruction to come and say their goodbyes to Papa. Gershom was the first. No one had told him in so many words that this was the last time he would see his father alive, but he knew.

"Papa..." He bent down and laid his cheek beside my father's. The blue-veined eyelids fluttered. Papa had lost at least half his body weight in these last weeks and his skin stretched over his bones like a fine woven cambric cloth. Beside him, the little boy's sallow complexion appeared positively ruddy with health and youth.

Now Gershom began to whisper urgently into Papa's ear, so quietly I could not make out what was being said. On and on he talked, becoming more agitated by the moment. No response from Papa.

Then all at once, before I could stop him, the little boy took my father's frail body by the shoulders and began to shake it wildly. "Say something, Papa. Talk to me. Please." And would you believe it, my father's eyes opened wide and he spoke. "Gershom, my son."

"Oh, Papa, I love you so much. I do not want to leave you. But Grazia says I must go to Ferrara. Must I go, Papa? Must I? Cannot I stay here with you and Grazia? I do not want to go on this journey."

"Nor do I, my son." I swear I saw a trace of a smile on Papa's lips as he uttered these ironic words. "But when the call comes..." His voice drifted off. Then just as he was sinking into a doze he roused himself up and held out his arms. "Kiss me, Gershom."

My little brother's name was the last word my father ever spoke. When Jehiel came in a few moments later with Ricca, Papa remained in his doze with nothing but an occasional twitch to indicate that he had not already passed over the bar.

Within the hour, all of them were gone: Dorotea, the children, and Asher, who was to see them as far as a bucentaur at Borgoforte and then return to my aid. And I was left with my dying father and two frightened servants. From the day they learned that we had been put out of our house by order of the *bargello*, they had quaked at every shout in the street and paled at every knock on our portal. When they realized that nothing stood between them and the *bargello's* pikes but a dying man and a defenseless woman, the last vestige of courage left them. By the end of the day I had had my fill of their bitten lips and twitchy eyes and told them to go.

So it happened that I was quite alone with my father when he breathed his last. He passed over so peacefully that I never knew the exact moment of his going. At about the fifth hour I took hold of his wrist to feel the pulse and felt — nothing. His heart had stopped beating.

37

MY FATHER DIED THREE DAYS BEFORE THE TIME allotted him by Marchesana Isabella. You might say he skipped away early so as not to inflict the embarrassment he would cause if he stayed too long at the feast.

I sat all night alone with him in the empty house in the Via San Simone. Some of the time I talked to him. And I believe I kissed his dear face many times and held his cold hands in my warm ones. Not with any idea of reinfusing life into him. Nothing so foolish as that. I did not even believe — or hope — that my words would reach him as he floated up to heaven. A born Jew does not think overmuch of the hereafter. I spoke to my dead father simply because my heart was full to overflowing and needed spilling.

When dawn came I kissed him for the last time, covered him with a soft blanket, and walked alone across town to the Finzi house. The old man Finzi stayed true to his word. A *minyan* of ten men — members of his *famiglia* — would be at the Casa dei Rossi for morning prayers, he assured me. And these mourners would form a procession that afternoon to see Papa to his last resting place.

A funeral is a funeral, no matter what creed you subscribe to — twenty percent grief, eighty percent arrangements. When I returned home from the Finzi house my first act was to turn the mirrors to the wall. Next I prepared a vat of pure water and a pile of clean cloths for the women who would wash my father's body. That was for God. For myself I took out all the candleholders in the great chest that held our family's treasures. I wanted my father's house blazing with candlelight on his last day there.

It was while I was searching for candles that Maestro Andrea's son appeared at the portal. His father had sent him to fetch me. My portrait was finished and I must come at once to see it. The fact that I was preparing my own father's funeral seemed not to register with him. After one or two verbal skirmishes, I gave up the struggle to make him understand why I could not come and shut the door in his face. Maestro Andrea would have to wait.

The funeral procession set out from our house at the eighteenth hour, just after noon. One of the Finzi sons offered me his arm but I preferred to walk alone through the streets, hoping against all sensible expectations that Asher would come flying back from Borgoforte in time to stand by me. And by God, he did. As we were crossing Saint George's bridge I caught sight of the familiar bandy legs flashing along the Porto Catena road. By the time the procession reached the end of the bridge, he was at my side, cloak flying, *berretta* askew, panting from exertion but there.

I leaned on him heavily during the brief service at the graveside and even more heavily on the way back to town. That night he helped me to prepare the house for mourning. We might have only one day for it but I was determined to render my father every last shred of his rightful respect.

Together, Asher and I took down the tapestries and draped the doors and windows with black cloths. Now we put away out of sight the cups and vases that adorned the mantel and all the candelabra I had put out the day before. Once the body is in the ground nothing must shine.

Soon after sunrise an assemblage of men—every adult male Jew in Mantova, I do believe—filtered quietly into the dark house for morning prayers. *"Yisgadal v'yiskadash,"* I heard them chanting from upstairs where I had retired. Women have no place in this ritual. The rabbis expect us to busy ourselves with more appropriate tasks: cleaning, tidying, cooking for the mourners. Very well. For the sake of my father's memory, I would find a suitable domestic task to occupy me while the men went about the serious business of mourning my loss.

Most of our domestic valuables were already laid out for the Finzi agent who would be arriving early next day to make his appraisal. But my father's personal effects remained unexamined. What better task could a loving daughter undertake than to catalogue her father's effects and consign each to its rightful place? *"Yisgadal v'yiskadash . . ."* I muttered as I reached into the *cassone* that held his clothes, determined to pray over each item and thereby cheat the men below of their exclusive right to petition God on my father's behalf.

His fine linen shirts must be packed up to be used by Jehiel and Gershom when they grew older. And Asher, I added mentally. My father had told him he was like one of his own sons. I must treat him as one. I put two of the shirts aside to pass on to him when I saw him later in the day.

Next I turned to the small velvet box where Papa kept his most valued possessions. And it was there, nestled in the folds of his prayer shawl, that I found his will. In the confusion and haste of his last hours all thought of it had fled my mind. But I knew what it was the moment I laid my hands on it. Tightly rolled with a velvet band, secured with three different wax seals, there was no mistaking it. But I had no heart to read it. Let it wait, I thought. Papa would be a long time dead.

My father was not an acquisitive man. He left few mementos behind aside from his books. All that remained to be carried with us to Ferrara were his silver *Kaddish* cup, a diamond-studded gold plaquette which I had not seen on his hat in a decade, and a fine filigree amulet made in the shape of the temple of

Jerusalem. Not a single finger ring or a gold chain did I find. Poor Jehiel. It would have pleased him to adorn himself with his father's jewels. Unlike his brother, Gershom, he had not inherited our father's disinclination for ostentation.

Once the men had finished praying, the women began to arrive and I was permitted to take my place downstairs among the neighbors who had come to comfort the bereaved family. Young people tend to regard mourning as a sham; purists, as a pagan ritual. Do not fall into this trap, my son. Every word of condolence, every recollection, every compassionate gesture, nourishes the seed of memory. For in the nature of things, memory fills the gap left by loss. Which makes mourning one of the few genuinely humane acts we are given to perform. Heed me. Do as the Torah commands. Never neglect the obligations of mourning.

As a final courtesy to Papa, old Davide Finzi came himself next day to appraise our household goods. Old men know about dying. That old man knew that to have some bumbling boy underfoot chattering as he toted up the sum of my father's worldly goods would have broken me. In the gentlest of voices he asked me if I would please mark for him those items we meant to keep out for ourselves so that they could be packed separately.

"Begin in the *sala*," he advised me, experience having taught him that most of the sentimental objects would reside there. "After that, the rest will be easier."

I let the old man guide me through the entire house, pushing me firmly past the shoals where sentiment lay in wait to engulf me, until at last nothing was left to deal with except my father's bed, the bed he had died in.

"I wish to sell it," I announced firmly.

"Your father's best bed?" The old man was shocked. "You are certain?"

"The bed. The hangings. The linens. Everything. I am certain. I will sleep in this bed tonight. Tomorrow your men can take it away. But see that they come early. For the *bargello* is due first thing in the morning."

"You are certain that you want to see strangers sleeping in your father's best bed?" he insisted.

"We have no use for it," I answered. Dorotea had refused to share that bed when Papa most needed her. Why should she have the good of it now that he was gone?

I did not disclose these thoughts to old Finzi. Instead I haggled with him over the price, a pastime which put me back into some kind of spirits. We were two of a kind in that. Now all that remained was for him to make his inventory and tote up the appraisals we had agreed upon.

"You may rest here while I do it, little lady," he offered. "Or go out for a stroll in the fine day. I will send my man to escort you if you like."

Why not take a stroll, I thought. It was my last day in Mantova — my last chance to visit the house where I grew up, to walk through the great squares, to cross the Mulina bridge one last time. And on the way I would pass Maestro Andrea's strangely constructed house and — Maestro Andrea! Until that moment I had completely forgotten his summons to come and view the portrait that would immortalize me forever.

My clothes were laid out for the next day's journey. In a moment, I had them on and was urging Finzi's servant out of the house with the tip of my sunshade, much to old Finzi's amusement. "You'll have to run to stay even with this little lady, you lazy scullion," he shouted after the lad as we tumbled out the door.

I found the Maestro's studio as dirty and cluttered as I remembered it. He was also unchanged. "I sent for you two days ago," he growled.

"My father's funeral..." I began to explain. But he would have none of it.

"Did my son not tell you the portrait was finished?"

"How could it be finished without me?" I asked.

"I am an artist, madonna," he replied gruffly. "Not a monkey. I have a mind to remember with. Only an oaf needs to paint entirely from life. I could have done without you after the first two sittings."

"Then why did you keep me coming back?"

"I enjoyed the sight of you," he answered simply, as if his own pleasure was quite enough justification for my inconvenience.

"And may I see it now?" I asked.

"No."

"But you said it was finished."

"Finished and gone."

"Gone?"

"Sold to a gentleman."

"But you promised that I would see it, maestro."

"The gentleman who bought it was adamant. He must have it then and there, that very day. No delay. He was leaving Mantova. He made me an offer I could not refuse."

"You broke your promise to me for money, maestro."

"No, madonna. Not for money. For beauty. Did you not hear what I told you? That he made me an offer I could not refuse? Here. See for yourself."

He went to his table and picked up a handful of coins.

"Look!" he ordered me.

I looked and beheld four matching coins of the Roman period, each emblazoned with the face of Faustina.

"She looks like you," was all he said. Not a word of regret or apology.

For a moment my temper flared. Then I thought better of it. To me the portrait had seemed a chance at immortality. To him it was merely a thing he had made, a work of his own hand, not comparable to the work of one of the ancient masters he revered. He had traded my portrait for something finer.

But perhaps there was still a chance I might see it, if I could find the purchaser. "This gentleman who bought my portrait..." I began.

"*My* portrait," he corrected me firmly.

"Yes of course, *your* portrait of *me*, maestro. The gentleman who purchased it, could you please tell me his name?"

"No."

"May I ask why?"

"You may not. But I will tell you. My silence was a part of the bargain. I am sworn not to reveal his name or anything about him. Besides, the matter is not your concern. The gentleman saw the portrait, fell in love with it and wanted it, a not infrequent occurrence with my works, I assure you."

"Did he not inquire about the sitter?"

"He did not, lady. He has all of you he wants in my picture. Women never understand these things."

I walked back from Maestro Andrea's house at a meditative pace much more to the liking of my lazy escort than the breathless dash that brought us there. When I stopped at the gates of the Reggio and announced to him that I meant to sit on one of the stone benches for a few moments, he even spread his cloak for me.

What an ugly pile it was, this mismatched agglomeration of disparate buildings that I had once thought the most elegant in all the world. But my stay in Firenze had trained my eye. Now, Brunelleschi's harmonious proportions were so embedded in my skull that I would never again be able to look upon the barbarisms of the Dark Ages without a shudder.

Yet there was strength here. The sheer weight of the stones compelled respect. Ahead of me, Saint George's loomed up like a fortress out of the *Reale di Francia*. As I gazed up, the old magic began to work its spell on me. Mind you, I had not forgotten that beneath one of those elegant coffered ceilings, my happiness had been disposed of like a soiled rag. "My illustrious husband has made other plans for Lord Pirro." Their cruelty is so casual; their power to inflict it, so great. And yet, as I stood looking up at the candlelit windows, I was taken over by a longing to pass through the gates and enter into the golden world inside the walls, to find myself dancing one more *frotilla* in Lord Pirro's arms with a thousand candles flickering around us and beauty everywhere.

By the time I returned to the Via San Simone, Finzi's wagons were already loaded in the courtyard. Inside, the *sala grande* was bare. Before me on the mantel lay a sheaf of papers—the inventory. One large iron cauldron, ten *bolognini*. Three ladles, three *bolognini*...I never got beyond the first page. Asher, I thought. Asher would check up on old Finzi for me.

I found my cousin in the *banco* leaning against the shutter, lost in grief.

"Come away, cousin." I drew near to take his arm. "You must sleep and so must I."

I steered him across the courtyard and into the *sala*, a gloomy cavern now that all of its innards had been removed.

"Come upstairs," I urged him. "Old Finzi has left us the bed to sit on."

He hesitated. "Would it be proper, Grazia?"

"It would," I assured him, and led the way. "Papa would not want us to sleep our last night on the cold floor."

Darkness was falling fast and with it came the chill that descends on Mantova from its surrounding circle of lakes.

"You are shivering, cousin. You must get into bed and cover yourself over," he said.

"And what of you?" I asked. "Are you impervious to the night's vapors?"

"I will manage," he replied.

"You will manage to catch catarrh," I corrected him. "Come and lie by me. I insist."

I could see in his eyes that he longed to join me in the cozy warmth of the covers but modesty held him back.

"Please, cousin," I urged. "I do not wish to journey forth tomorrow in the company of sniffles and coughs. Come." I patted the pillows invitingly. "Bring the candle. I have Finzi's inventory here. We can examine it together. Then our last task will be done."

The suggestion of duty moved him. He did as I asked. And we did sit together and examine the inventory. At least, he did. I merely went through the mummery for his sake.

I have vowed to be honest in this *ricordanza*. Very well, honesty you shall have, to the best of my ability to reconstruct the events of that night. The initiative was mine. I was the one who intrigued my cousin into my bed on the pretext of working over the Finzi papers. I did believe, when I proffered the invitation, that I meant nothing more by it. But once I felt the weight of his body beside me and the warmth of his breath on my cheek, I began to feel stirrings.

At this point I could retreat into metaphorical vagueness and tell you that what happened between my cousin Asher and me was the assertion of the life force in the face of death. All of us court poets are masters of that sort of twaddle. But looking back, I understand that I wanted to lie in a man's arms that night; I wanted to be possessed by another, stronger being; I wanted to feel my weakness surrounded by a pair of strong arms, to be taken away, out of my sadness and loss. Asher struggled manfully against temptation. But he was no match for my desperate need to be loved.

It all happened quite easily. Quite naturally. Knees touch. Bones thrust. Bodies adjust, closer together with every move. I bury my head in my cousin's broad shoulder. Softly, he smooths my hair. I raise my face. He kisses my forehead. My cheek. He groans. I open my eyes. The longing in his eyes is unbearable. I kiss his lips. His teeth are clenched tight. Slowly I feel them open to the soft pressure of my tongue. His mouth is liquid. I drink in the nectar, tasting each drop with my tongue.

Passion is like lightning. A chain of reaction. The flame ignited by the kiss rages through our two bodies and down to the nether regions. I feel the hardness of his member and I long to be possessed. Taken over. Taken away. Another groan. "No, Grazia."

"Yes," I insist. And so we consummate the moment. And when that act has been performed we fall into a dreamless sleep.

THE *bargello's* MEN ARRIVED at our door before the light. At the first sound of their pikes against the portal, I jumped up out of bed, leaving Asher, a sound sleeper, safe in Morpheus' arms.

On my way down the stairs, I heard the sergeant giving orders to his men to fetch the battering ram. "No need for that, good sir," I shouted through the door. "I will gladly give you entrance just as soon as I unbolt this door."

It was a disappointed face that leered at me when, a few seconds later, I managed to disengage the bolt and open the door to him.

"Good morning, sir," I greeted him. "Please come in. We will be gone as soon as our horses arrive."

"And when will that be?" he growled.

"Any moment now. But pray begin. The courtyard is cleared. And the stables."

"We begin at the top," he blustered. "Those are my orders."

"Very well then," I replied. "We will conclude our packing with utmost speed. It will take but a moment."

The more accommodating I was, the more irritable he became. I daresay he resented being cheated of the use of his battering ram. "It will take whatever time I grant you, lady," he snarled. "Up the stairs..." He gave me the barest shove. "I will come along to make certain you do not tarry."

You cannot imagine Asher's face when he saw the uniformed sergeant glaring down at him, a pike held aloft like the devil's pitchfork. For a moment my poor cousin must have thought he had died and gone to hell.

"This gentleman is the representative of the *bargello*, Asher," I informed him. "He has come to help us pack."

"I have come to escort you out, lady," the irate sergeant sputtered. "And you too, whoever you are."

"This is my cousin, Ser Asher dei Rossi," I offered politely, as if we were all at a ball, after which neither of the two men had much choice but to salute each other, which they did with equal truculence.

I reached down to the floor where Asher's garments lay in a little puddle and handed them to him. "I am certain the sergeant will be patient while you say your prayers, cousin," I advised him. "Is that not so, sergeant?" It was hard to say which of the two was more ill at ease, Asher in his nakedness or the sergeant in his frustration.

"And what is to become of this bed, eh?" The sergeant poked my arm. "You can hardly carry it out on your back."

What a time for a grand gesture! I could hear myself saying, "You can keep the damn bed. Or give it to the poor. Or burn the cursed thing for all I care." But alas, deep down, I am a pragmatist and so I answered him that Ser Davide Finzi's men would be along shortly to take the bed away. And in fact, the Finzi wagon and our horses arrived together a few moments later.

In no time at all Asher and I were mounted and out the stable gate. I looked back only once, just in time to see the first thrust of the battering ram against the facade of the house. The last sound I heard in the Via San Simone was the clatter of a hundred bricks falling.

38

I SLEPT IN ASHER'S ARMS ALL THE WAY FROM MANTOVA to Borgoforte, where we stopped to transfer to the barque that would carry us along the Po to Ferrara. It was there that I vowed to forgo the easy refuge offered me by my cousin's affectionate embrace.

"Here begins a new life," I told him as we waited our turn to board the craft. "We must leave the past behind us in Mantova and go on with our lives."

"I have been thinking the same thought, cousin," he answered. "You are a married woman, much as I might wish it otherwise."

"Shh!" I stopped him. "We must not even speak of the matter. Let us go back to the way we were before Papa's funeral. Brother and sister."

"No use, Grazia," he replied dolefully. "That night is emblazoned in my memory as if branded there. I will never forget it."

"Oh yes you will," I assured him, with a confidence I did not feel. For I knew the hopelessness of trying to expunge memories of love. "Once I am gone from Ferrara it will be easier."

"Easier for you. Because you are blameless in this business.

But I took advantage of you in your moment of distress."

"No. It was I, Asher. I led you on."

"Do not try to lighten my guilt, Grazia. I know what I have done." Oh, he was contrite. No doubt of it. And guilt-ridden. But beneath his self-castigation, I sensed a deep current of pride and realized that I must give up my share of guilt in the cause of his manliness.

IF EVER I HAD imagined my grandparents' house as a refuge in my bereavement, I was quickly disabused of that illusion. My first sight of the portal sent a message to my brain that something was not right. But fatigued as I was, and nervy and drowned in sorrow, my mind could not capture the precise cause of my unease. That only became apparent after we had entered the house and been greeted by my brothers. As I clasped Gershom to my bosom my eyes focused on his little waistcoat. It was robin's-egg blue, not black. And his *calze* were parti-colored. Now it came to me what I had missed outside! Where was the swag of black which announced to the world that this was a house of mourning?

They have not heard of Papa's death, I thought. The messenger we sent ahead has not arrived. But Dorotea's first words dispelled that thought. "My sympathies, Grazia. We were all grieved more than I can tell you by the news." She made as if to kiss my cheek but I managed to sidestep her embrace.

"Where is your widow's veil, Dorotea?" I asked. "And why are not the boys dressed in black?"

"The rabbi tells us that my honored husband's house is the mourning place," she answered.

"But that house is half destroyed by now. And there is no one in it to light the candles or say the prayers."

"Then we are excused." She shrugged. "It is an act of God."

"Excused!" I shrieked. "Excused from paying respect to my father? Well, perhaps you are excused, madame. But I am not. Nor my brothers. Call the servants. I want black cloths placed on these windows. And over the door."

"But you cannot," she wailed. "Rabbi Abramo says—"

"To hell with the rabbi!" Dorotea gasped. "And to hell with you as well. For hell is where you will certainly be sent for this sacrilege. Now call the servants."

"I cannot call the servants." She was shaking now, edging herself out of the room. "This is not my house. Nor is it your house. It is your honored grandfather's house. And you can speak to him yourself."

With that she rushed out, followed by a smirking Ricca and leaving me with my brothers and Asher.

"You must go with her, cousin," I counseled him.

"I must do no such thing, cousin," he replied, bristling. "I must go with you to our grandfather and complain about this outrage. And the boys as well. We must all go. Come along, Jehiel. Gershom." And out they marched into the courtyard, leaving me to follow behind like a docile female.

What a change had come over my timid cousin in four days. I can only conclude that sex holds much more magic for men than it does for us women. For I have never seen a virgin bride transformed into a virago by having her hymen broken.

Across the courtyard and into the *banco* trod the little procession. Straight up the staircase to the strong room. In all this perambulating we saw no sign of La Nonna or of my old enemy, Giorgio. But I knew we would soon have the pleasure of seeing them. For Dorotea could be counted on to deliver an instant report of my rash words.

And sure enough, we had barely had time to greet my grandfather in his counting room when in rushed La Nonna—eyes smaller and more squinty than ever—followed by her minion. The years had not been kind to Giorgio. Bent over now with a back hump, his feet bandaged from gout, he shuffled rather than strode and would have presented an altogether pathetic sight had I not remembered the misery he inflicted on me in the days when he was strong. Such memories corrode the wellspring of pity even in the softhearted. I glared at him and uttered no word of greeting.

"Still making trouble, Grazia?" was my grandmother's greeting.

"More than ever, Grandmother," was my reply.

Obviously my father's death had changed nothing between us.

"Now, what is all this fuss about black curtains?" she demanded.

"I and my brothers are in mourning for our father, who died five days ago at Mantova. You and his father ought to be in mourning too. He was your son," I answered.

"Are you presuming to tell us our duty?" she demanded.

"It appears that someone must." To my surprise my voice emerged from my throat without a quaver. "All I ask is that you pay the proper respect to my father while I am in this house. When the month is up I will return to Firenze with my brothers and you can dance naked in the *sala* for all I care."

It was an unnecessary crudity. But I was mad with rage.

Now my grandfather spoke up. "Rabbi Abramo has counseled us on this matter."

"So I heard," I retorted.

"Do you presume to put yourself above a rabbi in interpreting the Holy Words?"

"When the interpreter is a bought toady, a virtual catamite, I do indeed put myself far above him. Had I not more important things to do with my time, I would initiate proceedings against him with the *Wad Kellilah*. I still may ask my honorable husband to do so when he returns from Napoli. For I believe that what this scurvy priest has agreed to here is sacrilege."

"And so do I," Asher added. Bless him.

"And I," echoed Gershom.

But not a word from Jehiel. The poor boy stood silent in the center of the room, uneasily turning his head from side to side.

"This house must go into deep mourning for one month," I announced firmly. "Out of respect for the loss of the eldest son. I will not see my father's memory shamed by anything less."

"And if we do not agree?" my grandfather inquired, icy and hostile.

"I will return to Firenze at once with my brothers and trumpet your sacrilege the length and breadth of this peninsula."

"Unfortunately, your reputation precedes you, granddaughter," La Nonna spat back. "Who will believe the word of a known *catecumena*, a girl who ran off with a Christian, who denied her religion and disgraced us all?"

"Perhaps they will not believe me, Grandmother," I answered, for indeed she had a point. "But what Jew in this peninsula would doubt the word of Judah del Medigo? Or in Constantinople or Cairo or even Jerusalem for that matter? Remember, my honored husband is known, respected, and trusted throughout the Jewish world. And I assure you he will be horrified by this disrespect to me and to himself."

"We meant no disrespect," my grandfather muttered.

"Certainly not to Messer Judah," my grandmother added, careful not to include me in her admission.

"If that is so, then have the humility to change your stance. Cover the windows of this house. Hang the crepe over the door. Close up the *banco*."

"Not the *banco*! That is impossible."

The *banco*. Money. Profit. Greed. That was what lay at the bottom of their intransigence. Now I understood. But understanding only made me more implacable.

"Either the *banco* will be closed or I will call Judah away from his service to the French," I announced. "But remember this: If you are excommunicated the dei Rossi bank may be closed forever, since no other Jew will do business with you."

"The girl is a witch," my grandmother muttered, just loud enough for me to hear.

"No, Grandmother. Not a witch. Only a loving child who insists that proper respect be paid to her parent."

In the end they capitulated. They had no choice. All my threats were backed with truth. Judah, a stickler for observances, would have been hugely offended. He certainly would have taken the matter up with the great rabbis of the large cities where he was so well known. And excommunication was a very real possibility.

That night, Asher was sent to me with their counterproposal. They would close up the *banco* and rent a stall in the marketplace in which to conduct dei Rossi business.

Only on condition that no blood member of our family worked in that stall, I rejoined, and sent Asher back to them with my condition.

After a pause of some time he returned. They had agreed.

The skirmish was over. I had won. But I knew the battle would go on. And so it did. For the entire month, the house was a theater of war: Gershom, Asher, and I against the rest, with Jehiel hovering uncertainly between the opposing forces. It was surely the most unpleasant month of my life. Only the thought that I would soon be able to leave, and leave with honor, sustained me.

But before that happy escape, there was the will to be attended to. I had given it over to the family lawyer for safe keeping with instructions that the seals not be broken until the thirty days of our mourning were done. Until then I had refused to discuss the matter. But sure enough, on the thirty-first day after my father's death—the very day that the *banco* reopened and the curtains came down—la Nonna summoned the lawyer and ordered all of us into the *sala* for the reading of Papa's will.

The document began with expressions of love and regard for his family and a wish to be pardoned for any wrongs he had done any of us; not an endless palaver of ethical platitudes like the introductions to some wills, but a clear straightforward message from the heart—very much in Papa's style.

Then came the bequests. As the old lawyer began to read in his sententious voice, everyone in that room leaned forward, each face a picture: Gershom, confusion; Jehiel, apprehension; Dorotea, avarice; Ricca, a smug satisfaction that I could not read.

"To my firstborn son, Jehiel, I leave my astrolabe..." Jehiel clapped his hands together in undisguised glee. "And my share of cargo in the good ship *Helena* bound this year of 1496 for the

Occident. Should she return safe to harbor in Venezia, he will be a rich man. Should she founder at sea, he must depend for his future upon his own wits and whatever patrimony comes to him upon the death of his grandfather, head of the house of dei Rossi."

At once all eyes turned toward my grandfather. But he simply nodded and kept his own counsel.

The lawyer continued. "To my beloved daughter, Grazia, wife of Judah del Medigo, I leave all my books and I urge her to share this treasure with her brothers at such time as either shows an inclination toward scholarship." I thought of that small library now residing in Finzi's warehouse, not more than twenty volumes in all but each beautifully made. The illuminated Maimonides I vowed to send for at once and to keep by my bedside so that I might read a little of the wisdom of that great sage each morning of my life in Papa's honor. For he valued Maimonides above all the wise men of Israel.

Lost in these lofty thoughts, I almost missed the second part of my bequest. "Also to Grazia, I bequeath my house in the Via Sagnola where she lived her early years. And I instruct her to share it with her brothers should they ever need a roof, an instruction I know to be unnecessary because of the great love these three children of mine bear for each other."

"You did well to worm the house out of him," Dorotea whispered sharply in my ear.

"What house?" My question was genuine.

"What house indeed! My house, that Daniele promised to me, as if you did not know it. Shame on you, taking advantage of a man too sick and weak to resist your pleas."

This time she forgot to whisper. And even my grandfather seemed distressed by her show of temper. "Control yourself, Dorotea," he cautioned. And to forestall any further outbursts, to the lawyer: "Continue, maestro. And speak up, please."

"I speak as loud as I am able." The lawyer sniffed twice through his thin, pointed nose and continued. "To my widow, Dorotea, and to her children, Asher and Ricca, I leave my present house on the Via San Simone and all the furnishings thereof—"

"But that house is condemned," Dorotea interrupted. "It is being torn down by order of the Gonzagas."

"My uncle could not have known that at the time he drew this will," Asher answered her evenly.

"Then we must have the other house in its place," Ricca announced, rising to her feet. "Is that not a fair interpretation of my uncle's will, maestro, since he meant us to have the better house?"

"I doubt that the law would see it that way, madonna," he answered quietly.

"But this arrangement goes against Uncle Daniele's wish." No triumph now on Ricca's face, only undisguised rage. "Uncle did not intend to see me and my mother on the street. He meant for us to have a fine house. Besides, Grazia does not need a house, do you, Grazia? You will give us the little house, will you not, Grazia?" she wheedled.

"How Madonna Grazia disposes of her inheritance is not the issue here, little lady," the lawyer cut in, somewhat testy now. "The terms of the will are clear. The house in the Via Sagnola is hers. And the house in the Via San Simone is yours. And if there is no longer a house in Via San Simone, that is God's will and you had best accept it."

Whereupon Dorotea shrieked, "*Dio*, You have made me a homeless widow and my children two homeless orphans. Why me? Why me?"

I could have told her, but even I had not the gall to pretend to interpret God's intentions. I simply sat silent, eyes lowered, and waited for the next *bombarde* from the lawyer. But before he could begin, my grandfather rose from his seat and, in a gesture of compassion unprecedented for him, placed his hand on Dorotea's head and patted it once or twice. "Do not weep, daughter," he said. "You will always have a home here with us. You and your children are dear to us. And remember, Daniele's is not the only patrimony in this family. I cannot live forever."

"Oh, Grandfather, do not even say that." Ricca sprang up. "I cannot bear to think of life without you and La Nonna. Remember you promised to dance at my wedding. And at the birth of my first son. Promise me you will not die."

Plautus could not have written her speech better. And the vain old man sucked in every false word like a bee sucking in nectar.

But Dorotea was not so easily distracted. She knew her father-in-law's capricious nature and the value of his promises. And one look at me must have assured her that she would get my mother's house away from me over my dead body.

When at last the list was done the lawyer took a deep breath and asked for a glass of wine, which he downed in one gulp as if to fortify himself for the next explosion.

"While my younger son, Gershom, remains short of his maturity," the reading went on, "I commend the management of his affairs to my daughter, Grazia, and her husband, the renowned physician del Medigo. It is my wish that they supervise his education and guide him in the way of an honorable life. To assist him in reaching his goal after he is grown, I bequeath to him my life's savings, a sum of some twenty thousand ducats on deposit at the dei Rossi *banco* in Ferrara. That sum ought to buy him a good wife and a house in which to put her when the time comes."

"But that is *my* money!" Once again Dorotea rose to her feet. This time her eyes were wild and her shout a shriek that could have been heard as far as the *castello*. "That money is mine. He has no right to it." And before anyone knew what she was doing, she had rushed across the room and grabbed the terrified boy by his hair. "Give it back, you little swine. Daniele promised it to me. You have no right to it."

It took all our efforts to subdue her. She clung to that child's hair like a drowning man to a raft, and left him in a state near to shock. I determined then and there to make self-defense a part of his education as soon as I took charge of him. No man should be defenseless against attack in this violent world. Nor woman either.

After some moments of confusion Dorotea was led off, still wild around the eyes and threatening to sue my hapless little brother, who crouched shuddering in the crook of my arm. And La Nonna glowered at me as if I were responsible for the entire farce.

"Is it true, Grazia? Did my son promise his wife the money?" she demanded.

"I have no idea, Grandmother," I replied tartly.

"Very strange. Very odd," she muttered. "But then my son always was a strange one."

"He was an honorable man, a fine husband, and a good father to his children," I retorted.

"Still quick to take offense, Grazia?" Her beady little eyes squinted over at me. "I had hoped that marriage would soften you."

"My honorable husband finds me the gentlest of wives," I replied. "But he would not expect me to stand by and hear my father slandered."

"Nor I." A little voice beside me piped up. Gershom.

"Be quiet, child," she grunted.

"At any rate you will not have to put up with my odious presence any longer. Now that our mourning is over, there is nothing to keep me here."

"As you wish," she answered coldly. "Can we finish up quickly, Ser Moshe?"

"There is little more to be read, Madonna Sarabella," he answered. "Only a few small bequests to some old servants and retainers. To a cook named Rosa, five gold ducats." Poor old Rosa with the red nose whom Dorotea had dismissed. "And to Uncle Zvai of Bologna, twenty gold ducats." Dear old Zio Zeta. I had a sudden longing to see him again. We would be passing through Bologna on our way back to Firenze. I made a note in my mind to inquire if we might stay in the little house on Jew Street. I would show Gershom the place where he had suckled at Gelsomina's breast. And Jehiel ... I turned to look at him. To my astonishment, his lips were red with biting and his breath was coming in short, angry bursts.

Did he too feel cheated by Papa's will? It seemed unlikely. And yet there he sat, his face working in a most agitated way. I must sort this out at once.

"Are you angry with me about the house?" I asked him as soon as the lawyer had left the room.

"How could I be angry? You deserve the house. You nursed Papa. You cared for him. Dorotea ran away. She deserves nothing."

"Then what is troubling you?"

As I had so often seen him do in the past month, he stood silent, shifting his weight uneasily from one foot to the other.

"Come, Jehiel," I urged him. "Tell me. Whatever it is, we will always love each other. Maybe I can help."

"No! You will not understand. And you will try to dissuade me. But I will not be dissuaded, Grazia. I have made up my mind."

"To what?"

"To stay here in Ferrara with La Nonna and Grandpa and to marry Ricca."

My face must have turned quite pale with shock.

"I love her, Grazia. We love each other," he went on, speaking very fast. "Everything is all arranged. Grandfather says he will persuade the Duke to give me a post in his foundry."

"A foundryman? Is that your ambition?"

"Papa understood me. I knew you would not."

"I do not mean to be hard on you. But you are my little brother." I leaned over to embrace him but he turned his face away.

"I am not a baby, Grazia, to be rebuked and then fondled and forgiven. I am a man."

"A man! At fifteen!"

"I will soon be sixteen. Old enough to do a man's work. And to perform a man's duties in the bedroom as well. Look. Look at this arm." He rolled up the sleeve of his *camicia*. "Do you see those muscles? They are a man's muscles. I am a man now, Grazia. I do not need a mother."

"Nor a sister? Nor a friend?" I asked.

"You will always be my sister. And I hope my friend. But you cannot run my life. I am not made like you and Judah. I know you despise me for it but I am not."

"We do not despise you."

"He does."

"Perhaps he expects too much, but he loves you as I do."

"No, Grazia. If we are to be true friends we must have truth between us. Your husband despises me because I am not a scholar. He regards me as an ignorant lout. But I have my own ideas, Grazia. I have already learned the watchmaker's art from a master in Mantova. And I have designed a small crossbow that catapults an arrow much more fiercely than a mere archery bow and is light enough for a man to carry in the hunt. It is almost done. And when I have finished it, I will present it to the Duke — you know he loves both hunting and new gadgets — and I am certain to get an appointment at his cannon foundry."

"You want to spend your life making cannons?"

"Not only cannons. Other machinery. Battering machines. And hoists. And fording craft. And even bridges. I like to make things, Grazia. You could never see that."

"You never tried to make me see it, Jehiel. You have avoided me ever since I came here. In all our days of mourning, never a smile from you nor a touch on the arm."

"That was wrong of me, Grazia. I felt you despised me and I feared your displeasure. But now that we have come together again, how about a hug?" He held his arms out enticingly. "And a promise to dance at my wedding?"

"That I will never do."

"Then you are no friend to me. Nor sister." He drew back.

"You must not marry her, Jehiel. She has her mother's sluttish nature and will do you the same ill her mother did our father."

"How dare you speak that way about my intended? What gives you the right?"

"I am your sister. I love you."

"And I you, Grazia. Although you do try my patience with your endless criticisms. Now listen to me, sister. I cannot make you love Ricca as I do. But I can insist that you respect her. Just as you insisted that my grandparents respect Papa."

"But Papa was worthy of their respect," I wailed.

"Enough, Grazia. There are sides to Ricca that you have never seen."

And that you will never see again once she has hooked you, poor fish, I thought. But he had decided. Even I could see there was no point in prolonging the argument. I could win nothing and stood a good chance to lose my brother's love. So I kissed him on the cheek, wished him good fortune in all his ventures, and went to my room to begin packing.

Now who came knocking on my door but Penina, another who had grown away from me in the past month.

"Come and comfort me, dearest Penina," I cried. "For I am sorely in need of a shoulder to cry on."

"You, Grazia? In need?"

"Do I appear to you so callused that nothing can touch my heart?" I demanded.

"You appear to me to have hardened your heart against the world," she answered in her painfully truthful manner.

"Even against you?" I asked.

"Even against me," she answered, looking me straight in the face, even though I knew how she shrank from any unpleasantness.

"It is these people," I explained. "La Nonna. She turns me into a viper. She —" I stopped myself. I who loathe excuses and justifications, blaming another for my own defects.

"I know how hard it has been for you here, Grazia." The gentle soul held out her hand to smooth my cheek. "I did not mean to castigate you."

"And I did not mean to snivel my way out of my wrongdoings," I answered, gentled by her touch. "If I have seemed cold to you, I apologize. It was inadvertent, I assure you. For I hold you as dear as if you were my own sister."

"I have never doubted that you love me, Grazia," she answered. "But I wish you had allowed me to help you more."

"Help me? How could you have helped me?" I asked.

"Probably not at all," she answered. "But I felt my uselessness keenly. It is not altogether comfortable always to be the one being helped and never the one to do the helping."

"Well, you can help me now," I said. "For I have rarely felt so low in my spirits or so hopeless. Jehiel insists he will stay here in Ferrara and marry Ricca."

"I know." She turned her face from me. "She fascinates him."

"She's a bitch and a whore," I ranted. "She doesn't care a fig for him either. It's only what he will inherit. Greedy pig!"

"Grazia, please. Could we speak of something else?" As she turned back to face me, she wiped a tear from her eye and I suddenly realized how unutterably cruel I was being, rubbing salt into her wound simply to expunge my own frustration.

"Forgive me," I cried. "I am stupid and blind. You still love him, do you not?"

She shook her head sadly. "I have tried to master my feelings but it is no use... living with him day after day... seeing his desire for her in his eyes..."

"You must get away from them. That will make it easier for you, my poor sweet. Come with me to Firenze. Judah will love to see you. And I will be delirious with happiness to have my dear Penina beside me once again."

"No. My life is here." When people who are normally tractable finally put their feet down and refuse to budge, the fervor of their conviction creates a kind of resonance around them, as if they had plucked a lute string with all their strength. "My life is here," she repeated in just that resonant tone.

"But you are not happy..." I began.

"Please, Grazia. Do not try to run my life for me. I am past fourteen years. I am a woman. It is time for me to be married.

To have children. To have my own life."

"So you too no longer need me," I said.

"As a friend I will always need you. And so will your brothers. But not as a mother."

"But you *will* leave me Gershom," I said, half in jest but with a bite.

"Not for long, Grazia. He too will grow to manhood. We are not your children. You must have your own children. That is what God intended."

I LEFT FERRARA TWO days later with my little brother, Gershom. Once I had confided to Asher my miserable memories of travel along the Reno, he insisted on accompanying us as far as Bologna. And perhaps because of his reassuring presence, the banks did not seem nearly so high nor the inn at Malalbergo half so grim as before. And when we got to Corticella I found that this time we would not have to transfer ourselves to a donkey train for the last lap of the journey. Giovanni Bentivoglio, a tireless improver like so many Italian tyrants, had completed the Reno canal all the way to the gates of Bologna.

At Bologna, the manager of the *banco*, doubtless on La Nonna's instructions and in spite of Zio Zeta's tears, refused us a bed in the little house I remembered so fondly. Our old uncle had gotten frail and was more easily moved to tears than ever. He wept to see us. He wept when the manager refused us a bed. He wept when we took lodgings at an inn. He wept when he heard of Papa's bequest to him. And of course he wept a flood when we bade him goodbye. I do believe that old man shed all the tears he had been holding back for a lifetime during the two days we spent in Bologna.

My parting from Asher was even more laced with pathos, albeit not dramatized by tears. He had been my best friend through the last weeks, at times my only friend. At parting he spoke of his feelings for me only indirectly.

"If I were Gershom's age I too could come to Firenze and sit at Judah's feet and learn from him and bask in the light of your smile. But alas..."

Alas, he was not a boy but a man. And I was no longer a girl but a matron with a wife's responsibilities.

My last sight of him was his heavyset figure, feet astride, his flat hat tilted by the wind and held by one hand to his head while the other waved us on, so solid that he looked to be planted there in the earth forever.

39

J UDAH RETURNED FROM NAPOLI CELEBRATED NOT ONLY
as the French king's personal physician but as the dis-
coverer of the mercury cure for the French boils, now
officially named syphilis after its first victim, the ancient
shepherd Syphilus. More in demand than ever, he found it all
too easy to fill up his days with patients and leave me to find
easy refuge in books, studying Greek along with my brother
Gershom and basking in the sunny warmth bestowed on me
by my friend Diamante. Thus life provided each of us with the
illusion if not the substance of a complete existence. But each
night as we prepared to retire, the becalmed marriage bed
stood before us as silent evidence that nothing had changed
between us.

When I journeyed up to Mantova, I left behind a metrop-
olis radiant with humanistic light. But the city of Firenze had
undergone an amazing transformation during my absence. I
returned to a theocracy ruled in the name of Christ (Whom
the citizens had crowned king of their city), with Fra Girolamo
Savonarola ensconced as His deputy. He staged his first Bonfire
of the Vanities during my absence. But I had a gallery seat for

the second. During my absence the Bonaventura family had moved to a house just off the Calimala, fronting on the Piazza della Signoria, and on the morning of the great event I sat at Diamante's side on her rooftop and watched the Florentines pile up their treasure for burning in the square below.

A seven-tier platform had been built especially for what the *frate* called the Scourge of Unclean Things. Everything was grist for Savonarola's mill—lutes and zithers and card tables and chessboards and statues both sacred and profane and panels of oil painting—all manner of rare and beautiful objects. Dotted in among them like the shiny sugar sprinkled on *confetti* we were able to count hundreds of dandy boxes and small objects—carved chessmen and etched bowls, jeweled casks and fine glass perfume bottles. All this beautiful mess was swathed in coils of women's hair and wrapped in bolts of silk and satin cloth like one enormous birthday gift.

Can you imagine the frugal Florentines throwing away wealth? They did. With abandon. Somehow Fra Girolamo persuaded them that they were trading mere baubles for everlasting salvation. With my own eyes I saw Fra Bartolommeo step forward and place four of his drawings on the pyre—red chalk sketches, they seemed to be, of nude women. Beside me, Diamante gasped. Even she, no patron of the arts, appreciated their beauty. After Fra Bartolommeo came Sandro Botticelli hauling a large panel of the Virgin with a saint at either hand. The *frate*, you understand, had condemned the artists for using their mistresses and wives as models for the Virgin and Her acolytes. Sacrilegious filth he called it.

Once the stage was set, the performance began. First came a hundred white-clad schoolchildren singing the *ave verum corpus*. Next, the four captains of the four main quarters of the city, each holding a flaming torch high in the air. In slow and measured steps, each took his place at one of the four corners of the pyre. The choir ceased to sing. A moment of silence. Then a flourish of trumpets announced the man of the hour, the Scourge of Christ, Girolamo Savonarola.

Like a king ascending a throne, he climbed the seven steps to the top of the pyre. Turning to face the crowd, he raised his right arm as if to pronounce a benediction. But no. Instead, his fist slashed through the air to give the signal to his captains: Let the conflagration begin!

As one, the captains stepped forward to light the corners of the pyre. In perfect symmetry, the fire rose to a single point and thence straight up to heaven.

In hindsight I recognize that moment as Fra Girolamo's apogee, the point at which his meteoric rise reversed its course and became his fall. There was an edge of excess to the spectacular bonfires that went against the prudent, calculating Florentine temperament. Two fires was one too many.

The friar's reversal of fortune began in Roma, where Pope Rodrigo Borgia divined that the time had come to pluck out the thorn that had nestled in his side for half a dozen years. He issued a papal bull excommunicating Savonarola. Heresy was the charge. Either ship the heretic priest to Roma to be dealt with by my inquisitors, he told the *signoria* of Firenze, or lock him up in your own *stinche*. Otherwise the whole city will be placed under an interdict.

Interdiction meant that Florentines could not get married, could not receive extreme unction, could not be buried, could not take communion. And take note: The Pope had the power to prohibit all the Christian cities of the world from conducting business with any Christian city under interdiction. With one decisive gesture the Pope had contrived to threaten the Florentines both in their pocketbooks and in their souls. Who was the Sword of Christ now?

From that moment on, Savonarola's star plummeted with startling suddenness. In April of 1498, Girolamo Savonarola was arrested by the Florentine Senate. Before they had stretched him twice on the rack, he confessed to everything—that he was no prophet; that God had not spoken in his ear; that his visions were lies. On the twenty-third of May, he was burned on a pyre in the Piazza della Signoria.

The very same day at Blois, Charles VIII hit his head on a low lintel as he came off the tennis court, and expired there and then. Rodrigo Borgia's enemies were all falling down at once.

On the day of Savonarola's burning, Diamante and I were up on the Bonaventura roof, the same place from which we had witnessed his Bonfire of the Vanities. All the Bonaventura *famiglia* were present, including the servants, many of whom had once been ardent supporters of the *frate*. Even Judah took time out from his busy life to witness the event. Who, he asked, could miss the burning of the greatest vanity of all—Era Girolamo himself?

The burning of the man himself was not staged with anything like the *bravura* of his Scourge of Unclean Things. Strange as it sounds, the event was much less solemn. There was much laughter and chattering in the crowd, even throughout the hanging of the two Dominicans who were condemned to keep the *frate* company in hell.

But at the sight of Era Girolamo being led up to the gibbet, the noise ceased abruptly and his stringing up took place as a dumb show in eerie silence. Then suddenly the air was fractured by shock after shock of earsplitting bombast. Some villain had conceived the idea of sprinkling gunpowder over the faggots so that when the fire reached them, they would explode with the noise of a hundred rockets, as at a fete. That trick reignited the holiday spirit. Coached by the signal, the people cheered.

They cheered again when the three twitching bodies were lowered into the flames. All of a sudden the rope that bound Era Girolamo's arms to his upper body burst asunder and his arms swung forward and out as if to gather in every mortal being in the piazza. And the crowd dropped to its knees in terror amidst cries of *"Miracolo! Miracolo!"*

Diamante and I did not last out the spectacle. We survived the agonized jerks of the martyrs and the bloodthirsty howls of the crowd. But once the smell of burning flesh began to waft up toward us, Diamante ran off to the comfort of her scent bottle. And I followed her, happy to fill my nostrils with anything other than that rank, cloying odor. Three times she had recourse to the night pail to vomit up her disgust. Even then she remained bilious, which surprised me. Ordinarily, she had the constitution of a hog butcher.

"I am going to call Judah down," I told her. "He can put a stop to this vomiting."

"No." She held her hand up weakly to stop me from going. "There is nothing he can do. I am like this every morning now."

"Have you spoken to Judah about it?"

"There is no need. My malaise is only temporary." She smiled. "I am pregnant, Grazia."

"Pregnant?"

"Why so surprised, my friend? It is quite a familiar state for me."

"Pregnant, yes," I replied. "But sick, no." Diamante's effortless confinements had made her the envy of her circle.

"Ah, but this one is different. This one..." She placed her hand gently over her belly. "This child is a girl."

"You went to the conjurer?"

"I need no magic man to tell me what I already know. She is a girl. And I love her as I never loved those boys. I even have a name for her. Fioretta. Little flower."

"And if these auguries of yours prove wrong and she turns out to be a boy, you can call him Fioretto," I joked. "That will certainly win him the envy of his playmates."

But she was not to be deterred by my jest. "I know I must sound a fool to you, Grazia. But I tell you I *know*. Those boys grew in me like great turnips, as firmly anchored in the soil of my womb and as easy to pull out when they grew ripe. This one is shallowly planted. Every time I make a sudden move she jumps in my belly like a skittish fish. A sudden change of position, a blow however slight, any upset of my temper, causes her to quiver as if she has been jarred to her tiny roots. There will be no gallops for us this summer, my friend. I dare not even dance the *moresca* around the Passover table." She clasped my hand tightly. "This one I love, Grazia. This one I love."

The first things to be given up for little Fioretta were our daily gallops. "Remember what happened to the Queen of Portugal," Diamante quoted her mother-in-law, but only half in jest now.

Next went our neighborliness. With cases of plague multiplying daily, Diamante felt she must leave her husband and take refuge in the country "for the sake of the little flower." Ever generous, she invited me to join her there. But to desert Judah and my brother seemed to me a dereliction of duty, and neither of them would consider abandoning the city.

Watching Judah pursue his calling in those days was a revelation. Each day, he dressed neatly and close-shaven (for he maintained that contagion might nestle in body hair along with fleas) and went out on his rounds protected only by a fine cotton mask he had devised to cover his lower face. That and a talisman of sweet herbs hung around his neck were the extent of his precautions. When I suggested that he confine his visits to private residences and not expose himself to the contagion of the pesthouse, he replied that if I would agree to seek safety in the country he would do as I asked. But I could not bring myself to leave him and my brother. Yet every day the city became a more dangerous place.

In August, the *signoria* ordered a pit to be dug just outside the Porta Romano. The press of bodies had finally overwhelmed the gravediggers. From then on, all Florentines of whatever class or situation were buried in a single mass grave each day and a single funeral mass was sung daily for them all. Judah took it on himself to head up a group of volunteers to bury the Jewish victims separately and pray over them in the traditional way. To his surprise—although not to mine—Isaachino Bonaventura became his strongest supporter in this endeavor, sometimes neglecting to visit his pregnant wife in order to perform these odious duties.

When Gershom announced his intention of joining

Isaachino's cadre I objected with all my strength. He was exactly the same age you are now, hardly the time of life to be hauling around pestiferous corpses from morning till night. To my astonishment, Judah disagreed. "He will never become a man, no matter how many pages of the Mishna he commits to memory, if you do not allow him to exercise his virtue," he insisted. And after that my two men left me each day to go out burying.

Each night, my fastidious brother arrived home smelling of rot and camphor. And each evening, we heated pot after pot of water and poured it over him and scrubbed at him with carbolic soap until I thought we would rub his fine pale skin right off his bones.

Next to him, Judah sat in another great tub, yawning and dozing through his cleansing like some Oriental pasha. Never before or since, I daresay, have those two been cleaner in the sight of God and man. But in spite of those who would tell us that those ablutions must have raised them to a safe place at God's right hand—for cleanliness is next best to godliness—I knew that each day they went out to do God's work, the risk of contagion grew. However, nothing I could say or do would move them from their self-imposed task and I, the least prayerful of women, was forced into the last refuge of the desperate: constant prayers to God to keep them both alive until an early frost put an end to the plague season. Perhaps He heard me. They survived.

I had intended to journey to the Bonaventura villa and be at my friend's side for the birth of her child. But the little girl— yes, it *was* a girl—true to her whimsical nature, arrived long before the frost. Thus I did not see her until she was already a month old, a preternaturally quiet little thing with translucent skin who looked to belong more to the other world than to this one. But I was more concerned for my friend, suddenly transformed into a woman obsessed to whom nothing mattered except her motherhood.

By then the plague had subsided and Isaachino wanted his

wife with him in town. But Diamante would not leave Fioretta. He could not understand her reluctance. After all, she had left her boys in the country for the early years of their lives and no harm had come to them. What was so different about this child?

The contention between them was exacerbated when Diamante's mother-in-law discovered that she insisted on nursing the child herself, resorting to the wet nurse only when she came up empty.

"Her milk is not rich enough," the old lady complained to me. "It is thin and blue, like the milk of a lady. What this child needs is a peasant girl whose milk gushes out like a geyser. My poor daughter-in-law has to squeeze hers out by the drop. Mark me, the child will grow up thin and sickly if this keeps up."

"But Diamante is healthy, madonna," I expostulated. "And perhaps if she drinks cow's milk and eats butter..."

"She can drink herself drunk," the old lady snapped back. "But she will never turn herself into a cow. Peasants are bred for that. We are not."

At last a compromise was reached. The child and the wet nurse would both move into town. In addition to considerable gold, this maneuver entailed the uprooting of an entire family—for the wet nurse would not go without her own nursing babe and her young husband. But even with the wet nurse at hand to feed the babe, Diamante insisted that Fioretta sleep in a cradle next to her, and was up and down continually in the night fussing over the child.

"She hovers over that cradle like some dark angel, listening to the child's breath," Isaachino told me. "It is not natural."

I assured him that the aberration was a passing one and urged him to hold his patience. But in my heart I wondered where it would all end. The small inner voice first heard by Diamante when her child was in the womb seemed to grow in its insistence with each day, until it was dictating her every move.

"It is love run amok like a cancer," Judah said.

"But cancer kills," I reminded him.

To which he gave no answer.

Within a week after Diamante's removal into town, a messenger came to our door with an urgent call for Judah from the Bonaventura family. I awaited his return with mounting anxiety. When he came back hours later his face was ashen.

"I have terrible news, Grazia," he began. "There is no way to soften this blow."

"It is Diamante..."

"Yes, Diamante and the baby. And the wet nurse. And her own child. A cruel blow..."

"Tell me."

Three times he took a deep breath and opened his mouth, only to close it again and shake his head. Then at last, with an enormous effort of will, he began his terrible story.

"I was called tonight to attend the wet nurse. A fever. Nothing much, it seemed. When I arrived she seemed fit enough. She was lying in bed suckling her own infant. But when I came close, I saw on her breast the sign of the..."

Don't say it, I begged him silently. Make it not so.

"The tokens were there on the nurse's breast. The woman is a tippler it seems. Every night after little Fioretta was put in her cradle beside Diamante, the nurse went out to some foul tavern nearby. She must have caught the disease there."

"Does Diamante know her nurse has the plague?" I asked.

"She knows everything. And she has taken little Fioretta to her own breast once again and will not let the child go. It is certain death for her, Grazia. Fioretta had been sucking in the contagion every time she was put to the breast of the wet nurse. The child is doomed."

"And Diamante?"

"Determined to die with her child."

"I must go to her," I mumbled.

"No, you must not. She is harboring the plague now. You go at risk of your life. She begs you not to come."

"But I—"

"Your friend Diamante is very determined. She is removing back to the country so as not to infect others. Very likely she is gone from the city by now."

"I cannot leave her to die alone," I insisted.

"She forbids you to come, Grazia. You must respect her wishes. Besides, she will not be alone. I will be with her." He took my hand and squeezed it. "I will be your representative. And I will make certain that she does not suffer unnecessarily. And that her wishes are respected, just as you would do."

Still, I was haunted by the specter of my friend facing death without a loving companion to send her on her way. "Will Isaachino go, then?" I asked.

"No. Like you he insisted on it. But she prevailed over him. For the sake of the little boys. 'Can I die peacefully knowing that I have left behind two orphans?' she asked him. She is very clear in her head, Grazia. Very logical." He shook his head, incredulous at such capacity in a woman. "And very brave..." he added quietly, blinking his eyes once or twice to rid them of moisture. "Also very wrongheaded and stubborn and foolish."

FAITHFUL TO HIS PROMISE, Judah went each day by horse to sit with Diamante and her babe, returning late each night stinking of the sulfur fumes he used to disinfect himself. Each night, he returned home with a bulletin. Little Fioretta was sinking. But peacefully. Still no signs of buboes on Diamante.

Then, one night, Judah did not return and I knew long before the messenger arrived the reason for his dereliction.

"I found the babe, Fioretta, in a coma when I arrived," Judah told me when he came home in the early hours of the morning. "When I bent to examine the child, there were the tokens on Diamante's breast. 'The moment she draws her last breath I will die as well,' she told me, quite calmly, not a quaver in her voice. And so she did. She and the infant departed this world at the same moment. I think that they will keep each other company in paradise. For I never saw such a beautiful death."

"There is nothing beautiful about death," I retorted with all the bitterness I felt. "Death is cruel. Arbitrary. Senseless. Unjust. Unbearable..."

"But we must bear it. For her sake. And for our own," he answered calmly.

"How can we act for her sake? She is gone. Dead."

"But her spirit remains in you," he answered patiently. "And her last wishes must be respected. Would you not agree?"

To that proposition, I could not say no.

"She left a message for you. 'Tell Grazia that she must take up life with renewed vigor after I am gone. For she must bear the child I lost, a girl child. And she must name this girl Fioretta. If she loves me, let her do that for me.'"

"She wishes me to bear a child?"

"She wishes us to bear a child. For her. A living memorial."

"But it takes two to make a child," I reminded him. "I fear my friend Diamante did not know what she asked."

"I think she did," he replied solemnly. "Yes, I do believe she did."

"But I never said a word..."

He placed his fingers over my lips. "I know you did not betray me. But I think she knew nonetheless."

"What makes you think that?" I asked.

"The way she looked at me when she spoke of this child you would bear. And the fact that she asked me to swear to it."

"And did you swear?" I asked.

"Most willingly. Such a charge from a dying woman has all the force of an instruction from God Himself. I could never disobey her wishes."

Without a word being spoken, we knelt together and exchanged new vows of fidelity and fruitfulness.

There can be love without passion. That night when we lay down together, we caressed each other's bodies for the first time. I felt... The word "vessel" comes to mind as we hear it in the Bible. Yes, I felt like a delicate vessel, precious, ordained to hold a life and consecrated to that purpose.

Next morning Judah suggested to me that we might do well to celebrate the true beginning of our marriage in a new place. I did not find it difficult to accede to his suggestion without argument. Even when it emerged that the place he had fixed on was Mantova, I did not dissent. "Whither thou goest, I will go..." I had finally taken to heart Ruth's vow as a Jewish wife.

40

OME WITH ME AS I DISMOUNT IN FRONT OF THE familiar portal of the house where I was a small child. Sniff the subtle odor of the sea from the fish market over the way. Pace out the garden, overgrown and neglected since Mama's time but still alive. Look there. A damask rose. Mama's favorite. Her spirit lies sleeping under the tangle of brush, waiting for me to revive it with a hoe and a rake. Oh, Diamante, how I wish you were here to guide me. To smell the lavender patch. To squeeze a borage leaf between your fingers and taste its leafy freshness.

The *sala grande* is empty, but my imagination quickly supplies the missing furniture. Here is the chair where my mother sat sewing with her women. Here the long table was placed with its covering of golden birds. These are the stairs I crept down the day of my shameful encounter with Fra Bernardino. Banish that episode. Think instead of the wine and biscuit dispensed each morning under the fringed canopy of the conjugal bed, of the sable touch of Papa's beard brushing my cheek as he lifts me onto the red velvet pillow on his reading chair.

I swear I hear his voice in my ear. "Treasure these books,

Graziella, for they are the most generous of friends. Faithful always, never changing. Love them and they will return your love a hundredfold."

Papa's books. I had asked Davide Finzi to put them where they belonged, each wrapped in a silk rag as Papa kept them.

Now I approach the book rack and begin to turn over the manuscripts. Maimonides, of course. Josephus on the Jewish wars. Papa's own Passover Haggadah, covered in red velvet with a border of opal jewels. And the grammars, less elegant but more marked by use. Virgil, Cicero, Terence, Horace, Catullus, and finally, the *Decameron*. No secular library—nor any cleric's library either, for that matter—would be complete without that masterpiece. And alongside, its less celebrated sibling, *De Claris Mulieribus*, Boccaccio's tribute to 104 great women.

My fingers find their way to the story of Dido, defended here against what the master calls "the infamy undeservedly cast on her honor," and rescued from her consignment by Dante to the second circle of Hell with other souls of the lustful.

"She gave the people laws and regulations for living," I read, "and, as the noble city grew, Dido became famous throughout Africa for her great beauty such as had never been seen before and for her virtue and chastity."

In Boccaccio's version of Dido's story, the union between her and Aeneas is never consummated. Aeneas is simply a visitor who happens by at the moment of her death. The real story is Dido's betrayal by her own people, who think to save their city by delivering her into the hands of the marauding African king, Jarbas. But Dido will not accept the usurper in her husband's place. "She cast aside womanly weakness and hardened her spirit to manly strength," Boccaccio tells us.

In full view of her people, the Queen climbs up to the high sacrificial altar to perform the slaughter of a lamb. "Citizens, I go to my husband as you desire," she informs her subjects with heavy irony. Whereupon she points the knife not against the animal but against her own chaste breast and falls on it.

"And for this she deserves being called Dido which in

Phoenician means heroic," states Boccaccio, putting the lie to both Virgil and Dante, who see her as the wanton lover of Aeneas.

Do these poets sit and squabble over their inventions up in heaven, I wonder, as we do on earth? Will readers in some future time who come upon my *Book of Heroines* dispute my vision of Caterina Sforza or Lucrezia Borgia or my friend Diamante Bonaventura, whom I numbered among the heroic women of our time? Perhaps. My only defense is that I have tried, with all my strength, to conform my work to Judah's precept: accuracy of statement. What I knew from my own experience I have verified against the recollection of others. What I did not know I sought to learn. Where the letter was missing I contrived it in what I took to be the spirit of the character I was limning with my pen.

I did not begin with a grand scheme for what became Grazia's *Book of Heroines*. Inspired by Boccaccio, what I wrote that first day in my father's *studiolo* was a modest poem on the life of my friend Diamante Bonaventura, modeled after the lives in his *De Claris Mulieribus*. But when I was done with Diamante's life—especially with her death, which still brings tears to my eyes when I contemplate it—my friend called out to me for comradeship. "Just a few more pages," she urged me. "One or two other women of courage to keep me company between the velvet covers."

The first companion I chose for her was Isotta Nogarola, a scholar who withdrew from friendship, from the life of the city, and from public view to work in solitude. Self-exiled to a book-lined cell in a Florentine convent, she gave up her life as grandly and generously as Diamante had, for a great love: the love of scholarship. Then came Ginevra Almieri, who fought her way back to life from the grave. Then the virago Caterina Sforza and the others. Without intending to I created a gallery of women.

Although I was guided by Boccaccio in my selection, I would not make myself his slave. Of the more than one hundred women he chose to extol, only six were women of his own time. All the rest he picked from the ancient world. His reason: that the merits of pagan women had never yet been set forth, even in their own time. When I came to select *my* heroines, circumstances had changed. Boccaccio himself had already chronicled the merits of pagan women. But the merits of the women of my own time had not yet been published. I determined to concentrate on the unpublished heroines of the present, both well known and obscure, following him in principle if not in the detail.

Where I did copy him slavishly was in my definition of what constitutes a famous woman. My women are not "virtuous" in the narrow sense. I sing the *virtu* of those who rise above others through their intellect, daring, or strength. Just as Boccaccio included Flora the prostitute and Pauline the idiot among his famous women, so I have included the likes of Giulia Farnese, the Borgia pope's whore, known to the Romans as "the bride of Christ." Just as the master allows space to Faustina because of her incomparable beauty and in spite of her lascivious heart, so I have made room for Lucrezia Borgia. Whatever her vices, she was a woman of power to be reckoned with in the world. And God knows that in her youth, she was renowned for her great beauty.

But those decisions came later. At the beginning I simply began to scratch out the life of my friend Diamante in as accurate and pungent a style as I could, not sparing her lapses nor overrating her courage, both of which I was tempted to do on every page. This task occupied my life pleasantly while I awaited the inception of my friend's other memorial: the child Judah and I had vowed to produce. Each morning after prayers he set off for the Gonzaga Reggio, leaving me his *studiolo* for my work. Each noon he arrived promptly to dine and to consummate our marriage, an act which quickly became a ritual observance for us both. And when I say ritual, I do not use the word loosely. I can still see myself filling a basin with the rose-scented water that would purify us for our labors and measuring out the sweet oil that would ease the passage of the life-giving ooze from Judah's body to mine, with the same dutiful care that I observed when I covered my head to repeat the Sabbath prayers. Looking back, it seems to me that I approached the task of lighting Judah's fire with the same hand and in the same spirit that informed my performance each Friday evening when I lit the Sabbath candles.

For many months Judah did not confide in me Marchese Francesco's purpose in bringing him to Mantova. And, as usual in our dealings with each other, I had not the nerve to ask. But such things will out, and sure enough, one afternoon as we rested from our baby-making chores there came an importunate knocking at our door that led, quite accidentally, to the exposure of Judah's secret. Not wishing to awaken him, I quickly dressed myself and ran down to put a stop to the noise at the portal. There I found one of the stablemasters from the Gonzaga stud threatening our porter with a beating if he did not fetch Judah at once. He even raised his whip to me, but when I informed him as grandly as I could that I was mistress here, he came off his arrogance far enough to instruct me that Messer Leone was wanted at once at the stud because Granturco had taken a tumble and injured his foreleg.

Could this be the same Granturco that had recently won a purple scarf at Brescia? Was Judah's patient a resident of the Gonzaga stud? Had the famous physician been hired by the Gonzagas as a horse doctor?

The answer to all of the above was yes, and Judah readily admitted it once I had caught him out.

"But you detest horses. You cannot bear to ride them," I reminded him.

"Curing them is another matter," he rejoined, slightly offended. "And now, if you will excuse me, I have a sick patient waiting." And with that he was off, but I barred the door to him and would not let him pass until he had revealed to me how this incongruous commission had come about. And here is his tale.

"You know that the Aragonese are almost as unhinged on the subject of horses as the Gonzagas. So you will understand how it was that the King of Napoli paid a small fortune for a book on the diseases of horses in the actual hand of Hippocrates. It was not until the book was in his hands that he remembered he was unable to read Greek. Nor, it seemed, could any member of his court.

"But by then, he was possessed by a notion that this treatise would enable him to produce the healthiest, thus the strongest, horses in Italy. All he needed was a translator to bring to light the veterinary wisdom in his ancient manuscript.

"He dispatched an agent to Athens with orders to acquire a Greek scholar at not too steep a price. The foolish King got what he paid for. The mangled prescriptions misinterpreted by the bargain-rate scholar killed off several valuable animals before the King gave up on Hippocrates.

"Now who should enter the scene but Marchese Francesco Gonzaga, come down to Napoli to wipe out whatever vestiges of the French army had been spared by the love disease. He heard about the Hippocrates manuscript and managed to buy it cheap."

"But this time the bargain was no sham," I remarked.

"Oh, it was a shrewd purchase," Judah agreed. "And I told him so when I ran up against him at Napoli. Hippocrates' veterinary text is known and much admired in Arabia. And you know the quality of their animals."

"Then the true fault must have been with the Greek translator," I surmised.

"Precisely what I told the Marchese in Napoli. Actually," he added, "I told him I would stake my life on it."

"Without even seeing the manuscript?"

"Hippocrates was the greatest physician who ever lived," Judah informed me, in that lofty tone he sometimes assumes when his judgment is called into question. "And since I am one of the finest physicians of the day and certainly among the great scholars of Greek in this peninsula, you can be assured that when the correct remedies are accurately applied by me they will prove most efficacious. That is why the Marchese has offered me an enormous stipend to translate the volume for his exclusive use and to test its efficacy on his animals."

"So you are body physician to the Marchese's horses." I still could not quite believe it.

"Disease is disease, Grazia, and anatomy is anatomy. I am not too proud to wish to cure any of God's creatures, be it horse or man." Oh, how Diamante would have loved that speech! "Besides," he added, "when I think of some of the human patients I have treated, I cannot believe that these equine subjects can possibly prove more difficult, more obdurate, or less grateful."

To Judah, I believe, the exposure of his secret came as a relief, for after that he joked often and quite merrily about his equine patients. Once, when I asked him what he did every afternoon at the stud, he answered, altogether serious, that he talked to the horses. What his patron might have made of this form of veterinary practice, he had no way of knowing. The Marchese was little seen in Mantova that year. Exactly what he was up to nobody knew, although everyone had ideas on the subject. Conjecture on his long absences fell into two categories: one, that he was dallying with his mistress, a certain Teodora, who had appeared publicly at his side in Brescia; the other, that he was conspiring at out-of-the-way places with agents of the new King of France, Louis XII, the heir of little Charles VIII who had beaned himself into eternity at the tennis court.

In her husband's absence Madonna Isabella occupied herself with running the Mantovan territory, adding to her collections and, I gathered, waiting for her husband to settle down long enough to give her the son they both so ardently desired. Was it not a coincidence, Judah remarked, that each of us sat waiting the same blessing, she in her palace across the square, me in my modest house near the fish market, "... but both equally humble before the magnitude of God's will," as he put it.

"She expressed a wish to see you," he added. "She calls you her little sister and asks when you will come to call on her."

"And what did you tell her?" I asked.

"That you were fatigued by the journey from Firenze and harassed by household duties."

"And how did she take it?" I asked, knowing that Madonna Isabella did not take kindly to being refused in the smallest matter for any reason.

"She seemed slightly annoyed," he replied coolly.

To be perfectly truthful, I was tempted. I am not immune to the seductions of court life. But neither was I prepared to forgive and forget.

"Give her what excuse you will," I told him. "Say I'm pregnant."

"And are you?" he asked.

"No. But I soon will be. Better that than the truth: that I cannot bear to look upon her face. Or the Marchese Francesco's. Together those two have brought me nothing but misery."

"They too have their miseries," Judah reminded me quietly.

"You refer to this mistress of his that he flaunts like a jewel?"

"That and her inability to produce an heir. The child she was carrying when you last saw her died within a few months of its birth."

"Was it a boy?" I asked.

"A girl, I think," he replied.

"Then the death of that baby was no misery to her. She cares only for boys."

"That is a harsh judgment, wife," he replied.

"Harsh but accurate," I retorted. "Like all princes, Madama is more of a dynast than a mother. Do you know she refused to use the golden cradle for her first child because the poor thing was a mere girl? I would not be surprised if the second daughter died of neglect with a mother like that."

"Sometimes women come late to a realization of mother love," he reminded me. "Think of Diamante..."

"You dare to compare Diamante Bonaventura to a cold-hearted bitch like Isabella d'Este!" The reproach came out of me harsh and loud.

"No need to shout, wife," he remonstrated gently. But, as it so often did in those days, the subject of bearing children grated on my nerves. A fear had begun to grow in me that the child I so confidently planned might not be so easy to conceive. And, to exacerbate my unease, life seemed to be stirring everywhere around me but in my womb.

At Roma a child was born to Lucrezia Borgia four months after her second marriage and named after her father, Rodrigo. The question bruited about the peninsula was: Who is the child's true father, her brother Cesare or her father, the Pope? Each of them had been seen kissing her full on the lips before, after, and in between her various marriages. But this gossip did not deter Alfonso d'Este of Ferrara from asking for her hand in marriage once the child in question was safely tucked away.

On the feast of Mathias we learned of the birth of a son to Philip the Handsome of Burgundy and his mad wife, Joanna of Spain, which brought to mind Isaachino Bonaventura's prediction of the dynastic consequences of this marriage. Born during their endless journeying between Spain and Germany, this child had been dropped off at his birthplace like a cumbersome package in the same manner that the addled mother had deposited her other children wherever they fell out in the various towns of Europe. At the time, this Habsburg pup was simply one more reminder of my own disappointed hopes. It turned out that, as Isaachino foretold, his birth did produce far-reaching dynastic consequences. Still, I doubt that the Libyan Sibyl herself could have foreseen a troublemaker of the stature of Charles V, our revered Holy Roman Emperor, when his mismatched parents were joined in matrimony.

From Ferrara came the news that the two dei Rossi marriages celebrated the previous year were about to bear fruit. My friend Penina, married at last to the German rabbi, was expecting a child in the spring, and my brother and his slut of a wife, having produced an heir six months after their hasty marriage, were now expecting another. I prayed every day for one small share of this rampant fecundity and copulated with rigorous regularity. Still, the year 1499 drew to its end without any sign of a child in my womb.

In December, Leonardo of Vinci passed through Mantova with his friend Luca Pacioli. To earn a few ducats he obliged Madonna Isabella by drawing her in chalk. I have never seen this drawing. Her husband gave it away to the first person who asked for it. Imagine! To toss away a work from the hand of Leonardo. That Francesco ought to have stuck to judging horseflesh.

Oddly enough, Madama regretted the loss of her portrait even less than her husband. It was not really a very good likeness, she confided to Judah. It made her look fat. Judah reported this to me with considerable mirth. Overweening vanity in high persons always did tickle him.

"Of course she looked plump to him," he remarked casually. "She's at least five months pregnant."

How had the *illustrissima* earned God's blessing? Which of my sins was greater than hers or my cousin Ricca's or Lucrezia Borgia's or the mad Joanna's? Among them, those women had committed harlotry, mendacity, desertion, incest, and tens of minor offenses against the Holy Writ. Yet God had judged them fit to be mothers and not me.

Rather than give way to despair, I cultivated a faith in numbers. I worked a sampler emblazoned with the number 1500 in purple and strung it up above my carrel like a banner to announce to myself that the new century would bring a change of fortune.

41

THE FIRST MONTH OF THE YEAR 1500 BROUGHT NEWS of a terrible accident in Ferrara and a double death in the family. The letter, signed by my cousin Asher and penned by his own hand, was brief. On the previous day my grandfather and Penina's young husband had drowned together in the waters of the Po en route to petition Duke Ercole at Marmirolo. The sled they were riding in had pitched through a weakened patch in the ice and sunk before help could be summoned.

Much as I dreaded the voyage, it seemed to me right that I should go to the funeral for Penina's sake, and, as it often does, what I anticipated as an onerous duty turned out a pleasure.

We traveled by sled as my grandfather had done on the day of his death, yet I felt no fear. After my long confinement as a staid housewife the bracing air exhilarated my spirit, infusing me with a zest I thought I had lost forever. And when the merchants I was traveling with asked if I was game to ride on through the night, I agreed without a qualm. By stopping only to change horses, we reached Ferrara in less than two days' ride, not far short of the speed of a dispatch rider.

Of the funeral there is nothing to tell. Of the subsequent

events, much. The reading of my father's will had revealed the greed that lurked in the shadows of our family's grief when property was at stake. This time, it took longer to surface, not due to any change of heart but because my grandfather's style was so prolix that it took an entire morning for the poor lawyer to wade through the ocean of platitudes that preceded the actual bequests. It is a style reminiscent of the poems you have heard intoned at Madonna Isabella's fetes written to mark the death of one of her little dogs.

But finally, in the early afternoon, after digging through a ton of verbiage, we came to the hidden bombshell.

"My house in the Via delle Volte and all its furnishings..." As one, the assemblage leaned forward, on the alert. "I bequeath to my grandson Jehiel and his wife, Ricca—"

That is as far as he got.

"My house! Never!" La Nonna's shout was loud enough to be heard by the eels sunning themselves in the Comacchio basin. Before anyone could quite grasp what was happening, the old lady fell on the floor and lay there gasping. "Not my house... No...no...no..." Whereupon her voice trailed off and she began to twitch and foam at the mouth.

If ever I had wished for revenge against La Nonna, I got it that day, watching her borne out of her *sala grande* held high in Jehiel's arms as on a catafalque, pursued by the two women she had trusted and who, it was now clearly revealed, had conspired to betray her. Yet I felt no triumph in my revenge. Only a faint disgust and a strong wish to get out of that house— Ricca's house now, it seemed.

Penina voiced the sentiments of us all when she murmured, "I don't envy Jehiel caught in the current of that filthy pool." The unaccustomed sharpness of her comment reinforced my conviction that in spite of her marriage she had not given up her hopeless passion for my brother. And who could blame her? He had grown into a wonderfully handsome man, all traces of boyhood plumpness erased, his body lithe and strong, with solid, broad shoulders and narrow hips. And all of this natural beauty was enhanced by the rich court clothes he had taken to wearing. Even his black mourning doublet was trimmed with fine lace. And the sheen of his costume remained untarnished by that damnable yellow circle that Duke Ercole had once again ordered the Ferrarese Jews to wear. Jehiel was excused from that humiliation by the special dispensation of Prince Alfonso, Duke Ercole's heir. Somehow my brother had become a member of the prince's inner circle...shades of my father. He would have been at court even now had it not been for the required mourning, Asher said. As it was, Este pages came every day to our portal with secret letters and messages for Maestro Vitale.

"What does he do at court?" I asked Asher.

"He claims to be employed in the cannon foundry."

"Do I take it you do not believe him?" I asked.

"He hardly dresses like a foundryman, does he?" was his rejoinder. "Nor does a foundryman generally sail the river on a prince's bucentaur or gallop at the prince's side chasing wild boars. And where does he get the money for these clothes he keeps buying? Not from a foundryman's salary." He stopped himself suddenly. "I sound envious, do I not?" he asked.

"You sound skeptical, as I am after what you tell me, cousin," I replied. "We both have cause to know Jehiel's recklessness."

"I do fear for him," he answered. "Yet I refuse to repeat idle gossip."

"By the time there is proof, it will be too late to save him," I replied. "You do him no disservice by telling me, Asher. I am his sister. I love him."

"Very well," he sighed. "They say he sells Hebrew amulets to the ladies and gentlemen of the Duke's court and that he forecasts the future from Tarot cards. If the *Wad Kellilah* proves that he is practicing magic with the words of the Torah, they will whip him in the synagogue and excommunicate him just as they did your father."

"Does he admit to selling amulets?"

Asher shook his head. "But it is the most likely explanation for his sudden affluence. Christians will pay any price for Jewish magic."

I knew he spoke the truth. Judah was constantly being badgered by importunate Christians for *brevi*—as these bits of gibberish were called—from *The Sword of Moses* or *The Wisdom of the Chaldeans.* "They think we Israelites have Jehovah by the tail," he explained.

Now it seemed that my brother was invested in the business of catering to this perilous fantasy. I knew I must speak to him at once—and firmly. But each time I saw him that day he was whirling in and out of the house in La Nonna's service and could not be stopped. First the doctor had to be fetched. Then the pharmacist was brought to purge the invalid, and the butcher to bleed her. Each time I passed the door of her room, I was assailed by groans of pain and noxious fumes.

By the time of the compline bells I had given up hope of cornering my brother. But after I retired, an opportunity unexpectedly arose. Hearing footsteps on the tiles overhead, I pulled back the shutters at my windows and saw him standing on the roof above me, peering through some kind of astronomical instrument.

Stealthily, so as not to alert Ricca, I made my way up to the third floor loggia and onto the roof tiles. There I found my brother, eye to lens, gazing skyward through a glass with such intense concentration that I had to pluck at his sleeve twice to alert him to my presence.

"Grazia, what brings you here?"

"I might ask the same of you, brother," I answered in the Talmudic style.

"I have come to look at the stars, as I do every night."

"You have become an astrologer?"

"Better say an acolyte. I am following up the studies I began with a certain master in Mantova."

"I do not like it, Jehiel," I stated flatly.

"You do not like astrology, sister? Or the master? Or the stars?"

"All three of those things. Only fools or people who wish to deceive others pretend to read a man's destiny in stars and cards. All wise men agree on this, men as far apart as Maimonides and..." My tongue stumbled as I said the name, "Pico della Mirandola."

"Yet the same Pico hired more than one Jew to teach him the secrets of cabala," he retorted. "So I must conclude that I am acting according to the precepts of wise men if I seek out numerical formulas for bringing rain or destroying an enemy."

"Are the stories true, then?" I challenged him. "Are you selling amulets to the Christians?"

"If I am?"

"This is no game, Jehiel. The Jews will excommunicate you if they catch you at it."

"Then I must take care not to get caught." He grinned.

I could have kicked him for his arrogance, and might have done so but for an interruption that put a halt to our debate: a series of taps on the ceiling below us as if someone was signaling with a long stick. And to be sure, Jehiel responded to the signal by walking over to the edge of the roof, where he lay down on his belly so as to lower his head safely over the side and, from that position, to conduct a whispered conversation with someone in the room below the eaves.

"My wife," he explained tersely when he returned to my side. "Like you, she objects to my study of the stars. It takes me away from my marital duties."

"But is she not keeping watch over La Nonna tonight?" I asked.

"She says the old lady is too much out of her senses to notice us and that conjugal life must go on. She has even prepared a pallet for us on the floor."

"She plans to copulate with you tonight with La Nonna lying hard by?" I asked, unable to believe what I thought I had heard.

"My wife cannot settle into sleep until I have done my marital duty by her at least once each night...sometimes more than once. Sometimes more than twice," he added. Was he complaining or boasting?

"Are you happy with your life, Jehiel?" I asked.

"Plato said that no man can call himself happy until the moment of his death," he replied with a shrug.

"*Sophocles* said that no man can call himself happy until the moment of his death," I corrected him. "Plato said that no man can call himself free. But my question stands. Are you happy?"

"Happy with what? With my wife? With my life? With my work?" He bit on his lower lip thoughtfully. How full it was. How luscious. And his eyelashes, a double row of them that framed his velvet eyes like black lace. And the way he carried his body. Even standing casually up here on the roof, he fell naturally into the graceful contrapposto pose of a Greek nude. What a figure he must cut at the Este court, I thought. Beauty is much admired at courts. And sought after. And rewarded.

"I hear you have become an intimate of the young prince Alfonso," I remarked.

"He is my patron," he replied simply.

"And just what in you does he patronize?" I asked.

"I have constructed a cunning little astrolabe that he can take around and hold in his hands," he replied. "And I have built a telescope for him. I am his Leonardo." There was an edge of mockery in his tone.

"Leonardo does not sell amulets," I retorted.

"You pay too much attention to gossip, Grazia," he answered calmly. "The truth is, there is more magic in jewels than in amulets. And more profit. If you like I will get you a turquoise that will protect you from all accidents, especially when riding a horse. I also have a stone which makes fountains spring up overnight." My face must have mirrored my disbelief, for he added, with some urgency, "I have done it, Grazia. I have the gift."

"The gift of what?"

"The gift of prophecy. The gift of magic. I have an angel in my head."

Now, Jehiel may have been reckless and naive. But he never was a liar. If he said he caused a fountain to spring up overnight, he had.

"What other magic do you perform?" I asked.

"I concoct certain potions with the aid of an apothecary of my acquaintance. But I prefer not to discuss that part of my work with the wife of a doctor. The medical profession seems to feel it holds a God-given right to dispense remedies."

"Do you have a remedy for barrenness?" I found myself asking.

"Why do you ask? Do you long for a child?" He asked the question in a voice quite new to me who had known him all his life. It was the voice of a sibyl issuing from a cave and it called forth in me the recognition of what I had never yet admitted: that I *did* long for a child, not only in memory of Diamante, nor in imitation of my female acquaintance, but to fill something in me that stood empty. "Yes," I confessed, "I do long for a child."

"Do you wish me to help you?" he asked, in the same distant, sepulchral tone.

"Yes," I answered in spite of myself.

"Very well then. But first I must read you."

"The Tarot cards?" I shivered.

"Perhaps. Perhaps the palm. Perhaps the face. I must think about it. Meanwhile, duty calls. I do have an angel in my head, but I also have a wife in my bed."

As if on cue the tapping started again below, this time more urgent than before. Not a tap, tap this time but a bang, bang.

"Go to your wife," I said. "I will stay here and look at the stars through your glass. Who knows? Maybe I too can find some profound truth up there in the vault of heaven." My remark was not entirely specious. Even though Judah refused to give credence to the influence of the stars, I knew that many wise men took an opposite view.

I leaned down to fasten my eye against the eyepiece of the instrument. The Chair of Cassiopeia loomed up, stunning me with its brightness. I could almost feel the cold northern rays of the double star entering my head, bending my mind.

Then a voice spoke within me. "Everything a man is to believe must be traced to three categories," it said. "First, things which can be proved by mental processes, such as mathematics and geometry; second, things of which the five senses can convince us; third, things known by tradition through the prophets and wise men. Only a fool would believe anything beyond these categories."

Those words of Maimonides came back to me with all the force of my father's adoration of that great sage behind them and reinforced by Judah's imprimatur. Compared with their clear, steady light, the brilliance of Cassiopeia paled. I set the instrument aside and scuttled off to bed, determined that if Jehiel proposed to me any further excursion into magic or astrology I would refuse.

But the next night when he whistled down to me, I went again to meet him on the roof. As if the moonlight had clouded over my reason, I took my place obediently on the little stool he had brought there and allowed him to proceed with his reading.

In preparation he had wrapped himself in a long tunic of white cloth, passed a red belt around his waist, and put on a helmet garlanded with drawn snakes that looked alarmingly lifelike in the moonlight. Then, setting a marble vase in front of him and lifting a sponge tied to a man's leg bone in his left hand, he drew a deck of playing cards from under his cloak, muttered some weird incantation, knelt, kissed the tiles, dipped the sponge into the vase, and whispered, "Let us trace Pluto's circle with this dragon's blood." Whereupon he proceeded to draw a large circle on the tiles with his reddened sponge.

I knew all this to be nonsense. Yet I waited, subdued, obedient — caught up in the magic.

Now began the laying out of the cards. First he divided the deck card by card, discarding a good number. "Those are the common cards of the Minor Arcana," he explained. "They are unsuitable for divining."

"What are they suitable for?" I inquired, ever curious.

"For gaming, what else?" he answered impatiently. "Any fool can place a bet on a ten of staves, sister, but few men can read the future in the Tarot."

The explanation was meant to put me in my place and it did. I remained quiet while he shuffled the cards of the Major Arcana, all the while mumbling some odd-sounding gibberish. Gypsy talk?

Finally he ceased to shuffle and mumble. "Draw five cards," he ordered me, "and lay them out in the shape of a Greek cross."

I did as I was told.

"Now you must turn them over one by one, starting at the top and going around the clock."

"And the one at the center?" I asked.

"That is the one which will seal your fate."

Before you judge me a gullible fool, think of the scene. The pale backs of the cards glowing within the blood-red circle. The telescope standing by as a conduit to the stars. My brother, solemn, white-robed under the vault of heaven, suffused with that serene certainty that emanates from saints and fortune-tellers. And I, your mother, desperate to fill my barren womb with a child.

I reached down and turned over the top card. It showed a man and a woman, their hands joined, under the sway of Cupid, blindfolded and nude, preparing to launch an arrow.

"This Card of the Lovers shows the struggle between sacred and profane love," my brother advised me. "It forecasts the coming of a test. You will subject yourself to a trial. Turn the next card."

When I turned the card over to lay it in position, I saw that it was upside down and began to turn it right.

"No!" Jehiel snatched it from my hand and laid it down as it had lain in the shuffled deck. "You must not defy Fortuna, Grazia. An upside-down card reverses the meaning."

"Is that bad?" I asked.

"In this case, yes. The obverse meaning of the Lovers is delay, disappointment, and divorce."

"Divorce?"

"I do not create these portents, Grazia," he advised me sternly. "I merely divine them. Delay, disappointment, divorce," he repeated. "That is what threatens you, unless..."

"Unless?"

"Turn the next card," was his answer.

Now appeared an amazing card, much decorated, with a winged, blindfolded figure at its center turning a golden ring balanced on the back of an aged man in a ragged white garment, his stockings worn through, and festooned with the legend *"Sum sine regno"* — "I do not rule."

"This is the Wheel of Fortune," Jehiel explained. "It tells you to believe in the signs. You are not the master of your own fate, no matter how much you wish to be."

The fourth card revealed a youth in green hose hanging upside down by one foot, whom Jehiel identified as the Hanging Man. "He predicts reversal of the mind. Rebirth. He orders you to reverse your thinking and to prepare for the approach of new life forces. He orders you to surrender."

"To what?" I asked.

"To Venus," he answered without hesitation. "You and your husband have incurred her wrath. How you offended her I do not know. Look up, Grazia," he instructed me. "She is there among them, looking down, cursing you with barrenness. Ask her what you must do. Repeat after me, 'I conjure you, luminaries of heaven and earth...'"

"I conjure you, luminaries of heaven and earth," I repeated.

"'And in the name of the twelve hours of the day and the three watches of the night and the thirty days of the month and the thirty years of *shemitta* and the fifty years of Jubilee and the name of the angel Iabiel, who watches over wombs, and of the angel Anael, ruler over all manner of love, to look into her mirror and find there a child for me.'"

"...and find there a child for me," I repeated.

"Now touch the last card and kiss it," he ordered me. I did.

Then he placed the card faceup in the middle of the red circle and I saw staring up at me a golden woman, big and luminous, with green hands.

"This is the Empress," he announced. "She stands for fruitfulness and fertility. But she demands powerful purification." He paused, breathing deeply as if preparing to deliver himself of some awesome truth. "Fortuna smiles on you, sister. I have recently made a similar reading of the cards for the wife of my Duke, the lady Lucrezia Borgia. Like you, she longs for issue in her new marriage. Like you, she has offended Venus and remains barren. With the help of a chemist, I mixed a potion for her of secret ingredients handed down from the ancients. I will bring home a vial of it for you to take. Once you have purified yourself Venus will be propitiated. Both you and the lady Lucrezia will produce healthy sons."

Of course it was out of the question for me to take up his offer. Even had I wished to test the efficacy of the remedy, for the wife of a celebrated physician and observing Jewish scholar to accede to the power of magic even by swallowing a potion was unthinkable. That I could even have considered it proved to me that the time had come for me to go home. My life with Judah may have been joyless. But life in this house was mad.

One thing remained for me to do. I must see my grandmother for the last time. Much as I detested her, she was my father's mother and I knew he would have wished me to maintain filial decorum toward her, as he always had.

I presented myself at the door to her room just before dinner and announced to Dorotea that I wished to see La Nonna. "She is resting and cannot be disturbed," was the answer I got. "Perhaps this afternoon."

Of course that afternoon I was told that the old woman was too agitated to see anyone. At dusk, the doctor was with her, and by nightfall, a sleeping potion had been administered. In between my attempts to storm the citadel I packed my baskets and washed my head in preparation for my departure. Now that I had made up my mind, I could not wait to shed the heavy conspiratorial air of the place. But I was determined not to leave without first seeing my grandmother.

Next morning I confided my plan to Asher. Not only did he prove sympathetic, he offered to come with me. "It is my duty to visit my grandmother as well as yours, Grazia," he informed me in that endearingly serious manner of his. "I might have remained remiss had it not been for this suggestion of yours." Then he added, shyly, "You are always in the forefront when it comes to courage and probity." Interesting that each of us thought the same of the other.

Even with Asher doing knightly service at my side, it was no easy thing to gain access to La Nonna. Dorotea and Ricca formed a solid phalanx across the portal. But Asher possessed a formidable battering machine: Grandfather's will had named him custodian of all bequests. Always alert to the main chance, his mother and sister both knew that their future depended on his goodwill.

From within we heard the unmistakable rasp of La Nonna's voice shouting. "Grazia! Grandson! Come to me! Respect! Respect!"

"You see, she's deranged," Ricca announced. "Nothing she says makes sense."

"Do I not hear my grandson? Is it Asher?" the voice rasped out from behind the curtained portal.

"Yes, Nonna," he shouted back, loud enough to be well heard through the thick curtain. And to his sister: "Step aside, Ricca. Else I shall be forced to lay hands on you."

The threat worked. We walked past the gorgon and into the dimly lit room.

It was a proper witch's cave. A single candle burned beside the bed. A pot of some noxious stuff boiled over a small brazier that had been brought in for the purpose. And huddled up in one corner of the bed lay the old lady, her pockmarked cheeks glowing red and a bluish stain outlining her loose lips.

I tapped her lightly on the arm. "Nonna," I whispered, "it is I, Grazia, come to see you."

The little eyes opened to a squint. "Grazia..." She held a hand out to be kissed. "What has taken you so long? I have been asking for you."

"You were too fatigued to see people, Nonna," Asher explained.

"Fatigued?" Her voice dripped with the accustomed sarcasm. "I am not fatigued, foolish boy. I am dying. Can you not see it?"

With a sudden and unexpected show of strength she reached up, grabbed his head with both her hands, and forced it down to a level with her own, as if to show him the face of death.

"You must not speak of dying, Nonna..." Asher murmured.

"Why not?" Her voice came through at least twice as strong as his. "I *am* dying and I must get my house in order. *My* house. You are soft, boy." She glared at poor Asher accusingly as she let him go. "No match for your sister. She should have been the boy."

"Cruelty and a hard heart and cunning do not make a man, Nonna," I cut in. "Asher is honest, loyal, and clever."

"Still talking back, are you, Grazia?" she snapped.

"Still speaking out for justice and the truth," I replied.

"Haven't lost your spirit?" she inquired, almost civilly.

"Hasn't lost her spirit," Asher replied on my behalf.

Oddly enough, this mutual defense seemed to please her. For she smiled a lopsided grimace and inquired, "What have we here? An alliance?"

"A friendship," I replied.

"You will need more than friendship to best your enemies in this house. Fine man or not, this boy is no match for his damnable mother and sister. They are fiends from hell."

She paused a moment, as if waiting for one of us to deny her. But neither of us did. So she went on, talking quite lucidly, you understand, and in a strong, steady voice. "That whelp Ricca sucked around my vain old husband whispering all manner of flattery into those old ears while she pretended to clean them, and touching him, touching him, washing his head and paring his nails. He took these attentions as devotion. But all along she was conspiring to supplant me. Listen to me, grandson." A pudgy hand shot out from under the coverlet and waggled under Asher's nose. "Watch out for your sister. She is a witch. She will spirit everything away from you."

"She may try, Grandmother, but she will not succeed," he answered.

"Promise me," she demanded.

"I promise."

"Not that way. On your knees. Swear on your father's grave. Down. Get down."

A long look passed between us. Her mood was turning dangerously febrile. This was no time to deny her. He sank to his knees at the bedside and swore.

Now it was my turn. But first she dispatched Asher to watch at the portal and keep Dorotea and Ricca out.

As soon as he was beyond earshot she beckoned me down to her as she had him. "There are things you cannot tell a brother about his sister," she whispered. "Things too horrible..."

Things I do not want to hear, I thought. "You must rest now, Nonna," I began. "I can return later—"

"Now. You must hear it now." She grasped me firmly by the hand. "You are a good girl, Grazia. I was mistaken in you. I should not have beaten you." Could I be witnessing a softening of that hard old heart? "I should have beaten her instead," she went on. So much for the change of heart. "She was the imp all along. The devil was in her, not in you. If only I had beaten it out of her then, when she was soft and pliant. My poor Ricca. I let the devil take her."

"Ricca is not such a witch as all that," I replied, hoping to calm her. Instead, my defense of Ricca only exacerbated her excitement.

"Come here. Put your ear next to my mouth." She pulled me down with amazing strength. "Listen to me," she whispered. "She fornicates with the devil every night. Here. In my room. She puts out a mat for him. She calls to him. She teases him into her insides. He groans with fatigue but she goads him on and on and on. *I hear this!*"

Then, as if this outburst had taken all the strength she had, she fell back, eyes closed, and let loose my hand, and I thought that was the end of it. But no. After a moment she rose up and, with a great heave, threw herself out of the bed. "Cover me with something," she demanded. "They will soon return. I feel it."

Her will was still irresistible to me. I pulled the coverlet off the bed and wrapped it around her bloated, naked body.

"Now, take my arm," she instructed.

With each step we took across the room, I felt the weight of her swollen body threatening to pull me down. Yet I held firm and so did she. And thus, step by painful step, we reached the washstand that stood in the far corner of the room.

"Pick up the ewer," she ordered. "Turn it over."

There, pasted against the bottom, lay a carved brass key.

"Get the key off," she ordered, leaning heavily on the edge of the little wooden stand. But try as I might, I could not pry the thing loose.

"Give it to me." She grabbed the ewer out of my hand and dashed it against the stand, spewing broken shards in all directions.

"The key. Pick it up. Quick," she ordered. Then, heedless of the sharp shards underfoot, she led me over to a small cask secreted in a niche in the wall. By the time we reached the chest, blood was dripping from the soles of her bare feet. But when I bent down to see to her wounds, she smacked me smartly on the head and rasped, "Open the cask. Quickly."

"But your feet…"

"Later." She was breathing heavily now, almost gasping. "Open it," she repeated.

My fingers trembled as I twisted the key in the lock. Turn. Turn. Click. The lock was undone.

"Good. Bring it to the bed. Quickly."

I placed the cask in her lap. Her swollen fingers closed around it like fat worms and slowly lifted the lid. What a sight greeted my eyes. Gems of all shapes and colors. Golden chains and barrettes and earrings. A king's ransom in jewels. "Hold up your *gonna*—make a little well in it," she rasped.

Out in the corridor, there arose a swelling of angry voices. Above the din, I recognized the familiar voice of Dorotea. "You dare to forbid me, your own mother?"

"Hold firm," the old lady ordered me. "Spread out your *gonna*."

Then, all in a rush, she dumped the entire contents of the cask into my lap. "Go now. Leave this place. Tell no one. Guard the jewels. They are the dei Rossi treasure. Go."

For a moment I hesitated. Then, because my heart prompted me to it, I turned back and laid my cheek against the flushed, mottled one on the pillow. "Goodbye, Grandmother," I murmured. "May God keep you."

"Grazia..."

"Yes, Grandmother."

"Pray for me."

I prayed for her that night, and when I was done I took my first sip of Jehiel's potion.

My grandmother died two days later. By then, I was on the road to Mantova, the jewels fastened around my waist, Jehiel's potion in my belly.

42

THE YEAR 1500 PRODUCED A CROP OF CHILDREN WHER-
ever I looked. On the eve of *carnevale*, the bells rang out
all over Mantova to announce the birth of a Gonzaga
heir. Having produced two girls, Madonna Isabella finally got
her heart's desire, an heir named Federico. Just before Passover,
news came from Ferrara that Ricca and Jehiel had been blessed
with twins (not even one child for me but two for them!). A
few weeks later Penina bore a daughter, a true comfort to her
widowed mother, named Sarabella after La Nonna (now there
is true generosity of spirit for you).

But I no longer greeted these evidences of other women's
fertility with a rush of black envy. For now I too felt life stirring
in my belly.

The moment I felt life I rushed a letter off to Jehiel. No mention of miracles or divine intercession, of course. Nor did he
in reply refer directly to his magic potion. He did inform me,
however, that his princess/client — as he referred to Madonna
Lucrezia Borgia — had also been touched by God's bounty, and
added, "No matter if I am chosen or not, I will always feel a
godfather to these two babes." I certainly intended to name

him godfather to our babe, no matter how Judah might object. But I doubted he would be accorded that honor by the parents of the Este heir.

Summer came early that year and by June it seemed that everything was fecund and growing—the trees and flowers outside my door, the babe in my womb, and the manuscript in my *studiolo*. The writing of my *Book of Heroines* moved swiftly, as if buoyed by Zephyr's breezes, with little effort on my part. By the end of summer my heroines were prepared to meet the world. But now I began to find little reasons why the manuscript was not ready to be seen. Something held me back, something far deeper and stronger than the natural reticence of authors. I knew I had offended God when I swallowed the devil's potion, and I feared exposing anything I loved to His wrath.

The first confirmation of my fears came from Ferrara. In the seventh month of her pregnancy—and mine—Lucrezia Borgia produced a stillborn infant and lay in a delirium in the Este palace at Ferrara with little hope for her survival. In my mind, she and I were bound in our pregnancies by my brother's potion. We had both solicited Venus's favors and had seemingly been blessed by her. But now my fellow suppliant lay feverish in Ferrara with only a dead infant to show for her traffic with the cursed magic. My pregnancy, which for seven months had provided me a refuge, now became a prison of uncertainty and I prayed to know my fate.

This time God did answer my prayers. Your sister, Fioretta, came six weeks before her time, but not without travail. Some days before her delivery she turned herself upside down in my womb, and the midwife's attempts to reverse the position came to nothing, even with Judah to help her.

They worked over my swollen belly for hours, turning the little creature a finger's length at a time. But each time they stopped to give me a bit of respite, the little body slid smoothly back into its preferred habit—feet facing out. They were still working at it when my pains began. After that, all their efforts were directed to extricating the little creature before she either suffocated or strangled to death within me.

Like Madonna Lucrezia, I too fell victim to feverish delirium after the birth. Like her, I languished in some limbo land of velvety blackness that descended, then lifted, then blackened again, until one morning I was able to make out a circle of heads ranged around my bed, looking down on me like a circle of Mantegna's *putti*.

I held out my arms for my little Fioretta.

"She wants the child," I heard someone say.

I saw Judah turn away from my gaze and I knew the worst. "My baby is dead," I said. "Is it not so?"

His silence confirmed what I already knew.

The next time I saw the light, only one face was there to greet me: it was my brother Jehiel, bent over me, weeping.

I must have groaned inadvertently. For he looked down at my face and, suddenly ashamed, turned his head aside to brush away the tears with the corner of his *camicia*.

"What time is it?" I asked. "What day?"

"Wednesday, just after compline," he answered.

Wednesday. I remembered feeling my first pains on the Sabbath. "Have I then been unconscious for five days?" I asked.

"More like twelve," he answered. "But you are healing, Grazia. Judah says you will be well."

"My baby is dead," I told him.

"Oh, Grazia, I am so sorry. I believed that I could lift the Venus curse, but she was too strong for me." In an effort to hide his tears he threw himself against my breast, holding on for dear life while he mumbled his bitter remorse into my ears.

How long we stayed that way I cannot say. But when we drew apart, my tears had washed away whatever bitterness I might have harbored toward my brother as the architect of my woes.

"You must not blame yourself for my travail," I told him. "Whatever heresy I committed I did of my own free will. If God wished to punish me for it, that is between me and Him and no affair of yours."

"You have a large spirit, Grazia." He leaned over and kissed my cheek softly. "But will you always keep your tender feelings toward me, no matter what?"

"Of course," I answered. "You are my brother and I love you more than my own life."

"But will you always? Say that you will, Grazia. Swear it."

"I swear it," I replied. The idea that I could stop loving my brother was unthinkable to me. Yet even after I had sworn, he still appeared pale and distraught.

"Is there something else, Jehiel?" I asked.

He nodded. "Many things, sister. But the chiefest of them is that I have left Ferrara forever. I came here to say goodbye. I am a man pursued. Alfonso d'Este has issued a summons for me to meet his inquisitor. I am accused of witchcraft and blasphemy — crimes of the first degree — on account of Madonna Lucrezia's dead baby. She has denounced me. I must be gone before the Duke's men find me here."

"Where will you go?" I asked.

"South to Roma. After that, somewhere out of reach of Lord Alfonso. I cannot face the torturer." He shuddered. "Perhaps I will go to Greece. I do not know. I only know that... I will never see you again." He buried his head in his hands but could not stifle the sound of his sobbing.

"No, it cannot be," I cried out. "Asher will speak to the Duke. He will make things right for you."

"No one can ever make things right for me, Grazia," he answered, from under the shock of hair that had fallen over his bowed head. "All there is left for me now is flight — or the fire."

Brushing the forelock aside, I took his face in my hands and looked deep into those warm velvet eyes with the dancing yellow lights. But no lights danced there. The eyes were cloudy, like the eyes of an old man with the beginning of cataracts.

I held out my arms. "Kiss me on the lips as we used to do to horrify the rabbis. Come now. A lover's kiss for the sister who loves you."

I had always been able to tease him out of his moods. But

not this time. This time he turned away from my embrace and went on in a deadly serious tone. "I have a request of you."

"Anything," I answered.

"My wife. I know how you feel about her. But I must ask you. Will you watch over her and my little boys. Will you, Grazia?"

"I promise to love your sons and care for them as if they were my own children," I answered without hesitation. "As for Ricca, I cannot say that I will love her as a sister, for she will never be a sister of mine. But I will respect her as your wife and the mother of your children. More I cannot promise, Jehiel."

"More I cannot ask," he answered. Then he finally leaned down and kissed me firmly on the mouth, as if to seal our bargain. "Now I must be off." He straightened up. "But first I have something for you." He reached into his pocket and took out a small filigree case.

"This is an amulet to bring you good fortune." He placed the little case in my hand. "Is something wrong, Grazia?"

THREE DAYS AFTER JEHIEL's flight from Mantova we received a coded message from Roma announcing his safe arrival and we all rejoiced, even Judah. Our jubilation was short-lived. The next day the dispatch rider from Ferrara brought us news that the dei Rossi *banco* and all its assets had been confiscated by the Ferrarese *bargello* and that my cousin Asher was a prisoner in the dungeon of the *castello*, accused of conspiracy to commit treason.

Judah announced at once that he was going to Ferrara to seek Asher's release.

"Then I shall go too," I announced.

"I will go alone," Judah replied in a firm voice which brooked no argument. "There are scholars close to the Duke who know me, one old Greek in particular who might be persuaded to speak for us."

"What use is reason with a man like Alfonso d'Este?" I argued. "He is whimsical and cruel just like his sister."

"Can you suggest a better alternative, then?"

"Bribery?" I suggested.

"The Duke already has confiscated the *banco* and the warehouses. What have we left to bargain with?"

"I have some gems," I replied. "Entrusted to me by La Nonna. Perhaps for just such a purpose. Will you take them with you?"

Judah nodded his assent. "And husband," I added, "do not hesitate to give every last one for my cousin's life."

"I will do everything within my power to rescue our beloved Asher," he replied. "But you, in return, must make a pledge to me."

"And that is?"

"Not to give way to premature grief," he answered. "It is an offense to God to mourn the living. Remember that God is just and keep believing that, no matter how dark the future looks. Your faith and virtue will be rewarded."

And our sins too, I thought to myself with an aching heart. For I could not help but feel that the taking of Asher was God's price for Jehiel's apostasy and my own.

Six anxious days went by without a word from Ferrara. On the seventh day, Judah arrived home leading a ragged column that included my brother Gershom; Penina, cradling a sleeping Sarabella; two nurses, each with one of Jehiel's twins on her arm; and Ricca, carrying her older boy, his jacket wet with the tears that gushed from his mother's eyes in a never-ending stream.

The moment they came to a stop Ricca shoved her older boy into my arms. "Here. Take my poor orphan, Grazia," she instructed me. Whereupon the child, terror-stricken already by the fright of the journey, took one look at my astonished face and began to squall loud enough to wake a deaf beggar in the Piazza San Pietro.

Of course his cry was all that was needed to signal to his brothers. Until that moment they had appeared quite the serene little pair. Now, having gotten their go-ahead from him, they joined in the caterwaul. This in turn set off Sarabella, no mean wailer. And of course shutters flew open all up and down the street to give the neighbors a good view of the dei Rossi circus. The only thing to be said for this absurd scene was that it silenced Ricca for a short time. But the moment the infants had been quieted and put down for the night, she took center stage and commenced a peroration worthy of Antigone or some other great wronged heroine.

"Woe is me! Woe is me! Everything gone. My beautiful house. My fine silver service. My beautiful rock crystal vessel with the ormolu mounting." And on and on until every last item had been individually mourned. After that, without taking a breath, she went on to part two of the lamentation: "What will happen to me now, tied to a renegade, deserted, my poor children unprotected? How could he leave me here buried, neither wife nor widow? I cannot mourn, nor can I marry." Not a single word of concern for her brother, incarcerated in the Este dungeon, nor of the death sentence under which her husband now lived. Nothing but her lack of money and a man.

It was not until this geyser of ill will ceased to erupt that I was able to talk to Judah alone and get a report on his mission to Ferrara. The news turned out to be even worse than I had feared. Quite simply, the Estes were not approachable on the subject of the dei Rossi family. Judah had not even gotten close enough to the Duke to offer him the sack of jewels.

"Feeling in Ferrara is running high against Jehiel," he told me. "Not only at the court but among the people as well. Everywhere I went I heard men cursing Vitale the Jew-Witch, as they call him."

"And Asher?"

"He is in the custody of the inquisitor. They question him every day. My friend at court tells me they are convinced he knows Jehiel's whereabouts."

"But that is not true!" I cried.

"You and I know that. But the inquisitor does not. There are witnesses against Asher."

"What witnesses? Who could hate him enough to lie about

him? He never did a moment's harm to anyone."

"They've got some blind old stableman who babbles any slander that comes into his head about your family."

"Old Nachum?"

"I believe that is the name. And there's another one. That rascal Giorgio who used to be your grandmother's steward."

It seemed poetically just that these two who had been favored for their evil ways should end by turning their malice on the masters who had trained them to it. But why must Asher suffer for the sins of others, he the most honorable, the most innocent?

"Were you able to see him?" I asked.

"I could not, but Dorotea is allowed in. She takes food to him every day."

"How is he?"

He did not answer.

"Tell me, husband, I must know."

"There are some things better not known."

"In your philosophy, not mine," I retorted. "I want to know."

"Very well," he sighed. "His heart is not strong. They put him to the torture every day. If the inquisitor does not give him relief soon, then God surely will. That is the judgment of my friend, the Greek physician who attends him. Meanwhile we must put our faith in God's mercy."

But I had not his serene faith in God's beneficence. Asher was still alive. There was still time to act. And one last resort remained to me.

The next morning I wrote a note to Madonna Isabella requesting an audience. She had wanted me to humble myself. Very well, I would. I would have bowed down before the devil to save my cousin.

A reply came from the Reggio within the hour. The *illustrissima* would be pleased to grant me an audience that afternoon. The language penned by Madama's secretary was cold and formal. But the readiness of the reply bespoke a warmth that gave me hope.

I was not delayed in the anteroom, nor was I required to make my petition in the presence of the full court. The moment Madama caught sight of me she beckoned me forward and extended her hand to be kissed in a most cordial manner. Then she dismissed her entourage saying, "This lady, Madonna Grazia Ebrea, is an old friend whom we have not seen in many years. We will speak to her in private."

As you know, the meaning of the word "privacy" is not quite the same in courts as in everyday life. When the court withdrew, we were still left in the company of some half-dozen of Madama's maidens and two footmen. Nevertheless the easy familiarity of her manner suggested that she would not rub my nose in my capitulation now that she had me back in her orbit.

"Grazia..." She held out her arms, the fingers bejeweled as ever but more pudgy than I remembered. "Come near and tell us of your literary work. We have heard it praised extravagantly."

"The *illustrissima* is too kind," I replied.

"How can I be, not having seen the pages? I can only repeat what I hear. Maestro Judah speaks highly of this scholarly work of yours."

"He is my husband, ma'am. How could he speak otherwise?"

"Oh, he could. And would. I have known your honorable husband longer than you have and I know him incapable of uttering a falsehood even if he wished to do so. Now tell me what this work is to be called."

Of course the last thing I wanted to talk of was my damned book. But if I was to do my cousin Asher any good, I must not only endure the prattle but pretend to enjoy it.

"It is called simply *The Book of Heroines*, ma'am," I replied. "It deals with the lives of heroic women."

"You mean virtuous women?"

"No, ma'am," I answered. "I mean women who abound with that quality of *virtu* that men strive for so mightily."

"You speak of courage, then?"

"Courage, yes. And constancy. And boldness."

"And have you found many of these women to extol?"

"The problem I have faced is not so much who to put in as who to leave out," I answered. "The world abounds with women of spirit: the Amazons, the Sibyls, the goddesses of the ancient world..."

"You mean to include goddesses?"

"I take my position with Maestro Boccaccio, madonna. As he explains it, these goddesses and seers were women like ourselves. But because of their surpassing beauty or intelligence or courage, ignorant folk tended to impute supernatural powers to them. Abetted by the poets, of course."

"And you intend not to fall into that error?" she inquired with only slight sarcastic edge.

"I am using Maestro Boccaccio's method as my guide," I replied. "But in some respects I have followed my own inclinations. For instance, since he has already covered the great women of the ancient world, I will include only the ones I cannot bear to leave out, such as Dido."

"Ah yes, Dido," she sighed. And then proceeded to quote from Virgil's version of the story Dido's final curse on Aeneas:

If there is any power for righteousness in Heaven,
you will drink to the dregs the cup of punishment...
and, as you suffer, cry "Dido" again and again.
Though far, yet I shall be near, haunting you
with flames of blackest pitch. And when death's chill
has parted my body from its breath, wherever you go,
my specter will be there.

"I was in love with Virgil's Dido when I was a girl," I told her. "But lately I have come to prefer Boccaccio's version of her story."

"And to what do you attribute that lapse of taste?" she inquired with some asperity.

"Lapse of taste it may be, madonna," I agreed sweetly, "but I find I can no longer accept a love slave for my heroine. Virgil's Dido is a woman so enamored of a man that when she is spurned by him she chooses to immolate herself rather than live with the loss. That woman is a man's creation," I asserted.

"And is the divine Dante, who chose to view Dido in a similar light to Virgil and condemned her to the second circle of Hell for her lustfulness — is he also a mere man in your eyes?"

"A sublime poet but withal, yes, a man," I asserted boldly. "After all, the poet chooses his angle of vision. Dante and Virgil chose a Dido spurred on to her frightful death by lasciviousness. Boccaccio chose a queen who went to her death rather than betray her true husband. I throw in my lot with Maestro Boccaccio."

"And against Dante and Virgil together," she reminded me. "Such an audacious author will need the protection of a powerful patron when the Dante-worshippers unleash their arrows at her."

That this advice concealed a tentative offer of sponsorship I could not doubt. Now the question was: What price did she set upon her endorsement? And her next question clearly indicated the direction of her interest.

"Tell me, Grazia," she drawled, stifling a yawn to indicate her indifference to the subject. "By what process have you selected your heroines?"

"I mean to include many more modern women than Maestro Boccaccio did in his time," I answered. "With only a sprinkling of the ancients, as I say, to establish the model."

"And these modern women, who are they? Who, in your judgment, exemplify heroism in our time?"

"Caterina Sforza, the Virago of Forli, is one," I replied.

"Poor woman." She managed to work up the appropriate expression of compassion. "I fear she is no longer the heroine she once was. Her encounter with Cesare Borgia apparently took the starch out of her. I hear her looks are quite ruined since he ravaged her."

"But not her great heart, *illustrissima*," I answered. "The woman who so courageously defended Forli against two rapacious popes cannot be ignored when one totes up a list of heroines."

"I suppose not," she answered, somewhat petulantly. "But surely all your heroines need not ride around brandishing swords and wearing breastplates in order to prove their *virtu*."

"Not at all. I merely mention the lady of Forli because her exploits are so astonishing."

"*Si, si, si*." She tapped her finger against her palm impatiently. "But who else?"

"A young woman I knew in Firenze who is the inspiration for this book. A Jewess of no particular talent or notoriety who gave her life for the love of a child."

"Another dead one," she pointed out. "Who else?"

"I have considered your illustrious sister of beloved memory, Duchess Beatrice of Milano."

"Quite so." She nodded.

"Considering that she had not yet reached the age of twenty-two when childbed fever took her, her accomplishments are all the more admirable. I believe that she was barely seventeen when her illustrious husband sent her to represent him before the Venetian Senate."

"Eight days short of eighteen," she corrected me.

"And the court over which she presided..." I continued.

"Shone with a light that illuminated all of Italy," she finished the sentence for me. "Ah me, if we who love so much to spend money had but half of the wealth that my honorable brother-in-law lavished on my honorable sister." She sighed deeply, moved by her own valiant efforts to achieve her sister's illustriousness with so much less in the way of resources. Then, because she has never been a woman to waste time or emotion on regret, she went back to her subject with renewed vigor.

"But Grazia, my honorable sister is, alas, dead like so many of your candidates. Even Caterina Sforza of Forli is more dead than alive right now. Who do you have that is alive and breathing?"

"A young scholar in Firenze whom I met but once and who has immured herself in a convent for life in order to pursue scholarship. Her father has completely disowned her because she refuses to marry."

"A decision I find quite incomprehensible," she rejoined. "For surely we women are meant to be married. Why else has God arranged the race in two sexes?"

Dio mio. Would I now be obliged to enter into a prolonged *disputa* on the subject of scholarly abstinence? But no. In one of those whimsical reversals that characterize her nature, she left off sparring with me, leaned forward in a most confidential manner. "I saw an old friend of yours last week in Bozzuolo."

I was damned if I would rise to the bait.

"He was very eager for news of you. Don't you want to know who it is, Grazia?" I knew perfectly well, but I refused to be trapped in her snare. Whereupon she shrugged and in an abrupt change of subject asked, "What news do you have from Ferrara? I understand that your brother Maestro Vitale has landed himself in serious trouble with my brother the Duke."

At last.

"But it is not Maestro Vitale who has reaped the punishment," I hastened to explain. "The one being tortured in the dungeon is my cousin Asher, who is totally blameless in the affair."

"And this cousin is very dear to you?"

"As dear as my brothers," I answered. "Oh, madama, could you, would you intercede for him?"

"I could and I would, Grazia," she replied. "But that leaves unanswered the important question: Will my intercession do your cousin any good? My brother is bitterly disappointed by the death of his heir and full of vengeance against your family."

"But the soothsaying was my brother Jehiel's doing, not Asher's."

"When it comes to satisfying a *vendetta*, one member of the family is as good as another," she remarked. "Were the little children of the Ordelaffi family responsible for the assassination of Girolamo Riario? Your heroine Caterina Sforza knew them to be blameless. Yet she slaughtered them all, babes and women alike, in vengeance for her husband's death. That is the way of a *vendetta*."

Of course she was correct. That is the way of vengeance.

But just this once I prayed, just this time, let it be different.

"By the way, Grazia..." I was jarred out of my supplication by the hard drawl of our earlier conversation. "About your *Book of Heroines* and who is to be in it... I would be disappointed to learn that you did not consider me fit company for the spinster scholar of Firenze and the rest. But I wish you to understand that my offer to petition my brother on your cousin's behalf in no way represents a bid for membership in your sisterhood. I make the offer as a disinterested act of sympathy for one who, like me, is bound by indissoluble bonds of love for her family. I do not need to be bribed to be kind."

MADAMA'S GENEROSITY HAD GIVEN me a shred of hope to cling to. But that last shred was severed when just two days later we had word from Dorotea that her beloved son, Asher, had died after an application of the strappado. As the Greek physician had predicted, my cousin's heart gave out from the shock of the tremendous blow. His death united all the surviving members of our family under my roof (except Jehiel who, as Ricca reminded us daily, might as well be dead).

Dorotea brought her son's body by river from Ferrara to Mantova, and together she and Ricca and Penina and Gershom and Judah and I buried him. Then we settled down for the mandated thirty days to mourn.

I never knew how much I had depended on my cousin or how much I loved him until he was gone. The one person who would always come when I called, who would always love me no matter what, was gone, never to come back. I feel his loss to this day.

Prayers were said for him for thirty days. But on many of those days we were compelled to forgo the memorial prayer service because we could not gather up the ten men needed to form a *minyan*. Mind you, our Jewish neighbors had much to lose by public demonstration of friendliness toward us: cancellation of their Ferrarese *condotta*; seizure of their persons. Still these considerations did not stop Davide Finzi from joining in our prayers. He was always present both morning and evening, along with his sons and his two grandsons. Nor did the Norsa family desert us for fear of Alfonso d'Este's wrath. But in the middle of the month, they were off on their annual journey to the Champagne Fair, and after that, my beloved Asher was mourned or not depending on whatever stray Jewish travelers the barges washed up on the shores of the Lago Superiore who could chant *"Yisgadal v'yiskadash"* with my brother, my husband, and our few loyal friends.

One of the Mantovans who did make haste to convey condolences was Madonna Isabella. Granted, unlike our Jewish neighbors, she stood in no danger from her brother Alfonso for expressing sympathy with us. On the other hand, she certainly had nothing to gain by her kindness. For the second time in as many weeks I was touched by her compassion and resolved to call upon her at the Reggio as soon as our mourning period ended. I felt certain she had honored her promise to petition her brother on Asher's behalf. And, in the event, I was proven right. For Dorotea later informed us that Marchesana Isabella's petition arrived in Ferrara on the very day that Asher expired in the arms of the torturer.

IF EVER YOU WISH to put a truly vicious curse on anyone, wish him to be locked up in a small house for a year with your Aunt Ricca. That I did not mangle her to death during her daily lamentations for herself is a credit to my forbearance. But eventually I began seriously to question my own ability to continue living in such proximity to her. Yet I had promised Jehiel to care for her.

I might simply have left the house to her and fled. Judah had been offered a fine appointment — as body physician to Count Giovanni Sassatello, General of the Republic of Venezia — which included as is customary a house, a mule, an allowance of oil, fish, and grain, and an astronomic stipend of twenty-five ducats a month.

After a year with Ricca and her brats, the offer to move to Venezia appeared to me as a dispensation from the Almighty Himself. But there were Gershom and Penina to consider. Could I in conscience inflict the burden of Ricca's custody on them?

I never thought to consult Gershom on the matter. To me he was still a boy even though he already had served an arduous apprenticeship as a fledgling banker and had emerged with glowing testimonials. Here I digress briefly to warn you against myself, my son. No matter how old or how wise you grow, I fear I will always consider you in some sense a boy. And I strongly advise you to stake your claims as a man whenever the opportunity arises and to pursue them vigorously in spite of my opposition. It is a task that children born of strong-willed parents inherit.

Your Uncle Gershom needed no such instruction. Not only did he have the nerve to oppose me, he was born with a banker's sense of timing. During the preliminary skirmishes between me and Ricca he stood by, allowing the boil to grow and fester until the day it burst. When that happened, he stepped in as healer.

Ricca and I had long detested each other. She felt I had cheated her of her birthright. I resented her disloyalty to my brother. But when we joined battle in the sewing room it was not over such substantial issues but over a small piece of lace I had been saving to trim a bonnet for Penina's little Sarabella.

One day, without a by-your-leave, she picked it up and began to trim her cap with it. As I sat watching her stitch, it was as if her needle plunged into me each time she ran it through my lace. The first day she wore it, the sight of that finely worked filigree entwined in her coarse black plait set me on fire. I went for her like a wild thing. She lunged for my face with her nails. I grabbed her hand and bent the fingers back until they cracked.

Alerted by our shrieks, Gershom rushed downstairs from the courtyard, convinced, he later told me, that someone was dying in the sewing room. What he saw was two grown women rolling around on the tiles locked in furious combat, with hair and blood flying. He had to enlist the help of our manservant to pry us apart but he finally did put a stop to the joust. Ricca stalked off muttering curses and I was left to the pitiless judgment of my little brother.

"Oh, Grazia." He could barely contain his amusement. "I am astonished at you. Where is my lady sister, the devotee of the ancients? What has become of the golden mean and 'Above all, no zeal'?"

"Even I can be driven beyond endurance," I replied crossly.

"So I see." He came closer to inspect the river of blood that Ricca had dug into my cheek. "This wound must be attended to. Shall I call Judah?"

If there was anyone I did not wish to see me in this sorry state, it was Judah. So I persuaded Gershom to fetch a certain unguent from my beauty box to cleanse the wound of infection. "She is as likely to be rabid as any other mad bitch," I explained, my vengeful spirit still at the boil.

Until then I had tended to his blackened eyes, bruised limbs, and other childish hurts and had never missed the opportunity to preach to him the virtues of restraint and self-control. Now the roles were reversed. He not only spread the healing unguent on my burning cheek, he also added to the treatment a dollop of wise counsel.

"I have heard the expression that no kitchen is big enough to accommodate two women, but for you and Ricca a refectory would not suffice. You two cannot live under the same roof, Grazia. You will end up killing each other."

"What's to be done, then?" I asked.

"Obviously one of you must yield place to the other," he answered.

"If it were that simple I would happily leave this house to her and Penina. And you, of course, brother," I replied. "But who then will take care of you?"

"Take care of *me*?"

"You and the women and children," I replied, still quite

unconscious of the implied insult to his manhood.

"Might I suggest to you, sister, that I no longer need taking care of, in your sense? And that I might even be capable of taking care of the others?"

I admitted that the thought had never entered my mind.

"Are you ready to hand over the reins, Grazia? Think before you answer. For if you are, I am willing to take them up and lead this ragtag little dei Rossi force from now on."

"Can it really be that simple?" I asked.

"For me it is," he answered gravely. "I have only one condition to make, Grazia."

"And that is?"

"I refuse absolutely and categorically to marry either of those women."

Marry? It was becoming clear that he had a completely different picture of himself than I did. "Do you have your own bride picked out, then?" I asked, half teasing but half serious.

He blushed and denied it. But something in the denial, some trace of braggadocio, hinted that this fledgling had already made his initial voyage into Venus's orbit. Maybe more than once.

That day he and I struck our bargain. From now on he would be head of the family. I would leave the house and its inhabitants under his protection and follow my husband to Venezia.

Once decided, our move to the Veneto was accomplished with astounding ease and quickness. To Ricca it must have seemed as if God had reached down from heaven to pluck out a thorn in her side—namely, me. To Gershom my departure spelled a change in his status from boy to man. Even to Penina, who I thought would regret my departure most, the new arrangement promised certain advantages.

"This time things will be different between me and Ricca, Grazia," she told me. "I am finished playing the mat under her feet. My daughter demands more of me. If not for myself, I must contest Ricca for little Sarabella's rights. And I will."

The only one who seemed to regret my going was, of all people, Dorotea. She actually wept when she heard the news of our imminent departure.

Mindful of her service to me, I paid my final visit to thank Madonna Isabella. I had in addition a second purpose: to offer her a place in my humble pantheon of heroines, should she be gracious enough to accept.

"And when will I see what you have made of me with your wicked pen, Madonna Ecritus?" she asked playfully. But I detected an urgent undercurrent beneath the casual question. We all wish to know in advance what will be said of us by our historians—and to make editorial revisions if we are allowed. But I was not about to fall into that trap.

"One of the great disadvantages in undertaking biographies of living people," I explained to her (as if she did not already understand this), "is that they may claim the right to censor what one writes. Dead people are too moribund to do much else but turn over in their graves."

She laughed thinly at the jest.

"In fact," I went on, "if I were not able to enjoy as much freedom in writing of the quick as I can when writing of the dead, I would give up on the living entirely."

"I see." She rubbed her little finger up and down against the side of her nose several times, a habit she has when she is making calculations. "Well..." The rubbing stopped and a new decisive tone took over. "In that case I wish you luck in your ventures and look forward to seeing the completed manuscript before we are both too old and weak-eyed to read it."

VENEZIA

43

PERMIT ME TO INTRODUCE TO YOU MESSER ALDUS Manutius: scholar, printer, self-appointed guardian of textual integrity, founder of the celebrated Aldine Press of Venezia. Like many men of prodigious accomplishment, Ser Aldo was consumed by a single overwhelming passion: to publish on his new printing machine all the great works of the Golden Age, not only Homer, Plato, Aristotle, and Cicero but also lesser-known writers whose manuscripts had lain moldering in the libraries of ancient abbeys during the Dark Ages. His passion to find and publish these lost texts was exceeded only by his will to publish them in faultlessly authentic translations.

This obsession led him to establish his press in Venezia where he hoped to find a bottomless pool of translators, grammarians, and copy readers. But he quickly learned that although there was such a pool, it was hardly bottomless. Thus he was forced to spend whatever time he could spare from the press trolling the canals for Greek scholars to aid him in his noble endeavor.

From the moment we arrived in Venezia, Judah became Ser Aldo's quarry. Through his humanist friends the printer approached Judah for a new translation of Plutarch's *Moralia*. Judah declined the commission, explaining that his duties to his new patron, the General, prohibited such a vast expenditure of time.

Undaunted, Ser Aldo lowered his sights. He had heard of Judah's translation of Hippocrates' veterinary treatise. Might not that translation be acquired by the Aldine Press? Judah doubted Francesco Gonzaga would be willing to share the secrets of that arcane work with other breeders. The truth was that Judah wanted no commerce with printed books, which he viewed as a means of duplicating the most stupid ideas in a moment and spreading trash throughout the world, to use his own words.

What Ser Aldo finally had to settle for was Judah's membership in the *Neakdemia*, that group of earnest patricians who met regularly at the Aldine Press to converse in the ancient tongues. One among them was Pietro Bembo, then a rising star in the humanist firmament. It was to Bembo that Judah mentioned his learned wife, Grazia, and her immaculate hand.

Now this Bembo was neither better nor worse than others of his stripe—that is to say, haughty, snobbish, and prejudiced against Jews. Yet at the sound of the word "Greek," his bigotry evaporated and he became as eager for information of me as a besotted suitor.

"Does this wife of yours write Greek as well as Latin?" he asked Judah.

"Impeccably," Judah replied proudly. "I taught her myself."

"Then she is the one we need for Ser Aldo's edition of the poems of Sappho. A woman's delicate touch would not go amiss in that maze of ambiguities. Besides, you will be there to assist the work, for you need only walk across your bedchamber to correct your scribe."

This suggestion put Judah into a quandary. To mix the roles of provost and husband, he felt, was to court disaster in both endeavors. "If my honorable wife wishes to take on the task, I have no objection," he told Bembo. "But you must find her another editor. When it comes to scholarship, Madonna Grazia is, so to say, her own man."

Looking back, I realize what a generous gesture Judah made that day. A different husband would have kept his wife bent over her script as if over a spinning wheel and then taken all the credit for the product of her labors...and the payment as well. By forcing me to meet Ser Aldo on my own, Judah laid the basis for any reputation which I now enjoy as a scholar. I see that now. And I praise him for his generosity of spirit and purse. But at the time, my insight was clouded by my timidity. I had no wish to be "my own man." I was flattered by Judah's confidence in me of course. But I was also intimidated by the stern air of pedantry that hung over the Aldine circle. I would be honored to do the work, I told Judah, but I was truly terrified by the prospect of coming face-to-face with the formidable Aldus.

"Aldo is not the bear people take him for," he assured me. "He is a man with a mission. A man on fire. And, occasionally, those who approach him closely may get a bit singed. But never burned, Grazia."

"Scorched is more like it, from what I have heard," I replied. "They say that this Aldus exhibits a *terribilita* of temper equal to that of Michelangelo Buonarroti."

"There is only one way for you to find out," he answered. "Meet with the man. See for yourself. Then make an independent judgment. I have arranged for you to call on him this coming Monday. He expects you at the stroke of noon."

"But what shall I say?" I wailed. "What shall I do?"

"Do and say whatever comes naturally to you," he answered, quite untouched by my perturbation. "Haggling over wages is no different from haggling over a tapestry or a goblet. Believe me, Grazia, in the matter of bargaining, Aldo is a child in comparison to you. And besides..." He leaned forward and tapped me playfully under the chin. "You and he have something in common. You both believe that the printed book will be the salvation of the human race."

His arguments were persuasive. But even more enticing to me was the promise that a gondola would be hired to take me to the appointment. We were living on the island of Murano then and the prospect of being whisked across the lagoon and wafted past the great palaces on the Grand Canal lured me into agreement.

The Grand Canal did not disappoint. Bordered like a Byzantine illumination by shimmering golden palaces called Ca' d'Oro or Ca' Rezzonico (ca' being short for casa in the Venetian dialect), that waterway is surely the most magical in the world, especially when the sunlight dances on the surface, as it did that day.

At the time, Venezia was a city of women. Courtesans of both high and low estate constituted some ten percent of the population of the city. As soon as my gondolier turned off the canal I began to see women hanging out of windows, their bare arms perched on velvet pillows, their strong perfume wafting down to the water below, their ever-present songbirds perched beside them in golden cages, echoing the seductive serenades of their mistresses.

In due course we made a sharp turn into the small rio spanned by the renowned Ponte delle Tette, the Bridge of Tits, which I had heard much of but had never seen.

The Ponte delle Tette lives up to its reputation. Try to imagine layers of women stacked in rows from one end of the bridge to the other, each one naked from the waist up, their jeweled white hands cupping their milky breasts, thrusting them out at all comers as if to say, "Come and suck, you sons of women."

Observing my distaste, the gondolier was quick to inform me that this spectacle was sanctioned by the Venetian Senate. "It brings trade to the city," he explained, as if the benefits of trade excused any transgression of morality or taste. There speaks a Venetian.

Hardly had I begun to recover from my astonishment at the bridge than we drew up before Maestro Aldo's establishment.

Here a shock of a quite different sort awaited me. Nailed to the post that served to anchor the gondolas that came to his establishment, the proprietor had posted a notice printed in the elegant cursive script for which the Aldine Press is celebrated, and addressed to Whoever You Are. It read: *"Aldus begs you once and for all to state briefly what you want and then leave quickly, unless you have come, like Hercules, to support the weary Atlas on your shoulders. For that is what you will do when you enter this door."*

Not encouraging. But I gathered my courage and jangled the bellpull. No response. I tugged at the thing again. Again no one answered. Altogether I had to signal four times before the door curtain was pulled aside.

There stood a man, slim and sprightly, with bright eyes, round spectacles, and a very bushy head of wiry hair which stood out in all directions. I introduced myself and was invited to enter by this person, who did not seem to recognize me even when I identified myself as the wife of Leone del Medigo. But when I mentioned Greek, the bright eyes lit up.

"Oh yes, the lady scholar." Suddenly, he was all attention. "Welcome to Aldo's domain, madonna *ebrea*. I hear you are a meticulous grammarian with an immaculate hand."

Of course I went tongue-tied at the compliment like a bashful milkmaid. But I needn't have worried about what to say to Ser Aldo. He took care of all the talking. Words flowed forth — gushed is more the accurate word — from his lips like a spring torrent, almost all of them complaints. He was, he explained, beset by two main problems — "among six hundred others," to use his own hyperbolic term — which interrupted and hindered his studies.

"First of all, there are the numerous letters of learned men from all over demanding answers. If I were to reply to all of them, I would spend the rest of my days and nights on earth writing letters, do you see?"

I nodded my understanding.

"Then," he went on, "there are those who visit me. Some come to greet me. Some come to find out what is new. Others — and this is by far the largest number—come for lack of anything else to do. 'Let us go and visit Aldus,' they say. They come in droves and sit around idly like leeches that will not let go the skin until they are engorged with my blood."

I interrupted with an offer to leave at once if that would release him for his more pressing duties. But he brushed aside the suggestion and went on with his laments.

"I pass over those who come to recite their poetry or some prose composition they want published by our press, and this very often clumsy and unpolished since they cannot brook the toil and tedium of the file." He stopped suddenly. "You do not have a poem you wish me to publish?"

I assured him I had not.

"Nor a prose piece?"

"Nor that either," I answered, a not entirely genuine answer since I did secretly harbor a draft of my *Book of Heroines* in my *studiolo*. But I kept this information to myself and shook my head energetically back and forth to deny that I was in any way, shape, or form an author.

"Thank God." He breathed a deep sigh of relief and took my hand. "You, madonna *ebrea*, will allow us to say these things to you since you are at once very learned and very kind."

I opened my mouth to deny these exaggerated compliments but was cut off. "When I speak to you," he went on, "I speak to one into whose hands these books of ours may come." He turned away and, without ceasing to talk for a moment, grabbed a sheaf of proofs in what seemed to be a totally haphazard way. "Read the brief introductory discussion I have written for the books of Cicero." He pressed the sheaf of papers into my hand. "And do not judge me reproachfully as Hannibal did Formio. For I have been more pressed and harassed than usual these past two months. So let me off kindly when you have read them."

In this circuitous way, I was given to understand that my first task for the Aldine Press would be to correct the proofs of the writings of Maestro Aldus himself. No mention was made of payment. I was ushered out as volubly as I had been ushered in, the gentleman exhorting me to the end. As we sailed out of the *rio* his strong, passionate voice rose above the waves. "Remember, madonna, that those who cultivate letters must be supplied with the books they need. Until this is done, we cannot rest..."

In the brief space of an afternoon my gondolier had whisked me up to the heights of Venetian life and down to its dregs. As we floated back under the Bridge of Tits, I looked up at the courtesans packed in like so many carcasses in a meat market, and reflected that but for an accident of fate, I might well have spent my afternoon up on the bridge instead of palavering at the Aldine Press over the niceties of authorship. And there welled up in me an immense gratitude for the fortunate endowment that enabled me to sell the works of my own hands rather than the use of my body and to gain satisfaction from a respected craft.

Editing Ser Aldo's introductions had merely been a test of my skill. As soon as he had satisfied himself that I was competent, he set me to real work rendering the poems of Sappho into the Tuscan tongue. "For it is most appropriate," he informed me on granting me the commission, "that the lady poet be interpreted by one of her own sex."

Now, I have never been an enthusiastic admirer of Sappho. Among the ancient lyricists Catullus is more to my taste. But Ser Aldo cared more about Greek than Latin in those days. Besides, he and his circle believed that such robust fare as Ovid and Catullus fell naturally into the province of male translators. They would have been amazed to know bow many of my sisters have committed to memory Catullus's passionate plea to his Clodia. I can scarcely count up the number of dreary evenings Madonna Isabella and I have enlivened by declaiming in unison Catullus's wild words:

Come, Lesbia, let us live and love
Nor give a damn what sour old men say...

Give me a thousand kisses, then a hundred,
Another thousand, another hundred,
And, in one breath, still kiss another thousand,
Another hundred...

After Catullus, Sappho's love lyrics are tame stuff. But conscience overcame my indifference and *I* set about to serve the
poet of Lesbos with all my heart and mind, both of which were
needed since I was assigned three different texts, one in Greek
and two in Latin translation, from which to derive her authentic compositions.

The Greek text had been written with a stylus on some kind
of papyrus and lent to us by a rich collector from Crete who
absolutely believed that it had been written by the hand of the
poet herself. Both Messer Aldo and Pietro Bembo were convinced it was a forgery, but we never let on to the collector.
When I asked why, Ser Aldo replied in a manner perfectly char-
acteristic of him, "Why break his heart?" Without stopping for
my answer he added, "He would not believe us anyway."

So we treated the borrowed manuscript with all the respect
due its supposed provenance but relied mostly for purity of
text upon two others, each copied by the hand of a monk in
the Dark Ages. One came from the monastery at Corvei and
the other from Augsburg, of all places. The one from Corvei,
which I judged to be the less corrupt of the two, was the plainer,
with only the initial letter of each page illuminated. But it was
written in a fine even script that only a fellow scribe could fully
appreciate and was remarkably lacking in grammatical flaws.
Of course, given the vulgar taste of our times, it had been
valued at one quarter the price of the illuminated text from
Augsburg. Very fancy, that one, with little pictures of the *F*'s
and the *H*'s in the margins and several fully drawn pages plastered with ultramarine and gold, showing that a lot of money
had been spent to decorate it.

As the work went on and I became more and more immersed
in it, I came to love both the poetry of Sappho and the modest

little Corvei manuscript equally. And at the end of the task, I arranged through Messer Aldo to buy it. After much soul-searching, I decided to sell one of La Nonna's smaller jewels for the purpose. That little volume was the first acquisition of my own library.

I also reaped another reward from Sappho. Ser Aldo was so pleased with my work that he offered me a selection of the comedies of Aristophanes — lighter stuff than the great Greek tragedies which, of course, constituted the natural province of male interpreters. But I accepted what came to me under his patronage and settled into the detached life of a scholar on the isle of Murano, seeing very few people other than Judah and going almost nowhere except for the occasional visit to Ser Aldo's press.

Never before or since have I lived more satisfied with my lot. The pangs of childlessness were somehow driven off by the regular scratching of my quill. And when I began to feel myself slipping too far beyond the family circle, a few days in Mantova gave me back what I missed. There, in my father's old house near the fish market, my brother ruled over what he laughingly called his harem. Actually his jest contained much truth, for he took as much pride in the family of which he was unquestionably the head as any sultan. Certainly none of his four fatherless nieces and nephews suffered from the lack of a father. And, in return, the children adored their Uncle Geronimo (for some reason they preferred to call him by his Italian name).

Even Ricca found a place in this newly constituted family. She was much subdued now and, from everything I observed, had come completely under my brother's domination. At the slightest nod from him she would break off in the middle of a sentence and inquire, "Is that not so, brother Gershom?" in a most maidenly and modest way. Her deportment toward Penina had become equally respectful although not nearly so subservient, quite proper from woman to woman, I thought. To me she returned cordiality for cordiality. Jehiel's name was never mentioned between us. In short, we managed to throw a bridge of *cortesia* over the muddy waters that swirled below the surface of our relationship. And I left that place each time regretting that my visit had come to an end and promising to come back soon.

But always my quill beckoned. And the pile of rag vellum sheets waiting to be filled with the wisdom of the ancients. The sentimental might opine that since I was childless, the books I produced for Ser Aldo became my children. But that is twaddle. Books are books and children are children. The wonder of the printed book is that it can disseminate knowledge at such a small cost compared to a written manuscript that even the poor can afford acquaintance with Plato or Cicero. And the charm is that this is a new thing in the world, a weapon of incalculable potency in the battle of the poor and ignorant to raise themselves up. This possibility is what gave me pleasure and satisfaction in my work for Ser Aldo. Believe me, a woman, whether she has children or not, still needs to feel herself capable of worthwhile work just as a man does.

In the year 1506, I translated *The Flies* and received much credit for it. My translation of *The Birds* the next year brought me even more acclaim. At the onset of each negotiation with Ser Aldo, I bargained for better financial terms and the opportunity to tackle the *Lysistrata*, a work which amused me with its ingenious solution for balancing out the unequal powers of men and women. My monetary requests were always granted—albeit with some grumbling—but my request to bring the breath of life back to the *Lysistrata* invariably elicited a negative response. "For it is scurrilous stuff," Ser Aldo cautioned me. "And might even be considered seditious."

IT TOOK MADONNA ISABELLA to ruffle the calm surface of my scholarly life in Venezia. I had given the Gonzagas almost no thought since the time of my father's death. That part of my life was over, I thought. So when I heard that Francesco Gonzaga had traded his Venetian generalship for a high-paying commission from the French, I merely took note that in addition to his other virtues, he was a turncoat. But when I heard that he had been taken prisoner by his erstwhile patrons while sleeping in his campaign tent and was being brought into Venezia in chains, I made the effort to hie myself across to the Grand Canal to witness the spectacle along with half the city.

The day he was brought into town bonfires were lit in the *campos*; masses were sung in the churches, and cries of "Kill the traitor!" rang out everywhere. Looking down on the flotilla from General Sassatello's loggia, I felt that history was passing in front of me as it does in Mantegna's "Triumphs."

The Marchese was accorded a barge of his own, as befits a prisoner of consequence. He was not caged in a crude sense but set up on a box high enough for all to see, surrounded by the unsheathed swords of the splendidly equipped guards massed at the base of his platform. His scowl when he passed below me was so ferocious I would not have been surprised to hear him growl like an animal at bay.

Following the prisoner came the booty that was captured with him. One barge displayed his silver plate and his splendid suits of armor; another the sumptuous hangings that had lined his tents; yet another his furnishings, including the spacious bed in which he was sleeping when the Venetians captured him. After this came five huge barges loaded with some of the finest horses in the world.

For weeks after her husband's capture stories came to us at the Aldine Press—like any hive of intellectual activity, it was a major center for gossip—of Madonna Isabella's efforts to cheer her raging bull of a husband and to effect his release. Like the others, I was amused. Nothing more. It was almost a decade since our lives had intersected. In the interim I had managed to create a gap between the time in my life when the Gonzagas mattered to me a great deal and the present, when they mattered not at all.

Then came a letter from Madama herself which put the lie to that comforting fiction. The purpose of the letter was to demand a reduction in the price of a packet of books she had ordered from the Aldine Press. But it not only contained column after column of what she characterized as pricing errors (each one of which she claimed entitled her to a discount), it also made reference to an obscure work of scholarship—authored by a Jewess residing in Venezia—for which she had long cherished high hopes. To my complete stupefaction, the work she cited was my *Book of Heroines*, which at that moment lay unedited and almost forgotten in a dusty *cassone* in our boxroom. To me, the letter came as a shock. To Ser Aldo, it added an item to his long list of grievances.

"I am vexed that I should be the last to know of this egg you have been hatching here under my roof," he reproved me, waving the letter under my nose. "May I ask why you have been keeping this treasure from me? Is it that you do not consider the Aldine Press a sufficiently distinguished repository for your precious words?"

Could he have forgotten his stern interrogation of me on the day we met and his adamant detestation of authors' solicitations?

"To hear of it from a third party..." he sniffed. "It is an affront."

"Oh, Ser Aldo, I am sorry," and indeed I was, for it was plain the old man had quite forgotten his diatribe against authors and was genuinely hurt that I had not confided in him.

"And what am I to make of this, lady?" He thrust in front of my nose the postscript of Madama's letter and I read with astonishment, "Since I believe the work to be a distinguished extension of Boccaccio's *De Claris Mulieribus*, I am prepared to sponsor Grazia dei Rossi's *Book of Heroines* should the Aldine Press decide to publish it." How typical of her highhanded ways to address herself directly to Ser Aldo and to overleap entirely the insignificant person of the author.

The lady's arrogance was somewhat mitigated by a second letter, addressed to me this time, inviting me to attend on her at the Reggio in Mantova to plan the progress of my *Book of Heroines*. Notable by its absence was any mention of the long silence between us, nor did she express the slightest doubt that I would jump at her offer. Even Judah assumed I would go. He was as importunate as the habitués of the Aldine Press who descended on me en masse after the invitation arrived to offer advice, most of it having to do with ways to collect my travel expenses and my authorship fees in advance.

But in the end it was the prospect of seeing my family that drew me back to Mantova. I missed my friend Penina, and my brother Gershom, the only brother I had left. So, leaving Fingebat behind as hostage for a quick return, I set off, full of misgivings, for Mantova.

I walked into one of the most severe crises in the life of Madama Isabella. Her husband's incarceration in Venezia had been an ordeal for her from the beginning. Now the Venetians conceived a plan whereby before her husband could be ransomed, she must give over their ten-year-old son, Federico, to stand as hostage for his father's promise not to engage against Venezia once he was released. And her husband, the gallant Marchese, was threatening to cut her vocal cords if she did not comply.

So far, she had managed to hold on to the boy. But just as I reached Mantova, the Pope insinuated himself into the negotiations with an offer to house the little hostage in the Vatican palace under his own personal supervision.

"I will continue to resist the demands of my husband," Madama told me. "And I will find reasons to keep Federico out of the hands of the Doge. But my will is powerless against the Pope and his saints. That monster means to take from me my last and finest treasure — my son — and I hope that God will soon ruin him and he will die."

Then, almost without taking a breath, she quickly abandoned the detested Pope to the judgment of heaven and set herself to the practical problem of how to hold on to her son.

"The best line of approach we can take is to plead a mother's love. Besides, it is the truest thing we can say and truth is always the best argument, is it not?" Then, without waiting for an answer from me, she went on. "You know how to phrase such letters, Grazia. Messer Equicola is hopeless, like all men." That is the closest I came to being hired officially as her secretary. But for once I did not feel badly used, for I found myself in total sympathy with her, especially after I had read the despicable correspondence between her and the three men who, between them, had turned a beloved little boy into a pawn in their power struggles. I was also flattered that she had asked me, a humble scribe, to speak up in her name against a marchese, a doge, and a pope.

FROM DANILO'S ARCHIVE

TO MARCHESE FRANCESCO GONZAGA IN THE DOGE'S PRISON
AT VENEZIA
Most Revered and Respected Husband:

Have patience, I beg you. Know that I and our brother Cardinal Ippolito think continuously of your liberation. We will not fail you. Someday I hope to make you understand why I cannot in conscience give Federico over to the Doge as hostage for you. Even if your Excellency were to despise me and deprive me of your love and grace, I would rather endure such contumely, I would rather lose our state, than deprive us of our children. I am hoping that in time your own prudence and kindness will make you understand that I have acted more lovingly toward you than you have to yourself.

Pardon me if this letter is badly written and worse composed but I do not know if I am dead or alive.

Isabella, who desires the best for your Excellency.

Mantova, May 14, 1510.

TO THE DOGE OF VENEZIA
...as to the demand for our dearest, firstborn son, Federico, besides being a cruel and almost inhuman thing for anyone who knows the meaning of a mother's love, there are many reasons which render it impossible to hand over to strangers a

child of his tender and delicate age. And you must know what comfort and solace we find in the presence of this dear son, the hope and joy of all our subjects.

However reluctant I am, I must frankly inform you, once and for all, that we will suffer any loss rather than part from our son, and this you may take to be our deliberate and unchanging position.

Most respectfully,

Isabella, Marchesana of Mantova

May 12, 1510.

TO POPE JULIUS II
THE VATICAN, ROMA

... and although we are quite sure that his person would be well cared for and protected in the Vatican palace, to deprive ourselves and Mantova of our son and heir would be to deprive us of life itself and of all we count good and precious. If you take Federico away you might as well take away our life and state at once.

FRAGMENT OF A REPORT
FROM THE MANTOVAN AMBASSADOR TO THE VATICAN
TO MARCHESANA ISABELLA D'ESTE DA GONZAGA AT MANTOVA
JUNE I, 1510.

... I have never seen the Pontiff in a worse rage. He shook like a vessel in a great storm, twisting his wrists together as if to tear his hands off and quite truthfully foaming at the corners of his mouth. "That whore of a Marchesana refuses my offer!" (These were his words, madama, not mine, I assure you.) "I will never forgive this defiance. And when her husband comes out he will punish her, I promise you. Poor Marchese Francesco is the prisoner not only of the Venetian signoria but of a rebel wife. She is a whore..."

44

As Madama feared, our efforts to keep her son were finally overcome by the unholy alliance against her. Not one to waste her rage, she instantly turned to delaying Federico's departure by every ruse she knew. There was so much to be done; so many letters to be written; so many arrangements to be made. Grazia the scribe soon became indispensable.

In the pressing urgency of these multitudinous tasks my heroines slipped from the notice of their sponsor. But every so often the purpose of my visit did rise to the surface of her attention and my heroines were most fondly recalled, only to be confided to the ministrations of Messer Equicola.

"Confer with him, Grazia," Madama urged me. "Hear his opinions on the selection of your women. Regard him as your tutor. Take his advice in matters of taste as I do." But ten minutes with this arbiter was enough to convince me that what passed for his taste consisted mostly of an unerring instinct to ferret out any word or phrase or, indeed, any anecdote or even any of the heroines of my choice who might incur Madama's displeasure.

On the inclusion of Diamante he expressed doubt, "...for with all respect, Madonna Grazia, what place has a no-account Jewish matron between the same pages as our own illustrious princess?"

And discussing a recent addition of mine, a certain Christine di Pisan, "...as you yourself admit, madonna, she lived in Paris, and you know our honorable patroness's opinion of French letters."

It was only a matter of time, I felt, before he would suggest replacing Caterina Sforza with Madama's little dog Aura, "...for she is a female, after all, and a great pleasure and delight to the *illustrissima*." These traveling humanists write by the yard for whoever offers them a hearth and a living. Like chameleons, they change the color of their views to suit the landscape. Were there a single motto on the escutcheon of all humanists, it would surely be "Never offend."

Obviously between Maestro Equicola and myself a meeting of minds was impossible. Not being a stupid man, he quickly realized it and became as assiduous to avoid meeting with me as I was with him. In truth neither of us wished to offend Madama. And in the hysteria that mounted as the day for young Federico's departure for Roma came closer, we found reason enough to avoid each other.

My Sabbath absences also contributed to the cause. From the beginning of my visit I insisted that one day of the week belonged to my family. Each Friday after dinner I cleaned my quills, scrubbed the ink stains off my hands, donned my *tabi*-cloth gown, and, accompanied by one of Madama's hulking palace guards, walked through the town to the house on the Via Sagnola to spend the Sabbath with my brother and his harem, of which I quickly became a delighted member.

I might never have known how fragile this structure was had not Madonna Isabella offered me some fishes fresh from the waters of Lake Garda one warm summer day. Anxious to preserve their freshness, I set out to deliver them to my brother's household without troubling to announce my visit.

I came upon Penina in the garden with all four children gathered around her. Where, I asked, was Ricca?

To my surprise, I got no straight answer but a series of obfuscations and evasions that only exacerbated my curiosity.

"Oh, Grazia, it would have been better for everyone had you not come here today," she finally admitted.

"You mean I have intruded in some way? Am I not welcome?"

"Welcome in your own house? Of course you are. That is a silly question, Grazia, and you know it."

"What then? Why would it have been better had I not come?"

"Because now you will have to know," she answered. "And because we had decided not to trouble you. But now..."

"Now what? Where is Ricca?" She turned her face away. "Tell me," I urged her. "I have a right to know."

"Very well." She sighed. "But believe me, Grazia, nothing can be done. Gershom and I have tried every way to persuade her out of this madness but we cannot. And if we cannot you surely cannot."

"What madness?"

"Ricca no longer lives here. She does not live in this house any more than you do. She only comes on Fridays, as you do. And she stays over the Sabbath, as you do. And on Sundays, just after you have left she leaves. And we do not see her again until the next Friday."

"Where does she live, then?"

"With a merchant. A rich German. From Dusseldorf. He has taken over a big house in the Via San Giacomo. She lives there. With him."

"She lives with this man openly?"

"Well, we haven't exactly sent forth a *grido* to that effect," she answered tartly.

"But people know?"

"People understand. They see her as a deserted woman, neither wife nor widow."

"Still, when the children go out to school they will be the butt of jokes and scorn," I surmised.

"We reminded her of that," she answered.

"What excuse does she offer?" I asked.

"That if she had to live one more day in this nunnery, she would slit her own throat."

"Not a bad solution," I remarked.

"Grazia! Bite your tongue!"

But I could not apologize. For I believed then as I do now that death is preferable to dishonor. If that makes me a turnip of a woman without sweetness or juice, so be it.

We left it there, Penina and I agreeing to disagree for the sake of family amity. And the next Friday, I managed to greet Ricca cordially although I would sooner have spat in the harlot's face than clasped her hand. But I did extend my hand to her and so we trudged along in sweet hypocrisy. But even that tainted sweetness was not destined to last. For, not more than two weeks later, a letter was forwarded to me from Venezia which fractured the little household into so many jagged pieces that not even that expert diplomatist Gershom could put it back together.

I recognized the hand at once from the flourish that embellished the G in my name. Only one person besides myself made such G's — my brother Jehiel.

His letter, sent from Salonika, was short and to the point. He was homesick for Italy and wished to return. He missed his family. Would I intercede on his behalf with Madonna Isabella? The letter read as if he had been away on a pilgrimage or a pleasure trip; no mention of his offenses, of the pain he had caused others, or of the cousin whose life had paid for his folly. Still, he was my brother and I loved him. So, I laid plans to trap Madama at a time most felicitous for my presentation of his case.

The opportunity came a few evenings later when she invited me into her *grotta* to sing and make music with her and some of her ladies. "For even a virago like me must temper her embattled life with some beauty, Grazia," she explained. It was there after the music was done that I managed a moment alone to beg her to intercede with her brother Duke Alfonso on Jehiel's behalf.

"And what makes you think that what I have to say will move my honorable brother the Duke?" she asked, not sourly but as a practical question. "You remember that I did intervene once on your cousin's behalf with no result."

"But time has passed since then, *illustrissima*," I urged. "Perhaps your honorable brother has softened. By now his Duchess has given him two healthy boys. Does that not make a difference?"

"In logic perhaps," she replied. "But men such as my honorable brother are not ruled by logic. You do not understand princes. Let me remind you that my honorable father was named for the god Hercules. Such men think themselves at least half gods. They do what they will and brook no interference, not from counselor nor from wife nor from sister."

"But a good word. A plea for *caritas* . . ."

"*Caritas!*" She shook her head from side to side in exasperation. "Have you learned nothing of the world from observing my failure to save my son from the clutches of that beast of a Pope? Come. Sit here. Close. I will tell you a tale. It is a tale that must not be repeated, you understand."

I nodded my obedience to her command. And I have not repeated her story from that day until now.

"Some five years ago," she began, "just after my honorable brother Alfonso had succeeded to the dukedom of Ferrara, a terrible quarrel broke out between two of my younger brothers, Don Giulio and Cardinal Ippolito. The cardinal had fallen under the spell of a little Borgia witch named Angela who attends upon my sister-in-law the lady Lucrezia. Not content with refusing the cardinal, this Angela took pains to inform him that she preferred my brother Don Giulio and, out of sheer bitchery, added that his whole person was not worth Don Giulio's eyes. I need not tell you what came out of this wicked tease. You must have heard of it at the Aldine Press."

I confessed that I had not and begged her to finish the story.

"My brother Cardinal Ippolito was wild with jealousy and hurt pride," she continued. "The next day, as Don Giulio was riding home from the hunt, he was attacked by a bunch of ruffians whose clear aim was to put out his eyes. And they very nearly succeeded. He did lose the sight of one eye and most of the sight of the other, poor fellow."

"His own brother hired men to put his eyes out?"

"It was the Borgia bitch who goaded him on to it and of course my brother the cardinal has inherited the Este temper and the Este pride," she replied, as if somehow this excused him.

"Quite correctly, my wounded brother Don Giulio appealed for justice to my brother Alfonso, head of the family and of our state," she continued. "But the Duke did not act and that is where folly took over. Don Giulio entered into a conspiracy with my unfortunate half brother Ferrante against Alfonso."

"No wonder," I commented, "with such provocation..."

"Perhaps no wonder, but treason nevertheless," she retorted in a censorious tone. "Treason of the worst sort," she went on, "because my younger brothers were inept at the game of conspiracy and their plot was discovered. Ferrante was caught. Don Giulio escaped and took refuge with me here in Mantova."

Now the point of the story was beginning to emerge. "So you were torn between your loyalty to one brother and another," I commented.

"I felt a sisterly duty to shield Don Giulio from Alfonso's wrath," she replied primly, then added with a sudden softness, "He did have the most beautiful blue eyes."

"But Duke Alfonso would not be moved..." I prodded her.

"I wrote him long letters. I pleaded. I begged. But in the end I had to turn Giulio over to the Duke's justice."

"Is he dead, then?" I asked.

"Not dead but might as well be. On the eve of his execution he and Ferrante were marched to the scaffold and blindfolded, to prepare them for the executioner's axe. But at the last moment my brother the Duke relented and altered the sentence to life imprisonment in the dungeons of the *castello*. And that is where they languish now and will until the day they die."

She paused. "I see them through the bars when I visit my honorable brother's court at Ferrara. They are a most pathetic pair. Pale. Ragged. Forsaken." She paused again. "I tell you this, Grazia, in greatest confidence. It is a subject not easy for me to dwell upon. But I have recollected it today for your sake so that you may understand how limited is the influence of women over princes. Though the woman be called *La Prima Donna del Mondo* and rule as marchesana, still she has no weapons to fight the outraged pride of a prince even if he be her brother."

45

T HE EVER-WHIMSICAL MADAMA, HAVING SPENT A morning giving me the best reasons in the world why a plea from her could do my brother's cause no good at all, then spent an afternoon dictating a letter to her brother Duke Alfonso, putting forward an excellent case for Jehiel's reinstatement at the Este court. She even went so far as to suggest that in his present embattled state the honorable Duke might have use for "a foundryman of proven ability with not a little genius for making siege machines and designing earthworks."

Wonder of wonders. A letter flew back from Ferrara exonerating Vitale the Jew on all previous charges and reappointing him to the position of chief foundryman at Alfonso d'Este's cannon foundry. Whether it was the compassionate argument or the practical one that reached the Duke's heart, we will never know.

Of course, Fortuna is never as generous as she likes to appear. To give with one hand while she takes with the other is her way of going. Less than a week after I announced Jehiel's rehabilitation and only a few days before his expected arrival, I received an urgent summons from Penina to come at once to the house in the Via Sagnola. My only thought was that one of the children must be ill. I left off my copying and ran all the way there.

When I arrived Penina and Gershom were seated side by side at the table in the *sala grande*, their faces grim. There was no mention of children. Ricca was the subject.

"She has bolted," Gershom announced. "Taken off without even a goodbye to her own children."

"To where?"

"We do not know," Penina answered. "She has gone off with the German."

"What will we tell Jehiel?" I asked them.

"The truth, of course." Gershom's tone was as hard as a note from Tromboncino's trumpet. "That his wife is a whore and that he is well rid of her. That is what we all feel, is it not?"

Penina and I nodded our agreement although neither of us would have stated the case so baldly.

"What about the children?" Penina asked. "What are they to be told?"

"The children are already delighted that their father is returning to them," Gershom replied in the same metallic tone. "As for the loss of their mother, Penina is more a mother to them than the harlot who bore them."

I could not argue the point. But I promised to be present when Jehiel arrived, so that we might share the burden of breaking the news to him.

It was a strange welcome. We must have expected the old Jehiel to gallop up in his laughing way on a fine steed, for none of us recognized the slack figure sauntering toward us on a reluctant mule until he waved. Of course, once he had identified himself we adults shouted halloo and the children followed suit. But when he dismounted and went to pick them up and kiss them, they turned shy and ran away and hid behind Penina's skirts.

"They will need time to get to know me again," was his only comment. Surprisingly, he displayed little distress when told that his wife had run off. Nor did he put up even a token resistance to Gershom's suggestion that he get a divorce at once. What consumed his mind was his determination to arrive in Ferrara in time for the feast of Rosh Hashanah.

"From the time of Ptolemy until now," he explained, "men have sought out the most propitious moment at which to embark upon new ventures. This year the New Year commences on my most favorable day. For the Hebraic and the Ptolemaic calendars to coalesce in this way is extraordinary. I take it as a sign that my new life will be blessed with prosperity and success if I commence to live it on that propitious day."

"Surely you are not still looking for guidance in the stars," I berated him. Whereupon he flushed red and went silent. The wild spirit in my brother was not completely extinguished yet.

He *had* changed in some ways. No longer did he defer to my judgment. Coming hard on the heels of Gershom's recent emancipation, I found this uncharacteristic independence difficult to accept. And my feeling of being cast aside was exacerbated by my discovery that without telling me he had made plans to take Penina with him to Ferrara. Between themselves my little brother and my mouse of a cousin agreed to set up house together in Ferrara, and had made that decision without asking for my advice or even bothering to inform me. Even though the pill was sweetened by their obvious happiness, it was a little hard to swallow.

After that there was nothing to keep me in Mantova except the ostensible purpose of my visit: the preparation of my *Book of Heroines*. And my hopes for that project had receded with each week that passed. If it was true, as Madama insisted, that Ser Equicola's mind was a mirror of her own, could I in conscience cut my creations to suit those two mentalities? No. I could not lend myself to the corruption of my own words, however unworthy they might be. Perhaps I had spent too long at Ser Aldo's fount imbibing the doctrine of textual integrity. Whatever the reason, I resolved to announce my departure to Madama, the sooner the better. And to be sure, Fortuna obliged.

That very evening a summons was delivered by a smirking lady-in-waiting with the admonition to be quick as Madama had a special surprise for me. What surprise? Another humanist "tutor" to adulterate my text and disarm my heroines?

As I approached Madama's private suite a roar of laughter echoed down the long bare alley, a man's voice, teasingly familiar. Ghosts. Would I never be rid of them?

As I stood there, the curtains parted and one of Madama's little beauties slipped out, still giggling. "You had better go in at once, Madonna Grazia," she whispered as she passed me. "Madama has been inquiring after you all evening."

"Who has she got in there?" I asked.

"One of the gentlemen who are to accompany Prince Federico on his journey to Roma," she replied. "Just arrived home from the French court."

By then I had had a bellyful of courtiers with their pomades and their exaggerated manners and their cold hearts.

I hesitated, searching for a way to excuse myself from yet another tedious display of courtly wit. Then I heard my name. "Madonna Grazia…" No doubt about it, the man was talking about me. "Does she still…" The speaker must have turned his back to the door for I heard no more of his question. But I did hear Madonna Isabella's answer quite clearly. "She is still slim and pale and pliant as a reed. I'll tell you, cousin, I am taking my life into my hands to reintroduce you to her, for you are quite certain to fall in love with her all over again…"

With quivering fingers I carefully drew the door curtain aside just wide enough to peek through the crack with one eye.

Dio, it was he. "The last time I encountered her she was on a horse and she cut me dead," I heard him say. "Perhaps she will not be happy to see me."

"Perhaps yes. Perhaps no. We shall see," Madama answered lightly. "Whatever comes of it, I have promised her a surprise and if you are nothing else you most certainly are that, cousin."

Gazing through the frayed edge of the curtain, I was Narcissus at the edge of the drowning pool. God knows I wanted to stay. But my feet obeyed my command and delivered me from temptation. Without stopping even to gather up my possessions, I ran down the great staircase, out the great gates of the Reggio, and through the dark streets to the Porto Catena with nothing more by way of baggage than the clothes on my back and the little leather pouch fastened around my waist in which I carried La Nonna's jewels.

A pearl from that hoard bought me my passage. A cameo set in filigree gold procured me bread and wine for the voyage and one night at Padova. There I took passage on the *burchiello* at the cost of a gold bangle, with enough left over to finance a gondola ride in great style from Saint Mark's to Murano. But my little bubble of joy was quickly pricked for, on arrival, I found my life's companion, the gallant Fingebat, had suffered a stroke in my absence.

His ravaged little body ceased to draw breath that very night. "The only thing that has kept him alive these last few days was the hope of seeing you one last time," Judah told me. "If I were a believer in the movements of the planets, I would say that your lucky star brought you home at just the right moment."

MY BOXES WERE SENT from Mantova some weeks later with only the briefest note to accompany them.

"Do you know the story of Anaxarete, who disdained her suitor Iphis out of misplaced chastity?" I read. "The heartless girl was turned into a stone image by Venus. Venus hates a hard-hearted maiden. Be warned and prepare to yield to your prince." It was unsigned but I recognized Madama's hand.

However, I was safe from her meddling and mischief by then and confident enough to fire off a poem of my own.

> May you never, oh never, behold me
> Sharing the couch of a god,
> May none of the dwellers in heaven

Draw near to me ever.
Such love as the high gods know
From whose eyes none can hide,
May that never be mine.
To war with a half-god is not love.
It is despair.

To this riposte I received no reply nor did I hear further about my *Book of Heroines*. And I put them to rest in my *cassone* without regret. Better unpublished and unseen than tailored to the taste of this whimsical lady and her paid humanist. To inquiries as to what had transpired during my stay at the Reggio, I responded with such a ferocious scowl that even Ser Aldo ceased to ask.

THE MILLS OF THE gods grind slow. It took almost three years for Madonna Isabella to get her son back, but Pope Julius finally fell in one of his many battles and Federico was returned to Mantova the most worldly thirteen-year-old in all Italy.

The happy mother was not the only one delighted by the death of the Pope. By then Italy had had a bellyful of war. Even the cardinals had become pacifists. To prove it they elected as their next pope a man of peace, a man of compromise, a man of commerce, a son of Lorenzo *il magnifico*, Giovanni dei Medici, who took the name of Leo X.

They said that when this tenth Leo received the news of his election to the papal throne he confided to his Medici cousin, "Since God has given us the papacy, let us enjoy it!" But his papacy was by no means all self-indulgence. To his credit this first Medici pope devoted the initial two years of his pontificate to playing the role of peacemaker. Unfortunately for him and for Italy, just when he finally got all his counters lined up, there came to the throne of France a young man of war, raised in the tradition of chivalry and as besotted with the vision of glory as his ancestor Charles VIII. This one was a Bourbon who became Francis I of France.

He was crowned at Rheims cathedral on the twenty-fifth day of January 1515 and set about at once to raise a vast army. His goal: to cross the Alps and take possession of the duchy of Milano. Dreams of conquest never die. The basis of Francis's claim was a marriage between his ancestor the Duke of Orléans and Valentina Visconti of Milano that had been celebrated over a hundred years earlier, a claim about as legitimate as the claim of his ancestor Charles VIII to the crown of Napoli.

Aided in this vainglorious scheme by his doting mother, Louise of Savoia, Francis quickly assembled the finest and best-equipped army in Europe. Only one thing held him back, a miserable malady that prevented him from sitting a horse for long periods.

Young, virile, and a patriot, what disease other than the French disease would he have contracted? And what physician would be called upon to help the King regain his seat, so to speak?

The letter of appointment — more properly, the summons — to treat the King came not from the monarch himself but from his mother, Louise of Savoia. By then Judah and I between us had had so many farewells and welcome-homes that I hardly regarded the journey as anything unusual.

Judah embarked for Paris directly after the Chanukah celebrations, promising to be back for Passover. Who could have predicted that by the time he was done with his royal patron he would be practicing medicine from a battlewagon?

FROM DANILO'S ARCHIVE

TO GRAZIA DEI ROSSI DEL MEDIGO AT VENEZIA
Beloved wife:

When I look back on how I have spent the last few years, crossing and recrossing the lands of Europe in response to this or that entreaty or bribe or threat, I begin to believe that every important personage in Europe has somehow gotten himself a dose of this foul plague now named after Niobe's son Syphilus.

The young King, my patient, arises at eleven o'clock, hears mass, dines, spends two or three hours with his mother (that Louise who persuaded me to come to France, for which I will never forgive her), then goes hunting (since I have forbidden him whoring until the course of his treatment is done), and finally ends the night wandering here and there. This means that nobody can get an audience with him by day.

It is his heart's desire to mount a campaign in Italy this spring and he swears he will not set off until I have eradicated the pustules that cover his private parts both without and within and which cause him much discomfort when he urinates. "A fighting man in the midst of a battle cannot stop every half an hour to get out three drops of piss," he advised me.

He is very cheerful in his infirmity and I would number him among my more agreeable patients did he not insist that I attend his damn court. He tells me that he loves men of learning. He believes that scholars bring a prince more glory than battles. It is my misfortune that I am learned and thus an ornament to his entourage.

I rave on in my vain manner when the task before me is to clean out the King's urinary tract so that he can go comfortably to Italy and kill a thousand Swiss mercenaries to satisfy his vanity. Vanity, vanity, all is vanity, so says Koheleth. And should you take it that because you care neither for glory nor fame you are exempt from his judgment, I remind you as I close this letter that he also tells us: "Of the making of many books there is no end. And all is vanity and a striving after wind."

Pay no attention to this dyspeptic oratory. It is but empty talk from a lonely man who misses his own bed and his own dear wife and wants only to be in Venezia with her and not here at Blois.

My compliments and a kiss.

Your devoted husband, J.

Blois, May 12, 1515.

Beloved wife:

The King is cured. He can piss without fear or reproach. Still I am with him and his army at Lyon. Why? His mother, that witch Louise, insists that I remain at his side while he crosses the Alps. She reminds me that I am protected from highwaymen and bandits by thirty thousand of the finest fighting men in Europe. The woman has fallen in love with me. But I am warned. They say at court that Louise's embrace can be the kiss of death.

While we lodge here at Lyon, an advance party led by the venerable general Trivulzio has sniffed out an old shepherd's path through the Alpine mountains which would deliver our army into Italy behind the Swiss mercenaries who are said to be waiting for us at Suza ten thousand strong. The King is tempted to chance it. But I hear from a corpsman in the reconnoitering party that this new pass is hardly more than a series of defiles with only room on the path for a single horse; and that torrents swollen by the melting snows run so fast no horse can keep his footing in them; and that when a horse falls it falls half a league down. I assume this estimate applies equally to a falling man, such as myself.

If the King gives this reckless venture a go-forth I mean to separate myself from him at once and make my way back to Italy through the Mont Cenis pass like a rational man. I will inform the King that we must go our separate ways because we pursue separate ends. He is after glory; I wish to save my own life. Only one other is dearer to me and that is yours, my exemplary wife.

Your devoted husband, with the King at Lyon, July 31, 1515.

These may be the last words you will ever hear from your husband, Grazia.

My reasons for being where I am I will not try to explain. I have been misled by a mother with lies on her lips and a king with stars in his eyes. Now it is too late to turn back.

This is the fourth day of our passage through the Alpine mountains. For three days we have lived on bread and cheese and slept on the bare mountainside with only the mountain torrents to drink from. Even the King has gone without wine. But he has no need for it; he is drunk on glory. All he talks of is how the world will marvel at this exploit. And that his mother will be proud of him.

These paths have not seen the footprints of men on them since the time of Hannibal. And, by the way, if my life is extinguished in this mad venture I trust you to set the record straight in my name. No elephant ever came across these mountains. I will stake my life on it. I have staked my life on it.

The ascent was terrifying. Nothing to see but dark pines and giant peaks, nothing to hear but the roar of the swollen streams and every once in a while a strangled cry, a whinny, a screech as a man or a horse lost footing and plunged into the abyss.

Today we reached the top and started down. The descent is worse than the ascent. Climbing, one could look up at the sky and think of God. Descending, all we see is the void.

The King's engineer, Don Pedro, and his men have constructed a series of bridges out of logs and ropes to enable the men and carts to traverse the ravines. They are so delicate that each time I step foot on one I recite the prayer for the dying and commend myself to God for I fear that such a fragile structure will not hold my weight. But thus far not one of the bridges has broken.

The cannons are swung across on swings operated by an ingenious set of pulleys also designed by Ser Pedro. (This Spaniard is a genius.) Since we can only go in single file, we proceed like ants down the face of each defile with interminable waits for slinging the cannons. The boredom is excruciating. Yet the King appears to be enjoying himself. Clad in full armor except for his helmet, he manages to be everywhere — encouraging, cursing, laughing, lending his great strength here to swing

a cannon, there to quiet a panicked horse. Everybody adores
him. He is irresistible. But when he smiles at me, I want to
cry, "Can you not see, sire, that I am too old for these knightly
antics?"

Oh, my dear wife, I long for a world which recognizes
something other than jesting, jousting, and boasting.

My folly has brought me to this. I swear that if God allows
me to cross these mountains alive I will never again curse the
gondola, that perfect cradle of a vehicle, or General Sassatello,
that prince among patrons, nor stray farther from your side
than the winged lion of Saint Mark's. Only let me live that I
may demonstrate my deep love for you with more than words.
Until that day, I am your devoted husband, J.

From the French HQ at Col d'Argentière, August 20, 1515.

TO GRAZIA DEI ROSSI DEL MEDIGO AT VENEZIA
Still not home, wife—

Today is the King's twenty-first birthday and I am still
riding his wagons like a camp follower. Have I become a
war lover? No. It is not combat that entices me. I have succumbed to a much more insidious infection: tenderness. I have
appointed myself godfather to this great boy of a king. All my
homeless father-feelings have come to rest on him. Today was
his twenty-first birthday. And I worried that he would eat too
many sweetmeats and give himself a bellyache before the battle.
He needs protection both from his excessive appetites and from
his excessive valor. And who is there to protect him besides me?

We are camped amid the swampy rice fields of this plain
on the only high, dry ground for miles around. Constable
Bourbon (I still marvel that Montpensier's little son has grown
into a formidable general) is the King's tactician as well as
his second in command. He has chosen our position well. We
stand some forty leagues from Milano waiting for the Pope's
Swiss mercenaries to decide whether to do battle or no. They
are democratic, it turns out. They vote on whether or not to
fight. Last week our King offered them an enormous bribe to

turn tail and march themselves back to their cantons. Some twelve thousand of them took their booty and went home. But the Swiss of the eastern cantons have thrown in their lot with Cardinal Schiner, one of those warlike churchmen, who just yesterday preached a sermon in front of the Milano cathedral announcing that he wanted to wash his hands and swim in French blood. Our spies tell us that this Christian sentiment had its desired effect and that, as I write, the Swiss are preparing to descend upon this valley and gratify the saintly bishop's wishes. Remember the name of this place: Marignano.

Do not worry over me. I will stay far behind the lines to tend to the wounded and to be of service to my patron should his reckless courage land him in trouble. After this battle, home.

Your devoted husband, J.

In the field at Marignano, September 12, 1515.

FROM FRANCIS, KING OF FRANCE, AT MARIGNANO
TO GRAZIA DEI ROSSI DEL MEDIGO AT VENEZIA
WRITTEN THE 18TH DAY OF SEPTEMBER, 1515.

Madame:

It pains me to inform you that Maestro Judah has been wounded in the field at Marignano while succoring me. With God's grace, he was spared the terrible fate of many on that day and my physician assures me that his wounds will heal with time and no ill effect of them be felt. Take it as a measure of our regard for him that he leaves here today in the care of one of my most valued lieutenants. God willing, their party should reach Venezia in ten days' time.

Maestro Judah took the field at Marignano in the company of heroic men. Be proud that he acquitted himself no less nobly than the noblest knight. Accept the thanks of a grateful King.

46

I T WAS A HOT SHINY DAY SUCH AS VENEZIA OFTEN enjoys in late autumn. A gondola emblazoned with the arms of the Brotherhood of San Rocco skittered along the *rio* below my balcony like a swift, black snake. I knew that this brotherhood volunteered its services to the dead, and was convinced that Judah had died on the way home from Lombardia and that this death craft was carrying his body home. The black curtains that sealed the occupants from view played directly into my fears.

As I watched, the gondolier guided the craft out of my sight to dock at the landing stage below my balcony. Moments later there was a pounding on the stair and our servant broke into my room without knocking. "The maestro..." he panted. "They've brought him home from the war. Oh, madonna..."

I thrust him out of my way and rushed down the stairs. I recall the sun streaming in through the open gates at the end of the *sala*, blinding me. Silhouetted against the sky, two men were climbing out of the gondola, half carrying a bent-over figure, a moving frieze.

As I stepped forward to meet them, they moved from the

sun's glare into the shadow of the door canopy. Now I could make out the hunched-over figure. It was Judah. A pale, weak-kneed figure, but alive. At the same time, a third man who had been giving orders to the other two emerged out of the glare and turned to face me.

I rubbed my eyes to make certain the sun hadn't tricked me. But no. The fine wrinkles at the edges of the eyes had broadened into furrows. Long days in the saddle had darkened the fair complexion. And the bronze sheen of his hair had faded to a golden brown. But the eyes were still as blue, the teeth as white, and the form as straight and sturdy as ever. The years had been kind to Pirro Gonzaga.

I gaped, mouth hanging open like a cretin, as the trio passed slowly before my eyes and up the narrow staircase to the *piano nobile* while I remained fixed to the spot, stunned.

When he returned to the *sala* some moments later, Lord Pirro's greeting to me was punctilious to the point of coldness. As if we had never met, he introduced himself to me as a personal envoy from the King of France. My honorable husband had borne the rigors of the journey with much courage and strength, he reported. A doctor consulted at Milano had predicted he would recover completely albeit slowly. A Venetian doctor should be brought in to confirm that opinion. Regretfully, he was unable to see to that last task as he had not yet paid his respects to the Doge. But with my permission he would return that evening. Then like a wraith he disappeared, leaving me to question if indeed it was he who had carried my wounded husband into my house or a figment of my imagination.

Later that morning the Venetian doctor came and pronounced his opinion. Maestro Judah had been treated skillfully at Marignano. There was no inflammation of the wound, no fever. All the patient needed was rest and plenty of licorice tea, licorice being beneficial for the brain, and to keep his head swathed in a wet bandage soaked in a tisane of comfrey and linden leaves.

"And do not worry yourself if his mind seems to wander," he cautioned me. "The shock will wear off in time and he will regain his senses and his balance." Would I? I wondered.

I will not dwell on the balance of that day, the longest day I have ever endured. Two apprehensions vied for my anxiety: first, that Lord Pirro would not return; second, that he would. Teetering like a rope dancer between these two possibilities, I so wore myself out that by vespers I was entirely overcome by fatigue. And I did indeed withdraw to my room and ready myself to retire. But I did not get into bed. Instead I placed myself on the sill of the window wrapped only in my *gamorra*, peering out into the *rio* from behind the half-open shutter, allowing the soft mists of the descending night to cool my fevered body.

Just after dark I heard the soft swish of paddles under my window. Mercury himself must have put wings on my feet, for I dashed down the stairs so quickly that I arrived at the gates before our porter.

I cannot imagine what that sedate old man made of the scene—his mistress in a loose *gamorra*, her hair flying, her feet bare, leaning out into the black water like a deckhand to grab the rope from the gondolier while he whose task it was to secure the vessel stood by at a loss.

"Off with you," I muttered to the porter. And the old fellow discreetly took his leave. Just in time. A moment later, I hurled myself into the arms of the descending passenger, knocking his *berretta* into the canal and almost catapulting his own precariously balanced body after it.

What I write for you now are the secrets of a woman's heart. I invite you into my grotto, my secret place, the place where my most beautiful and dangerous memories are kept. Come back with me in time and learn of the exquisite, tender, powerful currents that swept you into being.

Up, up we went. Up the stairs. Past the room where sleeping Judah lay, forgotten. And there in full view of all Venezia—for neither of us had the presence of mind to close the shutters—I undressed him and reaped for my services a cadenza of kisses on the neck, the ears, the mouth, the breasts, as I unlaced the doublet, then the *camicia*, then knelt to the task of removing the boots; he all the while draining my lips of their sweetness the way the hummingbird sucks the nectar from the deep throat of the nasturtium flower.

I kissed his toes. He kissed my ears. I squeezed his calves. He caressed my shoulders. I stroked his thighs, those marble pillars that I had adored from first sight. He cupped my breasts in his hands and buried his head between, folding them with little, delicate wanderings of his fingers.

We sank to the floor. And there on the cold stones he took me over, master to slave, pounding my willing body ceaselessly into the hard tiles as if his Venus rod were a hammer.

We did not speak. We simply lay face-to-face, our fingers soothing each other as if to smooth out the coruscating lines that unappeased longing had etched on our two spirits. Then slowly the pace quickened. Gentle fingers gave place to not so gentle teeth, nibbling, nipping, biting. Arms, legs, belly, ass, every part of me was rubbed and kneaded until no part was left unexplored.

Then it was my turn to play coachmaster. And I rode him the way Pantesilea, the Amazon queen, rode her charger into battle against the Greeks—free and wild, using my long plait as a whip to spur him on.

After many hours, when the field was drenched with sweat and spent seed, I left him and went in search of wine and rose water and fresh linen. When I returned we drank together and washed each other all over, part by part, limb by limb, cleaning and oiling those poor worn orifices that had been so well used.

And then a vagrant phrase from the pen of Koheleth came to my mind: "Stay ye with me, dainties. Refresh me with apples, for I am lovesick." And I brought a bowl of small fruits to the bedside and some jelly that I myself had made out of quinces. For a lark he dipped his fingers into the jar and dabbed some of that jelly on my nipples. Not to be outdone, I brushed it on his lips and kissed it off. Then we fell into an orgy of dabbing and licking in every sweet place there is, and laughing at our foolish selves licking up jelly with our two tongues like greedy rabbits. And still we had hardly spoken a word to one another excepting for the formal salutations of the day before. But we needed no words to tell us that our hearts were as firmly entwined as our bodies.

Toward dawn I placed my sticky fingers over his eyes so that he might enjoy a brief sojourn in the arms of Morpheus. But the moment his eyes closed, my hands found their way back to his outstretched body, and with Koheleth again as my tutor I reached for a jar of sweet oil beside my bed and began to anoint him with it, running my fingers back and forth in the grooves between the toes, then circling the ankles, next the calves which curved into my hand as if made to fit there, then the thighs, and finally his private instruments of pleasure, squeezing and teasing them back to life with the oil but also now with little licks and nips until he awoke and taking me firmly in his muscled arms laid me upon my back, and thus we ended our long night as we had begun, with him the rider and me under his great weight, utterly mastered by him. A steed, true, but a triumphant one.

When two equals join in giving pleasure to each other, that and only that is true love, my son. The more delicate the balance, the greater the tension, the richer the pleasure. I think that, that night, we came as close as imperfect beings can come to perfect equilibrium. Should I regret the achievement of such perfection? I cannot. I took it as a brief return to Eden after more than twenty years of being cast out. And so God must have meant it. For the seed of that sowing which came into flower nine months later was you, my son.

THERE IS LITTLE MORE to tell of this blessed encounter. At dawn we dressed so as to present a correct picture to the household, and spent a brief time sipping watered wine and saying our farewells. There never was the slightest doubt that we would say goodbye. We both knew better than to ask for more than one night in paradise. Sufficient unto the day, says the Holy Book.

But before he left, Lord Pirro did make a brief explanation of how he had come to bring Judah home to Venezia.

"I have known for a long time, Grazia, that I owed you a debt," he began. "At Marignano I found my chance to begin repayment. The King was casting about for someone to conduct Maestro Judah back to Venezia—"

"But a lackey would have done for that task," I cut in.

"Exactly," he replied. "I volunteered for the lackey's job in order to serve you. For I felt that it was not enough to give a gift or to make a speech or to ride up in full armor and sweep you off your feet...though I admit I thought of that often..." Here he reached under the table and squeezed my hand tightly. "I felt the need to humble myself before you, to truly make restitution for the indignity I had inflicted on you. And God gave me the opportunity when he put the life of someone you cherish into my hands."

And in so doing He created a rift in my heart that no amount of time will erase, I thought.

The sun was full up by then and the boatman waiting. Our time in paradise had run out. But at the last second, just before he stepped into the waiting craft, he turned and beckoned to the gondolier to hand him a wrapped package lying on the seat.

"You are ever in my thoughts, Grazia, and will ever be as long as I draw breath. For proof I leave you this." He placed the packet in my hand. "I spent my last penny on it when I was young and it is still the dearest thing I own."

So saying, he boarded the craft, drew the curtains, and was whisked away.

For once in my life curiosity did not lead me into haste. I continued to stand on the landing until the gondola had disappeared in the mist. Then I took the package up to my room, where I would not be disturbed.

Slowly I peeled off the wax seals that secured the parcel. Then I untied the strings that bound it. At length the coverings were loosened and I peeled them away layer by layer. Paper on the outside. Then linen. And finally a silk jacket, gathered with a silk cord.

I sat with the silken bag in my lap for several minutes, savoring the moment. Then slowly I pulled at the cord and uncovered the object that was my lover's most valued possession: Messer Mantegna's portrait of me as Faustina's twin.

From that moment until this one the portrait has never left me. It sits opposite me on an easel as I write for you the story of your beginnings. When I die it will be yours (if Madama does not get her hands on it first). Guard it well. It is a talisman of the splendor of your birth and of the great love that brought you into being.

47

FORTUNA DOES NOT OFFER US MANY OPPORTUNITIES to take our lives into our own hands. The moment of your conception was one such opportunity. Once I was certain of my pregnancy, I could have seized the moment to confess my indiscretion to Judah and set the course of our lives on an honest path. But instead I announced my condition as if it were an act of God and waited to see if an explanation would be demanded. None was. Judah could read the calendar as well as any man. He knew that the child growing in my womb could not be his. But, like me, he chose to treat my pregnancy as a sign that we had been forgiven our transgressions against God by being given a child.

Anything I might add to this confession of the great lie we foisted upon you... and Lord Pirro... and ourselves... could only be read as self-serving justification of an act that cannot be justified. When the moment of truth came, we stepped aside and let it pass in the most cowardly way. For that cowardice I beg you to forgive us. There is nothing more to say.

In March of the year you were born, a merchant by the name of Zacharia Dolphin rose up at a meeting of the Venetian *collegio* to demand that the Jews be prevented from contaminating Christian citizens. It was the presence of Jews that had brought on Venezia's financial woes, he said, and pointed out that the moment Spain and Portugal had expelled the Jews from their lands, God showed His approval by showering on them the good fortune He had previously bestowed on Venezia.

Why had the Venetians fallen from favor? he asked. It was God's punishment for allowing the perfidious nation of Jews to flourish in their midst. He cited a canon of the Third Lateran Council of the year 1179 which forbade Jews and Christians to dwell together. The Jews must be sequestered. Messer Dolphin had even chosen a location for them: the area of the New Foundry—the Ghetto Nuovo—in the parish of San Girolamo where, not inconveniently, he owned many houses.

When Judah brought home this news, I took it the way Jews have learned to do over centuries—with a shrug. If a Jew trembled at every Christian threat, the whole race would have palsy. Nor was Judah unduly distressed. He recalled that as far back as 1385 various *condotte* between the Jews and the Serenissima, as the Venetians called their state, had called for a place where Jews could live apart from the Christian population. But nothing had ever been done to enforce these provisos, he reminded me, and no doubt the same inaction would prevail in the future.

He did not figure into his calculations the disquiet of the people or the venom of the priests or the cupidity of the property owners. On April first of the year 1516, the Venetian Senate issued a proclamation that the Jews of Venezia were to be settled into the Ghetto Nuovo within ten days. Dolphin and his henchman, another property owner called Bragadin, had carried the Senate by eighty-six votes.

The news came to us via no less a personage than Rabbi Asher Meshullam, the one you hear spoken of as Anselmo del Banco. He came to our door on the night of the vote of sequestration, banging and shouting to be let in after we had locked up for the night. At first we mistook him for a housebreaker. But when Judah recognized the old rabbi's voice he immediately ordered the locks undone. Meshullam, the wealthiest and most powerful Jew in Venezia, was at that time close to eighty. Nothing less than a catastrophe would have brought this frail old man out on a cold, wet night.

With Rabbi Asher came his son Jacob, one of those sons of rich men who are continually getting into trouble on one account or another but always wear a dapper smile because they know that at the final hour their rich papa will step in to save them. But tonight Jacob was not smiling.

The talk went on far into the night. Strategy was discussed. What bribes to offer and to whom. Much anger was expressed. Old Meshullam swore that he would never live behind sealed walls. "Rather live in the burned-out ruins of Mestre...rather die," were his words. And his son echoed him. Judah remained silent. And I kept my counsel as befits a humble Jewish wife. But after the Meshullams had left, I did not hesitate to engage my husband.

"Are we really as threatened as Meshullam believes?" I asked.

"I think yes," he replied gravely. "Because it is not just current events that have exposed us to danger. Or bigotry. Or greed. This crisis in Venetian affairs has been building for over a decade. Now the forces of history, commerce, religion, and geography have found common cause against our people."

"Geography?" That inclusion puzzled me.

"Probably the most powerful factor in the equation," he replied. "Remember, my dear, that the goods which are the stuff of trade travel over geographical terrain. For centuries wealth has flowed into the Venetian lagoon over sea routes from Byzantium, the Levant, and the Black Sea. It is in gratitude to the sea god who makes this trade possible that the Doge sails out to sea in the state bucentaur on Ascension Day to cast a gold ring into the waves. The Venetians see this ritual as the wedding of the bride, Venezia, with the god Neptune. But about ten years ago, the Serenissima came under attack from the Italian princes and was forced to divert her attention from the sea to her holdings on the mainland, the so-called terra firma. As the mythologists would have it, the sea god proved to be a jealous mate. When Venezia lost interest in the sea, Neptune found himself a new darling, Portugal."

"But we have prevailed in the terra firma," I reminded him. No one who lived in Venezia could ever forget the celebration of that victory.

"Too late. By now, the arteries that pumped gold into the heart of Venezia have dried up. When Vasco da Gama found a short route around the Cape of Good Hope, geography took over. The lordly Serenissima is now no better than any other small Italian state scrapping for bits of territory in the terra firma."

"And for this they blame the Jews?"

"Who else? They can hardly blame their own shortsightedness."

"But surely the Venetians will not act on this monstrous plan to lock up hundreds of people who have done them no wrong." My imagination could not conceive such a thing. "And even if they do, the Jews will soon buy their way out as they always have... will they not?" I asked.

"Perhaps." He sighed deeply. "But no matter what comes of this proclamation, I fear that the climate of Venezia is no longer conducive to our good health. Tomorrow I will begin to search for a new post. The Sultan has written to me again."

"No, Judah, not Constantinople!" I protested.

"We must go where we can, Grazia," he admonished me gently. "I will do what is in my power to satisfy your desires, but I urge you to remember that we are not in the same position as Meshullam. He is a man of vast wealth who can pick and choose his refuge. I am a physician and scholar with vast resources of skill and intellect—which I lay at your feet—but without estates and wealth. I will go at once to beg the General to intercede on our behalf. But I warn you that if my best efforts fail we may be forced into this ghetto. Your time is close, little wife. At least there you will be with people who love you and your child will have a roof over his head."

Judah is the seer in this family, not I. As he predicted, ten days flew by without a change of heart on the part of the Senate. On April 10, every Jew in Venezia was required to present himself at the gateway to the cannon factory in the district of San Girolamo. No exceptions. Not even our patron, General Sassatello, was able to get us excused from the order.

As a consolation the General had sent his gondola to carry us on our journey through the canals. I brought with me only one small hamper, for I knew we would be out of that place within a few days. Paddling along under the gold fringe of the General's *baldacchino*, it was easy to think that way. But when we reached the Grand Canal and saw before our eyes the mournful cavalcade bound for the ghetto, my foolish optimism began to fade.

Most of the scows and barges that made up the flotilla bore aloft huge piles of possessions, for most of the families brought with them everything in the world they owned, including dogs and cats and birds and even whole dovecotes of pigeons. We took a position directly behind a rag seller who had managed to pack his wife, five children, and all their possessions onto one small scow. There we were joined by the Meshullam family's train of gondolas and barges.

As the flotilla moved haltingly along the Grand Canal, I was reminded of the Venetian processions painted by Vittore Carpaccio. On both sides of the water you have housewives leaning out of their windows to view the spectacle. The bridges become the bleachers for the courtesans. Everywhere there are young boys larking about among the housemaids. And all the faces are lit up with joy to see the spectacle...the casting out of the hated Jews.

The pace of the procession was funereal. But after some hours, we turned off the Grand Canal and entered the district of San Girolamo, a marshy and insalubrious part of the city as far removed as one can get from the Piazza San Marco. There, many years before, had been established the cannon factory, the ghetto. The spot was clearly marked by a stone ball perched on top of the iron gateway now manned by two tall Venetian guards wearing the Doge's insignia. The fortresslike aspect of the place was emphasized by recent repairs on the buildings that faced the canal. During the previous week all the windows on the side facing out had been bricked up. Even our gaze was anathema to the Venetians.

At the first sight of that prison—it *is* a prison for all they still call it ghetto—children and adults alike began to weep and then to sway and then to pray as we do when mourning the dead. How appropriate, since we were engaged in burying ourselves.

As the long day wound down, our craft edged slowly toward that implacable wall where we awaited our turn to disembark. Then just before sunset the decorum of the occasion was disrupted by the arrival of a sleek gondola bearing a patrician crest, which swept around the bend of the canal and sped past all the other craft like an arrogant dowager who claims the place at the head of the line as her right.

At first all we heard from under the canopy was a series of imperious commands.

"Pass them by, pass them by," the mistress of the craft commanded her boatman. And then: "Pull up there. No, not there, ham hock. Can you not see the mud? I wish to be put off on the dry part. There. In front of that dirty barge. Tell those people to move. If they will not, ram the barge. Move, curs." Obediently the gondolier rammed a dirty barge out of his path and maneuvered his craft into its place.

By now everyone within sight of the gondola was holding his breath, waiting for the sight of the person about to disembark.

First came a large fan, shoved out from under the canopy by an arm covered with jeweled bracelets. Next came a rather large foot bound in the highest *pianelle* I have ever seen. More like stilts than *pianelle*, they were calculated to lift the wearer at least two hands above her normal height. We now had a foot and a hand. Next, in response to a terse command from behind the curtains of the *baldacchino*, one of the boatmen leapt off the gondola and with a great flourish opened a parasol, presumably to shield the passenger's delicate skin from the rays of the setting sun.

Now a book bound in gold and red velvet was thrust at the gondolier by the bejeweled hand. And finally the lady herself emerged, giving the crowd a fine view of her ample bosom. She was as good as naked from the waist up. Mind you, for modesty's sake, she held a half-mask over her upper face to conceal her eyes. But I would have recognized that nose and that chin and that voluptuous mouth anywhere. It was my former sister-in-law, Ricca, followed by a wizened crone, her *ruffiana*, her female pimp...Dorotea, come to roost in the Venetian ghetto.

In the craft beside us, pushing forward for a better view, young Jacob Meshullam licked his lips. "Amazing, is she not?"

"Who is she?" asked his father.

"Why that is Bellina Ebrea, the Jewish courtesan, Papa," his son explained. "You have heard me speak of her. She is the one who goes about the streets reading Psalms from her little gold Bible. It never leaves her hand. Not even at the certain moment."

"It is Ricca," I whispered to Judah.

"I know," he whispered back.

With her two boatmen following, her Bible in hand, and her mother following along like a maidservant, she sailed past the officials and their clerks, tossing out orders in a deep contralto voice clear as a basset horn.

"I am to have the top story in the building at the left corner. My things will be arriving later tonight. And mark you, make certain that no harm befalls my lute. It is a treasure from the hand of Lorenzo de Pavia and is the very favorite thing of a most important gentleman of my acquaintance."

With that she rounded the corner and was lost to our view.

"Much as I loathe them both, I am saddened by what they have come to," I confided in Judah.

"Do not waste your pity, Grazia," was his reply. "That woman has accomplished what few of us are privileged to do in this life. She has found her true vocation and is practicing it with notable success."

MY FIRST LOOK AT the quarters in which I was destined to spend my confinement brought instantly to mind my mother's birth pangs in that hellhole of an inn at Governolo long ago. Dark, cramped, and filthy, the single room meant to serve us for living, sleeping, cooking, eating, and study seemed cut off from all the light in the world. Yet Judah assured me that this suite was the best to be had at any price. We were among the fortunate. Less spacious rooms were being made to accommodate whole families. In my mind I understood I should be grateful. But my heart was flooded with despair. "They mean to bury us here," I told Judah. "We must escape from this place or I will die here."

But the possibility of escape retreated farther with each day's passing. As always Judah's faith in God's ultimate wisdom sustained him. He was even able to discover a benevolent intent behind our incarceration in the ghetto at this particular moment.

"Perhaps being born in the Venetian ghetto is God's way of marking your child as one of His chosen people," he suggested. What my heart heard was that if you could not be his child, you would at least belong to his God.

YOU WERE THE FIRST boy child born in the Venetian ghetto. Was it an honor or a shame? If you are looking for God's answer, I give you the evidence of it herewith. You were a child of the sun, born after a single night of laboring just as the first light suffused the sky. Our neighbors wanted us to call you Mithras because you had bested the sun god in entering the world. I clung to my first choice, Danilo — little Daniele — in memory of my father. But the gods had their own *imprese* to bestow: a pair of eyes bluer than the vault of heaven. All babies are born with blue eyes. But not eyes of that particular cornflower blue. And, as if they were not enough to mark your heritage, a thatch of golden hair graced your broad little brow.

"You really ought to call him Apollo," said my neighbor, the seamstress who saw me through my labor. "He is a golden boy."

Since we were denied the services of wet nurses in the ghetto, I nursed you myself. Why do women so easily relinquish this pleasure? I wonder. You had the habit of closing your eyes as you sucked and opening them wide when you had gotten your fill. Those were the moments I treasured, moments that made everything unbearable about the ghetto—the crowding, the racket, the stink—bearable.

Also there was kindness within that maze of hovels. And even without. Judah's patron sent box after box of oil and wine to celebrate your birth and more wine and candles and sweetmeats to celebrate your circumcision. And he worked assiduously to help us escape into the light once more. Perhaps as a Venetian he felt shame at what he had brought us to. Whatever the cause, he wrote to Pope Leo a glowing encomium on Judah's behalf and I am certain that it, along with others by such luminaries as Pietro Bembo, helped Judah to gain the post of body physician to the Holy Father.

When the news of the appointment arrived I literally jumped for joy, spilling out milk all over my chemise. I had tried to hide the depth to which my spirit sank each evening at sundown when the huge gates of the ghetto swung shut on us and the clang of the three massive locks announced to the world that the Jews of Venezia were safely locked in for the night. But, once we had bade goodbye to that hateful place and were sailing out the *rio* to freedom, I gave voice to my emotions and Judah in his turn disclosed to me a despair as black as my own which he had hidden for my sake.

"This ghetto has engendered in me visions that turn my blood to water," he confided, as we drifted away from the forbidding facade with its patchwork of blind windows.

"But surely the Senate will relent in time." I could not bear to think that others less fortunate might be immured there for all of their lives.

"I wish I could share your optimism," he replied. "But I fear my vision of the future is much more bleak than yours. In my prospect, this ghetto in Venezia is only the first. Soon another will spring up in some other city—Parma perhaps or Trento—then another and yet another until finally there will be a ghetto in every city. At this moment Venezia is no longer a place where Jews can live freely. Soon Italy itself will not be a fit country. And not long after, other nations will follow suit and there will be no place for us in all of Christendom."

"Oh, that could never happen!"

"Oh yes it could," he corrected me. "And my bones tell me it will. Today the Venetians say the sight of Jews is an offense to God. But I say that the sight of many people is an offense to men and that once you begin to enclose the outcasts in some place set aside, there is no end. For, even as a Jew is an offense to God, a poor man is an offense to one with a full belly and a madman is an offense to one who has all his wits about him.

"Here in this cursed year of 1516 the Venetians have put their Jews aside out of sight in an enclosure where they cannot offend the pious eyes of Christians. But Jews are not the only pariahs. Mark me, we will be followed by other despised groups. Would it not improve the landscape of the city if the citizens were not forced to smell the filth of the poor or to expose themselves to the anguish of the mad? Why not enclosures for them?"

There was a terrifying logic behind his argument that drove me to follow him down a dark path where I had no wish to go. I placed my hand on his arm in a pathetic attempt to stem the flow of his imaginings. But he was not yet done.

"I predict that as certainly as the night follows the day it will not be long before these pariahs—the sequestered ones—are seen to be the authors of their own misfortunes. That will be the means of perpetuating the enclosures. Mark me"—he was thundering now like an Old Testament prophet—"it will not be long before the victims of these sequesterments will be blamed for the crime of having brought misfortune upon themselves. They will be accused, jailed, whipped, like common criminals. After many decades—or centuries—they will be gathered up like a crop of rank weeds and burned."

From where, I wondered, did such thoughts come to him, thoughts so morbid, so fantastic? It was too bleak a vision of the future for me. But that night I fell asleep wondering, Supposing what he foretells comes to pass? Who will want to live in such a world?

ROMA

48

O UR FIRST MONTHS IN ROMA WERE ALL DELIGHT. The Tiber did not overrun its banks in 1516, so we were spared the annual flood. And Judah's new patron, Pope Leo, received him with all the pomp and ceremony due a chief body physician. Unfortunately, the physician did not possess an instant cure for the Pope's painful anal fistula; but he did concoct an unguent to calm the suppurating wound. For this the grateful patient rewarded him with an additional emolument, an appointment to the Pontiff's own university, the Studium Urbanum.

Judah was only one among the many accomplished men attracted to the service of this magnanimous patron. As soon as the Pope was elected, he announced the appointment of two Latin secretaries, Pietro Bembo and Jacopo Sadoleto. Both were distinguished Ciceronian Latinists and between them they set the humanistic tone of the court. He enticed the singer Gabriele Merino into his service by making him an archbishop. From his predecessor he inherited the glorious duo Raffaello Santi and Michelangelo Buonarroti. Buonarroti's tempestuous nature proved too much for the easygoing Medici pope.

But Raffaello became the instrument he used to accomplish extensive improvements of the Vatican and of the city of Roma. Under Leo, Roma shone like a beacon, beckoning every artist, poet, and humanist in the peninsula to join the ever-widening Leonine circle.

Even those of us on the periphery were touched. Buried in their dusty *cassone*, my heroines began to stir. "Release us, Grazia," they whispered to me. "We are cold and stiff from this long interment. Every half-baked Minerva is allowed to warm herself in Leo's sun. Why not us?"

I could not resist the call.

"Courage, Grazia," I muttered to myself as I lifted the lid of the *cassone*, unopened since the day I had consigned my creatures to death rather than dishonor at the hands of Madonna Isabella and her henchman Equicola.

What did I fear? That the interred heroines would rise to revenge themselves for their long incarceration? Or that I would find them beyond resuscitation?

When I touched the pile of vellum leaves, wisps of pale dust rose as if from a desiccated corpse. But these bodies were not dead. Reading the pages brought them instantly to life. Before long my heroines had regained their former vitality and were pressing to have their stories presented to the world at last.

If ever there was a time and place for them, Leonine Roma was it. The city was teeming with enlightened printers and publishers. Surely there must be one among them willing to bring out my *Book of Heroines* despite its lack of patronage. Newly inspired, I set about to polish up my portraits, taking as my mentor in portraiture Maestro Mantegna. If my subject had a wart on her nose I would describe it. If she was fat I would limn in the folds. If she was a wanton I would list her lovers. With one toe rocking the cradle beside me as I worked, the work of revision became a joyful task. Never was a poet more inspired by his muse than I was by your wide, unblinking blue eyes peering up at me as I composed.

I also regained my brother in Leo's Roma. By the time we took up residence in our new home under the ancient Portico d'Ottavia, your Uncle Gershom had established himself as an agent for the great Sienese banker Agostino Chigi, and was living across the Tiber on a property adjacent to Chigi's newly built Villa Suburbana. Once we had settled in we urged him to join our household, but he quickly and decisively rejected the offer.

"Ser Chigi is always in fine spirits at the villa. The very sight of it sets him to smiling. In that benign mood he often stops to chat when he catches sight of me. Thus, living where I do in such close proximity to him when he is at his most expansive, I receive all the news of Roma firsthand."

"Do I take it that getting the news of Roma is more consequential to you than being in the bosom of your family?" Judah inquired stiffly.

"For a banker, dear brother-in-law, the answer is a reluctant yes," my brother replied cheerfully. "News is the lifeblood of banking. I would never have made my investments in the Campo Marzio had I not known in advance that the Pope was planning expansion in that area."

"You own a palace in the Campo Marzio?" I asked.

"Not yet. But I do own land there which someday will be worth a fortune," he replied with cool assurance.

He had good cause to be confident. Before the age of thirty, he had achieved by his own efforts a success unmatched by any Jew in Roma. Dressed in the finest brocades and velvets, treated by the Pope's banker as an intimate, flattered and fawned upon by men twice his age, he had every reason to believe that his star would continue to rise forever. But will it? I wonder, sitting here in the heart of a city that is every day increasingly threatened with despoliation. My father always put his faith in movable property—bags of gems, easy to hide, easy to transport. I wonder if history will prove him a cleverer banker than his clever son.

Do you remember how sweet life was in our little house among the ancient pillars of the Portico d'Ottavia? True, the Tiber came much too close for comfort and safety. And the fish in the market below did stink in our noses when the wind blew in the wrong direction. But I learned early in life to tolerate the odor of dead fish, for I grew up close by a fish market just as you did.

Fishy as it was, I quickly came to love the life around us in the Jewish quarter. I loved my Jewish neighbors even if most of them were, as Judah pointed out by way of apology, poor ignorant ragpickers. I loved the garlands of tattered garments they festooned on the walls behind their stalls. I loved having our own neighborhood ruin, the ancient Portico d'Ottavia. From the moment we took possession of the little house the Pope had provided for us, I felt protected by those sheltering arches.

It was months before a bizarre upheaval turned my view of Leonine Roma upside down and revealed to me its scabrous underbelly. The revelation came in the person of one of the many leeches who wax fat on the body of the papal Curia, a certain Marc Antonio Nino, secretary to Cardinal Petrucci.

This flunkey made quite an impression striding across Ottavia's square with a white plume flying from his *berretta* and a heavy gold chain hanging from his neck. I felt I ought to shout down and warn him against wearing such an ostentatious collar in this quarter. Already two Gypsies were edging close to him as he walked. They materialize by magic at the sight of gold. But then I noticed at his right hand a hulking servant type, sword unsheathed, and I ceased to worry for his safety from the Gypsies and began to worry for our own well-being. Visits from courtiers with armed guards rarely bode well.

I got little indication from this Nino if he meant us good or ill. His business was far too confidential to be divulged to a mere wife; he made that quite clear when I met him at the door. And after he left, Judah remained locked up in his *studiolo* with a chair barring the portal, always a sign that he was perturbed.

When he emerged late in the afternoon, he did not mention the visitor. And when I asked him who the man was, he changed the subject abruptly. But the visit had disturbed him.

That night he tossed about the bed like a rudderless ship, bumping against me, then shoving off a distance, then throwing off the coverlet, then pulling it back up. Not a word did he utter about the afternoon's visitor. But in the morning, after he had put on his phylacteries and said his prayers and washed himself, he turned to me and without warning announced, "We must leave Roma immediately."

When I asked him why, he as much as told me to mind my own affairs. Still, I was not about to be torn from my home and scattered to the winds without knowing the cause of it.

"I will not budge until I know the reason for this upheaval," I announced firmly.

"Better for you if you don't," he muttered.

"It has to do with that courtier who came to see you yesterday, does it not?" I pressed.

"Yes," he replied, and nothing more.

"What did he want of you?" I asked.

No reply.

"Judah, look at me." He turned toward me reluctantly. "I am your wife, Grazia, not some cretinous slave. I deserve your confidence."

"I had hoped to keep it from you." He sighed. "But if you must know, one of the cardinals has concocted a scheme to murder the Pope. This Nino is his secretary. They want me to apply a series of poisoned bandages to the Pope's fistula when I treat it."

"Would that kill him?"

"Oh yes. His wound suppurates constantly. It is as good an entry for poison as any mouth. I told this Nino no, of course. But he would not accept my no, and in the end, I had to force him out the door with his sackful of ducats. But none of that matters. I am implicated now in a plot to kill the Pope. If this plot is discovered, Cardinal Petrucci and his friends will certainly look for a place to lay the blame and I am the logical candidate. Men will say anything under torture. The rack makes cowards of us all."

The fear in his eyes, his pallor, the beads of sweat that dotted his forehead, all worked on me like a contagion, infecting me with the same terror. If the Petrucci plot succeeded, Judah's position of trust would certainly place him first in the line of suspects. Yet some inner voice of reason reminded me that to run away is often considered an admission of guilt, and warned me against a hasty flight. We needed time and thought. And a cool head.

"I believe we should consult with Gershom before we take any irrevocable action," I told Judah.

"Your little brother?"

"He has his own identity now, Judah," I reminded him. "He is a part of the great world and understands its workings. Besides, he has an orderly mind, and—not the least—we can trust him. We risk nothing in seeking his opinion."

"Very well," Judah conceded. "But Grazia, we must be on the road by dawn tomorrow. That is my final word." Clearly it would take a more powerful lever than I possessed to move this boulder.

I dressed quickly and, enlisting my maid as companion, set out to find my brother. We had yet to be invited to Gershom's house. All I knew of it was that it abutted Chigi's property across the Tiber somewhere between Trastevere and the Borgo, a long stretch of uninhabited wasteland at the edge of the river. Why on earth, I wondered as my girl and I tramped around bogs and over pastures, had a clever man like Ser Chigi chosen such a wayward spot for his villa? Like Judah, I am an urbanist and would pitch my tent in Saint Peter's Square if the space were to let.

I had imagined my brother living in a tiny cottage on the periphery of the estate. Instead, I discovered a spacious guest house within shouting distance of the villa itself. In answer to my ring a steward appeared, all in black, with what I took to be the keys for the wine cellar hanging from his neck on a golden chain. Even the servants were ostentatious in this place. I introduced myself and asked to be announced to Ser Geronimo. This put the flunkey into a quandary. Clearly the protocols of his position did not provide for unexpected visits from unknown relations with muddy boots. He shuffled uncomfortably, then, suddenly decisive, announced that he would fetch Madonna Pantesilea.

Now, my knowledge of the ladies of Roma's half-world was limited, but I did recognize a typical courtesan's name when I heard one. Pantesilea, Imperia, Hortensia, Cassandra, Lucrezia (a singularly inappropriate choice but apparently a great favorite) were names I had heard bruited about. Presumably Roma brought out the classicist in these women. *Dio!* My brother was living openly with a Christian whore.

Waiting for her to appear, I constructed a vision of this creature who had named herself after the Queen of the Amazons. Buxom. Coarse. And most likely with a small overfed dog waddling in her train.

"Good morning, madonna," trilled a high, girlish voice. "We were not expecting you, else I would have left instructions at the gate." She was slight beyond slimness, with pale skin and hair so fair that I recognized it as nature's own work. Although her chemise was cut low enough, I was hard put to find a trace of bosom above the lace. In fact her flat bosom, flat belly, and flat ass gave her the appearance of a young boy in spite of the corona of curls that wreathed her doll-like face. Oh yes, I might add that she had no chin whatsoever and wore a large jeweled golden cross around her neck.

I was about to apologize for intruding and then I thought, Why apologize to a tart? So I merely explained that we had had some disquieting news, and requested her to send word of the emergency to my brother, wherever he was.

Geronimo was at the villa conferring with Ser Chigi, she explained. But, knowing his deep feelings for his family, she would send for him at once. Then, as she left the room, she touched my arm ever so softly and, in her sweet, girlish voice, begged me to take heart. "Whatever crisis has brought you to us, Geronimo will have a solution at hand," she assured me. "For as you know, he is prodigiously clever and extremely well connected." A tart she may have been, but a tart with more grace by far than I had shown toward her.

My reverie was interrupted by the sound of voices at the door. My brother had returned.

"Grazia, what an unexpected pleasure." He came forward to embrace me.

All credit to Pantesilea, she made haste to disappear at once, leaving me free to explain quickly to my brother what had brought me there.

"...So I have come to you, Gershom, because Judah and I are both distracted beyond sense. Much as I would like to run away, I feel that a hasty flight will undo us."

"I agree with you completely," he answered without hesitation. "To run away would put the worst complexion on the matter. You must not leave Roma, at least not before the Pope is told of this conspiracy." He paused. "Yes, the Pope must be warned. And the sooner the better."

"Must Judah go to him, then?" I asked.

"Perhaps. Although Judah may not be the best man for the job. But wait." I could almost hear the click of the abacus inside his head as he paced back and forth weighing out the options. Then at last he stopped, turned to me, and announced: "Ser Chigi. Yes, Agostino Chigi is the one to do it. He will tell the Pope for us. That way the report will come from an unimpeachable source."

"What makes you think he will do it?" I asked. "Why should he?"

"Because it will serve his interests as well as ours. You see, Ser Chigi's brother is married to Cardinal Petrucci's sister, a mite close for comfort if this conspiracy is brought to light. It will be in my master's interest to expose the plot and thus place a corridor between himself and the plotters. Yes, Ser Chigi will be pleased to warn the Pope for us."

"What if Chigi chooses to warn his kinsman Petrucci and names Judah as the villain of the piece?"

"Out of the question." He took my hand and looked deep into my eyes. "Grazia, for your own sake try to understand this much of the great world. Agostino Chigi holds patents granted to him by the Pope that make him the richest man in Roma. We maintain offices in London, Alexandria, Constantinople, Lyon, and a half-dozen Italian cities. By his own estimate Ser Chigi numbers his employees at over twenty thousand. And this vast edifice is built on the Pope's confidence. Can you believe that Chigi would risk all that to protect a wild crazy boy who has proven nothing but an embarrassment to him from the beginning?"

"This Cardinal Petrucci is young, then?"

"Not over twenty-two. And until recently a playmate of the Pope's. But they got into some dispute over Sienese politics and it is common knowledge that the cardinal has been in correspondence with the Duke of Urbino. You *do* know who he is?"

I ignored the insult for I knew it was not maliciously intended. "You have become so worldly, Gershom, that I sometimes feel I do not even know you," I told him, hoping that he would open his heart to me just a little so that I might catch a glimpse of the sweet affectionate boy I once knew. Instead, he took me firmly by the shoulders as I had often done to him when he was a child, and explained, "Sister, know me as a brother who loves you and who wants above all to protect you and your husband and your little boy from those vultures that nest in the Vatican. I have learned much from Ser Chigi and much about him. Whatever you may think, he is our man for this occasion. Believe me, he will happily tell the Pope Judah's story and put Judah in the most favorable and innocent light, because it will be to his advantage to do so."

"Very well," I concurred. "But who will tell Chigi the story?"

"You will. At once. There is no time to lose. We must get a true account of the plot to the Pope before one of the conspirators loses his nerve and goes running to him with a false version that implicates Judah."

Any other day, the prospect of a visit to Chigi's villa would have filled me with pleasure. The building itself was the talk of Roma and had everyone in town vying for an invitation, if only to see the magnificent fresco cycle being painted on the walls of the atrium by Raffaello Santi. But I walked by that master-work as if blinkered, my entire concentration on the test ahead of me. If I did not succeed in convincing Chigi of the veracity of my report and of Judah's innocence, God knew what peril lay in store for us.

The great man greeted us upstairs in the informality of his bathroom, seated in a deep copper tub of steaming water. Leaning back against a pillow, eyes half closed, inhaling the perfumed vapor, he reminded me of a sleek, reddish-brown otter baking in the sun, his body encased in a layer of fat, his fingernails polished to a high gloss, his hair combed over back-ward to cover his bald spot. But the moment I mentioned the name of Cardinal Petrucci, the sea animal was transformed before my eyes into a jungle cat. With a snap of his fingers he motioned a servant to wrap him in towels. All languor banished, he strode across to a giant ebonywood bed, settled himself on the pillows, and nodded curtly for me to approach closer to him. That was when I noticed the ice-blue eyes, wide open now and clear as a pair of pale sapphires in the flushed face. One look told me that were I to attempt any manner of prevarication or falsehood, those eyes would surely find me out.

I told my story as plainly and accurately as I could and was rewarded with a little nod of approval. Then came his ques-tions. Had Nino mentioned a specific time? A specific sum of money? Where was Judah to obtain the poison? Was he expected to prepare it himself? Had any other conspirators been mentioned? Had Nino mentioned any names at all? That was most important, the banker assured me, and urged me to agitate my memory.

As it happened, I did remember a name because Judah and I had wondered over it.

"The courier in this plot is to be a Sienese soldier who goes by the name of 'Poco in Testa,'" I told him. "I remember the name because my husband pointed out to me that anyone who agreed to lend himself to such a venture must, indeed, have very little in the head."

"Very amusing, madonna," he replied with a thin smile. "But I would prefer you to remember the name of a cardinal or a bishop or a prince who might have been mentioned."

"Would not such information come more readily from one of the underlings, such as the secretary who came to corrupt my husband or this 'Poco in Testa'?" I asked.

"Never fear, madonna, all avenues will be explored. I have certain connections in Siena and you can believe me I will not hesitate to use them no matter who stands to suffer. For I find conspiracy to be the most despicable of all crimes, and poison the slyest of all methods. Besides, I have my own reasons for seeing young Petrucci brought to justice. He is a beast and the world would be well rid of him."

From then on I never doubted the wisdom of putting ourselves into the hands of Agostino Chigi. But Judah had also to be convinced and, as you know, Judah is not an easy man to move once he has dug himself into a position. But, using Gershom's wiles, my tears, and both our wits, we finally prevailed. That night when my brother left our house long after it was safe to be out in the streets, he took with him Judah's promise to remain in Roma trusting God and Agostino Chigi. Thenceforth we were to communicate only by letter, in Hebrew, and destroy each communication after it was read.

The following Monday a courier decorated with Chigi's crest came to our door with a brief note. What it said was: "Marc Antonio Nino arrested today and put to the torture. Stand fast."

We stood fast for a month of rumors and alarms. Then one day Judah came home from the Studium white as chalk but composed. "They have named a doctor," he told me. "We must trust in God and hope for the best, but prepare for the worst."

Judah did not let you leave his side that day. He used the pretext of telling you stories to hold you tight and cover your little head with kisses. And for once, you submitted to sitting still for the caresses and sat in his lap stroking his face with your fat little fingers.

Just before dark a masked messenger clattered up to our portal at full gallop and requested entrance in the name of Ser Geronimo dei Rossi. Wild to hear the report of our fate, both Judah and I ran out into the street and would have begun to question him there in full view had he not warned us off with an admonishing finger to the lips. Even after we were safe in our own *sala*, the messenger waited until the servants were well out of sight before taking off the mask. Off it came with a tug and who should I behold but Pantesilea!

"Ser Geronimo has sent me to announce the end of your long travail," she panted. "A physician has been named and arrested. He is called Giovanni Battista da Vercelli. Ser Chigi has it from the Pope himself. Maestro del Medigo" — a deep curtsy to Judah — "is safe from suspicion."

Welcome words. But if Judah was completely safe, why send a masked messenger with the news?

"Why did not my brother-in-law bring the good news himself?" Judah asked, echoing my thoughts.

"Discretion to the end is his motto," she replied.

"In other words, the case is not yet closed," I concluded.

"With three men under torture in Castel Sant'Angelo, the case is far from closed," Judah declared solemnly. "But sufficient for this day is the bounty thereof. Let us simply accept that God has granted us a stay and let us celebrate it." He turned to the courtesan in his most courtly manner. "Can I offer you a glass of wine, lady? Or shall I call you sir?"

"Call me not at all," she replied airily. "For I must be off lest I miss vespers at Sant'Agostino's church." And with a smart click of her spurs she was gone.

Judah's comment—the only words he spoke on the subject after meeting his brother-in-law's Christian mistress for the first time—was so Judah-like that I must pass it on to you. "Tell me, Grazia," he inquired with a puzzled expression, "does she always dress like that?"

After the physician Vercelli was seized, arrests followed one upon the other. Within days, young Cardinal Petrucci was arrested by the Pope's guards and taken to the Maracco, the most horrible of Sant'Angelo's dungeons. There he was joined a week later by old Cardinal Riario, so petrified with fear that he had to be carried to his cell in a litter. The old man had been named as a fellow plotter by Perrucci. A week after Riario's detainment, two more cardinals were arrested. "But no more doctors," Judah remarked with a half smile.

On June 16, Petrucci's captain, Poco in Testa, the armed man who had been seen entering our house with Nino, was hanged in the prison of the Torre de Nona and his body put on view. Hanging there, rotting and stinking, the body was hardly a sight to calm our agitation—or anyone else's. Ordinarily, the bodies of criminals are taken down after three days. This one was left out to poison the air of Roma until the flesh fell off the skeleton. For this horrifying spectacle my brother had an explanation.

"The Pope has now evidenced openly what Ser Chigi and I suspected would happen," said Gershom. "He has managed to turn this conspiracy into a gold mine."

"That thought is too cynical even for a banker," I reproved him.

"Perhaps, dear sister. But I tell you, this Medici pope leaks money like a sieve. A man in that position can ill afford to neglect an opportunity to replenish his treasury if Fortuna provides it. And, as Ser Chigi says, a stone could more easily fly up in the air of itself than Leo can keep possession of a thousand ducats. His treasury needs constant replenishment."

He calculated that Leo had gleaned a clear profit on the minor cardinals of seventy-five thousand ducats in fines plus the subsidiary profits accruing from the resale of the benefices they were stripped of. He further estimated that these revenues, added to Riario's fine, had brought Leo a fortune exceeding that of any individual in Italy with the possible exception of Agostino Chigi.

"I think that with this coup the books on the Petrucci account can finally be closed," my brother advised us, stroking his chin in the manner of a shrewd old banker. "At last we can all rest easy. By the way," he added, "Ser Chigi is not unaware of your contribution to our success, sister. He has spoken to me many times of your quick wits and your discretion. I do believe he intends to express his gratitude in some material way."

"I do not want his money, brother," I snapped. "We merely did the honorable thing. There has already been too much talk of money to suit me."

In truth the unfolding of the Petrucci conspiracy had left me disillusioned with the great world, so much so that even when Zacharias Callierges, a publisher of Greek texts, invited me to meet with him, I refused. I had had my fill of Leonine Roma. Fortunately Judah did not abandon me to my folly. He insisted I must at least hear the Greek's proposal, if only for the sake of courtesy. He reminded me that Callierges' edition of Pindar sat on my own shelf and that, as a proponent of the printed book, I owed the man my respect.

Like you, I have never found it easy to deny Judah his way. Two days after our conversation I found myself face-to-face with the Greek publisher. No longer the terrified girl who had feared to negotiate with Aldus Manutius, I sat down to the meeting calmly confident that if I did agree to it, I would end up with the commission on my terms. But my calm confidence was totally destroyed when, instead of offering me some Greek translation, he proposed to publish my *Book of Heroines*.

"I have heard from reliable sources that this book of yours takes up where Boccaccio left off," he informed me. "And that your authorship is of a quality that will bring distinction to our press."

Caught so by surprise, I had all I could do not to collapse into a puddle of accommodation. But I did keep enough possession of myself to inform him that, honored though I was by his offer, I must insist on certain conditions before I could accept it; namely, that I would submit to no editorial interference either with the selection or with the rhetoric of my text. To my astonishment he agreed without demur and we shook hands on it. And from that moment dates the long-awaited debut of my heroines and the beginning of whatever small celebrity I have achieved as their author.

A FINAL NOTE ON the Petrucci conspiracy.

I once asked Madonna Isabella what she made of the affair. Here is her answer: "If I had known that Pope Leo was selling off cardinals' hats for ten thousand ducats, I would have bought one for my son Ercole. By the time I got to Roma, the price had doubled."

49

O N MY FIRST VISIT TO THE VILLA SUBURBANA,
apprehension and fear had blinded me to the gorgeous works of art that Ser Chigi had commissioned
for the little palace. I had failed even to notice Il Sodoma's
frescoes in the room in which I was interviewed, scenes from
the life of Alexander the Great, considered by many to be his
masterpiece. Now I was offered a second chance, an invitation
to sup with Agostino Chigi at his villa. This time I would not
pass up the two loggias on the ground floor said to be frescoed
by the finest artists in Roma—Sebastiano del Piombo, Giulio
Pippi (whom they call Romano), Baldassare Peruzzi (Chigi's
architect), and, at the pinnacle of this array of stars, Raffaello
Santi, the prodigy of our age.

My plan was to beg a few minutes to repair my toilet before
being announced. Thus would I give myself time to feast my
eyes on the gorgeous swirls of color and form before my gaze
and above my head, for I meant to fix them so firmly in my
memory that even if I never saw them again they would be
with me until I died.

Although the design was Raffaello's, only one figure in

the entire panorama had been executed by the master's hand, Gershom told me. "Try to determine which one that is," he dared me.

What was I to look for? I asked.

"Look for the same quality you would seek in a great poem, where grace and life are implicit in every line," was his answer.

Now, although I had been exposed to poetry since early days, I had had no opportunity to live with works of art, so had little basis for judgment. But, never able to resist my brother's teases, I determined to somehow find out the one figure above all the others that exhibited grace and life in every line. I went so far as to lie down on the tiles and study the ceiling straight up, thinking to give myself a more revealing perspective from that position. But no one figure on that vault jumped out at me and announced, "I am by the hand of Raffaello."

The more I beheld them, the more they all looked slightly puffy and just a little too earthbound for gods and goddesses. Confused and out of patience, I rose and was ready to give up when a figure in one of the lunettes caught my eye, a female posed with her back to the viewer. The curve of her back, one beautiful long line especially enthralled me.

"You have a good eye, madonna. That is indeed the one."

I turned to face Agostino Chigi, his sallow face wreathed in a smile of pleasure. "Not a few connoisseurs have failed this test. Or were you prepared in advance by your brother Maestro Geronimo?"

I assured him that, quite the contrary, my brother had put me to the test.

"In that case allow me to congratulate you. And with your consent to conduct you into the loggia of Galatea where you can peruse the master's hand to your heart's content."

So saying, he led me into an adjoining loggia where, grasping my shoulders, he spun me around to face the interior wall. "Allow me to direct your eye to the masterwork of this house."

What greeted my eye was a triumphant Galatea aloft in her scallop-shell chariot, driving a team of dolphins across a froth of waves at flying speed. No puffy goddesses here. This was indeed a scene with grace and life in every line.

"Magnificent, is she not?"

I nodded my assent.

"I knew the lady," he continued. "Believe me, he does not do her justice."

"You knew Galatea?" I asked, foolishly.

"I speak of the model, madonna. Every poet in Italy has tried his hand at describing her. Even I took my poor turn at it. But none of us has succeeded in capturing her ineffable beauty. Not even my Raffaello has done her justice."

"May I know the name of this paragon?" I asked.

"Imperia," he replied.

Now Imperia's fame was so widespread that even I had heard of her—a legendary courtesan, dead by her own hand, pursued by every great man in the peninsula; among them, Agostino Chigi.

"It is on her account that I invited you to sup with me," he told me. And before I had a chance to pursue this cryptic statement, he held out his arm and asked, "Shall we go in?"

He spent the entire course of the meal extolling the virtues of Imperia—her swanlike neck; her broad brow crowned with golden hair; her breasts, the most perfect of any woman in Italy; her talents: her mastery of the viola da braccio; the sweetness of her voice, her poetry. She was a second Sappho, he rhapsodized, with the ability to create grace and harmony wherever she laid her hand. And if that were not enough...He waved the servants off, moved closer to me, and whispered: "What I tell you now, Madonna Grazia, are intimate secrets. I speak to you of the tenderness of a woman's heart and of the callousness of a man. You may have heard that Imperia committed suicide..."

I confessed that I had heard of it.

"She swallowed poison," he continued. "For three days and three nights I stood at her bedside hoping and praying, but to no avail. The divine Imperia died for the love of an unworthy man." He leaned closer, close enough for me to see the beginnings of mist cloud over his crystalline eyes. "And I am that man. This woman who commanded the most highly regarded and powerful men in the land wanted only the one she could not command." He turned aside to dab at his eye. "I broke her heart."

We had begun to sup while the sun was visible in the sky. By now the moon had risen and was shining overhead. Yet I still had no clue why I had been singled out to hear this tale of love and loss. Now, it came.

"Do you not agree that this lady's story cries out to be told?" he asked. And when I did not agree instantly, he added, "Is she not the perfect model of a modern Dido?"

Given my lifelong devotion to Dido, it was an unfortunate choice of persona. Pathetic though his story was, I certainly could not see this Imperia reaching the stature of my queen.

"I have asked you here to beg a favor, madonna," he went on. "I would give much to see my Imperia enshrined in your *Book of Heroines*. That is my request."

I cursed myself inwardly for not having guessed the destination of this pathetic tale, and cursed my brother for sending me there.

"Do I sense a reluctance, madonna?" he asked very quietly. "Have I invaded your private preserve? Have I offended the independence of your spirit?" he asked.

He seemed so sympathetic, so understanding that with no further thought for the enormous risk I was about to take, I launched into a breathless history of my battle to control the fate of my heroines, of my soul-destroying afternoons with Mario Equicola, of my vow to consign my creations to oblivion rather than abandon them to molding by another hand.

To my astonishment he proved an entirely sympathetic listener.

"I understand, madonna." He took my hand in his. "Let us leave the matter for now. From what I understand, the *Book of Heroines* is likely to find a large public. If so, there will be amendments, corrections, new editions. Perhaps then..."

"Perhaps, signore," I allowed, more persuaded by his understanding than by his sad tale.

We parted without rancor, having reached a bargain of sorts. If my *Book of Heroines* did go into further printings, I would seriously consider adding Imperia to their number. If there were no future editions, he wouldn't care since he was seeking a literary memorial secure enough to outlive him at the very least. My father would have called the outcome an excellent *condotta*. Neither got exactly what he wanted but we each got enough to satisfy the other.

When I told my brother of the conversation he was aghast.

"You refused Ser Chigi?" he asked, unable to believe his ears.

"I told him I would seriously consider including Imperia in the next edition," I corrected him. "And by the way, I did pick out the Raffaello. Furthermore, you owe it to me to admit that you were entirely in error about the purpose of the interview. He never once offered to do anything for me. It was altogether the other way around."

"But Grazia, he has already done you a great service."

"By giving me supper?"

"No, dunce, by publishing your book."

The answer made no sense to me. "My book is being published by Callierges, the Greek."

"But everyone in Roma knows that Ser Chigi set up the Greek press for Callierges. Grazia, how could you?"

Now, the enormity of my ingratitude struck me full force. If I were Chigi, I thought, I would stop the publication. But I still had something to learn about Agostino Chigi. My *Book of Heroines* was published by the Callierges Press with each word as I had written it, no additions, no excisions. It brought me enough acclaim so that a second edition was ordered. Among the many congratulatory letters I received was one from Madonna Isabella. Apparently our estrangement was over.

You could say that this note more than any other thing signified that I had won the battle for my integrity. But my heart told me that in the final reckoning, Agostino Chigi had won the war. He gave his patronage to me freely with no strings attached; whereas I, in the grip of a mean-spirited rigidity, had rejected without consideration a reasonable request to include a lady who could have shared pride of place with the likes of Lucrezia Borgia or Giulia Farnese without shaming the more "respectable" ladies in my pantheon.

I made a vow there and then to include Imperia in all subsequent editions. That vow I kept. But, sad to tell, by the time the second edition came out, Agostino Chigi was beyond caring whether his Imperia was in my book or not. Had I known how ill he was on the night of that candlelit supper, I would not have waited. But not even Gershom knew that. Chigi shared his secrets with no one. He died in the spring of 1520 only a few days after his protégé, Raffaello.

First Chigi. Then Raffaello. Of the Leonine triumvirate only the leading light, Leo himself, was left. And very soon that beacon began to flicker.

50

T
HE PERSON LEAST SURPRISED BY POPE LEO'S EARLY
death was Judah. "He will not live to see his forty-fifth
birthday," he had predicted gloomily after his first examination of the patient. "And nothing I can do will delay his end."

"Because you cannot cure his fistula?" I asked.

"Men do not die of fistulas, they only suffer," he replied. "No,
this Medici is at risk from birth — all the Medici die young; it
is bred in the bone — and he compounds the inheritance by
his manner of living. Everything I observe in his constitution
spells death: his corpulence, his bloat, his chronic catarrh, all
demand that he follow a regimen of moderation. Instead, he
alternates fasts with gorging and bouts of violent exercise with
torpor. And every excess brings him nearer to the diseases that
carried off his father and brother."

Leo died on the second of December in the year 1521, in
the forty-sixth year of his life, cheating Judah's prediction by
six months. His death blasted apart the fabric of Roman life
like a broadside from one of Alfonso d'Este's *bombarde*, leaving
the tattered shreds of the golden years fluttering in the winter wind. At his death every cup, every chalice, every crucifix,

every altarpiece, every valuable object in his treasury lay in pawn. He was in debt over 850,000 ducats.

Like lice we Romans live off the body of the Curia. When the Pope rides high on the hog's back we gorge ourselves. When his fortunes wane we all go hungry. With Leo's death Roma entered on a prolonged fast. Everyone felt the pinch at once—bootmakers, butchers, courtesans, muleteers, innkeepers, embroiderers, actors, musicians, even the Jewish rag peddlers—all lost custom.

Our family was doubly hit in that twelvemonth. With the death of the Pope, Judah lost his patron. With the death of the Pope's banker, my brother lost his sinecure, his home, and his mistress. When he announced he was retiring from the world of banking to live frugally on his investments, Pantesilea took off for greener fields with no hard feelings on either side. In fact, Gershom continued to advise her on her investments and she continued to call me sister and visit us on those occasions when her conscience led her to her favorite sanctuary, the Church of Sant'Agostino.

She and my brother were two of a kind, I tell you. It took more than hard times to knock them off their pins. Gershom accepted his reversal of fortune with a shrug and a smile.

"Remember what Koheleth tells us, that everything has its season," he reminded me. "In time, this harsh climate will give way to fair weather and the barren bushes of this city will blossom once again with lush fruit. When they do I, Geronimo dei Rossi, will be there to gather in the harvest. Meantime I will take a lesson from Signore Bear, go into hibernation, and live off my fat."

Others simply fled. Bembo, the exquisite, felt a sudden need to commune with nature and withdrew from Roma to a secluded spot near Padova, taking with him as a memento of his Leonine days a beautiful concubine named Morosina and all the wealth he had accumulated as Leo's principal secretary.

Many prelates joined the exodus. Cardinals who had not laid eyes on the source of their benefices for twenty years heard the call of duty and sped off to give succor to their distant flocks. The Academicians wandered into exile. Sadoleto, our finest Latinist, retired to Carpentras, Castiglione to Mantova. The Florentines who had been nibbling away at Leo's treasury like clever mice for a decade skittered back to Toscana with wagon-loads of loot. Of the inner circle only Paolo Giovio remained— a diligent scholar of history marking off the daily defections.

It seemed that God was determined to exact retribution for every golden moment of Leonine indulgence. While the car-dinals were locked up debating who they would elect as Leo's successor, a new menace appeared in our midst: the plague.

Overwhelmed by their misfortunes, the Romans looked to the Vatican for a savior. What they got for their Holy Father was Adrian of Tortola, tutor to Emperor Charles V, a man so mindful of his obligations to his Emperor that he would not leave Spain even to attend the consistory that elected him pope.

When the cardinals emerged to announce the election of a German to the throne of Saint Peter, the streets filled with people hissing and booing to express their indignation. With a world of candidates to choose from, these men had elected a barbarian, a poor dependent of the Emperor, a man from whom no one could expect a favor.

Only Cardinal Gonzaga had the courage to face the howl-ing crowd. Putting on a brave smile, he thanked his clamor-ous attendants for contenting themselves with words of abuse. "We deserve the most rigorous punishment," he told them. "I am grateful that you choose to avenge your wrongs with words and not with stones."

By the day of the new Pope's coronation as Adrian VI, the plague was claiming victims at the rate of thirty or more a day. Judah said he had never seen it more virulent, not even in Firenze in the nineties. "I fear lest God should completely annihilate the inhabitants of this city," he confided in me. Was it God who had it in for us, I wondered, or the devil? Demons and furies infected the Roman imagination that plague season and I was not immune to the contagion.

There was a Greek called Demetrius who paraded the city with a bull he claimed to have tamed by spells. He came to our piazza one morning, and despite Judah's warning, I found myself down in the street with the gawkers come to touch the miraculous animal and thus to achieve immunity from the pestilence.

A few days later Judah told me that this Greek had sacrificed his holy animal at midnight in the Colosseum. "The scoundrel professes to appease the hostile demons that have taken over the city and persuades half of Roma to join him in the sacrilege. We have reverted to the worst excesses of the Dark Ages." Then he added with the thin smile he habitually assumed when mentioning Jehiel, "Too bad your brother Maestro Vitale the Occultist cannot be spared from Duke Alfonso's service. He could earn the mint selling his spells and amulets to these lapsed pagans."

In truth, your fortune-telling uncle *would* have done well in the Roma of Adrian VI. Romans never have been more than a step away from their pagan roots at any time. Seeing the physicians powerless against the contagion, they understandably — one might almost say, reasonably — turned to the magicians for help. It was a rare citizen who dared walk out into the street without an amulet hung around his neck to protect him from the evil spirits. I might have worn one myself had I not feared Judah's contempt. Your Uncle Gershom, always one to hedge his bets, did send off to "Maestro Vitale" at Ferrara for a precious bit of ancient writing to keep on his person. And the lady Pantesilea came around with charms and talismans dripping off her ears and wrists and waist and neck, the way jewels had in safer times.

"We must no longer kiss, madonna," she warned me one day when I leaned forward to embrace her. "For there is contagion in kisses."

I reported this advice to Judah, who pronounced the lady amazingly intelligent for an ignorant tart. I did not enlighten him as to the pharmacopoeia of potions and charms — all procured from various sorcerers—with which this "intelligent" lady doctored herself. Nor did I bother his mind with the information that she was everlastingly after me to embrace her thaumaturgy and join her in patronizing its questionable practitioners.

There was in particular a procuress of her acquaintance who she swore knew all the secrets of Venus *and* Averroës both.

"This woman is in touch with the infinite," she assured me with utmost conviction. "Even if you do not need the benefit of her love potions—which *work*, believe me, for I have tried them—you should benefit as I do from her profound understanding of female skin. She understands how the skin breathes and through those breaths she can expunge wrinkles and turn those ugly brown spots to which we women are prone back to their rosy hue. She can make your hair curl like one of Maestro Melozzo's *putti*, and she tells the future better than any astrologer. Allow me to bring her to you, madonna, I beg you."

I would have allowed it gladly but I dared not welcome this creature into our house. In Judah's pantheon, witches and sorcerers stand lower than snakes.

Pantesilea persevered. She brought a tooth whitener made by the prodigious procuress out of ground-up pearls; then came a breast cream extracted from the umbilical cords of infant boys. And, knowing my softest spot, she brought for you a painted mask of monk's cloth, special protection for "the little warrior" to wear when you ventured outside. This you instantly added to your wardrobe, along with the tin helmet—a gift from your Uncle Jehiel—that you donned when you galloped around the square on your hobbyhorse brandishing your wooden sword and shouting "Charge!" at the top of your lungs. But much as you loved the gift, I still could not bring myself to meet with the donor, out of respect for Judah's feelings.

"I see that there is no moving you, madonna, and I will cease to try," she finally announced. "From now on, the name of Dido will not pass my lips."

"Dido? This *ruffiana* calls herself Dido?"

"What would you have her call herself? Puttana? Zoppina?" she replied crossly. "Have I not told you that this woman is not some ordinary procuress? Do you suppose that the divine Imperia would have employed some vulgarian as her *mezzana*?"

"Imperia?" The name had never been mentioned in all our conversations.

"Yes, Imperia, mistress to two popes and God knows how many cardinals, toast of three cities..."

The same Imperia I had so cavalierly banished from my company of worthy women. "You never told me that this Dido was *ruffiana* to Imperia," I reminded her.

"Not *ruffiana*," she corrected me. "In those golden times, Dido was a *mezzana*, the only female *mezzano* in Roma, perhaps in the world."

At this point I must interrupt briefly to clarify the cloudy distinction between these two degrees of pimpery as I came to understand it that day. The *ruffiana* is essentially a procuress, but also a hairdresser and beauty expert with a specialty of hiding defects and concealing the ravages of age. Many of these paragons also tell fortunes by cards and by the stars, concoct love potions, make charms, and cast spells.

The *mezzano*, who occupies a step up on this greasy ladder, is also a procurer. But he is often a musician as well. He knows all the latest love songs and, in emulation of a gentleman of the town, never fails to carry a copy of Petrarch's sonnets in his pocket. But above all, he is a negotiator. It is through the mediation of her *mezzano* that a courtesan of the first rank conducts the long and complicated negotiations—often beginning with a song or a sonnet supplied by the *mezzano*—which, if successful, result in the suitor being received in the courtesan's salon. Need I add that this road is paved with expensive presents frequently chosen—or at least specified—by the *mezzano*. After all, he knows the lady's taste.

On the face of it there does not seem to be much to choose between the status of the *ruffiana* and the *mezzano*. A pimp is a pimp. But to those who patronize courtesans (which includes cardinals, ambassadors, and all the wit and learning of Roma), the distinction counts.

To me it mattered not a whit what status this Dido had achieved in the ladder of pimpery. What decided me that I must meet her was her name and her association with Imperia. In the tumult of post-Leonine Roma, the name Imperia had slipped beneath my notice along with my resolve to pay my debt of honor to Agostino Chigi someday. Now Fortuna had brought this self-named Dido into my orbit. I felt I must reach out to her. It was foreordained.

"I will see her," I told an astonished Pantesilea. "But not here." That much I owed to Judah.

It took her only a moment to find a solution. "You must come to my *vigna*." She tossed off this newly acquired property as if it were a new cloak. "There we three can meet unobserved in the cool of the arbor and explore the mysteries of the great unknown. It is the perfectly discreet place."

I agreed.

On the day of the outing I received from her a pomander consisting of a ball of resin stuffed with lavender, wrapped in a note cautioning me not to open the curtains of the *baldacchino* under any provocation, "... for the air of Roma is thick and vitiated by plague demons," in the words of my counselor.

"The city is like a giant tomb," Judah had told me. So I was prepared to ride through the streets in silence. But what I heard through the heavy curtains of my *baldacchino* sounded more like *carnevale* revelry. The incessant ringing of bells, loud music, pistol shots, and the crackle of grenades filled the air. Puzzled at first, I then remembered that explosions were ignited in order to stir up the air and thus dispel the demonic pall. That odd bit of reasoning accounted for the tambourines and the volleys of gunfire. And there was no mystery in the moans and shrieks of the dying. But as we moved along the Via Lata, a new sound began to intrude itself upon the cacophony. It occurred irregularly and seemed to issue from the windows of certain specific houses. Sometimes uttered by a single voice, more often by several, the repeated cry was, "See my body, see my body..."

My curiosity thoroughly aroused, I bade the litter-bearers stop and, against all wisdom, parted the curtains of the *baldacchino* a slit. Directly in my line of sight a barricaded door displayed the huge red *X* that marked a plague house. My eyes traveled up the facade of the house, past the *piano nobile*, past the shuttered windows of the attic floor to the top loggia. What I saw there I shall never forget: a young girl, completely naked, turning slowly around and around, her arms raised high to show that she had no buboes in her armpits where those tell-tale signs first appear, and chanting as she turned, "See my body as healthy as yours, Madonna...see my body...save me, for God's sake."

As my gaze widened, I saw that the entire loggia was peopled by naked bodies all turning, turning, with their arms pointed to heaven. Old men with unkempt beards, old women with breasts sagging to their knees, a small child chewing on a tit rag, boys and girls, men and women, some calm, some frenzied, all gyrating like mad herons, all begging to be delivered from that house of death.

Now I remembered the heartless (but necessary) decree that if a single member of any household, servant or master, was stricken, the entire *famiglia* must be quarantined whether they be sick or well—a virtual death sentence on the healthy ones. These twirlers on the loggia above me must be the healthy members of a *famiglia* immured within the house, parading their lack of buboes in the vain hope of being rescued from starvation, infection, and death.

I closed the curtains quickly and plugged up my ears with my fingers to silence the cries of the doomed ones. But their miserere continued to ring in my ears long after we had left that street. "See my body...healthy as yours...see my body..."

After a while the sound of the voices receded and the curtains began to undulate, then to flutter in the breeze. Gradually, coolness suffused the litter. We were ascending the Quirinal hill.

"Welcome, welcome…" Swathed in some version of a toga, Pantesilea flung open the curtains of the litter.

"Come look. Come see. How do you like my *vigna*? Is it not a paradise? Come bathe your face in my fountain. Never fear. The water is pure *acqua vergine*."

I barely had a chance to investigate that claim before I was hauled off to the crest of the hill to admire the prospect.

"See my view of Mount Auria. I chose this spot for the panorama." With a sweep of her draped arm she described a wide arc across the horizon. "There below us is the garden of the Palazzo Colonna. How I envy them their ruined tower! It is the very place where Nero stood to watch the barbarians come to burn this corrupt city, you know."

I need not recall for you the attraction of this ruined tower, you who have often looked down upon it with me from the windows of my *studiolo*. But that was the first time I ever saw it and I was quickly lost in the contemplation of its past. On that spot Nero had stood watching the conflagration. Had he truly plucked at the strings of his viol while he watched? If so, what was he thinking of while he played upon his instrument?

It took the bray of a donkey to awaken me from my reverie. Then came a series of bawdy oaths. Finally a bright painted cart rounded the bend, piloted Roman chariot style by a blackamoor all naked except for a band of linen caught up at his hips and an orange turban. Behind him, sitting on a pile of straw and swathed in veils, rode a Gypsy woman in fifteen shades of crimson with gold flashing from her fingers, ears, and teeth. She alighted from the cart, assisted by the blackamoor.

It is difficult to describe the impression she made, at once tawdry and majestic, full of wind and yet carrying an air of authority, and most surprising, tinged with an edge of familiarity.

"Hail, mistress." She bowed low before Pantesilea. "I have come to bring you the wisdom of the ancients, to ease your heart's ache, to beautify your face and form, and to forecast for you all that is about to befall. Dido, at your service."

Pantesilea led her forward to meet me. "Allow me to present the illustrious scholar and poet Madonna Grazia dei Rossi del Medigo, wife of the miraculous healer Leone del Medigo."

"Grazia? Dei Rossi?" With a single sweeping gesture the *mezzana* pulled off her veils and stepped close to me, breathing garlic as a dragon breathes flame.

"Do not retreat from me, little Grazia. It is Zaira, your own Zaira."

With the iteration of that name, I forgot about the garlic, the plague, Pantesilea, and the blackamoor (both struck dumb with amazement) and threw myself into Zaira's arms.

We covered each other with kisses. We hugged until both of us were breathless. And then, as you can imagine, we began to pelt each other with questions.

"Have you been in Roma all this time?"

"Have *you* been in Roma all this time? Tell me everything."

I spoke first, telling her much of what you have read here in this *ricordanza*. Then it was her turn.

"I left Firenze with a man who got me out of jail and promised to set me up in Roma as a respectable woman," she began. "But instead he took me to the fair at Foligno and tried to sell me."

"As a slave?" I asked.

"No, although a slave is what I would have become. No, he tried to sell me in the street."

"Swine!"

She seemed to harbor less malice toward her betrayer than I did. "It was his profession," she explained. "He was a pimp."

"I still say he was a swine," I insisted.

"As you like, Graziella. But he paid dear. They caught him stealing chickens at the fair and cut his hands off. Whereas I walked out of that town unbound and unmutilated and made my way to Roma. Mind you I was full of mange and dressed in an old sack, but I was free."

"What then?"

"Knowing no better, I went to work for a Spanish laundress.

Do you remember my hair, my beautiful hair, how thick it was and burnished, like a fine copper kettle?"

I did remember the beauty of her hair and said so.

"I lost it all in that filthy place. The humid air loosens the roots and it falls out in clumps."

"What brought you to this Spanish laundress in the first place?" I asked.

"It was either the laundry or the Ponte Sisto for me," she answered. "And no whore spreads her straw on that accursed bridge if she can help it. There is no lower place on earth, except the Hospital of San Giacomo."

She shuddered. And I shuddered with her. I had heard stories of that foul hospice where infected prostitutes were sent to die. And I vowed that as long as I was alive to prevent it, such a thing would never happen to Zaira.

Then, full of my own *caritas*, I proposed there and then that she should come and live with us in the Portico d'Ottavia. "The house is not big, but it is comfortable and there is a little room beside Danilo's."

She held up her hand. "Not so fast, Graziella. Think what you are suggesting."

"I do not have to think. My heart tells me..."

"Your heart is soft as mush. Always has been. But you have a brain. Use it. You have eyes, use them." She reached out her hands and twisted my head on my neck until my eyes were locked with hers. "Look into my eyes and tell me what you see."

"I see a woman, honest and honorable, and loaded with virtues."

"You see an old whore with a face like a cauliflower and a body riddled with French boils," she corrected me grimly. "I told you that I lost my hair in the Spanish laundry. That is a lie. I lost it from syphilis. I steal the lamps out of churches for the oil that is in them. I sell lies to credulous dupes. I am everything you detest, Graziella. How I got to be this way no longer matters. What does matter is that I am who I am. And I would rather be taken to San Giacomo in a cart and end my days befouled by pus and vomit than soil your life and loved ones with my corrupt presence."

No words of mine could dissuade her of her own unworthiness, not even my threat to include her in my *Book of Heroines.*

"Don't you dare, Grazia." She waggled her finger in my nose like an old nurse in response to the suggestion. "It would make a mockery of us both."

"But you would be —"

"I would be made a fool and so would you. If you want to shock the public, I have a candidate for you, a genuine heroine, my old mistress, Imperia. Let them know that even a fallen woman can be undone by feeling."

"Did she really die for love?" I asked.

"Killed herself for the love of a man she trusted, who promised to marry her, then ran away like a craven coward to marry a woman with a name, position, and money."

"Chigi," I whispered.

"What has Chigi got to do with it?" She looked puzzled.

"The man who broke her heart..."

"Did he tell you that?" she asked.

I admitted that he had.

"He would have had you believe that he was the villain who betrayed her?" She smacked her thigh with her open palm. "That old cock!"

"Who was it, then, that broke her heart if not Chigi?" I asked.

"That is her secret... and mine, to the grave. But be certain it was not Agostino Chigi. Chigi was her slave until the end. For three days and three nights he paced the floor of her *sala* praying and hoping while, upstairs, she lay dying for the love of another man—a faithless knave who never even came to her funeral."

WHEN I WROTE THE story of Imperia for the second edition of my *Book of Heroines,* I did not name the man for whose love the great courtesan gave her life. That it was not Agostino Chigi was hardly essential to the tale. Let the world believe that he was the one who broke the great courtesan's heart. Chigi had valued my discretion. If he chose to go down in history as a blackguard rather than a cuckold, I would not be the one to rob him of that dubious distinction.

51

T HE ROMANS HATED ADRIAN VI FROM THE BEGIN-
ning. They took his cautiousness for feebleness of will;
his thrift for avarice; his asceticism for barbarism.

When he was shown the "Laocoön," he turned away saying, "What else are these figures but heathen effigies?" They
said he compared the Sistine ceiling to a filthy *stuffa*, planned
to whitewash Michelangelo's magnificent nudes, and meant to
have all of Leo's precious statues reduced to lime for building
Saint Peter's. And the Romans believed every mean thing they
heard about him.

Perhaps if the unfortunate Pope had not spoken Latin with
that barbaric guttural accent or if he had spent a few more pennies, even on himself...But no. Adrian set himself up in the
Belvedere Palace of the Vatican like a pauper with no staff but
a valet and an old woman he had brought with him from the
Netherlands who attended to his washing and cooking. To her,
they said, he gave from his own pocket the wretched sum of
two ducats a day to be spent on his table saying, "This is for
tomorrow."

"The Romans will kill him," my brother Gershom predicted.

"He is no match for them." He hit the mark.

When Adrian died after only eighteen months in the Pontiffs chair, there was dancing in the streets. With my own eyes I saw a garland that had been affixed by grateful Romans to the doorway of the Pope's body physician, bearing the legend "To the liberator of the country, the Senate, and the people of Roma." Never before or since have I seen a doctor publicly lauded for killing a patient.

The conclave which met to elect Adrian's successor sat for fifty days. Moving with stealth and craftiness, Cardinal Giulio dei Medici lured supporters to his side one by one with promises of benefices and gold, much of it supplied by the new Holy Roman Emperor, Charles V. Charles had recently bought the office of Holy Roman Emperor using gold lent to him by the Fugger banking house. Why not buy himself a pope by the same means? Certainly the Medici was eminently buyable.

Did Giulio dei Medici comprehend the risk of putting himself so deeply in the Emperor's debt? Perhaps. But he had inherited his cousin Leo's empty treasury, and the Emperor's ducats relieved him of that embarrassment.

To further weaken his position, the new Pope also fell heir to the enemies that his cousin had not succeeded in either buying off or fending off. It was an impressive list: Martin Luther, pledged to destroy the Catholic church, which he called "the whore of Babylon"; Suleiman of Turkey, equally determined to decimate what he called "the scourge named Christendom"; Francis I of France, who regarded the Pope as his personal chaplain by divine right and thus subservient to his royal self. And the new Holy Roman Emperor, Charles V, who having bought himself a pope, intended to get full value for his money.

"It will take a pope stronger than Julius and wiser than Pius to protect Roma from these overgrown bullyboys, but Giulio Medici is up to the task," my brother Gershom asserted, with all the buoyant confidence that the election of a second Medici pope instilled in his followers.

I believed Gershom implicitly. Judah kept his counsel.

Giulio Medici was crowned Clement VII in the waning months of the year 1523. Within weeks of the coronation Judah was called to the Vatican to resume his former role as body physician to the Pope. He returned home with the news that Clement had granted more favors in the first month of his reign than Adrian had during his entire term of office. He also observed wryly that Jews were back in style.

Now there came to us a letter from Ferrara that made my joy complete. My brother Jehiel was coming to Roma. He had taken a leave from Duke Alfonso and was setting off on a pilgrimage in the company of a most remarkable and holy man named David, a descendant of the ten lost tribes of Israel and very learned in cabala. The word ought to have warned me.

Jehiel himself arrived about a week after his letter, heavily bearded, with filthy feet and matted hair. You were always a brave child, but he sent you cowering into the kitchen crying that a mad preacher was at our door. Even I did not recognize him until he spoke.

"It is I, Grazia, your brother Jehiel," he announced. "Am I such a stranger that you will not open your door to me?"

What had transfigured my strutting peacock of a brother into a mendicant?

The answer is simple. He had given himself over body and soul to a new Messiah, an Israelite named David Reubeni who claimed descent from the princes of one of the lost tribes of Israel and authority from God Himself.

"This David draws thoughts as pure and sparkling as spring water from the depths of the cabalistic well," my brother explained, serenely forgetful of Judah's detestation of the very word cabala. "Wherever he goes people flock to listen to his wisdom. Of course some come to try him with questions. But they do not succeed. For nothing is hidden from him."

"And how came you to this paragon?" I could sense Judah trying with all his strength to keep the scorn out of his voice.

"Quite simple," my brother answered, with all the innocent assurance of the woefully woolly-headed. "I was sent to

Venezia by my prince to collect a panel painting he had ordered from Tiziano. But when I got there that lazy rascal had not finished the work. He claimed he could not get his Aphrodite right, which I took for procrastination. That was before I understood that the delay was a part of God's plan."

"You understood that the painter's procrastination was engineered by God?" Judah had the appearance of a man who could not believe what he had heard.

"I am afraid we do not quite understand the connection between this holy man and Maestro Tiziano's hand, brother," I told him.

"I saw that God had stayed the painter's hand until the moment I was destined to meet the holy man," Jehiel answered, in a patient, condescending tone that irritated even me, who loved him dearly. "Reubeni was on his way to Roma, but by way of Ferrara. Imagine it! Both of us on the same barque and all because God stayed Tiziano's hand. It was the first day of the new moon of Adar." He paused to allow the import of this statement to sink in. "In other words, we came together at the very moment when my planets found themselves in the most fortunate conjunction."

"Ah yes, the first day of the moon of Adar..." At this point Judah gave up and retreated into a kind of trance, as he often does when the conversation bores or annoys him. Now it was left to me to make sense of my brother's non sequiturs.

"And what brings this holy man to Roma, brother?" I asked.

"He comes to Italy not only as a holy man but as an emissary from his brother, King Joseph of the tribe of Reuben."

"Is that not one of the lost tribes of Israel?" I had been taught that the tribe of Reuben was lost along with the other nine.

"We have all been misled, Grazia," was the astounding reply. "The tribe of Reuben did not perish with the others. It flourishes in the wilderness of Chabor and is engaged even as we speak in constant warfare against the Turk. It is this war which conjoins Prince David with the Pope and all the Christian princes of Europe. They stand together against the infidel."

This last was too much for Judah. He literally choked on the alliance between the Christian princes of Europe and this suddenly rediscovered lost tribe of Israel, and rose to leave the table. But Jehiel bade him sit and listen to an important proposal.

"I have consulted my master, Prince David Reubeni, and he agrees to accept you as our translator at the court of the Vatican. It is a great honor, brother. For the first time, a Jew will be received not as a suppliant or a servant but as an ambassador equal to any Christian."

At this suggestion, there passed over Judah's face the look of a drowning man. "Quite beyond my powers," he sputtered.

Then, as if someone had thrown him a rope, he bobbed up quite cheerfully. "But I do know of someone eminently suited for the job," he announced, gaining spirit with every word. "A scholar of great repute among both Jews and Christians, someone of your own blood who will bring honor to your house."

"And who is that, brother?" Jehiel asked, all unsuspecting.

"Why, your own sister, Madonna Grazia, she of the silver tongue and the immaculate hand."

Just wait until I get you alone, Signore del Medigo, I thought. But the die was cast. I had been nominated. I could not refuse my brother. Besides, I did harbor a curiosity as to the personage my brother had chosen to follow to the ends of the earth.

David Reubeni's audience with the Pope was fixed for two mornings hence. Jehiel insisted I must wear my finest clothes and jewels. "Remember, Grazia, that we do not go as beggars but as the equals of princes," he admonished me.

"What about you?" I retorted. "You look lower than the scurviest street sweeper."

"But there is a purpose to it, sister," he replied. "We who surround Prince David must not rob him of his allure."

"And will Reubeni appear barefooted in a filthy cloak with matted hair?" I pressed him.

"He will appear as grand as any Christian prince astride a

white horse, clad all in white wearing the jewels that the faithful have donated to his crusade."

And indeed, when I did lay my eyes on him, the charlatan was dressed like a prince. But he sat his white horse like a dressed-up monkey, a shriveled little monkey at that, reduced to skin and bones by fasting.

If this is the savior of the Jews, God help us, I thought. But I was alone in my judgment. When Reubeni rode into Saint Peter's Square he was followed by a great mob of at least a hundred Roman Christians as well as his personal escort of Jews, each one of them trudging behind him in worshipful silence.

At the gates of the Vatican, the Swiss guards parted ranks to give passage to the little dark man on the white horse. Into the Vatican we walked in solemn procession, past the gardens, past the fountains, past the Belvedere Palace, through Raffaello's sunlit loggia, into the sanctum sanctorum: the Pope's private apartments.

Here, waiting to greet us, stood a smallish man in a red hat. It was Cardinal Egidio de Viterbo, Jehiel whispered to me. How he was able to identify the cardinal I do not know, since he kept his eyes half lowered at all times as if to avoid being blinded by the rays of glory that emanated from the holy Reubeni. And when the little monkey-man beckoned in our direction for assistance in dismounting, my once-graceful brother fairly fell over his feet in haste to render this lowly service.

Whatever else this Messiah might or might not be, he *was* a master of ceremony. Everything proceeded at an even, majestic pace. I saw my brother kiss the roe of his idol's holy boot before offering his clasped hands to receive the holy foot. Then, when he had performed his groom's task and safely deposited the little fellow on the tiles, I saw him reach for the hem of his master's sleeve and kiss it. His obeisance rendered, he raised himself slowly, leaned into the master's ear, and began to whisper.

At that moment the smooth flow of the procession was interrupted by Reubeni himself. Uttering a vicious hiss, the little man raised his brown hand high in the air as if to smite my brother like an avenging angel.

Jehiel fell to his knees, an abject creature.

The holy man spat a great gob of spittle full upon my penitent brother and turned to look at me. Steel is not colder nor more unforgiving than that look.

All at once a hundred pairs of eyes were fastened on me. Hard eyes filled with accusation.

Jehiel came staggering toward me through the crowd, panting and sobbing, and pushed me out into the adjoining corridor.

"Oh, Grazia, I have offended my master mightily. He will never forgive me," he cried.

"What have you done?" I asked.

"I have dishonored him and defiled this holy mission. I ought never to have listened to Judah and brought you here." Whereupon he sank to his knees beside me and, hands clasped, fell into the cadences of the morning prayer. Only when he got to that passage in which every Jewish man thanks God every day of his life for not making him a woman and began to beat his breast wildly and to beg forgiveness for staining Jehovah's escutcheon with the touch of a woman did I begin to understand the bizarre display I had just witnessed.

Jehiel's offense was to have brought a lowly woman to serve as his master's voice; and I was that woman. I had brought my brother down in disgrace. I was the stain on Reubeni's escutcheon.

For some reason this understanding did not provoke me. Instead, I felt a rush of pity for the ruin of the man who was my brother, sobbing beside me as if his heart was forever broken.

"Go back and make your peace with him," I urged.

"And you?"

"I will stay here and wait."

"You are not offended?"

Offended? I prayed he might never know how happy I was to be rid of his wailing and of the sight of the pious fraud he had pledged his loyalty to.

Assured that I would nor hold it against him, he was off in a moment to demean himself even further before the little brown monkey, and I was left to my devices.

I looked around me. It was a small room empty of furniture, but every wall surface was covered with jumping, writhing, twisting figures so lifelike that even my untutored eye recognized the hand of a master. Directly facing me bright red flames were consuming a building from which naked men fled while a woman leaned over the roof at a treacherous angle to lower her baby to safety. This must be Raffaello's "Fire in the Borgo," the latest of the masterpieces he had so nobly begun with the "School of Athens." Yes, for a certainty it was. In the deep background I made out the Pope, hand raised, damping the fire below the walls of the Vatican with a benediction. There on the left I found the bent figure of Aeneas carrying his old father to safety with his son Ascanio by his side.

"Grazia." I felt a man's grip on my arm. Not Jehiel's hand, yet a touch familiar to me.

"Grazia...turn. Look at me. You need not speak. One look in those eyes is all I ask. Then if you wish I will leave you."

I turned. He was in some kind of uniform with a black band wound around his arm. I touched it softly with my fingers.

"I am in mourning," he explained.

"I am sorry," I said.

With great tenderness he drew me over to a bench nearby. "I cannot believe even now that I am seeing you." He shook his head as if in wonder at some miracle. Then without any words he reached over and traced with his two index fingers the outline of my face, my nose, my lips... "We must leave this place. Come with me, Grazia." His voice was soft but urgent.

"No. I cannot. My brother..."

"Will you not grant me one hour?"

"I have a new life," I stammered.

"I have no designs on your life, madonna," he replied with infinite sweetness. "I simply ask for an hour of your time."

I could not find voice to explain that with every passing

minute in his presence I was giving up ground, that within an hour I could easily become altogether lost.

As we walked out into the Borgo he inquired what had brought me to Roma.

I replied that I lived here, that I was a Roman now. "We lost our taste for Venezia," I explained.

"Ah, Venezia," he repeated. And sighed. And I could not find in me the strength to pursue the subject as I might have done. Instead I asked what brought him to Roma.

"Only this month the new Medici pontiff, Pope Clement, seconded me from the French court," he replied.

"Then I take it you too are a Roman now."

"Not Roman nor Parisian nor Spanish nor any other species," he answered. "I am that nomadic animal known as a roving ambassador, meaning that my master, the Pope, can and does move my person around Europe as if I were a chessman. No, much as I regret it at this moment, I cannot call Roma my home."

"Is Roma that seductive?" I inquired.

What I longed to hear from his lips was that Roma had suddenly become a paradise because I was in it... that I made the old stones sing with my smile and turned the pale Roman sky into a heavenly vault with my gaze. But instead he talked of Madonna Isabella, whom he had seen recently, and how unkindly the years had dealt with her.

"Is she ill?" I asked, surprised to find as I mouthed the polite inquiry that I harbored a real concern for the woman.

"She is not ill in body," he replied, "but in spirit. You know of course that Marchese Francesco has died. I fear that since his father's death, my cousin Federico's hat no longer fits his head. He does not pay his mother the respect owing her."

My own opinion is that the only way that boy will ever grasp the reins of state firmly in his own hands is to run over his mother with a battlewagon. But I do not say that. Instead I suggest that the young Marchese might have felt it necessary to assert his authority strongly in order to become his own man.

He agrees. "Unfortunately," he adds, "Federico is *not* his own man. He has simply transferred his obedience from one woman to another, a young woman and beautiful. Also named Isabella."

"Does he mean to marry this other Isabella?"

"Alas, the other Isabella is already married. But that has not stopped Federico from conferring on her all the honors and privileges of a consort. He has made her his Marchesana in everything but name. And the court to its eternal shame has followed his lead. These days when young Isabella Boschetti rides out into the streets of Mantova the nobles follow her train as if she were a princess. Isabella d'Este, *La Prima Donna del Mondo*, can barely attract the allegiance of one or two old men."

"Poor Madonna Isabella." I find myself remembering how valiantly she fought, for her boy against her husband, the Doge, and the Pope. To have him turn away from her now when she was beginning to get old; worse, to see another woman—a mistress—installed in her place... No apothecary could have concocted a pill more bitter.

"With your permission, I will carry your regards to her when I next visit Mantova," he said. "She always speaks to me of you."

"What does she say?" I asked.

"She admires you. Your intellect. Your talent."

And what of you? Do you admire me? Have you thought of me since that night in Venezia? How many times? Are you reminded of me when you pass through the Piazza San Andrea in spring? And when you gallop past the Sacred Wood on your way to Marmirolo, do you remember how we lay together on the damp ground beside the Bosco Fontana and pledged our vows through eternity?

We had passed under the Porta San Spirito in our meander and were headed into that wasteland between the Vatican and Trastevere where my brother used to live on Ser Chigi's estate. When I felt a slight tug at my shawl, I thought some field animal—perhaps a mouse—had jumped up on me. Then, in rapid succession, a slight pressure against my thigh where my *borsetta* hung from my waist; the quicksilver movement of a pair of hands; a flash of red velvet; a smart smack; a cry of pain. We had fallen into a nest of Gypsies.

Of course the mere sight of Lord Pirro's sword sent them flying off. But the spell was broken, the sacred spring forgotten. I was not a fourteen-year-old heroine risking all for love. I was Madonna Grazia dei Rossi—wife and scholar.

"Have you been in good health?" I inquired, to cover my embarrassment at being surprised in paradise.

"Of course I have," was the brusque answer. "And so have you from all appearances. Grazia, we have so little time. Let us not waste any of it on politesse."

He reached for my hand. I drew it away.

He stepped close. "Have you forgotten Venezia, lady?"

It was my second opportunity that day to confess that no day passed without my remembering that rapturous encounter. I could have told him then that a son had been born of that wondrous night, a beautiful boy who bore a likeness to him. But no. Instead, I found myself answering coldly, "We cannot simply climb into a convenient bed every time we encounter each other."

The bitter tone of my rejoinder cut short his smile. With nothing more than a slight grimace to indicate how precisely my arrow had hit its mark, he held out his arm and bowed in a courtly manner. "May I accompany you back to the Vatican palace?"

"Thank you," I answered, just as formal as he.

By the time we reached the San Spirito Gate I began to regret my outburst. "I thought we understood that there could never be anything further between us," I began. "My husband...your wife..."

"My wife is dead, madonna," he replied coldly. "Dead of the plague this year at Bozzuolo. She was a virtuous woman and a good wife, even though there was no love between us. Nor could she produce a living child. Only five dead ones. But she bore the lot of a soldier's wife with fortitude and I owe her my respect."

We were back in the Borgo by then. Do it, Grazia, I told myself. Beg his forgiveness before you lose him forever.

"There was no call for me to speak to you as I did," I admitted, but without looking him in the eye.

"Quite the opposite," he answered. "I was presumptuous to believe that I would hold the same place in your heart as you do in mine. Who am I to impute feelings to you, a woman I have twice over seduced and abandoned?"

I opened my mouth to answer the question but he seemed determined not to hear me.

"For a moment today I believed I had been given one last chance. But today is not my fortunate day."

"You sound like my brother the stargazer," I berated him.

"There are moments of decision in this life, Grazia," he went on. "Any soldier will tell you that in every battle there comes an opportunity that must be seized or all is lost. Hence the motto 'Carpe Diem.'"

"Is this a war between you and me, then?" I asked. "Are we adversaries?"

"So it would seem," he answered, grim-faced.

The Vatican gates loomed up ahead. We entered, silent, and parted without a further word, our moment lost.

52

LTHOUGH I DID MY BEST TO MAKE LIGHT OF MY humiliation in the Pope's apartment, Judah was furious at what he took to be an insult to his wife, his house, and himself. Since he laid all the blame for the debacle on Jehiel, my brother's remaining time with us became a casus belli. (Your Uncle Gershom, with a banker's instinct for being—or not being—in the right place at the right time, managed to have to spend the entire duration of Jehiel's Roman sojourn away from Roma on "important business.")

One night at supper Jehiel let slip an admiring reference to Lazzarelli's *Epistola Enoch*. It was as if he had slapped a stinking fish on the table. Judah's nostrils quivered with distaste and disdain.

"Accursed cabala!" he thundered. "I will not hear it spoken of in my house!"

"And on what grounds do you base your objection, brother?" Jehiel inquired, with an unctuous mildness he must have copied from his holy man and which drove Judah even farther into rage.

"As a Jew, I object because the cabalists create deities in these seraphim of theirs contrary to the law of Moses, which tells us plainly as the first and fundamental command that there is only one God. And as a scholar and a thinking man, I object because these transformations from men into gods that the cabalists claim to generate with their magic directly contradict all human reason."

That slur silenced Jehiel for the moment. But the war continued.

Each Friday when Jehiel arrived to spend the Sabbath with us, Judah invited him to take part at evening prayers. And each time he did so, Jehiel declined politely without giving his reasons. But my brother was never able to hold his tongue, and finally, one Friday evening, he followed his refusal to join Judah in prayer with the explanation that he preferred a spiritual understanding of the Torah to blind ritual observance.

"Blind observance!" If Judah had had any tendency toward apoplexy, he would certainly have had a fit at that. As it was, he exploded into a series of epithets, calling my poor brother in turn a Christ-lover, an ingrate, and an idiot and ending up by showing him the door.

"These fools dare to question the laws of Moses," he fulminated. "As if their addled brains had a better grasp of truth than the Prophets. Believe me, Grazia, that brother of yours is halfway to conversion without knowing it. Today he favors spiritualized understanding. Tomorrow he will dunk his head into the baptism font. Then he can wallow in his spiritualized understanding to his heart's content and never be obliged to perform any observance ever again."

"He does not mean half of what he says," I tried to explain. "His mind has been consumed by this Reubeni."

"What mind?" Judah grumbled.

"Just because he does not think like you . . ."

"He does not think at all. Can he not see where these heresies will lead him?"

"You mistake him," I insisted. "He has no intention of leaving our faith."

"It is not his apostasy that frightens me. I fear for his wretched

carcass. Try to understand, Grazia. Jehiel babbles about 'regener-
ation.' He quotes Lazzarelli like a parrot: Man was created to
know divine things and to dominate all creation. What does that
sound like to you?"

"Heresy," I admitted.

"The Hermetic fallacy is nor new to me," he explained. "I
heard it from the lips of Ficino and . . ." He paused. "Others."

"Others?"

He paused again.

I waited.

"Oh, Grazia, I have lived too long and seen too much," he
burst out.

"What is the danger to my brother that you foresee?" I asked.
"Tell me."

"Very well," he replied. "Jehiel is flirting with a dangerous
philosophy. Simply put, it is the belief that man through his
own capabilities — albeit under the guidance of a magician —
has the power to become a terrestrial God."

This was indeed diabolism.

"Pico della Mirandola." A shadow passed over his face when
he spoke the name. "Pico was called to Roma and came close
to burning for less heretical sentiments. And he was clever, rich,
respected, and a Christian. What do you think the church will
do to a Jew who publishes it about that any man can reach the
level of Christ once he has mastered the effluvia of influences
pouring down from the stars?"

"Jehiel believes that?"

"Lazzarelli promulgates that doctrine and your brother has
taken up Lazzarelli."

"*Dio!*"

"Believe me, Grazia, it is not your brother's apostasy that
concerns me. Jews have deserted the ship of Moses before and
will again. No, my dear, your brother is flirting with a flame far
more damaging than apostasy, a flame that may consume him
literally. The Catholic church has its own system of sanctified
miracles to preserve, exclusive to them and mediated through

their priesthood. There is no room in the house of their God for secular magic. That, my dear, is why magicians and sorcerers burn."

Plainly I had misjudged the quality of his concern. "I see now that Jehiel is in real danger," I admitted.

"He puts us all in jeopardy," Judah answered gravely. "It was one thing for him to tinker with fancy hunting weapons and to predict at what hour the Este whoremaster should inject his sperm into his Duchess in order to produce a boy baby. But now he is in Roma, where the flame of orthodoxy burns brightest. For all our sakes, I pray he leaves soon and goes back to Ferrara to turn dross into gold."

IT WAS DURING THESE tempestuous times that Zaira chose to reconsider my offer of hospitality, or so I took to be her purpose when she turned up at my house. No doubt the rigors of existence had finally caught up with her. Otherwise she never would have come to beg a favor of me. That I knew. Nor was I surprised that the request presented itself in the form of an order from the gods.

"The oracles instruct me that I must accept your offer of aid, madonna," she announced without any formalities. "If I refuse you, the consequences will be grave for all of us."

Good, I thought. Let her move in at once. Judah will understand. "Shall I hire the muleteer or will you?" I asked.

"I do not understand, madonna," she replied, looking puzzled. "What use will I make of a muleteer?"

"How then will you move your boxes?"

This question appeared to throw her into even greater confusion than my previous one.

"You do intend to move into our house, do you not?" I asked.

"Never," she replied. "I thought we had settled that."

"Then perhaps it is I who do not understand," I suggested with a trace of irritation.

"Indeed you do not, Grazia. What can you know of my life?"

"I know that you have been buffeted by fate, that you are forced to find your bread in low places, that you are ill."

"Not so fast, madonna. Do not bury me yet."

My stricken look must have told her how deeply the accusation cut me. She took my hand in hers and, very much the Zaira of old, said gently, "This disease I suffer from is not the plague, you know, which kills in a day. I have a few good years left before the French devil claims me."

"But how will you live?"

"Just as I do now," she answered cheerfully.

"I want to take care of you," I cried.

"But I am quite capable of taking care of myself," she answered, with the same maddening aplomb. "I have a life of my own. Perhaps it is not the one you would wish for me. Perhaps not the one I would wish for myself. But it is the life I have made and it has its consolations."

"What consolations?" I was beyond patience now. "Poverty? Filth? Humiliation? Disease?"

"The first is mother of all the rest, believe me, madonna." She said it so softly that I barely heard, carried away as you know I can be by my own passion.

"I do not want you to die alone," I wailed.

"But I am not alone, madonna." Again, she spoke softly. But this time I heard her. Not alone?

"You have a . . ."

"Two," she replied. "An Italian and a Spaniard. Buying them both presents is quite a strain on my budget. But worth it."

Not yet ready for the grave indeed. That was putting it mildly.

"I think of them as my *famiglia*," she added, with an unmistakably salacious leer.

"Is it because of this . . . *famiglia* that you refuse to come and live with us?" I asked.

She paused, pushed out her lower lip, and chewed on it for a moment. "No," she answered at last. "Although I would miss them, especially the Italian. He is an Adonis." She sighed softly, then shook herself out of her regret and continued. "It is for my own sake, madonna, that I do not come to live in your house as a pensioner, for the sake of my own life which I mean to live — what there is left of it — according to my own lights. To sleep where I wish, with whom I wish, to take my pleasure where I find it. And if misery comes along as a companion, to accept that in the same spirit."

I had heard men speak so. But never before a woman.

"Now about the money," she continued without missing a beat. "I will need money for the house and food until I am established..." (*Dio*, I thought, she wants me to invest in a bordello.) "And wood and ashes and soap and baskets and water and clotheslines. Is that asking too much?"

"You mean to go back to the laundry?"

"I am too old and sick to play the *ruffiana*," she replied. "And too honest for a witch. What else is left?"

"But you told me that the laundry was a hole in hell."

"That was the Spanish laundry," she answered. "I would not shame you by cheating my customers and abusing my girls as that Spanish bitch did, feeding us wine all day so that by the end we never knew if we had gotten paid or not."

"She did that?"

"Kept us tipsy all the time. Then beat us when we fell asleep at the tubs. If you like I can show you the marks."

I begged her not to trouble herself. I could tolerate her words. I could not tolerate her wounds.

"Tell me how you propose to operate this honest establishment," I asked.

"For one thing, I will use both soap and lye in the true Spanish way, not delude the customers with the tall tale that leaving the lye in the clothes gets rid of stains."

"Does it not, then?"

"Madonna, do you not look to see what happens in your washhouse?"

I had to admit that I did not.

"Your mother taught you better," she admonished me. "But

you needn't worry about that now. For my laundry will give you perfect service. We will soak the clothes and soap them and put them in a basket and drain them and leave them all night in the basket so that the lye can drain out, which is what that Spanish bitch never took the time to do."

"It sounds like a good method," I commented.

"It is the *only* method for an *honest* laundress. Do you agree then? On the money?" I gave her my hand on it.

From that time on she arrived each Monday to collect our laundry and to deliver the previous week's hamper. But she refused to meet you or Judah, or even to see Jehiel. At first I insisted. Then I understood that in spite of her claims not to be ashamed of her state, her pride would not permit them to see her so degraded. And I no longer pressed her.

Nor did I have any success in reconciling my husband and my brother. The savage discord that had erupted between them over Lazzarelli destroyed whatever little trust they had built up out of their mutual love for me, leaving only bitterness and stubbornness on both sides. And thus things remained until Jehiel left Roma for Portugal to accompany David Reubeni in soliciting funds for a crusade against the Turk.

Loyalty to my brother took me to the embarkation point to salute the holy band as it set off. By then Reubeni's brief celebrity with the fickle Roman mob had run out and his party consisted only of ten raggedy Jews without so much as a horse among them. But their leader appeared more resplendent than ever. He had given up white (had he lost his purity in Roma? I wondered) and was clad in a gabardine of red damask and a black velvet cap embroidered with gold and pearls—personal gifts to Prince David from Pope Clement, Jehiel whispered to me proudly. My brother, alas, still wore the same shabby cloak in which he had arrived at our portal. To see him so dilapidated, his face gaunt, his body shrunken—for he had taken to fasting in emulation of his idol—was a sight to tear your heart from your body.

Yet he was happy on that day. His eyes shone with high

hope and optimism as he described for me the glorious days ahead. With Judah's forebodings buzzing in my brain, I begged him to be prudent, if not for his own sake, at least for the sake of his motherless boys.

"Promise me," I begged him, "that you will not tell fortunes. Or sell amulets. And, above all, that you not theologize disputatiously with Christians."

He took the request as an insult.

"What do you take me for, a simpleton?" he demanded.

No, not a simpleton, I thought. Worse. You are the son who has not even the capacity to inquire.

He walked off to join his crusade without a backward glance or a final embrace. It was a bitter parting.

FROM DANILO'S ARCHIVE

TO GRAZIA DEI ROSSI DEL MEDIGO AT ROMA

My dearest and most beloved Grazia:

I am now at liberty to reveal to you a secret I have concealed over this past year. Prepare yourself for a shock. I am married. Sit down, Grazia. Take a deep breath. Now read on.

Your brother Jehiel and I were married in a private ceremony on the eve of his departure with the holy David. In one stroke God granted me two of my most ardent prayers: to be married to the man I love and to have you as my sister. May I begin again and salute you correctly:

My dearest and most beloved sister: (Ah, it is good to write that word.)

I know you will forgive me for holding back my news. It was not my design but my Jehiel's. He made me promise a solemn oath not to reveal this marriage to you until he had left Roma. Now he is halfway to Portugal and I am released from my oath. Rejoice with me in my happiness, Grazia, I beg you.

Perhaps you guessed that we lived in this house as man and wife long before we went to the rabbi. That was a secret

· 612 ·

I had no difficulty in keeping from you. I lived in shame of it every day. My only excuse is that I could not help myself. You above all people know how long I have loved your brother When I finally found a way into his heart through his children, I took it. I knew that all I was to him was a nursemaid and a bedmate, but I was content with my portion. To me, he is everything.

I pray every day for my husband to come back safely. On that day, after all the years of waiting, I will begin to live the life I was meant to live. Pray with me, Grazia.

Your loving sister, Penina dei Rossi, at Ferrara, July 20, 1525.

TO THE FAMILY OF JUDAH DEL MEDIGO AT ROMA

Greetings from Portugal, dear sister, brother, and nephew!

Already this land is a second home to me. In every great city we enter, there come Jews and Gentiles too, men and women, great and small, so worshipful of my master that he must warn them continually not to kiss his hand, since that honor is reserved to the King, and my master does not wish to steal glory from any man.

This King of Portugal is a real Christian; he loves all the Jews. But unfortunately we have a powerful enemy at court, a certain Don Miguel who seeks to alienate my master from King John. Night and day he whispers in the King's ear that our party is come to restore the Marrano conversos to the faith of the Jews. But the King loves us. Of that there can be no doubt. Two days ago he invited our party to celebrate a joy day with him in the open air. When we arrived, there were many guests sitting upon the railing of the loggia watching the dancing below. And the King called to one of his officers, "Drive away the men who are sitting between the arches..." (Mind you, they were great lords, every one.) "And arrange for the Jewish ambassador and his party to have seats." Does that not bespeak his love and respect for my prince? Still, we are in the midst of suspicion here.

The King, a very forthright man, spoke plainly what was

on his mind. *"His Majesty hears,"* the interpreter informed us, *"that Prince David has come to restore the Marranos to the Jewish religion and that the Marranos pray with him and read in his books night and day and that he has made of the house I gave him a synagogue for the use of these Marranos and that they all kiss his hand and bow to him. I am pleased that he has come to help me, but listen to this: he is ruining my kingdom with his presence."*

Whereupon my master, now very angry at these slanders, said to the King, *"How can your heart harbor such ill suspicions of me, I who come here in God's service to do a meritorious deed? Have you forgotten, sire, that I too am the son of a king, a king of the seed of David, son of Jesse?"*

And the King bowed his head in shame and tried to pacify my master with good words. But Prince David was no longer satisfied with words. He had come for firearms and weapons and help against the Turk, he said. From here he proposed to go into Germany to make the same request of the Holy Roman Emperor, whose hatred of the Turks was beyond question. The barb hit home. The King promised to supply us with eight ships and four thousand large and small firearms to use against the infidels. And all he exacted in return was the master's promise to tell the Jews not to kiss his hand.

Rejoice. Sing Hosannahs. The land of Ishmael will return to Israel. The Word of the Prophet will come to pass.

Your brother in Jehovah,

(signed) Jehiel dei Rossi at Almeida, Portugal.

August 23, 1525.

TO GRAZIA DEI ROSSI DEL MEDIGO AT ROMA

Beloved sister and brother:

Today my master, Prince David Reubeni, has gone off to work his wonders in Germany and who do you think he has left behind to sail the King's eight ships to the Holy Land? My proud answer is that I, your brother, have been deputized to lead this historic armada. Yes, the master has named me captain of his flotilla with eight ships under my command carrying four thousand firearms for the destruction of the Turk.

Dear sister and brother, I will yet make you proud. All my life I have been wandering in a desert of confusion as barren of hope as the lost tribes of Israel. At last like them, after forty years of wandering and waiting, I am let into the Promised Land. Finally I know why I was put on earth. My entire being sings in ecstasy. Lazzarelli spoke the truth: We are all gods if only we would act like gods.

Your brother (signed with the initial "J.") at Tavira.
October 18, 1525.

TO GRAZIA DEI ROSSI DEL MEDIGO AT ROMA

Dear sister:

Four months in this stinking port and still no sign of my promised ships. But I do not lose hope nor must you. The King is a man of honor, I am certain he will fulfill his promises. Meanwhile I seem to have taken the place of Prince David in the hearts of our people. They call on me to make peace between them when they are in dispute and wherever I go they listen to my voice. I begin to believe that God has decreed this delay so that I can perform His work among these people. Be assured that whatever task He asks of me, I am willing to perform it.

Yours in the service of our Lord. (signed "J.")

TO GRAZIA DEI ROSSI DEL MEDIGO AT ROMA

Beloved sister:

The worst has come to pass. Only a miracle of haste and generosity can save me now.

How this came to be, there is no time to tell. It is enough for you to know that I am held here under house arrest by the magistrate of the town in ransom of five hundred golden ducats. Find this money for me, Grazia. Get it to me quickly before they hand me over to the King's Great Inquisitor. Once the churchmen get their hands on me, I am doomed. They burn Marranos every day here for crimes less serious than the one of which I am accused.

My life is in your hands, trusted sister. Do not throw it away through dilatoriness. Hurry! Hurry! Each day brings me closer to the pyre. At night in dreams I can feel the flames licking my toes. The agony. The terror. Save me, sister, for God's sake.

(signed) Jehiel dei Rossi at Tavira.

June 3, 1526.

53

THE MORNING WE RECEIVED JEHIEL'S DESPERATE PLEA for help, Judah took up my brother's cause. He was packed up and on his way to Portugal before the sun set. No matter that he considered Jehiel an irresponsible fool. He was our fool and needed help.

With Judah's departure for Portugal a cloud of despondency settled over me. The sensible part of me told myself that Jehiel was an agile cat who always leapt to safety at the last moment. Another more insistent voice whispered that my brother Jehiel had finally exhausted his credit with Fortuna and that this time nothing could save him. Days I sat by the window waiting for news of his fate. Nights I dreamed him on the rack screaming, the torturer towering over his broken body.

God knows where these unhealthy fantasies might have led me had not Madonna Isabella reappeared in my life. Whether or not she knew of my situation I had no way of knowing. How she found my whereabouts in Roma is another mystery. These people have ways of finding out things. All I can report to you is that one afternoon a servant appeared at my door commanding me—there is no other word for the tone of that summons—to present myself at the Palazzo Colonna in the Piazza S.S. Apostoli the next morning. Years had elapsed since the woman last laid eyes on me. Yet the possibility that I might be unable or even unwilling to materialize at the snap of her fingers was not even suggested. Then again, Madonna Isabella has never seen the need to consider the personal feelings of anyone below the rank of duke.

Mind you, she did rise from her dais and come forward to greet me when I was ushered into her presence. And she did hold out her arms, but whether to embrace me or to observe me more closely, I could not know.

"Time has been good to you, Grazia," she crooned, looking into my eyes in that way she has of making you feel that she cares for no one else in the world. "Your waist is as small as it was the first day I laid my eyes on you. Do you remember?"

Did I remember? Who could forget such a terrifying moment?

"And now you are famous, celebrated throughout Europe. Why, I have heard you referred to as Boccaccio's daughter. Come closer. Let me look at you. It has been too long."

As she spoke she reached down for a pair of spectacles that hung between her breasts on a gold chain, and put them up to her eyes to see me better. "Hardly a wrinkle." She pinched my cheek softly. "The flesh still firm as a young girl's." She sighed. "Would that I could say the same for myself."

I assured her that she had not changed any more than I had. But we both knew this to be a lie. What I saw before me was an old woman, very fat, with gray hairs sprouting out of her *balzo*, a protruding belly which no dressmaker's art could disguise, and a set of fingers puffed up like pastry balls.

Seeing Madonna Isabella, whom I had known as a slim girl with a step as light as a nymph's, sunk so far into decay, I felt a welling up behind my eyeballs and the next moment I was dissolved in a saltwater bath.

"Grazia, what is it, my dear?" She put her hand on my shoulder, a sure sign that she was truly moved.

Between sobs I told her of Jehiel's misfortunes at the court of the King of Portugal and of my fears for his life.

"Maestro Vitale always was a wild one," she observed. "There seems to be one such in every family. And they are the ones we cherish the most..."

The slight quiver of her lips told me she was speaking from her own painful experience. But, being Madonna Isabella, she would not allow herself to dwell overlong in the unfamiliar haunts of sisterhood. However, she did commiserate—in her way.

"Your brother's fate is in God's hands now, Grazia," she advised me. "There is nothing we can do to help him. But there is an elixir vitae for your melancholy. To act, to do, to read, to write, to busy oneself with work, these are Nepenthe's remedy for your disease. Perhaps you should enter our service. As you know, we have always felt a certain closeness to you, especially now with your honorable husband so far away. Besides..." She leaned over, dropping the royal rhetoric in the descent. "It doesn't do for a woman to stay locked up with only a child for company. It rots the brain. How old is your son now?"

"Ten years," I replied.

"You must bring him to us one day. We will be pleased to audience him," she announced, back to being the *alta donna* again. Have I mentioned the whimsicality of this woman?

"So it is settled then. You will attend us on Mondays and Wednesdays. We can surely find something for you to do."

She may have lost her figure and her smooth complexion, I thought to myself, but she has kept her arrogance intact. Nonetheless, I did agree to the proposal. To turn her down twice in one lifetime was courting catastrophe.

After that I waited on the lady in her borrowed palace twice each week. The subject of my brother's incarceration was never raised between us again, but from time to time as I bent over my writing table I felt the light touch of her hand on my shoulder and I did find those occasional touches comforting in the weeks of waiting for news from Judah, especially so since

Madama is not a great one for touching, particularly those of the lower orders.

The previous year had been a tumultuous one for Italy. The French army was decimated at Pavia and King Francis himself taken to a Spanish prison where he languished for almost a year before his mother, Louise, was able to negotiate the terms of his release with the Emperor.

While these momentous events played out on the world stage my attention was riveted on Portugal. Living with the realization that as each week passed, my brother's folly and carelessness were drawing him closer to disaster, the misfortunes of kings and emperors hardly touched my mind. But every day in Madama's service I was pulled back into the great world of affairs, like it or not.

Normally a robust woman, she developed a permanent headache on the day she first heard rumors that Georg Frundsberg, an obscure Swabian feudatory of the Emperor's, had gathered up a force of German soldiers, called landsknechts, and was preparing to cross the Alps into Italy to teach the Pope respect for his feudal lord, Emperor Charles V.

Remember that traditionally the Marchese owed his feudal loyalty to the Emperor. At the same time, he held a contract as a mercenary captain in the opposing army, the Pope's army. Each day, I witnessed the tremendous exertion of will with which Madonna Isabella banished her worry over this intractable problem from her mind and, instead, bent that marvelous instrument to what she believed to be its proper function: devising ways to keep Mantova balanced on the high wire of neutrality, above the fray.

Out of sorts with her principal secretary, she now insisted that all her voluminous communications must be composed in my immaculate hand. Not surprisingly, my two days of service per week extended to four, then five. Before long I found myself spending more time at the Palazzo Colonna than in my own house under the Portico d'Ottavia.

Thus enmeshed in Madama's feverish maneuvers to shore

up her state and her house, I barely had time to supervise my own little household, and as a result hardly noticed that Zaira had ceased to appear with her laundry cart. Even when the maid brought it to my attention, I took the dereliction as one of Zaira's vagaries and told myself that her life, as she had reminded me more than once, was her own business.

Then one day when Zaira's affairs were the farthest thing from my mind, I was interrupted at my desk in the Palazzo Colonna by a caller. I could tell by the distaste with which the flunkey pronounced the word "caller" that this surprise visitor did not live up to his standard. "Just the type a Jewess would drag in," I could almost hear him say to himself as he announced my guest. It is always the underlings who cling fastest to snobbery.

Now this mysterious guest appears. He is someone I have never seen. Medium height. Swarthy. Corsican, perhaps, with Herculean shoulders and very big feet. Scruffy to be sure but with a most engaging smile.

"Forgive the intrusion, madonna." He removes his cap respectfully.

I forgive him at once and inquire his business.

"A delicate matter, concerning my friend Dido." He seems actually embarrassed. "She has taken herself to the Hospital of San Giacomo."

"San Giacomo?" I cannot believe what I am hearing.

"Last week she went blind. I reached my hand out to help her and she hounded me out of the house. Then, while I was out, she hired a litter and took herself to that pesthole of a hospice at Santa Maria Nuova. It took me until today to find her. She is lying in a long room with fifty other prostitutes on a straw pallet drenched with piss. Oh, madonna, if you ever loved her, get her out of that sewer."

"What must I do?"

"All that is needed is a doctor's permission and a place where she will be cared for, a haven..."

The haven I could and would supply. The doctor's permit

was not so easy to come by. Judah could have written such a document handily. But Judah was somewhere between Italy and Portugal. And my brother Gershom was hibernating in the Ferrarese countryside.

Considering who else I could enlist in Zaira's cause, I thought at once of Madonna Isabella. She was the most powerful person I knew and she sat in a suite of rooms less than a hundred steps from me.

Without even asking the page at the door to announce my presence, I pushed my way into the little sitting room that served as her dressing room and, begging her pardon most humbly, requested her help in a matter of life and death.

What I presented was a colored version of Zaira and her affairs. Zaira's story, after all, was not a matter of my authorship and I felt no shame in tailoring the tale to the lady's taste. Throughout my recital I referred to Zaira as my nurse, painting her as a woman of uncommon virtue with whom life had dealt harshly (all true), and managed to abridge certain details such as the fact that Zaira had been blinded by the French disease and was now dying of that affliction. Eyes ruined by years of embroidering in bad light seemed a much more appealing detail. Mind you, knowing Madonna's fascination with celebrated personages, I did cobble up as tasty a dish as I could out of Zaira's servitude to Imperia and Messer Agostino Chigi. Chigi was dead. How could gossip hurt him now?

I must have done a fine job of sweetening my tale, for when I came to Zaira's present pathetic condition Madama, her eyes quite misty, volunteered her interest. "We are touched by the story of this unfortunate widow, Grazia, and would help her if we could. But how? Shall we send our steward?" She rejected that idea with a nod of her head. "No. What is needed is a man of authority and presence. I have it. My kinsman Lord Pirro of Bozzuolo is in Roma at this moment conferring with the Holy Father. Soldiers know how to accomplish these things, do you not agree?"

In my many weeks in her service this was the first mention

I had heard of Lord Pirro. Now she simply let the name fall at my feet like a rose.

"Yes, Lord Pirro is definitely the one to take care of this matter," she went on. "I will send for him at once. And you must go home and make a room ready to receive the invalid. Lord Pirro will bring her to you before this day is out. You can depend upon it." Then she added, "One can always depend upon Lord Pirro, Grazia."

The litter that brought Zaira out of the hospice arrived at the Portico d'Ottavia long after you were asleep. Just as well. The bundle of bones under the dirty blanket was not a sight I would wish you to see. When I bent over to lift the black veil that covered her face, Lord Pirro reached out to hold me back.

"Believe me, Grazia, it is better if you do not look," he warned. But I thrust aside the restraining arm, drew back the veil, and saw what words can barely describe... wide, staring eyes sunken into what once had been a face but was now a mass of running sores oozing pus and blood. Almost imperceptibly, the mouth moved. Simply a back-and-forth sawing of the jaws. No sound. But enough to tell me she wished to speak.

I felt for her hand under the blanket, not even bothering to brush off the army of fleas that attacked my arm when it reached into their stronghold. Mindless of the vermin, I began to stroke her arm and to murmur words of which I have no recollection. And after a while she began to respond with sounds even more incoherent than mine, mutterings and mumblings interlaced with bits of prayer played against a constant iteration of my name... "Grazia. Grazia. Grazia." And finally, a sentence: "Thank God you came to me, my little Graziella." Mark me. No one wants to die alone.

Sometime during that long night a basin was brought and her poor wasted body washed and the flea-filled blanket exchanged for clean linen. After that I remember a pair of powerful arms lifting up the fragile body and carrying it into a small anteroom, where I laid myself down alongside, the better to hold her in my arms.

As dawn was breaking she sat up as if resuscitated and asked in a perfectly clear voice, "Am I forgiven?"

"Of course you are," I reassured her. "God has mercy. He forgives." At a loss for words of comfort, I riffled through my mind. "The Lord is my shepherd..." The Psalm came to me unbidden. "I shall not want. He maketh me to lie down in green pastures..." Before I came to the end, a tap on the shoulder alerted me that this life—so entwined with mine for so many years and in so many ways—had ended.

All through the long night I had felt the life oozing out of Zaira's worn body, draining my own vitality with it in some kind of sympathetic union. Now a strong, callused hand took hold of mine and I began to feel a steady current of strength flowing back into me. Eyes closed, I clung to the vital force as I allowed myself to be lifted up and carried to my bedchamber.

Need I tell you more? Lord Pirro was back under Judah's roof, back in my heart, in my arms, in my bed. Time enough for shame tomorrow.

I awoke in a sea of pleasure, with a muscled arm holding me safe as in a cradle. Then I remembered where I was and whose arm it was, and like Eve at the instant she bit into the apple, I knew at once the corruption of my body and pulled up the quilt to cover my nakedness.

"Do not start off this day by shaming your body or our love, Grazia, I beg you."

I dared not look at the speaker.

"Allow me to feast my eyes for just one moment more." He always seemed to be asking for just one something—one look, one hour, one moment. Still I made no move to stop him when he slid back the coverlet and once again exposed my nakedness. I may be an adulteress but I am not such a hypocrite as to deny by day that which I condone by night.

Once or twice I made an effort to disengage, but the power of our passion held us both in thrall to the point of total exhaustion. Finally toward nones we fell back for the last time on linens by then soaked through with the sweat of our labors.

We did not awake until the bells chimed for vespers. When we did, Lord Pirro announced without any preamble, "You must marry me, Grazia. There is no other way for us."

I made a vain effort to protest. I spoke of Judah, whose absence in my cause had given us this opportunity. I spoke of ingratitude. I protested that I could not steal away from Judah in the night like a thief.

"Write him a letter," was the implacable answer.

Dismiss Judah from our lives with a stroke of my pen? At the very moment that he was on an errand of mercy to save my brother's life? It was unthinkable. The dissolution of this marriage, if it was to be, must be discussed, planned, prepared for. I owed Judah that. "I need time," I explained.

"You are not prepared to entrust your life to me, is that not the sum of these excuses?" he demanded in his usual forthright way. And I could not deny it.

"For your lack of faith in me, Grazia, I have no remedy. After what I did to you in our youth, I can expect no better. But if you believe that it is all tumbling about in the grass with me, you are wrong. Perhaps it was true once, but the years have taught me lessons. To prove it, I wish to declare my intentions toward your son. When we marry, I expect to adopt the boy and bring him up as my own. For I love every part of you, Grazia, including everything that you love."

Why did I not tell him the truth at that moment? That he was offering to adopt his own son, the son I had kept from him for ten long years? I wish I could give you the answer.

He was that day departing for Lombardia. Much as he wished it, he could not tarry. Milano—that elusive prize—was once again under siege. Only this time it was the Pope's allies who were clinging desperately to their hold on the starving city, and the Emperor's troops who encircled them in the iron ring of a blockade. Lord Pirro's mission was to light a fire under the Duke of Urbino, Captain-General of the Pope's League, and inspirit him to come to the aid of his besieged allies.

"That man has more lead in his feet than in his cannons," he quipped without a smile.

This was the first mention I had heard of the dilatory tactics of Madama's son-in-law, and I listened with only half an ear. Milano seemed far away, the Imperial army a chimera, and Urbino's cowardice of much more concern to his proud mother-in-law than to me. What did matter to me was that I had a reprieve.

"But I must know my fate soon, Grazia," he warned me earnestly. "Now that I can see happiness within my grasp, it would be cruel of you to tease me with it only to refuse me at the end. When you decide, decide firmly and finally. I will expect your decision the day I return to Roma."

By my reasoning his liaison to Urbino's camp was sure to be the work of weeks. By then Judah would have rescued my brother and returned to Roma. It seemed a virtual certainty that I would have the opportunity to make a clean and honorable break with him before Lord Pirro returned to claim me as his bride, if such was to be my fate.

Man proposes. God disposes. Lord Pirro did not return from Milano within weeks. Milano fell to the Imperials before he arrived at Urbino's camp. In the wake of that disaster he was ordered to proceed directly to Paris to solicit aid for the Pope from King Francis.

Nor did Judah return triumphant to Roma. Instead, duty and a good heart set him on a detour to Ferrara with a new role: the bearer of bad tidings.

FROM DANILO'S ARCHIVE

TO GRAZIA DEI ROSSI DEL MEDIGO AT ROMA
Beloved wife:
Prepare yourself for the worst. Your brother is dead. I arrived too late to save him.
I can see the shock in your eyes. The moment of disbelief. The refusal to accept what God has decreed. But He will not

be gainsaid, not by all the tears in all the eyes in the world. Somewhere the end of Jehiel's life was written. Now it has come. All we can do is trust in God and believe that what He does is for the best.

I made several vain attempts to negotiate with the Inquisition using the five hundred gold ducats I brought with me, but there was no use to it. Once the magistrate relinquished him to the inquisitors, all hope of negotiation was dead. "We do not bargain for souls here," I was told when I offered my bribe.

I could not save him, Grazia. But I did see him once in his cell. We communicated through a small opening in the door. He thanked me for coming. Not a word of reproach that I had come too late. He begged us to take care of his widow and children. I assured him we would. He told me that a confessor came each day to ask him to recant his faith but this he refused to do even at the end. Small comfort though it may be, your brother died a martyr.

You will want to know the circumstances of his death. The charge was that he performed a circumcision upon a scribe in the King's court. Your brother swore to me that he had not performed this ritual, that the scribe had circumcised himself.

"This scribe came to tell me how he dreamed of being circumcised and of seeing God's angel write his name in the Holy Book. He asked me to circumcise him as had been forecast in his dream. I refused, I swear it, Judah," he told me. "I warned this scribe that even to talk of such a thing was to put himself and every Marrano in Portugal into danger. But to talk to him was like talking to a deaf man. He was crazed in pursuit of circumcision."

Your brother told me his side of the story with a great show of sincerity, but there remains a question in my mind as to how the circumcision actually came about. Jehiel claimed that all the Marranos knew the scribe had circumcised himself but were too craven to tell the truth to the inquisitor. We will never know. The scribe too is dead, burned in the same pyre as Jehiel.

Oh, my Grazia, it pains me to write so coldly of the end of your brother's short life. I know you cherished him with a special love. Perhaps my acting on your behalf better expresses my deep sympathy for your anguish than any words I am able to find.

I have put off writing to Penina at Ferrara, but last night I had a dream that showed me the way I must go. I saw myself in a large armchair in your grandparents' house, my lap full of little children. More children sat at my feet, innocent faces looking up at me, waiting for me to speak.

The dream ended without my knowing what I had said to these children. But this morning I understood all. I must go to Ferrara and tell Jehiel's sons face-to-face that their father is dead. To send them such news by messenger would be a slothful and derelict act. I must make the effort. I must soothe them and comfort them. I must let them know that, even fatherless, they are loved and will be protected and taken care of. It is my duty.

I will sail from this port by the first fair wind to Genova and thence will make my way across the peninsula to Ferrara. God willing, I will be there by the High Holy Days.

Bear up, my brave Grazia, God works in mysterious ways. We must be grateful to Him that your brother, always so troubled and so tumultuous, died at peace.

There is no more to say save to call on God to comfort you in this terrible loss and to watch over our brother Jehiel, who, in his martyrdom, must surely have achieved a stay in paradise.

God bless and keep you, my beloved wife,

(signed) Judah del Medigo at Tavira.

August 10, 1526.

54

J UDAH'S LAST LETTER FROM PORTUGAL ARRIVED
toward dusk on a Friday. Everything about the moment
is clear in my mind: the Sabbath candles waiting to be lit;
you in a fresh *camicia* looking at least a hand taller than
you had the month before (you are growing up too fast for a
doting mother); the enticing aroma of the Sabbath pie, which
I continued to bake even though there were only two of us to
eat it. I remember thinking how fortunate I was to have a son
so close to manhood to recite the prayer over the wine... and
to read the letter to me. I pleaded tired eyes but in truth I could
not bring myself to read what I knew Judah had to tell me.

"Oh, Mama..." From your face, I knew that my fears were
confirmed. "It's Uncle Jehiel. He's dead." The word hit me like
a body blow and knocked the breath out of me.

What would I have done without you there to carry me
upstairs (so strong for one so young) and to sit by my bed and
comfort me (such a warm heart)? I will never forget that long
night when I was lost in grief and you were the rock I clung to.

At first I cried for a day and a night without stopping. After
that the cataract erupted only intermittently. Whatever unseen

hand turned the spigot, its touch was sudden and irresistible. Even your good efforts to cheer me could not overcome my terrible sense of loss.

So it went in the early weeks of my mourning and may well have continued for God knows how long, but, once again, Madonna Isabella intervened, this time not by messenger but as a living presence come to pay a condolence call in her fabulous coach.

She found me dirty, disheveled, and completely given over to grief—that is to say, everything her strong spirit despised. Yet when I apologized for my unbuttoned state she waved my explanations aside. "If we do not lose countenance at the loss of a much-loved brother or sister, when then?" she inquired. "The day Maestro Vitale's soul departed this earth a part of you went with him." She touched my arm gently. "The feeling is no stranger to my own heart."

My expression must have given away my surprise; one does not associate Madonna Isabella with deep grief.

"Perhaps you forget, Grazia, that I too have lost brothers. Not to the pyre, I grant you, but to a living death. The auto-da-fé contrived for them is not hot but cold; not quick and brutal but slow and subtle. However, they are equally lost to me, equally removed from life, equally banished from my sight, as Maestro Vitale is from yours. And I too was able to do nothing to stop it."

An expression came over her face that I had never seen before, a look of despair so close to my own state that I felt at that moment as if we were sisters.

"Oh, madonna." I grasped her hand, heedless of the presumption of the gesture. "I do not think I can bear this."

"Yes you can, Grazia, just as I can and have learned to do. Every time I visit my old home in Ferrara I hear the voice of my brother Giulio calling out to me from the dungeons, 'Save me, sister, for the love of God and our father...' But I cannot save him nor ever could. I cannot even visit him to pray with him or to comfort him. My esteemed brother the Duke forbids it."

"But surely, madama, after all these years your honorable

brother can find a morsel of forgiveness in his heart for his brothers."

"His heart is a stone," she replied. "To him his brothers are traitors, disgraced, forgotten, as good as dead. But in my heart, they live. When I dance in the ballroom where we all practiced our steps together under Maestro Ambrogio's wand, each step I take reminds me that directly below me lie the dungeons. And in my mind I see my brothers partnering each other in some grotesque charade of our *moresca*. Ferrante loved to dance. Even as a little boy, he was the best dancer among all my father's children, more graceful even than I."

She half smiled. "Is there room for him to dance in his cell in the dungeon? I ask myself. Do my Giulio's beautiful eyes ever see the glow of the sunset or the beams of the moon? No. My brothers are as deeply planted in the dank earth as your brother's ashes and I can do as little as you to bring them back. There, you see, you have stopped weeping."

To be sure, I had. "You have helped me to bear my burden, madonna," I told her.

"And you have eased my pain, Grazia," she responded. "Your tears opened a chamber in my heart that I thought was sealed forever."

In that spirit I agreed to follow her advice and attempt to return to life as soon as my month of mourning was finished. "Maestro Vitale loved life and hated gloom," she reminded me. "If you wish to honor his memory you will make yourself a monument to his spirit, if not for your own sake, for that of your son." She hardly paused before adding, "By the way, where is the boy?"

"He is at a private *scuola* that Judah arranged for him," I replied, happy to be able to offer a truthful excuse why she could not meet you. My cub-mother's heart warned me that if once she set eyes on you, so fair and sturdy of limb and so obviously a soldier's son, she would find a way to suck the story of your parentage out of me. And this revelation I was determined to withhold for a time and place of my own choosing.

But I did gratify her wish to have me return to her service the following month—just in time, as it happened, to become an unwilling participant in one of the most scurvy plots in the history of this peninsula.

I believe that we in Madonna Isabella's household got word before anyone else of the Colonna brothers' plan to raid the city of Roma in the name of Emperor Charles V. In fact, Madama was the one who warned his Holiness of the impending danger. How did she gain intelligence of this highly secret plan? Through the indiscretion of a lovesick swain under the spell of one of her *donzelle*.

You who now consort with these young girls daily and who often sport with them in the garden perhaps do not understand how it is that such wellborn young ladies have given Madama's court its slightly raffish reputation. You know her view: that, just as boys of good family are sent as pages to the courts of kings for their worldly education, so her girls come to her court to finish their education as women. You may not have heard the accusation by her enemies that she uses these human adornments to decorate her court in the same way she uses works of art to decorate her *grotta*—that is, to enhance her status in the world and for nefarious political purposes. Madama is hurt by these slanders, for, as she said to me in a confidential moment, "I do not impress these young women into my service, Grazia. They beg to come. Their parents know that at my court they will learn the ways of the world and be launched into the marriage market under the finest auspices. And everyone knows I take good care of them."

She spoke the truth. After less than four months in Roma four of the current crop of *donzelle* were already promised to eligible husbands. But there is an obverse to this pretty picture, the side that Madama prefers to turn to the wall, so to speak. These *donzelle* do not receive their education free. They more than pay their way by acting as magnets for the rich, powerful, and clever men who typically patronize a renowned salon. Furthermore, the girls perform as sponges, albeit delicate and subtle ones, who sop up information and pass it on to their benefactress to be used for the advantage of herself, her family, and her little state.

You may remember that when we first came to this palace, there lived here among the *donzelle* a distant connection of Madama's, Giulia Gonzaga, celebrated as the most beautiful virgin in Italy. Whether or not she was the most beautiful—or indeed a virgin—this jewel of a girl sparkled with enough brilliance to capture the heart of Vespasiano Colonna. The bride was fourteen years old. The grizzled groom was a widower over fifty, very rich, brother to Cardinal Pompeo Colonna. It was considered by all a brilliant match.

Now with the wedding less than a month away, the besotted bridegroom found himself about to attack the city where his beloved bride was tucked away under Madonna Isabella's protection. Passion overcame reason. Fearful that the shock of waking up with troops outside her window would alarm his bride, the old campaigner threw discretion to the winds and sent the girl a note warning her that a secret raid on the Vatican was in the offing.

"Stand fast and have no fear, darling," the foolish man wrote to his Giulia. "You will always be safe in the stronghold of my family where you now reside and soon you will rest within the sheltering arms of your knight, Vespasiano Colonna."

I saw the letter with my own eyes, for of course Giulia made haste to bring it directly to Madama. And from that document Madama, no mean reasoner, not only learned of the raid but was able to estimate when to expect it.

"Vespasiano's dispatch rider tells me he has ridden post from Anagni in sixteen hours. Surely it will take the Colonna troops twice that time to make the same trip," she calculated aloud for my benefit. "So we must tell the Pope that he has one day to prepare himself and the city. And we too must prepare ourselves for the visit of this lovesick cur of a Vespasiano and his marauders."

She was in a terrible rage against Colonna.

"Only weeks ago, Vespasiano signed an honorable truce with the Pope. The Pope trusted him. *I* trusted him. He has proven himself unworthy of our trust."

There are some loyalties she cherishes with utter consistency. I have never seen her turn her back on a member of her own family or the Holy Father. This latter allegiance may not be unrelated to the number of favors she wants from him, but I credit it at least partly to a good Catholic's reverence for the office if not the man who fills it. Whatever her reasons, she did take immediate steps to warn the Pope of what she perceived as a serious danger. And he showed sufficient confidence in her assessment to order the gates of the city closed and to enforce a troop levy at once.

The only one without enough sense to pay attention to her wisdom was your mother. When Madama urged me to bring you to the palace the next day so that you and I would both be safe, I refused. Whatever the meaning of Vespasiano's warning to his bride, I could not believe that he and his brother Pompeo—a *cardinal*—would go to war against the Pope for the sake of the Emperor. The more Madama attempted to persuade me that our safety—perhaps our lives—stood at risk, the more obdurate I became in my refusals to bring you to the palace. I did have my reasons.

Of course she could not force me to take refuge with her. So she finally gave up trying, but not without having the last word. "Go back to the Portico then if you will not be dissuaded," she ordered me. "But be sure to lock your doors and hide your valuables." With that she turned away to other matters as if to say good riddance, but as I backed out of the room in the customary way, she added with a disapproving shake of her head, "You are as stiff-necked and reckless as you were when you were a girl, Grazia. I hope for your sake and that of your son that you do not live to regret your obstinacy."

She had offered help. Her offer had been scorned. Another woman would have left me to stew in my own juice. But Madama is not small-minded. That night she sent her coach to offer me a second chance. Knowing my obstinate nature, she also sent along the letter she had received only hours before from Cardinal Pompeo Colonna himself, wherein he had advised her that he and several of his staff would be occupying the west wing of the palace within a few hours. She was not to be alarmed. But it was made quite clear that she had better clear her possessions out of the west wing—some thirty-odd rooms including the main salon and all the fine reception rooms—on the double quick.

"We stand only twenty leagues from Porto San Giovanni," the letter concluded, "and will be at the Piazza S.S. Apostoli in time for supper tonight."

If indeed Roma was the target of the Colonna brothers, there was hardly a safer place to wait out this raid than in their own palace, which, despite its being on loan to Madonna Isabella, they apparently meant to use as their headquarters. In the face of that undeniable reality even my obduracy gave way. I bade the coachman wait and ran upstairs to awaken you.

I know that in your eyes that night was all adventure. The midnight awakening. The hasty toilette. The wonderful golden coach. The ride through the streets of Roma at break-neck speed. The sight of the shimmering facade of this great palace by moonlight.

I was not so charmed. I entered the place full of misgivings. You must have sensed my panic. I remember that you offered me your arm as we passed slowly under the grinning *putti* carved into the lintel over the portal.

In no time you were fast asleep in the trundle that was set up for your comfort in my workroom. But I did not find such ready ease within the sheltering walls of the Colonna Palace. Sleepless, I paced back and forth across the chamber, driven by restlessness and confusion.

What my mind could comprehend my imagination still could not encompass: that thousands of Imperial supporters and hirelings were even now converging on the city; that, in the name of the Holy Roman Emperor, these "Christians" were prepared to penetrate the heart of Christendom with their swords and to violate its Holy of Holies.

What I did not know that night—just as well for my fluttering peace of mind—was that the raid on Roma was only a feint, a rehearsal, so to speak, for a serious assault on the papacy to come, this to be led by the Emperor's strong right arm, Constable Bourbon, not long since the strong right arm of the King of France.

My mind kept returning to that little boy who could not decide which toy soldiers best suited him and who, when he was grown and became Constable Bourbon, had the same difficulty deciding which real troops deserved his loyalty. What decided him to desert Francis and go over to that German weasel the Emperor? What turned this chivalrous knight into a traitor? Madonna Isabella, who has known him since he was a child—he being her nephew on her husband's side—admits herself puzzled by his willful pursuit of self-destruction. It took Lord Pirro, our mole hidden deep inside the French court, to ferret out an explanation.

FROM DANILO'S ARCHIVE

TO GRAZIA DEI ROSSI AT THE COLONNA PALACE, ROMA
Good news, my love! My petition has been granted. The Holy Father has released me from my bondage to bloody Francis and bloody France. I leave for Lombardia within the week, and thence to Roma.

This letter comes to you from Chambord, the site of the King's most recent burning enthusiasm. Here he is building a grand new palace upon the design of our own Leonardo. He has shown me drawings of the plans and I have pronounced them excellent although I have as little right to speak on architecture as on the movements of the planets in their orbits. If he had shown me da Vinci's plans for fortifications or siege machines, I could have responded with confidence. But alas, I am not a soldier here. Nor, I fear, much of a diplomat either, since I have not achieved a single one of the objectives I was sent here to attain. No navy blockades the port of Napoli; no Swiss have been levied; not a white piece has been sent to protect Roma.

As for the King's mother, Madama Louise, whom I hoped to enlist on our side because of her well-known hatred of Constable Bourbon, she does indeed hate him. I even know why. If I did not love you so much I would leave you there suspended. But knowing your appetite for the secrets of the human heart, I will give you one juicy enough to satisfy all the gossips of Europe.

It seems that all these years, without anyone knowing of it, the King's mother, Louise, has harbored a mad, incestuous passion for her nephew the Constable. This is the genesis of all that follows. Surely you can already guess how it had to go.

Bourbon's young wife dies. She was an angel. He is heartbroken. In the midst of his heavy mourning he receives a condolence letter from his aunt, Louise, in which she urges him to resume his duties to life, to France, to the noble house of which they are both members and . . . to marry. Her!

Bourbon is appalled, enraged, insulted. He bursts into a furious rant in the presence of the lady's emissary. "Does your mistress actually believe that I, who have been married to the finest woman in the world, would stoop to marry the worst woman in the world?" he rages.

Posthaste, the messenger relays Bourbon's message to Louise. In a rant equal to Bourbon's she calls upon her son — Francis, the King — to avenge this insult to his mother. "If you do not redeem my honor from the stain placed on it by Charles Bourbon, I will disown you and consider you a coward king."

A coward king is, of course, the last thing Francis wants to be thought, especially by his mother. From that moment on Bourbon, the King's strong right arm and best friend, becomes anathema. He is humiliated at court, his lands threatened, his advice ignored, his will thwarted at every turn. After two years of this treatment he throws himself into the willing arms of the Emperor, avowed enemy of France and rival of King Francis. How do you like that for a footnote to history, Messer Guicciardini?

A personal note. Armed with what I thought to be the key to Louise's heart, I sped to Paris to fan the flames of her rage and thus, I hoped, to swell the Pope's empty coffers with French ecus. Alas. Much as Louise hates Bourbon, she loves money even more. What I received from the lady was a paltry offering which stands to our need as a fly to an elephant.

How can I have been so blind to the profligacy and vanity of this life of courts? When I think how I berated you for your opinions on the subject, I am ashamed. Do you forgive me, my love? Say this for me at least. My lesson was long in the learning but is in the end well learned. I tell you this so that you may know that I love you for your fine mind as well as for your sublime body. And sign myself forever your friend, lover, pupil, and at last to be husband.

(signed) Ever, P. G. at Chambord, France.

January 10, 1527.

55

THERE IS NO NEED TO RECALL FOR YOU THE AMAZE-
ments of the Colonna brothers' raid on Roma last
September. You saw their arrival in the square below us
with your own wide eyes and thrilled to the blast of the trumpets when they sallied forth to sack the Vatican palace.

Your head is filled with battles and glory. Don't bother to
deny it. With each day that passes I see increasing evidence
of your father's blood in you—his daring spirit, his soldier's
appetite for the joust. Do not mistake a mother's concern for
disapproval. If anything, finding these qualities of his in you
makes me love you more—and fear more to lose you. I do not
want my son to perish in a burst of chivalry.

Look at the underbellies of these bold knights whom you
admire: Cardinal Colonna, who connived secretly to unseat
his master, the Pope, in the hope of securing the triple crown
for himself; his brother Vespasiano, who suffered no qualm
of conscience when he betrayed his oath of fealty to the Pope
within weeks of swearing it. And what of the so-called *Holy
Roman Emperor*? Madama explained the Colonna raid to me
as a family quarrel—those were her words—between the

Holy Father and his loving son Charles: a warning to the Pope to cease treating with the French. The Emperor would never countenance a genuine attack on the city. So she said.

But Caesar tells us that once a city reveals itself to be soft and ripe, it is bound to be picked off. Now tell me, my son, if you were an emperor who craved to be lord of Europe, and the Colonnas revealed to you a plum as ripe for picking as the Vatican, would you not be tempted to gobble it up?

To Madama the Colonnas are the real villains of the piece. She will never forgive Vespasiano for breaking faith with the Pope. "When I think that I have promised my beautiful niece to that dishonorable cur..." she raged. It was too late to break off the marriage agreement but she vowed that she would refuse to attend the wedding. Then she added, quite proud of herself, "One must maintain some principle." As though refusing a wedding invitation ranks as a major act of defiance. If this travesty of ethics is what we get from a woman who has enjoyed the finest moral education in Italy, what can we expect from the European rulers who were not exposed to the humanism of Vittorino's school?

Judah is right, I thought. This palace—this world of pomp and *lusso*—is maintained by compromise and opportunism, the worst place to bring up a child. I made plans to spirit you out of this sink and back to the Portico d'Ottavia the moment the Colonnas were safely gone from Roma. But before I could commandeer a *bravo* to accompany us, Madama summoned me. She has read my mind, I thought. But no. She simply needed my services to whip up dispatches to her son and her brother telling them of Cardinal Colonna's one-day campaign.

"And mind you, he did not even trouble himself to apologize for upsetting my household and disturbing my rest." I remember the outrage in her voice as she dictated.

"There is something of the brute in these Colonnese, Grazia," she remarked thoughtfully. "With all their pretensions to ancient lineage, they are at heart bandits from the hills who cannot resist a call to pillage and rapine."

Note that nowhere in this outpouring of indignation did Madama talk of relinquishing the cardinal's loan of his palace for the duration of her stay in Roma. That idea never came close to her mind. It is so pleasant and comfortable here in the Palazzo Colonna with its delightful gardens. And the alternative—her son-in-law Urbino's palace, low-lying and damp without a garden to speak of—would not do, not at all.

Long after her letters were dictated the lady continued to fulminate against the Colonnese, but the tirade was finally brought to a close by a yawn. "I am tired, Grazia. So must you be." She raised her hand to her brow. "Rest awhile. I will do the same."

I moved quickly toward the door. But no sooner had I reached the portal than I was recalled.

"I am remiss. How could I have forgotten? Your son slept under our roof last night and I did not even inquire after him. Was he comfortable in his little trundle bed? I hope it was not too short to accommodate his frame. Since I have never seen the boy, I have no way of knowing his height. How old is he now?"

"Ten years," I replied.

"Does he resemble you or his father?"

"In certain respects, both; in some, neither."

"Hmm." Madama knows when she is being put off. "I hope the young man will forgive me for not welcoming him myself on his first visit to our court, but the events of yesterday…" Her hands fluttered. "Perhaps next time…"

I drew a breath of relief.

"On the other hand he might take it as a sign of my disrespect for you and his father if I did not welcome him personally."

"Not at all, madonna. He will understand," I hastened to reassure her.

"No. It is not right. I must see him and greet him if only for a moment. Quickly, Grazia, fetch the boy."

What you remember of that interview is the gracious princess on the raised gilt chair that she affects even in her dressing room…her welcome, her warmth, her gracious invitation to come to the palace any time, even to attend her fencing school.

What I remember is how she beckoned you closer, ever closer, and how, when you were no farther than three feet from her face, she pulled up her spectacles, attached them to the bridge of her nose, and murmured, "Let me see your eyes." Those eyes. Bluer than cornflowers. A dead giveaway.

"And when did you say you were born?" she asks.

You, already half a courtier through some combination of observation and blood, do not remind the lady that you never did say when you were born. Instead, you answer courteously, "I was born in the year 1516."

"Ah yes, the same year as the battle of Marignano."

"Oh no, madonna," you correct her, overproud of your fine memory just like your mother. "I was born in 1516. The battle was fought at Marignano in 1515. I know because my father was wounded there while in the service of the King of France."

"In 1515, of course," the lady concurs graciously. "I remember being told of Maestro Judah's wounds and of how he was carried home more dead than alive just after the battle, carried all the way to Venezia." She pauses. "And you were born in the year 1516, some nine months later…"

Her voice trails off into a knowing smile.

FROM DANILO'S ARCHIVE

TO THE ESTEEMED MARCHESANA ISABELLA D'ESTE DA GONZAGA AT ROMA

Illustrious, Brave, and Honored Mother:

You are quick to inform me of the Colonnas' dastardly attack on the Holy Father—for which I thank you many times. But nowhere in your dispatch do you speak of plans to leave Roma. I agree with you that Pompeo Colonna is a pig and that his brother Vespasiano is a cur. But with all respect, Mother, the point of the exercise is that the Emperor has his eye on Roma.

Wishing not to alarm you, I may have spoken too softly of the German hordes camped in my territory these past months. Trust me, the rumors you hear are only too true. Georg Frundsberg does keep knotted at his saddle side a silken rope with which he intends to hang the Holy Father. To him, the Pope is the Antichrist. Yes, Mother, the commander that the Emperor has sent down into Italy to save us is a flaming, believing, bloody Lutheran! He worships two idols: his feudal lord, Emperor Charles, and his spiritual lord, Martin Luther; for them he is prepared to sacrifice fortune, honor, his very life.

This is a man out of the Dark Ages, a knight the like of whom we in Italy know nothing. He has mortgaged all of his lands in order to mount this campaign with no help from the Emperor. The whole of his personal fortune has gone into this expedition. Listening to him talk, it is as if we were living five hundred years ago and he was setting off on a Crusade to the Holy Land.

Let others disdain his barbarian ways. I do not. I urge you, Mother, remove yourself from his path, for he is a prodigious force entirely capable of overrunning this peninsula like a tidal wave. Let me remind you that his men are Protestants and bear no respect for a Catholic princess. To them, you are simply a rich marchesana loaded with clothes and jewels and molti soldi. Your fame, which has spread throughout the world, has made you a tempting target.

Go anywhere—to Urbino, Pesaro, Venezia, wherever pleases you if Mantova no longer does—but leave Roma now, for the sake of a son who loves you more than he loves his own life.

(signed) Fed. G. at Mantova.

January 3, 1527.

56

JUDAH RETURNED FROM FERRARA A MAN OBSESSED with one idea: The Italy we knew was doomed. The Colonna raid had confirmed his worst fears. The barbarians were upon us. We must leave Italy at once to escape the holocaust.

Without even consulting me he wrote a letter to Suleiman the Magnificent agreeing to enter the Sultan's service if he was still wanted. When I questioned the move he replied, "If this country were my patient, I would tell his relatives that the time had come to say goodbye to him. That is exactly the course I propose to follow with Italy." He then added, in a much stronger tone, "The matter is decided. You must obey me in this, Grazia."

His high-handedness neither reassured me of his wisdom nor allayed my fears. I had heard tales of the life women led in the Sultan's seraglio. Would I be expected to live there? To take the veil like a nun? Where would you be brought up? Would we be permitted to have our own house?

To all my questions, he answered brusquely, "It will all be arranged. There is no time to waste on details." Details!

"I cannot agree to go and certainly not to carry my son back into the Dark Ages because of some phantom in my husband's imagination," I confided to Madonna Isabella, who stepped into the role of my counselor in that troubled time. "He asks too much."

"Far too much," she agreed.

"And he will not be moved," I went on, "even to the extent of writing another letter to the Sultan to request answers to my questions. I cannot go. He leaves me no choice but to refuse."

This time I heard no sly digs from her on the subject of Jewish nerves. She listened attentively, considered thoughtfully, and when she volunteered advice, it was prudent and conciliatory.

"Why not let Maestro Judah go on ahead to Constantinople as a sort of advance party?" she asked. "He can write and tell you what life would be like there for you. And in the interim, you can move in with me and become my confidential secretary."

Her suggestion seemed to me a solution worthy of Solomon. But when I carried the proposal home to Judah, he rejected it out of hand. "You don't know the Germans as I do," he explained. "They are fanatics and always will be. Without them in the picture, the Emperor and the French king might have gone on bickering over Italy until the next century. But Luther has transformed the Emperor's cause into a jihad. Now that the Colonnas have exposed the soft underbelly of this city, it is only a matter of time before the Imperials swoop down on us. And when they come, they will make the Goths and the Vandals look like benign visitors by comparison."

Could we not simply leave Roma for a time, until the worst was over? I pressed him.

"You think the worst will be over once these new barbarians have seized the Vatican? Ha!" he barked. "An attack on Roma is only the beginning, my dear. The worst comes when the church rouses itself to fight back. Do you need a picture? Think of Spain since 1492. The Inquisition is master of all, even of kings. Heresy-hunting is the favored sport. The auto-da-fé has replaced feasting and dancing. And God help the Jews.

"You tell me you fear to lose your freedom in the seraglio," he continued. "How much freedom will you have in the new Imperial Roma? You told me once you would suffocate and die in the air of the Venetian ghetto. I remind you of that and beg you to allow me to save you from such a fate here in Roma."

How well he knew me. The city of his vision — stern, repressive, pitiless — could never serve me as home. Even were I to convert and save myself, I could never stand in a crowd cheering while a man burned to a cinder the way the Florentines did when they burned Savonarola. Or as I have no doubt the Portuguese did when they burned my brother Jehiel in the public square in Tavira.

When I advised Madonna Isabella of my final and irrevocable decision to leave Roma with my husband, her first response was to berate me as an ingrate for rejecting her munificent offer. But her pique quickly gave way to serious questions as to why I was willing to give up the opportunity of a lifetime.

"To be the confidential secretary to a princess is an honor never yet vouchsafed a woman and not likely to be offered to a Jewess again," she pointed out. "Think before you refuse me. Think of your son's future and of the honor you will bring to your people."

I *had* thought. I had thought so much that I had no thoughts left that I could call my own. So, like a dumb puppet, I simply repeated Judah's prophecy: that bad times were upon us and that the Jews would be the first to suffer.

"Underneath that Platonism of his your Judah is just another old Jewish soothsayer crying doom and gloom," was her response to his prophecy. "But let us give him the benefit of the doubt. Let us agree to his case. If the Jews are doomed to suffer, why be a Jew at all? Why cling to this cursed faith?"

"He is too old to change now, madonna, too embedded in Judaism," I replied.

"And you? Just because the world is finished for him, must that mean that it is over for you as well? And for your son?"

I had asked myself that question too many times in the pre-
ceding weeks to find a ready affirmative answer.

Encouraged by my silence, she continued. "Think of the
boy, Grazia. Why subject him to such a hard life? With his
looks, his bearing, he would be instantly accepted as a member
of my household, a student in the Pope's *sapienza*, an apprentice in the fencing corps of noble young men. With those blue
eyes anything he wished could be his." Then as if it were an
afterthought, she added, "I never could understand where he
got those angel's eyes. If I did not know you better, Grazia, I
would suspect some..." She raised her eyebrows knowingly.
"Why, Grazia, you have turned all rosy. Have I touched a chord?
Have I uncovered a secret? Come, Grazia, tell me, is the father
someone I know?"

I turned my head away to ward off the attack I knew was
coming, but she simply leaned over, took my face firmly in her
hands and turned it toward her own. "Let us have a game," she
cooed. "I will ask you questions and you will answer them. But
you must tell the truth."

"That is a child's game, madonna," I retorted. "And what
you speak of is not a childish matter."

"But of course it is," she disagreed sweetly. "For it is something that happened long ago, as in a fairy tale...and with
someone known to me...Have I not hit the mark?"

"Yes, madonna," I confessed wearily.

"But not a Jew," she went on. "The blush has already told
me that. A Christian most certainly. Handsome. He must be to
have fathered such a son. Known to me...known *well* to me...
a member of my family, perhaps...a kinsman...That narrows
the list."

Why does she not pounce and be done with this cat-and-
mouse game? I thought.

"A kinsman of mine who was in Venezia directly after the
battle of Pavia," she went on. "A kinsman of mine who was in
your house nine months before your son was born...The boy's
father must be...How stupid of me not to have guessed."

Of course she had already guessed. But years of playing *scartino* had taught her to save her trump card for the final trick. She played it. "Now that we all know the truth, it is out of the question for you to take this boy away from his father, is it not?"

"Do you refer to my husband, madonna?" I asked, knowing well she did not.

"I refer to my kinsman, Lord Pirro Gonzaga of Bozzuolo," she replied directly. "Who it appears is the boy's father by blood, a man who proposed marriage to you even before he knew your boy was his. It would be wrong by the canon of any religion or law to keep this father and his son apart, Grazia. You know it in your heart."

These plain words penetrated the layers of false reasoning that Judah had laid on me. The insoluble problems — whether to go to Turkey, whether to seek a divorce, where my loyalties lay, how best to serve you, Judah, Lord Pirro, myself — all crystallized in an instant and I knew what I must do.

Ten years before, Judah and I had made an unspoken pact to keep the truth of your fatherhood hidden — from the world, from you, from ourselves. As I dragged my feet homeward past the ancient Portico d'Ottavia I prepared the words that would blaze a path through that deep silence, words as simple and direct as Madama's to me. "Danilo is not your son, Judah. You cannot take him to Turkey. He is not yours to take."

These were the words I delivered. They tore through the air like arrows and hit their target in the heart. I heard Judah groan with pain. But for me there was no turning back.

"I will not go with you to Turkey," I continued, pounding away at the stricken figure slumped in a chair across the room. "Nor will Danilo. He will stay here with me. He will be told the truth. It is his right to know his father."

"I am his father," he croaked in a broken voice.

"No, you are not," I insisted, relentless. "His father is—"

He raised his head and held up his hand. "Spare me that knowledge, Grazia. The name is not the issue here, nor the man."

"But Danilo is our joint concern, Judah," I told him. "We have deceived him with our silence. We have kept him from his true father. We must give him back."

He shook his head violently. "I will not give him up. I cannot. He is the only son I will ever have."

"You have no choice," I replied, made strong by my belated conversion to the cause of truth. "I mean to tell him tonight with or without your assent." Even as I spoke the words, I regretted my intransigence. "Judah..." I moved close to him, the better to engage his eyes. "You and I have suffered grievously from the lie that came between us once. We must not allow a second lie to come between us and our son. All I ask is that we tell him the truth."

"The truth is..." He straightened his shoulders and lifted his chin as an adversary might do. "The truth is that according to the law of Israel, being the son of a Jewish mother, he is a Jew."

"Then tell him that," I replied softly, my harshness somehow mitigated by his will to fight this hopeless battle to the end. "And tell him how much you love him. For that is surely as important as any law. But tell him the truth."

"Very well." Thank God, I thought. "But not yet."

This time his intransigence only served to try my patience. "You are bargaining over Danilo like a pawnbroker, Judah. I will not have it."

"Oh yes you will." His reply came back harsh and bullying. "Let me remind you that I too have a stake in this boy, Grazia. I have nurtured him. I have taught him. I have trained him in the rituals of our people. I have dreamed of standing at his side on the bimah and seeing him welcomed into the community of Jewish men. I have earned the right to fight for my son, have I not?"

I nodded my assent.

"Danilo stands little more than a year from the time he must prepare to become a man by the laws of Israel. Let us make that waiting period a time of probation for him in the Christian world. I propose that we adopt Madonna Isabella's plan. I will go to Turkey. You will introduce Danilo to all the delights of the life you have chosen for him and for yourself... Oh yes, you have. If we are after truth, let us have the whole truth. I know that I am fighting for both you and my son."

In honesty I could not deny it.

"At the end of a year, you will divorce me or not as you choose. Danilo, with all the facts laid out before him, will choose either his blood father and the Christian life or me and the life in which he has been raised. But until the year is up, there will be no talk of divorce, no conversions. All I ask is one year to make my case."

"And what of his blood father? Now that Madonna Isabella knows who he is, he is bound to find out. There are no secrets in courts. Is the man to wait for a year to claim his son?"

"Perhaps if you remind him of the tender care his son has received at my hands, he will take pity on me. Can you, Grazia, will you plead my case with him?" It would have taken a harder heart than mine to deny this proud man reduced to begging a favor.

So it was agreed. And two days later you and I journeyed to Ostia in Madama's golden coach to say our goodbyes to the man you had known all your life as your father.

FROM DANILO'S ARCHIVE

TO GRAZIA DEI ROSSI DEL MEDIGO AT ROMA

Grazia:

I left France a happy man, headed for home and the woman he loved and trusted with his whole heart. But a letter awaited me here at Piacenza that tore my happiness to tatters. I know you will find this intemperate expression foreign to my usual manner, but I assure you that when I take stock of my years on earth, I will mark this fourteenth day of February in the year 1527 as the low point of my life.

The letter that greeted me on arrival here, written by a member of Madonna Isabella's court who need not be named, was so loaded with innuendo and malice that my honor as a gentleman bade me destroy and forget it. Still, the possibility of a betrayal of my heart and my honor torments me.

Can it be possible that the boy I offered to adopt is indeed my own son? That you have hidden this boy away from me for the eleven years of his life? That you are capable of such a monstrous deception?

If this sounds to you like the raving of a madman, if you have no knowledge of it, forgive me my doubts. But if by some godforsaken chance you do, please do not wound me any further with evasions. Only the truth can cauterize this festering sore.

Everything in me longs to rush on to Roma, to look into your eyes and to hear from your lips that these slanders are the inventions of a vicious mind. But, to rub salt into my wound, my mission has been extended. I am ordered to make a detour to Urbino's camp, there to insinuate myself into his confidence and to ferret out precisely what the man is doing at Milano. As you know, he has led the world to believe that, in his words, he has the Imperials blocked up there tighter than a virgin's hymen. But my master, the Holy Father, suspects that all is not what it seems with the blockade. So I, the failed diplomat, am now seconded into the spying game, for which I have even less heart than for diplomacy. You know that I am not an admirer of Urbino. In fact, I find him personally unpleasant and professionally incompetent. Nonetheless he is a fellow officer. He is also son-in-law to my kinswoman Madonna Isabella, and the idea of using his hospitality in order to spy on him stinks in my nostrils.

I will, of course, do my duty. But I am crippled in my resolve by a wretchedness of spirit unlike anything I have ever known. I trusted you, Grazia. Have I been deceived by someone so close to my heart?

Signed with a heavy heart, P.G.

Piacenza, February 14, 1527.

Greetings from Ferrara, dear sister:

As Koheleth says, "Vanity, vanity, all is vanity and a striving after wind." Truly, a man struggling to make his own fate engages himself in a futile enterprise just as a sailor does who strives after a fair wind. It will come when it will come, or not, as God wills.

On Tuesday, the fifth day of March, I will marry Penina. I could have held out indefinitely against all human persuasion, but against God's will I am powerless. My duty is clearly prescribed in the Holy Book. I must take my brother's place in his widow's bed without delay. Wish us good fortune, Grazia. Congratulations, I do not deserve. I am simply doing my duty as a Jewish man.

During the days of settling the accounts of our beloved brother, God bless his memory, my mind seized the opportunity to dwell on matters far removed from the loan bank and the counting table. Perhaps it was Jehiel's martyrdom that set me free from my worldly life. All I know is that some force entered my brain and, as if drawing aside a curtain, exposed to me in a flash the true meaning of a point of argumentation between your honorable husband and my late lamented brother which I never wholly understood.

"A Jew must be an observing Jew; there is no other kind; for ours is a religion of practice, not transcendence." How many times I have heard Judah expound this view. Yet only in these past weeks have I come to a true understanding of it. A man cannot deny the practice and pretend to embrace the faith any more than he can live the life of a Christian by day and the life of a Jew by night. For me, the issue has come to this: Am I a Jew or am I not? If I am, then I must observe the law.

In this instance my obedience takes the form of marriage to my brother's widow. Since I have made that decision others crowd in on me at a rapid pace. No longer will I submit to being called Geronimo. My name as it is written in God's book is Gershom. Men must either call me that or cease to address me. No longer will I stumble through life half blind, showing one side of my double face to the synagogue, the other to the city. I am a whole man at last. A Jew. A banker. Soon to be the husband of a Jewish wife and, God willing, to produce Jewish sons.

I believe in God and His commandments. I find graven images abhorrent, even those I once adored as the essence of beauty. I am finished with Geronimo, with the divine Raffaello, and with the flesh of the pig. And my spirit is the lighter for it.

Had God not seen fit to take our brother from us and to force me to this decision, I might never have known relief from the agony of the double life. I can only believe that it was my destiny finally to live the life of an observing Jew, just as it was Jehiel's to die a martyr's death. I mourn him. But in between the teardrops I glory in my release from the curse of Janus. There is a logic and clarity in this life that far better suits my nature. Geronimo is now a dead man. Gershom alone lives.

God's blessing on you, Grazia, from your brother who at last knows his rightful name.

(signed) Gershom dei Rossi, in his own hand.

Ferrara, February 20, 1527.

57

TODAY IS THE DAY OF LORD PIRRO'S RETURN FROM Urbino's camp. The moment of truth is upon me. If you are ever tempted to practice deceit, my son, remember this: Only shame ensues and a pain in the heart.

I have good reason to believe that the man I love is hurrying home not to embrace me but to accuse and reproach me. This time I will not flinch from admitting my deceit. I vow not to write in this book again until I have told your father that in the Venetian ghetto I bore him a child and that you, the boy he knows as the child of Judah del Medigo, are in fact his son. My hand shakes as I write these words.

LATER.

The deed is done. Lord Pirro knows all and forgives all. Back from Lombardia he came to me, his beard powdered with the dust of the road and his *camicia* damp from the exertion of a day's ride. But that sweat smelled like civet perfume to me. I do love him, Danilo, not only for his fine figure and his flashing smile but for the man within—open, frank, and plain-dealing.

He did not prolong the moment of truth as others might have done; nor did he force me into blurting out my confession by maintaining an austere silence. Those mean-minded ways are not his. Instead, he first took me up in his arms and embraced me to show his love for me; then he spoke at once of the matter in both our minds.

"Is it true, Grazia, that Danilo is my son?" he asked.

And I answered, simply, "Yes."

He must have rehearsed the moment in his mind, for his words came out in the way an actor speaks a speech, as if prelearned.

"It is a cruel thing you have done, Grazia," he began, not in a reproachful way but, rather, as if saddened by my deceit. "To keep a father from his son and a son from his father...it is a cruel thing." He paused a moment, shaking his head as if he still could not believe the depth of my deception. "When I received the letter at Piacenza hinting that my son was being passed off as another man's, my heart flooded with rage. But I have had a long ride down to Roma and time in the saddle to reflect. And that time has led me to see that I cannot blame you. Abandoned by me, how could you be other than wary ever after? You and your son had a good home with the Jew del Medigo. You only did what any mother would have done. You looked first to the safety of your babe. I must respect that."

"You forgive me, then?" I asked, not quite believing that I would be so easily let off.

"On one condition. That you divorce the Jew and marry me at once. And this time, I will not be denied."

But denied he was. I could not—would not—go back on my undertaking to Judah: a year of consideration before arriving at a final decision. "It is the very least I can give the man," I explained. "In repayment for all the years he has taken care of me...and our son. All he asks is this small gift of time."

"A year is no small gift," he corrected me. "In some lives, a year can be forever. We are no longer young."

"But we are together with our son," I reminded him. "Judah

is not asking me to retire to a cloister. Only to put off the divorce and my baptism and marriage to you."

"And what of my acknowledgment of my son? Is that to be delayed too?"

"The decision is up to us," I answered. "I will understand if you insist on telling Danilo at once. But my heart tells me we had much better approach the subject cautiously. Let him get to know you as a man before he is forced to accept you as his father."

In some ways this was a harder condition even than the delay of our marriage. His whole being clamored to say the words "My son," and to hear you answer "Father." But for your sake he agreed—albeit reluctantly—that for the present at least he would devote himself to becoming a part of your life and making you a part of his and leave the moment of revelation to some future day.

Blood calls out to blood. You took to each other like a falcon and its fledgling. Before long it was, "Lord Pirro has invited me to go hunting. May I go, Madonna Madre?" Next: "I should like to go for a walk in the garden with Lord Pirro after supper, Madonna Madre. He has promised to tell me about the siege at Marignano." Then: "Lord Pirro has invited me to accompany him to the Vatican tomorrow. May I, madonna?" And finally: "Madonna Madre, I wish to ride to the northern battlefields with Lord Pirro as his page. He is heading the Pope's party to negotiate with the Imperials. I will get to see the landsknechts and that Bourbon they call 'the French Devil.' Tell him I may go, madonna. Please."

I might have found the resolve to make you unhappy for your own good. But the prospect of denying both of you was beyond my will. I said yes to the proposal, with reservations.

"You must promise never to let him out of your sight," I cautioned Lord Pirro. "Milano is a city under siege. They say that Urbino has it bottled up tighter than a . . ."

"Than a virgin's hymen?" He finished my sentence for me. "Well, my love, here's a piece of highly confidential information for you. Bourbon was out of Milano four days ago. Like many other virgin hymens, Urbino's barrier proved illusory at the moment of penetration. It never was the army of the Papal League that kept the Imperials blocked in Milano. Bourbon's own men held him back. They refused to budge from Milano until they were paid the two months' back pay they were owed. Charles Habsburg may claim the titles of King of Spain and King of Burgundy as well as Holy Roman Emperor and ruler of God knows what lands across the seas, but apparently he is no more solvent than our own poor Pope."

"But now you say the Imperials are out of Milano. Who paid off the troops?"

"Bourbon did, out of his own pocket," he replied, then added with a rueful smile, "Nothing requires a more bound-less infusion of money than war. And apparently nobody has enough money to fight this one."

"Still they keep on fighting," I reminded him.

"War is a fact of life, Grazia." He was not smiling now. "It is also a fact that I am a soldier. Any day now Bourbon will join his army to Frundsberg's in Lombardia. I am delegated to treat with them as an emissary from the Papal League. I want to take Danilo with me and show him history being made."

"You wish to take him to a military camp? To consort with ruffians and soldiers?" That was even worse than Milano.

But he had an answer that silenced my objections. "Why not, Grazia? He *is* a soldier's son."

FROM DANILO'S ARCHIVE

Madonna Madre:

This dispatch is being written all in a rush to reach you by the fastest courier. Please do not judge my grammar or the carelessness of my pen. I wish you to know of the events of this day from no other person than me, your son who loves you and respects you and thanks you for permitting me to make this amazing journey in the company of Lord Pirro of Bozzuolo so that I may experience history at first hand and thus further my education.

Today I saw history made before my eyes. I witnessed a mutiny and I saw the great German general fall into a fit from the exertion of trying to subdue his men, called landsknechts. But these Germans would not be stayed. They roared and stamped and raged like wild beasts, screaming, "We want money! Give us money!"

With tears streaming down his face in rivulets (I do not exaggerate, Mama), old Frundsberg begged them to serve the Emperor and wait patiently for their pay. He called them his children. But they were past listening. Two in the front lowered their halberds at him. At him, their leader! He reached for his great sword. But even as he drew it from the scabbard, he fell back upon a drum behind him and lay still as a corpse before our eyes.

As soon as the apoplexy struck him, the soldiers began to see how wicked they had been to treat the old man with so little respect. Now it was their turn to cry. But it was too late. They raised him on their shoulders and carried him to his tent. Then we left the camp to return to Piacenza. Now we hear that he is dead. You and the Holy Father will be the first in Roma to hear of this.

Lord Pirro is very kind to me and reminds me to inform you that he watches over me so that no harm comes to me, and that I sleep under two heavy wool mats and drink no more than three glasses of well-watered wine a day.

Lord Pirro says the death of General Frundsberg has made his task here easier although it is very regrettable. The old man was very gallant even though he was fighting on the other side. Now Lord Pirro has only one general to deal with: the Duke of Bourbon. We saw him today too but not in audience. Our audience was to be with General Frundsberg but he is dead.

The dispatch rider is about to leave for Roma. If I witness any more historic events, I will write you a complete description immediately for I know you will love to hear such reports.

From what I am able to deduce, all the soldiers on both sides are very brave except for the Duke of Urbino, who commands the Pope's forces here in the north. Please do not tell Madonna Isabella I said this. I know that this duke (whom we have not seen for he is off somewhere hiding from danger) is married to Madama's daughter, the lady Leonora, and I do not wish to bring her distress or shame. But oh, Mama, you should hear how they speak of his cowardice. It would sadden you as it does me and Lord Pirro. A cowardly soldier, he says, brings disgrace upon the whole profession. And I agree.

Now I must pour on the wax and seal this dispatch. Lord Pirro has given me his signet so I may use it for a sealer. He was surprised that I had no signet of my own and says that when we get back to Roma he will have one made to my own design by Benvenuto Cellini. What shall I adopt as my escutcheon? Please, Mama, help me to decide for I am wanting in knowledge of ancient lore and you are very wise and learned in such things.

Lord Pirro also plans to have made to my measure a suit of armor for me to wear into battle if I choose to embrace the profession of soldier. I explained that my honorable father hoped for me to enter the university and become a scholar and rabbi like himself. Lord Pirro says there is still much time for me to make up my mind. But he believes, knowing my father and you both, that my parents would not want to force me into a profession against my wishes. And I agree. I was correct to agree, was I not, honorable mother? It would not make Papa angry if I became a soldier, would it? Of course it is much too early to tell. Lord Pirro says that, above all, I must not make a precipitate decision but oh, Mama, I do love war.

Your obedient and affectionate son, Captain Danilo del Medigo. (Do not be offended, Mama. Here in camp, there is much jesting and I have taken up the habit.) March 14, 1527, Piacenza.

Most beloved mistress, soon to be wife:

We arrived in time to witness the death of Georg Frundsberg. They say he died of apoplexy but I tell you he died of a broken heart. Driven mad by hunger and cold and filth and wet, his men turned on him. Danilo witnessed this bit of history.

Now I begin to deal with the Duke of Bourbon, another vein of metal from the German. This one is deeply buried yet mercurial in its substance. In spite of my loathing of all traitors, I cannot help but admire his resolution and fortitude. He led the Emperor's Milanese forces through a blockade of troops far superior in numbers and did it without ammunition, without any assurance of provisions or any sign of support from his master the Emperor. To unite with Frundsberg he made a daring crossing over the Trebbia. Does this ring a bell in your learned head, my love? It is the very Trebbia where Hannibal enjoyed his great victory in, I believe, the year 218.

Today, only two days after Frundsberg's death, the landsknechts converged on Bourbon's tent like a band of cannibals, out for blood. To his credit, Bourbon faced up to them squarely. He assured them that he was their leader now and that he would care for them as much as for his own men. He invoked "Mahomet's law" on their behalf, giving them the right to take their pay in plunder and pillage. And to back up his rhetoric he brought out from his tent every silver vessel and ring and jewel and treasure he possessed and offered to share his possessions with them, reserving for himself only the clothes he had on and the gleaming surcoat of silver he wears over his armor by which his men can recognize him in the turmoil of battle. The landsknechts were won over. They ended their mutiny swearing to serve him until the end even if it led them to the devil.

Between the world as it is here in the camp and as it is imagined in Roma stretches a chasm so deep that I cannot find the words to fill it. This army is rapidly approaching the point of no return. Each mile they advance takes them farther from home and closer to the Holy City. Yesterday Bourbon consulted with his astrologers and was assured by them that all the omens are in his favor. Today he makes preparations to break camp and march south into Toscana. Perhaps when this deadly war machine of his is pointed at the heart of Firenze the Pope will see the light and send the 150,000 ducats needed to avert the sack of his own city.

On a lighter note, Danilo adds a postscript to his previous letter. What a boy we have made together, my love. His beauty and modesty make me the most enviable of fathers and you, of mothers. Is it too late for us to duplicate our triumph in producing him? I mean to test the proposition with the utmost perseverance on my return — nightly, if it please you.

Oh, lady, be proud. You have conquered this fierce warrior. First, I was captivated by your grace and courage. In time, I began to value your wisdom. But always, I remained my own man. Now a barrier has been breached within me. I am yours, Grazia, forever.

(initialed) P.G.

Postscript:
Dearest Mama, I forgot to tell you that even before we visited the German camp, we audienced with the Duke of Bourbon. He greeted Lord Pirro in a brotherly way. They are old companions in the service of the French king and distant kinsmen as well through the Gonzaga connection. It made no matter to either one that they now fight on different sides of this conflict. Lord Pirro says that a true knight ranks kinship and friendship above partisanship. Is that not a noble sentiment?

To be frank, Mama, I find this Bourbon a disappointment. He dresses himself poorly and is most unkempt. The only garment he wears that is worthy of his rank is his silver surcoat. But for it, you could easily mistake him for a common captain. Nor is his manner commanding. He speaks low and looks sideways. For my part, I would more willingly follow Lord Pirro into battle than this Bourbon, even with his silver surcoat.

With deepest respects and most affectionate love, Madonna Madre, I am your obedient son, (signed) D.

TO GRAZIA DEI ROSSI DEL MEDIGO

Grazia, most treasured wife:

There is no heaven on earth, but if there were, it would be this fair city of Constantinople. Fear not, I will not attempt to beguile you with pictures of flower-laden bowers and perfumed gardens. Instead, I will describe for you an oasis of peace, dignity, and freedom unimagined even by me until now.

In our first meeting, the Magnificent Suleiman received me standing up. This is a wonderful compliment for a Moslem to pay an unbeliever. He then seated me at his right—an expression of his trust, I am told—and begged me to consider him as a father. Indeed, he has treated me like a son since my arrival, sending me almonds and sugared sherbet, fruit and sweetmeats twenty times a day. Jewish physicians are traditionally held in the greatest esteem in this court. The Sultan himself confessed to me that the Ottoman kings have always preferred us to Christian doctors and even to Mohammedans. What they value is our skill, education, secrecy, and discretion. These are Suleiman's words exactly.

Although newly arrived, I am elevated to coequal status with his first physician, Moses Maymon, whose father, Joseph, held the same post with Suleiman's father. Here is what Moses Maymon had to say to me at our first meeting. Listen, Grazia.

"The Sultan has opened this country to us with the wand of his mercy," he said in his old-fashioned, formal way. "Here the gates are ever open to equal position and the unhindered practice of Jewish worship. Here, thou canst renew thine inner life, change thy condition, recover thine ancient truths, and abandon practices thou hast been compelled to adopt by the violent nations among whom thou wast an exile. Welcome to great Turkey, wanderer."

You belong here at my side, Grazia. Roma is becoming an increasingly dangerous place. My son deserves to be safe.

He belongs in the synagogue in which he was raised. Do not betray us, I beg you.

(signed in his own hand) Judah del Medigo

By sea from Constantinople, February 18, 1527.

58

THE NIGHT JUDAH SAILED AWAY TO SEEK SAFE HARBOR with the great Suleiman I sat at this table and, quill in hand, made a vow to trace for you the long road that has led from my own childhood through your birth and up to the present. Tonight when I took up my pen I realized that I have come to the end of the journey. My *libro segreto* is done. My tale is told. You know all. What you make of it and how you use it is up to you.

This year, 1527, is a year of decision for Italy, for me and for you. When it is done you will have chosen a religion and a father. I know you will choose wisely. You need only follow your heart. It is a good heart, sturdy and brave and wise. Trust yourself. Whatever you decide, do it with your whole heart. Remember: *carpe diem*. Seize the day. With both hands.

Tomorrow you will return from the camps of Lombardy having fallen in love, you say, with war. Lord Pirro has begun the long process of claiming the son he was denied. Judah continues to hold out the promise of heaven on earth in Turkey and the threat of hell on earth in Italy.

I will admit to you that Judah's arguments weigh heavily on

me. He, not Jehiel, was the oracle in the family all along. Before anyone else, he foretold the threat we now face from Charles V and his armies. He heard the hoofbeats of the Colonna raiders and the echo of trumpets as Frundsberg's *landsknechts* crossed over the Alps, heard it louder as they forded the treacherous Po and scaled the wintry peaks of the Apennines, and louder still as they rolled southward, painfully and at great cost but ever closer to us here in Roma. I was too occupied living out my own odyssey of love and betrayal, of friends lost and found, and of opposing loyalties to hear those warning flourishes. But looking back, I see that this gathering chorale of violence has been a part of my tale from its beginning. Reading your fine letters to me from the battlefield tell me that it is a part of your story, too, a story that is about to begin as mine reaches its end.

EPILOGUE:
THE SACK

59

APRIL 6, 1527

The Via Flaminia is awash in the flood that deluged Roma this noon. But Lord Pirro of Bozzuolo, impervious to his splattered cloak, his lagging companion, and his weary horse, spurs the animal on faster, ever faster, through the river of mud. His weeks in the Imperial camp have turned him sour. He cannot wait to get home.

Pressing the horses to their limits, the weary riders manage to gain the Porta del Popolo just before it closes and to arrive at the Piazza S.S. Apostoli as the last rays of sun are falling behind the Janiculum hill.

"Go to your mother, Danilo," Pirro instructs the boy gruffly but not unkindly. "I must pay my respects to Madonna Isabella." Pirro Gonzaga may be more a soldier than a diplomat but he has a firm grasp of the etiquette of courts. He knows that, while his kinswoman plays at being a romantic, in her heart of hearts the forms of obeisance to her station take precedence over all, including the imperatives of true love. She would be seriously insulted if he were to pay his first respects to her confidential secretary rather than to herself. The best he can hope for is that she will let him off with a brief audience and not keep him nodding until midnight while his lady waits above.

The greeting he gets from his kinswoman does not encourage his hopes. Madonna Isabella's eyes devour him with curiosity. And her manner indicates a willingness to stay up all night if need be as long as there is information to be extracted.

"Do not even waste a moment kissing me, cousin. Only answer the questions that have been burning in my brain." This is his welcome after an absence of five weeks. Then she remembers herself and, in a most cursory manner, remarks, "I assume all went well. You look fit enough. Now tell me: Is Frundsberg really dead? Is my nephew Constable Bourbon in sole charge of the Imperial forces? Did you meet with him? What is his temper? He does not seriously intend to besiege Roma, does he?"

And to think that this woman has a reputation for subtlety.

"In answer to your first query, yes, Frundsberg is dead," he replies in a manner as direct as her own. "To the second, also yes. Your nephew is the sole commander of the Imperials now. Spaniards, landsknechts, and whatever Italians remain in the Emperor's hire all fall under his command. Third, I did meet with Constable Bourbon. Fourth, he informed me—and I believe him—that the Emperor has authorized him to do whatever he likes in Italy, including an attack on Roma if he feels strong enough for it. As to whether he intends to use that authority, all I can tell you is that he has doubled the price for moving his troops out of Italy. He is now asking a quarter of a million ducats."

Isabella shivers. Even she, a celebrated spender of money, is intimidated by such a sum.

"And what course will you advise the Holy Father to follow when you convey Bourbon's new terms to him?"

"Pay it," he answers without a moment's hesitation. "Pay it before he goes to three hundred thousand. And pay it to Bourbon himself, not to the Emperor's viceroy."

"Well, the Pope has made a different plan. The viceroy left

two days ago for Firenze to collect enough Florentine gold to bribe the Germans away."

Pirro's heart sinks. "How much is he offering Bourbon?" he asks.

"One hundred and fifty thousand."

Pirro sighs wearily. "As usual, too little and too late."

"Oh, do not be so sad, cousin." She chucks him under the chin fondly. "Tell me, does the Emperor continue to send supplies and money to his army?"

"Not a penny, not a man, not a joint of meat nor a single weapon," he answers. "Bourbon swore it to me."

"That confirms my suspicions. It is the stratagem of starving the lion before he enters the arena. These moves are tactics, feints of the épée if you like."

"To what end?"

"Do you not see it? The Emperor's object is to get hold of enough money to pay his troops and to wring from the Pope the most favorable terms possible. Only then will he call off his dogs."

"And that day will be . . ."

"The day our poor Pope against all his better instincts is forced to sell off a few red hats," she replies.

"He swears he would rather give up the Holy See than sell cardinalates."

"But sell them he will," Isabella replies. "Oh, he will kick and he will squirm, but the Emperor will keep threatening him with Bourbon's army and one day very soon a messenger will come to my door with word that his Holiness has graciously consented to bestow upon my honorable son Ercole the red hat of a cardinal of the Holy Church. And I—along with heads of the Accioli, the Gaddi, the Spinola and the Grimani families— will dig into my strongbox and retrieve the ducats I have kept sequestered for just this purpose. And I will ask you, my loyal and trusted kinsman, to deliver forty thousand ducats into the Pontiff's hands—his and no others—and to bring me back a box with a red hat in it."

She pauses to take a deep breath—her great bulk prevents her from breathing as easily during her long elocutions as she used to do when she was younger—then continues in a low, almost conspiratorial voice: "I swore to my son the Marchese Federico that I would not leave Roma without the red hat for his brother Ercole. I have waited two long years. But I always knew the day would come. And so it will. On that day, cousin, I will leave this city and not before."

THREE DAYS LATER, THE Emperor's viceroy, Lannoy, arrives at a little town some thirty leagues from Firenze with orders for the great army which it is his mission to satisfy and dismiss. He carries with him in a brassbound oak chest 150,000 gold ducats, most of them contributed by the Florentines, fearful that their city will be sacked if the Imperials are not paid off.

Heavy downfalls of rain have turned the Imperial camp into a swamp. Lannoy cannot help but notice the condition of the men, their clothes in tatters, many without shoes, all sullen and angry-looking. He was told in Firenze that these men have taken to prowling the countryside like packs of emaciated crows, grabbing whatever stray bit of bread they can out of the mouths of peasants too startled and frightened to resist.

"And you tell me that these men are to be thrust out of Italy like beggars with no more than the pay that was owing them two months ago!" Bourbon emits a sharp bark that parades as a laugh.

"Those are the terms of the truce agreed upon by the Pope and the Emperor. Do I take it that you refuse my order to abide by them?" Lannoy asks mildly, appearing not to care overmuch what answer he gets.

"It is the men who refuse." Bourbon corrects the viceroy. "Have I not made myself clear, Lannoy? This is no longer an army of soldiers. It is a land armada of pirates, long severed from their Emperor. We have turned them into freebooters whose only loyalty is to their own skins. All that keeps them together now is the belief that in Firenze or Roma they will find warmth, food, wine, and riches beyond their dreams."

The viceroy is not moved by Bourbon's impassioned speech. He rises to his feet and signals to his aide to pick up the oak chest.

"In that case, Constable Bourbon, there is no more to be said. His Holiness has assured me that the hundred and fifty thousand ducats I bring to you today represent the last of his resources. In his own words, it would be as easy for him to join heaven and earth together as to raise another ducat." With that he bows low in the Spanish fashion and takes his leave.

That night Bourbon and his captains convene to debate whether or not to attempt a siege of Firenze. The attack would drain the strength they need to reach Roma. Still, the city is a close and tempting target for the weary, footsore army.

In the midst of their deliberations a messenger arrives with a bizarre piece of intelligence. The Duke of Urbino has arrived at the gates of Firenze at the head of the Pope's forces, with an offer to defend the city against Bourbon's Imperials.

At first the Imperial staff takes the dispatch for some kind of joke. Urbino has chased Bourbon's tail all the way down the Apennines, managing with great deftness never to engage with him. Now, suddenly, this reluctant commander seems to have hauled his army to the site of a battle and is even offering to fight. Incredible though it is, the intelligence is confirmed before dawn. Thus Bourbon's decision is made for him. Backed up by Urbino's army, Firenze is no longer a soft target. The Imperials have no choice. Without a dissenting voice, the captains vote to bypass Firenze. On to Roma!

The next day, Bourbon's army breaks camp and swings out across the Arno down the Val d'Ombra into the state of Siena, which has promised them hospitality. There, over the curses and mumbled threats of the entire force, Bourbon abandons his carriages, heavy baggage, light artillery, and camp followers, save for three prostitutes per company. By a series of forced marches of incredible hardship, the Imperials reach Viterbo on the second day of May. There, a mere fifty miles from Roma, they can all but smell the women and taste the wine and count the ducats that will rain down on them after they have scaled the walls of the Holy City. Newly infused with hope, they hit the road next morning like a pack of wild dogs, and God help the poor bastards who get in their way.

With the enemy almost literally at the gates, the Pope has become strong and decisive. After indulging in months of self-deception, he has finally allowed himself to think the unthinkable: that within two or three days, his city may be under siege. As Madonna Isabella d'Este predicted, he is left with no way to finance the defense of his city but the practice he detests above all: simony, the sale of offices of the church. His captain, Renzo da Ceri, has guaranteed that two hundred thousand ducats will buy enough troops to make the city impregnable.

On May 3, saying he would rather lose his right hand than do so, he nominates five new cardinals on condition they provide him with forty thousand gold ducats each. In an hour, Madonna Isabella d'Este da Gonzaga has placed the required ducats in the hands of her trusted kinsman Lord Pirro Gonzaga with strict instructions to deliver them into no other hands than the Pontiff's own. By the day's end, each of the nominees has graciously taken up the Pope's offer. The total amount raised—two hundred thousand ducats—is fifty thousand more than Bourbon demanded less than a month before to satisfy his army and turn them back over the Alps.

His mission accomplished, Lord Pirro guides his mount back from the Vatican to the Colonna Palace. Under his arm he balances a large, round hatbox—in it, the red hat destined to grace the head of Ercole, as of this day Cardinal Gonzaga. Lord Pirro also carries concealed on his person a document signed by his master, Pope Clement VII, offering two hundred thousand ducats to redeem Roma from the Emperor's troops. His orders are to ride out at dawn to the Imperial camp at Viterbo and deliver the offer to Constable Bourbon personally. If the offer is refused, he is to proceed directly to Urbino's camp south of Firenze.

Time is of the essence. But midway across the Ponte Elio, Lord Pirro reins in his horse for a moment of reflection. On his right the Ponte Sisto forms a sturdy arch against the darkening sky. Built by that prodigious papal builder Julius II, it is the first bridge to span the Tiber since ancient times. Lord Pirro looks down into the murky brown river. What he sees pleases him. Fast-flowing water. Whirling eddies that augur treacherous currents. When the Tiber lies low and runs sluggish, a man or a horse can make his way across with little danger of drowning. But turbulent and strong as it is now, the river presents an almost impenetrable barrier to the old Roman city.

If I were in command here, thinks Pirro, I would blow those bridges tomorrow without waiting to see if Bourbon accepts the Pope's bribe. That way the heart of Roma will be protected no matter what. Of course it is unthinkable that Bourbon will refuse the Pope's offer. But what if...

A trained soldier has a mind conditioned to think in terms of contingencies. What if the Imperial troops have been so maddened by hunger and rage they refuse their leader's order to turn back? What if they press Bourbon to attack Roma? What if they succeed by a superhuman act of will in scaling the thick walls? What if they take the Vatican palace and occupy the Borgo? Even so, the river will stop them from piercing the heart of Roma...once the bridges are blown. Yes, if I were in command here, I would most definitely blow those bridges, thinks Pirro.

The horse kicks his right front shoe impatiently on the cobbles. It is getting late and, in his horsey way, he is signaling it is time to go home. But the rider is not ready. He is still nagged by the question what if? What if, against all the odds, the Imperials do penetrate the heart of the city where his lady and his son live under the protection of the Marchesana Isabella? If they stand in peril, where does his duty lie? With his master, the Pope, or with those he has promised to love, cherish, and protect? In sum, can he in conscience ride off tomorrow morning and leave them to whatever fate and the Holy Roman Emperor have in store for Roma?

GRAZIA HAS ALWAYS BEEN an early riser but this morning she is at her desk even earlier than usual, writing by candlelight before sunup. Back to the quill and the inky fish. Back to the pristine vellum pages.

"My beloved son and confidant," she writes.

"When I told you in these pages that I had reached the end of my *ricordanza* and that all my secrets had been told, I did not reckon with the events of this night, which draws to a close as I write. You now know the disappointments, deceptions, and betrayals that have for so long tainted my love for Lord Pirro. Tonight all these were expunged, for tonight he laid before me a proof of constancy beyond all doubt.

"Under orders to ride north to the Imperial camp and beyond if need be to beg reinforcements, he informed me that he would not go, that he could not leave us — you and me — bereft of his protection in this uncertain time. Think of it. For us, he was willing to sacrifice his career, his reputation, his conscience, and his honor. In the face of this sacrifice, any lingering doubts that remained buried in my heart burst out and flew away. I am decided. I will marry him. This time there will be no turning back.

"Of course, I cannot allow him to make a ruin of his life for our sake by defecting from his duty. He must go as he is ordered to do. I have promised that I will marry him on the day of his return. In his absence I will prepare myself for a Christian marriage by being baptized. At last Madama will have her chance to stand beside me at the font and become her sister in Christ.

"As for my promise to Judah that I would wait a full year, I have given him half of his twelve months. More I cannot afford. We live in precarious times. Life is short and pleasure fleeting, as the magnificent Lorenzo taught us in his laud. The dishonor that falls on me for breaking my word to Judah and his disappointment in me, I can bear. It is you who are most dear to him. Me, he lost long ago.

"The moment I made my decision a great heaviness was lifted off me. This is not a matter of whether I be Jew or Christian or whether Roma or Constantinople is the safer haven. It is a matter of the heart. Quite simply Pirro Gonzaga is the only man in the world for me and ever has been. And this decision brings to me the promise of a happiness I have dreamed of since I was a girl.

"We will marry by special dispensation the day he returns from Urbino's camp. On the same day he will acknowledge you as his son. But I am not to tell you of it. He wishes to reserve that pleasure for himself.

"The only blot on this fair horizon is that damn Bourbon and his army. There does remain a stray chance that, as my beloved brother Maestro Vitale would have put it, the planets that oversee our lives may come into disastrous collision, and that we will be caught in a city under siege. Should such a catastrophe occur, I swear to you as I swore to Lord Pirro that not the Pope's stinginess nor the Emperor's venality nor Bourbon's extraordinary soldiering nor any other act of man or nature will break my will to marry. If siege there be, you and I will withstand it. When the opportunity comes, we will escape. And I will keep my vow unto death to the man I love that when next we meet, I will become his wife.

"I beg your blessing on this enterprise."

NOW THAT MARCHESANA ISABELLA has the red hat in her possession and is prepared to leave Roma, the roads are no longer safe for travel. She can afford to be amused by the irony. Her good sense tells her that very soon now the Imperial army will approach the walls of the city, blow loudly on their trumpets, make their final demand, grab the enormous bonus that their Emperor has so cleverly negotiated, and march away rich and happy.

In case for any reason this scenario does not play out, Isabella has prudently made contact with her nephew Constable Bourbon, Commander of the Imperial Forces, and with her son Ferrante, a captain in that same army, and been reassured by both that her comfort and safety will be their first concern when—neither gentleman admits to if—they take the city.

Was ever a woman better situated to withstand the rigors of a sack?

FROM DANILO'S ARCHIVE

TO THE HONORABLE DUKE CHARLES OF BOURBON, CON-
STABLE, ETC., IN THE FIELD AT MONTE MARIO
Most esteemed nephew:

I thank you exceedingly for your expression of concern for our safety and must tell you, in return, of my admiration for the honor and glory you are gaining in the service of His Imperial Majesty, Charles V.

Those of us here behind the walls of Roma continue to hope for a truce between your Imperial master and the Holy Father, but, as you remind me in your most gracious letter, it is prudent to prepare for the worst while hoping for the best.

In accordance with your advice I have garrisoned this palace, not forgetting a special guard for the well. We are bountifully provisioned and prepared to await rescue at your hands should matters come to that. I commend myself to your protection and my dear Ferrante to your care.

Isabella, Marchesana, etc., Colonna Palace, Roma, May 5, 1527.

TO CAPTAIN FERRANTE GONZAGA, IN THE FIELD AT MONTE
MARIO
My dear son:

I thank you more than I can say for your letter and I beg

of you to take care of yourself for I am always anxious when I remember you are in the camp, even though this is where you wish to be. We pray for your safety as you do for ours and await your arrival eagerly.

From her who loves and longs to embrace your dear self.

(signed) Isabella G., Colonna Palace, Roma, May 5, 1527.

60

MAY 5, 1527

Constable Bourbon has refused two hundred thousand ducats in ransom. Already on the march when the offer reached him, he informed Lord Pirro Gonzaga coolly that his men could do better by sacking Roma. Such confidence in a general virtually without weapons, totally without siege machines, and lacking supplies of any kind leaves Lord Pirro dumbfounded.

The Imperial soldiers are even more ragged and weary than Pirro remembers them. Slogging doggedly through the muddy countryside, they resemble nothing so much as an army of ghosts, with wild eyes like holes in their gaunt, starved faces. Even the vast sum offered them in exchange for a retreat has lost its meaning. Privation, suffering, and betrayal have leached away both reason and sentiment. There is only one emotion left in them—hatred.

Somewhere outside of Firenze the Duke of Urbino is waiting with fresh troops for God knows what. If this is not the time for him to bring the Pope's army to the Pope's aid, when will that time come? The task of putting this question to the reluctant warrior has fallen to Pirro Gonzaga. Having failed to save Roma by bribery, he is ordered to press on to Toscana and instruct the Captain-General of the Pope's Holy League to come to the aid of the city at once. Lord Pirro's orders do not say how he is to accomplish this miracle.

IN ROMA THE GREAT lords—nobles, cardinals, and merchants—have been making themselves secure in their palaces. Those who do not maintain private armies have recruited mercenaries to guard their possessions and themselves. Cardinal Cesarini has raised 200 men; Cardinal Piccolomini, 150.

Benvenuto Cellini, who, with his customary modesty, claims to be even more talented as a soldier than as a goldsmith, has graciously accepted a commission to defend his wealthy friend Alessandro del Bene. Even now, Cellini is giving last-minute instructions to the fifty young *bravi* he has recruited on Alessandro's behalf. Alessandro is confident that with Benvenuto to defend his property he has nothing to fear, come what may.

HIGH UP ON THE Quirinal hill, seated on the loggia of her borrowed palace, the Marchesana Isabella d'Este gazes westward toward the Via Cassia. No sign of the Imperials yet. But when and if they come, Madonna Isabella is ready for them. So confident is she of her position in the beleaguered city that yesterday, when she knew an attack was imminent, she offered the protection of her palace to a number of noble Roman ladies and gentlemen not as well connected as herself. By evening there were some three hundred guests under her roof including Felice Orsim, the daughter of the late Pope Julius, and the ambassadors of both Ferrara and Urbino.

"How many did we take in last night, Tommaso?" the lady inquires of her chamberlain.

"Three hundred and twelve ladies, Excellency," he replies.

"Two cardinals. Twenty bishops." Tommaso squints over his record book, hard-pressed to make the calculation in his head. "Forty-one clerks of the Holy See, or is it..."

"Never mind." Isabella waves him away from the book. "You must prepare to welcome twice that number before this day is out."

Tommaso sighs audibly.

"Who would you have us turn away? Messer Landriani, the Milanese ambassador?" she challenges him. "Or Messer Lippomano and his family?" Lippomano represents Urbino at the Vatican. "We can hardly deny our largesse to such august persons when they choose to accept our hospitality, now can we, *Messer* Tommaso?"

In truth she herself is somewhat alarmed at the response to her invitation. She had meant only to put out a discreet word to a chosen few, never anticipating the horde of "friends" that has been streaming through her doors.

At the same time she is secretly pleased at the turnout. She knows that this prodigious display of hospitality will be the talk of Italy and bring great honor to the house of Gonzaga. She also knows that the gaining of honorable repute is inevitably followed by more substantial rewards such as dukedoms, lands, and emoluments.

"The gunpowder, has it been delivered, Tommaso?" she asks the dour old man.

"Yes, madama. It arrived last night. In a covered wagon, as you ordered."

"And the pikes?"

"Lined up in the antechamber."

"And the men? Where are they garrisoned?"

"Up at the top of the *giardino*, madama. At the Torre de Mesa." The Torre de Mesa. Isabella shudders. She knows her history. That tower is the spot from which Nero watched the burning of Roma. Now her own men are positioned there. Is this a sign that they are destined to witness a similar conflagration? She shivers again. A footman with no knowledge of history to burden his soul steps forward with a shawl and wraps it around her, murmuring something about a nip in the air. She graces him with a dazzling smile. He has told her what she wanted to hear. That her shivers were brought on by a chill in the air. Nothing more. Isabella orders a draft of warmed spiced wine and proceeds to get on with her tasks.

A glance at her account books tells her how much she has already spent on the defense of this palazzo.

Fifty gold ducats for fifty armed men.

Ten gold ducats for gunpowder.

Five ducats for pikes.

Her treasure chest is running low. But the unpleasantness will be over within a few days and she will be on her way back to Mantova, having finally gained the prize for which she came to Roma two years ago. It is as she always told her children. The key to a successful life is perseverance. Next to piety, of course. She crosses herself, recites a quick Paternoster, and turns back to the matter at hand.

Forty barrels of wine.

One hundred pounds of sifted wheat.

Twelve casks of oil.

"What say you, Tommaso? Are we well provisioned for the siege?" she asks.

The graybeard shakes his head dolefully. "They do eat, madama," he reports sadly. "In between their tears, they are eating our larder bare."

"Perhaps weeping stimulates the appetite," she suggests facetiously.

"Oh no, madama," he replies quite seriously. "Essence of ginger is a far better remedy for loss of appetite than tears."

Isabella smothers a smile and asks him to get on with his report from the *cucina*.

"We used forty pounds of fish at yesterday's dinner," he tells her sadly. "Not a herring bone is left. My boys are at the market at this very moment with orders to buy anything that wriggles, just as you instructed." His thin lips register disapproval of this profligate spending.

"We are sharing our bounty as Christ commands us to do," Isabella admonishes him. "Now be sure your scullions get plenty of smoked fish. It keeps and we may use it on the journey home. And extra flour. And candles. And send Costanza to fetch the boy Danilo. She will find him with his mother in the Room of the Fishes."

The more she sees of Grazia's boy, the better she likes what she sees. The brightness of his mind, the modesty of his spirit, the eagerness with which he embraces life, are all qualities that attract her. By some miracle he has managed to avoid the contagion of that deep pessimism endemic to his mother's race. This boy is his father's son. Already he has done credit to his blood—and, one must add, to his upbringing—by his exemplary behavior on the tour he took with his father of the camps of Lombardia. She reminds herself that when the present disruption is over, she owes it to her house to take a closer interest in his education.

But why wait to enjoy a preceptor's pleasure in the company of such a charming boy? History is in the making this very hour. Why not take him up to the top of Nero's tower and impart to him a lesson in living history? Together they will enjoy what may turn out to be the most spectacular event she is likely to witness in a life replete with spectacular events.

ON THE OTHER SIDE of the Colonna Palace, the little maid Costanza picks her way through the mass of bodies sprawled along the walls of the covered loggia of the *piano nobile*. *Dio*, what a mess there will be to clean up when this lot decamps. She swerves to avoid a puddle of urine that has overflowed the slop bucket Madama thoughtfully provided for her guests. Are they too lazy or too proud to carry their pisspot out to the courtyard? she asks herself, then shrugs off the question. Let them wallow in their own slop if they like. She has too much work today to bother over Colonna's marble floors. Serves him right if the stains never come out, the old goat.

Costanza has no sympathy for the highborn refugees who have crowded into these halls, not even for the women that follow after her begging milk for their babies. If they'd nursed their own brats rather than sending them off to wet nurses, they'd have plenty of milk handy now when they need it.

She shoves a clinging child aside impatiently and turns toward the Room of the Fishes. Each time she approaches this portal, she pauses to eavesdrop, hoping to overhear some bit of information that will clarify a mystery that has plagued her ever since Madama took in the occupants: What does a great lady like Madonna Isabella find to love in this no-account Jewess and her brat?

"Remember, Madonna Madre, that a thirty-foot wall stands between them and us and that scaling such a wall is a very risky venture," she hears.

"Risky but not impossible," the woman Grazia answers.

"Mama, you worry too much. Have I not told you that with my own eyes I saw the abandoned Imperial artillery lying along the road all the way down from Lombardia? And did you not hear Lord Pirro explain that even if Bourbon does manage somehow to break into the Borgo, the city bridges can be cut and the city saved?"

"Yes, I heard. But—"

Costanza marches into the Room of the Fishes. "Madonna is calling for Master Danilo," she announces without ceremony.

Grazia looks up. "She wishes to see my son?"

"At once."

"Then I must go," the boy announces. "At once."

"One minute, my son. How fares Madonna Isabella on this terrible morning?" Grazia asks the maid.

"Seemed like her regular self to me, lady," is the surly answer. "You know Madama. It would take an eruption of Vesuvius to shake her up."

"She is as good as her motto," Grazia remarks. "*Nec spero, nec metu.*"

Costanza recognizes the phrase as the one she has seen

embroidered on Madama's linens and engraved on some of Madama's medals. She has often wondered what it meant but is damned if she will give the Jewess the satisfaction of asking.

"*Nec spero, nec metu* means 'without hope or fear,'" the boy answers her unasked question. "A very valiant motto for a lady, do you not agree, Costanza?"

As always, the maid is mollified by his winning ways. "I suppose so," she answers grudgingly.

He smiles, bows to his mother, and with a knightly sweep of his arm, beckons to the maid. "Lead on, Costanza. Madama is not only without hope or fear, she is also without patience and does not like to be kept waiting."

But Grazia, reluctant to relinquish her son, recalls the pair before they have passed through the curtain. "Tell me, Costanza, what news do we have from the town?"

"They say a vast army is approaching from Viterbo."

"And that doesn't trouble you at all?"

"It's all one to me, lady, who sits on Saint Peter's throne. If the Imperials do take Roma, they say the Emperor will leave Spain and come and live here with us and the city will prosper more than it has under these greedy-gut priests." And off she goes.

If this girl's cynicism is any indication, Grazia thinks, how can the Romans be depended on to rise to the demands of this day? What is to stop them from running from the fight and making common cause with the looters? It is all very well for Danilo to speak of impregnable walls and irresistible firepower, but in the end battles are fought by men and half of Renzo da Ceri's men are cooks and priests and scullions and other come-lately soldiers. The thought that her life and the life of her son may end up in such hands brings on a wave of despair.

61

AY 7, 1527

MAt dawn two suns are rising in the Roman sky. This is not an astronomical phenomenon. The second sun glistering on the crest of Mount Auria is the reflection of twenty-two thousand steel helmets and twenty-two thousand brass breastplates. Last night the Imperial army took up a position just outside the walls of Roma high on the Janiculum hill. Yet no alarms are sounded. No bells ring out warnings. The citizens of Roma—those who are awake this early—look up at the Janiculum and point and comment, but there is no panic in the streets.

Why are the citizens of Roma not more alarmed? History has lulled them into sanguinity. This is hardly the first hostile army to assemble under the massive brown walls. Again and again over the centuries, armies have shown their mettle to the Romans. Only last fall, the rambunctious Colonna clan led a force of some thirty-five hundred Imperials through the city gates virtually unopposed and straight into the heart of Christendom. But they were done away in a day by a series of quick negotiations. That autumnal sortie is still fresh in the minds of Romans, those experts at eleventh-hour reprieves.

True, this year's Imperial army is formidably large. But it is known to be in a terrible state of dilapidation. The soldiers have long since lost everything but their armor. They have been forced by the winter's privations to save their lives at the expense of their heavy weaponry, which lies abandoned all along the route from Bologna to Roma. Against such an enemy, a well-provisioned city can hold out almost indefinitely.

THE SAME CONFIDENCE POSSESSES Pope Clement. Despite the great army arrayed against him across the river, he refuses to withdraw to the security of the Castel Sant'Angelo. No member of his retinue dares to interrupt his morning devotions; but the moment he emerges from the small chapel adjoining his private apartments, he is besieged by his advisers.

"Excellency..." Paolo Giovio, Clement's chief secretary, begins the importunings. Giovio may be a mediocre historian but he is a first-rate courtier. In a single flowing gesture, he manages to glance the papal ring on the way down, touch his lips to the hem of Clement's cape, and cross himself on the way up. "I beseech your Holiness, on behalf of good Christians everywhere, to leave this palace and secure your person in the Castel Sant'Angelo."

Clement dismisses Giovio by simply turning his head away in the direction of his military commander for the defense of Roma, Renzo da Ceri. "Is all in readiness, captain?" he asks.

"Every man at his post, sir." The old soldier stiffens to attention.

"Well armed?"

"As you ordered, Holiness."

"And the bridges?"

"Well guarded, Holiness."

This answer does not please the Pope. For days he has been agitating for destruction of the bridges that connect the Vatican city with old Roma. But Renzo is held back by the inhabitants

of Trastevere whose houses along the riverbank would collapse with the bridges. "The Romans love their bridges, sir,"
he explains. "If we destroy them, we destroy the morale of our
troops."

"And if the Imperials manage to gain the Vatican, what then
will stop them from crossing the river into Roma?" the Pope
inquires with some asperity.

"I will stop them, sir. I and my men." This is no pose. The
man means every word he says. "The day the Imperials enter
Roma, you have my permission to take my head from my
shoulders."

Renzo's sincerity is irresistible. Besides, the Pope wants to
believe him.

"My city is in your hands, my son." Clement holds out his
ring to be kissed. Renzo falls at the Pontiff's feet to be blessed.
Everyone present is convinced that, with two such valiant
characters at the helm, their cause will prevail.

CONSTABLE BOURBON FALLS ASLEEP at midnight, lulled into
restfulness by the quiet of the great city. He awakens after a
brief but profound sleep, dons his silver surcoat, makes his confession, and orders his drummers to sound the stand-to

An experienced tactician, he is fully aware that the ideal
point of attack on the Borgo is from the west where the
Vatican itself would offer his men protection from the guns of
Sant'Angelo. But the western wall presents a sheer thirty-foot
cliff and, as the aspiring strategist Danilo dei Rossi pointed out
to his mother, the Imperial army has long since been forced to
abandon its siege equipment. Now, the only advantages that
remain to Bourbon are the numerical superiority of his troops
and his own nerve.

In a classic maneuver, he dispatches his second in command,
the Prince of Orange, to create a diversion by feinting an attack
on the Ponte Milvio. Then he mounts his huge charger and,
serenaded by the beat of drums and the blare of trumpets,

sallies forth to bash his way through the impregnable walls of Roma at San Spirito.

AFTER AN HOUR OF hard fighting at San Spirito, Renzo da Ceri's men have knocked down the makeshift scaling ladders mounted against the wall and killed a hundred landsknechts.

"Victory!" shout da Ceri's men, "Victory to the Holy Father."

Da Ceri himself cannot quite believe how easily this bunch of summer soldiers turned back the Imperial assault. But, not being overly thoughtful by nature, he simply thanks God for His help and dispatches a small squad to the Vatican bearing the five standard flags captured from the vanquished enemy. Caught up in the panoply of the banners that swirl above them flaunting the Habsburg double eagle—now humbled—the crowd that has assembled to watch the battle cheers wildly.

None of this commotion disturbs the concentration of Benvenuto Cellini, out for a spot of reconnoitering with his patron, del Bene, and now busily at work bringing the battle scene to life in his sketchbook. The goldsmith works quickly, using only a crayon; he has caught the terrible stillness of the dead who lie draped over the wall in grotesque attitudes and the contrast of their presence with the tensed muscles of the papal arquebusiers, who continue to pursue the fight against their defeated enemy.

Suddenly the goldsmith pauses, crayon in air. A subtle change in the light has caught his practiced eye. He turns toward the Borgo, where the Castel Sant'Angelo stands with its back to the river. A thick fog is beginning to rise from the marshes.

"If this mist continues to rise, the Imperials will soon be invisible to the Pope's falconets," he tells his friend. "It will give them all the cover they need. *Dio*, I fear this victory may be turning to defeat before our eyes."

A sinister quiet has fallen over the battle scene. Cellini, ever curious, wriggles his way up onto the parapet which supports two of Renzo's arquebusiers. Cautiously, he raises himself on his haunches between them and peers down. The thick fog has created an indistinct blur of bodies. From the gray mass below, a commanding voice rings out. "God has manifested Himself to us, men. He has covered us over. Up the ladders once again! Follow me! This time we cannot fail."

"It's the Bourbon traitor," Cellini shouts, and grabbing an arquebus from one of the astonished gunners, he aims at the clearest target he can find: a human form that looms up over the top of the wall, so camouflaged by the fog that it appears as nothing more than a floating, ghostly-white surcoat.

Cellini shoots.

The figure falls backward, hit.

Then comes a wailing and an outpouring of curses from the other side. Cellini peers down for a look. He can just make out a still figure on the ground, surrounded by a crowd of Imperial soldiers gesticulating wildly.

"He is dead. The Constable is dead." An anguished voice rises out of the mist.

"Dead...dead...dead..." The word echoes in the stillness.

"Dio!" Agile as a monkey, the goldsmith jumps down from the parapet and lands beside del Bene. "I have killed Constable Bourbon, Alessandro," he announces, his voice quivering with pride and excitement. "I, Benvenuto Cellini, have killed the Imperial army."

But the Imperial monster does not die so easily. Like Hydra, the moment one of its heads is lopped off, others spring up to take its place. Out of the fog, young Ferrante Gonzaga materializes to lead the charge anew. The death of their leader has inspirited the Imperials. Spurred on by Ferrante's exhortations to avenge their leader, they hurl themselves once more at the ladders. This time, they reach the top unimpeded. Then, slowly, one by one, they drop through the fog and down into the Borgo like wraiths from heaven.

Renzo is the first of the defenders to spot the ghostly cadre. Are these men or the shades of men? Terror-stricken by what he takes to be an invasion of spirits, he begins to shout like a madman that all is lost and every man must save himself.

IN HIS PRIVATE CHAPEL, the Pope is "harvesting prayers," as his historian Giovio puts it, refusing to accept the fact that the Imperial army has broken through at San Spirito and is headed directly for him. Over his protests he is dragged out onto the balcony and forced to look down into the streets of the Borgo. All he can see is the thick fog that God has sent to nourish his enemies and punish him. But his ears tell him the tale his eyes cannot comprehend—screams of alarm, cries of rape, supplications to God, vilifications of priests, of Roma, of himself, and steadily louder and louder, the zzzip, zzzip of deadly arquebus shafts.

Time is running out. Giovio propels his master, compliant now and sobered by the pitiful sounds below, to the walkway that will lead them to safety in Sant'Angelo. The Pope's escape is so narrow that, as one Spanish cardinal has it, had he tarried for three creeds more, he would have been taken prisoner in his own palace.

Thank God for old Borgia, who built this passage for himself in case of just such an extremity. He knew something the Medici never understood: that it is as easy for a pontiff to be hated as to be loved.

It occurs to Giovio that should any one of the landsknechts happen to look up and see, through the fog, the unmistakable white-clad figure of the Pope, it would present a tempting target. He throws his purple cape and hood over the Pontiff. No longer identifiable, Clement is now merely another refugee fleeing from the spawn born of Habsburg pride and Lutheran hatred.

IN THE BORGO, CHAOS. The Swiss fight to the last man. But most of Renzo's citizen-soldiers throw down their weapons and rush to join the exodus from the Borgo. Cellini has forecast accurately: the victory at San Spirito has turned into a rout.

Using Alessandro del Bene's body like a battering ram, Cellini is trying to force his way through the mob that jams the streets leading to the Castel Sant'Angelo. But the young nobleman pulls back, his mind still fixed on the idea of defending his palace.

"Forget your goods, think of your life, man!" Cellini exhorts him. Using their combined strength, they force their way to the gate of Castel Sant'Angelo just in time to see the castellan emerge and order the portcullis lowered.

"Jump, friend!" Cellini propels del Bene onto the drawbridge as it pulls up, and together they leap under the descending grill-work of the portcullis, which closes behind them with a reverberating clang. Safe!

Fat Cardinal Armellino is not so fortunate. He delayed too long defending his palace against looters and now arrives breathless to find himself locked out.

"Let me come in." He raises his hands imploringly.

The Pope, who has seemed to be in some sort of daze since his arrival at the fort, is now aroused by the sight of the flapping red sleeves waving out their distress signal.

"Lower a basket," he instructs his captain, Pallone dei Medici. Even in this extremity he refuses to abandon his friend.

"But surely they will not harm him, not in his cardinal's robe, Holiness," the captain expostulates.

"I would not wager on it," Clement replies, for once a pessimist and for once accurate in his assessment of the situation. "Lower the basket."

Pallone calls two of his men away from their posts to handle the basket. Watching this most unlikely deus ex machina jerk its way down the rough curved wall, Giovio the historian mutters, "Even Attila the Hun respected bishops."

His honor in shreds, Renzo da Ceri drags his reluctant feet down the Capitol hill to the Sistine bridge. With the day not half over, the Borgo is lost and the Imperials have overwhelmed neighboring Trastevere. Now they are preparing to hack their way through the three hundred knights gathered at the Ponte Sisto, who represent all that is left of the city's defense. They are men of heroic stripe, many carrying in their minds the image of Horatius facing the Etruscan hordes, and are ready to defend this last bridge to the death.

With these survivors of the age of chivalry Renzo finally finds his place. He may have lacked the will to destroy this bridge, but he does not lack the courage to fight for it.

In the corridors of the Colonna Palace, while the babies squall and the mothers moan and certain gentlemen try to hide the trembling of their limbs, Madonna Isabella d'Este makes certain for the tenth time that day that her citadel is impregnable.

The thick wooden doors have been bolted for hours. Her mercenaries are deployed along the north-facing loggia, with a second layer stationed at the windows of the rooms in the *piano nobile*. These men are far from the company her guests are accustomed to keeping, but she has heard no complaint from the occupant of any room in which a *bombardiste* is stationed.

To Madonna Isabella, this is the time of greatest trial. For hours now, a blanket of fog has cut off her view from the top of Nero's tower. But her nose tells her that this mist is at least partly compounded of smoke — an ominous sign. Defending armies do not set fire to their own cities.

"It is always best to prepare oneself for the worst," she counsels her young companion. "So let us make the worst case: that the Borgo is taken, that the Tiber has been crossed, and that the Imperials are already streaming through the streets of Roma grabbing what they can where they can, as soldiers do. My honorable nephew Bourbon is too experienced a commander to permit them to sack the town until they have their position secured. Rest assured there will be no looting tonight."

Danilo intuits that she is speaking more to herself than to him and does not reply, but merely nods companionably.

"My honorable nephew promised to come to us within hours of the fall of the city," she continues. "If this smoke we smell presages that catastrophe, a troop of his men will arrive here to reinforce our own *bravi* before midnight and to watch over us once his troops are let loose to loot the city. So even if the worst has come to pass and Roma has fallen to the Imperials, we have nothing to fear, do you understand?"

"I do, madonna," Danilo answers. "But I cannot say the same for those people in there." He points in the direction of the palace behind them

"I know. I know," she cuts him off. "But sad to say, not all men are brave, Danilo."

"Nor all women beautiful," he adds, bringing a smile to her harried countenance.

By midnight the drunken songs of the marauding soldiers are clearly audible to the inhabitants of the Colonna Palace and the acrid smell of gunpowder and burning buildings has begun to sting the linings of their nostrils. At two hours before midnight a basket was lowered into the Piazza S.S. Apostoli to give entrance to a Spanish officer, Don Alonso de Cordova, dispatched by Madama's son Ferrante to inform his mother that her nephew Bourbon is dead and that with his dying breath the Constable gave orders that the Colonna Palace was to be protected even at the sacrifice of lives.

For two hours now the Spaniard has sat listening courteously to the lady's recollections of Bourbon's youth, of his mother, Chiara, of the happy times they spent together at her favorite villa, Marmirolo. But his patience has run out. It is time for business. However, Cordova is bound by orders and honor to await the arrival of Captain Ferrante Gonzaga, the lady's son.

At last the young man arrives and is hauled up in the same ignominious basket as the Spaniard. Now he can take up the task of comforting his mother and leave Cordova to get on with the true purpose of his visit.

But no. First there must be a reunion. This mother and son have not laid eyes on each other since he set off for Madrid to serve at the Imperial court of Charles V three years ago. In place of the dashing young *cavaliere* she waved off then, Isabella now welcomes back a gaunt and haggard man smelling of blood and gunpowder who looks several years older than his twenty years. But in his heart he remains his mother's loyal son and is overcome with embarrassment at the role he is about to play.

Cordova opens the subject with a blunt demand for one hundred thousand ducats.

"And in what cause, sir, am I expected to contribute one hundred thousand ducats?" Isabella inquires icily.

"For your ransom, señora," the Spaniard replies, equally frigid but with a smile. "Roma is a captive city. You and your"— he waves his arm in a great arc to indicate the numerous guests she has taken in—"friends are the spoils of war."

Whatever treatment she may have expected from her rescuers, this is not it. "Ferrante! Do you hear this fellow?" she demands of her fidgeting and uncomfortable son.

"I do, Madonna Madre." All the courage he displayed this day at the barricades dissolves at the sight of her anger.

"Then why do you not remind him that he is here as the representative of my dead nephew, cut down in his cause this very day and leaving him with orders to protect me?"

"We will protect you, señora," the Spaniard cuts in smoothly, "but for a price."

This Spaniard is not making Ferrante's task easier. But the young man gamely takes up the challenge of explaining to his outraged mother why it is necessary for her to pay ransom to her own son.

"It is the men, the soldiers, Madonna Madre," he stammers,

every minute more the erring boy and less the cool captain. "They have followed us here with the expectation that we will assess the ransoms available in this palace and exact them. If they do not get what they feel is coming to them, they will sack and burn this place as they are doing at this moment all over the city."

"You have that little control over them?" she asks.

He nods, silent and ashamed.

"If what you say is true, if these barbarians really do answer to no one or nothing but their own bestiality, then I thank God my poor dead nephew did not live to see this day," is his mother's impassioned reply. But the Spaniard will have no traffic with rhetoric.

"It was your poor dead nephew, señora, who drove these men on with the promise that they would collect their pay, now owing to them for more than six months of hunger and cold and betrayal—that they would collect all that was owed them and more when they reached Roma. Constable Bourbon gave them Roma, señora, Roma with all of its treasures. Unfortunately, you are one of those treasures."

"I fear, Madonna Madre, that your generosity has proven your undoing." Her son takes up the argument. "It is reported in the camp that more than two millions in valuables are concealed in this palace. Your hospitality has made you not only a prize but a glittering prize. Believe me, madonna, ransom is far preferable to a sack of the palace. Let each of your guests pay what they are assessed, and out of the money collected we will engage a cadre of stout and loyal men to stand guard over you. And when the violence ends three days from now, those *bravi* will accompany you out of this city to the sea and safety."

It is scandalous, of course. Unconscionable and wickedly opportunistic. Isabella plays her outrage to the hilt. Again and again she turns to her son, at times imploring, at others demanding. But her game is up and she knows it. By dawn, it is tacitly agreed that ransoms will be paid.

A table is set up in a vault behind the kitchens, covered

with green baize and equipped with a small weighing scale. Seeing it, Grazia is reminded of the table she sat behind in her father's *banco*. The difference is that here the *banchieri* are two high-ranking officers in the Imperial army and one dowager marchesana.

Now a long line of clients forms outside this bizarre *banco* to make their offerings to the unlikely *banchieri*. Isabella fights the Spaniard on every case. She wins some small victories but for the most part her guests must pay with every ducat they can raise, every jewel, and indeed every valuable thing they own. For some an armed escort is provided so that the client can retrieve assets he or she has hidden away and bring them back safely to the palace.

By the end of the first day so much treasure has piled up that the assessors, threatened with suffocation in the packed vault, are forced to move to larger quarters. There the assessing goes on as before, slow, methodical, tedious—in striking contrast to the scenes in the streets outside, which by now have begun quite literally to run red with blood.

THE THREE ALLOWABLE "DAYS of violence" come and go, but there is no cessation to the savagery. In vain the Prince of Orange, who has fallen into leadership of the unruly force by default, sends his heralds through the streets to announce the end of the sack. He might as well have blown his trumpets into deaf ears. The landsknechts continue to kill every priest or nun they lay their hands on and to loot every church, convent, and monastery.

In the whole city there appears to be not a single person who does not have to purchase his safety, babies and infants excepted because, whenever found, they are simply tossed out of high windows to splatter on the street below in view of their horrified mothers. Whereupon the mothers themselves are forced to copulate with pigs—a favorite entertainment of the Germans—or are driven through the sewers naked to forage for treasure that the crafty Romans are reputed to have buried in human excrement—a favored diversion of the more gold-oriented Spaniards.

These are the scenes that greet the eyes of Captain Ferrante Gonzaga as he rides dutifully across Roma every morning to play his role of *banchiere* to his mother's guests and incidentally to beg her to let him spirit her away to a safe place outside the city. But Isabella remains firm. She will not leave the palace until every soul she had taken under her protection is released at a place beyond the walls where they will have a reasonable hope of safety.

"I have promised these people my protection," she reminds him. "You know, my son," she chides gently, "men are not the only creatures who hold their honor more closely than their lives. We women too are jealous of our word."

Not for the first time Ferrante wishes that he had not been blessed with the *prima donna del mondo* as his mother.

For her own part, Isabella confides in Grazia, she would gladly have run into the arms of the devil if he offered to lead her out of this hell. But honor holds her at the bargaining table trading lives for gems and ducats. She spends her evenings with Grazia who, to keep her own sanity, has begun to lead her son on a voyage along Herodotus's winding paths.

To the two women and the boy the Room of the Fishes has become a sanctuary of learning where they can wrap themselves in the cocoon of the past and there find peace and comfort.

"I, Herodotus of Halicarnassus, am here setting forth my history," Grazia hears with pleasure the still-reedy voice of her son translating from the ancient tongue. "So that the great deeds of men may not be forgotten, whether they be Greeks or foreigners and especially to show the causes of war between them..."

As Madonna Isabella never tires of pointing out, no one who collects books and reads them is ever totally bereft of comfort.

62

MAY 10, 1527
The last prayer offered in the Sistine Chapel
before the Imperials entered Roma on the seventh
day of May was a plea to God to save His city, offered by a
pope with tears running down his cheeks. Since that day, the
strains of Kyrie and Agnus Dei have given place to the dissonant neighing of the Prince of Orange's horse. The Prince has
chosen to stable his horse in the chapel next to his new headquarters in the Pope's private apartments in order to prevent
the animal from being stolen. There it stands tethered at the
foot of Perugino's ideal city, gazing up at Michelangelo's Adam,
the first man, at the moment of his release from the hands of
God.

The Prince of Orange is impressed by the Sistine ceiling. He gives it his undivided attention for at least two minutes each day when he comes to the chapel to visit his horse.
These visits aside, no one else has shown the slightest interest in Michelangelo Buonarroti's vision of the Creation. After
all, there are no jewels embedded in the ceiling of the Sistine
Chapel. Its frescoes cannot be scraped off and sold. A single

horse gives sufficient protection to this treasure.

But wait. What of the ten panels that hang below it—those elegant tapestries designed by Raffaello, worked in Brussels by Pieter Van Aelst and valued above all his other possessions by Leo X, the Medici connoisseur? In the present climate the perfection of their design, the beauty of their colors, their meticulous workmanship, count for little. But the gold and silver threads worked into the weave are another story. Tapestries have been burned before now to salvage the precious metal of their threads. These tapestries are at risk.

Harried though she is by her Spanish captor, the Dowager Marchesana of Mantova cannot get the thought of Raffaello's tapestries out of her mind. The negotiations at the green baize table are winding down. The last of the refugee women under her roof will be conducted to the Nomentana gate the next day. Then, finally, her honor will permit her to leave Roma. Her position as mother and aunt of two of the city's conquerors has wrung at least one concession from the rapacious Cordova. She and the members of her household will be escorted out of Roma unransomed, their possessions guarded by a special contingent of *bravi* handpicked by the Prince of Orange.

Again and again the lady's thoughts return to the tapestries. How easy it would be to pack them in boxes and send them to Mantova along with her own possessions. As she puts it to herself, God has given her the opportunity to rescue the tapestries from certain destruction. They will be safe in her baggage train, guarded by the barbarians themselves. And in time, when Roma once more becomes a secure depository, they will of course be returned to the Pope. But for a time—who knows how long?—the tapestries will be hers.

IT IS IN ORDER to discuss the matter of the Raffaello tapestries that Ferrante Gonzaga pays a visit to his commander, the Prince of Orange, in his billet—Raffaello's *stanze*, the apartments known to the world by the name of the genius whose frescoes adorn the walls. There, enthroned in the Pope's audience room, the fair-haired young commander of the Emperor's army finds himself quite at home in the company of the great minds of the ages assembled by Raffaello to populate his "School of Athens."

Captain Ferrante Gonzaga is a welcome guest here. By virtue of the levelheadedness and courage he displayed at San Spirito, the twenty-year-old has earned himself a place in the Prince's inner circle and a seat on the Council of Ten appointed by Orange to rule the city. Once he has apprised his commander of his celebrated mother's wish to rescue the panels in the chapel, Orange is happy to oblige. But alerted now to their value, he decides to set aside a few for himself.

"Refresh my memory. How many of these panels are there?" he asks.

"Ten in all." This is a detail Ferrante came by only yesterday. In fact, until his mother brought up the subject, he had not even been aware that there were any tapestries from the hand of the master. Had he been trained at an Italian court, he would have had implanted in his mind a complete inventory of all the great treasures in the peninsula together with their location and approximate value. Since the time of the first Sforzas, Estes, and Montefeltros, an Italian *condottiero* has been expected to master not only the martial arts but the fine arts and the humanities as well. However, Ferrante Gonzaga was torn from his roots at a young age and sent to Madrid to learn chivalry at the Emperor's court. Like Orange, he is the product of the Habsburg code. Honor, courage, and skill with the sword are the virtues prized among the Spaniards and the ultramontanes. In Spain and Germany it is no disgrace for a knight to be clumsy at the galliard. And singing, lute playing, and quoting Virgil are best left to priests and women.

So these two young men, hardly more aware than the common soldiers they command of the inestimable value of their booty, set about quite casually to divide the spoils: two panels for Isabella; three for Orange himself; and five for the pleasure of his Majesty, Charles V.

THAT NIGHT AFTER DARK the two tapestries assigned to Madonna Isabella are hauled up by rope into the Colonna Palace. They have been packed as carelessly as if they were bales of hay; in fact, some of the hay that lay on the floor of the chapel still clings to the gold and silver threads. But no manure. Madonna Isabella thanks God for small mercies.

She cannot wait until daylight to see them. A porter is called, and with his help and that of Costanza, the chandelier is pulled down and all of its candles lit to illuminate the first panel to be rolled out onto the marble floor: Saint Paul preaching at Athens.

Isabella's eyes devour the deep red and gold folds of the saint's cloak with the voracious hunger of a predator. To her, every detail is a separate dish to be tasted and savored. But it is a lonely feast.

Many of those incarcerated with her in the palace are sufficiently cultivated to recognize the magnificence spread out on the marble floor of the salon, but not, she fears, sufficiently scrupulous to be entrusted with such a secret. There is only one person in her entourage both cultivated and trustworthy enough to share the moment. "Call Madonna Grazia," she orders.

Together the two women walk the perimeter of the huge tapestries, which, laid side by side, leave only a narrow margin of the tile flooring as a walkway. Occasionally one or the other will comment on the vitality of a gesture or the perfection of a line. Mostly, they remain silent in the presence of such beauty.

At last the sputtering candles announce the end of the show. Regretfully, Isabella orders the tapestries to be rolled up and locked away. Far from exhausting her, this orgy of visual pleasure has calmed her spirit and brought the light of life back into her eyes. She appears to be sated and utterly content, as if she had spent the long night in the arms of a lover.

The following evening, under Madonna Isabella's personal supervision, a long caravan forms up outside the Colonna Palace, cordoned off from the crowd by two hundred of Ferrante

Gonzaga's most loyal *bravi*. Ever attentive to the smallest detail, Isabella sees to it that Grazia dei Rossi and her son, Danilo, are accorded a position of honor hard by her litter, "to help protect me from any harm that may befall," she explains to a beguiled Danilo. As always, the lady assumes that any mark of her favor is its own reward. In fact, what the forward position offers is the first look at unspeakable horror.

Five days of Imperial occupation have transformed a city of palaces and pleasure gardens into a charnel house. The streets are strewn with bodies, many of them headless or limbless; palaces are reduced to piles of rubble, blocks of houses to smoldering ashes. More pitiful even than the dead are the survivors who wander through the streets dazed—fathers searching for daughters, husbands for wives, jostled and pushed about by street wenches parading in ermine, toothless hags bedecked with coronets, and soldiers reeling about drunk on wine or blood or both.

The route to the port takes Isabella's party into the Via Giulia, the broadest avenue in Roma. Tonight Isabella's cortege can barely squeeze its way between the piles of detritus that line the road on either side—beds and mattresses, broken pots, broken bodies, dead cats, all tossed carelessly into heaps during the height of the looting.

Straight ahead, blocking the road, a motley group of low-lifes cluster around a bonfire. Silhouetted against the wall of Farnese's garden they make an eerie dumb show, dancing a jig around a figure hidden to Grazia's eyes.

"Open your mouth to receive Christ's nourishment, priest," she hears. A space clears in the circle, permitting her to see one of the dancers stagger forward and proceed to urinate on a fat man with a crucifix around his neck who sits on the ground weeping.

Then comes the chant, "Drink, priest, drink. Drink the wine of the people."

Grazia manages to keep her composure until the blasphemous ritual runs down and the crowd disperses. But farther along as Madonna Isabella's party is crossing the Ponte Sisto, she makes the mistake of peering down at the Tiber, where a sight greets her eyes that shatters her composure. Directly under her gaze the nude body of a girl floats slowly by faceup, her long auburn hair fanning out behind her like a train, her young body skewered from her vagina to her mouth by a pike. She recognizes the girl at once as one of Domenico Massimi's redheaded daughters, a young woman she had seen dancing at one of Madama's fetes less than a month before.

"Don't look, Mama." Danilo turns her face away and places his arm around her shoulder to steady her. From then on, she walks with her eyes down.

At length the party arrives at the Ripagrande, where a group of barges stands ready to receive them. Now the pace picks up. The loading is accomplished expeditiously. Of all the party the only one who can bear to look back at the ruin of the once-great city is the youngest member, Danilo del Medigo. The despair that has taken root in the hearts of the others has not penetrated his. As the barge pushes off for Ostia, he turns to look at Roma for what may be the last time and salutes the city with a jaunty wave.

Sliding noiselessly across the glassy surface of the Tiber, Grazia is reminded of another escape by river. Will Ostia prove to be another Borgoforte? Will Messer Andrea Doria keep his bargain and have a vessel waiting for them at the dock to carry them out to the Tyrrhenian Sea? Or will their party be insulted, refused help, turned away?

Grazia reaches for her son and, wrapping him in the fold of her shawl, clasps him in a tight embrace.

WHEN THE REFUGEES FROM Roma first began to arrive at the port of Ostia, the hands and hangers-on at the port rushed eagerly to the quayside to observe each contingent. That was before the people of Ostia realized that the Imperials had shaken these people loose of every ducat they possessed before allowing them to leave. Highly placed though some of them may have been—and might be again—they are at this moment just as much beggars as the lowliest derelict on the waterfront, with not a ducat among the lot to pay for a loaf of bread. Even worse, their presence constitutes a menace to the town.

Paolo, the porter, is one of the first to have perceived the danger of giving aid and comfort to the refugees. "What if word gets to the Imperials that we took their enemies into our homes or gave them food?" he put it to his fellows. "In war, a man can get strung up for aiding the enemy. Do we want to risk our lives for these Romans?"

In company with the others in the audience, Nobilia found her protector's arguments persuasive. Why risk reprisals from the fierce landsknechts for offering *caritas* to their enemies? Besides, there is little point in soliciting clients if they cannot pay. So Nobilia has remained shut up behind a window at the inn, avoiding all contact with the tainted souls who stream forth daily off the barges that ply their way between Roma and Ostia. But now and then, for distraction, she does steal a peek at the collection of human misery that has washed up at the port.

Sitting sideways at her window, the better to see out through the crack she has opened between the shutters, Nobilia watches the day's dismal parade. There is the usual comple-ment of barefoot ladies and gentlemen with tattered *camicias* and slashed trunk hose. And she notes that today the armless and legless and noseless and earless are present in dispropor-tionate numbers. Is it the Germans who cultivate this fancy for cutting off body parts or the Spaniards? she wonders. Most likely the Spaniards. Word has it that the Germans are more brutish, the Spaniards more cruel.

Her musings are interrupted by the glimpse of a golden head bobbing up and down on the deck of the barge tying up below. Fair hair is rare in these parts. And these golden curls, caught in the sunlight, are so beautiful. She draws her eyes into a squint, trying to make out the face beneath the curly thatch.

Something about the nose looks familiar. She pushes aside the shutter and leans over the sill to get a good look.

Now she recognizes him. It is the page who came last autumn with the old Jew and the lady in the carriage. And there she is, the lady herself, not quite so grand now but not as bad off as some Nobilia has seen this past week. At least this lady has managed to hold on to her boots.

The boy and the lady descend from the barge and join a party of several others on the quay. As Nobilia watches, an even grander lady waddles down the plank and joins the party, a lady so grand that she keeps her entire face hidden under a long black veil. To give her passage across the quay, the group divides itself into two halves. It is as if Moses came back down to part the sea of people so that the lady could walk unimpeded to the door of the inn.

Before the grand dame reaches the portal the blond page pops up out of the crowd and with a deep bow and a flourish, throws open the door of the inn. Nobilia claps her hands with delight. She appreciates a gallant gesture.

The great lady is inside the inn now and Nobilia creeps out of her room and crouches at the top of the stairs to eavesdrop. The innkeeper claims to have no rooms. The lady calls him a liar. The innkeeper declares himself slandered and orders the lady off. The page marches up to face the publican toe-to-toe and demands an apology on the lady's behalf. But before a fracas can develop, an old man wearing the chain of a steward shuffles his way forward swinging a velvet bag that jingles the tune of coin against coin.

To this accompaniment, the rooms materialize as if by magic—the attic for the men, the second floor for the ladies, and the innkeeper's own room for the Marchesana and her attendants—all, including the host's own, dank, dirty and dismal. But by now the party is so worn out by fatigue and fear that no one complains. They simply lay themselves down head to toe on their lumpy pallets and thank God for their deliverance, the Marchesana included.

After dark, when the refugees have settled into sleep and the inn is quiet, a perky figure darts into the hallway and skips up the stairs to the attic where men are lying all around on pallets, snoring. Silent as a cat, Nobilia slips under the blanket that covers all of Danilo except for his golden thatch.

"Shh..." she warns him when he stirs to the touch of her body. "I've come to carry you to paradise."

"But I have no money for the fare," he murmurs sleepily.

"Never mind," she whispers. "We all must give a little bit of *caritas* now and then."

63

AY 20, 1527
Huddled in a dank corner of the Marchesana's room in the Atlantis Inn in Ostia, Grazia writes: "Five days in this filthy pesthole held captive by storms so fierce and winds so wild that even Andrea Doria's Genovese seamen fear to set sail. Madama reminds me how much better off we are in port—even in Ostia—than we would be at sea. I wonder. This place has the smell of death about it. I find myself making plans. Tomorrow I will consign to you, my son, the two items of value I am carrying with me, my portrait by Maestro Mantegna, which I wish you to wear rolled up under your *camicia* like a bellyband, and my *libro segreto* made for you to read when you reach manhood. Together, they constitute your inheritance. Common sense tells me that nobody ever died of cold and lice. Still, I will turn over the portrait and the manuscript to you tomorrow."

GRAZIA IS NOT THE only one to have lost heart in Ostia. After five days without fresh air or water on a diet of moldy bread and maggoty meat, locked up with a greedy-gut host who has begun to charge even for washing water, most of the members of the Marchesana's party have fallen into despondency, personal filth, foul temper, or some combination thereof. The only one who remains in perfect spirits is young Danilo.

"You can be proud of your boy, Grazia," Isabella tells her secretary. "He is a model of fortitude for us all." And indeed, the boy goes about with a smile on his face, whistling all day long.

What can there be in this hellhole to keep him so happy? wonders Grazia. Isabella, a light sleeper, has more than a suspicion. But she keeps her counsel.

On the seventh day of their Ostian captivity, the sun breaks through and calms the Tyrrhenian waters. Christians though they are, the entire party sends up a cheer for Apollo.

"My prayers have been answered," Isabella tells Grazia as they clamber up the gangway of Andrea Doria's four-master the *Hesperion*. "Next stop, Civitavecchia. Then Genova. And finally, Mantova and home." She crosses herself out of reverence for the god who has arranged this itinerary for her.

It does appear that God has answered someone's prayers. But did He answer my call, Grazia asks herself, or was it Madama's Christian prayers that moved Him to call off His storm and give us passage out of Ostia? This is no idle question from a woman preparing to desert her own God for a more expedient one.

Aboard the *Hesperion* on the twenty-third day of May, Grazia writes:

"Apparently apostasy does not come easy to me. Madama, who I think has never suffered a qualm of conscience in her life, attributes my perturbation to the rotten eggs we were fed at Ostia. Now that we are safely under way, she assures me, the sea air will cure my malady. But what if it is not a disorder of the gut that disturbs me? What if I am suffering from a crisis of the soul?"

She stops. Something about this sentence bothers her. Crisis of the soul? "The sea air seems to have infected me with a touch of grandiloquence," she continues. "In plain language, living through the sack has shaken my faith in the rightness of my decision to cut myself loose from my past. And seven hellish days in Ostia have done little to restore my confidence in the venture. Can a woman who abandons her God expect anything but sorrow and disappointment in repayment?"

As if in response to her question, the wind shifts abruptly, overturning her ink bottle and making a large black stain on her cloak.

Summoned by the winds, the storm quickly reappears, even wilder than before. This time no one in the party has the stomach to face it, not even the indomitable Isabella. Crowded into the airless saloon of the vessel, the refugees must deal not only with the press of bodies that threatens to suffocate them and the crash of thunderbolts that deafen them but also with the relentless roll of the ship as it tosses from side to side, sickening the most robust stomachs and turning the ship's mess into a sea of vomit.

After a full night of this, Isabella emerges from her private cabin, worn and haggard in the yellow light, in search of her secretary, who had elected to ride out the storm on deck.

"There is no one else I can say this to, Grazia." The lady's hand trembles as she touches Grazia's shoulder. "I am past my endurance. I cannot bear one moment more of this cruel sea. I have taken a potion which will give me the relief of sleep. When I awake we will be at Civitavecchia. From there I mean to continue the journey by land."

"I'm sure we will all be glad to quit the sea," replies Grazia.

"But I do not mean you to come with me, Grazia," the lady explains. "I am relying on you to shepherd my treasures safely back to Mantova by ship. I cannot abandon all my goods."

"But you can abandon *me*?" Grazia cannot conceal her distress.

"Not abandon. I am entrusting you with the things most dear to me in the world, excepting of course my children—the medals which I value so highly, my antique marbles, and the divine Raffaello's tapestries which we hold in trust for his Holiness. You are young, Grazia. You can withstand the rigors of the sea. And you are clever and brave. Of whom else in my entourage can I say those things?"

"Madonna..." Grazia reaches impetuously for the lady's hand and grasps it in her own. "I would do anything for you. But please do not ask me to leave your side."

"I had no idea you were so affected. You hide your fear well, Grazia." The lady nods her approval.

"Your example has given me the will to overcome my fright," Grazia answers truthfully. "No, madonna, it is not fear that binds me to you. If that were so, I would try to overcome it for your sake. But I gave my solemn word to Lord Pirro that, come what may, I would not leave your side until we were safe. And much as I love you, madonna, I love my honor even more."

This sentiment should have the power to move Isabella, but she does not yield. Instead she fondles the hairs that bristle out on her chin and, after a long pause, presents one of her characteristically self-serving arguments.

"I fear I fail to grasp the cause of your dilemma, Grazia. Have I not brought you out of Roma and into the safe waters of the Tyrrhenian Sea?"

"But our journey is not yet over, madonna. We must still undertake the voyage to Genova and, after that, there remains the trek across Lombardia," Grazia points out.

"You have the mind of a lawyer, Grazia," is the petulant reply. "But common sense tells me that if what you promised was not to leave my side until you were safely out of Roma, your promise has been fulfilled. Therefore your honor will not be sullied if you undertake to repay me by minding my treasures." Isabella nods, pleased with her own logic. "You look puzzled, Grazia. Am I not clear?"

Only too clear.

"Why so glum?" Capitulation is not enough for the lady. She demands surrender with a smile. "With a good wind behind you, you will be in Genova in four days and in Mantova in time to greet me when I arrive saddle-sore and bone-bruised from traversing the mountains. It is not as if I am condemning you to the stocks, Grazia. The captain assures me this is a freak storm. From now on, you will have easy passage. And I have booked my private cabin for you and the boy. There are people who would consider a private cabin on one of Andrea Doria's ships a privilege. And all I am asking in return is that you keep a good eye on these precious children of mine." She waves her hand carelessly at the baskets and barrels and *cassones* piled high on the deck beside them.

Such a reasonable request. Such a fair exchange. Impossible to refuse.

THE STOP AT CIVITAVECCHIA is brief, the farewell rushed. Unencumbered now by her baggage train, Isabella skips off the ship lighter in spirit as well as lading, with barely more than a wave for Grazia.

But for Danilo, perched high on top of the highest *cassone* to view the scene, she does have a moment.

"It pleases me that you are so attentive to my goods, young Danilo," she shouts up to him. "See you guard them with your life, for they are dearer to me than my own."

With that she is off to barter for horses and mules and the equipage to carry her large party through the Tuscan valleys, and thence across the Apennines to the waterways of the Po and finally home to Mantova. She bears with her the one treasure she would not entrust even to Grazia's trustworthy care: the red hat. That, she is determined to carry triumphantly into Mantova not only as a gift for her son Ercole but as a token of her victory over all the vicissitudes Fortuna has caused her to endure.

UNDER FULL SAIL IN a calm sea, the *Hesperion* is a different vessel than the hulk that creaked and groaned its way from Ostia to Civitavecchia. It has been transformed by the calm water into a great cradle that rocks its occupants gently as it skims along the Etruscan coast. Tucked away on the lee side of the four-master, Grazia gazes up at her son, who has adopted a post atop Isabella's *cassones* as his station. There he sits, guardian of the lady's treasure, serenading his mother in wonderfully dulcet tones:

> Oh beauteous rose of Judea, oh my sweet soul,
> Do not leave me to die . . .

Where did he learn this song?

She beckons him down. "I have not heard that tune since I was a girl," she tells him.

"Lord Pirro taught it to me while we were riding to the Tuscan front," he answers. "He wrote it for a girl he loved and lost when he was young."

Grazia turns aside to hide a sudden rush of color to her cheeks. She needn't have bothered. Her son is too intent on his knightly tale to notice that his mother is blushing for no reason.

"He called her his wild rose," he goes on, "because she had the same purity, the same pungency, and the same sharp thorns."

"He said that bit about the thorns?" she asks.

"He meant it in the nicest way, Mama," he hastens to explain. "The prickers were what made her irresistible."

"Doesn't sound like a very nice girl to me," she teases him, smiling.

"Then I've told it all wrong." He frowns with concentration and finally finds the words he has been looking for. "It is the contrast between the delicate flower and the piercing thorn that creates the excitement."

"Are those your words or Lord Pirro's, Danilo?"

"Oh, Mama." Now it is his turn to smile. "I could never think such a thought myself. I believe it was his way of warning me about love — that it can be oh so sweet and still make you bleed."

"That's what the poets tell us," she remarks thoughtfully. "But I never thought Lord Pirro cared overmuch for poetry."

"Then you don't know him as well as I do," he answers, once again rising to the defense of his mentor. "We talked about many other things besides battles while we were riding, Mama. He told me how it was for him when he was young, how he lost the love of his life because he was confused between love and duty. How he learned too late that fealty to his lady is a man's first obligation, even ahead of his oath to his liege lord."

"You did indeed talk of other things besides battles," Grazia observes. Then, half to herself: "I wonder why he told you all this..."

"Because he doesn't want me to make the same mistake he made when he was young. I will always remember the advice he gave me."

"What was that?" she asks softly.

"A woman who loves you with all her heart is a treasure beyond glory and fortune. A man can count himself lucky to know one such love in a whole lifetime. He says he wasted years learning that lesson."

How can the boy know how she has longed to hear those words? Or that they are twice as precious coming from him, a boy without guile who has no idea that he is his father's messenger?

She feels a strong urge to spill out the whole story there and then, on the deck of the *Hesperion*, and not wait for him to read it at the appointed time. Her son's trusting eyes have put her to shame.

She leans down closer to him. "Danilo..."

Before she can continue, a short, sharp crack rends the air. Then another, a gunshot straight across the bow. Next, a series of bloodcurdling whoops.

Danilo thrusts his mother into the wheelhouse for safety. Then, before she can stop him, he has clambered up to his post atop Madonna Isabella's *cassones* to protect her treasures, with his life if need be.

THE PIRATES WHO ATTACKED the *Hesperion* struck viciously and without warning. Almost before the captain sounded the alarm, they had come along the port side and descended, fifty strong, each man armed with a long curved weapon like a scythe and a dagger in his mouth.

There was no time to prepare a defense. The Corsican marauders had the captain at knifepoint in three minutes and the crew in irons a quarter of an hour later.

What to do with Grazia posed the marauders no problem. Even Corsicans do not shackle respectable ladies belowdecks with common sailors. But they felt no such constraints when it came to the boy perched up on the pile of *cassones*.

Twice the pirates called him down. Twice his mother ordered him to obey their command. Twice he refused to descend. Instead, he reached for a small dagger he had concealed in the folds of his sash at the beginning of the journey.

"Do not harm him, he is only a boy," his mother begged.

For answer, the leader, a black-bearded giant decked out like a Janissary, shouted up in a rough Corsican accent, "Boy or man, jump down, or I will shoot you like a dog!"

The boy raised his dagger in the air, meaning to aim it at the Corsican's heart. The Corsican raised his arquebus to his shoulder.

"No!" Without a thought, Grazia hurled herself at the pirate.

The boy heard a roar and saw his mother clutch her breast and fall at his feet.

Her heroism, the immediate unthinking bravery of her act, must have been something the Corsicans had never seen before, for they hovered over her as she lay on the deck bleeding, and brought cloths to cool her head and sweet water to moisten her lips and pillows to prop up her head and beautiful blankets of silk to cover her. And all that day they stood vigil beside the boy, taking turns to wait on his mother as if they too were her sons.

She suffered no pain, but she weakened quickly from loss of blood and had little strength to move or talk. Then toward the end she rallied, looked up at her son and spoke his name.

"Lean closer, Danilo." Her voice was low but firm. "It is time for us to say goodbye."

"No!" His mind, his body, everything in him, resisted.

"Only fools and knaves deny what they know to be the truth, my son. Come now."

This time, he did as she asked, leaned down and bent his ear to her lips.

"Listen carefully." Her breath was labored but her voice was clear, each word distinct. "It was my choice to take the Corsican's bullet. My doing, not yours, do you understand?"

No, he did not understand. His folly had caused this to happen. He should be the one bleeding out his life on that deck.

She paused to gather her strength, then went on. "No one chooses the moment of his death, Danilo. The lucky ones get to choose the manner of it. Try to understand this. I am blessed to die for the only cause I would have chosen, my love for you. You have made me, in the end, noble and brave. You have made me a heroine like the women I wrote about but never was... until now. Do not rob my end of its purpose, I beg you. Be gracious. Forgo the blame."

He agreed—how could he refuse?—although with only a dim understanding of what a gift she had given him. In one move, she had taken away his guilt and turned it into a kindness. But all he could think of was that she was leaving him.

Stay with me, Mother, he begged her silently, bowing his head to hide the tears forming in his eyes. Don't leave me.

"I know what you are thinking." Her voice was weaker now. "Lift up your head and look into my eyes."

He did as she asked, and what he saw in those eyes was a corona of devotion so radiant that he could no longer restrain himself and, as his mother spoke her last words, his tears fell unchecked.

"As long as you live I will be with you. If you are troubled or confused, call out for me. I will answer from a deep place inside of you." Through his tears he saw forming on her face that cunning half smile that so often followed one of her sly jests. "Can you doubt that I will answer? Could I ever resist giving advice?" Then, smiling, she closed her eyes for the last time.

THEY WRAPPED HER BODY in a silken shroud, the boy and the pirates, and consigned it to the sea, according to the custom of sailors. For the rest of the voyage, the crew allowed him to roam the ship unfettered. Perhaps as a tribute to his mother. Who knows the ways of Corsicans?

AFTER TWO DAYS OF sailing, Danilo felt bold enough to ask when the ship might expect to land at Genova. Only then did he discover that the pirates had turned the *Hesperion* about the night they boarded her and were bound for Constantinople to sell off their booty at the bazaars and their prisoners at the slave market. God must have the mind of a trickster, he thought, to make me the instrument of my mother's death and then to deliver me to the one port in all the Levant where my redemption is assured.

The pirate king, as the boy had come to think of him, came himself to attach the leg irons. He also permitted the boy to write a note to his father, Judah del Medigo, at the Sultan's harem and undertook to have it delivered as soon as the ship docked so that he might be quickly ransomed. "I do you this courtesy out of respect for your mother," the pirate told him. "She was a woman of valor."

The boy did not see the fabled spires of the city as they rounded the Golden Horn. He was down in the hold with the other prisoners, waiting there until the *Hesperion* was securely moored. But he did hear the cries of the mullahs summoning the faithful to prayer. It was this strange, dissonant wail, so foreign to his ears, that told him he was in a place different from any he had ever known. During the Mediterranean crossing, things seen and heard had registered only dimly in the great void that was his loss. Now, suddenly, the cries of the mullahs awakened him and he felt the stirrings of a call to adventure which had always been a part of his nature.

With his mother's portrait strapped tightly to his chest and her book, which he was enjoined from reading until he crossed the threshold of manhood, safely tucked under his arm, he fell in beside his fellow prisoners. *Carpe diem*, he repeated to himself as he began the deep descent down the gangway and into a new life. Seize the day.

AUTHOR'S NOTE

THE REAL HEROINE OF THIS NOVEL IS A YOUNG WOMAN OF THE Renaissance who lived out her life in obscurity and emerged from the shadows of history only once, as a footnote in Shlomo Simonsohn's *History of the Jews of Mantua*. There I found her name, Pacienza Pontremoli, and the provocative suggestion of a forbidden romance between the young Jewess and a Christian gallant at Isabella d'Este's court in Mantova.

The Simonsohn citation sent me on what I was certain would be a fruitless quest: to find a pair of letters printed in Bologna in 1923 in a journal, the *Rivista Israelitica*, which expired after the first two issues. But I live less than forty blocks from the New York Public Library and it seemed worth a walk.

Bingo! There in the card catalog was listed the *Rivista Israelitica*, preserved on microfilm. A dash upstairs to the microfiche room brought me face-to-face with two letters, one from Isabella d'Este to Pacienza Pontremoli, the other Pacienza's reply; and a third from a man named Pardo Rocque who claimed to have found them in his attic during a recent housecleaning.

It was no less than thrilling to read, in her own words,

Isabella's plea to Pacienza to give up her foolish attachment to the synagogue and enter into a proper Christian marriage with the young man who was dying of love for her. Then came Pacienza's reply, the words of a young girl terrified to offend the great lady yet unwilling to stand at the baptismal font and renounce forever her family and her God.

At that point the curtain descends and Pacienza disappears into the mists of history. But, for me, she had just begun to live. As her story took shape in my mind, she was transformed into Grazia dei Rossi; she acquired forebears and descendants, a famous husband, and personal distinction as private secretary to Isabella d'Este. She also acquired letters of her own, some real, some invented. But Grazia's heart remains the heart of Pacienza, suspended between the court and the synagogue, torn between love and duty.

Those who wish to read the original Pacienza/Isabella letters in full will find an English translation at the end of these notes. An edited version of Isabella's letter appears at the end of Chapter 16. In adapting this letter—in fact, all the documentary material—for the purposes of the story, every effort has been made to maintain the style of the original. In the same spirit of respect for the historical integrity of the story, no date or place has been falsified to satisfy the demands of the plot. If a certain battle or death or party or feast is described as happening on a certain date, that date is historically accurate. When Francesco Gonzaga threatens to cut his wife's vocal cords if she does not obey him, those are his own words as reported by a reliable bystander. When Benvenuto Cellini, the sculptor, takes a weapon in hand and hits the Imperial commander during the sack of Rome, I have given the scene as Cellini describes it in his autobiography.

For those who have seen Raphael's magnificent tapestry, "Saint Paul Preaching at Athens," hanging in the Vatican Museum in recent years and are led to question the authenticity of the episode in this book in which that tapestry is captured by pirates, rest easy. John Shearman, the eminent art historian, reports in his study of Raphael's Sistine tapestries that this and one other of the set did fall into Isabella's hands during the sack; were seized by pirates in transit; were sold, resold, and finally acquired by Constable Anne de Montmorency. It was he who bought them in Constantinople in the year 1554 and, being a man of honor, restored them to their rightful owner, the Pope.

So the gorgeous tapestry that you may have seen hanging in the Vatican Museum is the very one that was spirited out of Rome in Isabella's baggage train and then taken as booty by pirates. All I did to alter history was to put Grazia aboard the ship.

A complete listing of the source material for this book would, I think, be of limited interest. But, for anyone who wishes to venture a little farther into Grazia's world, Ludwig Freiherr von Pastor's *The History of the Popes, from the Close of the Middle Ages* was recommended to me early on by Professor James Ackerman as the seminal work on this period of history and I have leaned on it heavily throughout. (Incidentally, Professor Ackerman's short film, *Looking for Renaissance Rome*, is required viewing for anyone seeking to find what remains of the Renaissance in Rome.)

Julia Cartwright's two-volume biography of Isabella is fusty and Victorian but it is firmly based on documents from the Gonzaga archives. That family saved everything including shopping lists, and Mrs. Cartwright (a.k.a. Celia Ady) dispenses generous portions of the archive translated into English.

For an overall Jewish perspective, Cecil Roth's books on the Jews in the Renaissance are a good place to start. As with Mrs. Ady, modern scholarship has overtaken Professor Roth's research. But he was the pioneer and his work still has the power to lead you on to other books and articles which, in their turn, will point you in the direction of yet others and others and others... as they did me.

THE ISABELLA/
PACIENZA LETTERS

FROM ISABELLA GONZAGA

TO PACIENZA PONTREMOLI, THE MANTUAN JEW
OCTOBER 20TH.

*The fame that resounds all around about your virtue and good-
ness prompts me to write you and exhort you to convert to
Christianity so that as virtuous a soul as yours should not
remain deprived of heavenly consolations. By now the blindness of the Hebrew faith should be clear to you; so what are
you waiting for? Doesn't your prophet Rhau say that the hour
that your Messiah was supposed to come has already passed?
Haven't you read this more than once in the book entitled
Sanidrin? Are the seventy weeks of Daniel not already over?
Has the spectre of the house of Judah not been lifted? I myself
have read many times in that same Sanidrin that the Messiah
was born on the same day that the Temple was destroyed:
what are you waiting for then, to acknowledge Jesus Christ as
the true Lord and the true Savior of the world?*

*Oh! Please, think it over; please, cleanse yourself now in
the fountain which will be the stairway that will enable you to
climb to heaven and to eternally enjoy the resplendent face of*

the Eternal Father, Don't let yourself be deceived any longer by your doomed Rabbis ignorant of both human and divine doctrine: listen to my advice, because I'm advising you faithfully with perfect (Christian) zeal! Convert to Christianity. If you do so, for the one flesh-and-blood mother that you renounce, you will find ten more through the love of Jesus Christ! The Madonna of Mantova, mirror of pure sanctity, will be a Mother to you; my sister, both of my sisters-in-law, myself and many others will be mothers to you; nor will you lack a gracious husband because Marco Antonio Sidonio longs for you so much that the wretched man has been at risk of losing his head for love of you. The poor little thing is pining away and falling apart like a snowflake that the sun has discovered. And I am certain that you will find excellent companionship in him; and his being grateful to you will bring you honor and a fine reputation.

You will enjoy a husband who is wise and not fraudulent, courageous and not fearful of clear and flowing speech, not importunate or wearisome. Every time I hear his witty narrations accompanied by more well-executed actions than Roscio ever had, I'm afraid I'll die laughing just as Philomene the poet or Philistione the actor did. No melancholy humor will ever reside in your house; sad thoughts will keep far away from you. You will never suffer any discomfort for anything at all; on the contrary, it will seem to you that under your roof the goddess Amaltheia (Copia) is residing with her horn and whenever the whole world lets you down the generosity of your most revered Padrone will supply your needs because he feels an infinite lightening of his heavy thoughts due to his jokes.

I assure you even further, on my faith, that you will be even more loved by him than Euridice was by Orpheo, than Aspasia was by Pericle, than Orestia was by M. Plautio, or than Lisidica was by the poet Antimaco. Oh, don't delay, then, to make yourself a friend of Christ and to thus make our church happy and to render tearful the evil synagogue. Please, do not put off your sacred conversion any longer, do not put

*off increasing the number of the Elect in Heaven; and finally
do not put off making happy poor Marco Antonio, who loves
you fervently and has withstood for you as many hardships as
Hercules did in his own time. Nor will I go on anymore now
about his good qualities. Think, and examine well what I've
told you; pray to God that He might illuminate you with the
living rays of the Holy Spirit so that you will do the right thing.
Beautiful and pleasant thoughts to you. May God guide you.*

FROM PACIENZA PONTREMOLI, THE MANTUAN JEW

TO THE ILLUSTRIOUS SIGNORA ISABELLA GONZAGA
OCTOBER 23RD

*Yesterday I got the letter that it pleased you to send me, which
has very much troubled my thoughts. Your reasoning seemed
to me full of vigour and spirit and your persuasions were made
in such a way that they almost did violence to my intellect.
Your offers did not displease me; on the contrary, they made
me blush, because I realized I was unworthy of such a husband
as you proposed for me. On the other hand, I'm in doubt about
offending the Divine King by converting to Christianity. If I
confess Christ to be the true Messiah, I live in the anguish of
turning against me the disdain of Moses and the curse of all the
synagogue. I don't know (poor me!) where to turn for help and
advice. Your letters have moved me infinitely; and if certain
difficult steps had not held me back, I would have gone straight
to church and importunately asked for baptism. But I am considering, my lady, the sacred scripture's promise that when
the Messiah comes, Israel will be recovered. I read in the book
entitled* Badra *that in his coming, Jerusalem and the temple
of precious stones will be rebuilt—which, however, has not
yet happened. Furthermore, I see that our law was publicly
given by God through the hand of Moses on Mount Sinai in
the presence of frightening thunder and lightning—which you
Christians confess to be true without any reservations, there*

where your {law} is given secretly by the hand and the confession of twelve poor barefoot men. So I cannot help believing our Rabbis, who have a very different opinion about your Redeemer than you do. Let it not seem too strange to you, then, if I do not give in so quickly and if I seem somewhat stubborn. As for the husband that you speak to me about, I think — no, I clearly know — that he is even more worthy than you say; I know without a doubt that for his rare witness he would deserve to have a woman more beautiful than Deiopeia, than Amarilli, or than the fugitive Galathea. May God inspire me to do that which does him honor and glory; and meanwhile I beg you to pray that the Holy Spirit will reveal to me what I should do. I reverently kiss the beautiful and generous hand of your Excellency that had written me a most inspiring letter and beg you to pity the indecision of a weak and confused girl. Pray for me.
Signed Pacienza Pontremoli

(Translated by Kathleen Crozier Egan)

Read on for a preview of the sequel,
The Legacy of Grazia dei Rossi

Available November 15, 2014

ISTANBUL

I

RANSOM

AFTER A LONG AND SUCCESSFUL CAREER IN THE SER-
vice of the great and powerful, Judah del Medigo was
not surprised when out of the blue a courier arrived in
Rome ordering him to report immediately to his new master,
Suleiman the Magnificent, at Topkapi Palace in Istanbul.

Sudden arbitrary orders were the price the doctor knew
he would have to pay when he signed on as the Sultan's new
Chief Body Physician. Just as he knew that doctors do not say
no to sultans. So the doctor reluctantly kissed his wife and son
goodbye and boarded the first ship bound for the eastern Mediterranean, leaving his family behind in Rome to pack up and
follow him.

When news reached him at the Ottoman court that the city
of Rome had been sacked and burned soon after he left, del
Medigo was not unduly alarmed. He felt sure — with good
cause — that his wife and son would escape the sack unscathed.
He had left them in the fortified Colonna Palace in Rome under
the protection of his wife's patroness, Isabella D'Este, the
Marchesana of Mantova, and he knew Isabella to be a woman
of infinite resources and a practiced survivor.

Not until the doctor had heard nothing of his family for some weeks did he begin to worry. Even then, he mentioned his concern only casually to the Venetian *bailo* when they met at the Ottoman court. He knew that the Venetians made it their business to pick up odds and ends of information, and sure enough, that very evening the *bailo* presented himself at the Doctor's House with a rolled-up dispatch from one of his informants.

Wordless, the Venetian pressed his spy's report into the doctor's hands, gently patted him on the shoulder, turned on his heel, and left without a word. When the doctor unrolled the document and read it, he understood why.

Madonna Isabella D'Este reached home safely, he read. *Sadly, members of her household were captured by Mediterranean pirates off the Isola D'Elba. Their ship, the* Hesperion, *put up a brave defense, but its crew and passengers were lost at sea.* Then, being Venetians, they added, *Most of the lady Isabella's valuable treasures were also lost.*

The blow hit the doctor with the force of a pole axe. He had never doubted that the indomitable Marchesana Isabella would protect his dear ones. Isabella was an Este by birth and, say what you will about the Estes, they take care of their own. Now suddenly the Marchesana was apparently safe in her palace in Mantova, but her confidential secretary, the doctor's wife, Grazia dei Rossi, and their son, Danilo, had been lost at sea.

Judah del Medigo was an observant though not a believing Jew. The day he received the news, he locked his doors, covered his mirrors, and settled down on a low stool in the basement of the Doctor's House in the Third Court of Topkapi Palace to weep and grieve. Being a realist, he did not pray to have his loved ones brought back to him. There was no reason to hope they might still be alive. The Venetian report had left no doubt as to their fate. Yet before dawn on his sixth day of mourning, the Sultan's Chief Body Physician found himself scrambling across the dark silent streets of Istanbul in response to a ransom note that had been slipped under his door on the previous night.

The woman is dead, the note read. *The boy is safe. You have until dawn to appear at Pirates Cove with 2,000 gold ducats. If the ransom is not paid at sun-up the boy will be delivered to the Istanbul slave market and sold to the highest bidder.*

The ransom note read like a fraudulent ruse to extract money from a grieving parent. And the doctor knew better than to trust any bargain made with the Corsican pirates who prowl the waters of the Mediterranean. But what if just this once, the Corsicans proved to be as good as their word? What if his son was still alive? He could not afford to risk that chance.

So the next morning, well before sun-up, the Sultan's Chief Body Physician was found plodding through the sleeping city of Istanbul clutching a pouch full of gold coins. When the doctor clambered down the bank of Pirates Cove he saw no sign of life in the woods that ringed the shore or on the beach. Only one small portion of the landscape moved in the stillness: a deserted fishing boat bobbed up and down against the small dock anchored in the curve of the cove. If anything, the tattered sail that fluttered from the flagpole of the abandoned skiff underscored the flat emptiness of the scene.

By now a rim of sunlight had appeared on the horizon. The witching hour had come and gone, but there was no one there to collect the ransom.

As the doctor stood gazing into the void, reluctant to give up his last remaining glimmer of hope, he heard what seemed to be the sound of a twig breaking behind him in the silent woods.

When he turned his head toward the sound, he was taken from behind by a pair of unseen arms and felt hot breath on the back of his neck.

"Did you bring the gold?" The question was voiced in a growling, deeply accented Corsican dialect.

The doctor nodded his assent.

"Hand it over."

He reached into his pocket for the pouch, only to find it yanked from his fingers by a hairy hand that made immediate use of it to rap him smartly on the back of his head. A sharp pain flashed through his body. Then blackness.

When he opened his eyes his attacker had made off with the gold, and the woods behind him were as unruffled as they had been when he first arrived at the rendezvous. He had been duped. How could he have been such a fool as to put his faith in a passel of Corsican pirates?

But wait. Out of the corner of his eye he became aware of something moving on the deck of the abandoned skiff. Transfixed, he watched as a trap door was slowly thrust into view from below the deck of the craft and two pairs of bronzed, muscled arms emerged bearing what seemed to be a black-hooded body wrapped in a tarpaulin.

Mesmerized by what he took to be a mirage brought on by the blow to his head, the doctor stumbled to his feet expecting that at any moment the illusion he was seeing would disappear into the wind. Instead, the sailors carrying the wrapped figure moved forward to the prow of the ship where they propped it up against the mast and began to unwind the straps that enclosed it.

They did say he was alive, the doctor reminded himself. But could he take them at their word?

One of the sailors pulled out a knife. *Oh my God, they are going to kill him in front of me.*

But no. The sailor used his knife to slit the black hood at the neck, releasing a single golden curl onto the forehead. Then a nose. Now a chin appeared. Above it, a mouth. Then a pair of clear blue eyes. At last a whole living boy was revealed, arms stretching out toward the shore.

The sailors led their captive down a small gangway from the deck of the skiff to the pier. And, with a gentle push, Danilo del Medigo was released into his father's waiting arms.

It was at that moment that Judah del Medigo became a believer in miracles. And if a battle-scarred, somewhat arthritic old campaigner can be said to have floated through the streets, the Sultan's Chief Body Physician floated home from Pirates Cove that day to the Doctor's House in Topkapi Palace, cradling his son in his arms.

There he settled his son on a pallet beside his own bed and wrapped him in a lavender-scented quilt. But not before he had washed and barbered and massaged the boy into a state of cleanliness and ease.

At the same time, the physician in him managed to conduct what he hoped was an unobtrusive examination of his son's physical condition. And Judah del Medigo fell asleep that night with the miracle boy nestled beside him, confident that, considering the shocks he had suffered, the boy was amazingly fit. No broken bones or bruises, no signs of being starved or beaten.

Not until the next day did Judah become aware that, although his son was healthy enough, he seemed to exist in a state of passivity, hardly moving, not speaking unless spoken to. Perfectly obedient and accommodating, never rebellious or defiant, this pale wraith bore little resemblance to the vigorous, lively boy his father had left in Rome just a few months before. When the doctor tried to distract him with tempting morsels of food or chat, the boy accepted the offerings with a nod but showed no sign that he enjoyed his father's pleasantries any more than the eggs and meat and pilaf that Judah poured into him, hoping to renew the energy that had always been so much a part of his nature.

Certainly the doctor was beyond joy to be reunited with his lost son. He thanked God every morning in his prayers for the boy's miraculous delivery. Yet he couldn't shake off his awareness that come spring, he was bound to the Sultan on campaign and would have to either leave the boy behind or take him along. Could he in good conscience leave his troubled son behind in the care of strangers? Or expose him to the hardships of campaigning? Or must he now resign his position in order to devote himself to the boy's rehabilitation?

While he was struggling to come to a decision, a note from the Sultan arrived. Suleiman was proposing that during the upcoming campaign, the doctor's son join the royal children in the so-called Princes School attached to the Sultan's harem, where he would be as well taken care of as a prince. The offer was tempting. But after two sleepless nights and many prayers, Judah regretfully tendered his resignation as Chief Body Physician, pleading pressing family obligations.

In the interim he would bend his efforts to find a replacement body physician to serve Suleiman on the battlefield. Knowing that his decision was the right one put his mind at ease.

But Suleiman the Magnificent was not a man to be denied his will by a mere doctor. Like the popes at Rome and certain Christian princes whose instinct for self-preservation exceeded their religious scruples, the Ottoman sultans favored Jewish doctors. Unhampered by medieval Christian screeds against "pagan science," Jewish physicians had continued to practice the teachings of Asclepius and Hippocrates. Armed with this knowledge, they had emerged from the Middle Ages as an elite cadre of medical practitioners, Judah del Medigo foremost among them.

The Sultan had pursued the renowned Jewish physician through the courts of Europe for several years before finally bagging him. And he was not about to allow the unexpected appearance of a motherless boy to rob him of his campaign physician. Certainly not at this moment when the gout that it was said only Jewish doctors had a cure for was beginning to make it uncomfortable for him to mount a horse.

To initiate what he confidently expected to become a fruitful dialogue, Suleiman called in his physician for a friendly chat, reminding him that the campaign season would not commence for many months, that there was no urgency to make such an important decision, and urging the doctor to take some time to reconsider resigning.

"You have my assurance that in the Harem School your son will do his learning as a part of my own family under the watchful eye of my own mother, the Valide Sultan," he coaxed. "Surely," he went on, "that would be a much safer arrangement than dragging the boy off to the battlefield or leaving him behind with strangers." Then, to add a little sweetener to the sherbet, he offered to assign the boy an armed guard to escort him from the Doctor's House in Topkapi to the Princes School in the harem each day that Judah was absent on campaign.

The prospect was tempting. Judah wavered. His head told him that the Sultan's offer was a solution to his problems. But his fatherly heart told him that the boy was not yet ready to deal with yet another abandonment by the only parent now left to guide him through the labyrinth of dark memories that haunted him.

What the Sultan was offering the doctor was time to ferret out what had happened during the boy's captivity on the pirate ship, and to find the key to his son's despair. A boy's natural grief for the loss of a much loved mother could account for weeping, fainting, even vertigo—but not for virtual paralysis. What cruelty had the damned Corsicans inflicted on Danilo to cause such damage?

That question might never have found an answer had not some lost soul stumbled in the dark into the Sultan's personal domain, a swampy moraine outside the wall of the Third Court. If an interloper ever managed to get anywhere near the Sultan's *selamlik*, a warning fired from a Janissary's musket would have scared him off, pronto. Which is what happened that night. But as the shot reverberated across the palace wall into the Third Court, it also shattered the silence in the Doctor's House, where Judah del Medigo and his son lay sleeping.

At the sound of the shot, the boy sprang up from his pallet as if he had been hit, clutching his heart in terror. "Stop, don't shoot!" he pleaded. "Noooooooo..."

Then came a blood-curdling shriek of anguish. "Not Mama. Not her, I beg you. Take me... take me."

The musket-shot had released a flood of dammed-up memories. And finally, between the sobs, came a confession.

"It was all my fault. The pirate ordered me to abandon my perch guarding Isabella's baggages. Mama begged me to climb down. I wouldn't listen to her. If I had come down the pirate wouldn't have aimed the gun at me and she wouldn't have thrown herself in front of me to take the bullet. She would be here now. Alive." A long pause. "I killed her."

A glance at his son's face told Judah he could not allow this madness to go on. Gently but with great firmness he took the boy's pale face between his hands and addressed him sternly. "Did you have a gun?" he asked.

When no response came, he demanded with fatherly authority, "Answer me."

"No." The answer was barely audible.

"So who did have a gun?"

"The pirate they called Rufino."

"Then it was the pirate Rufino who killed your mother with his gun. Not you."

"No. No." The boy wrenched himself from his father's grasp. "You weren't there. You don't know what happened."

"Tell me," the doctor urged him softly.

Somehow Judah had struck the right note. His son took a deep breath, straightened his shoulders, and began to relive his memory.

"Madonna Isabella left the *Hesperion* to finish the trip to Mantova by land because she was seasick," he began, hesitantly at first but with increasing assurance as he went on. "Before she quit our ship she asked me to guard her baggage with my life and bring her things home safely to Mantova. There were treasures packed in those cases—a tapestry by Raphaello that she said meant more to her than her own life. When the pirates attacked the *Hesperion*, the crew put up a brave fight, but the ship sprang a leak in the hold and started to take on water. That was when Rufino and his crew began to remove Madonna Isabella's valuables from our ship to theirs. All I could think of was my promise to watch over her goods. I climbed up on top of her cases to guard them. Rufino ordered me out of the way. I didn't move. He said he would count to three.

"'One.' The pirate raised the musket to his shoulder. I saw Mama moving toward us.

"'Two.' He placed his thumb on the trigger.

"'Three.' He squeezed. The shot rang out just as Mama threw herself into the line of fire. Nothing seemed to happen...then she fell at my feet."

There were no tears in the boy's eyes when he spoke. Simply a blank emptiness. "That bullet was meant for me. I killed her."

"That bullet was shot by the pirate, not by you," Judah insisted.

"But if I had stepped down..."

"It would still be the pirate that killed your mother. There is no pity in these men. Murder is their business. When I first saw you at Pirates Cove you were tied up in a tarpaulin. They had bound your ankles, taped your wrists, and covered your head in a hood. You were their prisoner. They would have killed you."

"You don't understand, Papa. They never would have killed me. They tied me up to save me from drowning. They saved my life."

"Are you telling me that these bandits rescued you out of pity?"

"Of course not. I may be confused, Papa, but I am no fool. I know they saved me to sell in the slave market in Istanbul. But they did fish me out of the sea and save me."

"After they threw you in?"

"No, after I jumped in. They put Mama's body in a wooden box and shoved it off the side of the ship. When I saw her body sinking under the waves I wanted to follow her, to be dead like her. So I jumped in. That's when they tied me up, so I wouldn't try to do it again."

Judah had convinced himself that if he learned the secret of his son's suffering at the hands of the Corsicans, that knowledge would guide him to a cure for the boy's malady. But having relived his ordeal, the boy remained pale, silent, and still. Clearly reliving his nightmare had done nothing to alleviate Danilo's guilt and pain. It would take months, even years, to rescue his son, Judah thought, from the pit of despair into which he had fallen. If there had been any doubt in Judah's mind, there no longer was. There would be no campaigning this year for the Sultan's Chief Body Physician. Danilo's needs were far greater than the Sultan's, and Judah's first duty was to his son.

ACKNOWLEDGMENTS

My work on this book over ten years on two continents has left me with a debt of gratitude that can never be repaid. My ledger of indebtedness begins at New York University, my university, and early conversations with colleagues, notably two distinguished scholars, Norman Cantor and Baruch Levine, who set me on a righteous research path.

Through the generosity of the Art History department, I got a crash course in Renaissance art that led to a series of wanderings in Italy to see for myself what the slides had promised. The Italian department introduced me to the Italian language, now a lifelong study. An introduction from Professor Levine put me in touch with Professor Benjamin Ravid at Brandeis University whose vast knowledge of the history of the Jews of Venice is exceeded only by his willingness to share it.

From the Tisch School of the Arts I got encouragement and time off. My thanks to my former dean, David Oppenheim, and to the present dean, Mary Schmidt Campbell. Janet Neipris, my chairman and friend, continued to believe in this book at times when I quite lost hope for it.

I am not the first to recognize the New York Public Library, that astonishing repository of everything you ever wanted to know about anything. In my case, I found the beating heart of my story buried in their microfiche archives and am, for that, especially beholden. Living within blocks of the Bobst Library at NYU and the Hebrew Union College library, I took it as my right to use them as I wished. It took research experience in Europe to teach me that the vast network of free libraries in this country has no equal in the world and to learn to cherish them.

A stay at the MacDowell Colony enabled me to make my first efforts at writing fiction. The American Academy in Rome gave me a safe and friendly place from which to pursue my Roman researches. And the Canadian Cultural Council has offered advice and help over the years. To Gilbert Reid, who headed that office, and to Elena Solari who still represents Canada's cultural presence in Italy, my everlasting gratitude.

Everybody loves the Italians. And, like all lovers, we all believe that our relationship with the loved one is unique. I am no exception. I went to that country ill versed in the language and profoundly ignorant of Italian life, both in the sixteenth century and in the present. And to a man—and woman— the Italians I turned to for help offered me their time, their knowledge, their precious documents, their hospitality, their friendship. Who else but Tudi Sammartini, the greatest guide in Venice, perhaps in the world, would have undertaken to guide me from Ferrara to Bologna on a lunatic search for the long-buried Reno Canal—and helped me find its remains? Who would have handed over to me, without my asking for it, a private history of his family, as did Dottore Ugo Norsa of Mantova? Or have given hours of time out of his busy life to act as my interpreter as did Professor Vittore Colorni?

My knowledge of the Gonzaga *reggio* comes from a tour I was given by Sandra Sicoli of the office of the Sovrintendenza per i Beni Artistici e Storici. My acquaintance with the Venetian ghetto I gained from Sally Spector; with the Roman Jewish quarter from Bice Migliau of the Centro di Cultura Ebraica; of Italian Jews then and now from the late patron of the Jewish museum in Rome, Signore Fornari; and from Tullia Zevi, head of the Union of Jewish Congregations of Italy. The kindness and patience of these individuals and countless others has been simply boundless.

Finally, I must express my gratitude to the staunch crew of friends who read through this lengthy manuscript—some more than once, some more than twice—as it took shape: Zane Kotker, Susan Cartsonis, Michael Manzi, Sheri Holman, and Laurie Chittenden, who came aboard late but has been an unwavering support. My agent, Molly Friedrich, and my editor, Mary Ann Naples, have devoted themselves without stint to the task of steering this book to publication. To say that I thank them with my whole heart does not begin to express the gratitude and affection I feel for these two kind, smart, and generous women.

Jacqueline Park is the founding chairman of the Dramatic Writing Program and professor emerita at New York's Tisch School of the Arts. She lives in Toronto, Ontario.